Beth's gaze _____ *he stood at the altar.*

He was so handsome in his tuxedo—so tall, so broad shouldered, so…masculine. And within minutes he would be her husband.

They were entering a binding union, and the gravity of the commitment overwhelmed her. Exactly what would he expect of her, of their marriage of convenience?

The ceremony passed in a quick haze. Beth realized they were making promises to each other—important promises that would guide the direction of their lives. To have and to hold. To love and to cherish. Promises that were meant to last a lifetime.

And before she knew it the minister smiled and said to Nathan, "You may kiss your bride."

Dear Reader,

What makes a man a Fabulous Father? For me, he's the man who married my single mother when she had three little kids (who all needed braces) and raised us as his own. And, to celebrate an upcoming anniversary of the Romance line's FABULOUS FATHERS series, I'd like to know *your* thoughts on what makes a man a Fabulous Father. Send me a brief (50 words) note with your name, city and state, giving me permission to publish all or portions of your note, and you just might see it printed on a special page.

Blessed with a baby—and a second chance at marriage—this month's FABULOUS FATHER also has to become a fabulous husband to his estranged wife in *Introducing Daddy* by Alaina Hawthorne.

"Will you marry me, in name only?" That's a woman's desperate question to the last of THE BEST MEN, Karen Rose Smith's miniseries, in *A Groom and a Promise*.

He drops her like a hot potato, then comes back with babies and wants her to be his nanny! Or so he says…in *Babies and a Blue-Eyed Man* by Myrna Mackenzie.

When a man has no memory and a woman needs an instant husband, she tells him a little white lie and presto! in *My Favorite Husband* by Sally Carleen.

She's a waitress who needs etiquette lessons in becoming a lady; he's a millionaire who likes her just the way she is in *Wife in Training* by Susan Meier.

Finally, Robin Wells is one of Silhouette's WOMEN TO WATCH—a new author debuting in the Romance line with *The Wedding Kiss*.

I hope you enjoy all our books this month—and every month!

Regards,

Melissa Senate,
Senior Editor

Please address questions and book requests to:
Silhouette Reader Service
U.S.: 3010 Walden Ave., P.O. Box 1325, Buffalo, NY 14269
Canadian: P.O. Box 609, Fort Erie, Ont. L2A 5X3

A GROOM AND A PROMISE

Karen Rose Smith

Silhouette®
ROMANCE™
Published by Silhouette Books
America's Publisher of Contemporary Romance

To Lee, a courageous friend—Thank you for your
friendship and your ability to help me keep
my perspective.

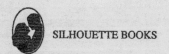

SILHOUETTE BOOKS

ISBN 0-373-19181-2

A GROOM AND A PROMISE

Copyright © 1996 by Karen Rose Smith

Printed in U.S.A.

KAREN ROSE SMITH

created scenes in her mind to fit popular songs when she was a teenager. Those scenes developed into stories. Reading romance books has been a favorite pastime throughout her life. Her love for the genre led her to apply the skills of her English degree to writing romance novels after back surgery. Now, she cannot imagine doing anything else. She says, "I try to write stories about hope and overcoming obstacles. My characters are as real to me as my friends. I share their pain as well as their joy and cheer them on as they resolve their conflicts."

Karen hopes you enjoy meeting Cade, Gavin and Nathan—the three special men from her THE BEST MEN series. She likes hearing from her readers. You can write to her at P.O. Box 1545, Hanover, PA 17331.

THE BEST MEN

*Beth Warren's Tips
on Finding a
Groom of Convenience*

1. Ask your best friend for a recommendation. Surely her handsome husband has some available buddies.

2. Never let on just how desperate you are.

3. Don't agree to move the marriage into the bedroom, unless your convenient husband proves too irresistible.

4. Remind your chosen groom that this is not a love match—but that you both have the option to change your mind at any time.

Prologue

"Mommee. Sw-wing."

As the hot Virginia sun beat down, Beth Warren chuckled, reached for the mail from the box and carried her two-year-old daughter inside their apartment. "We just spent an hour swinging in the park, Dorie. Now it's nap time. Would you like a drink of juice first?"

Dorie nodded, her fine blond curls bobbing along her cheeks, her blue eyes sparkling with the innocence, joy and mischief of a toddler learning to assert herself. "Ow-ange choos."

With a smile Beth set her daughter on the floor and plopped her purse and the few letters from the mailbox on the table. "Orange juice, it is." She pushed her own blond hair away from her forehead. Falling below her shoulders and much straighter than Dorie's,

Beth's hair had grown long over the past two years as she'd concentrated on her daughter rather than herself. Making Dorie the entire focus of her life had helped her deal with Mark's death and her grief. The past few months she'd finally felt as if she were emerging from the cloud that had overshadowed her for too long.

The air-conditioning cooled Beth as she gave Dorie her juice, changed her diaper and lifted her into her crib. With a nuzzle, two kisses and a giant hug, she wished her daughter a happy nap and closed the door partway.

Beth hated the idea of starting back to work in September. Well, actually, she didn't hate the idea of going back to work as a medical secretary—she hated the idea of being away from Dorie, missing anything, even a smile. But Mark's benefits would run out in a few weeks, so she had no choice.

Pouring herself a glass of orange juice, Beth sat at the round oak table she'd refinished when she and Mark were first married. She opened the top piece of mail—a note smaller than the remaining legal-size envelopes. As she lifted the blue flap, she grinned. A birthday party. Jessie Bradley was giving a surprise party for her husband. Jessie's listening ear over the past year had helped Beth tremendously. They'd met by accident in the park one day and become fast friends. A birthday celebration for her husband, who was as nice as Jessie, would be fun.

The address in the upper left corner of the next envelope made Beth frown. Mark's parents. Why were they writing, when they could pick up the phone and call? Although Mark had been estranged from them, after his funeral Beth had offered them visits with their granddaughter. They were overbearing, which was the quality Mark had fought all his life, but they did seem to genuinely enjoy and care about Dorie. Beth didn't want to deny them that link with their deceased son.

Curious as to what she'd find, Beth opened the letter.

Dear Beth,

We know you are trying to provide the best home for our granddaughter. However, we think we can do better. You yourself told us you need to return to work. We can't abide the thought of Dorie in day-care. Besides your work situation, you simply don't have the means we do to take care of Dorie. Your apartment is small; our house is large. You don't have a backyard; we have acres. We can buy her anything her heart desires.

Therefore, we have consulted with our lawyer, Richard Turnbell, about claiming custody of Dorie. He will be contacting you within the week. We felt you deserved to hear this from us before we went ahead with the proceedings.

Sincerely,
Ivan and Clara Warren

Beth stared at the letter in shock. Surely they couldn't be serious! Surely they didn't have a chance at gaining custody. Did they?

*　*　*

The next day Beth walked out of her lawyer's office into the sunshine, feeling as cold as death inside. Her attorney had been blunt. Precedent-setting cases were being won by grandparents who sued against working mothers.

Beth had been horrified and shaken by the facts and her lawyer's advice. When she'd asked the best way to safeguard her rights as well as her daughter, he'd leaned forward in his chair, stared her straight in the eye and advised her, "Find yourself a husband. Stay home and mother your daughter. Then your in-laws won't have a leg to stand on."

As Beth sucked in a deep breath of hot, humid air, tears welled up in her eyes. She would *not* give up her daughter; she *would not!* And if that meant she had to find a husband...

Then find a husband she would.

Chapter One

Nathan Maxwell tossed the horseshoe and felt the pretty blonde's gaze on him again. She'd been watching him for the past hour as guests at his friend's backyard birthday party mixed conversation with participating in outdoor games.

Nathan had noticed the blue-eyed, blond-haired woman from the moment he'd stepped into the Bradley's backyard. Jessie Bradley had apparently invited a variety of acquaintances—from Gavin's colleagues at the hospital to neighbors, to relatives. Some were dressed more formally than others even for a backyard party. He'd noticed the blonde because in her bib denim shorts, white T-shirt and tennis shoes, she looked as if she belonged in the backyard setting. Often the breeze lifted her long hair, tossing it. She didn't seem to mind. It had been a long time since Nathan had seen such a natural-looking woman.

Maybe too long.

The bite of desire was sharp as he turned and met her gaze squarely. She blushed when she realized he'd caught her looking, ducked her head and reached for a carrot stick on the buffet table under the striped canopy.

Nathan lifted the second horseshoe, aimed and threw. Metal clanged on metal. A ringer.

As he finished the game, he noticed the blonde disappear into the house with Jessie. He might have to ask Jessie about her.

Do you really want to do that?

The voice that had safeguarded him since his divorce seemed intrusive this time. The breakup of his marriage and the reason behind it had made him cautious and reluctant to start dating again. Yet he still wanted a family more than he wanted anything in his life.

Nathan got caught up in another round of horseshoes before he glimpsed the blonde again.

A short time later Beth walked beside Jessie across the yard. "I must be crazy for even considering this. Nathan Maxwell's a complete stranger! He's—"

Jessie stopped and laid a comforting hand on Beth's arm. "Gavin has known Nathan since college. Over the past year since Gavin and I married, Nathan has become a friend to me, too. He's a kind man with the integrity I never thought I'd find in anyone *but* Gavin."

KAREN ROSE SMITH   13

"Does Gavin know you and I have discussed this?"

Jessie smiled. "He knows I'm going to introduce you. And that's all I'm going to do. Anything else is up to the two of you."

"The man will think I'm out of my mind," Beth murmured, wondering if she was.

"Even if Nathan doesn't want to get involved, believe me, he'll understand your desperation in wanting to do anything to keep Dorie with you."

"You said he likes children."

"He's great with Lisa. He takes her horseback riding and in-line skating."

Lisa was Jessie and Gavin's nine-year-old daughter. Being with a nine-year-old was much different from being with a two-year-old, Beth realized.

They started walking again and Beth became more and more nervous as she stared at Nathan Maxwell's broad shoulders. He wore a navy tank top, and his tanned skin gleamed. He carelessly tossed a volleyball from one hand to the other as he talked to another guest. His navy shorts emphasized his long legs, his powerful thighs. He'd played football in college, Jessie had said. The dark brown hair on his legs was slightly lighter than the hair on his head.

Beth attributed the tingles running through her at the sight of him to her anxiety. Attraction to a strange male was foreign to her. Eight years ago, when she'd fallen in love with Mark, it was as if she'd turned off her sensors to any other man. And that hadn't changed since Mark's death. She just didn't think of men in that way.

Jessie called to Nathan. As he turned, his gaze slipped from Jessie to Beth . . . and held.

"Nathan, I want to introduce someone to you. This is Beth Warren, a friend of mine."

A smile tilted Nathan's lips. "Hi, Beth." He extended his hand. "Nathan Maxwell. Great party, isn't it?" His hand was large, engulfing, but the press of his fingers was gentle.

Beth's mouth went dry. The tingles that she had relegated to anxiety suspiciously felt like something else.

Before she could answer, or figure out how to ease into a conversation she was terrified of having, Gavin clattered two horseshoes together. His gray eyes twinkled as he pointed to the stack of burlap bags he'd piled near the horseshoe pit. "Time for the three-legged race. Grab a partner."

As groans met him, he laughed. "If you need an incentive, the winners get first place in the line for a steak from the grill. C'mon. Forget you're adults and have some fun." He beckoned to his daughter. "C'mon, honey. Let's show them how it's done." Holding out a burlap bag, he waited for Lisa to step into it. "Let's go, everybody. Suit up."

Jessie said to Nathan and Beth, "I have to referee. Why don't you two pair up?" Then she was gone, leaving them to make the decision.

Nathan Maxwell arched his brows. "Are you game?"

A three-legged race would be a cinch compared to what would come after, Beth thought. "I like a good steak as much as the next person," she said.

As Nathan smiled, he motioned toward the starting line. "Then let's give them a run for their steaks."

Jessie handed each pair of runners a burlap sack.

Nathan took the burlap, opened it and held it at one side. "I suppose it's better if we do this at the same time."

His eyes were very green ... intense, strangely mesmerizing. Beth's heart fluttered as she took hold of the other end of the sack. She put one leg in, then waited for him to do the same.

The edge of their shoes touched, his so much bigger than hers. When his leg grazed hers, she could feel the brush of masculine hairs. He was so tall—at least six-two to her five foot five. He smelled male and dangerous, and her heart pounded faster.

Jessie blew a whistle to get their attention and pointed to the finish line. Grinning, she called, "Everyone knows how this works. I count down. You go. Ready?" She waited until a few of them cheered, then she yelled, "Three. Two. One," and blew the whistle, signaling the start of the race.

Nathan said, "Put your arm around my waist," as his encircled hers.

For a moment the sensation of a strange masculine arm around Beth immobilized her. But then they were moving forward and she clutched onto him. Hot, hard muscles registered under her fingertips, then her palm, as she secured her grip.

When they hobbled forward, her hair swept across her cheek, and she tossed it back.

Nathan groaned, hoping Beth Warren would think the exertion was his problem—not her. He hadn't been this close to a woman in a long time. Well, he had hugged his friends' wives, but that was different. Entirely different. Hugging Jessie or Randi or Katie was *not* the same as circling Beth Warren's waist—a very tiny waist—with his arm, feeling the hint of softer flesh as his hand accidentally slid over her buttocks— femininely curved buttocks, or being aware of her breast grazing his chest each time they hopped forward.

And when her hair and the sweet scent of her caressed his cheek . . .

The race. Maxwell. Win the race.

How the hell could he win it when he couldn't concentrate on it?

To Nathan, the gift of concentration usually came easily. He'd mastered it during his chaotic years in foster homes, when focusing on a book or studies or football was his means of surviving. But right now, with Beth Warren tucked into his side, baser instincts kicked him in the gut, making concentration practically impossible.

He'd never had a problem concentrating when Elaine was around. Even before making love had become a marathon exercise to conceive and all the romance had flown out the window, a simple look from her had never bothered him as much as Beth Warren's gaze on him—making his blood run fast.

Maybe he just didn't remember.

Yeah, and Christmas will come in August this year.

As other pairs of runners fell or couldn't regulate their gait, he and Beth hopped, jumped and ran as if they'd run this race a hundred times before. They moved together so well. Instantly Nathan pictured them moving together in another way, her beautiful blond hair across his pillow, her blue eyes glazed with desire for him....

They reached the finish line. Someone smacked Nathan on the back. "You won!"

Nathan grinned and hugged Beth. "I guess those first steaks are ours." She felt so right in his arms.

She returned the hug, leaned back and asked, "Will you marry me?" As soon as she'd said it, she turned red. "That just came out. I didn't mean...I mean...I was thinking—"

At first Nathan had thought the question was a joke, a means of making flirtatious conversation. But as he looked into Beth's eyes, he realized something much more serious was going on. Instead of being shocked, he was intrigued.

Stepping out of the burlap bag, he waited until she did the same. Then he took her hand and tugged her toward the shade of a tall sycamore. He laid the burlap on the ground, gestured for her to sit, then sat across from her. "What's going on?"

She was obviously embarrassed. Her cheeks were still rosy from more than exertion. But she gazed directly into his eyes. "You must think I'm insane. *I* think I'm insane. But I don't know what else to do, and Jessie said you're a good man and kind, and I thought if I could get to know you just a little..."

He held up his hand and smiled. "Whoa! Slow down. I don't think you're insane."

Brushing her hair from her forehead, she sighed. "That's a relief, I guess. Though sometimes I think desperation and worry can make a person feel insane. My mind's been spinning for the last two weeks and—'' She suddenly stopped. ''And now I'm not making any sense.''

''Tell me why your mind's been spinning for two weeks,'' he suggested, knowing all about desperation. He and Elaine had been desperate for a family, trying procedures that were anything but natural. When he'd realized their marriage was breaking up *because* they couldn't conceive, he'd become more desperate, spending days and nights worrying. Yes, he knew all about desperation and worry.

''I'm afraid I'm going to lose my daughter.''

As Beth's hands fluttered in her lap, his gaze landed on the ring finger of her left hand. There was a thin line, white against her tan. ''Are you married?''

''Widowed,'' she answered. ''Two years.''

Relief swept over Nathan. ''How old is your daughter?''

''She turned two last month. Mark died two weeks after she was born.''

The sadness in Beth's voice told him she'd loved the man very much. ''I'm sorry.''

She nodded, accepting his condolence. ''His parents are trying to take Dorie.''

The idea of anyone trying to take a child from her mother outraged Nathan. ''Why would they do that?''

Beth squared her shoulders and lifted her chin defensively as if the question was an insult. ''Mark was never very close to his parents. They had expectations and demands for him he didn't want to fill. When he decided he wanted to be a teacher rather than going into his father's business, they cut off his funds. His father disowned him after he graduated and took a teaching job."

Nathan shook his head. "I can't understand parents doing that."

"I don't think his mother wanted to, but it was his father's way of trying to control him. Ivan Warren is wealthy, and he thinks that money gives him power. Clara goes along with him because she doesn't know what else to do."

"She must be very weak."

Beth sighed. "I used to feel sorry for her...for them. I had Mark, we had a wonderful life, and they could have shared it. But now I'm so angry at what they're doing. I've been home with Dorie since she was born. Because I felt it was important to both of us, I used Mark's benefits to live on so I didn't have to go to work right away. But now I do have to go back. Ivan and Clara insist they can make a better home for Dorie than I can."

"Why don't they just baby-sit for you?" Nathan asked with the pragmatism that had gotten him through life.

"Even if I'd let them, and I'm not sure I would because of the cold controlling atmosphere Dorie would be exposed to, they want more than that. My lawyer and I met with them and their lawyer. It's as if they want some kind of second chance. Mark is gone, so they want to raise Dorie!"

"But, Beth, if you're a good mother—"

She didn't let him finish, but pushed herself to her knees. "I *am* a good mother," she said succinctly.

"This was a crazy idea, thinking I could take my lawyer's advice and marry a stranger for convenience and the law's sake. I might as well run off to Alaska. It would be easier."

As she stood, Nathan caught her hand. "Now wait a minute. Don't even consider a life on the run, moving from one place to the next. *That* certainly can't be the life you want for your daughter."

Beth didn't move as her eyes glistened with her inner turmoil. "I can't imagine life without Dorie. And if I have to run..."

Nathan stood, still holding her hand. "A judge can't decide to take her away from you simply because you have to go back to work."

"My lawyer says he can. There are precedent-setting cases happening more and more often. We can fight, but I don't have the money my in-laws do."

Nathan ran his finger over Beth's knuckles, appreciating the softness of her skin, the beauty of her, standing before him, baring her heart because she had no choice. He thought about a precious two-year-old with no father and how very much he wanted to be a father and have a family. It had been a lifelong dream that had never materialized.

He cocked his head and studied her. "Marriage would be better than running, if you can find someone who wants the same things you do."

"The same things?" she asked, her voice breaking.

"A home, a family, children. Jessie knows they're important to me."

"You wouldn't actually consider..."

He smiled because she couldn't say it. Would he actually consider marrying a stranger? He was attracted to her—no doubt about that. Her situation grabbed his heart. No one should have to face losing their child.

It was mind-boggling for him to consider marriage again. Yet, if marrying Beth could give him the family he'd always dreamed of... Searching her face, he admitted, "Maybe I'm considering lots of things I never would have considered this morning."

Beth's eyes grew wide and even bluer. "Um, I'm not sure what to say or do next."

He chuckled. "I don't think there's an instruction sheet for this one. Maybe before we put any more thought into this I should meet Dorie."

Beth snuck a surreptitious glance at Nathan as he guided his forest green sedan down the streets of Four Oaks toward her apartment. "I really don't know much about you. Jessie told me you've lived in Roanoke since you graduated from college and you own a sports equipment store."

"That's right." After a pause he asked, "She didn't tell you why having a family means so much to me?"

"No. She said I should ask you the personal questions myself."

He nodded. "That's Jessie. I'm glad she and Gavin managed to find their way back to each other."

Beth knew Gavin and Jessie had fallen in love in college and lost touch. Nine years later when Gavin discovered Jessie had borne him a child, they'd fallen in love again. But at the moment Beth was more interested in Nathan's history. "So why does having a family mean so much to you?"

He pulled into the parking lot of her apartment complex and switched off the ignition. "As I've heard it, my mother died when I was four. Six months later my father decided he didn't want to take care of a kid on his own, and he put me in foster care. He never came back from a trip out West. I went from foster home to foster home, never feeling as if I belonged, most of the time living with people who didn't care if I did. The idea of having a family someday became more than a dream—it was a goal."

"Jessie did say you were divorced," Beth said softly.

Unlatching his seat belt, he faced her. "And you want to know why."

She could see the pain still lingering in his green eyes and realized she had no right to pry. "It's none of my business."

Tilting his head, he studied her for a long moment. "Considering the question you asked me, it could become your business. But for now let's just say it fell apart—like lots of marriages do these days."

She felt like leaning closer to him, stroking his jaw.... "I'm sorry," she said.

They were in complete accord for the moment, both of them sharing a loss. Nathan bent toward her, brought his hand up as if to touch her, but then dropped it and reached for the keys. "Which apartment did you say you live in?"

With a feeling of disappointment mingled with relief, she opened her door. "Four."

Beth led Nathan up a few concrete steps to the path that passed apartments one, two, and three. Stopping at four, she took her key from her purse and opened the door.

"Mommee . . . Mommee," Dorie called as she ran from the kitchen to the living room.

Beth scooped her up into her arms. "Watcha doin', cupcake?"

Dorie shrugged and nestled into her shoulder.

Rosa Panetto came into the living room. "She just helped me fold some laundry. You want I—" Seeing Nathan, she stopped.

Beth said, "Rosa, this is Nathan Maxwell. Nathan, this is Rosa. She's one of the few people I trust to look after Dorie. When I go back to work, she's going to baby-sit for me."

Rosa looked Nathan up and down. "Nice to meet you, Mr. Maxwell. Beth, you want me to stay or go?"

Beth had to smile. One thing she liked most about Rosa was that she didn't mince words. Opening her purse, Beth took out the appropriate amount of money and handed it to the elderly lady. "You can leave. We're going to take Dorie back to the party with us, if she wants to go."

Rosa closed Beth's hand over the money. "You weren't gone long enough for me to do anything. Save your money for better things."

"But, Rosa . . ."

She went to the door. "Call me if you need me. ¿Capisce?"

Beth smiled at the woman who had been so kind to her since Mark's death. "I will."

Rosa took a last look at Nathan and then closed the door behind her.

"Why do I feel as if I've been X-rayed by an expert?" Nathan asked good-naturedly.

Beth laughed. "Because you have been. I'll probably get an earful as soon as Rosa gets a chance. She's become as protective of me and Dorie as a mother grizzly." As Beth talked, she crossed to the sofa and sat her daughter on her lap. "Honey, there's somebody I want you to say hi to. This is Nathan. He came here to meet you."

Dorie stuck her thumb in her mouth and looked up at Nathan's face.

He must have realized his height would seem overwhelming to a little girl. Angling around the coffee table, he crouched beside her so she could look down at him.

With one large finger he traced over the ice-cream cone embroidered on her shirt. "Do you like ice cream?"

Dorie kept her thumb in her mouth but nodded. He grinned at her. "Good. Because there's a party going on right now where I'm sure there'll be lots of ice cream and cake. Would you like to go with your mom and me to get some?"

"Icin'?" the two-year-old asked.

Nathan looked to Beth for help.

"She wants to know if the cake will have icing. Sometimes I make cakes that don't."

Nathan chuckled. "Do you like icing?"

Dorie nodded again.

"Then let's go get some," he suggested.

Dorie looked up at Beth and said firmly, "Icin'."

Beth laughed, shifted Dorie to the sofa and stood. "All right. Icing and cake and ice cream but you have to eat some real food first. Let me go pack a few things in your bag, then we can go." As Beth headed for Dorie's bedroom, she waited for the patter of footsteps behind her. When she didn't hear them, she stopped and turned, peeking around the wall into the living room. Nathan was sitting on the sofa beside Dorie, and she was letting him tie her shoelace.

Beth watched as Nathan murmured something to Dorie and she giggled. Beth's gaze fell to the coffee table and the picture of Mark and her. Suddenly she realized no matter what did or didn't happen with Nathan, nothing would ever be the same again.

Chapter Two

Nathan lifted Dorie to the top of the sliding board and held on to her as she glided over the surface and giggled with the pleasure of the motion. She stared up at him and grinned. "I . . . gin."

He was catching on to her language. So when she scampered off the edge of the sliding board and ran to the ladder, he was prepared for her quickness. Catching her around the waist, he lifted her to the top.

She seemed to like him. And she'd already captured his heart. It was obvious Beth gave her plenty of love, affection and nurturing. Dorie was a ray of sunshine, and her smile reached a place inside Nathan that had been sad all his life.

And then there was Beth. She was watching him closely. Who could blame her? Even now as she stood a few feet away talking with another guest, her gaze was never far from her daughter. Throughout feeding Dorie bites of hamburger and cake, she'd let her own food get cold. Finally, with her permission, he'd held Dorie on his lap and fed her ice cream. Beth's blue eyes had followed his every move and Dorie's interaction with him.

As Beth finished her conversation and walked toward him now, he wondered what she was thinking. His own thoughts raced, examining possibilities, glimpsing a future much different from yesterday's.

Scooping her daughter into her arms, Beth smiled at Nathan. "I'm going to get her something to drink."

Beth's smile touched the same place in his heart as Dorie's. Trying not to be distracted by it, he saw Dorie's face was flushed, her hair damp on her forehead. He suddenly realized the responsibility of taking care of a child who was too young to know or express what she needed.

He tapped the tip of Dorie's nose. "Save some for me. I'll be over in a few minutes." He needed some time to absorb what was happening and to decide what he wanted to happen next.

The expression on Beth's face was uncertain as she nodded and headed toward the striped canopy. Maybe she'd already dismissed the idea of marriage as too farfetched to consider. Maybe Alaska was looking better and better to a woman with a child she was determined to protect.

As Nathan leaned against a tree, he watched the flutter of a robin's wings in the bird bath. Suddenly he sensed he wasn't alone.

"This is *my* birthday. *I'm* the one who should be contemplating life," Gavin joked as he came up beside Nathan.

Nathan had been friends with Gavin since college. Although Gavin's years at med school had caused limited contact, his friend's move to Four Oaks to practice as a pediatrician at the hospital had reconnected them once again. "Not contemplating life. Deciding if I want to take a risk with it."

"Uh-oh. Does your stockbroker have a hot tip?"

"No, I'm wondering if a marriage of convenience has a better chance these days than the traditional method."

Gavin looked astonished. "What are you talking about?"

"Do you know Beth Warren's situation? She needs a husband to keep her daughter."

His friend shook his head. "Jessie told me about the custody suit. But, Nathan. Are you crazy? A marriage of convenience? You don't *know* her!"

"I knew Elaine. And look what happened."

"But, Nathan..."

"I want a family, Gavin. You know how much."

Gavin raked his hand through his black hair. "You're *not* going to jump into this."

"No, but I'm going to give it plenty of thought." Nathan's intrigued gaze found Beth under the canopy.

Beth was aware of Nathan's gaze on her. She didn't feel uncomfortable, but rather disconcerted, and if she had to admit it, a little proud. There was appreciation there for her as a woman. She'd forgotten about being a woman the past two years and had concentrated on being a mother.

After Dorie drank water from the cup, she wrapped her arms around Beth's neck and laid her head on her mother's shoulder. Beth knew her daughter was getting tired.

Nathan ambled across the lawn toward them, his long legs moving him with an athlete's gait, smooth and controlled. He picked up a cup of soda and drank half of it, his eyes staying on Beth and Dorie.

Then he smiled. "She looks sleepy."

Beth rubbed her cheek against Dorie's hair. "I should be going."

When Nathan didn't respond, she figured her crazy proposal had been just that—crazy. Finding a husband was difficult under the best of circumstances. Asking a man to take on a wife and child for nobility's sake was sheer absurdity.

She shifted Dorie higher on her lap. "I have to say goodbye to Jessie and Gavin. It was nice meeting you...."

"I'm ready to leave, too. I'll walk you to your car."

After their goodbyes—including Gavin's raised brows and Jessie's compassionate smile—Nathan walked beside Beth, matching his pace to hers. At her car she stopped.

He smiled and tapped her daughter's sneaker. "It was nice meeting you, Dorie."

The two-year-old grinned up at him then stuck her thumb in her mouth.

Beth opened the back door and strapped Dorie into her car seat. When she reemerged and closed the door, Nathan was very close, so close she could feel the heat of his body.

"What's next?" he asked, his green eyes intense. "Alaska or finding a husband?"

She shook her head. "I was fooling myself, thinking I could do something so outrageous—"

He reached out then and touched her. A simple stroke of his thumb on her cheek. But she felt the heat, comfort and excitement from it in every fiber of her body. This couldn't be a natural response. She was reacting to the circumstances.

"Do you want to see me again?" he asked. "Because if you do, I'd like to spend time with you."

There was something about Nathan that pulled her toward him. It wasn't his looks or his personality or the sense of confidence surrounding him. It was a combination of everything that made up the man.

Not usually an impulsive person, nevertheless, she felt she needed to act impulsively now. "Would you like to come to dinner tomorrow?"

His smile widened into a grin. "Yes, I would. What time?"

"Around five?"

He nodded, then gazed into her eyes with a power that immobilized her. The breeze lifted a strand of her hair. The scents of August heat, summer and Nathan surrounded her. The world became the two of them, standing there, contemplating what could happen next.

Nathan lowered his head and suddenly Beth was more afraid than she'd ever been in her life. Of losing Dorie. Of Nathan. Of moving on.

She backed away and bumped the car door with her elbow.

Nathan took a step back as if he realized she needed the space. He said, "I'll pick up some ice cream for dessert. What's Dorie's favorite?"

Beth took a deep breath, trying to slow her racing pulse, trying to tell herself her world wasn't spinning out of control. "Chocolate marshmallow."

"My favorite, too," he said. "Don't go to a lot of trouble tomorrow. I'm easy to please."

Was he? In other areas besides food? How would he kiss? What kind of response would he expect? What if *she* couldn't respond?

Stop it.

The questions, the light in Nathan's eyes, the pulling she felt toward him made her scurry around to the driver's side of the car. Over the hood she said, "I'll see you tomorrow." Then she quickly opened the door, slid in and switched on the ignition.

When she pulled away from the curb, she glanced in her rearview mirror. Nathan was standing there, watching her drive away.

On Sunday evening when Nathan rang Beth's doorbell, a sense of anticipation made him shift from one foot to the other. Already drawn to Beth and her child, he realized what a big step marriage to Beth would be. Could it work out? Would she decide the idea was too insane to consider? He tried to tell himself not to be too hopeful. Hope had led to disappointment too many times to count, over the past few years. Still, the idea of seeing Beth and Dorie again brought a hum to his heart.

As the moments ticked by and Beth didn't answer the door, he frowned and rang the bell a second time.

Finally the door opened. But Beth wore a worried frown, not a smile that said she might be glad to see him. She was holding Dorie. "Hi. Come on in. I'm a little behind. Dorie's not feeling well."

When Beth backed up, he stepped inside. Dorie's cheeks were rosy. She'd tilted her head against her mother's shoulder, but she stared up at him with her big blue eyes.

Beth looked as if she could use a break. "What's wrong, little one?" Without hesitating, he held out his arms to her.

Dorie watched him for a moment, then leaned toward him, her arms outstretched. Nathan cuddled her against his chest, relishing the feel of her small arms around his neck. A lump formed in his throat.

"She hasn't eaten anything since the ice cream last night. She doesn't want to drink, either, but I've been coaxing her with grape juice. Her temperature is 100. I gave her children's acetaminophen this morning, but she's not feeling any better. I was hoping she'd eat some supper. If she won't, I'm going to take her to the emergency room."

Nathan gently patted Dorie's back. "What can I do to help?"

Beth raised her gaze to his. "Are you sure you want to stay?"

He felt the heat from Dorie's cheek through his white polo shirt. Handing Beth the bag with the ice cream he'd brought for dessert, he answered, "Yes." He'd never been more sure about anything except his desire for a family.

Appreciation lit Beth's face for a moment and then was gone, as if she was afraid to feel it, as if she was afraid to depend on anyone's help. As she turned away and headed for the kitchen, Nathan noticed the straightness of her back. The patterned blue-and-green silk blouse and shorts molded to her, enhancing her curves. But her squared shoulders made him realize this was a woman who carried her own burdens.

He held and tried to occupy Dorie as Beth mashed potatoes and removed the roasted chicken pieces from the oven. She'd set the table with blue-and-white-flowered china that he suspected she didn't use every day. In the center of the table sat a milk glass vase with three pink rosebuds. She liked flowers. He'd have to remember that.

After Beth set the meal on the table, she opened her arms to her daughter. "Come here, baby. Let's try to eat some supper."

Beth's expression grew more worried as she offered Dorie small bites of chicken, then a cooled dab of mashed potatoes. Dorie just shook her head and turned her face into Beth's shoulder.

Nathan managed a few mouthfuls but could see Beth was getting more upset. "Try the juice again."

Dorie took a few swallows of the juice.

Beth patted Dorie's leg. "Good girl. How about some more?"

Dorie shook her head, her lips pursed together.

The doorbell rang.

Nathan asked, "Are you expecting anyone?"

Beth shook her head. "No."

As she started to rise with Dorie in her arms, Nathan pushed his chair back. "Stay put. I'll get it."

When he opened the door, he found an older couple, their expressions serious. The man wore a suit even on a day as warm as this one. Sweat beaded above his bushy gray brows and along his receding hairline. The woman, whose black hair was obviously dyed, wore a slim green dress with heavy gold earrings and matching necklace. They both looked astonished at Nathan's appearance at the door.

"We're here to see Beth," the man declared. "Who are you?"

"I'm a friend of Beth's," Nathan answered smoothly. "Who should I say is looking for her?"

The older man pulled open the screen door and tried to step inside. "Tell her her father-in-law needs to talk with her."

Nathan blocked the man from stepping into the living room. "She might not want to see you. Wait here." He shut the screen door, keeping the couple on the outside.

In the kitchen again, he said to Beth, "It's your in-laws. Do you want me to tell them you can't see them?"

Beth shook her head and stood with Dorie in her arms. "I'm afraid that will make the situation worse. Maybe they've come to work something out," she said hopefully as she headed toward the living room.

Beth had always considered herself an optimistic person. Although she'd lost her father when she was a teenager, and her mother a year after she'd married Mark, she'd felt as if her parents had given her a solid foundation of love and support that she still carried with her now. Mark's parents' attitude toward their son had baffled her. She'd never stopped hoping they'd eventually support Mark's decisions and reconcile with him.

But as she approached the door and saw the hard expression on Ivan's face, she knew the Warrens hadn't turned up on her doorstep to work anything out. Still, she opened her door to them. "Come in. We were just finishing dinner."

Dorie became restless in Beth's arms and fretted.

Clara examined her granddaughter closely. "What's wrong with her, Beth? She looks flushed."

Beth smoothed her hand over her daughter's brow. "I think she has a sore throat..."

"You think?" Ivan bellowed. "What kind of mother are you that you don't know what's wrong with your child? Like I told you, Clara, she belongs with us."

Ivan's loud voice bothered Dorie and she squirmed in Beth's arms, hugging her tighter around the neck. Beth took a step away from the Warrens closer to Nathan. "She does *not* belong with you, she belongs with me. I thought you came today because you realized that."

"We came today," Ivan announced, "to tell you you don't stand a chance. You know that as well as we do. You don't have the money to fight us in court. We can keep it going, you can't. You *will* lose. Don't you think it would be better for Dorie—"

Not easily pushed to anger, Beth had to come to grips with the rage swelling inside her. Who did these two think they were, judging her, deciding what was best for *her* daughter? "I know what's best for Dorie. I love her. You don't. You see her as some sort of prize. You lost your son so you want her. Well, you won't get her. Not today, not tomorrow, not ever. You wanted to control Mark, to manipulate him until he became what you thought he should be. Fortunately he was too strong to let you do that. Dorie and I are just as strong."

"Money makes a man strong. Not ideals," Ivan said tersely.

Beth shook her head. "In your world. Not in mine."

Ivan stepped closer to her. "You're a foolish woman if you think you can win against me, and—"

Dorie started crying.

Beth raised her chin and her voice. "Please leave."

Ivan didn't budge. "I'm not going anywhere until I'm good and ready."

Dorie cried harder, and Beth stroked her daughter's hair.

Silent during the interchange, Nathan now stepped forward. "Beth asked you to leave."

Ivan glared at Nathan. "This is none of your business."

Nathan pointed to the door. "Don't make me do more than ask you to get out."

Clara tugged on her husband's elbow. "C'mon, dear. This is Beth's home. We'll call Richard."

From what Beth had seen since she married Mark, Ivan didn't listen to his wife. But the name of his lawyer seemed to calm him. "All right, Beth. We'll leave. But you'll be hearing from us. Soon."

As Dorie cried louder, Nathan crossed to the door and waited.

With a last glare at Beth, Ivan turned and walked out, leaving his wife to follow. Nathan closed the door behind them.

Suddenly Beth's knees felt shaky, and she sank down on the sofa, crooning softly to her daughter, trying to calm them both. As Nathan sat beside her, she leaned her head against Dorie's and murmured, "Thank you."

He shook his head. "I didn't do anything."

"I couldn't have made him leave without calling the police. He's a stubborn man."

Dorie restlessly moved her head back and forth on Beth's shoulder. No matter what else was happening, she had to take care of her daughter first. "I'm going to take Dorie to the emergency room. I'm sorry you were here for all this...."

"I'll come with you."

"Nathan, we're not your responsibility."

"I'll drive so you can take care of Dorie."

The determined expression on his face said his mind was made up. She was too concerned about Dorie to argue.

* * *

The emergency room was busy. Nathan stood beside Beth as she gave information at the registration desk. He even held Dorie for a while as she grew more restless and tired of waiting.

Beth watched him read to her from one of the children's books. His voice was deep and calm. Dorie had settled into the crook of his arm naturally. She pointed to the pictures as he read.

Finally a nurse showed them to a cubicle. Nathan lifted Dorie and carried her, as if he'd done it many times before.

Only a few minutes passed before the curtain opened and Gavin stepped inside. His surprise was obvious. Crossing to the table where Beth sat with Dorie, he gave Nathan a quick once-over. "What brings you here?"

Beth brushed Dorie's blond hair from her forehead. "She won't eat and is drinking very little. Her fever started mid-morning. I was afraid everything would get worse if I waited until tomorrow."

Gavin smiled at Dorie. "Hi, there, sweetheart. Can I take a look at your throat?"

Dorie nodded.

After checking her throat and ears and eyes, Gavin examined the rest of her gently, but thoroughly, probing her stomach, listening to her heart and lungs. Finished, he stuffed his stethoscope into his pocket. "Her throat is red and her glands are swollen. Hopefully, if we get her on antibiotics, we can prevent an earache from developing. Keep giving her acetaminophen for the pain and get her to drink as much as possible. Popsicles might go over well."

"I should have thought of that," Beth said.

Gavin smiled. "One person can't think of everything." He patted Dorie on the head. "Call me if she's not feeling better by Tuesday morning."

"I will. Thank you, Gavin."

He wrote the prescription, handed it to her and said, "You take care of yourself, too." With a lift of his hand, he left the cubicle.

Beth took the small paper gown from her daughter and slipped her pinafore over her head.

Nathan leaned against the corner of the table. "If we stop at the grocery store with the pharmacy, we can pick up the Popsicles."

Dressed, Dorie reached up to Beth for the comfort of her arms. "Nathan, I can't tell you how much I appreciate this."

He shrugged and smiled. "No problem. What else do I have to do on a Sunday evening?"

"I can imagine a few more enjoyable activities than sitting in an ER."

He came close to her and looked down at her with a gentleness she'd never felt before as he said, "More enjoyable, maybe. But not as worthwhile." Then he tapped Dorie's nose. "Come on, little one. Let's find you some Popsicles."

About a half hour later Beth unlocked the door to her apartment, Popsicles and prescription in hand. Nathan followed close behind, carrying Dorie.

After setting her in her high chair, Nathan took the Popsicles from the box and asked Dorie, "Orange, cherry or grape?"

"Chew . . . ee," she answered.

Beth quickly took the bottle of medicine from the bag, plucked a spoon from a drawer and gave Dorie her first dose of antibiotic. Her daughter made a face and swallowed. "Good girl," Beth praised. "Now, let's try a Popsicle. It'll make your throat feel better."

Nathan unwrapped the icy treat and handed it to Dorie. But it slipped from her chubby fingers.

Beth took a dish from the cupboard. "I'll chop it up and she can eat it as finger food. She'll do better with it."

As she set the dish in front of Dorie, she saw the light blinking on her answering machine. She pressed the button.

Ivan Warren's voice played. "Tomorrow morning, Beth, Clara and I will be talking with a representative from Social Services. We will not allow you to neglect Dorie's health or parade strange men around her. You might have pushed us out of your apartment but that's as far as you will be able to push. *I* have the clout and the contacts. We will get custody of Dorie."

The machine whirred, clicked and rewound.

Beth pulled out the chair beside Dorie and sat, her legs shaking. Ivan Warren *did* have clout. And contacts. How was she ever going to fight him?

Nathan reached across the table and covered her hand. "He's just trying to intimidate you."

"He's succeeding," she murmured, all of her attention on Dorie, the joy of her life. Finally she looked at Nathan. "He's pulling out the big guns now. Showing me just how tough he's going to make this fight. I don't know what I'm going to do. I don't have the money this will take."

Alaska was looking better to Beth. So was packing up all their belongings and leaving on a very long trip. In her mind she tried to find another option.

Then Nathan said, "You don't need money. You need a husband. Marry me."

Chapter Three

Nathan's words held a gentle command as his fingers tightened around hers. She couldn't believe how the deep vibration of his voice comforted her, how the heat of his hand sent tingles through her. But even if she was drawn to him, attracted to him, they were discussing something much more serious than attraction.

She pulled her hand away from his. "You don't know what you're offering."

Leaning back in his chair, he gave her a small smile. "If I remember correctly, you're the one who proposed yesterday."

Unable to prevent the heat flaring in her cheeks, she pushed back her hair and went to the sink for a washcloth to wipe Dorie's face and hands. "I don't know why it popped out like that. I guess I was desperate."

Although she didn't hear him move, she suddenly sensed him standing behind her. His proximity unsettled her and she turned on the spigot, taking her time soaking the washcloth and wringing it out.

"Beth, look at me."

Taking a deep breath, she faced him.

With a searching thoroughness that disconcerted her as much as his six-foot-two solid bulk only a few inches from her, he asked, "Because you were desperate, would you have proposed to just any man at that party?"

She didn't have to think about the question very long. "No."

Nathan touched her cheek with his thumb, sliding it along her cheekbone. "We connected."

The pad of his thumb on her skin made her tremble. Fear? Panic? Attraction? She shook her head. "Did we? Nathan, we're not talking about a date here. We're talking about our lives!"

"I know that. I know exactly what I'm proposing."

"Why? Why would you even consider taking on the responsibility of a woman you don't know and her child?"

"I want a family more than I've ever wanted anything in my life. We'd both have strong motivation for this marriage, Beth, and making it work."

Dorie started fretting.

Instead of being annoyed by the interruption, Nathan nodded to the melted Popsicle on the high-chair tray. "I think she's had enough."

Slipping from between Nathan and the counter, Beth went to her daughter and took the tray from the high chair, setting it on the table. "She's tired. I'm going to put her in her crib and see if she'll fall asleep. If you have someplace to go or things to do..."

"I left the evening open for us. Take care of Dorie. I'll wait."

Nathan heard Beth murmur to Dorie as she carried her to her room. Restless, he picked up dishes on the table and took them to the sink. Beth had stowed away the leftover food before they'd left for the emergency room but had let everything else sit. Dorie was obviously her main priority.

And if Beth agreed to his proposal, she and Dorie could be his.

He didn't consider himself a noble man. He'd asked her to marry him for his own selfish reasons. He'd taken the usual route the first time. He'd wanted to be financially secure before he married and started a family. At twenty-six, when he'd met Elaine, he'd felt as if the time was right. They'd been engaged for a year before they'd married. He'd meant his vows for better or worse, but apparently Elaine hadn't. He'd been bitter at first, but a month after their divorce, he'd decided bitterness was too big a price to pay for a failed marriage.

His almost instant attraction to Beth was uncommon. Elaine was a beautiful woman but she'd never provoked this base need Nathan felt to touch and kiss Beth...protect her...make love to her. Maybe it was the circumstances, but he'd reacted to her before he'd even known what they were.

And Dorie. Such a wonderful child any father would want to cherish and protect.

Was he crazy to consider marrying Beth because she needed a husband and he wanted a family? No. A marriage of convenience, if they shared the same goals, could be stronger than any traditional courtship and marriage. Now all he had to do was convince her.

By the time Beth returned to the kitchen, Nathan had loaded the dishwasher. She looked surprised. "You didn't have to do that."

He shrugged. "Did Dorie fall asleep?"

"After I rocked her for a bit. She didn't sleep much last night."

So, of course, Beth hadn't, either, he realized. She looked pale, with faint blue smudges under her eyes. During supper as she'd tried to get Dorie to eat, Beth hadn't taken a bite. "Are you hungry?"

She shook her head.

"It won't help Dorie if you get run-down," he remarked, his voice gruffer than he'd intended.

"Nathan, I don't need a keeper," she returned with a touch of defiance.

He realized how patronizing he sounded, how she must hate being in a position where she felt powerless. His taking over and trying to "fix" everything obviously wouldn't work with Beth.

He approached her slowly because he didn't want her to back away. "You don't need a keeper, just a reminder to take care of yourself, too. I could get you a magnet for the refrigerator."

The lightness of his tone coaxed a smile from her. Then it faded. "I'm sorry I snapped. I'm just feeling..."

"Overwhelmed," he said.

She nodded. "Nathan, your offer seems to make sense. At least right now. But I think we both need more time to consider it. Decisions made in desperation aren't usually good decisions. We both have to be sure."

Nathan wondered how happy Beth was with her life the way it was...if she'd even considered meeting and dating someone before this situation with her in-laws had come up. He'd seen the photographs in the living room of her and her husband. They looked happy. Was she still in love with him?

The idea unnerved Nathan. This woman standing before him with her silky blond hair, her heart-shaped face, her beautiful blue eyes, had gotten under his skin the way no other woman had. He'd lived long enough to know desire, its depth and its temptation. Maybe Beth needed to feel a little of that temptation. She trembled whenever he touched her. She didn't back away until she analyzed what was happening. Her eyes, her face, her blushes were honestly expressive. She was unique in that respect. Nathan dealt with men and women on a daily basis who wore masks and guarded their thoughts. Himself included.

Her blue eyes now held doubts, uncertainty and a vulnerability he found almost impossible to believe. Sliding his hand under her hair, he searched for a sign that would tell him she wasn't attracted to him. But he didn't find it. Her cheeks became rosier. He could feel her pulse increase under his thumb. The blue of her eyes seemed to deepen. She didn't startle; she didn't pull back; she waited. Maybe she was as curious as he was.

He bent his head slowly, his gaze on hers, giving her the opportunity to pull away. Finally her eyelids fluttered closed. As his lips hovered close enough to brush hers, he realized he could be making a mistake, but he was a realist now, and they both deserved to know exactly what kind of desire would or wouldn't flare between them.

When his lips first touched hers, every muscle in his body tightened. Her scent, both sweetness and woman, grabbed his chest and made his breaths short. Her mouth was soft and warm, her hair silk in his fingers. The temptation to take more, feel more, want more, was too strong to ignore. He slipped his tongue along her lower lip, and she let him in.

Nathan forgot gentleness and finesse and coaxing. The taste of Beth, her heat, her softness whirled around him until he was caressing her back and probing her mouth with deep strokes of his tongue. Her hands slid to his shoulders. She held on, then kneaded his muscles in rhythm with the cadence of the kiss.

He held her tighter, and when her breasts pressed against his chest, he groaned. Arousal should be old hat to a divorced man after a five-year marriage, but this blazing fire was different from anything he'd ever felt. Beth's response was as natural as everything else about her. And he knew he would push to know how far her natural response could go, if he didn't stop himself now.

Reluctantly he loosened his hold, stopped the kiss and raised his head.

Beth's expression was dazed.

He knew the feeling. Clearing his throat, he dropped his arms to his sides. "That will definitely give us something to think about."

If he didn't leave now, he would kiss her again. Gut instinct told him that would be the wrong move. When she didn't respond, he wondered if she was reliving their kiss or worrying about the future. Crossing to the door, he stopped with his hand on the knob. He wanted to say so many things...hopeful things. But...

Maybe Beth was right and they both needed time to think. He opened the door, then closed it behind him.

Beth slowly walked into the bathroom and stared at her face in the medicine cabinet mirror. Her cheeks were flushed, her hair slightly disheveled, her lips rosy and kiss swollen. Who *was* this woman?

She'd kissed a relative stranger... a man she barely knew. And she'd felt such a need, and a want, and an ache...

Oh, Mark. Why do I feel as if I've betrayed you? Why do I feel as if you're slipping away to a place where I'll forget about us and what we shared?

As her body still sung with the passion she'd so briefly shared with Nathan Maxwell, as she slid her fingers over her still-heated lips, tears began to fall. *Oh, Dorie, what are we going to do?*

* * *

When the phone rang Monday evening, Beth was feeding Dorie supper. She plucked the receiver from the wall. "Hello."

"Beth, it's Nathan. How's Dorie?"

She wasn't prepared to hear his voice. She wasn't prepared for the vivid sensations of their kiss that washed over her. Trying to ignore all of it, she answered, "She's feeling much better. She's drinking and eating again. Matter of fact, she has mashed potatoes smeared on her face and in her hair right now."

Nathan chuckled. "Good. And how are *you* doing?"

"I'm fine." What else could she say? *I've been thinking about you much too much, reliving a kiss that shook up my world?* Uh-uh.

"Are you thinking, Beth?"

At least she could be open about that. "Too much," she responded.

He was silent for a moment. "I won't keep you from Dorie. Take care of the two of you."

"I will. Thanks for calling."

Nathan said goodbye and Beth felt...disappointed. That was silly. She was the one who'd told him they both needed time to think.

So why would she rather see him than think?

The following evening Beth sat on a bench in the park, watching Dorie play in the sandbox. Her daughter had been content for the past fifteen minutes, scooping sand into a bucket then dumping it out. Beth opened her purse and removed the three envelopes that had come in the mail. Did she think carrying them around would make money drop from the sky? The utilities had to be paid first, along with the rent. She could only hold out a few weeks, and if she had to go to court—

Two girls whizzed by Beth on in-line skates. The third person stopped, and when Beth looked up, she realized Jessie was smiling at her. Her helmet, arm and knee pads decked her out for the sport she enjoyed with her daughter.

Flicking off the helmet, she sat beside Beth on the bench. "How are you doing?"

"I brought Dorie out for some fresh air. She was sick the past couple of days, and I've tried to keep her quiet. Did Gavin tell you we saw him at the ER?"

"No. But everything between Gavin and his patients is confidential. I understand that."

"Nathan was with me," Beth confided to her friend.

Jessie arched her brows. "A peculiar date?"

Beth explained how she'd invited Nathan to dinner, about Ivan and Clara's unexpected visit and Dorie's sore throat.

"So... are you and Nathan going to see each other again? Or did all that scare him away?"

Beth shook her head. "I don't think Nathan scares easily. You should have seen him with Ivan."

"You sound impressed."

"He was so... protective. I sort of liked it, yet I know I have to fight my own battles."

Jessie ran her hand through her hair. "A little help never hurts."

Beth stared at Dorie playing in the sandbox, confused about the best way to safeguard her. "Nathan asked me to marry him."

Jessie gave a low whistle. "That was fast. I saw the way he looked at you at Gavin's party. But still..."

"It's not me. He wants a family. He's very clear about that."

"What do you mean it's not you? He'd be marrying *you*. I would hope there would be a few sparks."

Beth felt her cheeks heat up.

Jessie searched her friend's face. "There are a few sparks, aren't there?"

"There are sparks. There's guilt because I feel unfaithful to Mark. There's confusion because I'm even considering such a crazy move." She picked up the bills in her lap. "And there's necessity. That's what bothers me most. I hate the idea of getting married so someone can take care of me!"

Jessie's tone was calm. "Maybe you should look at it differently. If you get married, you're doing it so you can take care of Dorie."

Beth thought over what Jessie said. "If it weren't for this custody suit, I wouldn't even be considering marriage."

"Because you're not over Mark?"

"Because I wonder if I can ever be as happy as I was with Mark. And to start like this...I need more time."

"Do you want time so you can avoid making a decision?"

"I want time to make sure I have to make *this* decision."

"And Nathan?"

Beth sighed. "I'm supposed to think about it...us...marriage. I don't do anything *but* think about it and hope and pray Ivan and Clara change their mind."

"Do you think there's a chance of that happening?"

Beth returned the bills to her purse, remembering Ivan's vehemence, the threat in his phone message. "All I can do is continue to hope they'll drop the custody suit."

Jessie patted Beth's hand. "I'll hope with you."

Waiting wasn't something Nathan did well. Especially when he had a goal. Especially when he'd decided Beth and Dorie were the family he wanted. Saturday morning he parked in front of their apartment and went to the door.

The weather had cooled to a comfortable eighty for the day, and the living room door stood open. He rang the bell.

When Beth appeared, Nathan's heart pounded faster. Her flowered skirt and white cotton blouse made her look feminine...and totally delectable. She opened the door and he stepped inside.

"Are you busy today?" he asked, impatient with preliminary conversation they didn't need but she might feel was necessary.

"I was just going to run some errands with Dorie."

"Go horseback riding with me."

Her brows arched, and her blue eyes widened. "I don't know how to ride. Besides, Rosa is away today and—"

"We'll take Dorie along. She'll love it."

"You aren't serious!"

He stepped closer to her, longing to do more than settle for kissing distance. "I'm serious. About more than horseback riding. Thinking things over apart from each other isn't as good as spending time together. If nothing else, that kiss told me that."

Beth's cheeks pinkened at the mention of their kiss. "But horseback riding? I don't know..."

"Some friends of mine own a stable. I can ride whenever I like. They even teach children's classes so they'll have a helmet for Dorie. She'll probably like being around the horses. If you decide you don't want to ride, we can just walk the grounds."

"I don't have riding gear..."

He wondered if Beth's excuses had more to do with riding or with him. As she looked up at him, her sweet scent surrounding him, he wanted to kiss her. Restraining the urge, he asked bluntly, "Do you want to spend some time with me?"

He saw the turmoil in her eyes as she made her decision. Finally she said, "Yes."

As Nathan transferred Dorie's car seat to his car, Beth packed Dorie's bag. It was much easier to put Nathan out of her mind when he wasn't around. Even then, it was difficult enough. Their kiss had been more than memorable. All she had to do was think about it, and she needed a cold shower. She also experienced more confusion than she'd ever dealt with.

"Horsee, Mommee."

Beth looked over at her daughter who'd plopped on the carpet in her bedroom with a stuffed horse. Beth had explained to her daughter where they were going.

She picked up Dorie's bag and offered her her hand. "Let's go see some *real* horses."

Dorie grinned, scrambled to her feet and clutched Beth's fingers.

As Nathan drove to Roanoke, Beth couldn't resist taking quick peeks at him. He wore jeans today and a pale blue T-shirt that had seen many washings. But it didn't matter what he wore. She was aware of his muscled arms as he turned the steering wheel, his taut thighs as his foot went from the accelerator to the brake, his sheer bulk taking up most of the breathing space in the front seat. And she remembered again their kiss.

Cedars zipped by in rows and groves as Nathan asked, "Did you hear any more from your in-laws?"

"No. And not hearing makes me as nervous as open confrontation. I wonder what they're planning. I expected to get a call from Health and Human Services after Ivan's last threat, but none came."

Nathan slid her a glance. "Maybe they'll back down."

"I hope so. But from experience, I know Ivan doesn't back down easily."

"Did you have many run-ins with him?"

"No. But Mark did. When Ivan cut Mark off, Mark was devastated. But he knew if he wanted his own life, what made him happy, he couldn't give in to his father."

"You sound as if you loved your husband very much. Were you happy?"

"Very happy."

At that, Nathan's jaw set and the conversation ceased. Beth wondered why he'd become so quiet, but didn't know him well enough to ask. Instead, she turned in her seat to look at her daughter. Dorie cooed to the stuffed horse. Beth wished Mark could see his daughter... could know her. But then, maybe he did.

As Nathan drove under the arch for Longmeadow Stables, Beth gazed at the manicured lawns, the white fence, the gently rolling hills surrounding the buildings. "Did you say a friend of yours owns this?"

"Actually, I'm a partner in Longmeadow. I was thinking about opening a second store when the opportunity to invest in the stables came up. I'm glad I did. Longmeadow is doing well, and I have a place to spend time off."

Nathan parked on a macadam lot with several other cars. When Beth looked over at the barn, she could see children on horses in the fenced-in area.

Beth unbuckled Dorie from the car seat.

Nathan held his arms out to her. "Do you want to go see the horses?"

The two-year-old reached up and held Nathan by the neck. "Horsees."

He laughed and lifted her into his arms.

The interior of the stable was cooler than outside. The smell of hay tickled Beth's nose. She followed Nathan to a stall housing a sturdy chestnut.

The horse neighed as they approached.

Dorie asked, "Horsee?"

Nathan nodded. "Yep. This is Molly." When he extended his hand, the horse nuzzled it.

Beth watched her daughter lean forward and hold out her hand.

Nathan saw the worried expression on Beth's face. He took Dorie's hand and gently smoothed it over the horse's nose.

Dorie giggled. "I...gin."

Nathan did it again. Then he stepped to the next stall where a gray horse stood with his nose in the feed trough. "And this is Smokey. He rarely moves faster than a walk. I thought I'd saddle him for you, and I'll take Dorie on Molly with me."

"I don't know, Nathan."

"We'll just walk them. If Dorie doesn't like it, we'll turn around and come back."

"I've never been on a horse..."

He grinned. "The hardest part is mounting, and with your little bit of weight, you won't have a problem. Trust me."

Trust him. Could she trust Nathan? She wasn't sure, and until she was...

Nathan searched her face, his green eyes serious. "If you can't trust me, think of this as a new experience."

"I'm not used to trusting someone else with Dorie...or her safety."

"What about Rosa?"

"Rosa folds laundry and plays patty-cake with her. That's different than putting her on a horse."

"With me, she'll be as safe as if she were sitting in a rocking chair."

Beth was torn between keeping Dorie safe and giving her an experience that might thrill her. They were here. Dorie didn't seem to be afraid of the horses. "All right. But if she starts to cry or squirm..."

"I'll put her safely on the ground."

Beth studied Nathan, her daughter nestled in his strong arms, the grin on her face as she watched the horse. Taking a deep breath, she said, "Let's saddle up."

Beth held Dorie as Nathan saddled the two horses. Then he took Dorie from her and held Smokey. "Put your left foot in the stirrup and pull yourself up by the horn. Then swing your right leg over."

As Beth tried to fit her foot into the stirrup, she mumbled, "I should have watched more Westerns."

Nathan chuckled.

Finally she pulled herself up and swung her leg over. The leather creaked, and she wondered if she trusted a few straps to hold her in place.

Nathan patted the horse's neck and let Dorie pet the horse, too. "Dorie and I are going to lead Smokey a little until you get the feel of the saddle. Go with the motion instead of trying to hold yourself steady against it."

The first few minutes Beth felt uncomfortable, as if she were perched on top of a mountain, ready to topple off. But then, she tried to relax. The motion soon became soothing, and she smiled.

Nathan glanced up at her. "What do you think?"

"It *is* sort of like a rocking chair."

He laughed and walked back to the fence where he'd tied Molly. Then he handed Beth the reins.

"This looks harder than driving a car," she said softly.

He covered her hand. "It's much easier than driving a car because if you direct Smokey gently, he'll sense what you want. Press your heels against him when you want him to go. Give a gentle tug to the right or left to turn. Pull back on the reins if you want to stop. We won't worry about reverse until your next lesson."

Nathan's crooked grin told her he was enjoying teaching her. The deep green of his eyes invited her to have fun and to get to know him better.

Dorie smiled and then giggled as Nathan set her in the saddle, put the smallest helmet he could find on her head, then swung himself up behind her. She let out a laugh of delight as he put his arms around her, jiggled the reins and started moving forward.

Beth was busy watching her daughter's enjoyment when Nathan checked over his shoulder and beckoned to her. She applied a bit of pressure with her heels, and Smokey moved forward.

As Nathan promised, he kept Molly to a walk. They rode on a trail that made a close perimeter around the buildings. Every once in a while, Beth would catch Nathan watching her, and she wondered what he was thinking. As the sun rose high in the sky, he led them back to the stables.

He dismounted, lifted Dorie from Molly and tied the horse to the fence. Then he held Smokey by the halter. "Well, what did you think?"

She smiled. "I think I like riding more than driving."

A slow smile crept across his mouth and lit his eyes. "Then we'll have to do it again. Soon."

There was something about Nathan's eyes that made Beth want to stare into them forever. She shook the ridiculous notion away. "What's the best way to get down?"

Amusement laced his voice. "Hold on to the horn. Swing your right leg over the horse's back while you balance yourself on your foot in the stirrup."

Beth did as he directed. But when her feet touched the ground, he was standing close, just in case she'd gotten hung up. She wasn't used to this type of protectiveness in a man. She and Mark had been partners. Even when she'd been pregnant, he'd been caring, but not overly solicitous. She had a feeling Nathan was the type of man who'd monitor a pregnant wife's sleeping, eating and working habits.

Now why was she thinking about that? It wasn't as if she intended to get pregnant anytime soon.

Yet when she looked up at Nathan, she realized his entrance into her life had made her think about tons of things she hadn't thought about before. Impulsively she said, "Why don't we go back to my place and I'll make us something for lunch. Unless you have other plans."

"No other plans." His voice was husky, and she couldn't help wondering if he was thinking about kissing her again. Because she was definitely thinking about kissing him.

During the ride back to Beth's apartment, Dorie cooed and gibbered about "horsees". Beth and Nathan's gazes met many times, and they smiled. Back in her kitchen Beth chopped chicken and celery, adding grapes and almonds with a dressing while Nathan sat on the living room floor with Dorie building towers with blocks.

Beth couldn't remember the last time she'd enjoyed herself this much. When the doorbell rang, she suspected it might be Rosa coming to check on them.

Nathan called to her. "Beth, you have to sign for a certified letter."

Her stomach sank. Ivan and Clara. What else could it be?

She signed for the letter, and as the postman left, she stood with it in the doorway as if it might explode in her hand.

Nathan went to her, his expression concerned.

She opened the envelope, slid out the letter, then read it. Her heart hammered in her ears, and she realized she had to make a decision. Now.

Lifting her head, squaring her shoulders, she met Nathan's gaze and said, "If your offer of marriage still stands, I accept."

Then she handed the letter to him and waited for his response.

Chapter Four

Nathan took the letter from Beth's hand. After a quick but thorough reading, he realized why she'd accepted his proposal. The custody hearing was scheduled for the end of September. She didn't want to take the chance of losing her daughter.

He held no illusions about why she was accepting. He'd seen the stack of bills on her coffee table. And he suspected she was still in love with her deceased husband. If she married him, it would be out of sheer necessity.

But he'd be getting the family he'd always wanted. That's what mattered.

"My offer still stands. When do you want to get married?" he asked in answer to her question.

She licked her bottom lip, and her hand trembled as she reached for the letter. After a moment she said, "I

guess as soon as possible. So Ivan and Clara drop their
suit."

"I think we should go all out, though. So they know
it's the real thing—a church, tuxedos, the whole
works."

"Nathan, I can't!"

He gazed into her troubled eyes, wondering if she'd
changed her mind. "Why not?"

"I . . . I don't have the money for a gown and flowers and—"

"I'll handle the cost," he offered.

"I can't let you do that."

"We're getting married, Beth."

"I don't want to be dependent on you."

He saw the turmoil in her eyes. Because of the situation, she must feel as if all her power was slipping
away, let alone her right to call the shots. "We're entering a partnership. You're giving me the family I've
always wanted. I'm providing support. This isn't one-
sided. Both of us will do whatever we have to do to
protect Dorie. The cost of the wedding is a small price
to pay to convince Ivan and Clara Warren to leave you
alone."

Beth's eyes glistened. "This is all happening so fast.
I usually take time to make decisions and think them
through carefully."

Nathan tapped the envelope in her hand. "We don't
have time."

Beth walked away from him and sank down into a
chair with the letter. After glancing at it again, she
raised her head. "What do you think we should do
first?"

* * *

"It's perfect," Jessie declared.

Beth turned on the carpet-covered dais to give her friend a complete view of her wedding gown. It was the Wednesday afternoon before her wedding, and Beth was having her final fitting.

But she wasn't thinking about the satin and lace dress; her thoughts were on the wedding which was on Saturday. "I can't believe we've actually pulled this together in less than two weeks. Nathan's moving some things over tonight. I've made as much room as I can. Fortunately I have the basement for storage."

"Have you and Nathan talked about getting a bigger place?"

"Since we decided to get married, we haven't talked much at all. Except about the wedding."

"Are you having doubts?"

Beth reverently touched the off-white lace on her bodice. "Every minute. But I have to go through with it for Dorie. Nathan is so good with her. He'll make a terrific father."

"And husband?"

Since they'd decided to get married, Nathan had backed off physically. He'd spent most of his time and energy with Dorie, getting her used to him being around. Beth found herself terrifically drawn to Nathan, but she wasn't about to make any first moves. She was still trying to get used to the idea that a virtual stranger would soon be her husband.

"Beth?"

Beth realized she hadn't answered her friend's question. "I don't know what kind of husband Nathan will be. But I'll soon find out."

* * *

That evening Beth opened the door to the basement. Its outside entrance in the rear of the apartment building was convenient. As Nathan carried his rowing machine through the door, she followed him inside. "Are you sure I can't help?"

He set the rowing machine in a corner of the room. "Yep. I have some weights, skiing equipment and a bicycle for down here. And my suitcases are probably too heavy for you to lift."

"Nathan, I'm not a weakling."

His gaze started at her forehead and took a lingering, appreciative pass over her face, her white T-shirt and turquoise cuffed shorts. When his eyes reached her sandals, he smiled. "I never said you were."

The heat he generated with a simple look flashed through her like lightning. Her mouth went dry, and she thought for sure he'd kiss her.

Instead, his smile faded. "Where do you want me to put the suitcases?"

"I made room for your clothes in the chest of drawers and the closet . . . in my bedroom."

Nathan did approach her then. In his navy shorts and red T-shirt, his broad shoulders blocking the light from the window, Beth couldn't focus on anything but him. Them. Alone in the dim basement.

His voice was low. "We're getting married, Beth. But nothing will happen until you're ready for it to happen—whether my clothes hang in your closet or not."

In a way she felt relieved by his words. But in another . . . All she could say was "Thank you."

His eyes searched hers, and she had the feeling he was trying to see into her heart. She wasn't sure what he'd find except confusion.

He gently pushed her hair behind her ear. "How long will Rosa and Dorie stay at the park?"

"Usually about an hour. They just left before you arrived."

He nodded and stepped away. "I'll get the ski equipment."

Beth shoved aside a pup tent she and Mark had used on camping trips, along with a tackle box and fishing rod. Mark had often roared off on his bike with his buddies and fished at a nearby lake.

When Nathan returned, he propped the skis against the wall in the space she'd made. One ski tipped and landed on the handlebars of a bicycle. Mark's bicycle. Hers stood propped beside it.

Nathan retrieved the ski from the man's racing bike and asked, "Your husband's?"

She nodded. "I just...haven't been able to part with it." She and Mark had explored the nooks and crannies of Four Oaks on the weekends he hadn't spent with his friends.

Nathan's jaw tensed and his shoulders squared as he faced her. "If you'd rather I didn't keep mine here, I can find room for it at the store."

Mark was a subject they needed to discuss, but Beth had to get her own thoughts and feelings straight before she could talk about them with Nathan. Somehow she'd figure everything out in the midst of all this. "Don't be silly. If you want to ride it, you'll need it here."

His gaze fell on her bike. "Do you ride much?"

"I used to. After Dorie was born I meant to buy a child seat for the back but never got around to it."

"I have them at the store if you'd like me to set up your bike . . . or mine."

The thought of riding with Nathan and Dorie caused such mixed emotions. He must have seen that because he said, "Think about it."

Something else to add to her list.

After Nathan stored his sports equipment, he and Beth climbed into his sedan, and he drove around to the front of the building.

"Have you heard anything from Ivan and Clara?"

Beth shook her head. "Not a word. With the invitations having RSVP on them, I expected something. Clara's very etiquette oriented. But Ivan might be planning their strategy."

"I don't know what strategy they have to plan."

"My lawyer said they'll probably wait until they witness the ceremony to drop the suit."

"My friends, Jeff and Katie, are coming from the D.C. area."

"You mentioned a couple in Montana."

"Cade and Randi. Unfortunately they won't be able to fly in this weekend because they'll be coming for Jeff and Katie's anniversary party in a few weeks. It's their third anniversary. They were married at the end of August, but they wanted to set a date when we all could make it. You'll be able to meet Cade and Randi then."

"Are these old friends?"

"I went to college with Gavin, Cade and Jeff. We belonged to the same fraternity. Cade and Jeff were two years ahead of Gavin and me, but we've all stayed in touch over the years."

"That's terrific. I lost touch with my school friends. I was thankful when I met Jessie."

"How long have you known Jessie and Gavin?"

"About a year. I met Jessie in the park one evening."

Nathan pulled into a space in front of Beth's apartment. While she unlocked the door, he pulled two large suitcases from his back seat.

As she led him to the bedroom, her heart beat faster. Going to the tall chest, she opened the top three drawers. "I hope this is enough room. I didn't know how much you'd have."

Nathan looked around the bedroom with its off-white walls, the dark-green-and-navy flowered drapes and bed spread. The bedroom suite itself was maple including a chest, dresser with double mirror and two nightstands. She hadn't changed anything in the apartment after Mark died. She'd needed the sameness of it to get her through her grief.

As he lifted his suitcase onto the bed, he asked, "Did you and your husband live here long?"

"From the beginning. We'd put a down payment on a house before he died. We were waiting for the loan to be approved."

"You decided not to move?"

"The mortgage payments would have been too high for me to handle."

"How would you feel about moving into a bigger place?"

There really had been no choice as to where they were going to live now. Nathan's apartment had one bedroom; hers had two. But she hadn't thought much about the future. She was too caught up in what was happening now. How *would* she feel about leaving the apartment she and Mark had found, furnished and shared a life in?

"I suppose we could look at some bigger apartments."

"What about a house?"

"Don't you think we should make sure the marriage is going to work first?"

The lid fell back on the suitcase as Nathan turned away from it. He approached her, a crease in his brow, his lean cheeks taut. "I have every intention of making it work."

Beth looked away from the intense green of his eyes, down to her clasped hands. "Don't you have doubts about what we're doing?"

He lifted her chin with his finger. "Of course, I do. I'd be a fool not to. But I also believe if we both commit ourselves to this marriage, we *can* make it work. Eventually."

Eventually. Just where did that leave them now? In the midst of preparation for a wedding that was a means to an end—to keeping Dorie. How different this was from her marriage to Mark, when she'd been head over heels in love and certain about their future.

Nathan dropped his hand and said, "You can still call this off."

And risk losing Dorie? No. She had the courage to go through with it. Somehow she'd put the past behind her and make it work.

Nathan saw the doubts in Beth's eyes, and the sadness, and the loss. She was still in love with her husband. The ache in Nathan's chest told him he cared. Too damn much. He wanted her to be looking forward to the future and the life they could have together rather than to the memories of the past. But there wasn't much he could do about it except to be patient.

He knew he was simply a solution to Beth's problem. But he had to hope that in time she'd recognize that the chemistry between them could develop into much more... something lasting. This time he was using his head rather than his heart to make decisions.

Beth's expression changed as determination replaced all the other emotions in her eyes. "I don't want to call off the wedding, Nathan. I have to do this for Dorie."

That was the same reason he was doing this, too, wasn't it? So a little girl wouldn't be torn from her mother. So he would finally have a family. "We have good reasons for this marriage, Beth. We *can* make it work."

When she stoically nodded, he wished—along with her determination—he'd see some joy and happiness, too. But they both might have to wait awhile for joy and happiness to catch up to logic.

As he turned back to the suitcase and lifted out a stack of T-shirts, a small voice whispered, *You haven't discussed having more children.* He could tell Beth that he and Elaine couldn't conceive and they'd never really discovered why. Neither of them had a problem to account for it, according to the doctors. But why give Beth something else to think about right now? *Why give her the chance to back out?*

There is no defined problem, he repeated to himself as he put his T-shirts in the top drawer of the chest. *There is nothing to tell.*

It didn't take him long to empty his first suitcase into the drawers. But when he opened the second one, he realized he was going to need more space. So did Beth.

She opened the fourth drawer in the chest. "I can move this stuff over to the dresser."

When he looked, he saw pale peach, blue and white silky things. As Beth lifted out an armful, one slipped to the floor. He stooped to get it the same time she did. It was a peach nightgown, silky and definitely see-through. Nathan didn't have to work his imagination very hard to picture Beth in it. His blood ran fast.

As their hands grazed each other on the delicate material, he felt an electric current shoot all the way to his feet. The shock must have startled Beth, too, because she dropped another nightgown. It was blue satin... the color of her eyes.

Aroused, he met her gaze honestly. "I look forward to the night when I can see you in this."

She blushed, grabbed both nightgowns and stood, hurrying to the dresser and stuffing all of it into a drawer. From what he could see, it looked as if she'd combined nightgowns with slips and bras. There was a basic innocence and shyness about Beth that attracted him as much as the chemistry between them.

Taking a handful of socks and underwear from his suitcase, he carried them to the chest and plopped them into the drawer. As soon as he did, he realized the drawer wasn't empty. Two men's sweaters sat on the left side. He didn't take them from the drawer but waited for Beth.

She lifted the sweaters out and held them to her chest. "These were Mark's. The last of his clothes. I donated everything else to the Rescue Mission."

From the way she was holding the sweaters, Nathan guessed she wore them when she missed her husband. Again, logic told him to be patient, while his heart ached with the idea of her wearing her husband's sweaters. Still, he said, "You can leave them there."

She slid open the sliding door of the closet. Standing on tiptoe, she lifted the sweaters to a shelf that also held a blanket and extra pillows. "You need the space. This is fine."

It would be even more fine with Nathan if she would donate those last two sweaters . . . if she would really believe the two of them could have a promising future. Maybe for now he'd have to believe for them both.

The following evening Nathan found himself contemplating his new living arrangements as he drove to Beth's apartment. Anything he couldn't fit at Beth's, he'd moved to the storage room at the store. There hadn't been much—a sofa and chair, a couple of lamps, his bed and nightstand. When he and Elaine had divorced, they'd sold their house and everything in it, and split the proceeds. She had a career as an accountant; he had his store. They'd left their divorce with no ties. His ex-wife hadn't looked back, but had moved on. The last he'd heard she was still engaged. It was a long engagement, and Nathan wondered why she hadn't yet married again. But it was none of his business.

After the divorce, he'd been shell-shocked, mechanically running his store and his life. But gradually he'd realized he had to move on, too.

Was Beth ready to move on to a new life? And what kind of marriage could they have if she wasn't?

Parking in front of Beth's apartment, he realized the questions were complicated and had no easy answers. Right now her biggest concern was protecting Dorie. Maybe when they conquered that threat, they could concentrate on what they both wanted for the future.

He rang the doorbell and was surprised when Beth didn't answer. He'd pushed the bell a second time when someone called his name. He turned and saw Rosa beckoning to him from her porch. He jogged over to her.

"Hello, Mrs. Panetto. Do you know where Beth went?"

"Rosa. Call me Rosa. Since you and Beth are getting married, it seems right."

"Thanks, Rosa. I know Beth considers you part of her family."

"Yes, she does. And I just want you to know you'd better not do anything to hurt her or you'll have *me* to answer to. That girl's been through enough. Too many nights she worried about that husband of hers on his motorcycle. She needs a good man who won't do foolish things."

"You say he rode a motorcycle?"

"That's how he was killed. You didn't know?"

"We've only known each other a short while, and our main concern has been Dorie."

"That it should be. Dorie belongs with her mother. Tell me something, Mr. Nathan Maxwell. Why are you doing this for Beth?"

"I've always wanted a family, Mrs. Pan— Rosa," he amended. "And Beth . . . well . . ."

"Ah-hah. So this marriage will be more than a piece of paper."

Nathan had to smile at the older lady's bluntness. "I certainly hope so. Do you know where Beth and Dorie went?"

"She said she was going to Jessie's. She took flowers with her. Maybe they're arranging something for the wedding."

As Nathan drove out of the parking lot toward Jessie and Gavin's house, he wondered about the flowers. He and Beth had made the list for the florist together because Beth had wanted to make sure Nathan knew exactly what he'd be paying for. She'd made lists for everything with the itemized costs. He thought she felt as if she owed him. He didn't like her feeling that way.

When he arrived at Jessie's, Beth's car was not parked in the driveway. He walked up the path to the two-story brick colonial, wondering if Rosa had been mistaken. After ringing the bell, he waited.

Gavin opened the door, still dressed in a white shirt and tie.

Nathan asked, "Just get home?"

"About fifteen minutes ago. Lisa is showing me everything she bought to go back to school."

"I'm looking for Beth. Her neighbor said she was headed here."

Gavin opened the screen door so Nathan could step inside. "Beth had an errand to run. Dorie's with Jessie."

"Do you know where Beth went?"

His friend hesitated.

"Gavin?" He and Gavin had no secrets.

"She went to the cemetery."

Beth knelt by Mark's headstone. She'd placed the bouquet of wildflowers she'd purchased at a roadside market underneath Mark's name.

Tomorrow was the day before her wedding, and she felt she needed to say a formal goodbye to Mark. She could have asked Rosa to watch Dorie, but Rosa would have asked lots of questions and probably disapproved. She'd disapproved of Mark's hobby—his motorcycle. The older lady had never understood that side of Mark that longed to break free and run wild. Beth had done her best to understand it and not judge it.

Mark had been raised in a controlled atmosphere. Ivan had held tight reins on his family. Mark had bought the bike his senior year at college and kept it a secret from his father until he graduated—until he asserted himself to forge his own life.

"I was so angry with you when you died," Beth said aloud. "If you hadn't been riding that motorcycle you would have lived to see Dorie grow up, to celebrate anniversaries with me. But that motorcycle was as much a part of you as your brown eyes. So I couldn't stay angry."

She picked up an orange daylily and touched it to her nose, then gently laid it down again. "But I have stayed *sad.* And I still miss you. I don't understand this pull toward Nathan. I wish you could somehow let me know if I'm doing the right thing. But it seems to be my only choice."

"So I came to tell you I'm going to look forward not back. I'll never forget you. You'll always be Dorie's father. And she'll know that. But for her sake, I'm going to try and make a life with Nathan. And anytime you want to give me your blessing, feel free. It really would help me to know I'm headed in the right direction. Whenever I had doubts about something, you'd put your hand on my shoulder and tell me to trust my instincts. I sure could use your hand on my shoulder now."

She waited, almost expecting to feel the sensation. But all she felt was the slight breeze against her cheek and the warmth still emanating from the ground.

She felt foolish, kneeling there... talking... waiting... hoping. Finally, with a sigh, she took a last look at the flowers, traced her fingers over Mark's name and stood.

"Goodbye, Mark." Her eyes filled with tears, and she didn't brush them away.

She drove back to Jessie's house slowly, under the speed limit, thinking, remembering...and praying for a peace that didn't come.

Recognizing Nathan's car, her heart beat faster. Coincidence? Or had he come looking for her?

When Jessie answered the door, she smiled but her eyes were concerned. "Nathan's here. We're out on the patio. How did it go?"

"All right. It was a ritual more than anything else. Does Nathan know where I went?"

"He asked, so Gavin told him. I hope that won't cause a problem . . ."

"I don't have anything to hide, Jessie."

Jessie gave Beth a hug, then led the way to the patio.

Nathan sat beside Dorie on a glider, reading her a story. Gavin and Lisa played pitch and catch farther out in the yard.

When Nathan saw Beth, he stopped reading. "I went to your apartment, and Rosa told me you came here."

From his tone Beth suspected he wasn't pleased when he'd learned she'd gone to the cemetery. But it was something she'd had to do. She'd just have to explain why. If he'd listen. If he'd try to understand.

Jessie asked, "Would you like something to drink?"

Beth glanced at her daughter nestled against Nathan, her eyes almost closed. "I'd better get Dorie home. But, Nathan, if you want to stay—"

"I'll follow you," he said, his voice carrying a tense edge that said, yes, indeed, they'd have a talk when they got to her apartment.

As Beth drove, she was aware of Nathan's headlights in her rearview mirror in the enveloping dusk. He pulled into the parking lot beside her. Opening her back door, he unbuckled Dorie and lifted her from her seat. He didn't say anything as Beth unlocked the apartment door and he carried Dorie inside.

"There's iced tea in the refrigerator. Help yourself while I put Dorie to bed."

Nathan's gaze met hers, but she couldn't tell what he was thinking. She took the toddler from him.

A few minutes later when she returned to the living room, he wasn't drinking iced tea. Rather, he was standing by the entertainment center, staring at a photograph on the shelf of her and Mark. She approached him and stood beside him.

"Rosa told me your husband was killed on his motorcycle."

"Yes, he was. Once a month he raced with his friends. Something happened and he lost control..." Her voice caught.

"Were you there?" Nathan's voice was low. He still gazed at the picture, not at her.

"No. Mark's racing was something private, something he needed that I couldn't be a part of."

"What kind of man was he that he'd risk everything he had for a few thrills?"

"You have no right to judge him," she answered, anger instinctively rising in defense of her husband.

Nathan faced her then. "I'm marrying you. I want to know why you accepted that kind of teenage behavior."

"I loved Mark. I accepted *him*. It wasn't teenage behavior. It was an outlet for all the freedom his parents never gave him." At least that's what she'd always told herself.

Nathan's scowl drew his brows together. "Aren't you angry he died that way?"

"I was. For months. But the anger kept me from grieving. I had a new baby to take care of. The anger could only hurt her and me. Mark and I had always had love between us. The anger didn't belong."

"Gavin told me you went to the cemetery." Nathan waited for an explanation from her.

Since they were getting married the day after tomorrow, he deserved one. "I went to the cemetery to say goodbye to Mark."

Nathan's gaze returned to the picture on the shelf then moved to the one on the coffee table. "You still have his bicycle. You can't part with his sweaters. I don't think goodbye is as simple as a visit to the cemetery."

She didn't want to feel defensive, but she did. "Maybe not. But it's a start, isn't it?"

Nathan was slow in answering. But finally he agreed, "It's a start."

He didn't touch her; he didn't kiss her. He moved away. She was left with the feeling that Nathan didn't believe it was much of a start at all.

Chapter Five

Candlelight, soft music and champagne should have created a romantic atmosphere for Nathan and Beth at one of Roanoke's best restaurants. Gavin had insisted on taking the couple to dinner after their rehearsal at the small church where the wedding would take place the following afternoon.

But Beth could feel the tension between her and Nathan ever since her trip to the cemetery last night. She didn't know how to cut through it or even to confront it. She and Nathan were feeling their way, both afraid to step outside of some imaginary boundaries.

Gavin and Jessie carried the conversation at dinner. Over coffee Jessie said bluntly, "If you two don't relax and smile a little, the minister will think he's marrying the wrong couple."

"Jessie," her husband chastised.

Jessie glanced first at Nathan then at Beth. "Are you sure you want to get married?"

Gavin rolled his eyes and set his napkin on the table. "This might not be any of our business."

"They're our friends. It's our business," his wife responded.

Beth met Nathan's gaze across the table. He seemed to be asking her the same question Jessie had articulated. "I'm sure," Beth said, knowing keeping Dorie was more important than any doubts she may have.

Nathan nodded in agreement. "I'm sure, too."

Jessie sighed. "Then maybe by tomorrow morning you could smile for the photographer?"

Nathan's lips twitched. "Okay, Jessie. We get the message. Beth, how about if I take you home and we'll practice smiling."

Beth couldn't keep her lips from curving up now. "That sounds like a good idea."

Nathan had insisted on picking her up and taking her home afterward, although it meant extra driving for him. As he drove her to her apartment, which would be "their" apartment come tomorrow, he commented on the good quality of their meal at the restaurant. She told him about Dorie's escapades that day. They both seemed to relax—a little.

As Beth thanked Rosa for watching Dorie, Nathan shed his suit jacket, tossed it over a chair and looked in on the two-year-old. Beth had just said goodbye to Rosa and closed the door when he returned to the living room. His gaze lingered appreciatively on her strapless black satin dress.

Ignoring the tingles his gaze induced, she asked, "Would you like some iced tea or—?"

He tugged his tie open. "Beth, as of tomorrow, this will be my home, too. You don't have to treat me like a guest." Crooking his finger, he beckoned her to the sofa. "Come here. I want to give you something." After he sat, he patted the cushion next to him.

Curious, she sat beside him, feeling that pull toward him again that both confused and excited her.

Nathan produced a long box from the inside pocket of his suit coat, then tossed the jacket back over the arm of the chair. "You refused an engagement ring. So... consider this a wedding present."

"Nathan, you didn't have to—"

"I *wanted* to." He set the package in her lap.

Surprised but pleased, Beth unwrapped the gold foil, then lifted the lid on the blue velvet box. A strand of pearls gleamed against the velvet. "They're beautiful!"

"I wanted to get you something lasting, and they seemed right for you. But if you already have pearls..."

"No! I don't have anything like this. Thank you so much. They'll be perfect with my gown."

His smile was gentle as he leaned toward her. "I have a feeling *you'll* be perfect with your gown."

The darkening of Nathan's green eyes was as seductive as the huskiness in his voice. She swayed toward him because she wanted another of his kisses; she ached to feel the excitement again.

Nathan realized he was jealous of Beth's deceased husband. He understood the feeling, but Beth wouldn't. It was too soon, too sudden. The budding friendship between them, the blossoming passion were too new and fragile to rush. Yet he wanted to rush. And this close to Beth, with her perfume teasing him, her blue eyes inviting him, he couldn't resist wanting to coax her into a new life.

He'd sworn to himself he'd give Beth and Dorie time to get used to him…to trust him…to depend on him. But Beth's lips, scent and sweetness were too beguiling to think about not kissing her or going slow or waiting patiently for her passion to match his.

She appealed to everything masculine inside him— his protective nature, his desire to be strong, his sexual appetite that had been nonexistent since his divorce. When he sought her mouth, he pressed gently, not wanting to scare her or take advantage of a surprise sensual assault.

His lips remembered the texture of hers. His tongue remembered her taste, and he couldn't wait to taste her again. But before he did, he nibbled her lower lip to prepare her. She moaned softly as his lips played with hers and her hands settled on his shoulders. He took the cue and wrapped his arms around her.

Slipping his tongue into her mouth, he caressed her back. When she stroked her tongue against his, he took the kiss deeper. Soon she laced her hands in his hair. Satisfied she was as involved as he was, he lay back on the sofa and pulled her on top of him.

Her body fit against his so perfectly. Her hair slid against his cheek. Her dress, a material as soft as she was, invited his hands to smooth, caress and linger.

With her body pliant and an arousing weight on his, he forgot all thoughts of caution or patience.

He found his hands on the backs of her thighs, stroking, arousing in the same way he was aroused. He pushed up her dress and felt the silky nylons. What he wanted to touch was her skin. The heat and softness under her hose was driving him crazy.

Abruptly Beth jerked up and away. She braced her hands on his chest and pushed herself up, only to land in his lap. One look at her face told him she was more than embarrassed. She was upset.

As she tried to get her footing on the floor, he held her arm. "Hold on. I'll stop. We'll stop. Calm down a minute."

Somehow he managed to swing his legs to the floor while she moved to the end of the sofa.

He picked up his tie from the floor and slung it around his neck. "Talk to me, Beth. We're getting married tomorrow and if there's a problem—"

"Yes, there's a problem," she said, her voice rising with the color in her cheeks. "I don't *know* you."

The desire still raging through him made his voice gruff. "What do you want to know? My medical history, past partners..."

"Yes! I mean, not this minute, but we need to discuss all that. And more. I can't...I can't make love with you until..."

"You trust me," he said, finishing her sentence.

"That's part of it," she responded, her hands clasped in her lap, her back straight, her expression wary, as if she was afraid he'd try to change her mind.

He wondered what the whole picture was for her, if the reason she couldn't make love with him had more to do with her deceased husband than with trust. Or maybe they were tied together.

"I know you probably have certain expectations," she went on. She picked up the box of pearls that had slid to the middle cushion of the sofa. "And if you gave me these expecting—"

That brought his head up and made his stomach clench. "Whoa, there. I gave you the pearls as a wedding gift. Period. They were *not* meant as a bribe so you'd go to bed with me." He couldn't keep the anger from his voice.

She studied him for a long moment then said, "I'm sorry."

Nathan ran his hand through his hair, stood and picked up his suit coat. "You're right. You don't know me. And realistically, I don't know you. But we're both going to get a crash course. Living together will do that."

He went to the door, but stopped before opening it. "I'm attracted to you, Beth. And you've given me reason to believe you're attracted to me. That's one of the reasons I thought this could work. While we're getting to know each other, keeping a lid on that attraction could be tough. Not impossible...just tough."

He opened the door. "I'll see you at the church. Unless you change your mind."

Outside he stuffed his hands in his pockets and took a deep breath of summer night air. He might have blown it. He might have given her one too many outs. He'd know tomorrow afternoon.

* * *

Beth stood in the nave of the church, watching Jessie walk down the aisle in her pale blue chiffon dress. It was tea-length and elegant. Perfect for a wedding at four—an odd time, but the only time the church was available. Finding a church for a wedding this time of year on short notice hadn't been easy. Beth's hands shook as she waited for the change in music—her cue to start down the white runner. Gavin had asked if she'd like him to give her away. But as Nathan's best man, she felt he had enough to do. Besides, she didn't need anyone to give her away. She'd made this decision on her own and she would walk down the aisle on her own.

Even after last night?

She couldn't believe she'd let kissing get so out of hand. She couldn't believe she'd almost... Nathan was right. It would be difficult to keep a lid on the attraction between them. But she would. Until she was sure this marriage would work. Until she...fell in love with Nathan? Was she even ready for love?

The door of the church vestibule opened. Beth glanced over her shoulder and saw Ivan and Clara Warren walk in.

Nervous enough, she clutched her bouquet tighter.

Ivan came ahead of his wife and stood by Beth's side. "So you're going through with this charade."

Taking a deep breath, she responded, "It's not a charade. Nathan and I are getting married."

"We came to witness the ceremony... to make sure nothing irregular goes on. Because if it does, our lawyer will jump on it. I wasn't born yesterday. So if this is all for show, you might as well not walk down that aisle. Our lawyer will study all the paperwork thoroughly.''

The organ music swelled, and Clara tugged on her husband's suitcoat. ''Let's take our seats, dear.''

He gave Beth a scowl and followed his wife into the church.

Beth's fingers went to the pearl necklace Nathan had given her. Squaring her shoulders, she started down the aisle.

At the front of the church, she passed Clara and a still-scowling Ivan. Rosa stood in the front pew holding Dorie. The little girl smiled at her mother and waved. Beth waved back with a calmness in her heart and the knowledge that she was indeed doing the right thing.

As she glanced at the other side of the church, she saw a tall man in a Western-cut suit and wondered if Gavin's friend from Montana had arrived after all. Beside him stood a couple holding hands and Beth guessed they were Nathan's friends from the Washington, D.C., area.

Beth was conscious of Jessie and Gavin at the altar, but her gaze was drawn to Nathan. He was so handsome in his tuxedo—so tall, so broad-shouldered, so...masculine. And as his eyes slowly swept from her curled hair, over the off-white satin and lace gown and stopped to pause at the strand of pearls around her neck, she heard his words again from when he'd given her the necklace. ''I wanted to give you something lasting.''

They were entering a binding union, and the gravity of the commitment overwhelmed her. Could she come to love this man? What were the feelings already stirring in her every time she was around him? Exactly what would he expect of her? Did he want more children?

Suddenly, as Nathan's green gaze deepened and held hers, the questions stopped. Only time would bring the answers.

Nathan extended his hand to her. She took it and stepped up beside him.

The ceremony passed in a quick haze. Beth realized they were making promises to each other—important promises that would guide the direction of their lives. To have and to hold. To love and to cherish. Respect. Fidelity. Enormous promises that were supposed to last a lifetime.

How did Nathan feel about the promises? What did they mean to him?

I wanted to give you something lasting.

Almost before she could breathe, think or feel, the minister gave them a blessing.

Then he smiled and said to Nathan, "You may kiss your bride."

When Beth looked up at Nathan, she felt the trembling begin. This man was her husband, and he was going to kiss her.

She expected the excitement, the curiosity to see if the desire was the same as the last time they'd kissed, even in front of these people. Once Nathan's lips touched hers and his arms went around her, she forgot about everyone watching. All she felt and tasted and breathed was Nathan. With the excitement, curiosity and cogent desire was an incredible gentleness on his part—as if he already cherished her! She responded to the gentleness with the hope in her heart.

Losing track of everything but the seductive draw of Nathan's kiss, she jumped when she heard the minister's voice. To the guests in the church he announced, "I present to you Mr. and Mrs. Nathan Maxwell."

Nathan lifted his head, draped his arm around her shoulders and faced their guests with a smile. Then he stared directly at Ivan and Clara Warren. The excitement and rightness of the kiss paled as Beth wondered if he'd kissed her so wonderfully for her in-law's benefit. After all, that's why she and Nathan had exchanged vows and wedding rings.

The recessional music swelled and urged Beth forward on Nathan's arm. Jessie handed her her bouquet, and she walked down the aisle into an uncertain new life.

At the back of the church, Nathan took her in his arms again. "Ivan and Clara are watching," he murmured just before he kissed her.

When he broke the kiss, she raised her head. They were surrounded by friends who congratulated them. Beth forced a smile.

A few minutes later the photographer urged the wedding party back into the church. Beth felt Ivan and Clara watching as she and Nathan posed with Jessie and Gavin.

Finally, the last photo taken, they returned to the vestibule where they heard the laughter and chatter of their guests outside the front door. Beth peeked through the casement window and saw Dorie holding out her hands to Rosa while Rosa poured rice from a box.

"Don't think this is over," Ivan Warren said as he appeared at her elbow.

Beth faced him and kept her voice calm. "I'd like it to be over, so you and Clara can be grandparents."

"I don't believe for a moment that you and Maxwell will stay together. You've bought yourself time. That's all you've done."

Nathan crossed to Beth's side and lightly rested his hand at her waist. "Beth and I made promises today. We don't take them lightly."

Ivan's mouth twisted into a cynical grimace. "We'll see how long those promises last. You've put on a good show here, but I'm not finished yet. Beth, you'll be hearing from my lawyer." With that parting shot, he went to the church door, waited for his wife who scurried over to him, and left.

The pressure of Nathan's hand increased on Beth's waist. "He's bluffing."

"You can't underestimate him, Nathan. I'm worried about what he's cooking up next."

Nathan frowned. "Until we have cause to worry, we've got to try and relax. It'll be better for Dorie."

Beth knew Nathan was right. They had enough to concentrate on with getting to know each other. But she also knew Ivan Warren wasn't a man to concede defeat.

Nathan gazed at his new wife as the chauffeur-driven limo took them to their wedding reception.

Dorie sat on Beth's lap and pointed to something outside the window. He knew her little girl was everything to her.

When Dorie had reached for Beth after the rice throwing, Beth had looked up at Nathan with a question in her eyes. She wanted her daughter with her. Did she really think he'd object to bringing Dorie with them? How long had he wanted a child? Prayed for a child?

But Beth doesn't know that. She doesn't know you could have a problem and this is the only child she'll have.

He should have told her. They should have discussed the years he and Elaine had tried to conceive. But once he and Beth had decided to get married, the ball had rolled right over both of them with plans for the church, reception, moving in together.

You should have told her.

Yes, he should have. But he'd been a breath away from having the family he'd always wanted. He'd been reluctant to jeopardize that with something hazy and not even clinically factual.

Dorie swiveled around on Beth's satin gown, her black patent shoes brushing Nathan's knee. "Par-tee."

"Yes, we're going to a party," he responded. He'd made arrangements for a room and private dinner at one of Roanoke's finest hotels.

Beth said, "I really didn't get the chance to talk to your friends. I take it the tall man in the cowboy hat is Cade?"

Nathan remembered his surprise when he'd seen Cade sitting in the church with Jeff and Katie. "He said no matter how he turned it around, he couldn't miss my wedding. Randi stayed back at the ranch with their boys. You'll meet her in a few weeks.''

A few weeks. Would he and Beth truly be man and wife in a few weeks? Could she forget about her first marriage or at least relegate it to a memory? Maybe he was expecting too much. He did know he couldn't push her or he'd push her away. He also knew what happened last night on her sofa couldn't happen again until Beth wanted more than kisses...because the next time he might not be able to control the desire that rushed through him at the slightest provocation.

As Nathan exited the limo under the veranda of the hotel, he noticed the gray sedan slipping into a guest's parking spot. He was relatively sure it was the same gray sedan he'd seen parked outside the church. It didn't belong to any of their guests. Maybe Ivan Warren had more in store than another trip to his lawyer.

Inside the hotel, with Dorie in his arms, Nathan led Beth to the room where all their guests had gathered. Three rectangular tables were arranged horseshoe fashion for the small gathering.

As soon as they were seated, Gavin clinked his spoon against his champagne glass and toasted Nathan and Beth, wishing them a long and happy marriage. Cade and Jeff seconded the toast. Throughout dinner Nathan's gaze never strayed far from Beth as she listened to conversation coming at her from all angles and attended to Dorie sitting in a high chair beside her. Whenever her arm brushed Nathan's or her knee grazed his, she managed to look away. He wished he could read her mind. He caught her glancing at him and then at the wide gold band on her finger.

When it came time to cut the cake, Nathan accompanied Beth to the small table set up for that purpose. She took the knife, and he covered her hand with his, murmuring, ''I think we're supposed to do this together.'' He felt the tremor run through her and wondered if it was from desire, the excitement of the day, or the uncertainty of what would happen next.

After they'd cut the wedge of cake, Beth broke off a small piece and lifted it to Nathan's mouth. He opened his lips, and as she placed the cake inside, he tasted her fingers as well as the sweetness of the dessert. Their gazes locked, and time stood still.

Someone called with evident amusement, ''It's your turn, Nathan.''

Beth dropped her hand and blushed.

Nathan licked the icing from his lips and broke off a small piece of cake. Beth's eyes were wide and vulnerable . . . he knew he had to be careful every step of the way. Holding the cake to her lips, he waited.

When she opened her mouth, he gently placed the cake on her tongue. Her eyes on his, she ate the dessert and swallowed. The pulse at her neck fluttered rapidly. A tiny dab of icing had caught on the lower edge of her lip. Nathan traced over it with his finger, then brought the taste to his lips.

Beth's color heightened, and his own heart pounded in his ears. *Slow down. Slow down. Slow down,* he repeated like a mantra, hoping the message would get through to the impatient longings he was trying to rein in.

As he and Beth once again sat at the head of the table, the door to the room opened and a balding gray-haired man with a mustache stepped in. Glancing around the room as if he were looking for someone, his gaze fell on Nathan and Beth. Then he slipped from the room.

Nathan leaned close to Beth. ''Did you see the man who stuck his head in the door?''

''When?''

''Just now.''

She shook her head. ''Why?''

''I wondered who he was.''

''Maybe he was hotel personnel. Or a guest who was lost.''

''Maybe.'' Nathan didn't want to worry Beth unnecessarily by telling her his suspicions.

Jessie disappeared for a few minutes. When she returned, she wore a smile and carried a portable tape player. She set it on a corner of the head table. ''You decided not to hire a DJ or band, but I didn't think you should miss a wedding dance.'' She switched on the tape and it played a sentimental ballad.

Nathan pushed back his chair and stood. ''Leave it to Jessie to think of everything.'' He offered his hand to Beth. ''Would you like to dance?''

After she stood, he led her to the side of the room and took her in his arms. Everyone clapped.

Beth held on to Nathan's shoulder and felt the press of his fingers in the small of her back guiding her. It was easy to follow him...easy to get lost in the dark green depths of his eyes. The whole day seemed like a dream. Except for Ivan Warren, except for her own doubts, except for the feeling she'd somehow betrayed Mark.

But whenever Nathan touched her or looked at her as he was looking at her now, she forgot about Ivan and the doubts and the guilt.

Suddenly Beth heard Dorie fretting. Rosa was trying to occupy her with blocks, but the activity wasn't working. "She's getting tired."

Nathan smiled. "It's been a long day. Are you ready to leave?"

As Dorie's fretting turned to crying, Beth nodded. "We'd better."

Beth went to Dorie and picked her up. Everyone gathered around to say goodbye.

Cade shook Nathan's hand and smiled at Beth. "I hope you two are as happy as Randi and I. She's looking forward to seeing you at Jeff and Katie's anniversary party."

"I'm glad you flew in," Nathan said. "It means a lot."

"Where are you going on your honeymoon?" his friend asked.

Nathan's shoulders straightened. "We're not taking a honeymoon."

Beth jumped in. "We thought it would be better for Dorie if we...wait a while." Actually they'd never talked about a honeymoon.

The nerve in Nathan's jaw worked, and he remained silent.

Cade looked from Nathan to Beth, then back at Nathan. "Well, when and if you do want to consider a honeymoon, keep Montana in mind. It's beautiful country."

Nathan nodded. "We will."

As Cade moved away, Beth remarked, "You didn't tell him why we got married, did you?"

"I didn't feel it was necessary."

"You and Cade have been friends for a long time," she pressed. "If there's nothing wrong with a marriage of convenience, why are we so hesitant to talk about it?"

"Our marriage is no one's business but ours."

In a way Nathan was right. Yet she wondered if he was defensive because he had as many doubts as she did.

As they rode home in the limo, Dorie fell asleep against Beth's shoulder. At the apartment Nathan lifted the two-year-old from Beth's lap and carried her inside to her bedroom.

This night Nathan didn't wait in the living room while Beth got Dorie ready for bed. He shed his tuxedo jacket and asked, "What's the routine?"

Beth had to smile at his task-oriented tone. She unbuttoned her daughter's flowered party dress. "Tonight she's too tired to care about a story. I'll just put her into her nightgown and rock her a little."

"Would you mind if I rock her?"

Beth saw the longing in Nathan's eyes and realized he wanted to be a father as soon as he could. She finished undressing Dorie, changed her diaper and slipped a nightie over her head. "Dorie, would you like Nathan to rock you tonight? Since he's living with us now, he wants to take care of you, too."

"Mommee, tay?"

"Sure, I'll stay."

Nathan sat in the wooden rocker. Dorie climbed up onto his lap with a sleepy smile. He cuddled her in his arms and pushed with his feet.

Still in her wedding gown, Beth sat on the wooden toy chest painted with bears and books. It only took a few minutes until Dorie was fast asleep.

But Beth didn't move. She let Nathan rock and she watched.

Finally, he stopped rocking, stood and carried Dorie to her crib. Beth came to stand beside him and tucked Dorie's teddy bear by her side. "If she wakes up and he's not there, she'll cry."

"I'll remember," he said softly.

They went into the living room. Beth felt awkward, not sure what to say or do next. "I suppose I should change."

His gaze swept over her. "You're a beautiful bride."

She stepped closer to him. "I want to thank you for everything today. The wedding, the reception, the limo." She touched her pearls. "And for these."

"You don't have to thank me. It was my wedding, too. And now it's our wedding night. Where do you want me to sleep?"

Chapter Six

Beth's heart stopped. Thoughts galore zipped through her mind with vivid pictures to go with them. Yet she knew there was only one answer she could give Nathan tonight. "The sofa opens up into a bed."

"That's convenient," he said in a wry tone.

"Nathan..."

He gave a yank on his tie. "I told you I won't push you, Beth. And I won't. I *would* like to get comfortable. I'll get my things out of the bedroom and change out here."

Beth felt awkward and confused and totally unsettled with Nathan in her apartment. She followed him to the bedroom. As he took black silk shorts from a drawer in the chest, she picked up a small package she'd wrapped in silver on the dresser. She'd wanted to give it to him in private.

He would have brushed past her and left the room, but she clasped his arm. "I have something for you."

His eyes darkened. "You didn't have to get me anything."

"I didn't. Not exactly." She handed him the small package.

Nathan put his shorts on the bed and took the gift. Unwrapping it, he laid the paper and bow on the dresser, then lifted the spring lid on the brown velvet box.

"It was my father's," she said softly.

Nathan took the gold tie bar from the box. "Are you sure you want me to have this?"

"I'm sure."

He tilted her chin up, smoothed his finger over her cheek, and she knew they were headed straight into the storm of tingling awareness and electric vibrations that had swirled around them all day. When Nathan's lips met hers, they didn't ask, but demanded she respond. His tongue separated her lips, and she gave no thought to resisting. As Nathan held her tighter and kissed longer, she found herself drowning in the sensations.

Suddenly he broke the kiss and raised his head. His breathing was as ragged as hers. Stepping away from her, he said, "I'd better open the sofa bed." Then he left the room and closed the door.

It wasn't until she leaned against the dresser for support that she saw his silk shorts on the bed. She couldn't go out there right now. And she'd bet money he wasn't coming back in. Not until they both cooled off.

Beth hung her wedding dress in the back of her closet and changed into a cotton nightgown and robe. Belting the robe securely around her waist, she carried Nathan's shorts to the living room.

He was standing at the front window, peering between the blinds. His upper torso was naked. His tan skin, his muscled arms and shoulders and his dark brown hair created such a powerful image she froze by the open sofa bed.

Finding her voice, she asked, "Is something wrong?"

He turned, his gaze resting on the scoop neck of her nightgown under the V of the robe. "I heard a car."

Brown curling hair covered the center of Nathan's chest and wisped around his nipples. Without the cummerbund, his tuxedo pants hung low on his hips. This was her wedding night. This was her husband. A surge of heat flashed over her.

She laid his shorts on the chair. "I'll get you sheets and pillows."

At the linen closet she told herself to take a few deep breaths. If she just concentrated on making up Nathan's bed, she'd be fine.

When she returned from the hall, he'd closed the blinds and moved away from the window. She plopped the pillows on a chair and unfurled a sheet. He caught the edges and pulled it over his side of the mattress. They worked in silence until the bed was made.

She fluffed a pillow into place. "If you want to use the bathroom first, go ahead."

"No. You finish getting ready for bed. Will the television bother you if I turn it on?"

She shook her head. "Mark used to..." She stopped. "I can usually get to sleep pretty easily. But if you hear something in the middle of the night, it's me checking on Dorie."

"And if you hear noise, I'll probably be rummaging in the kitchen. If I can't sleep, a bowl of cereal helps."

"Do you have trouble sleeping?"

"Not usually. But tonight could be an exception."

She knew exactly what he meant. Everything seemed so strange...so unsettling. Just thinking about him bare-chested in the living room... She moved away from the sofa toward the hall. "I'll let you know when I'm finished."

He nodded.

This will get easier, she told herself as she headed for the bathroom. But as she closed the bathroom door and spied Nathan's shaving cream and razor sitting on the vanity, she wondered if it would.

The doorbell rang, causing Nathan to sit straight up. He'd tossed and turned most of the night, dozing off just before dawn.

Beth came rushing from the bedroom, her hair mussed, her robe slipping over one shoulder. As she hurried to the door, he grabbed her arm. "Wait a minute."

Startled, she froze. "Why?"

He released her, climbed from the sofa bed, and picked up the pillows stuffing them into her arms. "Put these in the bedroom. I think I know who's at the door."

The doorbell rang again.

He gave her a little nudge. "Go on. Better to be safe than sorry."

As she went to the bedroom, he folded the bed into the sofa. When she came back into the living room, he said, "Close the door."

She pulled it shut with a puzzled expression on her face. "It's probably Rosa."

"The morning after our wedding?" he asked with an arched brow. Then he went to the door and opened it.

The man standing there with gray hair and a balding head wore a blue uniform instead of a suit. But Nathan recognized him. He was the same man who'd peered inside the doors at the reception. The same man, Nathan suspected, who had been sleeping in a car in the parking lot last night.

The man smiled pleasantly and flashed an ID quickly. "I'm from the water department. We received a complaint from the apartment manager about rusty water in some apartments. Is that a problem here?"

The man's excuse was lame and no water department truck stood outside. The ID could very easily be fake. But to buy some time and make sure of his suspicions, Nathan played along. He turned to Beth. "Darling, come here a minute. The gentleman wants to know if we have rusty water."

When Beth joined him at the door, Nathan possessively curved his arm around her. He felt her tense. To the man in the uniform, he said, "We just got married yesterday so we haven't been noticing much but each other." He squeezed Beth a little tighter. "Have we?"

"No, I haven't noticed," she responded in a sleep-husky voice with a side glance for Nathan that told him she'd play along but he'd better have an explanation later.

The man tipped the bill of his cap. "I'm so sorry for the inconvenience. I'll check with your neighbors. Have a good day." With that he turned and started down the walk.

Nathan reluctantly slipped his arm from Beth and closed the door.

She pushed her hair away from her eyes. "What was *that* all about?"

"I think he's a private investigator Ivan set on our doorstep. I want to check something out." He went to the kitchen where he'd noticed a telephone book. He found the number for the municipal water company and dialed. All he got was an answering machine.

Beth stood in the doorway. "You really think he's a private investigator?"

Nathan hung up the receiver. "We're going to find out. How about a trip into the store? I'll show you around. That will give us the opportunity to see if we're being followed."

"And if we are?"

"Then we know we have to watch ourselves whenever we're outside the apartment, and when we're inside, we should keep the blinds shut. He probably carries a zoom lens in his hip pocket."

"As if we're not under enough pressure," she said softly as she ran her hand through her hair again. He

recognized it was something she did when she was
nervous.

"Are you having regrets already?"

Her gaze passed across his chest, over his silk shorts
and bare thighs. "Not regrets. Jitters. And it's harder
knowing we might have to live in a fish bowl."

Relieved, he smiled. "Is there anything I can do to
help your jitters?"

"Yes. Get dressed," she blurted out.

He laughed, and it felt so good to release some of
the tension between them. "I'll get dressed if you
make some coffee. We need to have our wits about us
today, and coffee will help."

She slipped past him to the coffeepot. He caught a
whiff of a sweet scent and longed to touch her hair as
it shifted over her shoulder. With a shy smile she
asked, "Weak or strong?"

"As strong as you can stand it," he teased as he
crossed to the bedroom to get some clothes. So his
being around her while he wasn't completely dressed
bothered her. He smiled. That thought made his day.

As Nathan drove to Roanoke, he checked his rear-
view mirror. "He's following, all right. Let's see what
we can do to shake him."

Beth looked worried.

"I won't do anything foolish, Beth. I wouldn't put
you and Dorie in any kind of danger."

She looked back over her shoulder at her daughter.
"I had visions of screeching around corners."

"Did you and Mark screech around corners on his
motorcycle?"

The stark silence in the car warned Nathan he'd hit a nerve.

"I wasn't fond of riding on Mark's motorcycle."

"Because he was reckless?"

"Mark knew how to handle that machine. It was part of him. It wasn't part of me."

"But you accepted it."

"I had no choice. I loved him."

The words stung Nathan. He wanted her love for the man to be over... finished. How could they begin to have a life together if Beth's past marriage had a hold on her?

"I know the side streets of Roanoke well. I'll just make a few turns. Nothing fancy."

Nathan managed to lose the private investigator without much effort. Afterward, he made a few detours to be sure. When the gray sedan didn't appear again, he drove to the store.

He pulled into a strip shopping center and parked in the back. It was becoming a habit for Nathan to take Dorie out of the car. She grinned at him and raised her arms. He lifted her out and walked beside Beth to the door with the Sports Center sign. Nathan used a key to let them inside. The store didn't open until noon. For security reasons he kept the rear entrance locked.

Nathan led Beth through a storeroom stocking every piece of equipment possible. Along one set of shelves sat his sofa and chair and a stack of boxes. Eventually, when he and Beth moved to a bigger place, he could get them out of the storeroom.

He introduced Beth to his manager who was sitting at the computer in the office. Then he took her into the store itself.

Nathan was proud of the business he'd built up. Elaine had been skeptical when he'd quit his job as vice-president of production at a printing company and made an offer on the sports store that had been under-inventoried, devalued, and losing money because of poor business management by the owner. In six months, with good public relations advice, an update on products and a widening of selection, he'd turned the store around.

Beth seemed to get real enjoyment out of experimenting on a putting green, trying on a set of in-line skates and rolling a colorful ball back and forth to Dorie. Dorie managed to pick up the ball and run with it down the aisle. Beth ran after her, laughing. When Nathan surprised Dorie at the other end of the aisle and scooped her up in his arms, she giggled and held the ball tight.

Nathan tickled her, and she giggled again. Tapping the tip of her nose, he asked, "Would you like to take the ball home with you?"

Dorie nodded.

Nathan gave her a hug and crooked his finger at Beth. "Come see the bicycle seats we can use for Dorie."

He showed her two different brands. After reading and studying everything on the boxes, she chose one. "I guess she needs a helmet, too."

"Absolutely. She can pick the one she likes best."

As Dorie looked at the helmets with various designs in assorted colors, Nathan suggested, "I could bring Mark's bike in here. I often get calls for second-hand bikes. I also know someone who fixes up used bikes and gives them to kids who can't afford them." As soon as he said it, Nathan knew he'd made a mistake.

Beth's eyes grew deep blue, and she bit her lower lip. Then she said, "When I'm ready to get rid of Mark's bike, I'll let you know." Turning away from him, she concentrated on her daughter and picking out a helmet.

Nathan raked his hand through his hair. That had been a stupid move. Gut instinct told him Beth would have to close past doors herself. But, damn, he wanted to give them a push.

Finished at the store, Nathan carried the bike seat, helmet and ball to the car while Beth held Dorie's hand. She buckled her daughter into her car seat and was much too quiet on the way home.

The gray sedan was parked at the apartment.

Beth saw the car the same time as Nathan. "There's no point in our trying to evade him."

"Unless we want a break from constant supervision. We'll just have to make sure we look like newlyweds when we go out."

Beth didn't comment. She also didn't take his advice as she opened her door, unbuckled Dorie, and took her into the apartment without waiting for him.

Lunch was strained. Afterward Nathan decided to attach the child's seat to his bike. When he returned to the apartment from the basement, he found Beth mopping the kitchen floor. Her movements were quick, jerky and agitated.

For too long he and Elaine had let thoughts and resentments and fears build up between them. Lack of communication had torn them apart, as well as lack of conception. He didn't want Beth to hide whatever was on her mind.

Unmindful of the wet floor, he crossed it and stood in front of her. "Is Dorie taking a nap?"

Beth kept mopping. "Yes."

Angling himself directly in her path, he waited for her to look up. When she did, he said, "I'm sorry if I upset you."

She kept her hands on the handle of the mop, holding it between them. "I won't wipe every trace of Mark from my life as if he never lived in my heart. He's Dorie's father."

Nathan's impatience surfaced along with the ache to have this marriage work, to make Beth his wife in every sense of the word. "But Mark's gone and I'm here now. I want to be Dorie's dad. And I want you to be as committed to the marriage as I am."

"It can't happen overnight, Nathan!"

He slipped his hand under her hair. "Can't it? The moment I saw you I knew I wanted you."

"I need time and some space—"

Lowering his head, he said, "I think you need to be reminded we're newlyweds, and a bride and groom don't mop the kitchen to pass the time."

Beth knew she was fighting, not only her attraction to Nathan, but her growing feelings for him, too. He was sexy—there was no denying it. The rugged planes of his face, his well-toned body, a sense of raw masculine power and confidence drew her to him. But there was so much more to the man. His gentleness and kindness were as seductive as his kisses.

Yet she felt as if she couldn't give in to any of it. The shock of Nathan's sudden presence in her life confused her and tilted her world.

His lips came down on hers, more demanding than coaxing. He didn't give her the chance to ease into desire slowly. The thrust of his tongue into her mouth made her let go of the mop and grab on to him.

His skin was hot under his polo shirt, and the material didn't begin to conceal the taut muscles underneath. His texture caused tingles in her fingers and a curiosity to know more. She moved the tips of her fingers slowly across his chest as his sheer maleness increased her excitement.

As her thumb grazed his nipple, he laced both of his large hands in her hair. He claimed her by tasting her deeply, exploring, holding her captive until she was shaking from the intensity of a need so overwhelming she felt consumed.

Nathan withdrew his hands from her hair and slowed down the kiss. Then he straightened, and she was standing on her own again. He didn't move but waited for her reaction. She didn't know how to react. She felt too disconcerted. But she also felt a battle between the desire to reach out to him and the caution of holding back.

To give herself a moment, she stooped over and picked up the mop. "Maybe after supper we could ride our bikes to the park and see how Dorie likes her new seat.''

"What about the P.I?'' Nathan asked as his gaze searched her face.

"We'll just pretend he's not there. As long as we're together as a family, what can he report? I'm not going to stay cooped up behind closed blinds because of him,'' she said.

"There is one place you'll have to make sure the blinds are closed all the time—the bedroom. If he finds out we're not sleeping together, Ivan will have the information he thinks he needs.''

"I'll remember.''

Nathan brushed his thumb over her chin. "We should have opened the blinds for that kiss.''

She blushed. "We would have broken his camera.''

Nathan chuckled. "While you finish mopping, I'm going to read the paper. If you want to open the blinds and join me on the sofa . . .''

When Beth didn't respond, his smile faded. "I know your memories of your life with Mark are special. Are you sure you want to ride to the park tonight?''

She nodded. "I'm sure.''

When Nathan moved away from her into the living room, she realized the thought of sitting on the sofa next to him created too much turmoil to contemplate. Bike riding would be much safer.

On an evening ten days later, Beth pedaled her bicycle into the parking lot of their apartment complex, glancing over her shoulder at Nathan and Dorie. The pull toward Nathan grew stronger as each day passed.

They had settled into a comfortable routine. At least it was comfortable when Nathan was at work. In the morning, if she ran into him going into or coming out of the bathroom or bedroom, his chest and legs bare, his shorts riding low on his hips, she took a deep breath. Except for his heated gaze, which seemed to stroke over her with a hunger she felt, too, he didn't touch her. He was giving her space, and she should be thankful.

But a contrary voice kept asking, "Don't you want him to kiss you again?"

Yes, she did. But she feared another kiss as much as she wanted it. At times she still ached for Mark and the life they'd shared. She was resisting giving up the part of her heart that belonged to Mark... Although, Nathan seemed to be encompassing most of her world.

His relationship with Dorie was patient, playful and caring. He fit the father role perfectly. He'd married her so he could be a father. But how long would that be enough?

Nathan pedaled his bike beside her. "No gray sedan in the parking lot. Maybe Ivan gave up."

She and Nathan kept the blinds closed at all times so Ivan's private investigator couldn't see whatever happened inside the apartment. Outside, she and Nathan usually kept their attention on Dorie, like any other couple would with a child. Nathan had predicted even Ivan would tire of paying an investigator who wasn't discovering anything that would refute their marriage. Once in a while they evaded the investigator for the freedom of knowing they weren't being watched. But most of the time they pretended he wasn't there. Though, whenever they were outside and Nathan dropped his arm across Beth's shoulders or curved it around her waist, she wondered if the gesture was natural or for the P.I.'s benefit.

Beth and Nathan stowed their bikes in the basement. Nathan carried Dorie to the apartment and unlocked the door.

In the kitchen, Beth poured glasses of orange juice for all of them and noticed the light blinking on the answering machine. While Nathan took a bag of animal cookies from the top of the refrigerator, she pressed the button.

A female voice, sweet and lilting, played. "Nathan, it's Elaine. I'd like to talk to you. But you obviously aren't home and I'm leaving tonight on a business trip. I'll be back Sunday night. I'll give you a call on Monday. Or you can call me. My number's the same."

Beth busied herself putting Dorie in her high chair. "Elaine's your ex-wife, isn't she?"

"Yes. We weren't gone long. Maybe she didn't leave yet." He went to the phone, picked up the receiver and dialed.

Beth thought it was telling he remembered the number.

When no one answered, he hung up.

"What does she do?" Beth asked, unable to quell her curiosity. They hadn't talked about his first marriage.

"She's an accountant."

"Do you talk to her often?"

"We haven't spoken since the divorce."

"You have no idea why she wants to talk to you now?"

"None." He studied Beth for a moment. "Does it bother you that she wants to talk to me?"

Beth opened the bag of cookies. "No. Of course not." Just then the phone rang and she didn't have to examine what she was feeling very closely.

Nathan answered it, then handed the phone to her. He said, "It's Clara Warren."

As Beth took the phone, Nathan gave Dorie her juice. The toddler smiled at him and he smiled back. She had the same blue eyes as her mother, the same silky blond hair, although it was a little lighter and a little curlier.

His gaze returned to his wife. His wife. He was trying to give her time and space. But it was damn difficult when what he really wanted was to carry her off to the bedroom—kiss her and touch her and bury himself in her. But he didn't want to just have sex with her. He wanted a life with her.

He couldn't imagine what Elaine wanted. He should use this opportunity to talk to Beth about his marriage. Why it broke up. Beth should know that if they made this a real marriage, they might not have more children. But questions and doubts prevented him from putting it into words. What if Beth wanted out of the marriage when he told her? What if she felt trapped because of Dorie? What if she didn't care enough about him to make a marriage work with or without more children?

Elaine had said goodbye so easily. . . .

Beth had been listening to Clara. Now she said, "I'll have to ask Nathan. I'll call you after we discuss it." She said goodbye and put the phone on its cradle.

"What's Ivan up to now?" Nathan asked.

Beth ruffled Dorie's hair and sat across from him. "They've decided that being enemies isn't good for Dorie. They would like us to spend the weekend with them at their house in the mountains."

"Their private investigator couldn't get any dirt so now Ivan wants to watch us himself," Nathan said angrily.

"Probably. What do you think?"

Nathan paused before answering. Finally, he said, "That depends on what you want. If you want to make peace so Dorie can know her grandparents, we have no choice. We have to accept their invitation. But if we do, we have to convince them we're happily married. That will probably mean at least sleeping in the same bedroom. Are you ready for that?"

Chapter Seven

Beth's face hid nothing. Neither did her wide blue eyes. Her lack of pretense, her complete honesty, was one of the things Nathan admired most about her. *So why can't you talk to her about your divorce?*

That wasn't the issue right now. This weekend was. "We can't ask Ivan and Clara for separate bedrooms. You realize that, don't you?" he pressed, hoping this could be a turning point.

The pink on Beth's cheeks told him she'd been thinking about the bigger picture. "So you don't think we should go," she said.

"I didn't say that. If we accept their invitation, maybe they'll accept our marriage and back off the custody idea permanently."

"But we'll have to sleep together," she said in a low voice.

Impatiently he pushed his chair back and stood, realizing that if Beth wasn't ready for a turning point, he couldn't pressure her. "You can stay fully dressed. I'll sleep on the floor. Do you think I won't be able to keep my hands off you?" His frustration spilled over into anger he knew she didn't deserve.

Her back straightened, and although her color was high, she met his gaze without wavering. "I imagine you can do whatever you set your mind to do. When you married me, I know you didn't sign on for subterfuge. I hate it, too. But if it will get Ivan off our backs..."

"Then of course we should do whatever we have to, to get through the weekend." He tried to keep his tone even as well as the emotions and sexual tension that simmered every moment he and Beth were together...and sometimes even when they weren't. "Call Clara and tell her we accept. *If* you trust me enough to sleep in the same room with me."

"I married you, Nathan, because I felt you were a man I *could* trust." She stood and went to the telephone. "I'll call Clara."

Nathan crossed to the freezer and removed a tray of ice cubes to add to his juice. He'd need more than ice this weekend, sharing a bedroom with Beth. Her words echoed in his head. *I married you because I felt you were a man I could trust.* Maybe so. But she didn't trust him yet. Not enough to go to bed with him. And he'd just have to accept that...for now.

From the passenger seat of Nathan's car Beth watched the gables of the Warren's home peek between the tall mountain pines. She had visited here once, years ago, when she and Mark had become engaged. But the visit had ended abruptly when Mark and his father had argued about Mark's teaching career.

After that, Mark's antagonistic attitude toward Ivan had contributed to the wedge between father and son as much as Ivan's desire to control Mark's choices. That thought surprised Beth. She had always been fiercely loyal to her husband. Yet now with time and perspective, she could see the part Mark had played in widening the rift.

As Nathan drove up the winding drive, Beth examined his expression. His shoulders were squared, his jaw set. He'd worked late at the store last night, and she'd missed his presence. She'd missed his deep laughter as he played with Dorie, she'd missed his inadvertent touches as they passed each other in the hall, she'd missed knowing he was . . . there.

Nathan parked in the curve of the circular drive. While Beth gathered her cosmetic case and Dorie's bag brimming over with toys, Nathan lifted the toddler from her car seat. They climbed the brick steps to the large porch.

Before Beth could ring the bell, Clara opened the door with a huge smile. "I'm so glad you decided to come." She held her arms out to Dorie, who was perched in Nathan's hold. "Oh, my, how you've grown. Will you come to me?"

Dorie ducked her head into Nathan's shoulder.

Clara didn't give up. "I know it's been a while since you saw me. But we have some surprises for you. Your grandfather bought you a merry-go-round with horses that go up and down. Maybe we can try it after lunch.''

Dorie lifted her head. "Horsee?"

"A pretend horse," Beth explained, relieved Clara was trying to make Dorie comfortable, but afraid outrageous presents could become a norm. To her mother-in-law, she said "Nathan has been taking us riding. Dorie's becoming very fond of horses."

"Maybe we can get her a pony..." Clara suggested.

Nathan interrupted. "Let's see how this visit goes before we make further plans."

Beth and Nathan had decided not to discuss the private investigator with the Warrens. They were going to take an hour at a time, a "wait and see" attitude with the weekend.

Clara looked from Beth to Nathan. "I hope you'll enjoy your visit. I just wish you could stay longer. Lunch is almost ready. I'll get Ivan. He's working in his study. Don't worry about your bags. I'll have the butler take them up to your rooms."

As Beth followed Clara inside, she decided to take the bull by the horns. "Rooms?"

Clara glanced over her shoulder as she led them through the foyer that was as large as Beth's living room. "I've put you in the guest room with a connecting door to the room we prepared for Dorie. I knew you'd want to be close. I made sure we bought a child-safe crib with the slats close together. I knew the one we used for Mark would never do."

Sliding a glance at Nathan, Beth realized this could be a frustrating stay for him. Not only did he have to deal with Ivan and Clara but with the fact they were Mark's parents. Yet his expression gave nothing away.

She was very aware of an escalation of tension between them since they'd decided to come here this weekend. Even more disconcerting was her inability to forget about his ex-wife's phone call. What if Elaine wanted a reconciliation with Nathan? Would he be interested?

Beth had never met a man who was as strong and confident in who he was and what he wanted. Or as caring. She had loved Mark dearly. But he'd had a selfish streak that had led him to race his motorcycle no matter what she'd felt about it, that often had led him to spend weekends with his buddies rather than her. He'd spent his life trying to separate himself from his family. Following that pattern, he'd tried to stay separate from her in many ways. Was it possible that since Mark's death she'd idealized him . . . and their marriage?

Nathan, on the other hand, liked being part of a family and took her plans into consideration before making his own. With Mark she'd often felt lonely. With Nathan . . . she felt excited stirrings and warmth and . . . love. Had she fallen in love with her new husband without realizing it?

As they ate lunch that knowledge fueled Beth's intense awareness of Nathan in spite of Ivan's cold stares and probing questions, in spite of Clara's attempts to smooth awkward lulls, in spite of Beth tending to her daughter's needs. It made Beth even more conscious of the night to come.

The afternoon passed with her gaze meeting Nathan's all too often. At the apartment they kept a length of a room between them ... or Dorie. Tonight there would be neither. Just the two of them and a bed.

Dorie loved the miniature carousel. She wanted to ride it again and again, giggling and laughing each time she did. Ivan produced a video camera and taped every smile and laugh. Beth almost felt sorry for him—his stiff attitude, his need to control, the years he'd lost with his son.

Dorie accepted Clara's overtures and was soon playing hide-and-seek with the older woman in the garden. Later they picked flowers. Dorie ran to Beth with each one, laying them in her lap. There was no way she was stopping for a nap. Beth decided not to push, but to take her signals from Dorie.

After a superb dinner on the screened-in porch, Beth and Nathan took Dorie for a walk. Nathan had become more quiet as the day progressed. Finally Beth couldn't stand the silence, which was as thick as the dusk falling about them. "Do you think Clara knows about the private investigator?"

Dorie ran ahead of them, and taking a few strides, Nathan scooped her up into his arms. "She might. She might not. You know them. I don't. But it seems to me Ivan's the type of man to keep secrets."

"Mark told me she doesn't know anything about their finances. Ivan expects her to do what he decides without any argument. I can't imagine a marriage like that—little communication . . . secrets.''

"I suppose you and Mark had no secrets and complete communication." Nathan's tone held a hint of sarcasm.

The truth was Mark had learned from his parents' example. But he'd soon discovered Beth hadn't been the type of woman to not speak her mind. "We tried, Nathan. That's all a couple can do." She wanted to leave an opening for him to talk about *his* marriage. But just then Dorie squirmed and squealed and wanted down again. Their conversation ended.

Clara met them on the patio as they returned from their walk. "Can I help you put Dorie to bed?"

Beth smiled. Clara truly did want to be close to her granddaughter. "If you don't mind getting wet. Bath time is more like a dip in the pool."

"Oh, I don't mind. I'll get plenty of towels."

Ivan stepped from the shadows. "I suppose you two will turn in, too? Or would you like some brandy?"

Nathan curved his arm around Beth's shoulders. "I think we'll skip the brandy."

He'd avoided touching her as much as possible all day. Now, his hand on her skin and the weight of his strong arm sent heat through every fiber of her being. But she felt the tension and restraint, too. His low tone and his possessive hold told Ivan they were newlyweds. She realized she wanted them to *be* newlyweds. But she had to ask Nathan a question first.

Nathan paced the guest bedroom. Clara and Beth had decided to bathe Dorie in one of the larger bathrooms with a sunken tub, rather than in the smaller one off their bedroom. He'd decided to stay out of their way. What he should do was go stand in the shower and let cold water beat on the part of him that was the hottest.

He stopped pacing and raked his hand through his hair. Frustration was becoming a nasty nemesis. How was he going to sleep next to Beth when sleep was the farthest thing from his mind?

But he'd made a promise—in fact several of them, and he didn't take them lightly. He'd keep all of them if he died trying. Beth and Dorie meant too much to him. He'd be patient. He'd be a gentleman. He'd keep his hands off Beth even if it meant sleeping in the bathtub!

He heard Clara and Beth in the adjoining room. Opening the door, he went inside to say good-night to Dorie.

Clara smiled at him. "She's almost asleep."

He took Dorie from her grandmother's arms and sat her in the crib. She reached up for a hug. Squeezing her, he said, "Mommy and I are right over there." Then he kissed her forehead and stepped away from the crib.

Clara went to the door. "If you need anything, just give a yell. I'll see you in the morning."

As she closed the door to Dorie's room, Nathan breathed a sigh of relief. But then he looked at Beth. Her cotton blouse was more wet than dry. He could see the lace of her bra through the material. His body responded and he groaned inwardly.

After Beth hugged and kissed Dorie, Nathan said, "If you want to get a shower, go ahead. I'll wait until you're finished."

"I think I'll take a bath. It might help me..." She hesitated. "Baths help me get to sleep faster."

He wished the solution to relaxation was as easy as taking a bath.

He'd brought a spy novel he'd started earlier in the week when dreams of Beth had awakened him with a need that wouldn't let him sleep. Instead of reclining on the bed, he settled himself in the bedroom chair. But it wasn't designed for someone as tall or restless as he was.

Determined to stay away from the bed until it was absolutely necessary, he opened the book.

Then he heard the water running.

Something fell over on the vanity.

Beth brushed against the door.

Was she removing her clothes? Of course she was. She was going to take a bath!

He could imagine her unfastening each button on her pink blouse. He could picture her unsnapping the waist of her shorts. He'd seen the silky underwear in the wash basket. White and a peach color—the color of her skin. Damn!

Although he had to read each page at least three times because of wandering thoughts, he didn't give up. Until Beth opened the bathroom door.

The rush of steam and scent of flowered bubble bath hit him first. Then the sight of her kicked him in the gut. He'd seen her in her robe before... almost every morning and every night as she scurried from the bedroom to the bathroom or vice versa. But tonight...

Her cheeks were pinker. The robe appeared to cling tighter to her body. The edging of lace on her nightgown seemed even more fetching. She'd pinned her hair up in the back but a few tendrils wisped along her cheeks. Desire surged through him hot and fast and demanding a release.

Someone knocked on their bedroom door. Beth crossed the room, the scent of flowers all around her, and opened it.

Clara peeked in and smiled at Nathan. Her gaze swiftly swept over the still-made bed, his shorts and shirt, and Beth's robe. "I'm so sorry to disturb you again but I wanted to ask you what you'd like for breakfast—eggs, pancakes, waffles?"

Nathan tried to hide his anger at the obvious, fact-finding interruption. "Anything you want to serve would be fine. Right now we'd like some privacy."

"Nathan..." Beth scolded.

Clara patted her daughter-in-law's arm. "It's all right, my dear. Newlyweds do deserve their privacy. I'll tell cook to present some of each. Good night again."

As soon as the door closed, Beth said in a low voice. "Nathan, that was rude. We're their guests..."

His frustration exploded and he stood, throwing his book on the chair. "Rude? I'll tell you what's rude. Clara Warren barging in here to see if she can catch us in bed for proof that we have a real marriage. Rude is setting a private investigator on our doorstep. Rude is inviting us here to scrutinize our every move."

Beth backed up a step. "I know this is difficult."

"*Difficult* doesn't begin to describe it." Suddenly his need for Beth, the aching to make their marriage real, became too combustible. He had to get away from the smell of flowers, the sight and scent of *her*. He crossed the room to the door. "I'm going for a walk and get some fresh air. Don't wait up."

"But what if Ivan or Clara sees you?"

"Maybe they'll think we had an argument like newlyweds sometimes do." With that he opened the door, then closed it behind him.

Nathan's hasty departure shook Beth. She'd wanted to talk to him, kiss him again, give in to the feelings she'd been fighting since she'd met him. But now maybe he wanted out. Maybe a family was more than he bargained for. At least this family.

Sinking down on the bed, she thought about his parting words. *Don't wait up.* Well, she was going to wait up, and there was nothing he could do about it.

An hour later Beth checked on Dorie. She was sound asleep, her favorite stuffed bear cuddled in beside her. Beth stroked her daughter's cheek, then, hearing footsteps in the hall, she returned to her room. The door opened and Nathan came in.

When he saw her, he frowned. "I'm going to get a shower."

"Fine. When you're finished we can talk."

"Beth, it's been a long day..."

"There's something I need to ask you." Her tone indicated she wasn't going to bed until she did.

He opened a dresser drawer and took out his sleeping shorts. "All right. Give me five minutes."

After Nathan disappeared into the bathroom, it was the longest five minutes of Beth's life.

Finally he opened the bathroom door and carried his clothes to the closet. As he hung them inside, Beth watched the play of his shoulder muscles, appreciated his taut buttocks as he leaned into the closet, tried to control the increase of her heart rate and the anxiety tightening her chest. Everything depended on his answer to her question.

"Are you thinking about reconciling with your ex-wife?"

He went still, then slowly turned toward her. "Where did *that* come from?"

"You left because of this fishbowl I've trapped you in. I understand you're angry about all this..."

He approached her when her voice quavered. "I left because being this close to you is driving me nuts!"

Her breath caught from the flare of naked desire in his green eyes. "I... I need to know, Nathan. Do you want out? Do you think you made a mistake marrying me?"

He tightened his hands into fists, and she could feel his restraint as much as the heat emanating from his bare skin. "I don't want out. *I* want to move forward. Why would you think I want to reconcile with Elaine?"

"Because... because our situation is so strange. Because you haven't talked to her in a long time and now you're going to get together with her. What if she wants you back?'' Beth tried to keep the proprietary note from her voice but couldn't conceal it entirely.

The nerve in Nathan's jaw worked. ''Do you care if she does?''

''Yes, I care. You're my husband!''

''And...?'' he pressed.

''And...and I'm worried. What if Dorie and I depend on you and then Elaine comes back into your life?''

''It's over, Beth. Whatever Elaine wants, I'm sure it's not a reconciliation. I'm not holding on to the past, but you are.''

Beth knew she had to take a risk. She knew she had to be the one to make the first move so Mark didn't stand between them any longer. ''What if I want to let go of the past? What if I want to move forward, too?''

When Nathan tilted his head, a lock of damp hair fell over his brow. He crossed his arms over his chest and said, ''You have to be sure.''

She took a step closer until her breasts almost grazed his folded arms. ''I am sure. I want to be your wife, Nathan. In every way.''

The guarded expression left his face, and he dropped his hands to his sides. His gaze held hers as he searched for any doubts. Finding none, he wrapped his arms around her and set his lips on hers.

The kiss was everything she could ever imagine a kiss might be...and more. It was the soft brush of lips, provocative strokes of Nathan's tongue, his desire inciting hers to riot, hers making him catch his breath. He broke the kiss for a moment to gaze into her eyes, to brush his fingers over her lips, to make sure she wanted more than a kiss.

Beth had never known a man this passionate, this gentle, this caring. She wound her arms around his neck and requested in a whisper, "Kiss me again."

A low groan sounded in his chest as his lips covered hers with the same hunger darkening his green eyes. Suddenly her feet left the ground. He never broke the kiss as he carried her to the bed and came down beside her.

Sliding his hand under the belt of her robe, he pulled it open. "I can't tell you how many nights, how many mornings I wanted to do this."

She smiled, put both her hands on his chest and slid her fingers through the soft hair. "And I can't tell you how many times I wanted to do this."

He closed his eyes for a moment, relishing her touch, then opened them. Taking one of her hands in his, he brought it to his lips and kissed her palm. Lightning bolts of desire flashed up her arm. First his lips, then his tongue, then his teeth nibbled her until she became restless and wanting and thoroughly impatient.

He looked at her expression, her other hand clasping the spread. "I want to do this slowly, Beth. I want you to remember this and never regret a moment of it."

Her love for him filled her heart and brought tears to her eyes. "I'll never regret it, Nathan."

He studied her for a moment, then he was kissing her again, touching her, creating a need neither of them could deny.

The sensual tension that had vibrated between them for the past month blazed into passion that consumed them both. Nathan's hands scorched through her robe and nightgown, but she longed to feel the fire on her skin.

Nathan wouldn't let her rush him. He kissed her face, her eyelids, her cheeks, her neck. With soft, slow caresses, he awakened every tingling spark of need in her body. Then when her skin rippled with sensitivity to his touch, he pushed her robe from her shoulders and helped her shed her gown. She lay naked before him, with no sense of self-consciousness, feeling freer than she'd ever felt in her life.

"You're beautiful," he said in a husky low voice that vibrated with desire.

She reached out and smoothed her hand over his shoulder. "You are, too."

He sucked in a breath. "Do you know what your touch does to me? How I've had to fight these past few weeks to keep my hands to myself?"

Sliding her hand to his neck, she caressed his jaw. "Now you don't have to fight anymore."

Nathan tried to control his ragged breathing, telling himself control was everything. Beth's wide blue eyes, her responsiveness, her innate sensuality, had pulled the reins on his desire so taut they could snap at any moment.

He hadn't been with a woman for a long time. It had been an even longer time since he'd participated in sex for the pleasure rather than the purpose. He intended to prolong the pleasure, to give them both a night they'd never forget.

"If I stop fighting, this could be over all too quickly," he reminded himself as well as warning her.

With a small shrug she smiled. "Then I guess we'll just have to do it all over again."

Beth's response broke the last vestige of his control. Skimming off his shorts, he sheathed her body under his.

His deep kiss and his hand skimming up her body had her moving sinuously against him until he thought he'd die from the pain of needing her. But he had to make sure she was ready. He shifted, sliding his hand between them. When he touched her intimately, she moaned his name.

"I don't want to hurt you," he murmured.

"Then make love to me, Nathan. Now."

Her breathless request took him over the edge. Control gave way to the desire for intimate union, for the need for a oneness he knew he could only find with this woman. He entered her with a prolonged thrust that made his heart pound and his body demand release. Beth's moan of pleasure, her hands on his buttocks urging him deeper, led him to a place he'd never been. The intense need, the aching for a family, the loneliness he'd carried from foster home to foster home exploded as he rocked against her, heard her cry of pleasure and followed her to the gates of Heaven.

Hours later bright sunlight peeked through the edge of the blinds. Nathan awakened, Beth nestled close beside him, with a feeling of total rightness but with an impending sense of dread. Beth had surprised him last night. He'd gone for a walk to get his control firmly in hand, fully expecting to return to a dark room where he would sleep on the edge of his side of the bed.

Her desire to make their marriage more than one of convenience had been a dream. She'd presented the dream to him like a precious gift, and he'd taken it. And now...

Now, after reaching for her again and again in the black of night, finding a harmony and passion he'd never imagined could exist, he had to shatter it. He had to talk to her about why his marriage had fallen apart. And he'd have to pray she could accept the unknown, the possibility of not having more children.

He should have told her before he'd married her.

He should have told her before they'd made love.

A sudden knock on the door broke the silence of the morning. Before he could even think of getting out of bed to answer it, the door opened.

Clara stood there, her expression uncertain. "Oh, I'm sorry. It wasn't locked so I thought you were up. It's already nine o'clock. Are you ready for breakfast?"

Nathan suspected Ivan had sent Clara to check on them, to determine if they'd spent the night together if she could. Before he could tell the woman how he felt about her intrusion, Beth raised her head from his shoulder and laid a restraining hand on his chest. "Dorie usually gets us awake. But she had a full day yesterday, so I guess she's catching up, too. Give us a half hour and we'll be down."

Clara's gaze passed over their entwined legs under the sheet and she gave them a tentative but knowing smile. "I'll tell Cook. And I'll also tell Ivan that bothering newlyweds this early is a bad idea. Take your time." With a wink she closed the door.

Beth ran her hand over Nathan's chest. "It's too early in the day to scowl like that."

His wife's fingers on his skin made him release a pent-up breath along with his anger. "Ivan might have sent her on the reconnaissance mission, but he's not going to like her report."

Beth's fingers stilled. "That breach of privacy might be the best thing that could have happened to us. Maybe now they'll leave us alone."

Nathan's thoughts returned again to the discussion he needed to have with Beth. Ivan and Clara and their spy tactics paled in comparison. Yet, Beth's warm body against his, the intimacy of her touch, the sight and feel and scent of her, urged him to wait just a little longer. After they returned home, they'd have plenty of time to talk. He wanted Beth. He needed her. And a day or two wouldn't make a difference.

He reluctantly moved away from her, slid his legs over the side of the bed, went to the door and locked it. "I'm going to make sure they leave us alone. At least for the next few minutes."

Beth smiled. "And what are we going to do with a few minutes?"

He climbed back into bed, took her in his arms and suggested, "Let's experiment and see just how much we can pack into them."

As he kissed Beth and she responded with a freedom that snatched his breath, he pushed his concerns away to concentrate on the moment and to pray they had a future.

Chapter Eight

Mark's bicycle stood in the corner of the basement. Beth went to it, flipped up the kickstand with her foot and wheeled the bike to the middle of the floor. As she set the tackle box beside it, Nathan walked in.

Her heart jumped then sped up. A true newlywed now, her skin tingled in anticipation of his touch. For three nights, after they'd put Dorie to bed, they'd caressed and kissed and lain in each other's arms. Nathan had made love to her as if nothing else in the world mattered. He still hadn't said the words, but she thought she could feel love in the tenderness of his strokes, the passion of his kisses. He didn't hold back his passion. Yet she felt he was holding back. Maybe it was just the newness of it all. And maybe he was waiting until after his meeting with his ex-wife. He and Elaine had played phone tag since Monday.

As Nathan came toward her, he smiled a slow sexy smile that told Beth he was remembering last night and anticipating tonight. Then he saw the bicycle.

"Supper's almost ready," Beth said. "I asked Rosa to watch Dorie for a few minutes so I could come down here."

Nathan stopped a good foot away, instead of taking her in his arms as he had the past few nights. "I saw your note. Do you need help or should I get Dorie?"

"I want to donate Mark's bike to that man you told me about. The one who gives them to children who can't afford them."

Nathan stepped a little closer. "And the tackle box?"

"Do you fish?"

He shook his head.

"Neither do I. Maybe you could take it to the store and give it to someone who wants it."

Nathan slid his hands under her hair and tilted her chin up. "Cleaning up the basement?"

"No, I'm putting my life in order," she said softly, hoping he'd get the message. She loved him. She wouldn't forget Mark, but she wouldn't hang on, either.

Nathan must have heard her, loud and clear, because he kissed her long and hard and deep.

When he raised his head, she gulped in a deep breath. "I have an idea for this weekend." They would be driving to Washington, D.C., for Nathan's friends' anniversary party.

"Gavin asked if we'd like to drive down with them," Nathan said.

Beth nodded. "Jessie called to ask me the same thing. She also said Lisa's not going. She's spending the night with a friend. I was wondering if you'd like to leave Dorie with Rosa."

The green desire in Nathan's eyes deepened. "You, me and a hotel room. We might not make it to the party."

Beth smiled. "Is that a yes?"

He rubbed his thumb along her cheek. "A definite yes."

A question had been gnawing at Beth all day. "Did you get hold of Elaine?"

"This afternoon. We're having lunch tomorrow."

"Did she say what it's about?"

"No. Just that she didn't want to discuss anything over the phone."

Too many thoughts chased each other in Beth's mind. "Does she know you're married?"

"I don't know. If she doesn't, she'll find out tomorrow." He traced his finger over Beth's bottom lip. "I think we have better things to do than talk about Elaine."

When he bent his head to kiss Beth again, she told herself not to worry. She told herself jealousy was *not* an attractive quality. Yet as Nathan's mouth seduced hers, she knew she would worry and feel jealous until after his lunch with his ex-wife. Until she was sure Elaine didn't want a reconciliation.

* * *

The next day Nathan saw Elaine sitting at a quiet, corner table positioned near three palms. Apparently she wanted privacy. Smiling at the maître d', Nathan strode toward her, curious as to why she'd called this meeting, eager to get it over with. Beth apparently saw Elaine as a possible impediment to their future happiness. She was wrong about that, and he wanted to reassure her as soon as possible.

In fact, maybe he'd go straight home after lunch. If Dorie was taking her nap...

Since Saturday night, when he'd first made love to Beth, he'd been almost afraid to let the happiness well up inside. He had everything he'd ever wanted. Telling Beth why he and Elaine had divorced had been inconceivable the past few days in the flush of passion and intimacy that was bonding them with each touch and kiss. All the years of loneliness, feeling rootless, aching for a family to love, had kept him silent.

As he approached Elaine now, he realized as he had many years ago, that she was a beautiful woman. Her sleek, dark brown hair, her perfectly applied makeup, her tailored suit, gave her polish and sophistication. Where once he had admired all that, now he thought of Beth—her natural beauty, her generosity of spirit and caring that Elaine could never match.

Pulling out the chair across the table from his ex-wife, he sat down.

Elaine scanned his casual dress, the knit shirt and khakis. "Hello, Nathan. It's good to see you again."

He noticed the large diamond of her engagement ring and remembered how Beth had requested a wide gold band. "I was surprised when you called."

"When I dialed your old number, I learned you no longer lived there. Your manager told me you'd married and moved. Congratulations."

"Thank you. Now why don't you tell me why we couldn't discuss whatever you wanted to discuss on the phone."

She picked up her glass of water, took a sip and set it down again. "Because the subject is too personal."

He waited.

"I'm engaged."

"I'd heard that."

She gave him a tight smile. "Brian's a wonderful man. We've been engaged for over a year."

Nathan crossed his arms on the table. "And what does that have to do with me?"

"I told Brian I wouldn't marry him until I got pregnant. I found out last week that I am. *And* it happened naturally."

He and Elaine had never discussed fault in their inability to conceive, because there was no clear evidence either one of them had a problem. But now the full brunt of Elaine's announcement hit Nathan.

She picked up her glass again and watched him over the rim. "I felt you should know."

Thinking about his marriage to Elaine, the way she'd walked out, he couldn't believe she'd wanted to meet with him for a purely unselfish motive. He would have learned about her pregnancy eventually. They still shared mutual acquaintances. "You didn't *just* want me to know. I think you want to shift the cause of our breakup to my shoulders. Now you can blame me for not getting you pregnant.''

Setting down her glass, she straightened in her chair. Her expression told him he'd hit the mark. ''It obviously wasn't *my* fault.''

He pitied this woman who'd wanted a child of her own so much she'd been willing to sacrifice their marriage. ''Tell me something, Elaine. What would have happened if you and your fiancé hadn't conceived?''

Her expression tightened; her eyes hardened. ''We wouldn't be getting married.''

Nathan shook his head. ''I feel sorry for your fiancé. Does he know he's expendable?''

She lifted her chin defensively. ''My biological clock is ticking. Men can't understand what that feels like. Now, thank goodness, I know I'm not the one with the problem.''

Nathan clenched his hands into fists. ''Marriage isn't something to believe in only when it suits your needs or gives you what you want.''

''Nathan, you knew children were important to me.''

''Having children was important to me, too. But so were you. That's where we differed.'' He pushed back his chair and stood. ''There's no point in my staying for lunch. I wish you luck, Elaine, and the life you want.''

''I felt I had to tell you.''

''And you did. Take care of yourself and that baby you're carrying.'' When he turned away, he felt his ex-wife's gaze on his back. He kept walking. Toward

Beth. Toward the discussion he couldn't postpone any longer.

With the radio turned on low in the kitchen, her hands busy peeling peaches for a cobbler, Beth tried to distract herself from thinking about Nathan's lunch date.

It's not a date, she reminded herself.

When she heard the front door open, she rinsed off her hands and reached for the towel.

A few seconds later Nathan stood in the archway of the kitchen, his serious expression scaring her as much as his silence.

"I didn't expect you till supper. Are you taking the afternoon off?"

He didn't move toward her. "Is Dorie napping?"

Beth nodded, more fearful than before that Nathan's lunch would shatter her newfound happiness.

"We have to talk."

"You're going back to her, aren't you?" Beth asked in an almost whisper.

"No, I am *not* going back to her," he said in an even tone. He moved then, shutting off the radio, pulling out a kitchen chair. "Sit. There's something I have to tell you."

She felt almost relieved as she took the chair he'd offered. If he wasn't going back to his ex-wife, what could be wrong?

After he sat across from her, he said, "I never told you why Elaine and I divorced."

The past few nights, in between the kisses and touches, they had talked. Beth had told him about her parents, confided how much she still missed them, even had admitted again to the anger she'd felt at Mark after his death. Nathan had asked questions, probed, drawn her out. She'd shared with him, hoping he'd do the same. He'd described a few of his foster homes, told anecdotes about his college days with Gavin, Cade and Jeff, but that's as far as he went. Unwilling to pry and bring discord to happy, passionate moments, she'd let the subject of his first marriage rest. But the grim expression on his face now told her that might have been a mistake.

"Why *did* you divorce?" she asked.

His gaze met and held hers. "Elaine and I both wanted children. We started trying right away. When she didn't conceive, doctors told us to be patient. After two years our patience ran out and we saw a specialist."

A foreboding settled over Beth.

Nathan went on, "We were hopeful again, but after two more years nothing had worked. There was no concrete evidence that either of us had a problem, yet we couldn't conceive. I wanted to adopt. Elaine didn't. A few months later she asked for a divorce."

Beth couldn't tell if the pain in Nathan's eyes was from the past or because of the present.

Before she could absorb the implications of what Nathan was telling her, he dropped the bomb. "I don't know if I can father a child."

Beth's breath caught, and she stared at him in astonishment.

He raked his hand through his hair. "I know I should have told you before the wedding. But safeguarding Dorie seemed more important."

Beth's shock quickly changed into a sense of betrayal that squeezed her heart. "Why did you decide to tell me now?"

"Elaine wanted to see me to tell me she's pregnant."

Pain sliced through Beth. Taking a deep breath, she stood and turned away from Nathan. Her life had changed again in the course of fifteen minutes. A little while ago she'd thought she and her new husband were building a marriage based on honesty. She'd been wrong!

She heard the scrape of his chair on the linoleum and felt him standing behind her.

He clasped her shoulder. "Beth, we can adopt. We have Dorie—"

Anger bubbled up inside her along with the hurt. She shrugged off his hand and faced him. "You don't understand what I'm feeling, do you? I'm not worried about having more children! I'm upset because you weren't honest with me. I have trusted you with everything about my life since the moment I met you. In the past week I've given you everything I am, all I have to give. And you didn't tell me about something this important? I thought I knew you. But I don't. Without honesty, Nathan, we can't *have* a marriage."

He clasped her arms and looked squarely into her eyes. "You *do* know me."

"No, I don't. Because now I wonder what else you're keeping from me. How am I supposed to trust you again?"

He dropped his hands as the full impact of her words hit him.

Into the stark silence of the kitchen came a small voice calling, "Mommee. Mommee. Mommee. Mommee." Each time, Dorie called a little louder.

"I have to get her up," Beth managed to say, turning away from Nathan, needing to think about everything that had just happened.

"Beth?"

She stopped.

"I'm going back to the store," he said. "We both need some space."

Space? There was enough space between them to fill the Grand Canyon. "Will you be back for supper?"

"I'll probably stay till closing. I should spend some time at the computer."

She couldn't tell him she wanted him to stay. She felt hurt, disappointed and so confused. . . .

Dorie called again.

Beth said, "I'll see you tonight then," and headed for Dorie's room before Nathan saw her tears.

After he locked the store and switched on the security system, Nathan called Beth. She picked up on the second ring. "Hello?"

He didn't know what to do for her; he didn't know what to do for him. He'd decided it might be better for him to stay away for a while; that's why he'd left. To think. To figure out a solution. To find a way to clear the pain of betrayal from Beth's eyes. Distance had always worked in the past. When he was a kid and a foster home didn't work out, the authorities moved him to another. Distance. When Elaine had said she'd wanted a divorce, the solution to the intensity of the pain had been distance. When he had a problem, to gain perspective, he needed distance.

On the other hand, if Beth wanted him to come home... "It's Nathan. I thought it might be better if I stayed at the store tonight."

"I see."

Her tone was cool. She was obviously still hurt and angry. If he went home, the tension would probably keep them both awake all night. "I'll come by in the morning to shower and change."

"Fine."

Although he sensed her reluctance to talk to him, he couldn't cut the connection. "I guess you put Dorie to bed already?"

"An hour ago. She asked for you. She wanted you to read her a story."

Bedtime had become a ritual he looked forward to on nights he didn't work late at the store. "Maybe I can read her one before I come back to work in the morning."

The silence between them was awkward and hurt like hell. "Get a good night's sleep, Beth. I'll see you tomorrow."

"Good night, Nathan."

The inflection in her voice couldn't have been more impersonal. She thought of him as a stranger again, and there was nothing he could do about it. Except give them both some distance.

He worked at the computer for a couple of hours to try and distract himself. But he kept seeing Beth's face on the screen. Finally he moved from the office to the storeroom and sat on the black vinyl sofa. All his life he'd felt set apart. Not having a family, a real family of his own, had always made him feel different from other kids. Most of the foster homes he'd stayed in wanted him there to help with the younger kids they took in. Some did it for the money. It was difficult to get attached to people who might not want you in the morning or the next day or next month. Temporary homes didn't give children stability. Yet, as children got older they were harder to place.

Nathan had never experienced the sense of belonging he'd craved. He'd thought he could find it with Elaine. He'd been wrong.

When he'd met Beth...

He'd sensed she understood about belonging.

Was he doing the right thing staying away from her? Would distance and time help or hurt them? This marriage of convenience had forced them to become a family. Is that what Beth still wanted?

He knew now he'd hurt her by holding back. So he couldn't push her. Maybe he'd pushed her into making love with him too soon and she regretted that, too.

Suddenly he realized spending the night here wouldn't solve a damn thing. His instincts told him distance might have been a solution in the past, but it wasn't a solution now.

He was going home.

* * *

The next morning Beth came out of her bedroom and stopped short. Nathan was stretched out on the sofa. He hadn't bothered to open the bed. She'd plopped the pillows and sheet out there earlier in the evening, in the midst of her tears, in the midst of her hurt and anger. When he'd called and said he wasn't coming home, she'd cried herself to sleep. Her eyes were probably still puffy.

Sitting up, he studied her. "Are you okay?"

She tightened the belt on her robe. "I'm fine. I thought you were spending the night at the store."

"After I thought about it, I decided it wasn't such a great idea. We have to decide what we're going to do about this weekend."

Jeff and Katie's party, the night in the hotel that was supposed to be special. Her logic told her she was asking for heartache if she went. Until she sorted all her feelings, being with Nathan would be fraught with tension. But her heart told her she was asking for heartache if she didn't make the trip with him. "I said I would go and I will. Most hotel rooms have two double beds. We don't have to spend much time there."

Nathan rose from the sofa and walked toward her. He seemed to take up most of the space in her world. "Jessie and Gavin will know something's wrong."

"Jessie and Gavin know our marriage for what it is—a convenient arrangement."

Pain flashed in Nathan's eyes, and she felt it, too. But she couldn't just set aside the feeling of betrayal, the doubts she had about their future.

He didn't contradict her. His expression became shuttered. It seemed neither of them knew where to start to put the pieces back together. In a neutral tone he said, "I'm going to get a shower. If Dorie's up, I'll read her a story before I leave."

With that he crossed to the bathroom. Beth felt the tears prick all over again.

Saturday night, in the reception room in the hotel where Jeff and Katie held their anniversary party, Beth looked around at the centerpieces filled with flowers and the host and hostess mingling with their guests. The conversation and laughter bubbling around Beth should have distracted her. But none of it did. All she could think about was Nathan and the terrible tension between them.

The drive to Washington with Jessie and Gavin had been an exercise in pretense. Neither of them had acted "normal," though they'd tried to carry on a conversation as if nothing had happened.

In the front of the room, the band started playing. Jeff and Katie were the first couple on the small dance floor. Cade and his wife Randi followed. Both couples looked happy and incredibly in love. Beth had talked to Randi earlier about her life in Montana, being a mother and practicing law, too. She and Cade had their hands full with three boys and the ranch. But it was obvious they loved their life.

Nathan stood across the room at the buffet table talking with Gavin. Beth looked at her husband... and hurt.

"What's going on, Beth?" Jessie gently nudged Beth's arm.

"What makes you think anything's going on?"

"I know you. I know Nathan. You might not have known each other well when you got married, but there's a wall between you today that was never there before."

"We...had an argument."

Jessie tilted her head. "Married couples argue."

"It wasn't just a disagreement. It's serious."

"And too private to discuss with me."

Beth nodded.

"Look, I don't know what's wrong between you and Nathan. But if you care about him, don't give up without a fight. We all make mistakes. We all have fears and insecurities that sometimes make us do stupid things. When Gavin and I were finding our way back to each other, I was so afraid he'd leave again that I couldn't see the love he was offering."

"Nathan hasn't even mentioned the word *love*."

"Have you?" Jessie asked.

Beth shook her head.

"Sometimes it's harder for men than women to admit what they feel."

"And sometimes it's only sex for men," Beth concluded, her voice low.

Jessie sighed. "You and Nathan need to have a heart-to-heart. Maybe when the party's over."

Beth thought about the hotel room waiting upstairs with the two double beds. Her gaze again found Nathan, and she realized she needed to know why he hadn't been honest with her. It could make all the difference to their future. She'd been too upset and hurt to ask why before. The question was—did Nathan care about her enough to give her the answer?

As the evening went on, Jeff and Katie's family and friends thinned out. After a slow dance Cade and Randi returned to the table but didn't sit. "We're going up to our room," Cade said. "It's rare Randi and I have time alone without our desperadoes."

Gavin stood and held his hand out to Jessie. "Sounds like a good idea."

Nathan asked Beth, "Are you ready to leave?"

She glanced at Katie and Jeff, who were standing on the other side of the room talking with friends. "We should say goodbye."

Her words seemed to echo between them, meaning something entirely different than she intended. Nathan's body tensed, his green eyes darkened, but his expression went blank. She thought about saying goodbye to Nathan and realized she couldn't. She loved him. She wanted to understand why he'd kept important information from her. She ached to know if *he* loved *her* . . . if there was more than desire and a need for a family on his part.

But right here, right now, she couldn't put any of that into words.

They said goodbye to Katie and Jeff, Cade and Randi, Jessie and Gavin. And then they took the elevator to their room.

Nathan stood beside Beth in the elevator, knowing he had to confront her about what was and was not happening between them. He knew he had to give her space, but now that space was becoming practically

insurmountable. He'd slept on the sofa bed last night.
She'd made no indication that that wasn't what she
wanted. If the tension between them pulled any
tighter, he was afraid they'd never find their way back.

If he'd realized how hurt she would be . . .

He never wanted to hurt Beth. He'd never considered this to be a matter of trust. But then maybe he'd
been in denial because all he could see was the family
he wanted and the risk of losing it. He glanced over at
her. Her simple violet dress shimmered, hugged her
curves, and all he wanted to do was strip it off
her...hold her in his arms again. But her hands closed
tightly around her purse told him she was uncomfortable being alone with him.

He'd thought about sending her flowers, giving her
perfume . . . something . . . anything. Yet he knew a
present, even a truck full of presents, wouldn't make
a damn bit of difference. Not with Beth. She had been
vulnerably honest with him from the moment they'd
met. He should have realized holding back the reason
for his divorce would tear apart the foundation they
were building.

Now, how could he build it up again?

When the elevator stopped, they stepped into the
hall. His suitcoat brushed her arm. From the look in
her eyes, the contact startled her as much as him. He
longed to take her in his arms and kiss the hurt away.

Voices drifted down the hall; a door banged.

Beth looked away.

Nathan walked toward their room, then unlocked
the door.

The room appeared untouched, as if they hadn't spent an hour there before the party. Beth had showered and dressed in the bathroom while he'd paced. She'd come out of the bathroom, her hair curled, dressed sexier than he'd ever seen her, and he'd wanted her with a desperation that had surprised even him.

But then she'd gone to the telephone, saying, "I'll call Rosa and tell her we arrived safely. She worries."

Nathan had closed himself in the bathroom, taking a long, cold shower.

Seeing Cade and Randi, Jessie and Gavin, Katie and Jeff, dancing, laughing, intimate in the way only happily married couples can be, Nathan realized all over again how much more he wanted than a marriage of convenience, how much more than living together and sleeping in separate beds.

Beth stopped at the dresser, opened the drawer and pulled out a nightgown and robe—the cotton set that had driven him crazy the first two weeks of their marriage. At least then, a door had separated them. Tonight, there'd be only space between their beds, space that could only make the tension between them worse. If he could remind her of the closeness they'd shared for those few nights...

He discarded his suitcoat and tossed it over a chair. "We can't go on like this."

Beth pushed her hair behind her ear. "I know."

When he went to her, she clutched her nightgown and robe closer to her. He could feel the wall between them. "We've been acting like strangers. And we're not. We know each other...intimately."

The flash of remembrance in her eyes said she wasn't immune to him or the intimacies they'd shared. Then a guarded look replaced the memories. "I *don't* know you, Nathan. Not if you could keep something so important from me," she said again, reminding him of the obstacle between them.

Unable to keep his distance, he placed his hands on her shoulders, remembering the softness of her skin, her touch when she'd reached for him in the middle of the night. "I was wrong. I'm sorry."

The pulse at her throat fluttered riotously. "Why didn't you tell me?"

He knew he had to be as honest as he could be or she'd back away again. "I wanted a family. I wanted you. I didn't want you to walk away like Elaine did."

Beth searched his face, probing for the truth. If she found it, he couldn't tell. Finally she said, "I wouldn't have walked away."

"Then don't walk away now," he murmured as he took her into his arms.

But she remained tense . . . stiff.

Loosening his hold, he leaned back. "I can only give you the truth, Beth. I can only tell you I made a mistake that I won't repeat. But we can't have a marriage if you're not willing to forgive me. That's the bottom line."

He saw the doubts in her eyes. The indecision. All he wanted to do was make it go away. "Can you forgive me?"

Beth gazed into Nathan's green eyes and knew he was right. If she didn't forgive him, they couldn't have a marriage. And maybe that's why she'd reacted so strongly. Mark had kept so much of his life separate from hers. They'd been companions and lovers, but not united in body and soul. With Nathan she'd felt united. She'd felt as if she'd found a new kind of marriage—a new meaning to promises and commitment. Until she'd discovered he'd kept something from her.

But she loved him. She still wanted their marriage. She still wanted him. She'd missed him so, the tenderness in his touch, the strength and security of his arms around her. It sounded as if he'd held back out of fear, not because of a lack of caring.

Maybe she'd needed the last two days to see how much she did really love him. And with love came the ability to forgive.

He was waiting for her answer.

"I can forgive you, Nathan."

When his lips came down on hers—hard, demanding, persuasive—Beth knew she never wanted to think about life without him . . . another night without him. She relaxed her grip on her clothes, let them fall and wound her arms around his neck. Maybe his desire would transform into love, just as hers had.

In time.

Because desire wouldn't hold them together. Only love could.

So why can't you say the words?

If she did, she'd make herself even more vulnerable. She'd be risking everything, and maybe she didn't trust either herself or Nathan to risk that much.

Nathan broke away and gazed into her eyes. She watched him search for answers, search for passion, search for the key to bringing them back together. She couldn't say the words, but she could try to show him what she felt. Reaching up to his tie, she tugged it open.

He stood perfectly still.

She unfastened one button after another on his shirt until she reached his waistband.

He didn't even blink.

She filled her hands with the material of his shirt and pulled it from his trousers.

His gaze never wavered from hers.

When she laid her hands on his chest, he covered them with his and asked, "Are you sure?"

She could feel the tension in his hands...the restraint. "I want you," she whispered, longing for so much more than desire.

The dam broke. His lips crushed hers, his tongue thrust into her mouth, and he lifted her into his arms.

Tonight, they'd have desire. She prayed love would soon follow.

Chapter Nine

When Beth awakened, for a moment she forgot where she was. Then the heat of Nathan's body, curved around hers as they lay on their sides, reminded her she'd committed herself to him again. That's how she saw making love. Did he?

She moved her leg, feeling his rough hairs against the back of her thigh. Erotic. Exciting. But was there more than desire and excitement? For her there was, but she wondered about him.

He tightened his arm around her waist and murmured into her neck, "Good morning."

His tongue tickled her earlobe, and she felt a rush of pleasure. Shifting, she turned and faced him. "Good morning to you, too."

He tilted his forehead against hers. "I don't think we moved all night."

"I like having your arms around me," she confessed, loving the feel of his skin, the rakish droop of his hair over his brow, the beard stubble that made him look sexy and dangerous.

Tracing his thumb over her bottom lip, he said, "I even made love to you in my dreams."

"That must have been the same dream I had."

He smiled. "Maybe we should compare notes."

Beth loved the banter, she loved being close to Nathan this way, but she wanted more than physical closeness. "We could. Or we could ... talk."

Nathan's smile vanished, and he shifted on the pillow until there was some distance between them. "What do you want to talk about?"

"Your first marriage."

Silence fell across them until Nathan said, "All right. Exactly what do you want to know?"

"Just tell me about it. What was right. What was wrong."

He lay on his back and stared at the ceiling. "When I met Elaine, I thought we wanted the same things. I didn't realize that children were more important to her than marriage."

"The desire to have children usually binds a husband and wife together," Beth said softly.

"It should. But infertility can tear a couple apart. Especially if they don't work on the marriage through the waiting and the doctor's appointments ... and the anxiety that becomes part of the process."

"Did you know you weren't working on it?"

"That's the hell of it. We were both so involved with our jobs. Elaine worked long hours during tax season. When I first bought the store, my hours were extended, too. The charts, the temperature taking, having sex because the time was right, not because it was a spontaneous freedom that fulfilled a marriage, after a while didn't seem much different from a day at work."

"So you didn't want to go home."

He turned his head to look at her. "Oh, I wanted to go home. But I wanted it to be a place that was peaceful and comfortable, not turmoiled and strained. That's why I finally suggested adoption. And that's when I realized we didn't have the same goals after all."

"You and I married so quickly. Don't you wonder about our goals?" Beth asked.

Propping on one elbow, he caressed her cheek with his other hand. "Right now I have one goal. To make up for the time we've lost as newlyweds."

As he cupped the back of her head, he nudged her toward him. Had she learned anything from what he'd told her? He wanted his home to a be a haven. He wanted to focus on marriage rather than having more children.

Had he married Elaine out of love or out of the need for the family he'd never experienced? He'd definitely married Beth for the desire to belong to a family. So where did love fit in? Would Nathan let himself feel it?

And if not, where did that leave her and the love that grew inside her for him each day?

Nathan's green eyes flashed with the desire that had sparked between them from the moment they'd met at

Gavin's party. She'd fought it from the beginning, telling herself it was too quick, too hot, too alive to be good for her. But right now she wanted the fire and the life and the hope that love could be buried beneath it all.

"I want you, Beth."

When Nathan sought her lips, she gave to him freely. His mouth was hot and seductive and promised her pleasure. She pushed her tongue past his lips and felt his shudder, realizing she held the power to make him need her. It was a heady discovery and one she knew she had to handle reverently.

As Nathan passed his hands down her back, he brought her against him. Desire became more than kisses and touches. His throbbing heat, ready to find a home in the core of her womanhood, convinced her she couldn't hold back her needs or the intense pleasure she experienced with him. She thought she'd given him everything before. But now she realized she'd merely started to give.

With a deep breath Nathan told himself to slow down. Last night had been explosive, a reconciliation almost too fast to absorb. But this morning he'd wondered how complete it had been. Beth's questions about his marriage, the doubts still lingering in her eyes, told him the trust between them had been severely shaken. All he wanted to do was regain that trust, reassure her he'd never intentionally withhold anything from her again.

He knew building trust took time. But he also knew intimacy could build trust quicker than any conversation. Holding on to his control, when all he wanted to do was plunge into her and make them one, he brought his hand between them and circled her breast. Her lips parted, and her sweet, low sound of pleasure reinforced his knowledge that slow could be more erotic.

She was so vulnerable and beautiful, yet so strong and independent, as well. He'd never met a woman who could make him need, want and feel as she could. Circling her breast again and again, he finally let his thumb brush her nipple.

"Nathan!"

"Tell me what you want. Tell me what will give you the most pleasure."

She opened her eyes, and he saw so much longing there. "I want all of you," she murmured in a low voice.

He smiled and a second before his lips enclosed on her nipple, he said, "You've got me."

His tongue teased and taunted her until she raked her nails down his sides. But it wasn't enough. He wanted to make her tremble and gasp and moan only for him, until he was the only man who could satisfy her, until he erased the memory of her dead husband, until she trusted him without reservation.

He raised his head to kiss her again, to trail his hand between her thighs, to glide his fingers where her damp heat proved her arousal.

She moaned and clutched him.

Propping himself on his elbows above her, he slowly lowered his body, watching her expression, encouraged by the growing wonder in her blue eyes. He felt the wonder, too.

She stroked his back, urging him closer.

But he teased them both, prolonging the moment, making their joining the ultimate pleasure.

She arched toward him to hurry him, but he wouldn't hurry. "Slower is better. We'll remember it longer," he said, his voice raspy from maintaining control.

Her eyes widened, but he was sure he still saw doubts. There was only one way to take them away.

With excruciating slowness he entered her and watched the pleasure overtake her.

When she raised her knees to take him deeper, when he filled her and felt her contract around him, he lost control. As he thrust into her again and again, he heard her cry of pleasure, felt the quaking of her body and knew he'd finally found a home.

Sunday afternoon, about an hour out of Roanoke, Gavin stopped at a fast food restaurant for sodas. Beth and Jessie went to the ladies' room.

Jessie ran a brush through her hair. "I guess you and Nathan made up?"

Beth felt her cheeks color. "Is it so obvious?"

Her friend smiled. "I think there's a natural hum around a couple after they've made love."

Beth turned on the spigot and washed her hands, then patted cool water on her cheeks. "I just wish I could read Nathan's mind."

"He probably wishes he could read yours."

Beth shook her head. "I tell him what's going on in mine. At least most of it."

Jessie tucked her small brush back into her purse. "You have to remember you and Nathan are still finding your way. Most couples have the chance to do that *before* they get married."

"How did you know that Gavin loved you?"

Jessie leaned against the counter. "We'd fallen in love in college and those feelings never died. It's not just feeling the love or even hearing someone say it. It's trusting in it. I had to learn to do that all over again."

Beth's trust in the world had been shaken when her parents had died. First with her dad and then with her mother, she'd lost her grounding, a basic sense of security. Then Mark had died.

What *could* she trust in except her ability to take care of herself and her unborn child by using her intelligence and determination and every ounce of strength she possessed? But now, married to Nathan, she knew she had to learn to trust in more than herself. She had to trust him and their marriage.

Jessie straightened and picked up her purse. "Trust your instincts, Beth, rather than your doubts."

Her friend's advice was solid. But could she follow it?

Beth and Nathan rode their bikes to the park Sunday evening. They'd both missed Dorie and wanted to spend some time with her. Beth took in a breath of the September air. The days were already growing shorter. Before long the leaves would turn.

Nathan smiled at her as he put Dorie on the children's swing with the special seats so she wouldn't fall.

As he pushed the seat, Dorie stuck her feet out in front of her and tried to touch the sky.

When she tired of the swing, Beth sat with her on the wooden merry-go-round, holding her steady while Nathan gave the playground ride a push.

Dorie giggled and called, "More."

Nathan spun them a little faster.

Finally Beth called a halt, laughing. "Much more of that and I won't be able to walk a straight line."

As Nathan lifted Dorie from Beth's arms, a trio of kindergarten-aged children hopped on the merry-go-round. One of them said to the man with them, "Daddy, I want to go real fast."

Nathan chuckled. "I think kids can take a lot more motion than adults." He asked Dorie. "What next?"

The two-year-old pointed to the line of seesaws.

The grass brushed Beth's ankles as she hunkered on the end of the seesaw that was on the ground. Nathan settled Dorie in front of her and dropped a quick kiss on Beth's lips.

When she looked up, surprised, he said, "I couldn't resist."

She smiled. "I'm glad you couldn't."

After he positioned himself on the other end, he let his weight take him to the ground while her end went up.

Nathan's light blue T-shirt had seen many washings. She'd learned his softest shirts were his favorites. He liked comfort. The jogging shorts he wore molded to his buttocks and thighs in the same comfortable way. Except it wasn't so comfortable for her.

She caught herself looking...often. And with the looking came the desire for touching.

"A penny for your thoughts," he called.

How did he always seem to know? She knew her cheeks were turning red. "You'll have to wait until later. There's a minor nearby."

His grin was wicked. "I'll wait. And don't think I'll forget."

After they'd pushed up and down a few times, he asked, "What do you think about moving to a bigger apartment or looking for a house?"

The question took her by surprise. "I...I don't know. I like being near Rosa. And everything's close by...."

"We could stay in Four Oaks. Rosa wouldn't be far away. But it would be nice to have a yard for Dorie. And I could use an office."

"I don't know how Dorie would take to a move."

"If she's with us, she'll adjust," Nathan concluded, his tone firm.

"Let me think about it for a while," she suggested.

"It's time to let go of the past, Beth. That apartment reminds you of Mark."

"That apartment has been my home for years. It's not as easy as closing one door and opening another."

"Maybe it should be," Nathan said as he stopped the seesaw and held it steady. Straightening his legs, he let Beth and Dorie gently settle on the ground.

Climbing off the seesaw, he came to where they sat. Dorie scrambled to her feet. "Sand, Daddee."

Nathan froze and so did Beth as Dorie ran across the grass to the row of sandboxes.

Beth stood and spoke first. "It was only a matter of time. We read her books about families. She hears other children call their parents Mommy and Daddy."

"But how do you feel about her calling me that?"

"If we're going to be a family, it's only right."

His shoulders squared. "Mark's her father."

Nathan seemed determined to confront the issue head-on, and Beth knew she should, too. "Yes, he is. And someday I'll tell her about him. But you're the one who tucks her in at night, who pushes her on the swing, who helps feed her at breakfast every morning. That means you're her dad."

The nerve in Nathan's jaw worked as he watched Dorie climb over the edge of the sandbox and plop down inside. Then he curved his arm around Beth's shoulders and they walked toward their daughter. Beth realized it *was* time to think about moving... and moving on.

Nathan couldn't help whistling Monday afternoon as he rang up a customer's purchase and bagged it. Beth had agreed to look at bigger apartments. But most apartments wouldn't give Dorie a big backyard. So he'd convinced Beth to look at houses with him, too. Tonight they could drive around and decide what neighborhoods they liked best. Maybe they should think about building. That would take a lot longer until they chose plans, a contractor. But if they built, they could plan exactly what they wanted.

Last night when Dorie had called him Daddy...he'd never experienced anything like the feeling at any time in his life. Now if only Beth could let go of the life she'd had with Mark, put her trust in their marriage and the future...

The bell on the door dinged as a new customer came in. Nathan checked the mirror on the ceiling and frowned. Ivan Warren. What did he want?

Ivan approached the counter with a smile. Nathan was immediately suspicious.

"Good afternoon, Maxwell. Is there somewhere private we could talk? I have something I'd like to show you." He held up the manila envelope in his hand.

Nathan didn't want to talk to the man, and he sensed trouble, but he didn't intend to alienate him, either. "We can talk in my office."

After Nathan informed his manager he'd be in the back, he led Ivan to the room behind the store. "What can I do for you?"

"I think it's the other way around. I think I can do something for you that will make us both happy." He opened the envelope, took out a photograph and laid it on the desk.

Nathan stared at it for a moment. It was a picture of him and Elaine at the restaurant. "What does this have to do with anything?"

"That's your ex-wife, isn't it?"

Nathan kept his anger in check. "Yes."

"Looks kind of cozy to me. The two of you... hidden in the palms. It sets up the next picture quite nicely. Cause and effect." He flipped the second picture on top of the first.

Anger burned deeper in Nathan's gut. Apparently Ivan Warren hadn't called off his private investigator after the weekend Beth and Nathan had spent in the mountains. And apparently they'd been too absorbed in each other to realize the man was still on the job. So much for letting their guard down, for thinking Ivan would give up if he thought they were truly husband and wife.

As Nathan examined the photo of the open sofa bed, with him sitting on the edge of it in his sleeping shorts the night before Jeff and Katie's party, he longed to wring Ivan Warren's neck. But getting arrested wasn't on his agenda, and he was sure Ivan hadn't finished yet.

"What do you want, Warren?"

"Like I said, I'm here to talk about what *you* want. It doesn't look to me as if you've got much of a marriage. Especially if you're still having lunch with your ex. Never mind spending nights on the sofa. So I have a proposition to make."

Nathan waited.

Ivan took something else from the envelope and laid it on top of the pictures.

Nathan stared at it, not wanting to believe the man would go this far. Ivan had made the check out to Nathan. It was for five hundred thousand dollars. "Just what will this check buy you?" he asked Beth's father-in-law.

"A divorce. You divorce Beth. The marriage was too short for her to win alimony. Dorie's not your

child, so there'd be no contest on child support. Beth
would have to go back to work, and we can pursue our
custody suit for Dorie.''

"You think I'm the kind of man who will accept a
check from you." Nathan tried to keep all emotion
from his voice.

"I believe no one in their right mind turns down
half a million dollars.''

Anger turned to rage that Ivan Warren could do
something like this to Beth and his granddaughter. But
Nathan couldn't give in to the rage. No amount of
money could make him turn away from Beth and Dorie. Nothing could. Yet if he played along with Warren, maybe he could kill the idea of a custody suit for
good.

Nathan picked up the check and looked at it as if he
was fascinated by it. "Your offer is tempting. Five
hundred thousand dollars invested properly could set
me up for life. I need time to think about it.''

"All right. You've got twenty-four hours. I'll leave
the check with you. My bank has orders not to cash it
without my authorization. Look at it, feel it, imagine
what you can do with it. I'll stop in, the same time tomorrow." Ivan walked to the door. "Five hundred
thousand dollars can buy one hell of a lot of happiness. Consider that while you're thinking.''

Nathan went to the door and watched Ivan leave the
store. Then he reached for the telephone to call Beth's
lawyer.

Beth stood at the sink peeling potatoes as Dorie
played on the floor nearby with pots and their lids and

her blocks. Beth wanted to have dinner ready when Nathan came home, so they'd have time to drive around, looking at houses. As she thought about it, she became excited about the prospect of more space, decorating rooms to suit them, having a backyard for Dorie.

When the doorbell rang, Beth glanced at Dorie, saw she was occupied and nothing was in her reach that could hurt her. Going into the living room, she spotted Ivan Warren standing on the porch.

She had talked to Clara after their visit to the mountains about setting up play time for the Warrens with Dorie.

Beth opened the door. "Hi, Ivan. Clara isn't with you?"

"Not for this."

Goose pimples pricked Beth's arms but she told herself she was a worrywart. "Dorie's in the kitchen."

"I didn't come to see Dorie. I'll have that opportunity very soon on an unlimited basis."

Fear squeezed Beth's chest, and she wished Nathan was standing beside her. "Now what, Ivan? Don't you think you've disrupted our life enough?"

"You always were too spunky for your own good. You're the one who drove Mark away from us. You're the one who filled his head with nonsense about being independent, living his life for himself. He had responsibilities to me, to carry on the business I put blood and sweat into for years."

Beth had never known that Ivan blamed her for his separation from his son. "I supported Mark's dreams. He made his own decisions. If you had decided to live with them instead of fighting him every step of the way, you wouldn't have been estranged. Don't blame me for your failure to accept Mark for who he was."

Ivan's face flushed. "Look here, missy, Mark was *my* son, and I had a right to tell him what to do. He could have been rich beyond his wildest dreams. I just underestimated your influence on him. Love made him foolish."

"Mark wanted to be a teacher before I met him."

"I could have washed that nonsense out of his head if it hadn't been for you."

She could stand here and argue with the man all day. It wouldn't do any good. "I'm making supper, Ivan. And Nathan and I..."

"Nathan and you are no more."

The fear banding her chest became as cold as ice. "What are you talking about? We're married. We have a life together."

"Not anymore. Unlike my son, Nathan Maxwell is a practical man. He's considering an offer I made him. If he divorces you, I give him five hundred thousand dollars. He likes the idea."

"No!"

"It seems Maxwell's not willing to give up his dreams for yours."

"Nathan would never—"

"Nathan has the check. Maybe he'll show it to you. Or maybe he'll just ask you for a divorce without telling you about it. It's what you deserve for putting together this ridiculous marriage. My private investigator is good. He couldn't find anyone who'd seen you and Maxwell together before some party your friend gave—only three weeks before your wedding. A stranger, Beth. You married a stranger. How could you possibly think it would work?''

Her heart hurt so terribly she couldn't speak.

''I feel sorry for you, Beth. If you play your cards right and don't fight us, we'll give you liberal visitation rights. But if you fight us—'' He shook his head, went to the door, and let himself out.

Beth's legs wobbled and her hands shook. She rushed to the kitchen to Dorie and took her little girl into her arms. Then she thought about Nathan. He couldn't betray her like this. He wouldn't.

Five hundred thousand dollars.

No.

He's never said he loves you.

No.

You married a stranger.

Yes, she had. And now she was going to suffer for it.

Nathan usually came home at six. He usually came in, called her name... Six o'clock passed. Seven came and went. No phone call. He always called if he was going to be late. Maybe he'd gotten a hotel room. Maybe he'd rented an apartment. Maybe he was planning the best way to ask her for a divorce.

Beth had asked Rosa to keep Dorie. Rosa had been concerned, but Beth had simply told her she would pick up Dorie later.

Pacing the kitchen, her heart thumping erratically, Beth's emotions alternated between hurt and anger, a sense of betrayal and despair. Yet she knew no matter what happened with Nathan, somehow she would protect Dorie. She couldn't compete with five hundred thousand dollars, but if she meant anything to him, maybe she could convince him to stall Ivan until she and Dorie could get away. She had to stay calm, she had to stay clearheaded, she couldn't let emotions get the best of her.

When the door finally opened, her heart pounded. She went to the living room, saw him and knew staying calm was highly unlikely.

He stopped when he saw her.

She couldn't keep the hurt inside or the sense of devastation. "I know you want a divorce. Five hundred thousand dollars is a lot of money. But can you at least wait until I can come up with a plan for Dorie and me to get away?"

Chapter Ten

"I should have known," Nathan said, his voice steel-like, his eyes harder than Beth had ever seen them. "Ivan couldn't stop at offering me the check. He brought his venom to you and you swallowed it."

Beth shook all over. "He said you were a practical man. You have dreams."

"Yes, I have dreams. But they have nothing to do with five hundred thousand dollars!"

"You took his check!" she shot back.

"Dammit, Beth, are you so willing to believe the worst? What kind of man do you think I am? Haven't you learned anything about me? Don't you realize family means more to me than money ever could?"

What was he saying? Ivan had made it sound as if it was a done deal. Ivan...

Ivan. A master at control and manipulation.

"You didn't take the check?"

Nathan's expression was grim, the lines around his mouth cutting deep. "Oh, I took the check. So I could show it to your lawyer. That's where I've been, Beth. Making sure Ivan's threats don't cost you another night's sleep. Judges don't look kindly on bribery."

Chills quaked through Beth. She'd made a horrendous mistake. "Ivan said you were going to divorce me, and he and Clara would take Dorie. I thought—"

Nathan's green eyes became shuttered, and he looked at her as if he didn't know her. Fury vibrated in his voice. "You thought wrong. What happened to everything we've shared the past month? What happened to the promises? You think I'd break them because of a check from Ivan?"

"Nathan, I'm sorry."

He held up his hand, effectively cutting off anything more she might say. "How can we have a marriage if you don't trust me...if you take someone else's word over mine?"

She had to make him understand why she'd doubted him. "When you didn't tell me about you and Elaine, it shook up my faith in what we could have. If you could keep something so important from me..."

Cutting in, his tone was sharp. "The point is, Beth, I *did* tell you. I *didn't* keep it from you. Maybe I should have discussed it with you before we were married. But I wanted you and Dorie. I was afraid to take the risk of being too honest too soon. I was wrong. But I didn't want to lose you."

Nathan's point was well taken. He *had* told her. And if he didn't want to lose her, didn't that mean...

He shook his head. "The problem is you were never mine. You still belong to Mark. Dorie has accepted me as her father, but I don't think you've accepted me as your husband. We were wrong about a marriage of convenience. *Marriage* and *convenient* don't belong in the same sentence. There has to be a hell of a lot more."

For a moment she glimpsed the pain in Nathan's eyes—the pain of disappointment and sadness and loss. Then he shut her out. He turned, strode to the door, then closed it behind him, leaving a silence that brought tears to Beth's eyes and an incredible ache to her heart. Sinking down onto the sofa, she let the shock of the past few hours wear off. As her tears fell, she clutched her arms around her, knowing she'd made the biggest mistake of her life.

He was in front of Gavin's house before he even realized he was headed there. Switching off the ignition, Nathan wished he could switch off the emotions churning inside him as easily. He climbed out of his car and slammed the door with enough force to shake the peace in the quiet neighborhood.

Then he went to Gavin's side door and rang the bell.

Gavin answered and let his friend into the kitchen. "Uh-oh. You look rough. What's going on?"

Nathan exploded. "I've reached a dead end. That's what's wrong!"

"A soda or brandy?" Gavin asked, going to the cupboard for glasses.

"Neither." Nathan paced back and forth on the tile floor. "I can't believe she thought I'd take Warren's money and bail out."

"Whoa. Start at the beginning," Gavin suggested as he took a liter of soda from the door of the refrigerator.

"Ivan Warren offered me five hundred thousand dollars to divorce Beth. He paid her a visit to stir things up and told her I'd accepted the offer. She believed it. She believed it!"

Gavin just arched his brows. "Things haven't been exactly smooth between the two of you, if last weekend was any indication."

Nathan hadn't discussed what had happened between him and Beth with Gavin, but apparently his friend had felt the tension. "I thought we'd resolved it. I thought..."

"Women remember *everything*," Gavin offered. "At least Jessie does. Tell me something. Why do you think Beth believed her father-in-law?"

Nathan stopped pacing. "Because I'm not sure she wants to *be* married to me. I think she's still hung up on her dead husband."

"I don't know Beth as well as Jessie does, but from what I've observed, from what Jessie has said, Beth doesn't seem the type of woman to wallow in what used to be. Tell me something. Do you love her?"

Love.

Nathan hadn't given much thought to the word in years. He'd known little of it growing up. He'd thought he loved Elaine. She'd said she loved him. But what had that love meant? She'd left.

He'd decided kindness, patience and, lately, desire were much better concepts to hold on to. They were more concrete, easier to grasp. Yet when he thought about everything he felt for Beth—the want, the need, the caring, the aching to be so much a part of her, for her to be so much a part of him nothing could separate them, he realized he needed a much bigger word, one that encompassed all of the emotions.

Love.

"Yes, I love her," he admitted to himself as well as Gavin.

"Does Beth know?"

Suddenly he realized why Gavin had asked the question. There could be a good reason Beth had doubts. He'd never put into words how he felt about her. Oh, he'd told her he wanted her. He knew what he meant by it. He wanted her desire, her kisses, her thoughts, a life with her that would last through every promise they'd exchanged. He wanted her love because that's what he felt for her. Love. So deep it hurt to think about living without it.

But what did Beth think he wanted? Her body? Sex? The family he'd never had? Sure, he wanted a family. But he wanted a family bonded together with love. How could she know that when he'd never told her? How could she trust him when she didn't know he loved her?

Beth had taken him into her heart by marrying him, by inviting him into her bed, by trusting him with Dorie . . . by forgiving him. She hadn't said the words, either. But he'd felt her love when she welcomed him home with a hug and a kiss, when she awakened be-

side him with a smile and a soft tender look in her
eyes, when she took him into her body and tightened
her arms around him, glorying in the passion they
shared.

With a startling flash of insight, he realized Beth's
doubts had less to do with her ability to trust and
much more to do with his inability to share what he
felt for her.

"She doesn't know I love her. I didn't realize how
much it meant. I didn't realize..."

"That saying the words is the final step of commitment," Gavin finished.

Nathan's gaze met his friend's. "Yes."

As the shadows lengthened, Beth pushed her hair
away from her face and wiped away her tears. After
Mark had died, she'd known that sitting on the couch
crying wouldn't bring him back. So she'd decided to
hold on to the memories, concentrate on Dorie and
make a life for the two of them. She'd never expected
someone like Nathan to come into her life, never expected to burn and ache for a man or fall in love again.

But she had fallen in love again. And made a mess
of it. She hadn't trusted her heart...she hadn't trusted
Nathan. She hadn't even told him she loved him. Her
doubts might have damaged their relationship irrevo-
cably. If she'd needed proof he loved her, the episode
with Ivan had given it to her. Maybe he hadn't said the
words, but if he was willing to give up five hundred
thousand dollars, play along with Ivan so he could
take the proof of her father-in-law's bribery to her
lawyer, he loved her.

The picture of her and Mark stared at her from the coffee table. Picking it up, she gazed into the eyes of her first husband. "Maybe Nathan was right. Maybe I was still holding on to you. But I've let go now. I know Nathan loves me, and I'm going to give him every bit of love I have to give. I'll never forget you, but I love Nathan now. I hope you understand."

Beth had talked to Mark after he'd died, poured out her feelings of grief and loneliness. But she'd never known if he heard her. Now, she felt a sense of peace fall over her like the enveloping dusk. As she sat on the sofa, she experienced a gentle warmth like the touch of Mark's hand on her shoulder. The feeling was familiar, comforting and . . . right.

She waited until the sensation passed, then she set the picture on the coffee table face-down. Soon she'd replace it with one of her and Nathan. As soon as she convinced him her trust was as free a gift as her love.

When she got into her car, she realized she didn't know where he was. But there were a few places she could look. And if he wasn't at any of those? She'd move on to plan B. Because she wouldn't give up. Not until she wrapped her arms around him and told him she believed in his promises because she believed in him.

First, Beth drove to Nathan's store only to find he wasn't there. Her next stop was Jessie and Gavin's. Breathing a sigh of relief, she saw Nathan's car parked in front of the house.

Before she could knock on the front door, Gavin opened it, his expression serious.

"I'm looking for Nathan," she said bluntly.

He motioned toward the kitchen. "In there. I'll go sit on the patio. If Jessie and Lisa come home from their Girl Scout meeting, I'll head them off until you two are finished."

"Thanks, Gavin."

He waved her thanks away as he went through the dining room toward the sliding glass doors.

Beth's palms sweated and her heart thumped as she made her way to the kitchen. All she had to do was get the words out and convince Nathan she meant them. Her husband pushed back his chair and stood when he saw her.

Trembling, she walked right up to him and stood close. He frowned, and she was afraid he might turn away. So she rushed into what she had to say. "I'm sorry, Nathan. I know that doesn't mean much. I hope it means more when I say I love you and I want to spend the rest of my life with you. I don't know if you can forgive my lack of faith, but..."

He clasped her shoulders. "Slow down. I'm not going anywhere."

Nathan's words reassured her, but she didn't know if he meant for now...or always. "I thought you might want to leave. I was afraid you'd give up on me. I'd like another chance if you can forgive me—"

He gazed deep into her eyes and said, "There's nothing to forgive. I've been an idiot. First, by not telling you about Elaine and me. I was afraid you'd think less of me, less of who I was as a man. And I hurt us by not telling you."

"It's all right. I understand," she said softly.

His voice was gruff. "It's not all right. You forgave me. When I found out you believed Ivan, I shouldn't have gotten so angry." He shook his head. "It was my own fault you doubted my commitment to you. Since the day we met, I've felt all these strong feelings for you. I called it desire because I was afraid to call it what it's really become. I love you, Beth Maxwell. And you don't have to worry about me leaving...ever...because I'm exactly where I want to be—married to you."

His words embraced her as surely as his arms surrounded her. She lifted her lips to his.

Nathan's kiss was everything she could ever imagine a kiss could be. It was filled with love and promise and so much passion that she yearned for union right here, right now, in the middle of Jessie and Gavin's kitchen. Throwing all good sense aside, she laced her fingers in Nathan's hair, pressed her breasts against his chest and met each thrust of his tongue with one of her own.

With a groan Nathan broke the kiss and raised his head, keeping his arms tight around her. "We'd better take this home," he said, his voice husky with unfulfilled desire.

Keeping one hand on the back of his neck, with the other she stroked his jaw. "I love you, Nathan Maxwell."

He caught her hand and brought it to his lips. "And I love you. I meant every promise I made to you on our wedding day."

She smiled. "Tonight we can celebrate the promises . . . and the love."

Nathan lowered his mouth to hers again for another taste of the future . . . for another taste of their love.

Epilogue

Fourteen months later

When Beth awoke on Thanksgiving Day, the sun was already pouring in the bedroom window, and Nathan's side of the bed was empty. Of all mornings for her to oversleep . . . their first day in their new home.

Scurrying out of the cherry wood, four-poster, king-size bed they'd chosen for their bedroom, she angled around boxes and went to Dorie's room. The single bed was empty. Nathan must have gotten her up. Beth smiled. He adored Dorie, and she adored him. Soon the adoption proceedings would be final, and he would legally be Dorie's father.

Beth pulled on stirrup pants and a violet thigh-length sweater. She was running a brush through her hair when the phone rang. Grinning, she picked it up. Their first phone call in their new home.

"Beth, it's Dr. Rathenburg."

Beth had seen her gynecologist the day before yesterday. She'd missed her period. Before she told Nathan or got his hopes up, she'd wanted to have a blood test to make sure. They'd been so busy, pestering their builder to have everything completed so they could move in by Thanksgiving, buying furniture and decorations, then yesterday with the move itself, she knew stress could have thrown off her cycle.

"Dr. Rathenburg. I didn't expect to hear from you until tomorrow."

"I tried to get you yesterday but your phone wasn't working. I had to come into the office this morning on my way to the hospital and thought I'd try again."

Beth's heart raced.

"Beth, you *are* pregnant."

After Dr. Rathenburg's announcement, Beth didn't remember much of their conversation. Congratulations. Goodbye. All she cared about was finding Nathan and telling him the news.

As Beth went from room to room on the first floor, she found them all empty except for boxes and furniture scattered this way and that. But she smelled coffee brewing in the kitchen, and the back door stood open.

Nathan was standing on the flagstone terrace that overlooked the enormous backyard. Dorie was chasing Buffer, the cocker spaniel they'd given her last Christmas. The dog and the three-year-old were practically inseparable.

Beth walked up behind Nathan and wrapped her arms around him, nuzzling her nose into his blue cable knit sweater. "Good morning."

He pulled her around to his side and gave her a thoroughly eye-opening kiss. "Good morning yourself."

"You should have gotten me up."

"We got to bed so late last night, I thought you needed the rest."

They'd spent all day moving. And then they couldn't just go to sleep last night in their new home, in their new king-size bed.... "Well, if I'm going to get extra rest I guess I'd better do it now. Because about eight months from now, I'll probably be getting much less sleep."

It took a moment for her response to register. When it did, Nathan took her face between his palms. "You're pregnant?"

"The doctor just called. *We're* pregnant."

With a whoop of joy, Nathan swung her into his arms. Then he set her back down and gazed into her eyes. "You are happy about it, aren't you?"

She locked her arms around his neck. "I'm thrilled. What about you?"

"More than thrilled." His eyes danced with amusement and the flash of desire. "I'd like to show you just how much, but our daughter and dog need a watchful eye right now."

"And we have a few boxes to unpack before we go to Jessie and Gavin's to dinner. Do you think we can corral Dorie and Buffer and make a few phone calls first?"

"To Cade and Jeff?" he asked.

"And Jessie and Gavin and Rosa," she said, feeling so much joy that she had to share it with the world right away. "And, if you don't mind, I'd like to call Clara, too."

After Ivan's offer of bribery, Clara Warren had called Beth. She'd said their lawyer had read Ivan the riot act. Clara had claimed she'd known nothing about the check. She'd told her husband if he ever pulled a stunt like that again, she'd leave him. And she'd promised Beth and Nathan that she and Ivan would never interfere in their lives again.

Over the next few weeks Beth and Nathan had decided it wasn't fair to Dorie to cut her grandparents out of her life. They were the only grandparents she had. Beth called Clara, and she started coming to their apartment one afternoon a week to visit Dorie. After a few weeks, with Beth and Nathan's permission, Ivan came with her. Clara had pulled Beth aside that day and told her Ivan had confided that he realized his need to control had almost lost him everyone he cared about. He couldn't admit his mistakes to Beth and Nathan, but he was ready to start fresh if they were.

Now the four of them enjoyed Dorie together. Clara was speaking her mind more, and Ivan seemed to be listening. It was difficult to teach old dogs new tricks, but not entirely impossible.

"I don't mind if you call Clara," Nathan answered her. "You can even tell Ivan if he answers. He's an arrogant old codger, but if anything can soften him up, it's grandchildren. Dorie has him wrapped around her little finger. And if last Christmas was any indication, we'll *need* all the room in the house this year for the presents."

Beth leaned her head against Nathan's shoulder. "But *we* know the presents that matter—faith, hope and most especially love."

Nathan closed her tighter against him. "Maybe this Christmas we can invite everyone here. Not only Rosa, Gavin, Jessie, Clara and Ivan, but Jeff and Katie, and Cade and Randi, too."

"That would be wonderful!"

After a pause, he confided, "I've been thinking a lot lately about Jeff and Cade and Gavin. Our college days. Where we were then and where we said we wanted to be by the time we were thirty-five. I think we've all finally found exactly what we wanted."

Beth stroked Nathan's jaw. "You're all best men. You were Gavin's, Gavin was yours and Cade's, Cade was Jeff's..."

Nathan leaned his cheek against her hair as they watched their daughter play. "All I care about is being *your* best man."

With his arm wrapped around her, and hers wrapped around him, she assured him, "For now and for always."

What had begun as a marriage of convenience had transformed into a marriage of love and commitment and sharing. Beth smiled at Nathan.

He smiled back.

And when his lips touched hers, it was a kiss for Thanksgiving and a promise for all the years to come.

* * * * *

The Calhoun Saga continues...

in November
New York Times bestselling author

NORA ROBERTS

takes us back to the Towers and introduces us to
the newest addition to the Calhoun household,
sister-in-law Megan O'Riley in

MEGAN'S MATE
(Intimate Moments #745)

And in December
look in retail stores for the special collectors'
trade-size edition of

THE
Calhoun
Women

containing all four fabulous Calhoun series books:
COURTING CATHERINE,
A MAN FOR AMANDA, FOR THE LOVE OF LILAH
and *SUZANNA'S SURRENDER.*
Available wherever books are sold.

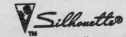

Look us up on-line at: http://www.romance.net

CALHOUN

FORTUNE'S Children™

Bestselling Author
BARBARA
BOSWELL

Continues the twelve-book series—FORTUNE'S CHILDREN—
in October 1996 with Book Four

STAND-IN BRIDE

When Fortune Company executive Michael Fortune needed help
warding off female admirers after being named one of the ten most
eligible bachelors in the United States, he turned to his faithful
assistant, Julia Chandler. Julia agreed to a pretend engagement, but
what starts as a charade produces an unexpected Fortune heir....

MEET THE FORTUNES—a family whose legacy is greater than riches.
Because where there's a will...there's a *wedding!*

"Ms. Boswell is one of those rare treasures who combines humor
and romance into sheer magic."
                                          —*Rave Reviews*

A CASTING CALL TO
ALL FORTUNE'S CHILDREN FANS!
If you are truly one of the fortunate
you may win a trip to
Los Angeles to audition for
Wheel of Fortune®. Look for
details in all retail Fortune's Children titles!

WHEEL of FORTUNE

Look us up on-line at: http://www.romance.net   FC-4-C

The collection of the year!
NEW YORK TIMES BESTSELLING AUTHORS

Linda Lael Miller
Wild About Harry

Janet Dailey
Sweet Promise

Elizabeth Lowell
Reckless Love

Penny Jordan
Love's Choices

and featuring
Nora Roberts
The Calhoun Women

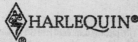

As seen on TV!
Free Gift Offer

With a Free Gift proof-of-purchase from any Silhouette® book,
you can receive a beautiful cubic zirconia pendant.

This gorgeous marquise-shaped stone is a genuine cubic
zirconia—accented by an 18" gold tone necklace.

(Approximate retail value $19.95)

Send for yours today...

compliments of *Silhouette*®

To receive your free gift, a cubic zirconia pendant, send us one original proof-of-
purchase, photocopies not accepted, from the back of any Silhouette Romance™,
Silhouette Desire®, Silhouette Special Edition®, Silhouette Intimate Moments®
or Silhouette Yours Truly™ title available in August, September or October at your favorite
retail outlet, together with the Free Gift Certificate, plus a check or money order for
$1.65 U.S./$2.15 CAN. (do not send cash) to cover postage and handling, payable
to Silhouette Free Gift Offer. We will send you the specified gift. Allow 6 to 8 weeks for
delivery. Offer good until October 31, 1996 or while quantities last. Offer valid in the
U.S. and Canada only.

Free Gift Certificate

Name: _____

Address: _____

City: _____ State/Province: _____ Zip/Postal Code: _____

Mail this certificate, one proof-of-purchase and a check or money order for postage
and handling to: SILHOUETTE FREE GIFT OFFER 1996. In the U.S.: 3010 Walden
Avenue, P.O. Box 9077, Buffalo NY 14269-9077. In Canada: P.O. Box 613, Fort Erie,
Ontario L2Z 5X3.

FREE GIFT OFFER   084-KMD
ONE PROOF-OF-PURCHASE
To collect your fabulous FREE GIFT, a cubic zirconia pendant, you must include this
original proof-of-purchase for each gift with the properly completed Free Gift Certificate.

084-KMD

You're About to Become a *Privileged Woman*

Reap the rewards of fabulous free gifts and benefits with proofs-of-purchase from Silhouette and Harlequin books

Pages & Privileges™

It's our way of thanking you for buying our books at your favorite retail stores.

PROOF OF PURCHASE

SR-PP189

Offer expires October 31, 1996

**Harlequin and Silhouette—
the most privileged readers in the world!**

For more information about Harlequin and Silhouette's PAGES & PRIVILEGES program call the Pages & Privileges Benefits Desk: 1-503-794-2499

Silhouette®

SR-PP189

WAT

He checked his calendar. Halloween was on a Saturday. "Trick or Treat . . . ," he murmured, making a neat box around October 31. Her treat was going to be something else again.

He knew where she lived. He knew how she lived. He had time to work out the logistics of getting her. That would be easy. A woman alone was a sitting duck. But first he wanted her to get real nervous. Then he'd make a move—throw her off. When she thought it was all over, he'd come back for her. He'd give new meaning to *Trick or Treat*.

Rikki didn't know that she and her children were being watched every moment. She didn't know that in the shadows someone was waiting for the right moment to come. But soon she would—fearfully soon . . .

SAFELIGHT

Linda Crockett Gray

A SIGNET BOOK

SIGNET
Published by the Penguin Group
Penguin Books USA Inc., 375 Hudson Street,
New York, New York 10014, U.S.A.
Penguin Books Ltd, 27 Wrights Lane,
London W8 5TZ, England
Penguin Books Australia Ltd, Ringwood,
Victoria, Australia
Penguin Books Canada Ltd, 10 Alcorn Avenue,
Toronto, Ontario, Canada M4V 3B2
Penguin Books (N.Z.) Ltd, 182–190 Wairau Road,
Auckland 10, New Zealand

Penguin Books Ltd, Registered Offices:
Harmondsworth, Middlesex, England
First published by Signet,
an imprint of New American Library,
a division of Penguin Books USA Inc.

First Printing, December, 1992
10 9 8 7 6 5 4 3 2 1

PUBLISHER'S NOTE
This is a work of fiction. Names, characters, places, and incidents either are the product of the author's imagination or are used fictitiously, and any resemblance to actual persons, living or dead, events, or locales is entirely coincidental.

To those who shared with me
their love of orchids, books,
photography, and life:
Robin, Toni, Darlene, Ed, Mike,
and Selby Gardens

Safelight: darkroom light of a color and intensity that will not noticeably affect light-sensitized photographic materials. Provides sufficient illumination to allow one to function safely without harming the work in progress.

Chapter 1

"Lady . . . Deliveries 'round to the side door." Donnie Rhule shut off the blower and said it again. Then he stepped toward the driver's side of the vehicle blocking the near lane of the Hilton's entry drive. "Read the sign. Deliveries. That way." He pointed.

"It's all right. I was told to pull in here. This won't take long." Without looking back, the slim, pretty woman in khaki shorts and a Selby Gardens tee-shirt slid out of the van and strode toward the front door of the Hilton.

"Hey. You can't leave that here . . ."

She was already on the gold-encircled capital *H* on the pressure pad that flung the hotel's glass doors open.

"Shit." Rhule turned and checked to see if she'd left the keys inside. She hadn't. She'd even locked the damn doors, so he couldn't slip it out of gear and push it. "Shit." He glanced around to make sure no one was looking, then he slid the broken handle of the blower down the door, leaving a jagged line scratched through the logo.

"There were supposed to be a couple of luggage carts out front. I'm Claire Hailey. Selby Gardens. Family Therapy Conference?" She watched the expression of the young man at the front desk for some sign of recognition.

"I'll be with you in a moment." He went back to conversing with whomever he had on the phone.

"Is there a manager around? Or anyone in charge?"

The young man held up a finger, urging her to be patient. She took a quick look back at the van, then headed down the corridor toward the conference center. "Janelle." She glided up to the registration table. "I've got the plants. I have to make a fast dropoff. Where's Rikki?"

The dark-haired, chubby social worker chairing the event looked up from alphabetizing a box of information packets, obviously a bit frazzled. "That way." She pointed farther down the broad, pink marble hallway toward the glass-roofed atrium that would serve as the social hub for the surrounding meeting rooms. Several exhibitors and conference staff were already there, setting up. The south concourse of Sarasota's Surfside Hilton had temporarily become an obstacle course, crowded with partially constructed display cases, crates, ladders, lights, and extension chords. Hotel maintenance crewmen wearing green knit shirts like the one on the young man with the blower out front were drilling and hammering in uneven cadence, rigging panels of lattice onto rectangular frames. Off to one side, a group of volunteers were assembling easels and pedestals. A few artists Claire recognized were already ferrying in and unloading their pieces, but she didn't go over to talk.

"Rikki," she called across the commotion.

A tanned, blonde athletic-looking woman who'd been wheeling in a handtruck loaded with flat crates immediately looked over her shoulder and grinned. "Claire."

"I need help."

"Be right there." Rikki Lundquist parked the load of artwork, spoke briefly to the construction crew, then came weaving through the workers toward her friend.

"Good to see you."

"You too." They hugged.

"What's the problem?"

"I hit a snag out front. I brought the orchids, but no one showed with the pushcarts. I'm pressed for time," Claire responded. "I'm parked in the circle."

"Let's go. We'll get it straight." Rikki fell in step with the other woman as they headed back up the corridor. "Andy said to track him down if we had any problem. We obviously have a problem."

"I asked for a manager, but the desk clerk put me on hold. All he had to do was point."

"Excuse me. Mr. Tubb said to call him personally if I need assistance. I need it. Now. Do you ring him or do we?" Rikki asked the desk clerk who was still on the phone. Tall, leggy, and elegantly muscular, the two women drew curious stares from a couple of men making transactions farther down the reception desk.

"Miss Lundquist. Rikki." Stocky, curly haired Andrew Tubb, the man in question, came bustling in from the opposite direction, clutching a hand radio. "Sorry for the inconvenience. We're already taking care of this." He had one porter with a flat-bed cart aiming for the door and another fellow wheeling a larger cart with a rack out of the elevator. "Sorry. We had a tour group checking out, the bus was late, and all our carts were tied up. The usual chaos. I didn't forget your plants. It's under control now." He waved the second porter outside as well. "I'll have another cart freed up in a few minutes if you need it. Meanwhile my men will help you unload. Sorry for the hangup." Tubb, shorter than either of the two women, kept smiling up at them as he walked them toward the van. "Donnie." He summoned the young groundsman with the blower. "These ladies have plants to unload. Give us a hand here."

"We've got plenty of help. We can manage now," Claire assured Tubb as she slid open the van door. "Just wheel that cart close."

Everyone else stepped back, giving the first porter more space. Tubb looked at the pavement underfoot, then frowned. "Donnie, be sure to make another pass at this drive after they're through here." He picked up a cigarette wrapper and a ticket stub the fellow had missed. "Don't leave bits of trash around. And don't just blast them into the garden. Pick 'em up." Tubb deposited his handful in the trash bin. His radio sputtered out some message. "On my way." He turned to Rikki again. "If you need the other cart, just tell the men. You guys stay with these ladies until they're all set." He nodded, then went off in another direction.

"Thanks, Andy. Okay, where do we start?" Rikki took a look inside the van at the dashboard-to-door sea of orchids.

"With the Paphs. I'll hand them out. You guys line them up. Keep them tight." Claire unwedged a clay pot from between two other plants, all with little pouched blooms on erect stems. "Just go easy," she told the porters. "We don't want the flower spikes to snap." She handed Rikki the first row. "Bell O' Ireland. Maudiae. And a nice bellatulum. See, I remembered you liked Paphs."

"They're cute." Rikki smiled as she set the pots, one after the other on the cart. The Paphiopedilums bobbled their impudent faces.

"Now lots of Phales. We've been doing some experiments forcing early fall blooms and we've got an unusual

number flowering like crazy right now.'' Claire lifted out
more pots. These were low leather-leaved plants with spectacular long, arched spikes ending with clusters of brightly
colored blooms, like great moths in flight.

"Very showy. We need showy. Very nice.'' Rikki nested
a purplish-pink Phalaenopsis between the more compact
Paphs, making sure none of the spikes collided. The porters
helped fill the empty spaces, then started loading the second
cart.

"Vandas.'' Claire gave Rikki four hanging baskets with
sprays of stiff arched leaves and long dangling roots. These
had spikes and clusters of pansylike flowers, splashy ones
from intense purples to brilliant orange, most with intri-
cately lined or mottled petals.

Rikki had the porters hook them onto the garment rack
on one end of the cart.

"And this.'' Claire handed out a cascading spotted rose-
lilac schilleriana wrapped in a protective foam collar. "And
more Vandas . . .''

Rikki passed them on to the second porter.

"I brought a huge Laelia superbiens. Mature, set in a
basket.'' Now she'd cleared a pathway, she slid forward the
tall cardboard box nearer the back. The sides of the box
kept the erect spikes of this particular treasure from getting
jostled. "You said you needed a centerpiece for the head
table. I thought this might do well.''

Rikki peered in. The massive plant inside had a number
of arm-length bloom spikes crowned with clusters of slim-
petaled flowers of pinkish mauve. It was like looking into
a bouquet of ripply, ribbon bows. "Perfect.'' She and the
porter each took a side and shifted the box to the cart.

"And a special bonus . . .'' Claire lifted out another
smaller box, this one with a squat clay pot wedged into the
center and surrounded with wood chips to keep it from sliding about. "I managed to get you one of our Cycnoches.''

Rikki sniffed its swan-shaped flowers. "This is heavenly.''

"Just don't let anyone walk off with it,'' Claire cautioned
her. "We're talking well-developed and expensive. I figured
it would perfume up the whole place. Most of the others are
unscented.''

"I'll guard it with my life,'' Rikki promised. Claire was
serious about protecting this one. This wasn't as large or

conspicuous as the Laelia or some of the Phales. But it was a highly awarded Panamanian species, bred from the grande dame of that genera in the Selby collection. Over the years, sight unseen, Rikki instantly knew whether the Cycnoches was in bloom whenever she'd stepped foot inside Selby's tropical showcase. Its distinctive scent would dominate the shifting currents of the greenhouse and hang in the humid air like none other. Pungent. Erotic. Tantalizing.

After hours, when there were no visitors and she had permission to set up her cameras, she'd photographed the Selby orchids. She'd shot the Cycnoches's luminous swan-like flowers repeatedly, never quite satisfied with the result. The visual image could only capture part of that orchid's presence. Its heady scent was the elusive other part that only firsthand experience could offer. "I'll take it to the meetings with me," Rikki added. "Maybe even to dinner. Make sure no one misses seeing it or smelling it."

"Don't go overboard. Just keep an eye on it."

"Of course." Rikki looked at the crowded carts, cleared a space, and set it down. "Okay, let's take this load in. Just park it off to the side and watch it until I get there."

"Fine with me." The first fellow guided his batch in through the front doors.

"That's it. On my next run, I'll bring a few baskets of Oncidium and some pots of greenery for filler, but it may be a while." Claire passed out the remaining plants. "We're beginning a new session with some kids from the juvenile detention center today. I need to be there to start them out." She didn't have to elaborate. Selby Gardens had several pilot projects in horticultural therapy that were quietly becoming models for similar programs nationwide. Some were directed at the disabled or aged. Some with abuse victims. Working with troubled kids was Claire's particular baby.

"So take off. We can handle these from here," Rikki assured her. "See you on the next installment. Whenever."

Inside, in the conference corridor, Janelle Givrey seemed more serene now that reinforcements had arrived to help with registration. "My God, those are gorgeous! Anything I can do?" she asked Rikki when she saw the orchid convoy passing.

"Everything here's just fine."

"Good." She gave Rikki a thankful smile and went back to signing in the latest influx of participants.

By seven-thirty that evening, the south concourse of the Hilton was transformed into a garden-art gallery for the initial icebreaker. The conferees—social workers, counselors, and family therapists who had arrived from all over the Southeast, had exchanged travel clothes for the specified "dressy casual," which seemed to encompass everything from sequined tops or tuxedos to leather bustiers or open-necked shirts.

"Congratulations. The exhibit looks great. Absolutely lovely." Janelle returned from the bar with a glass of wine for Rikki. "You did a fabulous job with this."

"Me, Selby Gardens, and a number of other volunteers," Rikki replied. The central area was set up like a tropical paradise. Lush plants as well as oils, watercolors, sculpture, fabrics, and photos lined the trellislike gazebos and walkways. A bearded musician played soft island music on a synthesizer, complete with birdcalls and the occasional rumble of thunder. Delighted hotel guests as well as the conference participants were browsing through the parklike arrangement. Some simply milled about, enjoying the ambience. Others stopped occasionally to read a title or examine a piece more closely. "I'm relieved that everything fell into place," Rikki confided.

"Nothing this good simply fell into place," Janelle said dryly. "You worked your ass off, just like the rest of us."

"A little advance planning helped," Rikki conceded, smiling a greeting to a friend across the way. Besides designing and orchestrating the overall installation and recruiting artists for this showcase of "resensitizing art," Rikki had to uncrate and set up her own photography for the exhibit. She'd also arranged interviews and press tours for reporters who had agreed to give the event some coverage.

"I do think the artworks are top drawer. If I didn't know these pieces were designed to be therapeutic, I'd still like them simply because they're beautiful," Janelle commented. "Not that being beautiful isn't a worthy accomplishment in itself, of course." She stopped talking and scrutinizing the traffic flow long enough to reapply her fuchsia lipstick.

"We do have some gorgeous pieces," Rikki agreed. "Good variety. Lots of tactile stimulation. Everything from silks and ceramics to oils and fiberglass. I'm sounding like a press release." She caught herself. "I must be more tired than I realized. It's been a long day." That comment prompted a nod from her colleague.

"Excuse me, but are these things for sale?" The question came from a short, paunchy fellow about seventy in a spiffy madras plaid shirt and bright yellow not-quite-matching Bermuda shorts.

"They sure are for sale. They're numbered. Price lists are at the registration desk and on those stands over there." Rikki pointed toward a pair of pedestals, like gateposts, at the entrance of the exhibit. "You can purchase any pieces you like anytime, but they can't be removed from the show until the end of the conference. Sunday," she told him.

"What about the plants? Are they for sale?"

"Sorry, no. They're on loan," Rikki explained. "Only the art is for sale."

"Sunday . . ." His bristly eyebrows arched.

"On Sunday the artists will all be here so the purchasers can meet them. We'll have refreshments and dismantle the show. Sort of a farewell party," Rikki elaborated.

"Really . . ." He nodded. "I'll be here. I'll bring the missus over. She likes stuff like this. You know, flowers and birds and things." He bobbed his head up and down approvingly.

"Purchasers also get a tax deduction," Janelle interjected with her typical attentiveness to detail. "A percentage of the proceeds is going to the Women's Center."

The eyebrows arched again.

Janelle continued without prompting. "These pieces are all by artists whose designs are used in therapy, particularly in abuse and co-dependency cases. They nurture the spirit as well as please the eye." She glanced out over the increasingly crowded area with obvious satisfaction at the attendance.

"Yeah? So that's what the resensitizing business means?"

"That's what it means."

The stocky tourist stopped and crooked his head like a plump-chested pigeon, contemplating. Then he nodded again. "Well, I'll be sure to tell the missus. She'd most likely buy this stuff anyhow. But the Women's Center support is a nice touch. We have grown daughters. One works with a hospital. One's a teacher. We've heard a lot about women's issues and things like women's centers. World sure isn't like it used to be." His smile diminished, stiffening a bit at the corners of his mouth. "Makes sense to do some good somewhere." He was looking up at both of them, chatting away amiably. "Especially if you've got a wife like mine. She's into all kinds of causes. A real goin' concern." He was nodding to himself and smiling as he moved on; he picked up a price list, then zeroed in on the first set of works in the show.

"Speaking of a goin' concern . . ." Janelle whispered, giving a sidelong look in the direction the fellow had gone. He had his reading glasses on now and was peering at the labels. "He's pretty feisty himself."

"Let's hope his missus comes back with him and likes what she sees," Rikki said. "It would be great all the way around if this were a sellout." Her soft dark eyes swept the crowd, then followed a quartet of affluent hotel guests who'd meandered into the area. They picked up the price sheets and continued on through the display. "These artists are good. They could all use a break, financial and otherwise."

"Ain't it the truth," Janelle murmured. "Speaking of artists and finances, how much are you asking for that one?" She pointed out one of Rikki's massive color prints, a feathery spray of orchids she'd photographed on her summer trip to Australia.

"The Dendrobium. Tetragonum. Two hundred and fifty framed. But I'll make a print for you if that one sells. No charge. Then you'll just have to pay for the framing."

"I wasn't angling for a bargain."

"You're turning it down?" Rikki kidded her.

"Of course not."

"That particular orchid really is huge." Rikki held out her hands to indicate the size. "I actually took the shot of it in the wild, but I also brought a tiny nursery-grown division home with me. I brought home several new plants."

"At least you get interesting souvenirs. You don't go for the coconut with a face carved in it," Janelle kidded her.

"When you come over, I'll show you what I did get. Granted, none of my new plants are much more than leaves and a few roots. But I've got slides of what they'll be like."

"How did your other orchids do while you were gone?"

"Basically, they went crazy. Eddie had time to run the sprinklers and fertilize, but he couldn't keep up with the potting. I've got a lot that need attention. Once I get at them, I'll have lots of divisions you can have, for absolutely free,'' Rikki offered. ''Pots included,'' she added.

''Speak with caution.'' Janelle rolled her eyes. ''Just because I haven't managed to annihilate the last few orchids you gave me doesn't mean you should risk handing over any more. You know me and plants.'' She grimaced slightly. ''Not a green thumb on either hand.'' She wriggled her stubby, neatly manicured fingers, stopping to erase a smudge of ink from one of them.

''Then just come and visit.''

''I will. I'll stop by as soon as this conference business is over.'' Janelle looked out over the concourse, then checked her watch. There was still thirty minutes until the opening banquet. ''I haven't been to see your place since your cookout in May, before you and the kids left for the summer. I could use a dose of your kind of horticultural therapy firsthand.'' She gave Rikki's photo of the whispy Dendrobium a covetous look. ''I've been too busy lately telling other folks how to nourish their psyches to take care of my own. And I've been unwinding with too many brownies,'' she admitted, patting her ample hips. ''Broadening the wrong horizons, I'm afraid.''

''Take it easy on yourself.'' Rikki reached her arm around the older woman's shoulders and gave her a gentle hug. ''This conference has been a big responsibility, especially on top of a full caseload. Next week, come and enjoy a sunset and dinner with the kids and me. We can go walking by the gulf, sit in the spa, and watch the boats on the bay side.''

''Sounds heavenly.'' Janelle sighed and glanced over toward the registration area. Several late arrivals were lined up. The woman rifling through the information kits apparently couldn't locate the one she needed. The older fellow in shorts was lining up, checkbook in hand, apparently ready to deal without consulting the missus. ''Later . . .'' Janelle patted Rikki's arm. ''And thanks. For this.'' She inclined her head toward the art display. ''And for the dinner invitation. I've missed you. I've got some ideas we need to discuss.''

''Over a sunset.''

''Over a sunset,'' Janelle agreed, then she was off with a

cheerful hello and a ready smile for the old chap as well as the newcomers.

"Please let me see you outside. Immediately. A. Tubb."

During the keynote speaker's presentation at the banquet, the hotel manager had a waiter hand deliver a note to Rikki at the head table.

"I'll be back," she whispered to Janelle, then exited as quickly and serenely as possible. She'd told her sitter to call if there was a problem at home. Maybe one of her kids was sick. Or maybe someone had an accident. But the instant she stepped outside and Andrew Tubb met her, she could see the problem was much nearer.

"Oh, my God." Rikki slowed her pace. "What happened?"

"Someone tore up the place," Tubb said, almost breathless.

Most of the zigzag trellis work around the periphery of the exhibit had been knocked flat. Like dominoes, each one had careened forward, taking the next one down as it fell. A few holdouts were grotesquely twisted and splintered. Separated by a walkway, the central section still stood with artworks and foliage intact, an oasis amid the surrounding devastation. Plants, moss, bits of charcoal and soil were strewn across the deep green carpeting. Shards of broken glass glistened everywhere. Hotel workers were lifting objects free and righting them.

"Watch out for broken glass," one cautioned them.

"Everyone back. Don't touch anything," Tubb called out.

"How could this happen?" Rikki stared at the dismal mass. "We didn't hear a thing inside."

"The meeting rooms and corridors are all acoustically insulated. For privacy," Tubb explained, shrugging. "All we heard down our way was a loud whoosh. The carpeting helped muffle the noise, I'd guess."

Rikki stepped over some debris to take a close look. The sculptures and paintings still standing were splotched and streaked with blue spray paint and graffiti. "Fuck." "Tit." The paint still looked wet where the letters had run. She freed one of her pieces, a closeup of the throat of an orchid, with "Pusy" written on it, punctuated with an exclamation point but misspelled. The glass was cracked, but the paint hadn't seeped through.

"We're sick about this. We can't figure how anyone could have pulled this off without getting caught," the assistant manager kept apologizing. "We had security making the rounds. We've got all the guards alerted. I've already called the police."

"I'll have to go in and tell everyone," Rikki said in a hushed voice.

"We've closed off everything. We've got staff searching every inch of the place." Ashen-faced, Tubb shook his head. "Our insurance will cover the damages." He licked his lips, then drew them into a thin line. "We figure whoever did this got damn lucky. Waited for a lull." He licked his lips again. "Son of a bitch timed it for just after the banquet started. The serving staff had just finished. Halls were empty. Up front, only a skeleton crew was on duty at the desk. Everyone was taking a breather," he went on, shrugging again.

"No one saw anything?" Rikki countered.

"One of the porters did say he saw a guy in there when he passed. But he only saw the legs." He pointed to one of the sections still standing. The artworks were hung at eye level, so they would block seeing the upper part of whoever had been on the opposite side. "He figured it was okay."

"I'd say he was wrong," Rikki muttered.

Tubb nodded. "A guest said she collided with a guy with a ski mask over his head. He ran down the hall just as she came around the corner. Knocked her over. She was startled and frightened. She couldn't say where he went from there."

Silently, Rikki listened to Tubb while she located another of her pictures in the rubble. "Cunt" was sprayed across this one. Pinned under it were two of the potted Paphs, beheaded.

"Mr. T." A woman's voice came over Tubb's radio. "Channel 10 is here. Sam called in from the parking lot."

"How'd they get wind of this? The police aren't even here yet," Tubb groaned.

"The police are here."

Tubb looked up. A woman wearing a blazer with the hotel logo was leading the way. Two uniformed officers were with her. Two more officers came in from the opposite corridor, off the parking lot.

"You folks stand back. We need to clear the immediate area. Don't touch anything. Just stand back." One officer waved everyone away from the site. Rikki put down her photo and did as he said. "You guys take an exit. No one in or out without an ID," he told the other officers.

A short, bespectacled man in a suit and a taller, uniformed police officer came walking briskly along the main corridor. The one in the suit, a slim, dark-haired man in his thirties, took charge. "I'm Detective Warnock. Where's the closest unoccupied room?" he asked Tubb.

"Right there." Tubb pointed to a set of closed doors across the concourse.

"Okay, all of you please go with the officers and take a seat in that room." The soft-spoken officer made it sound like an invitation to tea. "We'll let you all go back to work, or whatever, as soon as we can. We just want any information you might have."

"I didn't see anything. I'm working." One white-shirted waiter spoke up.

"Most of these folks are employees. We've got a banquet going on," Tubb told the man, with a trace of urgency in his voice.

"Okay. Just give your name to the officer, then you can go about your business." Warnock ammended his directive. "Ed, take care of the staff. The rest of you go into the conference room. Tell us what you can." The detective smoothed his moustache and tie in one downward motion while he scanned the area. "Now . . ." He took a notebook and pen from his inside pocket. Three other officers came in behind him. "Tape it off. Call the techs."

"We heard Channel 10 was here." The assistant manager glanced from one end of the hall to the other, rubbing his chin, his expression more resigned than anxious.

"They might have picked it up on the dispatch. Close off the halls and give me another perimeter," Detective Warnock calmly told one of his men. "Can't keep the press out, but for now they can keep their distance."

Rikki and Andrew Tubb were talking with the short fellow, Detective Warnock, a moment later when the television reporter, followed by a video cameraman, turned into the corridor. They stopped at the yellow crime-scene tape, tied doorknob to doorknob, blocking the hallway.

"Officer?" The lead man was in shirtsleeves, carrying his jacket.

His razor-cut hair looked synthetic.

Warnock raised a hand calmly, holding off any questions. "Okay. Details?" He got the basic information from Tubb.

"Brent Kendall." The reporter introduced himself once Detective Warnock offered him a break. "We got a tip that some sexy art was destroyed. What's the story?" He'd had time to slide on his jacket and straighten his tie.

"First, let's discuss this tip you got." Warnock stared at Kendall. Behind his glasses Warnock's eyes looked a bit too close together. "Elaborate, please." Despite his unimposing appearance, Warnock's subdued manner gave him a nononsense edge. Clearly, things would proceed according to his agenda or not pleasantly at all.

"I'm in the remote. The station got a call. Some guy. It's on tape," Kendall assured the detective. "He gave the name of the hotel and said there was some kind of protest over some sexy art. Porn, he called it. He said there was a hundred thousand dollars' damage."

Warnock looked at the clutter in the hallway. "Are we talking a hundred thousand here?" He asked Tubb, who blanched and deferred to Rikki.

"I wouldn't say that much," she answered, shaking her head.

"How much would you say?" Kendall prompted.

"I wouldn't," Rikki answered. "The artworks are all individually priced. But I'm not sure the pieces are ruined."

"But there is considerable damage," Kendall persisted. "The total here is easily in the thousands."

"Thousands." Rikki could go that far. "From what I saw, a lot may be salvageable. Spray paint can be scraped off most surfaces. The ceramics and fabrics can't be saved. Then there are the plants," she added, smoothing back a strand of pale blonde hair as she watched one of the officers lift up a basket of Vandas and rehang it upright. It seemed intact.

"What about the plants?" Kendall asked.

"They're on loan from Selby Gardens. Some of the orchids are very valuable. I don't think they're destroyed. Maybe roughed up a bit. It's hard to tell."

"So what about the guy's comment that this is sexy art? Obscene stuff. Pornography?" Kendall leaned forward, holding out the microphone. He'd moved to the side so the cameraman could shoot over his shoulder and focus on the attractive blonde in the ice-blue silky dress.

"This is sensual art. That means it appeals to the senses. It's intended to resensitize." Rikki replied, sounding calmer than she felt over the incident. "There was nothing obscene here until someone did this."

"Could you expand on that resensitizing part?" Kendall prompted her from off camera.

"Certainly." Rikki's lips felt stiff as she summarized what she and the others would be saying and demonstrating over the next few days. "These artworks are tools. They're designed to help fragile, damaged people heal emotionally. Actually, they can help anyone. They're intended to create a nonthreatening, positive bond with nature, one that carries over into a more positive self-image. They resensitize." She gestured with open hands in a sweeping movement as if she were drawing closer some invisible force.

The cameraman stayed on her.

"Having art like this in your home or office is like surrounding yourself with flowers. Only these require no care. There's no risk," she explained. "They ask nothing. These images consciously and subliminally remind us all we are all natural beings. We instinctively relate to their beauty, their texture, their vitality, and their vulnerability. They can help relax and calm us. They communicate with our senses and sense memories. They are sensual." She stressed that word again. "They help increase and restore our sensitivity. But they aren't sexy or sexual."

"What is your name and your connection to the hotel? And why is this art display here in the first place?" Kendall asked her.

"I'm Rikki Lundquist. I'm not connected with the hotel. I organized this display for the Family Therapy Conference. Most of the artists represented here have some background in psychology, or art therapy, or counseling."

"Are you a therapist or are you one of the artists?"

"I'm a photographer. I was a social worker for several years." She slipped in a deep breath, trying not to show how anxious she was to get out of camera range. She wanted to start picking up the pieces. "I do some photography and video work that therapists use as reinforcement with their clients and in their offices."

"So if beauty is in the eye of the beholder, what would you say happened here?" Kendall proceeded glibly.

"I'd say someone missed the point."

Listening and taking notes off camera, Detective Warnock looked up at her and smiled. He walked away before Kendall started in on him. Besides, the police lab technicians had arrived with cameras of their own.

Kendall drew an invisible cut line to end the taping. "Good." Rikki started to leave as well, but the reporter tried to stop her. "Wait a sec. We need to get a few wide shots of this. Could you stick around in case I have a few more questions?"

Detective Warnock was out in the concourse, talking to two officers. They were all stepping gingerly from open space to open space, occasionally lifting and examining the fallen items.

"I'm going inside for a moment." Rikki eyed the dismal scene in the hall. Police and hotel security were at every corner. Porters and other hotel employees were milling around again, some of them angling to get into the televised segments. Guests were backed up in the taped-off corridors, staring. Kendall's cameraman had started taping again.

Rikki straightened her shoulders, quietly collecting her thoughts so she could go back into the banquet hall and make the necessary explanations. Someone had to break the news before the other conferees came out into the chaos.

Rikki got home in time to watch herself on the eleven o'clock news. She'd peeled off her slinky dinner dress the moment she'd come in. Now she stood, wrapped only in a flower-patterned saronglike pareu, watching the report with Juli.

"Bad scene." Her babysitter, Juli Quinn, sat forward, elbows propped on her knees, staring at the TV. "Why would anyone do a thing like this?"

"That's what we've all been asking."

"What a waste."

"Agreed."

The newscast hadn't used everything Rikki said. Kendall had intercut portions of an interview he'd done with Janelle Givrey while Rikki was helping the other artists sort through the rubble. Fortunately, with the exception of a few of Judy Rodriguez's silk hangings and some of Lynda Abel-Smith's pottery, most of the works came through the attack surprisingly well. Claire had been there to help with the orchids.

"They'll come back," she'd said once she'd checked out the damage. "They'll come through this. We all will."

Rikki caught a glimpse of Claire in the background and felt her frown soften as she listened to the voice-over of Janelle's comments. "Most of us, consciously or otherwise, find peace and beauty and renewed strength through our contact with nature." They cut to a shot of one of the maintenance staff hanging a cascading Oncidium back in place. Then they cut to Janelle herself. "Sensual art is a reapplication of the restorative-nature principle, like a walk on the beach or a visit to a botanical garden. It is a type of self-help therapy." She was standing in front of Rikki's spectacular blowup photo of a cluster of rare cream- and rust-colored Paraphalaenopsis denevei, another specimen from the Australian trip.

"Your photo looks real good," Juli whispered.

"It sold. To a couple from New Jersey."

"Great."

Janelle's voice-over continued as the camera panned the scene of artists, police, and hotel security and maintenance workers tidying up side by side. "This kind of art soothes us on a very primal level. We feel better. We can relax and restore a beseiged part of ourselves." The camera came back to Janelle as she rested her small, almost childlike hand over her breastbone. "We must nourish ourselves." She did seem calmer now, simply articulating the principles, more so than she had when she began talking seconds earlier.

Now Brent Kendall's face appeared on the screen. "These artworks were for sale at the Hilton with part of the proceeds earmarked for the Women's Center. Because of the damage done here, that sale cannot be held. However, members of the community are already reacting positively to this outrage. Vicort Chambers, a well-known arts supporter who came down to assist with the cleanup, is rearranging his scheduled exhibits to hold a special showing of some of these artists' work next weekend. This special showing will take place at Chambers Gallery on the circle on St. Armand's Key. Again, the proceeds will be channeled to the Women's Center. We'll bring you an update on that event as it unfolds."

"He got the important part right." Rikki let out a small sigh. "Victor didn't just wander in. Andy Tubb called him and got him to come down and help assess the damage. It turns out Chambers has been a benefactor of the Women's Center for some time. He came up with the repeat show."

"Is his gallery the fancy one with the griffins out front?" Juli asked.

"That's it."

"I'm impressed."

"Hopefully, so will a lot of other folks. Chambers has been very influential in the arts for as long as I can remember. But his involvement in the Women's Center has been his behind-the-scenes story." Rikki hit the "mute" button on the TV. "One of Chambers's daughters was anorexic. Janelle counseled her and helped pull her through. Chambers said he owed her big time. So he helps the Center. Now, he said he's really going to do this opening right. Food, music, fancy dress. The works. And no commission." The news ended. A weather map filled the screen. Rikki switched off the set.

"Nice to have influential friends." Juli stretched.

"This is more than a friendly gesture," Rikki added. "This has to do with artistic outrage. Chambers knows most of us, or at least he was aware of our work. He was really shaken up by the damage. His hands were trembling as he walked through looking at everything."

"I'd be shaking too," Juli conceded. "But you did great. You looked really cool and collected. And gorgeous in that dress. Drats . . . I should have thought to tape this for the kids," she groaned. "They would have loved seeing you on TV." Rikki's two children, Lara and Jake, American-Polynesians she'd adopted as toddlers, were upstairs, long asleep.

"I'm not sure they need to hear that someone did something like this." Rikki shook her head. "I begrudge giving the creep who did it any publicity at all. It just might encourage someone else to do something similarly stupid."

"You've got a point," Juli conceded. "But Chambers's idea sure isn't stupid," she declared. "His show is a great idea for recouping the losses. Look at the publicity it got tonight. And that reporter said he'd be giving updates. There'll probably be a great turnout. You think he'll be there that night?"

"Chambers?"

"No, the reporter."

"He said he was planning on it."

Juli was swaying from side to side like she did when she was leading up to something. Lara had picked up a similar wind-up routine before she popped a question. The effect was difficult for Rikki to survive straight faced from a six-year-old, much less from a college freshman. "If I could tag along, maybe you could introduce me?" Juli cooed.

"To Brent Kendall? I could do that. But you won't thank me afterwards," Rikki told her as she went into the kitchen for a glass of juice.

Juli followed. "Why not? He's very cute."

"He thinks so too," Rikki noted. "I'd say he's more than a bit superficial. He comes across on screen pretty well." She uncapped the papaya juice. "He does that concerned part well." She paused, lining up two glasses. "Off screen, he's arrogant, pushy, and slippery. He tried putting some moves on Lynda Abel-Smith."

"The potter? I didn't think she was into men."

"She isn't. Her work was the most severely damaged. She was numb."

"So . . ."

"So Mr. Sensitivity started in on her, pouring on what he considers charm. She obviously wasn't interested. She kept ducking him. He kept following her. She finally had to tell him straight out to get lost." Rikki filled the glasses as she spoke. "Next thing you know, he's off starting his schmoozing routine with Olivia Mello."

Juli looked up abruptly and grinned. "Olivia?" She knew Rikki's circle of artist friends. Olivia Mello, a tiny, fragile-looking redhead, was no pushover. A reformed addict, Mello drove a Harley. She'd learned metalworking from a welder, a biker she'd lived with for years. Her large metal sculptures were energetic, stylized, and dramatic. But their delicacy, like her own, was an illusion. Olivia's temperament was volatile. Her fuse with smooth-talking, self-absorbed men was decidedly short, and her verbal karate could be succinct and emasculating. "She nailed him?"

"Appeared so." Rikki took a sip of juice. "I don't know precisely what she said. I was across the room and only caught part of it. Kendall's color faded. He quickly lowered his clipboard to cover his crotch. From then on he stayed close to Detective Warnock."

Juli chuckled. "I'll have to ask her what she told him.

Just in case I need a put-down one of these years, if *ever* anyone puts some moves on me," she added, with her typical shift to melodrama. At nineteen, Juli was getting edgy about losing her virginity. She had hoped for a passionate encounter with a handsome outback type when she agreed to go along with Rikki and the kids on the Australian trip as Rikki's technical assistant and Lara and Jake's part-time nanny.

Instead of meeting tempestuous romance, she'd met a very possessive, very proper Aussie graduate student who preferred to talk botany for hours and who, she lamented, "kissed like an anesthetized carp," not that she'd kissed a fish for the comparison. The only escape she had found was in jogging. This man abhorred sweat. Added to the hiking she and Rikki did anyway, the exercise had slimmed her down. She'd also started wearing her hair back off her face, most often in a French braid like Rikki wore. Now newly enrolled at the Sarasota Art Institute, and thirty pounds lighter than she'd been throughout high school, Juli was anxious to be discovered.

"Be careful how much of Olivia's vocabulary you acquire," Rikki teased her good-naturedly. "I think in most situations you'll encounter, a firm no is sufficient."

"I'd like to try out yes a few times first," Juli responded in her very breathy, very bad Monroe takeoff. "You have *got* to find me a man."

"I'll put one on my grocery list."

"Not a bag-boy. I want a man. Maturity, experience, a car, a real job, and all that good stuff," she said, bobbing her dark braid. "And a recent blood test." She picked up her car keys and flipped them in the air. "Gotta' cruise. See ya' tomorrow. Darkroom?"

"Nope. Upstairs. Production. We'll try putting together a tape. About noon?"

"Noon is good. Maybe a bit earlier. I'll be over right after class."

Rikki walked her out onto the front porch of the boxlike Caribbean-style house. Clouds obscured what little moon was out. The two other residences on the private cul-de-sac on Siesta Key were totally dark. Except for the neatly spaced rectangles of ivory on the ground, light patterns from the lower windows of her house, the two women were engulfed in still, black moist air, tinged with salt from the gulf.

"Sorry about the mess at the Hilton tonight. But you did look hot on the news," Juli said as she headed toward her car.

"Thanks." Rikki waited there, watching until the tail lights of Juli's hatchback disappeared behind the irregular vegetation at the turn leading out to the gate. She heard the car stop, allowed time for Juli to push the buttons so the electronic gate would open, then flinched at the skitter of crushed oyster shell as Juli hit the gas and turned onto Midnight Pass. The sound of the engine gradually faded.

Rikki stood outside a while longer, listening for other sounds, more subtle and serene. She could hear the wind rippling the branches of the mangroves and palmettos. From the rear of the house, she caught the soft beep and puff of dolphins playing out in Roberts Bay, the broad strip of Intracoastal Waterway between Siesta Key and the Sarasota mainland.

She breathed in the gulf breeze sweeping in from the other side of the Key. "Creep," she muttered, letting the night wind carry away the only comment she had about the man who trashed the art show. But the anger stayed with her and the unanswered questions kept coming. "Why would anyone . . . ?"

She locked the front door behind her, then turned off the entry-gate release, securing the one route into the peninsula. Only a keyholder could open it now until morning. She switched off all the downstairs lights, then sighed and rubbed her neck. In darkness again, she wished she could switch off the whispers in her head. "Why . . . ?" She hesitated at the foot of the stairs, remembering what Janelle had said about nourishing other psyches, but not taking time to nourish her own, about drawing strength and serenity from nature.

She was knotted up.

She'd take the time.

Rikki grabbed a towel on the way out the back sliders, then locked them behind her. "Be back shortly." She reached up and patted the long wooden fish carving suspended overhead. She strode down to the dock and stood there a moment, listening for the dolphins. The friendly beeps and puffs were more distant now. The towel and the pareu dropped silently at her feet. Naked, she dove in and let the salty water embrace her. She stayed under a long time, surfaced, took a breath, then rolled over and relaxed, floating effortlessly as the tension flowed out into the cool, dark water.

Dave McIver hadn't planned on attending the festivities at St. Armand's Key. He'd been out on Longboat Key showing a condo. It was five o'clock. He decided to avoid the rush hour chaos on the way back in to Sarasota, so he made his regular stop for a couple of drinks at Conroy's. The blonde bartender took his order and handed him one of the promotional flyers from a stack. "It's tonight." She said the local Art Alliance had sent them out to area businesses to publicize the event.

Dubbed the "Party in the Park," it was touted as an upscale block party honoring the nine artists from the Hilton show, with exhibits and ongoing live music on the central green. The main circle would be closed to vehicles, and the neighboring shops and galleries would remain open after hours. Surrounding cafes and restaurants would be offering complimentary sidewalk hors d'oeuvres and special prices inside.

Trafficwise, it would be a nightmare. McIver figured much of the crowd would just be parasites, coming for the free food and liquor and the ambience, all dressed up and trying to pass for the kind of people who really could afford the prices on the Key. Or they'd be the pushy liberal types, making a statement by showing up to support this current pop-psych fad the promo called "resensitizing art." Assholes. All of them.

Then he saw that one exhibit listed on the agenda that night piqued his interest. A video module sponsored by the Counseling Center would be showing some therapeutic tapes. Stress Reduction. Positive Imaging. By Rikki Lundquist. Somehow seeing it in print connected. That center. His wife. The tapes. That woman. He turned the flyer over and looked at the nine faces in two rows printed on the back. The blonde was labeled Lundquist. The bio said she was a photographer. He'd have chosen another word.

He'd been at Conroy's the night the news carried the story of the vandalism at the Hilton. He'd seen her on TV. He'd had a few drinks then and barely listened to what she said. He wasn't an art aficionado anyhow. But now the pieces clicked. Now he knew what part she had in all this.

He didn't give a shit that some "Trasher" had wrecked an art exhibit, and he sure as hell wasn't interested in buying anything any of them did. But he had to see her. Up close. Suddenly, making her real was important to him. He'd like to tell her face to face what her video bullshit had done to him.

He had another drink and worked out the parking logistics. St. Armand's was just down the road a bit. He could eat now, get there early, and be off the street before the wanna-bees clogged the route. He had a house a couple of blocks from the circle listed with the reality firm, so he could park his Mercedes in the driveway where it wouldn't get nudged or pawed. He had nothing else planned for the evening anyway.

He didn't bother moving to a table. He ordered a grouper sandwich and another drink at the bar. He read the flyer again, more closely than before. Chambers Gallery. He'd never been in it. It wouldn't hurt to put in an appearance, especially if the regular clientele showed up as well. Might give him a chance to revive some old contacts. Make a few new ones. Pass out some business cards. Maybe even run into his wife. Maybe with her sister. He hated the thought of the two of them seeing him walking around there alone. But not enough to stay away.

He ate slowly. Killed the drink. He thought about ordering another when the bartender came along, emptying ashtrays and food scraps in a dump sack under the counter. He kept a bottle of good Scotch and a glass in the car. He paid his bill, went to the john, splashed some water on his face, then took a leak before he left.

She was dropping the bag in the dumpster out back when McIver got to his car. He looked away. Traffic was thin. He poked along anyhow, feeling just a little looser than he liked when he was starting out for an evening on the town. He pulled into the driveway before dark, parked, poured a drink, then took it out back and waited until the sun set. He'd let the anxious-to-be-seen make the early rounds.

As he approached the circle, McIver could hear the music from the side street, some kind of electronic New Age stuff that sounded predictably artsy-fartsy. He halted at the corner for a moment, watching the flow of passersby. Most of them were young and thin and completely at ease. They were strolling past or standing in groups talking, dressed like advertisements for resort wear. He still had on his business suit. He felt conspicuously out of synch. His palms were sweating. He wanted to dissolve into the shadows. He needed a drink.

"McIver. Hey. McIver!"

He jerked his head toward the voice.

"Wait up."

"Charlie . . ." Grateful for a familiar face, McIver almost hugged the trim, white haired man trudging toward him. The fellow who'd spotted him was a Canadian retiree, a snowbird, who'd bought a condo unit from him several years earlier for a rock-bottom price. Drove a hell of a bargain. He'd checked in with McIver every few months since then, as he did with other beachside realtors, asking about available properties. But he was no easy sell. A former high school principal, at sixty-eight Charlie Forman had moved to Sarasota and taken a Florida real estate course. He didn't want to sell properties. He wanted to buy, judiciously. He made no bones about the fact that he was building a vacation-rental empire for him and his cronies.

"Ontario South," he called the Sarasota holdings. He had a lifetime of former students, now grown, as his vacationing clientele, and as a purchaser he was backed by a group of teachers nearing retirement, ready to invest their capital. Forman did his homework. He studied the market, jumped on foreclosures, "must-sells," and estate sales of waterfront condo properties. He'd put in a bid, always drastically low-balling the asking price. But the market was soft. He had up-front money to buy without having to qualify for financing. He was methodical and unflappable. If one seller didn't take an offer, he knew another would. Desperate people made deals. He'd buy, put the place in impeccable order, have it booked solid for the next five years, then go back for more.

"Haven't seen you in a while. Know of any good deals?" Forman asked, chuckling as he shook McIver's hand.

"I should be asking you," McIver replied, not kidding at all. He'd followed the progress of a few of Forman's transactions, enough to know that the empire the older fellow had spoken about was well under way. "You out here on business?"

"Not particularly. Thought I'd take a look at this art show. Maybe branch out a bit. Find another kind of investment,"

Forman said. Dressed in a navy blazer and yellow slacks, the dapper fellow glanced across the green. "Might even find a lady with some refinement at a gathering like this," he added with a glimmer in his eye.

"Maybe." McIver wished he'd worn an open-necked shirt so he'd look a bit more casual, more Palm Beach, like Forman. But he was taller, thirty years younger than his companion, and his dark custom-made business suit did signal a certain affluence.

"You interested in joining me in taking a look?" Forman asked.

"Sure." McIver was glad for the company. They crossed into the street, talking as they ambled toward the display windows of Chambers Gallery on the opposite quadrant. Huge pots of scarlet geraniums lined the curb front. The concrete griffins on either side of the door were newly gilded and gleaming. White jacketed waiters offered champagne or chilled mineral water to everyone who entered.

"If we get separated, we can meet out front by those statues afterward if you'd like and we can stop off for a drink." Forman spoke over his shoulder as they stepped inside. He picked up a copy of the catalog Chambers had put together for the show. He handed McIver the next one.

"Sounds good to me," McIver answered, nodding to a woman he recognized across the room. But the look he got in return was polite, noncommittal, as if she couldn't place him or didn't wish to. He finished the champagne he had in one hand and traded the empty for a full one before the waiter moved on.

He and Forman looked in the first room, then walked on without much hesitation. The room was hung with ceiling-to-floor silk banners in tropical prints, some vivid, some pastel. It all seemed to be moving. He caught a glimpse of the artist, a woman in a kimono outfit of a similar silk, standing with some prospects in the midst of the fabric maze.

The short, prematurely balding fellow in the next room appeared to be as insipid as most of the watercolors on display. Wimpy pastel things that looked like he hadn't used enough paint. Asshole.

McIver moved on with the easy flow, glancing past strangers into one room then the next, steadfastly maintaining some semblance of a smile and not meeting anyone's eyes directly. There were more drinks and hors d'oeuvres at a buffet table ahead. Chambers should have known it would cause a roadblock as the freeloaders bellied up to the trough. Assholes. McIver hated having to stand and wait for them like he was no more than part of the herd.

Forman disappeared into one of the side display rooms shortly after that. Some woman was in there with a lot of pots on pedestals. McIver remembered she was the one with a hyphenated name. Ass-Hole. That amused him.

He knew he was getting to the Lundquist woman when he saw the big flower photo dead ahead. More of her things were in a large white-walled room to the left. He could see her at the far side, surrounded by men, most of them shorter by a few inches. He stepped inside the doorway and stayed there watching her reflection in the glass of one of her photos, until some woman crowded up next to him.

"Pardon me, dear." She rested her hand on his arm and asked him to read the title for her. He gave her a sidelong look and guessed she was close to sixty, three face lifts, minimum. "I forgot my glasses." He could smell her cigarette breath.

"I don't think it's in English." He begged off, unwilling to risk butchering the word printed on the card. "But the price is three hundred bucks." He left her standing there and moved on. He didn't want the old dragon breathing down his neck.

One towering lumberjack of a man in a tux, steadying himself with crutches, was off in the far corner, talking intently to a slim black man with his hair in cigarlike coils. McIver knew the one with the dreadlocks was the other photographer, Lyman something. He'd been the third one in the top row of the flyer, only in that picture, he had the hair pulled back real tight. Now he was wearing a long African tunic thing. With Reeboks.

Asshole.

The big guy kept scanning the visitors, occasionally shaking a hand or exchanging a few words. From the similarity of their features, McIver knew he had to be Lundquist's father. Then the man caught her eye, and they both smiled. Something about that wordless exchange made McIver's chest go tight. Daddy's little girl. Come to Daddy. Just like his wife, running to the old man. He was sweating again. He needed a drink. He had to get out of there or he'd walk

over and bust her in the face. Or roll the catalog tight and
shove it up her ass. Up all of them.

"One little, two little, three little Indians . . ." McIver
didn't know what started the childlike chant running through
his head. "Four little, five little, six little Indians . . ." He
kept tapping the catalog against his leg impatiently as he
worked his way to the door. They were all in it. Nine of
them. He kept walking, not even pretending he was interested in anything else.

He bypassed the griffins and skipped the drink with Forman.

He went straight to the car. He held the catalog under the
beam of the dome light, sipping his own scotch and flipping
slowly from page to page. In truth, all the so-called victims
were to blame for someone's misery. They were all trying
to make a living interfering in other people's business.
Whoever trashed the Hilton show hadn't slowed them down
a bit.

But he sure as hell would.

"Nine little, eight little, seven little Indians . . ." He
was smiling as he flipped off the light and drove home.

"Hi, Dad. Hi, Ivey," Rikki called out from the kitchen
to the formidable white-haired figure coming up her walkway and the woman following behind him. "The kids are
out back if you want to help feed the parrots with them."

"We've got to talk." Swede Lundquist was sputtering
and swaying on his crutches as he came sweeping in the
front door like a sudden squall off the gulf.

"Not just yet, Swede honey," Ivey calmed him. "You
just go ahead and sit in the spa and I'll bring you an iced
tea."

"All right, but I don't like this business," Swede grumbled, but he kept on moving.

Rikki gave him a quizzical look wanting some clue for her
father's current uproar. Ivey winked and indicated she'd be
back to explain. First, she went along to open and close
doors and to get her husband settled. Rikki shrugged and
went back to chopping vegetables for the stir-fry.

"Okay, what's got Dad fuming?" she asked when Ivey
came back alone. They'd talked by phone, but Rikki hadn't
seen either of them since the gallery show the previous
weekend. Then, Swede, tanned and imposing in his tuxedo,

had stood in a corner, supported by his crutches, telling anyone who stopped to ask, about his new knee joints. "Retreads," he called them, delighted that after sixty-three years of mountain climbing and jungle trekking, his worn-out joints would be good as new within a few weeks. Not in time to go to Costa Rica on a fall bird-watching expedition with his old cronies, but enough to make diving off New Zealand at Christmas a possibility.

"You haven't heard the evening news?"

"What's happened?"

"One of your friends has been accosted." That brought Rikki's chopping to an abrupt end.

"Who?"

"Judy Rodriguez."

"What do you mean by accosted?" Rikki stiffened her stance. She knew accosting Judy Rodriguez wouldn't be particularly demanding. At thirty-one Rodriguez had her right arm severed near the shoulder in a water-skiing accident that threw her under the propeller of a speeding boat. Since then, not only had she undergone extensive surgery and therapy, but she'd resumed work as an artist. She handpainted designs on silk, singlehandedly, quite literally, as she'd point out herself. A cheerful, often irreverent woman, Judy ran a business and operated a vehicle on her own. The thought of anyone harming her had Rikki bristling.

"She's not injured." Ivey made that clear. "But that trasher guy with the mask apparently went into her studio while she was in the office part making calls. She had the CD on low. Someone turned it up. She figured it was her husband or someone she knew and came out. He was waiting. He swung a sack of garbage at her and knocked her down." A stage actress for years, obviously Ivey was framing her version carefully. "It burst open, but he had another one and emptied it on her too. Poured it all over her."

"No . . ." Rikki shook her head.

"It gets worse," Ivey went on. "On the way out, he pushed over some of her silk screens and threw around paint. The reporter said there was a lot of damage. But Judy is all right."

"And the guy got away?"

"Again." Ivey nodded. "Afraid so. They said the studio is set back too far for the neighbors to hear anything."

"That was the reason she put it there," Rikki recalled,

letting out an exasperated sigh. The studio was a converted guest house, Mediterranean style, beyond the pool in the Rodriguez's back yard. Its lacy wrought-iron balcony usually was dripping with purplish flowering bougainvillea and there was always some kind of classical guitar music on the CD player. Now the idyllic setting was altered into something sinister. "My God. I can't believe anyone would go into her yard in broad daylight . . ."

"At least she's not hurt." Ivey tried to sound reassuring. "The reporter said Judy didn't lose her cool. She went back in to the phone, called 911 and then her husband. She apparently stood in the shower, clothes and all, and showered off the residue until they got there." Ivey pressed her lips together, finding the telling more difficult than she'd expected.

"This guy is really sick." Rikki swallowed, editing whatever other comments she was considering. She stared at the meal she'd started preparing, suddenly having no appetite, nor any interest in food at all.

"He's sick, all right. And that means he could do it again. That's why your dad is concerned. Why I'm concerned too," Ivey stressed. "We both have a bad feeling about this person."

"They're sure it's the same guy?"

"Apparently he fit the description." Ivey responded. "Judy saw him. He was wearing a ski mask. One of the neighbor's pool men saw a guy, medium build, running down the ally behind the house. Wearing a ski mask. In Florida. In September. A tad suspicious. The guy yelled at him, then called the police too. But in all truth, I'm not sure what they can do." Ivey's expression clouded. "Your dad and I just want you to be careful."

"I doubt that anyone would pull something like that on me," Rikki replied. "I'm certainly not helpless. Or Olivia. She's small, but she's trouble. She'd have run him down and decked him, then carried him to the police station strapped across her Harley like a moose." Rikki rubbed her upper arms, not liking at all the negative energy that was building inside her. "I almost wish he would try it on me."

"Watch what you say. He might. That's the point," Ivey said in a low, concerned voice. "That's precisely what's got your dad worried. Me too. If it is that same guy, he's turned very nasty. That mean edge is really scary."

"I'll be careful," Rikki assured her.

"That's why we're here. I was thinking that maybe you'll need a few more locks around. Your dad already picked up a couple of those lights that go on when they detect any movement. You know how dark it gets here at night. Anyone could be out there." Ivey and her first husband had once owned the wood, tri-storey house Rikki now lived in. They'd divorced and she'd continued her theatrical career, leaving her son with a nanny and a housekeeper when she was performing out-of-state runs. After a short stint in a soap opera and a second divorce, Ivey came back to reside in Sarasota full time and immersed herself in local theater there. She eventually married Rikki's father, her friend and neighbor for years.

In a three-way shuffle the occupants of Mangrove Place had changed. Swede and Ivey had moved into a gulf-front condo. A bird-watching buddy, Harrison Ash, had bought the Lundquist home. Pat Simons, the director of the library, bought Ash's place, and Rikki moved with her two children into Ivey's house on the point that had the larger lot. Rikki had added on a darkroom and built a larger slathouse for orchids, consolidating their combined collections of plants. She'd expanded and partially roofed the back deck and had the spa installed and the gazebo built. But because of its isolation, Ivey knew the Caribbean-style house was as vulnerable as Judy Rodriguez's studio. She also knew Rikki rarely closed, much less locked her doors because she liked the cross-breeze through the screens.

"I don't see any reason for overreacting," Rikki countered calmly. "If we had motion-sensitive lights out here, I'd be caught stark naked on my way to the dock every night. Or a pelican or one of the parrots would set them off. The boys squawk and roam around at night."

"True," Ivey sighed. The "boys," a flock of wild parrots and macaws, considered the private peninsula of Mangrove Place their home too. Escapees who had found each other and banded together, they were spoiled, territorial, raucous, and occasionally nocturnal. Swede had started feeding and pampering them years before. Ash and Rikki had carried on the tradition, allowing them to use the area as a sanctuary.

"At least get more locks. Especially for the sliders. Upstairs as well as down," Ivey cautioned. "This guy might climb."

"He'd have to fly if I caught him on one of the balconies," Rikki muttered.

"Regardless . . . I had to say my piece," Ivey concluded with a dramatic flourish. "Now it's your dad's turn. Let's go out back and let Swede rant awhile. I promised him iced tea," she added hastily.

"I'm really not looking forward to this." Rikki inverted a bowl to cover the vegetables on the cutting board. She filled a glass and handed it to Ivey.

"Your dad thinks you might need some kind of bodyguard." Ivey braced her for the conversation ahead. "I swear, he'd have us both camping out here if he were more mobile. But there's not much a fellow on crutches can do. He's quite put out that he scheduled the knee surgery, and then this guy starts pulling his stunts. You know how carefully he organizes everything."

Rikki shrugged. She understood now Swede's huffing and puffing was because some upstart was making trouble while he was laid up with knee joint replacements. "I just hope Dad doesn't say anything to get Jake wound up. He thinks he's the man of the house. He'll start looking for ways to protect us. There's not much an eight-year-old can do in a situation like this."

"Perhaps you could ask Juli to move in for a fews weeks, just to have an extra set of eyes and ears. You know what they say about safety in numbers." Ivey kept talking as they started out back toward the tiered deck that spanned the rear of the house. "Or Eddie Sordo," she went on. Sordo, the middle-aged Melanesian gardener, was devoted to Rikki and the youngsters. He was unimposing, but he was solid as a pit bull.

Rikki kept a noncommittal expression and continued walking.

"You could move somewhere more protected for a few weeks," Ivey suggested. "There are a couple of unoccupied condos for rent in our building. I'm sure we could work out something." She let it drop, interpreting her stepdaughter's silence and uncompromising jaw set, so like her hardheaded father's, as "not a chance" in Lundquistese.

Swede was seated in the spa, submerged waist deep, under the gazebo on the south corner of the deck. From that thronelike vantage point, hung with flowering orchids, he could overlook both the wide Intracoastal Waterway and the mainland of Sarasota to the east and a row of cabbage palms, mangroves, and thick vegetation along the water's edge to the south.

Lara and Jake were sitting on the edge of the spa with him, bubbling their feet while Grampa's new knees simmered. From Jake's slack-jawed expression and Lara's wide eyes, the women knew Swede was deep into the retelling of some adventure or other, from chasing cockatoos in Australia or red shining parrots in Fiji to hanging from a treetop in a South American rain forest. He had an inexhaustible supply of tales from one photo assignment or another.

Already the reflected scarlet and mauve cloud bands above the city meant there was a magnificent sunset to the west, on the gulfside just a few hundred yards across Midnight Pass. But tonight Rikki doubted anyone would feel like putting on shoes, then circling around the front to cross over and watch the colorful finale. "How about you two going in to get a couple of slices of cheese to hold you over," she told the youngsters. "Dinner will be a little late. Grandpa and Ivey and I have to talk."

Lara looked at her mom and raised her eyebrows. "I'm not hungry yet." She knew something was going on, and she was revving up for one of her stalls.

"Please . . . we need a little private time." Rikki wasn't buying into it. "Both of you." Jake knew from the tone that he'd better cooperate.

"Maybe I'll just tag along and help," Ivey offered, shooing Lara and Jake ahead of her. "Play nice, you two," she called out over her shoulder as father and daughter settled in to negotiate.

McIver picked up the two sacks of grapefruit next door to a house he was showing. Whoever lived there had simply let them drop and lay there, so the yardman had bagged them and set them out with the clippings. McIver swung back by late that night and put them in his trunk. He put twisters around the necks to keep them from stinking up the car. "Variation on a theme," he mused as he drove off. He'd trash again, so the Trasher trademark would stick.

McIver had no idea what macro-photography was, some kind of ultra-closeup he guessed from the overblown description under Lyman Franklin's entry in the gallery catalog. "Franklin makes a dewdrop or the throat of a flower an accessible wonderland." Bullshit. Artsy-fartsy bullshit.

It took him three days to get a grasp of the guy's routine. Franklin lived in an older neighborhood off Bayshore with moss-hung oaks out front and his backyard running up to Jungle Gardens. Sitting there in his car the first morning he stood watch, McIver could hear the damn peacocks back there shriek. Some elderly woman came out in a flowered robe to get the newspaper and let her spaniel piss in the grass. Some kids with schoolbooks chugged up to the corner where another one was waiting. A school bus picked them up. A couple of women came past, powerwalking in spandex pants. A few neighbors in suits drove off in cars. Then Franklin came out on his bicycle wearing a backpack and some kind of knit cap, like a big green, red, and yellow-striped sock over his dreadlocks, and rode away.

McIver followed in his car, worrying all the while that Franklin would look back and spot him creeping along like that in the Mercedes, or one of the neighbors might wonder what the hell he was doing on their street at all. He didn't want anything to tip off Franklin that he was next.

Franklin only pedaled a few blocks to the camera shop he ran in a strip mall where Myrtle intersected the Tamiami Trail. McIver parked across the street, waited awhile watching him open up, and left. Just before closing time, McIver returned, better prepared than before. He parked the Mercedes down the Trail behind a supermarket, got his bike out of the trunk, and rode it, something he hadn't done in a couple of years. Besides making him less conspicuous, he figured the exercise would do him some good.

Problem was that Franklin didn't go straight home after work. He cut over to Bayshore and took off northbound, but he passed by his turnoff and kept going. McIver had to struggle to keep from losing sight of his skinny ass and the bright striped, swollen headgear. He was gasping and soaked with perspiration when Franklin turned into the University of South Florida's Sarasota campus, locked the bike to a rack, and went inside one classroom building. McIver sprawled on a bench across the way to catch his breath and wait.

Franklin didn't come back out again for two hours. It was almost dark. McIver was hungry. He'd found a water fountain, but he was starving and wanted a real drink. He followed Franklin anyway. The guy headed back along Bayshore, cut over to the Trail, picked up something at a funky restaurant advertising "natural foods," then he carried it to the camera shop and let himself in the back door. He turned on some lights and took the bike in with him.

By then McIver was spent. His leg muscles were cramping. He got back to his car and threw the bike in his trunk. He drove past the shop and circled around the back past the dumpsters from the neighboring shops. Like the other businesses in the strip mall, the rear end of Franklin's shop had no windows, but from the front he could see there were still extra lights on inside. Franklin was nowhere visible. He figured the guy must be in the back sorting stock or something. He wasn't going to wait around again. He bought Kentucky Fried, went home, and chased it down with scotch.

The rest of it was easy. McIver came back in his shirtsleeves at lunchtime the next day and looked around inside. He told Franklin he was interested in a good used camera. While the guy showed him what he had, McIver made small talk, commenting about the large color photos on the wall, knowing full well that the little guy had done them. He didn't buy a camera, but he did find out from Franklin while they talked that he did most of the photography as well as his own processing and printing there. His studio and darkroom were in the back half of the narrow shop.

"Must take a lot of concentration." McIver led him on.

"I do most of it at night after we're closed. Then there's nothing to distract me."

Asshole. McIver almost chuckled.

After work that day, he spotted the grapefruit and picked it up. Any garbage would have done the job. Then he had a couple of drinks at home, got a few essentials, and drove past the strip of businesses. Sandwiched between a vacuum repair shop and a baked goods thrift store, Franklin's place was dark as a cave. Same thing the next night. But the third try, he could see there was light inside. It was worth a shot.

He pulled in behind the strip and dropped the grapefruit off. Then he swung around the block and strolled back on foot, emptyhanded. Everything he needed fit in his pockets. This time, he'd even brought wire cutters for the phone line so Franklin couldn't call the cops right away like the newscast had said the Rodriguez woman had. Everything else would be the same. The Trasher strikes again, just like the newspaper said.

"Hey . . . anyone in there?" He banged at the back door. "Hey . . ."

No one came. He tried again.

Still no response. He pounded harder.

"Who is it?" Franklin finally answered without opening the door.

"Phone company. We've had line trouble coming into this strip. Backflow. It's burnt out a couple of units. Check to see if your phone is fried. If it's dead, I have a unit on the truck you can have now. I'd like a tradeout so I can drop it off with a technician. May not match, but it will work. Otherwise I'll put you on the list. May take a few days."

He waited. Of course Franklin's phone was dead. He'd cut the line and killed it. He'd made up the rest, the backflow, the burnout, and the tradeout shit. But he knew no one running a business wanted to be without a phone.

He was ready when he heard the lock slide.

Asshole.

"Rikki, dear. The fellow I mentioned is here. Can you break free for a few minutes? I'd like to bring him over and introduce you." Harrison Ash called Sunday, obviously eager.

Rikki was in her production studio on the second floor, trying to edit the video she and Juli had worked on over the past week. But her concentration was off. The Trasher had attacked Lyman Franklin and devastated his studio. The artist had been standing by a pay phone, reeking of rotting grapefruit when the police arrived. But bruised and shaken, he gave a thorough description of the assailant. Medium height, husky build, ski mask. The hands were encased in surgical gloves. The only visible flesh, the guy's neck, was white. Speculation now was he would hit again.

"Let him try it." Rikki refused to move off Mangrove Place like Swede had demanded this time. He'd come over bright and early Saturday, the morning after the Franklin attack, determined to press his case. While Ivey judiciously took the kids outside to help her water the orchids, Swede had paced and ranted in the kitchen, punctuating his comments by thudding his crutches on the tile floor. Rikki calmly fixed them all breakfast. "I'm not saying no to you," she'd finally told her father. "I'm saying no to him. I have a life here. My work is here. We love it here. I'm not going to give this guy the power to make me uproot the kids and go into hiding. The answer is no." Swede had sputtered on a while, but he had finally let it rest.

Now while Jake and Lara were across at one neighbor's house, helping Pat Simons reweb some lawn chairs, Rikki was spending the morning trying to be productive herself. But it just wasn't coming together. She kept replaying the sound track put together by Fuzzy Haight, the curly haired young musician whose job was playing flute for the symphony. But Fuzzy's real love was creating original music in his home studio, totally on synthesizers. Usually their efforts blended with more ease. Rikki wasn't content with the way a particular set of exotic flower images were supposed to dissolve into each other in sych with Fuzzy's music. Frustrated, she was almost glad to be interrupted when Harrison Ash, her other neighbor called.

"Sure. Five minutes. Meet you out back on the lanai."

Ash and his companion were an incongruous sight. Decked out in his Panama hat and color-coordinated shorts, jacket, shirt, tie, and knee-length socks, Ash was typically dapper as he led the way around the corner. His companion, however, was another fashion statement. A well-built man in his late thirties with sandy-colored sunbleached hair that hung over his collar, a deep tan, and a couple of days growth of beard, he wore print shorts and an open-necked shirt that he might have slept in. He also had his right arm in a cast. Mirrored aviator sunglasses masked his eyes. To Rikki he looked like an overaged surfer who'd had a decidedly unsuccessful encounter with a wave, or a bottle.

"Stuart Sullivan, your neighbor Rikki Lundquist," Ash introduced his housesitter. "With that damnable Trasher business and the possibility he or someone else may poke his nose into our compound, I thought it was best to have someone stay in the place while I'm gone. Stu is a bit laid up, but I figure he could keep an eye out and if need be, he could dial the phone with his good arm."

"Nice to meet you, Ma'am." Sullivan's voice was as disinterested as his expression. Rikki briefly considered underscoring the obvious by responding with "sir," then thought better of it. For the next six weeks, they were going to be neighbors, it seemed. She'd make the best of it.

"Call me Rikki. Nice to meet you, Stuart. Harrison said you live in town. His house should be a lovely change of pace for convalescing."

He nodded, sending her reflection skittering across his lenses. Then the lenses lost her completely as he scanned the layout of the back decking and the yard leading down to the Intracoastal.

"So. You leave tomorrow?" Rikki figured pursuing a conversation with the surfer would require more charm than she felt like generating at the moment. Ash was smiling and watching her closely. Without his glasses, he watched everyone closely, and today he'd apparently left them home. Swede loved to tease him, claiming Ash was too vain to wear his spectacles outside the house except for bird watching. He'd also claimed that the lanky Ash wore the knee socks only because he was too near-sighted to see what was in his path and had always had bruised shins from colliding with patio chairs and end tables. Rikki maintained the old fellow was simply absentminded.

"Tomorrow. Yes. I'm all packed. Can't tell you how glad I am that Stu will be here to water the plants and feed the boys." The parrot-macaw troop would line his upstairs deck railing at sunrise, protesting loudly if he didn't bring out chopped fruits for their breakfast. "I know you and the youngsters would take care of them, but this will save all that running back and forth, especially now. Until they get that guy, I do hope all of you will be careful."

"We'll be careful." Rikki stole a quick look at the surfer, wondering how enthusiastically he'd deal with the six-thirty fly-in each day. He didn't look like an early riser. "Would you like to sit awhile and have some tea?" She made the offer to Ash, but she included Stu Sullivan with a sweeping look. He was scrutinizing the dock and the water view, listening.

He turned their way again, but his expression remained impassive. The mirrored glasses obscuring his eyes were making her edgy. She liked to exchange some emotional energy when she spoke with someone. Sullivan didn't have to like her. But it would be less awkward if he registered some acknowledgement. Instead, he gave nothing and bounced nothing back, except an occasional fractured reflection that put her unnervingly out of context.

"I'd love tea. We both would," Ash answered for the housesitter as well. "I don't want you to lose track of whatever else you were doing. Speaking of which," Ash stammered, "I just remembered something I need to slip into my suitcase." He held up a finger as some means of securing the recollection of whatever elusive bit of paraphernalia had come to mind. "I must go. If I don't get back, would you mind showing Stu the slathouse," he suggested, clearly uncomfortable and flustered about walking out on them so abruptly. "He like plants." The finger was still aimed skyward, staunchly erect.

"Go. Pack. I'll show him around," Rikki said reassuringly.

"Good. I told him you have wonderful orchids. Worth seeing." Ash nodded to Rikki and exited quickly.

Sullivan was staring out over the water again.

"If you aren't really interested in orchids. you don't have to take the tour." Rikki wasn't about to expend any misdirected effort trying to interest the housesitter in her plants. "I could bring you a soft drink or a beer? You could stroll down to the dock."

"I like orchids. I'd like to see your collection." This time the voice had a different quality.

"You're sure?"

"I'm sure I like orchids. And I'm sure I'd like to see what you've got." His full mouth broadened into a half-smile. At least now he was trying.

"The showy ones are this way." Somewhat encouraged by his attitude, first she led him across the lanai to the spa enclosure where she kept the orchids that were currently in bloom. "I just got back from summering in Australia. I have a few new ones that I brought in." She'd hold the slathouse visit off until she could tell if he were really interested.

"Paperwork you have to do for importing can be a real bear. You don't get anywhere without C.I.T.E.S. certificates and phytosanitary documents."

She gave Sullivan a reappraising look, surprised he had any concept of what was involved in bringing in plants. "You've done it?"

He nodded. "A few times." He obviously didn't choose to elaborate.

"Over the years, I've tried to start the paperwork in advance," Rikki told him. "I'd never remove anything from the wild except on film. The actual plants I bring home are from licensed growers."

"Good approach." He was close behind her as they stepped up onto the raised area of decking with the gazebolike enclosure for the spa. From the way he favored one side as he moved, she realized he was in some pain. She tried not to stare as he lifted his glasses and propped them on top of his head. He squinted at the tag on one plant, then another. His greenish-hazel eyes locked onto hers a moment, registered something indefinable, then shifted again to the assorted pots and baskets of orchids suspended from hooks in the rafters or brackets on the latticed walls. "The Dendrobium. Australian?"

It took her a few seconds to respond. "Yes. I'm not sure how it will do out here." She followed him as he strolled over for a closer look.

" 'Scuse me, fellah," he said as they bypassed the skirted scarecrowlike figure she had in the corner.

"Beautiful plant." He reached up to turn the plastic label tied to the orchid so he could read the species name. Abruptly he checked the movement, retracted the arm, and clutched his other shoulder, above the cast. "Damn!" He breathed the word with just a slight catch. "Sorry. I forget that I can't move like I used to. I'm not good at maneuvering in all this crap." From his measured breaths and the way he cradled that arm, she knew he was suffering.

"There's more than the broken arm?"

"Broke a couple of ribs. Separated a shoulder. Bruises. I'm tied up like a mummy under here," he answered. "Tape all over. Some kind of harness thing. Big support dropped on me at work. When I screw up, I do a really good job of it." He was breathing in cautious, shallow breaths.

"Would you like to sit down?" She circled around, not quite sure what to do to help.

"I'm okay. This is really a nice layout back here." He quickly changed the subject. "Nice design. You get protection from the sun without sacrificing the view or the breeze." He was looking at the way the enclosed gazebo offered privacy on the south side, then the roofline extended in open slats above the upper tier of the deck, creating the lanai across the back of the house. From there the deck progressed, uncovered, in broad steps toward a long walk leading out to the dock on the northeastern curve of land.

"How's the fishing?"

"Pretty good. Jake is the fisherman of the family. He and the other neighbor, Pat Simons, like to fish together. You might talk to them about techniques."

"I like to fish." He still cradled one arm.

"I think I'll get some juice. How about you?"

"Juice would be good. Anything cold," he suggested. "I'll just look at the flowers and try not to flap my good wing too hard."

Despite his attempt at humor, Rikki could tell by the stiffness in Sullivan's expression that he was uncomfortable showing any discomfort in front of her. He obviously wanted some time alone. To recoup.

"Make yourself at home." She left him standing there. In the kitchen she took some extra time to slice fresh pineapple and rinse off some grapes, keeping everything easy to manage. When she went out again, she didn't want him to feel any more inept than he apparently already did.

"Stuart. It's Swede. For you." Harrison Ash was waiting, phone in hand, when Stu returned from Rikki's house. "He's already called. Three times."

"So. What do you think of my little fair-haired girl?" Swede demanded over the phone in his typical overblown style of discourse.

"She wasn't quite what I expected," Stu answered quite honestly. He'd read in the newspaper about the art show that was trashed. Several of the men on his staff had commented about seeing some blonde on the television in a blue dress talking about art the night it happened, a few days before his accident. The guys said that even if she said her art wasn't sexy, *she* sure as hell was. Then a crossbeam dropped on him while he was conducting an arson investigation and put him in the hospital. He'd had plenty of time to read the followup newspaper reports on the Trasher and his subsequent attack on the Rodriguez woman on Anna Maria Island.

He'd vaguely recognized Rikki's name when Victor Chambers called him to ask a favor the morning after the

second nasty incident, the one with the grapefruit in the
camera shop. Chambers mentioned showing some of the
controversial art that survived the Hilton vandalism, then
said in that roundabout conversation with Stu that someone
needed a bodyguard. For another photographer. A woman.
The daughter of a friend, Swede Lundquist. "He's an award-
winning nature photographer himself. You may have seen
his work."

"Never heard of him," Stu replied dully. He wasn't familiar with any of Chambers's art cronies. He'd met Chambers several years before through Plantworks, the nursery
business Stu and his younger brother started. On his off days
as a fireman, he helped with the plants and did some landscaping. Chambers was still a client, but Stu's connection
to Plantworks had become increasingly limited after he became the city fire marshal. Chambers knew he was out on
medical leave and would be home recuperating for a few
weeks at least. He offered him the opportunity to mend in
rather posh surroundings on Siesta Key. In the home of a
friend of a friend, he'd said. Protecting a woman who wasn't
supposed to know she and her kids were being protected.
Housesit and babysit. Stu already felt miserable from his
injuries and had balked. But since he and Chambers went
back a long time, he'd said he'd think about it.

He didn't have long to think. By midday, his boss, the
mayor, Robert Sloane, called him. Sloane and Chambers
were also old friends. Sloane had suggested Chambers call
Stu in the first place, to test the waters instead of having the
mayor or Lundquist approach him directly.

Stu had tried to bow out politely. He pointed out that
none of the trashing incidents were life threatening. They
were malicious pranks. They hardly called for a bodyguard,
much less a disabled one.

"If you're worried, why don't you just assign a police
officer to her?"

"There are seven artists from that group left, and we sure
as hell can't put someone on them all. We're tight as it is.
Can't spare anyone. You know we've had cutbacks."

"So have the father hire someone private."

"There's more to this than stopping someone from throwing grapefruit," Sloane told him. "This guy is stalking people. These are assaults, direct and personal." His retelling
was more ominous than the way it sounded in the news

reports. The Trasher didn't simply stroll in this time. He'd waited until after hours, when the nearby shops were closed. He'd cut the phone lines. He'd tricked Franklin, a small-boned, delicate-featured man, into opening a door. He'd burst in and driven Franklin into his stockroom, pelting the man with fruit. Some maggot filled. Some as hard as softballs.

Cornered and startled, Franklin didn't have the temperament or the body mass to fight back. He managed to break away long enough to blockade himself in his darkroom. Then the Trasher went into his studio and the shop out front, smashing anything he could get his hands on. Thousands of dollars' worth of equipment. "Looks like he went wild," Sloane said. "No telling what he might do to a woman and two little kids. They're six and eight, for God's sake," he added.

Stu could feel the pressure building. "Don't they have a relative or a friend they could move in?"

"Like I said, she's the independent type. She won't go along with it. And once we got a chance to talk with the detectives on the case, Swede agreed with Victor and me. We don't just want her protected. We want to get this guy. To do that, the Trasher can't know she's protected either."

"I've got a broken arm. What the hell good could I do?"

"Look helpless. Just hang around there. Watch. Call in anything suspicious. You're the trained investigator. You like to work. You're out of commission otherwise. This will keep you from getting bored," Sloane commented. "Off the record, if he attacks, I'd say shoot the son of a bitch. Officially, detain him. Immobilize him. Just aim low and do it inside the premises. And we all will be indebted to you. Consider it community service, with fringe benefits. I'd consider it a personal favor," he stressed. "At least give it a try."

Stu had finally consented to do just that. He'd stay at Ash's house, diagonal on the cul-de-sac to Rikki's. Reluctant to commit to any long-term agreement, he settled for a trial period of two weeks. After that, he and Swede Lundquist and Sloane would renegotiate, or find someone else if Stu wanted out. A lot depended on what the Trasher had done in the interim.

But in answer to Swede's inquiry about his "fair-haired daughter," Stu wasn't sure how to respond. He hadn't been prepared to like her. He expected her to be artsy, eccentric perhaps. Rich type. Probably arrogant. The guys at the office who'd seen her on TV had said she was a sexy broad. Nice tits. Showed well when the reporter, Kendall, interviewed her. When she came walking out to meet him and Ash in a bathing suit top and that Tahitian sarong thing, he was sure she'd be insufferable. Tall, lean, obviously in very good condition, she was a golden-haired version of one of those islanders in ads for Bacardi and the South Sea islands.

He just hadn't expected to like her.

She had a gentle way about her. She was somewhat reserved. And she wasn't arrogant at all. She treated Ash with a sweet, indulgent attitude despite the old boy's pretensions. And she didn't fuss. When he overreached and made his rib cage scream, she gave him the space he needed. Later, after the kids came back from the Simons house, they'd sat out back talking about orchids, and travel and Oceanic art. He watched her as her dark-haired children came and went. She was part mother hen, part cheerleader, part referee. Like a real mom. He hadn't expected that.

Rikki Lundquist wasn't the victim type. She looked strong, but she certainly wasn't tough. When she talked about her short stint as a social worker, her eyes were somber and distant. She said she hadn't been able to deal with the frustration of all the day-to-day abuse cases she encountered. "I had the education, but I knew I wasn't good at what I was doing. I don't like to do anything poorly. So I had to face my limitations and forgive myself for not being more resilient, and get on with something else. I wasn't the Superwoman I thought I was," she admitted. "I grew up trekking through jungles with my dad, stepping over snakes and hanging on slings, taking photos in the rain forests. I'm not cut out for housing projects and detention centers. But I always loved photography. My dad was an excellent mentor. So now I work with film. I use my skill as an artist to bring to people some relief from the world they live in. I'm very good at that."

He liked the way she said it with such quiet confidence. He figured what she said must be true. Not immodest. Simply accurate. So he'd asked to see her work. There were mostly family photos downstairs in a high-ceilinged living room with lots of Tiki figures and four loveseats in a bold batik print. Then she'd taken him into her second-floor production studio and showed him some of her large orchid photos, close up and firsthand. The amorphous term "sensual art" he'd seen used in the newspaper took on an entirely singular meaning. These were majestic and intimate and delicate. Without doubt, she was very good at what she did.

They spent the remainder of the afternoon together, talking, looking at her orchid slathouse, even taking a walkthrough of her darkroom addition across the back of the garage downstairs. He began to realize how vulnerable she was in that big, sprawling house. There was a lot of glass. Lots of doors. Balconies front and rear. Low trees and bushes on the perimeter for cover. Water access all around to this quiet world on one of several points across from the mainland.

"If someone wanted to get her . . ." He found himself running scenarios through his head. The thought of anyone getting close enough to douse her in garbage or pelt her with grapefruit or simply intruding into this oasis where she and Lara and Jake lived became increasingly repugnant. He couldn't let anyone terrorize her or her two sturdy, caramel-skinned youngsters. If the Trasher did show, he hoped he'd be able to do more direct damage than dial 911 and yell out a warning.

"She doesn't seem suspicious?" Swede asked him in the update over the phone afterward.

"Nope. It was relaxed. Real casual. I think she bought the story," Stu replied, not particularly comfortable that he'd agreed to edit some details about himself. When she'd asked about his work, he'd told her part of the truth. He said he was in landscape contracting, partners in Plantworks, the nursery-landscape firm with his brother Brian. She'd heard of the place. It was a few miles inland beyond the city limits. She even had one of their tagged orchids in her slathouse, a healthy Vanda with its basket netted in roots, with a spike but not in bloom yet. She didn't remember buying it, so she figured it may have been one that Ivey Currey had passed on to her, or something the gardener Eddie Sordo picked up. There were several hundred plants at least, he estimated.

After her being gone all summer, Rikki had shown him that many of her orchids had crowded pots and dried pseudobulbs and needed to be groomed and divided. "If you're ever looking for something to do, you're welcome to come over and help me repot a lot of these," she'd said, pleased to have someone knowledgeable at her doorstep. "I like to have a supply of giveaways for friends. It's fun to pass them on to folks and let them find out how easy orchids are to get along with."

He'd liked the way she'd said "get along with" instead of "grow." It had a nice, personal sound that suited her. He noticed the way she touched each plant with a special familiarity. Like a greeting. Like she touched Jake and Lara. It hadn't taken him long to realize he knew about the plants that grew well in Florida. But she knew more about the classification of orchids worldwide than he did. She'd photographed and brought home specimens from all over the globe, some he'd only seen mentioned in catalogs or horticulture books.

But he jumped at the chance to help with the plants. It gave him access to her and a reason to come and go. They agreed to start at one end of the slathouse and slowly work their way to the front, putting the plants and the place in better order. She'd get in extra pots and planting media, and he'd contribute his labor in return for a few selections from the new divisions.

"Let me give you her schedule," Swede said before he let Stu off the line. "So if she takes off, you'll have an idea where's she going."

"I'll get a pen."

"Tuesdays seven to nine she's teaching a photo class at the Art Institute," Swede dictated. "It's pretty open there. Campus security is around. Lots of students. I don't think he'd try anything there. On an open stretch, she'd run him down," he added with apparent smugness. "About every other Thursday she goes to the Safe House and switches off some plants. If there's anything at Selby—talks, special events—she likes to go. I'll get you a schedule. And she and the kids will be helping a couple of friends who are organizing a beach cleanup drive in a couple of weeks. Saturday, October third. Got it?"

"Got it," Stu replied, jotting each installment of Rikki's itinerary on the large wall calendar Harrison Ash had posted. He'd set up his "command headquarters" between the phone and the kitchen window. With or without binoculars, it afforded an unobstructed view of her front yard and the double front door. Because of the tall trees between the houses, he'd have to go upstairs to get a good view of the upper floors.

"Ivey will keep you posted about any other goings-on." Swede continued like a coach outlining a game plan. "You've got the school bus schedule?"

"I've got it." It was taped with the list of friends Swede supplied, along with their make of car if he knew it.

"Good. We don't want anyone unaccounted for." He hesitated, apparently going over some checklist he'd compiled. "Oh, yes. Rikki usually goes to any gallery opening that strikes her fancy. She's real good about rounding up folks to show up for any of her friends who are exhibiting. We tend to get drawn into those, sometimes at the last minute, but we'll call and let you know if one crops up."

"Fine," Stu replied, making a note to himself in the margin of the calendar to call the police headquarters to talk to Joe Warnock. He wanted to touch base and tell the detective that he was watching the Lundquist woman and her family. He had a few buddies in influential places too, and Warnock was one of them. He'd give Warnock his number there and ask the detective to keep him posted about how the Trasher investigation was coming along.

"Well, I guess that's about all I have for now," Swede said, sounding a bit less anxious than he had the first time they talked. He and Stu Sullivan still hadn't met face to face. "Just keep 'em all safe." There was a tremor of emotion in Swede's closing comment that signaled a depth of feeling that may have been more difficult for both men to handle in person.

"I'll do it, sir. I'll check in tomorrow," Stu answered. The shoulder hurt. He couldn't unclench his teeth. He needed a painkiller. He hated to admit how much they helped. But they made him groggy. He hated that more. He glanced at his watch as he hung up the phone to see how long it had been since the last one. Just that much torque set off a chain reaction.

"Fuck." He clutched his arm and hoped wherever Ash was was out of earshot. Then he almost smiled, remembering Rikki's comment about forgiving herself for not being a Superwoman. She could teach him a lot about letting up on himself for not being able to tough it out while the bones and muscles mended. "All right. I'm not Superman, either," he conceded, heading into the bedroom for the bottle of pills the doctor had prescribed.

Midweek, Dave McIver went in early and locked his office door at Suncoast Realty. He slid the cardboard box he'd brought in next to the file cabinet. More variations on a theme. He spread out on his desktop the map of West Central Florida. The GoldCoast. He'd checked all their street addresses and phone numbers. He'd marked each location in yellow highlighter, a simple bar of color. Most of them lived within easy driving range. Now he filled in with blue the Tampa one from the night before. That left six little Indians.

He'd eased up on the technique, though. This one was no risk, nothing personal. After the squalling in the press triggered by the Rodriguez dump, he'd intended to back off and cool things down a bit. But once he started tracking the little black guy, he got caught up in the gamesmanship of it all. Even the bike rides were exciting.

Then he connected with the first few grapefruit. Franklin let out those weird shrieks, like the fucking peacocks behind his house. Gave McIver a rush and made his skin crawl all at once. But Franklin wiggled away and holed up in the darkroom, and that really pissed him off. So McIver had a field day. He trashed the place, all of it. The point was to let everyone know the Trasher did it. Franklin saw enough to pass on to the cops the same details as before. The whole thing had given the press another hot headline. "Nine little, eight little, seven little Indians . . ." McIver would keep them guessing. But for his third hit, he'd decided to cool off the Tampa one, literally.

He'd driven over there to meet a business associate for dinner the night before. Only he went early, when it was light enough to make a drive-by and look the place over. He circled twice. Then he went on to Bern's Steak House and waited in the lounge.

There was nothing unusual about the dinner. Good food. Fine wine. Got a doggy bag for the bones in case the dog he'd spotted through the pickets on the drive-by was still out. Terrific dessert, chocolate something with raspberry sauce. Sinful. Stayed late. Had a Rusty Nail at the bar, lots of scotch with just touch of Drambuie. Afterwards, he'd gone back into the Old Hyde Park neighborhood and parked down the street from the garage-studio where the Greville guy did his work.

He pulled on the surgical gloves and threw the steak scraps through the gate to the bristly little mutt that was out there. It was the kind that yips in rapid succession until you want to grab it by its bony neck and strangle it. Not that McIver would hurt a dog. He liked dogs. Used to have one, part lab, part mutt. Taking the leftovers along was simply smart planning. When the pup showed its face, sniffing at the gate for more, he took it as a sign of sorts that it was worth a shot. So he pitched out a few more scraps, slipped into the yard, and dropped a whole bone. The mutt was in heaven. It hunkered down over its prize and didn't give a damn what McIver was doing elsewhere.

McIver simply whacked a small window pane with his elbow, enough to crack the glass but not shatter it. He used a penknife to pop out a corner. Ran Greville's own lawn hose in, and turned it on full blast. Then he pitched the pooch the second bone and left. With luck, the water would run all night. Whenever Greville went out and opened up, he'd get a nice, very wet surprise. And one hell of a water bill. It was neat, low-key, and nonviolent. Away from Sarasota. It would put the cops off balance. And it would make the rest of the ones left wonder, and sweat.

He wanted her to sweat. The cool, icy blonde with big Bambi eyes who made the videos. But she wouldn't be next. He had their attention. They were even capitalizing Trasher in the press. He could slow down the pace. One a week. He'd get the one in Venice next, the potter with the hyphen. Lynda Abel-Smith. By moving south, he'd get the one in Englewood and the one in Fort Myers nervous. "Sitting ducks," he muttered, glancing at the large cardboard box full of road flares that he'd picked up from a detour site. He'd simply pulled over and thrown them in his trunk.

All he'd have to do is light a couple of them and pitch them through a window. They'd be scrubbing the smoke scum off the walls for months. They'd have to dump all the drapes and furniture to get rid of the smell. He chuckled at the prospect. He hadn't expected this part of it to be so much fun. Exhilarating. It was like being a kid again, playing tricks on Halloween.

McIver checked his calendar. Halloween was a little over a month away, five weeks plus. On a Saturday. "Trick or treat,'' he murmured. He made a neat box around October thirty-first. *Bambi*. Her treat was going to be something else again. It would take some reconnoitering, so when it happened, it would look like a prank that got out of hand.

McIver knew the peninsula she lived on. He'd been to the neighbor's house, the Simons woman's place, by land once before, before she bought the place from Ash. Since the Hilton incident, he'd done a number of passes by boat, skirting the perimeter on the Intracoastal side. Despite the fringe of mangroves and palmettos around the edge, that waterside looked like the most promising route in. Because of the electronic gate, the problem with the street side was where to leave the car. Midnight Pass was the only main road down that side of Siesta Key. To get into the Mangrove Place compound, he'd have to park the car out of view, then walk back, climb over a low wall and through the overgrown barrier of palmettos and sea grapes, and work his way closer on foot. Parking was the issue. This time of year, locals out strolling would be nosy enough to spot a parked car that didn't belong. They'd be sure to notice his Mercedes.

From the water side, he couldn't use the big boat. It was too loud and conspicuous. He could plan ahead, drop off the canoe, and use it to come in at night. He'd just glide right onto the neighbor's dock and then cut across the yard to her place.

He had time to work out the logistics. He wanted her to get real nervous. Then he'd make a move, some pseudo-attack to throw her off. After she thought it was all over, he'd come back for her. He'd give new meaning to ''Trick or treat.''

McIver carefully folded up the map, took his bottle of scotch from his desk drawer, poured a short one, kicked back, and stared at the picture of his kids on the desk. Then he poured another scotch. ''Trick or treat,'' he muttered. She'd fucked up his life, his family, his finances. He damn sure was going to like the payback.

Chapter 2

"Shut the fuck up." The words were out of Stu's mouth before he squinted into the morning light and saw Lara Lundquist standing at the foot of his bed. She arched her eyebrows as only as six-year-old can do in the presence of an adult who'd clearly put both feet in his mouth.

"What the heck are you doing here?" He groped for the sheet to make sure he was decent, then he tried to right himself while the cast and chest brace held him partly immobile. Outside, something unearthly shreiked. "What the hell is that?"

"It's just the boys. They're hungry." Lara said patronizingly. "You were supposed to feed them." She was carrying a colander full of chopped fruit.

Instantly it all made sense. "I'm sorry. Sorry, honey." Stu started apologizing. "I forgot."

"Mom was right." She padded off, barefoot, onto the balcony to feed the row of parrots and macaws who'd milled around for almost an hour before starting to rant. Rikki had spotted them lining up even before Lara and Jake got up to eat breakfast. She'd apparently guessed Stu wasn't up to catering to the birds quite yet.

He knew the boys' routine. Harrison Ash had meticulously gone over the feeding instructions during his household orientation. Then before he left in the airport limo for his expedition, Ash had taken care of the boys himself early Monday morning. However, late Monday night, before Stu went to bed, he figured there was no real need to reschedule his sleep patterns to accommodate some birds. He'd outsmart them. Instead of setting his alarm for six fifteen as Ash specified, Stu took Tuesday's supply that Ash left prepared and spread it along the perimeter of the deck. It was cool out. And dark. He didn't think they could tell the difference.

He was wrong. After sitting out overnight, their breakfast wasn't as fresh as the pampered avian squadron were accustomed to getting. They'd grumbled. They'd stalled. But eventually they'd eaten it in relative silence, ostensibly willing to cooperate. Once. But this morning, there had been no food, limp or otherwise, and they'd griped and squawked in protest. When their patience ran out, they'd shreiked. It was that noise that jolted him awake.

He'd intended to feed them, but a few beers and some painkillers got in the way. When Rikki went to teach her class at the Art Institute the evening before, it wasn't even dark out. He needed to take Ash's car up the strip to a grocery store and load up on fruit and a few essentials. Then he heard a boat chug past. Then another. He started worrying. Not about her. Like Swede, he didn't think Rikki was in any real danger on campus. Too open. Too public. Too many people who'd enjoy bringing him down. Campus security was already alerted. He was worried about the baby-sitter and the kids. He knew the guy aimed at the studios. Hers was here, with them. He could hit anytime, anywhere. All it would take was one door left unlocked or unwatched.

For a while he'd moved from window to window, floor to floor, scouring the shrouded shoreline and watching the shadows on the compound blur as it grew darker. The problem was he couldn't see where the sitter or the two kids were. His neck was tight. His shoulder ached. He'd finally taken a painkiller, packed up his last two canned sodas, and gone over for a closer look. He could always claim to be visiting the orchids.

He'd knocked on the kitchen door just to find out if the babysitter had to unlock it to answer. He had to give her credit, it was locked. And she looked out the window at him before she opened up.

"I just wanted to let you know I'm going to be puttering around out in the slathouse awhile," he told her. He could see she and the kids were doing a jigsaw puzzle on the kitchen bartop.

"Can I go out and putter too?" Jake came up behind the young woman. "Please . . ."

"Sure. Won't bother me," Stu said quickly. "I could use a helper."

"You're sure you don't mind?" Juli asked him.

"I'm sure."

"You'll stick together?"

"We'll stick together." Stu was glad to have the company.

They spent all of three minutes in the slathouse. It was too warm, too humid, and the combination was making them both sweat. "Let's go look at the water. Got any breadcrusts? We could chum the fish." Stu figured from the dock he could keep an eye on the sliders out back, upstairs and down.

"Sure, I'll get some," Jake bolted for the door. "And I'll get some matches. We've got candles that keep the bugs away."

Stu picked up a wire plant hanger, followed him out, and pulled the door shut. Coming in, he'd noticed there was a loop for a padlock, but no lock. He threaded the wire through a couple of times then twisted it tight. Tomorrow he'd suggest she get the real thing.

"Hey. You guys interested in having pizza?" Rikki had offered when she returned and found him out on the dock with her son.

"Sounds great." Stu tried not to let on that he'd been anxious. And hungry. He was relieved that she was home.

"This place doesn't deliver, but the pizza is wonderful," she told him as she deposited her camera gear inside. "I've got to pick up some milk anyway. Anything you need?"

"Some fruit for the birds. Cereal. Beer. Bread. Cokes. Milk." He'd already been working on his list.

"You want me to pick it up? Or do you want to come along?" she asked. Ash had told her Stu had the use of his car, but in the two days he'd been staying there, the Buick hadn't moved.

"I'll come with you." He was noticeably eager.

Rikki laughed. "Island fever already? Listen, any time you're feeling trapped here, let me know. If you run low on groceries or need anything, I'd be glad to zip to the market."

"I'm not stranded," Stu answered a bit defensively. "I'm just taking a few days to get my bearings." The truth was he was having trouble adjusting to the everyday realities, private and public, that made him feel helpless or awkward. Like taking a shower. Or using the john. Or getting dressed. Or fumbling with a checkbook or a wallet. Or having to drive a grampa-style vehicle because he couldn't handle his own car one handed. He hated feeling awkward, much less dependent on anyone.

"Okay. But the offer stands."

He'd reminded her to double check the doors, then he'd gone home for his wallet. She was waiting out front in the van when he came out. "I called in the order. This won't take long." She turned south along the key to a tiny strip mall with the pizza place, a video rental, a laundromat, and an all-night supermarket. "Need anything else?" she asked.

"How about ice cream. My treat?" he suggested.

"Sounds fine."

"What kind do you and the kids like?"

"Anything chocolate. Preferably lumpy," Rikki answered with a smile.

"Like Rocky Road? Heath Bar Crunch?" He picked out a couple of pints of his favorites.

"After this, Jake and Lara may start camping on your doorstep."

"So these are good?"

"Those are great."

He picked up a couple of other cartons. "For backups. Now we're set."

They'd come straight back to Rikki's. Jake heard them coming and held the door open. "Drinks . . . napkins . . . plates. Let's eat out back." Rikki sent everyone scurrying after something while she hastily stowed all the cold food in her refrigerator, including the backup ice cream.

Juli Quinn stayed and ate three pizza wedges before she tore herself away. "Midterms," she lamented. Stu and the kids finished the rest. Then they'd emptied two containers of ice cream before Rikki called a halt. Jake and Lara both bathed, got pajamaed, and went off to bed, full and smiling like contented kittens. While Rikki made a final check on them, Stu took another painkiller and waited on the lanai.

"I was really pleased when I saw you and Jake on the dock," she told him when she returned. "My dad had a knee operation recently and can't get around yet, not like he used to. With Ash away, Jake is really outnumbered by all the females."

"I sure don't mind the odds," Stu said, grinning.

"I'm also glad Ash's house isn't sitting empty. Particularly now. I feel better having a conspicuous male around."

"You're calling me conspicuous?"

"You're big, sort of hairy, and you're wearing that thing." Rikki indicated the cast. "You're certainly not inconspicuous," she said, laughing.

"You make me sound like Bigfoot."

She laughed again. "I didn't mean to. I just meant that if the Trasher comes around, he'll have second thoughts when he sees you. You're a rather formidable obstacle, with or without the cast."

He almost smiled, hearing how much she sounded like her father.

"You also introduce some interesting complications," she added.

He glanced her way. "In what way?"

"Having you coming and going with no particular schedule makes it tricky to figure out the traffic patterns here. That's another reason I was glad to see you out there with Jake. I don't want the kids outside at night alone." She'd stopped then, and sat without moving, listening. Off shore a boat chugged past with its running lights on. Stu opened another beer, took a pain pill out of his pocket, tried to remember if he'd taken one earlier, chased it down, and leaned back. The coils in his neck were finally relaxing. So was he.

For a while the only sounds around were hushed, natural ones. Then a vehicle pulled off Midnight Pass, crunching the oyster-shell surface at the entry of the compound. It barely paused at the gate, then proceeded in.

"It must be ten-thirty," Rikki guessed.

She didn't wear a watch. Stu looked at his. "Ten-thirty-one. How'd you know?"

"It's Tuesday," she said simply. "Pat plays bridge with some women down the Key on Tuesdays and Thursdays. She's always home in time to bathe and catch the news at eleven." They listened again as the car noise came closer, stopped, and a door clunked closed. He made a mental note to add the neighbor's card playing to his master calendar so he wouldn't get unnecessarily alarmed some night.

They'd sat awhile longer. Sometimes talking. Sometimes in silence. Stu drank a couple more beers. Finally Rikki stretched and cleared away the drinks and cans. "It's time for me to call it a day." She blew out the candles one by one. "And it's time for you to go home. How's the arm?"

"Haven't noticed. Medication must be working."

"You sound very relaxed." He caught just a trace of concern in her voice.

Once he stood, he knew he was more relaxed than he intended. He'd had a few too many beers, especially on top of the painkillers. He took a couple of steps, feeling like the deck was flexing underfoot.

"I think I'd better walk you home," she said, catching him before he took a nose dive off the steps. "It's tricky in the dark." He didn't protest. He decided to salvage whatever dignity he could. He put his good arm around her shoulders and let her lead.

"You'll be all right from here on?" she asked at Ash's door.

"I believe so." He had some trouble getting the key in the lock. She helped.

"Do you want me to get you upstairs?"

"Might be a good idea."

She escorted him to the landing outside the bedroom door.

"I'll be fine now. Thanks for navigating."

"You're welcome." She waited. "Are you sure you'll be okay?"

"Absolutely." He hoped the word came out with the right number of syllables. "You go home now. I'll be watching. Make sure to lock your doors."

"I will. I'll get yours on the way out." She started back down the stairs.

"Thank you very much." He wobbled slightly. She glanced back up at him, but she kept on going. When he heard the door shut, he crossed to the deck, braced himself on the railing, and watched her like he said he would. He even waved when she looked up and saw him there. Then he peeled off his clothes and went straight to bed without a thought about the birds or the groceries or setting his alarm. Now, Lara was out there bright and early, making apologies to the squawking flock.

Stu finally pulled himself to his feet, wrapped the sheet around his hips, found his sunglasses to shield his eyes, and joined Lara on the deck. "Thanks for coming over." She was spreading the pieces neatly, scolding right back the ones who complained or crowded.

"Mom said she didn't think you'd remember," the youngster said without a hint of censure. "She said I could do this today because you were new. She said you were under the weather. And maybe you'd forgot to start setting your alarm.''

"Right on all counts," Stu muttered, feeling groggy and hung over.

She finished the job and turned to face him. "You don't usually get up this early, do you?"

"Not if I can avoid it."

"Mom didn't think you did."

"She's right again."

Lara was swaying from side to side, looking up at him with that arched-eyebrow effect as he stood there in mirrored glasses, his bandages and cast, and his bedsheet. "If you don't want to do this, we could make a deal."

"Your mom said we could make a deal?" Stu wanted to make sure he got this part straight. "About feeding the birds?"

Lara nodded. "Jake and I were going to take care of the boys while Mr. Ash was gone. He said he'd pay us every day. And he'd give mom fruit money."

"You'd come and take care of everything?"

"I'd bring the food. You'd have to clean up after."

"Sounds like a terrific setup to me. How much?"

"A dollar a day?"

"It's a bargain." Stu rubbed his face and shielded his eyes with one hand. Even with the glasses, he had to squint to protect them from the bright morning light. "By the way, how did you get in here?" He peered down at her.

"Mom has a key." She dangled it from a thin green ribbon. "Mr. Ash leaves it with us. So does Mrs. Simons. And they have one of ours. For emergencies." Lara's dark eyes widened guiltily. "Mom thought this time you wouldn't mind. She said you might need to sleep." She gave him a worried look. "But I wasn't supposed to come through your room. She told me not to wake you up. I really didn't mean to. I was just looking to see if you were awake." Now she was the one apologizing.

"No problem. I'm not angry at you. You did great. It was the boys who woke me up, not you," he assured her. "If your mom asks, I'll tell her that, for sure." He watched the concern on her face transform into a relieved half-smile.

"Good."

"Lara. Bus. I've got your stuff," Jake called to her from somewhere below. "Lara!"

"I've got to go."

"Same time tomorrow? A buck a day? Deal?" Stu said before she ducked back inside.

"Deal. Same time tomorrow." With a swirl of dark hair and a perfect white grin Lara Lundquist was gone.

Stu let the sheet drop and started into the bathroom

"Mr. Sullivan?" When he heard her voice, he grabbed a towel to cover himself.

"Yes?"

"I left your cereal and bread on the counter," she called back from the stairway. "And the milk is in the refrigerator."

"Thanks." He waited until he heard her shut the downstairs door on her way out before he let the towel drop.

"Such a deal," he muttered afterward as he eased himself onto the mattress, groaning with each twist and turn. He lay there a moment, studying the exposed rafters, feeling like a beached whale. He considered the feasibility of setting up a rope and pulley overhead to haul himself out each day, like one the deep-sea outfits had for weighing in fish on the docks. For a moment, the thought amused him. Then a midback spasm reminded him that screwdrivers, drills, hammers, and any work that required lifting either arm was out. Therefore, no pulley. "Such a deal," he grumbled, miserable again.

When he woke up the second time, he pulled on some shorts and went downstairs to make coffee. There was a car parked in front of Rikki's house, next to her blue minivan. It didn't match any of the ones on the list he had so far. He used the binoculars to read the license number, then he wrote it down. Phone in hand, he was ready to call over there to check that she was all right when he saw her and some woman cross from the kitchen to the slathouse. When they stood there fiddling with the door, he remembered wiring it shut. It didn't keep them out for long.

He kept watching for them while the coffee brewed. Then he took a mugfull out on the second-floor balcony. Already midmorning, the day was bright and sunny, and the surface of the Intracoastal glimmered like a blanket of metallic confetti. The birds and the chunks of fruit were long gone. But the boys had left mementoes.

"Bird shit," he grumbled and took out the hose that Ash had run up there to wash off the deposits they'd left behind.

He stayed upwind, grateful for the brisk breeze that carried off the odor. He'd kept looking up from blasting the bird droppings to check out the slathouse. The door was still open.

After about fifteen minutes of waiting, he saw them come out and cross into the kitchen. A few minutes later, they came out the front door and walked toward the car. He dropped the hose and went downstairs to get a better angle on them. Rikki was in her bathing suit, only without the pareu. The chunky, dark-haired woman had a small plant and a couple of videocassettes in her hands. She deposited them all onto the front seat. They stood and talked.

He watched.

He'd never seen Rikki in so brief an outfit. The same print as the twist-top, the bikini bottom bared something else he hadn't noticed before—a dark horizontal band around her upper thigh. He kept trying to focus in on the garterlike stripe, but the angle wasn't right. The visitor and the curve of the car kept getting in the way. Then the other woman got into the vehicle and left. Stu listened to the sound of her tires on the shell drive, but he kept watching the dark legband from the back as Rikki turned and went inside.

He wanted to jog right over for a closer look. But duty called. He called a buddy in Motor Vehicles, gave him Warnock's name for clearance, and had him check the visitor's plate.

"Car's registered to a Janelle C. Givrey." The fellow rattled off an address. Stu already had it. Givrey was number four on Swede's list of Rikki's friends and associates. He made a notation beside the woman's name. He felt hot and sweaty and uncomfortable. He paced. He stared out at her house. She'd said to come over any time. He wanted a close look at what she had on her leg. Finally he headed for the shower.

Prior to the injury, he'd showered at least a couple times a day. Once when he woke up. Once before bed. Sometimes he'd have a long hot one to relax after a hectic day, sometimes a short cool one just to freshen up. But now any shower was a clumsy, complicated procedure, something necessary but dreaded.

Every part of the process was slow and often painful. He'd get out of his clothes, undo the velcro strips that held his body brace, take off the regular sling, and put on the larger, waterproof cover the doctor had issued. Even then he couldn't stand in the spray. He used one of those hand-held hose-and-showerhead devices to avoid getting his rib-cage bandages soaked. Afterward, he had to drip and blot, rather than rub dry. It took almost half an hour to get into some shorts and a shirt, put the sling in place again, and comb his hair. By then he was usually sore, hot, and sweaty again, wishing for a miracle cure so he could start over and do it right.

He was almost put together when he spotted her carrying her sail down to the dock. She pulled out the sailboard from its resting place by the mangroves, put in the mast, then dragged the rigged board into the water. She climbed aboard without apparent effort, then stood, angled the sail to catch the wind, and glided off.

"Damn," he muttered, disappointed that despite the rush, he'd still missed her. He went out on Ash's balcony with the binoculars, so he could at least watch her skimming along offshore. The dark legband was still there, intact. Obviously waterproof.

Gradually the heat on the deck sent up an odor that reminded him he'd left the hosing job unfinished. So he sprayed the bird droppings and used the push broom one handed, pausing from time to time to watch her. He left the clean deck drying while he went in to wash off and change into a clean shirt. He had the cast into one sleeve when the phone rang.

"Mueller at Motor Vehicles said you needed a number checked. Got anything?" Detective Warnock asked.

"Nothing. Turned out to be a friend of hers. How about you? Anything?"

"Nothing real helpful. Could be another hit last night. We're not sure," Warnock reported. "Greville, the guy in Tampa, had his garage flooded. We're talking large can-vases, sitting on the floor, in about twelve inches of water. Major mess."

"Anyone see anything?"

"Nope. That's the problem. Anyone could have done this job."

"No signature?" Stu asked.

"Nope. No direct contact, except with a dog that didn't even bark. No telephone lines cut. Water damage, but no breakage except a window he shoved a hose in. No one saw him. Could be some jerk jumping on the bandwagon. Or could be our guy has shot his wad and is winding down. Or it could be him playing a fucking head game," Warnock said with equal emphasis. "But that still leaves us six potentials, whether it's his show or someone else is butting in. There doesn't seem to be any system to the targeting. Just random hits. All I can tell you is to keep an eye on your girl."

"I intend to." Stu finished dressing. He was waiting on the dock in the sunshine, wearing Ash's big Panama hat, when Rikki coasted toward shallower water, dropped the sail, then paddled in.

"You handle that thing very well."

"Thanks." She beached it on the small strip of sand she kept clear next to the dock. "It's how I unwind. I like being close to the wind." Her tanned body was striped in rivulets of salt water trailing down from her wet hair. She looked up in the midst of hauling the board onto dry ground and caught him staring.

One part of him wanted to ask if she knew about the Greville flooding. Another part didn't want to jolt her back to the Trasher if she'd been able to leave him behind for a while out there. "What is that?" He pointed at the dark geometric patterned band on her leg, figuring he'd better say something.

"A tattoo. I had it done in the Marquesas Islands." She pivoted so he could see the design that encircled her right thigh.

He wanted to say it was sexy. Because it definitely was. Unlike any tattoo he'd seen on other people, the band was elegant and exotic, like a strip of black lace with the natural color of her skin showing through. The impact was intensified by the fact she had to be nearly naked for it to be visible. The way it accentuated the contours of her leg made his mouth feel dry. He'd never had that kind of a response to a tattoo.

"It's unusual." He opted for polite.

"Not in the Marquesas. There they tattoo the entire body."

"Gluttons for punishment?"

She smiled. "They don't do it all at once. It goes in stages. Sometimes for special occasions. For them tattooing is part art, part ritual. There's sort of a communal ceremony when it's being done." She kept talking while she disconnected and rolled the sail.

Stu was watching her closely, his eyes screened by the mirrored glasses and shaded below the broad-brimmed hat. "Quite a step to take. Getting something permanent like that."

"I've never regretted the decision." She touched her fingertips to the band, a gesture he'd found himself wishing he could make. "I got this a number years ago, on a trip with my folks and me."

"A souvenir?"

"Actually it's a memorial. I had it done after my mother died."

Stu stood, stiff faced, wondering if he'd blundered into too personal a subject.

"Our plane went down and my mom broke her leg," Rikki elaborated. "We got her to a hospital, they put on a cast, and we thought everything was fine. She insisted we stay and finish the shoot. A few days later, a blood clot broke loose. She died in her sleep." Rikki's voice remained calm and gentle, as if the memory were one with which she had long been at peace. "The people at the hospital there were very loving, very comforting. One of them brought a tuhuna to speak with us."

"A tuhuna?"

"A tattoo master. Highly respected. They share the same rank as sculptors and carvers and priests. The tuhuna said this would help honor her and hold her memory. It's like carrying a talisman, only more personal. So we stayed and finished the shoot, just like she wanted us to do. In the daytime we took the pictures we were after. And in the evenings, we ate, someone told stories, someone sang, and the tuhuna worked on this. My dad has one here." She touched her right upper arm. "It was a special time for us," she said softly. While she talked, almost effortlessly she picked up the sailboard and put it under the overhang of the mangroves again.

"I'm sorry about your mother." Stu floundered for some response.

"Me too." She had stopped with her back to him and stood, staring off over the water, pausing while the roar of a passing boat momentarily intruded, making conversation futile. She waited patiently until the big powerboat was far enough away so she could be heard without having to speak louder. "Mom and the woman who owned this place, Ivey Currey, were friends and neighbors. After we came back, we all missed her. Ivey and my dad and I spent a lot of time together. Eventually they realized they loved each other, and they decided to get married. Mom would have liked that."

She still stared out, preoccupied. Stu simply waited for her to come back to shore again.

"Anyway, I've never regretted the tattoo, personally or artistically," she declared, finally turning around to face him. "The pattern is a traditional interpretation of life." Now they were both staring intently at the band. "The tu-huna said the open space around or within a design represents the natural world. It isn't background. It's the given that surround us, like water or air. The same pattern is on several of the wood pieces I brought back. It's done in shell inlay along the back of the shark, the one the kids named Oscar."

"Oscar? The black thing hanging out back?" He remembered a pronged-tailed wooden fish, about five feet long, suspended overhead by her back sliders. She'd pointed it out on the Oceanic art-and-orchid tour she'd given him the first night they'd met. He hadn't been paying much attention to artistic detail at the time; he just remembered it was large and the tail was pointed like a pitchfork.

"He's sort of a guardian spirit, protector of seafarers and fishermen," she explained. "The natives pat his belly for luck. So do I when I come out on this thing." She hoisted the sail over her shoulder and carried it toward the house.

"I'd need more than luck to handle that thing like you do," Stu said, hustling to keep pace with her.

"It just takes practice, and two good arms," Rikki said as she stowed the rolled sail in the corner of the gazebo behind the reddish rattan, goofy-looking figure she called the Sulka. It was propped on a stand like a scarecrow, wearing an expression of perpetual surprise. Unlike the shark or the Tikis around the house, this wasn't a heavy carved statue. It was a full body mask, a ceremonial costume, like an extended dunce cap with strawlike fringe. The wearer set it on his head and looked through the long grass skirt attached to the waist to find his way. The geometric pattern on the waistband matched the one around Rikki's thigh.

"Is this some kind of guardian spirit too?" Stu asked.

"It's more like a fertility figure. It's worn to celebrate health and growth and coming of age." Rikki picked up a towel off the deck railing. She seemed lost in thought as she stared out over the water.

"Speaking of celebrating . . ." Stu saw an opening and took it. "I'm sorry about last night. I feel real stupid. I overdid the beer and the pain pills. Thanks for getting me home."

Her dark eyes shifted to meet his. "I didn't mind."

"And thanks for sending Lara over to feed the birds. She said we could make a deal to keep it up, if it's all right with you." He kept talking as she toweled dry.

"What kind of a deal?"

"You get the fruit. She brings it over and feeds the birds. I pay for it and I pay her to deliver."

"How much are you paying her?"

"A dollar."

Rikki smiled. "Ash only offered fifty cents."

"So I've been had," he shrugged. "If it keeps me from having to roll out by six-thirty in the morning, she's welcome to it."

"If you're both satisfied with the deal, that's all that matters." Her eyes shifted to his cast. "You could probably use some extra rest anyway. How are you feeling today?"

"Okay."

"Have you eaten anything?"

"Not yet."

"I'm going to get lunch, then process some photos. You want to join me?"

"For lunch?"

"For either, or both. The only caution about the processing is that once we're in the darkroom, you can't leave until we're finished. I'm working with color today. I can't open the door and let the light or the temperature change."

"I won't be in your way?"

She gave him a quietly amused look. "If you ever are in my way, Sullivan, you'll know. I won't hesitate to send you home." She started toward the kitchen. "Let's fix some sandwiches. I'm starved."

For a moment he simply nodded, a bit unsettled by her honesty. Then he took off after her, following the black tattoo.

"I don't think it's made the news yet, but it looks like the Trasher did another job last night." She said it without emotion. He was spreading mayonnaise on four pieces of whole wheat bread while she sliced tomatoes.

"Really? What did you hear?"

"Someone put a hose in Steele Greville's studio in Tampa. His wife called. The police aren't sure it was the Trasher, but it seems likely. No one was hurt this time."

"That's something to be grateful for."

"I thought so too."

"Maybe he's slacked off." He gave her a sidelong glance.

"Maybe. At least we can all catch our breath." She managed a half smile. Her expression stilled and grew serious. "I was wondering earlier if he quit altogether, what we'd do. I wonder how long it would take us to shake the feeling of apprehension."

He didn't have an answer for that one. Obviously neither did she.

Later in the afternoon, Stu held his watch up to nose level in the darkroom, trying to read the time by the safelight. The youngsters got dropped off by the gate at three. It was two minutes till. "Shouldn't we wind up? Don't you need to get out there to meet the kids?" He recalled Warnock's comment about the change in tactics possibly being a head game. With the Trasher out there somewhere, he felt someone should make sure the kids got from the gate to the house safely.

"They'll be fine." She was concentrating on her work. "They'll knock when they get in. They can tell I'm in here."

"How?"

"Because my van is here, and the sailboard's in. I'm not upstairs editing. So I'm here."

"And they won't open the door?" He remembered what she said about needing to keep the conditions stable inside the darkroom.

Rikki lifted a photo from the chemical bath. "Of course not. There's a little amber light outside. It goes on when the safelight's on in here. That means I'm processing. If it's a real emergency, they could call. I have a separate line and a phone in here. It's under the counter."

"But the door doesn't lock, not from the inside, does it?" He remembered there was a deadbolt on the outside. "They could open it?" He wasn't thinking so much of Lara and Jake interrupting. He was remembering the Franklin incident. He got away by barricading a door. Swede said he'd asked her to put a lock on hers. She'd declined, pointing out the danger a locked door would present if there were an accident and she needed to make a quick exit. Or if she were hurt and someone needed to get in to help her. Stu's experience with fires made him agree with her logic, up to a point.

"The door's a bit warped and the handle is tricky," Rikki told him. "They'd have to rattle it a few times, and push in at the bottom. By then, if I were in the midst of something critical, I'd warn them off. But Lara and Jake have grown up around this kind of stuff. They don't make mistakes," she said with quiet confidence. "And if anyone else forced his way inside," she said quietly, "he'd be in more trouble than I would. This is familiar ground for me, with or without the safelight."

Stu let it drop at that. He checked the time again. Five past three. They should have reached the house by now. He tried to be patient. It was three-ten, and no knock. Three-fifteen. He was sweating, and not from the heat.

"I think it's time to take a pain pill." He lied.

"Almost done. Give me a second." Rikki finished up.

"I really should go."

"Done. You can open the door now." She switched from the safelight to the brighter regular bulb overhead. "I've got to clean up around here for a while. I'll see you later."

Stu almost leaped for the exit. Just as she said, it took three tries to get the doorknob just right, only from the inside, he had to pull as he turned it. He closed it quickly behind him.

Outside he glanced toward the roadway, then did a quick look around. There was a motorcycle pulled up in the walkway between the darkroom and the slathouse, in a blind section where it wouldn't be seen from the front. He stood still, listening, straining to hear kids' voices somewhere. He heard nothing but a few seagulls.

The slathouse door was open. Something inside it moved. Just a shadow, but he could tell it was too big to be Lara or Jake. He crouched and moved closer, peering between the narrow boards of the structure. There was a man inside, medium height, stocky build, white. In a helmet, not a ski mask. But it concealed enough to mean trouble. All he could think about was whether the kids made it in. Were they safe for now? If that was the Trasher in there, what was he doing to the priceless orchid collection?

Looking like an alien with his helmeted head, the guy was moving from bench to bench, carrying a small bucket. He didn't look particularly big. Silently, Stu groped around for some kind of weapon. The best he could come up with was a hand trowel. He could use the tool like a bayonet if he had to. He'd just wave it like he knew what he was doing and hoped it kept the guy at bay. But he had that damn sling with the cast and if they scuffled and the guy whacked his arm or twisted it, Stu knew he'd be reduced to Jello. He needed help. If he could get to Rikki, he could stall the guy while she called 911.

He stayed low and inched his way back toward the darkroom, trying to remember any karate moves he'd seen in old Chuck Norris movies. If the guy came out and tried to get away, somehow he was going to stop him.

He tapped on the door. He jiggled the handle. He tried to open it but the handle didn't catch. He didn't want to be seen or make too much noise. He rattled the handle again. Louder.

"I'll be right out." She'd heard but missed the point.

He didn't want to call out. He rattled the handle again, more frantically. Then he crouched and waited.

Rikki swung open the darkroom door, almost hitting him with it. She had a broom raised like a battle axe. "Stu? Are you all right?"

"Shhh. There's someone in there." He pointed toward the slathouse. "Some guy. In a helmet. He's got a cycle." His heart was racing, adrenaline pumping. "I'll keep him in there. You call 911."

She lowered the weapon. Her response was immediate and preceded by a sigh of relief. "It's Eddie. He's fixing dinner tonight."

"Who's Eddie?"

"Eddie Sordo. Family friend."

Stu vaguely remembered a couple of short last names ending with "o" were on the list Swede gave him. One was a female, one of the artists. The other had some kind of truck.

"Eddie used to be the gardener when Ivey lived here," Rikki said, turning to put the broom back inside the darkroom. "Dad helped him finance a greenhouse. He grows organic vegetables. Gourmet things. Mostly for restaurants."

"What's he doing in the slathouse?"

"He's probably checking to see if we made any progress with the potting. I told him you were helping. Or maybe he's just checking to see what some of his favorites are doing."

"With his helmet on?"

Rikki smiled and shrugged. "That's Eddie. The motorcycle is new. He thinks the helmet is hot stuff. He even prunes the bushes in it. Come and meet him. Eddie came from Saipan, the same island in the Marianas as Lara and Jake. But he left there as an adult, so he remembers a lot of stories that the kids were too young to pick up. So he comes around often, cooks, visits. He reinforces some sense of their mother's culture. I think that's important."

Stu discreetly ditched the trowel when she wasn't looking, wiping his hand on the seat of his shorts as she led the way.

Eddie turned out to be a muscular fellow, a few years older and a foot shorter than Stu. "Eddie, this is the visitor I mentioned. Stu and his brother run Plantworks," Rikki said as she introduced them.

Sordo shook Stu's hand and fixed the slightly long-haired, unshaven newcomer with a solemn, appraising look. "Good to meet you." He made no attempt at small talk. His fingers were large and calloused and his grip was iron hard.

"Good to meet you too," Stu replied, glad he hadn't gone into the slathouse and started anything with the man. One armed, he wouldn't have stood a chance.

For a moment the two of them simply stared at each other. "I saw some fire ants on the way in. Thought I'd better check around and put out some powder," Sordo explained the bucket in his hand.

"Where are the kids?"

"Washing vegetables."

"Good. I guess you met them out front?"

"I was there."

"With the cycle?"

Sordo grinned and shrugged. "Had to. You know they like it."

Rikki shook her head, explaining the routine to Stu as

they all stepped inside out of the sun. "Eddie sits there on the cycle, runs the motor, and lets Lara and Jake climb on," she explained. "Once the bus leaves, they get off and they all walk the cycle back. All the other kids go wild with envy."

"But no riders without the helmet." Sordo tapped his headgear. "And not till I get real good on my machine."

"I'd rather you involve the children in other things you're already good at."

"Like cookin'?" He grinned, finally removing the helmet.

"Exactly."

"We'll do that soon as I take care of the ants. I saw a bunch out by the hose."

"It's hot. I'll have a glass of tea waiting for you," Rikki told him. He bobbed his head and left.

"You want some tea?" Rikki turned to Stu.

He was dripping sweat by now, but his pulse rate was settling back to normal again. "I'd love some."

Stu sat at the counter with his chilled drink, watching while Rikki set the bamboo steamer out and talked with the kids. Lara and Jake had lined up the scrubbed vegetables. He enjoyed the running conversations and the activity around him. He'd been a bachelor for years, and often ate out or sandwiched in rather than cook for one. The few home-cooked meals he'd had lately were those at his mother's or his brother Brian's. Usually when he'd had someone else in at his place, it had been a woman, and cooking dinner hadn't been the focal point of the evening.

But here, the time spent preparing the meal was a cheerful, sociable occasion in itself. He listened to Lara talking about her teachers and her classmates, Jake discussing his math woes and some dispute on the bus, and numerous other bits of information that he filed away.

Sordo came in and parked the helmet on the counter. He and the family moved about the kitchen with an easy rhythm that made it evident their preparing a meal together was a familiar, frequent thing. From time to time, Sardo would give him a stern look, not quite threatening, but not particularly welcoming either. Then he'd flash his big knife and chop with deliberate flourish.

Stu nursed along the tea, feeling increasingly cumbersome and out of place. There was an intimacy here he wasn't part of. He was about to leave when Rikki squeezed a lime and a lemon, added some oils and spices, then handed him the bottle of dressing to shake. "You're welcome to stay. Eddie's meals are always wonderful. And don't ask if you'll be in the way." She cut him off before he said what he was thinking. "You are welcome to stay," she repeated with added emphasis.

"Then I'll stay. Thanks." He accepted, avoiding looking Sordo in the eye.

"Good." Without ceremony, she gave him five sets of utensils and put him to work setting things on the outdoors table. Suddenly he was part of the process, not a bystander on the fringe anymore.

The whole food preparation procedure was quick and efficient. Sordo sprinkled minced herbs on the fish and wrapped the pieces in banana leaves. Jake set them neatly into the bamboo steamer. Lara was in charge of the rice and cold drinks. Rikki fixed a salad, including the assortment of plants Sordo had brought along. Stu recognized a few of them. One handed, Stu helped ferry several trays with small bowls of spicy dips and relishes to the patio table on the deck out back. Then he lined up the glass-globed scented candles Rikki gave him. As the sun set, Rikki lit them, so their soft, aromatic glow would keep away insects as well as illuminate the tabletop.

There had been a peculiar normality to the dinner conversation that dealt with plants one moment, then the attacks and the Tampa hosing the next. In the aftermath of the flooding incident, they all felt the pressure ease, at least for a while. When Stu told them about mistaking Sordo for a prowler, the kids had giggled.

Sordo grinned. "Sure, it's funny. But I could'da been that guy," he said with all seriousness. "We all just got to be a little more careful, and keep an eye out," he cautioned them. "You see anyone 'round here, you just make sure you're all locked up and phone the police. They're big guys. They know what to do. You know how to call 911?'

They nodded.

"That's what you do. Call 911, and they'll come get him. So what if he makes something wet or messy? It's just stuff. But you be safe and be smart, and everything will be fine," he said, trying to coach them without making them frightened.

Rikki had watched their faces. She knew full well it was useless to try to hold back information. The TV and the paper were carrying updates on the investigation. She'd been interviewed. The Tampa hosing would make the rounds. Even the kids at school would be talking and imagining.

"This guy is a bully," Stu spoke up. "Just like some of the kids you know. But there are lots of big people here, and he'll have to deal with us. So you guys watch and we'll be watching for him too. He wouldn't be too smart to come around here."

"Right." Jake nodded. "He'd be in big trouble if he messed with my mom."

"Right," Rikki agreed, smiling across the table at him.

Later they all cleared the table then the kids went upstairs to get ready for bed. Sordo packed all the vegetable scraps and fish bones in his compost sack and strapped it to the back of his cycle. "If that Trasher fellow showed up now, I could give him a dose of his own medicine," Sordo said, patting the bag. "You be careful, Miz Rikki," he said earnestly. "Lock up tight. You call if you need me."

"I will."

Stu walked out with them to the breezeway where Sordo had parked the cycle. The fellow gave him and his encased arm an earnest look. "You be careful too," he added without his previous reserve. Throughout dinner, his attitude toward the bearded housesitter had warmed. "You let me know if anyone messes around with anything or anybody here. If you see anything funny, you call me," he told Stu. He pulled on his helmet, revved the motor, and rode off.

"Don't forget to switch the lock on the gate," Stu said, realizing that it had to be open earlier when Sordo picked up the kids.

"You're starting to sound like my father."

"I just wanted to remind you. Sorry," Stu said, stopping himself before anything else slipped out. He was concerned about her. Locking the gate at night was a simple precaution. But he didn't want to sound like Swede. Now that he had her alone again, he wasn't feeling particularly fatherly. She was wearing that draped thing, the wrap she called a pareu. He'd been catching glimpses of her legs and that lacy tattoo all through the evening. He felt tantalized, and distinctly aroused. Nothing paternal at all.

"You want to come out back and sit awhile?" She hesitated, waiting for his answer.

"Sure. Nice night." He wasn't ready to go home alone.

The silence closed in around them as they walked between the slathouse and the kitchen and turned toward the lanai together. Some of the citronella candles were still aglow. Rikki peeled off the pareu and draped it over the back of a chair. "I'm going to get a towel and go for a quick swim."

"Now? It's nighttime."

"I noticed that."

He shrugged, realizing he was "fathering" again.

"It's lovely swimming in the dark. When you get your cast off, you should try it. Very restful. I'd think the way salt water makes you buoyant would help your muscles. Good therapy."

Just seeing her this close in her swimsuit helped his muscles and set his mind racing with other therapeutic suggestions. "You want me to keep an eye out while you swim?"

"Actually if you don't mind, I'd rather you stay close to the house in case the kids need anything. You can answer the phone if it rings. Hearing a man's voice might give a few friends a start, but it would put off the Trasher if he decided to call and check if I'm home." He saw the preoccupied look and remembered what she'd said about unwinding. He could give her a little time off duty. Regardless, he wasn't about to leave her or the kids remotely vulnerable.

"Okay. Be glad to keep an eye on things and listen from here." He managed a slightly stiff smile and went inside, ostensibly to refill his iced tea.

After she took the towel and walked down to the deck, he watched from the darkened kitchen window. He saw her glance back, then quickly step out of the bathing suit bottom. Then she dropped the top onto the deck next to it. She told him she liked to get close to the wind. Apparently she liked to get very close to the water as well.

"When my arm gets better . . ." he mused, speculating what could happen between the two of them over the next few weeks. There seemed to be some subtle chemistry between them already. At least he could feel it. He just hoped he wasn't misreading her neighborliness as something more personal.

After catching a glimpse of Rikki on her return to shore, wet and naked, just before she wrapped herself in the towel, he'd done a quick inventory of his own anatomy. The woman was in very fine shape. And he'd decided there was just too much of him. If he ever stripped down like she had done, he doubted she'd be equally impressed. The lack of exercise was showing, and the beers he'd been drinking lately had done more than make trips to the bathroom frequent and occasional mornings difficult. They'd added pounds and softened his contours. So he'd started in on the case of diet sodas Ash had in his pantry. And he'd dragged out onto the deck a stationary bicycle the old fellow had in one of the unused bedrooms upstairs.

Then he called Detective Warnock for an update. The Trasher had only made one full daylight hit at the Rodriguez place. Then after dark at the camera shop. Even later at Greville's garage studio.

"Maybe he's getting more cautious and likes the cover of dark," Stu suggested.

"We figure the guy works days. Maybe on some kind of shift, so he gets off before rush hour," Warnock agreed. They were going over the time sheets of every employee at the Hilton. And the lab was sifting through what was left of the garbage from Rodriguez's place, doing a comparison with the Hilton Lounge. Warnock's first instinct was that only an employee or a regular delivery person would have balls enough to pull off a stunt like that. He had to know the place to have an escape route and the timing down so well. Warnock figured the perpetrator may have looped back and gone about his business. He never left the premises. That's why none of the outside staff saw any vehicle exiting from the lot.

And right after the trashing, someone had called the TV station to tip them off, before the Hilton managment even called the police. Like pyros who set fires and stayed to watch the commotion, Warnock figured the Trasher made the call and hung around and got some rush from watching the aftermath.

"We'll keep asking. Make whoever it is edgy. Give 'em all time to think. Someone will remember something. Someone will talk," Warnock said.

But he'd agreed that the Trasher was twisted. He obviously wanted them to know he was out there. He'd let two victims see him in the ski mask. Once he had their attention, he changed tactics. "The guy is unpredictable," Warnock said. "Which in layman's terms means crazy as shit. He could pull anything. One of the artists has decided not to stick it out. He's taken off to visit friends out of state for a while. Not that I blame him," he added. "All we can do is increase patrols in the areas. Alert the neighbors. We don't have the manpower to do more. So we wait."

"I thought all the fuss about watching out for her was pretty stupid at first. Now I'm glad I'm here." Stu had already felt the same apprehension as Warnock that anything could happen next.

"I'll bet you are," Warnock chuckled. "Tough life keeping watch on the blonde," he chuckled. "Just keep me posted. I'll do the same."

Later, Stu had gone out on the balcony of Ash's house and watched the last light go out at her house. "Okay, where the hell are you?" he muttered to some faceless phantom in a ski mask and rubber gloves. He sipped a diet soda and pedaled away. As long as he was staying up and keeping watch, he would at least pass the time doing some self improvement.

The view, sure as hell, couldn't be improved on. Now, at night above it all, he felt like Tarzan overseeing his jungle compound. There was an exquisite otherworldliness to the peninsula after everyone was asleep. From his tree house, he could hear sounds that he never picked up by day. Birds. Frogs. The splash of a fish. Then the porpoises came by, three of them. One was just a baby. They played in the moonlight, sending up sprays of silver when they puffed air from their blowholes. Their skin, wet and smooth like pewter, reminded him of another sea creature. Only this one had an ivory bikini outline on her posterior and a leg band on her thigh to hold her mother's memory. Just thinking like that made his body respond. He gave a few slow rubs over the pleasurable tightness in his crotch. He took a few deep breaths then started to pedal again.

Just before he went to bed, he saw a few pelicans swoop in and settle on the Simons woman's upper deck across the way. They squatted for a while, spread their long wings, and glided out of sight. He guessed they had a nesting site in the mangroves farther down the key. He gave a rough, one-armed approximation of a stretch and headed in, closing only the slider screen to let the wind blow through. He gathered the pillows to prop his arm, eased back on the mattress, and was deep asleep in seconds.

He'd barely got the coffee brewing the next morning when he heard the car sound outside. He grabbed the binoculars, hoping it wasn't more bad news. From the kitchen window, he saw a sporty white Cadillac, rental tag, pull up in front of her house. The fellow driving was tall, tanned, blonde like her, and lean. He looked as if he'd just stepped out of a Palm Beach menswear window. Dark blazer, cream slacks, green and cream striped shirt, open at the neck. Casual, but impeccable. He unloaded an upended cardboard box from the backseat and lifted the upper portion carefully, uncovering the plant it had protected, a multibloom firey red orchid. Stu took a good look at it. Strong color, established plant, mature. Undoubtedly expensive. Apparently a Prince Charming had arrived.

Stu watched stiff-faced through the binoculars while Rikki came out and wrapped her arms around Prince Charming's neck. They didn't kiss, not mouth to mouth. He figured that may not be her style, but the hug was sufficiently enthusiastic to make his chest constrict. Then Charming gave her the orchid. She seemed thrilled. Arm in arm, they went indoors.

Stu pulled out a beer. Then he looked at the twenty cans of diet soda still left in the refrigerator. He put the beer back. Instead, he grabbed the soda and a few sticks of celery. He stood by the window, sulking and watching, munching away and wondering how long Charming would stay.

He stayed an hour.

After the first fifteen minutes, Stu had taken the peanut butter and the rest of the celery and dunked until the peanut butter ran out. Then he paced. He drank another diet soda and tried another window. Finally, he got a beer. He was outside, wide-open on the balcony, when they surprised him by coming around the far side of the house from out back. Rikki looked up and spotted him standing there, binoculars in one hand, the beer in the one in the sling.

She waved. Charming looked up, grinning with a flash of

white teeth that Stu knew up close would be perfect. He waved too.

Stu flopped the binoculars in reply. Then he focused them out over the waterway, pretending he'd been absorbed in something offshore, so she wouldn't suspect he'd been watching her or her man friend.

Shortly after the white Cadillac pulled out, with only Charming in it, his phone rang.

"Hi. This is Rikki. If you're not busy, come over and see my new orchid." He stood there, caught off guard, not expecting a female voice, much less hers. "It's really a knock-out."

His first instinct was to head right over. But he'd been skulking around, up and down the stairs, indoors and out, sweating. He needed a shower. He didn't want to show up on her doorstep like he was, not with the image of Mr. Perfect fresh in her mind. Besides, he had to show her that he had a life too.

"Can't right now. I've got a few calls to make." There was some truth to that. He needed to phone home and check the messages on his answering machine. He could phone her father and fish for some information about the blonde guy who brought his fair-haired daughter flowers. Or he could call his brother or his mother. Or check in with his office. Or he could phone one of the women he'd been dating. He was too stubborn to bolt over there just because she had a lull in her schedule. "Maybe later?" He was weakening.

"Okay. Whenever you're free, if you feel up to it, come over. I'm going to work on some videos, so I'll be upstairs. The plant is out back. Make yourself at home."

"Thanks. I just need to tie up some loose ends," he hedged, already knowing he'd rather be there close to her than where he was now.

"By the way, there'll be some extra traffic tonight. I'm going out for dinner, and Juli will be watching the kids. She's nervous about the Trasher, so if you decide to drop over later give her a call first or just make sure she sees you coming," Rikki cautioned him. "She'll be locking things up tighter than usual."

"I'll be out for a while myself, but I'll check on your place when I get back," Stu said. "I shouldn't be too late." He was lying again. He had no plans. But he wasn't up to watching Rikki and Prince Charming ride off into the sunset, or, worse yet, return all mushy and get romantic right under his nose. Or his binoculars. If he stayed around, he knew he wouldn't be able to resist looking.

He called his mother. Helen Sullivan was already booked. "Stu, I wish I'd known you were at loose ends. Ruthie Simpson called and wondered if I'd like to go to a movie. Mel Gibson." She didn't have to elaborate. She'd said yes to Ruthie Simpson, of course. For years she'd had a crush on the blue-eyed Gibson who, according to her, looked just like Stu's dad had when he was young. "Would you like to come with us?" she offered.

"Thanks Mom, but I think I'll pass." He wasn't eager to tag along with two widows who'd be sighing at one perfect man while he was worrying about his weight and the progress of Charming and his neighbor.

"Brian and Vicky called. They're going to shop for a new washer. They don't think their old washer will make it through another year of diapers now that Vicky is pregnant again. They're getting it replaced before it succumbs." Disappointed, he knew that ruled out calling his brother next, hoping he and Vicky would be in the mood for company.

Afterward, Stu sat and stared at the phone book. He resisted the knee-jerk reaction of contacting any of the women he knew. Lately, his exchanges with females were limited to a few drinks, maybe dinner, and some horizontal recreation.

His ex-wife, Terri Lynn, had left a couple of calls on his machine. Usually that meant she was separated from number two again and generally receptive to whatever arrangements Stu could offer. Hearing her voice on his recorder only dredged up old memories, almost all but the physical ones unpleasant.

The only woman he wanted to see was the one next door, and she was spending the day working, then having a night out on the town with someone else. He couldn't even blow off steam by taking his own car out for a run. Ash's Buick wouldn't do the trick.

"Fuck it," he muttered. None of this was like him. He wasn't the sit-and-wait type. He'd been there four days and he was already losing track of who he was.

"Kenny, my man." He called Kenny Putnan. "This is Stu. I was wondering if you could send someone over to pick up my car and drop it off to me. I'll run them back myself." Putnam ran the custom auto shop where Stu had his car worked on over the years.

"Stu, sure, where is it?" No matter how frantic work was at the shop, Kenny always made it sound like he had all the time in the world.

"At home. You should have a set of keys from my office on file."

"If it's at your place, where are you?"

"I'm on Siesta Key. About a mile after Higel turns into Midnight Pass. Private road on a peninsula called Mangrove Place."

"All right," Kenny drawled. Stu guessed he was checking his wall map, figuring out a logical itinerary. "You know I'd be glad to drive that baby," he finally responded. "How about I bring the car myself later tonight? I can do it if you can wait till after work. I thought you were too banged up to work the stick shift anyway."

"I'll manage." All he wanted was to get his car and get out of there before the action started at Rikki's.

Kenny didn't argue. He just took down Stu's address on Siesta Key.

It was almost seven when Stu heard a car on the shell drive. It wasn't his. Juli Quinn's green Escort. It was almost time.

The next car noise was the Cadillac. Prince Charming pulled in beside the green car just as Rikki came out the front door. It didn't help that she seemed a bit overeager. Or that she looked decidedly regal with her hair pulled back in a pale braid that hung down between her shoulders.

He'd never seen her dressed up in "city" clothes. She wore a full-skirted ivory dress, one with a low neck that showed off her shoulders and her flawless tan. Stu watched them drive off toward the gate, feeling the knot in the pit of his stomach tighten.

"And I had to be so damn smart," he grumbled, wishing he'd at least gone over there during the day and talked to her face to face. Maybe he'd have picked up an idea how serious this romance was with Charming. And if it wasn't serious, he could have at least let on he was interested.

Instead, he'd stayed put. The deck was completely birdshit free.

He'd ridden the bike, going nowhere. He'd even got one

of Ash's bird-watching books and looked up a few types he'd noticed around. He'd watched her go out to the gate and walk the kids home. They were talking and laughing and holding hands. As the sky darkened, some of the Lundquist house lights went on. Then Prince Charming was at the gate, and it was impossible to do anything but watch.

He called Swede once they were out of sight, determined to find out who this guy might be. Ivey answered the phone, pleasant enough, but definitely in a hurry. "Could Swede call you back later? We're on the way out." They were running late. She'd already started Swede and his crutches toward the elevator and didn't want him to get too far without her. "You want him to call you back?"

"If he has time later. Sure. No rush. You two have a nice evening."

Ivey wished him the same in return, then said good-bye.

Stu stared out dismally at Rikki's house. He looked at the clock. He tried all the channels on cable, then turned off the TV. He poked in the refrigerator at the packages of sandwich meats. In the freezer there were steaks, and fish, and burgers to defrost. Ash had left his refrigerator well provisioned and said for Stu to make himself at home.

Stu was downstairs waiting when Kenny Putnam pulled the red 'Vette into the carport area under the house. Next to the low profile and rounded lines of the classic '61 convertible, Ash's newer Buick looked even more like a matchbox on wheels.

"Got hung up. Sorry."

"Better late." Stu sounded more philosophical than he felt. "You want to go eat pizza? On me? How about it? Mama Mia's? Just down the strip?"

"I'd sure love to join ya'," Kenny answered, shaking his head glumly. "But I'm runnin' darn late as it is. My wife has dinner cookin'. You know how it is." He shrugged. "I gotta get back to the shop, get my truck, and get myself home. Are you sure you oughta' try drivin' this thing?" He looked at Stu's rigid cast uneasily.

"You want me to drive you back in that?" Stu pointed to the other car.

"How 'bout I drive us both back in this one. So I get there on time," Kenny suggested. "Then you can get yourself all the way back out here in first gear if it comes to that."

"Okay, you drive." Stu surrendered, just relieved to have his own car back again. Still determined to have pizza, he called Mama Mia's from Kenny's office. Then he eased into the familiar leather bucket seats, leaned back and sighed, feeling more like his old self than he had in weeks.

By the time he reached the second intersection, he'd managed to get the cross-armed gear-shifting technique down smooth enough. It was awkward, sometimes it made his breath catch, but it worked. "Pepperoni, black olives, mushrooms." He tried to buoy up his spirits. The wind and cool night air helped. Pizza. Then he'd have a pint of Ben and Jerry's New York Super Fudge Chunk ice cream. And a diet Coke.

Stu began to dread how serious the outing really was when Prince Charming brought Rikki home. He'd heard the shell drive crunch and saw the headlights coming in time to step around the ground-level deck into the dark. He'd have a better vantage point from there.

The car stopped, its passengers silhouetted by her porch light, and he could see the four of them sit and talk awhile. Rikki was in the backseat with Ivey. He guessed Swede was riding up front with Charming so his legs and crutches had more room. It looked like a meet-the-family event, or, worse yet, dinner with the future in-laws. He was slipping up. He could have brought the electronic ear from the office so he could hear each word they said. But he had the binoculars and he could see enough to make him hurt.

Eventually Rikki got out of the car. But Charming didn't walk her to the door, and there was no good-night kiss. He didn't leave right away. Lara and Jake came bounding out with Juli right behind them. From the way they poked their heads in the window for kisses, it was evident they knew him very well. Then Charming and the others waited while Juli Quinn got in her car. Everyone waved and said goodbye. Rikki took the kids back inside. Juli drove off, with Charming and his passengers right behind her.

Maybe twenty minutes passed, then Swede returned Stu's earlier call. "I was just over at Rikki's. But I guess you were watching."

"I was watching."

"Good. That's why I enjoyed our dinner. Figured I didn't have to worry with you there," Swede responded. "Seems like you made quite a hit with my daughter.'' He became more expansive, adding with some amusement that Rikki had mentioned the Sordo-slathouse incident at dinner. ''She seems to feel comfortable with you around.'' She didn't seem to suspect anything more than neighborly concern. Swede was relieved and pleased.

''I was wondering about the car. The Cadillac. I don't have it on the list.'' Stu figured that was a reasonable way to ask about the fellow in the rental car.

''That was Ivey's son, Steele. He's an officer in the Navy. He's in town for a few days.'' Swede said that Steele Currey had taken them all to dinner, partly as a celebration of their anniversary which was still a few weeks off. He was also celebrating getting engaged to a marine biologist in Hawaii, where he was stationed. Stu stood listening, feeling the muscles in his face slowly relax. ''He had pictures of her to show off,'' Swede went on. Steele was family. Stu could breathe again.

Family. He'd stood there afterwards, feeling stupid. He could have spent the afternoon with her. Instead, he read bird books, and worried, and stuffed himself till he felt bloated on pizza and ice cream and soft drinks. Except for the drive taking Kenny back, he'd spent the entire day alone.

He went out on the balcony to pedal the bike in penance for a while. Her bedroom lights were still on across the way. He was tempted to phone her and blurt out how relieved he felt, but it was late. Anything he had to say could wait until tomorrow. Then he'd say something. He wasn't sure what. Maybe just that there was something nice between them. Even knowing she talked about him at dinner with her family was encouraging. But there could still be another Charming somewhere. If he procrastinated, she still might drive off into the sunset with someone else. He couldn't put himself through another day like today, not without giving it a shot.

Stu sat astride the bike, scanning the compound through the binoculars. He anticipated the night sounds, the distant plunk of a leaping fish, the flapping of pelicans convening, the low gossipy chatter of a couple of parrots strolling under the fruit trees next to Rikki's house. He could hear the rustle of creatures in the palmettos near the gate, a family of opossums, according to Jake.

He was sweeping her house again with the binoculars

when he thought he saw her pause by her bedroom window on the second floor. Then she was gone. The upstairs lights went off. Only one in the downstairs foyer remained.

A few seconds later, he saw the flutter of white out back. She was walking down to the dock with her towel. He watched the towel drop, the pale streak as she dove into the Intracoastal, and the ruffle of silver-white that closed behind her. Then the water was still again.

He waited and watched and listened. Finally, far out, she surfaced. Mermaidlike, she dove under and glided beneath the surface, breaking through with a flash of skin like alabaster in the moonlight.

He had to see her. Up close. He had to say something. Now.

Ash had set out a broad-beamed flashlight in case the power went out. Taking it and grabbing a pack of matches, Stu strode across the grassy space that separated their houses, zig-zagging the streak of light across the ground before him so if she looked that way, she'd see him coming. Then he cut along the back of her house to the lanai, relighting the citronella candles that were still out there from dinner the night before. He spaced them out across the deck.

He made sure he sat where she could see him when she climbed out. But he faced the other way, listening to the even strokes that suggested she was swimming in toward shore. He could tell when she got there. Over the beating of his own pulse, he heard the swooshing sound when she pulled herself out onto the dock. Then there was only silence while he waited for her to dry off and come his way.

"Hi. You're up late. Are you feeling okay?" Rikki circled behind him and came around the table so she'd be facing him. She was wrapped in the oversized white towel, apparently with nothing underneath. The beads of salt water on her skin caught the candlelight and sparkled, diamond-like. Stu looked up at her, feeling his mental agenda slip away.

"I'm fine." Whatever it was he'd planned to say to her was totally lost.

"Good." Her eyes glimmered with amusement. And curiosity. He was sure she knew the effect she had on him. "Do you want a drink or something?"

"No, thanks."

"You want to talk?"

"Sure." He nodded.

"Let me get my robe and some juice. I'll be right back."
She left him sitting there, trying to figure out how to mentally shift out of neutral every time she was near, especially
when she was wet.

"Try this." When she returned, she placed a glass of
chilled cranberry juice in front of him, keeping a second
glass for herself. She'd put on a thick terry robe, emerald
green, large enough to fit her father. Or a boyfriend. He
was beginning to perspire.

She sat and tucked her feet up under the hem of the robe.
"I missed seeing you today." He could hear the ice cubes
clink.

"Me too."

He sat very still, wondering what was coming next.

"Sullivan, I think a large part of this is purely physical,"
she said simply.

He wasn't expecting that one.

"I'm talking about this attraction that's going on between
us," she elaborated, arcing her hand back and forth between them, inscribing an invisible bridge.

He stared. She'd either read his mind or caught him drooling. He felt his color deepen, then heat up even more at the
realization that he was blushing. He hadn't blushed since
grade school.

"I'm concerned that the warm flashes we're feeling might
be more lust than anything really personal." Her clear, dark,
intelligent eyes met his steadily. "Not that I'm opposed to
lust. In the grand scheme of things, it has its place."

Speechless, Stu simply looked at her. He'd obviously underestimated how perceptive she was. And how straightforward.

"I'm not into casual body contact," she went on after
taking a long, thoughtful sip of juice. "And I'm not usually
attracted to large, hairy men. I'm more into rawboned, sinewy types with noble feelings." She gave him a slow, approving smile that made his breath catch. "Regardless, the
thought of making love with you has occurred to me. There's
a lot about you that I like, Sullivan. There's a lot more that
I'm not so sure about."

He figured he'd better say something. "I didn't realize
you were feeling anything toward me. Other than being
friendly. Not that I haven't had those feelings you men-

tioned. I just thought you and this guy you went out with tonight were an item.'' He couldn't tell her that Swede had told him otherwise.

"I wondered what you'd think when I saw you were up there watching,'' she said without any hint of censure. "That guy tonight was Steele Currey, Ivey's son.'' Her smile broadened. "He brought me a great orchid. Masdevallia. Crimson flowers. Really spectacular. He always adds something to the collection whenever he comes to town.''

Stu arched his eyebrows. "He seemed very friendly.''

"He is. Steele's like a brother to me,'' she said, beaming with a particular delight as she talked about him. "We were both grown when Ivey and Dad married, but we spent a lot of time as kids together. Buddies. He just got engaged, so he caught a government flight in and took us all to dinner to celebrate. All except his fiancée. She's still in Hawaii. He's been footloose for years. I'm glad to see him so happy.''

Stu nodded, trying to show that he was interested. But all he wanted her to do was to get back to the part about them and feeling attracted and getting physical.

"Relationships are precious to me.'' Rikki spoke in a low, deliberate tone, studying his face so she'd be sure she wasn't misunderstood. "When things really get personal, I'm into souls, not organs. I don't let one confuse the other.''

"I'm not just after a warm body, either,'' Stu responded. But the way the words rang true was a bit intimidating. Since his divorce, his relationships with women had been deliberately superficial and short lived. But if he'd wanted one of them this evening, he could have called one. He hadn't. He couldn't. And he wasn't sure he liked admitting that, even to himself.

"The kind of intimacy that interests me isn't easy to develop,'' Rikki stressed. "It requires an openness, a kind of sensitivity training. There's a lot of groundwork to do. We need to see each other clearly enough to make the decision whether to get involved in each other's lives in a significant way. I don't want either one of us to make a mistake.''

"Neither do I.''

"If you're interested and patient, we can spend some time getting to know each other and respect each other. Then if we feel good about it, we can get physical.''

He took that as a possible yes. "Maybe we should go out to dinner. Or take in a movie."

"I don't need to be entertained. We can get to know each other doing normal things, here, without distractions. It just takes unrelenting honesty."

"I can be honest." He almost choked on that one. He'd been fudging to her about the whole housesitting thing, easing around who he was and what he was doing there.

She leaned back, unfolded her long legs, propped her feet on an adjacent chair, and gave him a dubious look. "I hope you mean that." The robe slid open, exposing the black lace tattoo. "This is very serious business."

Stu took a drink to moisten his lips. "I realize that."

"I don't know what kind of romantic situations you were in before this. You have a past, just as I do. We don't just leap into something without knowing each other's history. So," she paused, contemplating his expression, "before we let this go any further, why don't we both sleep on it. Figure out where you are in your life," she said quietly, her dark brown eyes doelike and mesmerizing. "Think about this. Then let me know what you're really after. Decide how much of yourself you're willing to invest. And if you decide what I'm asking is too much, don't feel badly about saying so. I won't hold it against you. We can still be neighbors. Maybe friends. Just not lovers. I'll just windsurf a few more times a day." She took another drink of juice without breaking eye contact.

Stu could barely feel the glass in his hand. He stared at this magnificent creature who sat there, calmly setting all her cards out on the table. No games. No half-measures. He took another sip of juice himself, barely aware of any taste at all.

"One more thing. Keep things straight with the kids. For now be a pleasant, temporary neighbor. Don't get too buddy-buddy with them," she said, cautioning him, her assessing look a bit like that of a mama bear, quite placid on the surface but quite willing to use whatever tactics needed to protect her young if anyone made a wrong move. "They're very vulnerable. They disappoint easily. They have very active imaginations. Whatever we do is between you and me until we set other parameters. Don't mislead them."

He knew the game she meant. She didn't want him to play temporary daddy to win them over or to impress her.

But it was a technique he'd sunk to on occasion in the past. And he hadn't liked that about himself.

"Go home. When you reach a decision, come on over and we'll talk." She swung her feet to the deck and made the dark tattoo disappear.

Uneasy, excited, frustrated, Stu stood, collected Ash's flashlight, helped her blow out the candles, then waited for her to go in and lock the door.

" 'Night." He couldn't hear her response, but he could read her lips from behind the glass.

"I'll say . . ." Stu let out a long breath as he left.

He walked home slowly, smiling part of the time, intermittently stopping to shake his head, benumbed.

"What the hell are you getting yourself into, Sullivan," he muttered. "Decide how much of yourself you're willing to invest." He'd never had it put to him like that before. Except for the marriage, he'd just schmoozed in and out of couplings. He'd given that his best shot, at least he thought so at the time. That was back when he was a fireman with a typically weird work schedule. On his off-duty days, he was helping Brian run the nursery and trying to get a landscaping business started. Terri Lynn, his wife, had worked for the power company in the data processing department, around men who wore suits and always had clean fingernails. Ones who smelled of cologne, not smoke or fertilizer. Ones who got off at five and stopped for a drink, conversation, and munchies at a nice lounge before coming home or dining out. Ones who came to bed every night.

One day Terri Lynn told him she liked the office type better. She wanted a normal life and a regular routine. He couldn't blame her. It was easier to plan around someone with nine-to-five hours. Someone who didn't come in after a long shift and sleep for most of a day. Someone who didn't need to down six beers or more to gear down after a close call.

He told her he wasn't angry. He was disappointed.

She moved out. They divorced.

He found out later she'd moved in right off with some suit from work, someone she'd known for awhile. How well and how long, he hadn't asked.

After that, he'd settled for playing the field. He decided that as long as he was a firefighter, any semblance of a normal family life was out of the question. He took extra courses and trained to be a fire marshal. He worked with Brian and Vicky at Plantworks when he could.

He got promoted. He moved into a new condo. But his relationships with females were hit and run. He was big, athletic, good looking in a teddy-bear sort of way. Plenty of women found him appealing. But he wasn't rawboned or sinewy, and looking back now, he couldn't remember feeling anything "noble" for years, outside of work. Certainly nothing came close to the way he felt when she smiled at him and said she was into souls, not organs. Succinct. Very clear. And scary as hell.

Chapter 3

Stu didn't sleep well at all that night. He'd gone home and kept replaying what she'd said.

"Decide how much of yourself you're willing to invest."

He remembered cracking his eyes and noticing the sky was getting lighter. He heard the flap of wings when the boys flew in. He pretended to be sleeping when Lara Lundquist came and put out the food for the parrots.

He must have dropped off for a while after that. It was nine-thirty when he got up and showered and dressed. His hands were sweating when he walked over to her house to talk. At thirty-eight and single, he'd decided it was time to try again.

"I've thought it over."

She was out back in her bathing suit with the pareu knotted around her hips, misting the orchids that were in bloom in the gazebo.

"And . . ."

He glanced up and gave Oscar, the shark, a pat for luck. That made her smile. "I'd like to try this your way."

"Good." She sounded relieved. For a moment they looked at each other, smiling. She looked a little tired, as if she may not have slept so well either.

"Any news bulletins from the grapevine?" He wondered if she'd heard something from one friend or another.

"No. Nothing happened. Pour yourself a glass of orange juice."

She went back to misting the orchids while he got the juice and followed along after her.

"So, when do we begin?" He figured there was no smooth way to start.

"Let's start with you. Tell me about your relationships with women so far, good bad and indifferent," she responded.

He was ready for this one. He'd spent most of the night ruminating over bits and pieces of his past. He told her mainly about his marriage and the divorce and the disillusionment. She got the point that it was work schedules and life-styles that didn't mesh.

He admitted that he hadn't been particularly proud of his romances since then. She studied him with her typical intensity as he spared very little detail about what was wrong with them, and him. He even told her about regressing, and having a fling with Terri Lynn once when she was separated from the suit. "I think I was just getting even," he conceded. "I wanted to show her what she was missing. Rather immature, I know. I haven't done it since."

"But she's still available?"

"She calls." Stu nodded. "She's separated. Maybe divorced by now."

"Any unfinished business there?"

"I don't think so." He hesitated. "I know I was more hurt at the time than I let on. Last night when I was thinking about all this, I realized there was a lot of buried anger," he admitted, verbalizing the truth for the first time. "We were very civilized about it. Maybe too civilized." He'd tried to pass off that tempestuous one-night reunion with Terri Lynn as passion. But, he knew now, it was fury. He'd been blindsided. Even before he knew they had serious problems, she'd found a replacement and figured out her strategy. "The rematch was a backlash."

"So how are you now?"

"I've got my head on straighter." He said it with authority. It was easier to look Rikki in the eye now that he'd got that much off his chest.

"How much alcohol do you drink?" She put aside the mister and treated the orchids to a dose of fertilizer from a long-snouted watering can.

A momentary look of discomfort crossed his face. He'd run that past himself as well. "Probably too much. I'm not an alcoholic," he said, shrugging. "I just like beer. Too much beer. Since the injury, I've been overdoing it, more from habit and boredom than from any real interest in it. I'm into diet cokes now."

"Why? Because beer makes you loose?"

"That," he conceded. "And because beer makes me fat. And lazy." He said it right out loud, wincing. "I'm embarrassed to see how much of a spare tire I've picked up. I have a similar problem with ice cream. If it's there, I eat it.'' Even the bluntness of that admission made him feel better. "I need to take better care of myself."

"I saw you out there pedaling Harrison's exercise bike the other night. That's a start."

He paused and glanced at her. Her house had been dark that first time. He'd guessed she was asleep. It never occured to him that while he was out there in the dark watching her, she might be in the dark somewhere else, watching him.

"I noticed you were at it again last night before you came over."

He grimaced. "Penance. I'd just killed a pizza single-handed. And a pint of ice cream. Paybacks are a bitch," he said, patting his midsection. He didn't mind so much that she saw him exercising. He was hoping she hadn't seen him watching with the binoculars as well.

"You take this Trasher business very seriously, don't you?" She gave him a sidelong look.

He nodded.

"Harrison would be pleased to know you keep a close eye on all of us. It took some getting used to, but I'm glad you're there."

Stu let out a small breath. She'd seen him. But he was relieved that she hadn't read any more into his binocular routine than she apparently had.

"By the way," she said, softening the comment with one of her half-smiles. "You need to fill in blanks about me too. Aren't you curious why a nice girl like me isn't married? Or why I adopted two Polynesian-American children? You need to know my romantic triumphs and failures. Ask me anything."

The first two interested him. The third, he wasn't sure he wanted to hear. He was already feeling jealous of any man who'd been with her, and envious of whatever they had felt and done. He wasn't ready to get into specifics.

"I'm curious. I'm just not sure how curious."

"Well, I was almost married once." Rikki started without needing to be prompted. "I used to be very much in love with a German ethnologist. He was studying Oceanic art in the islands. I met him when I was traveling with my dad," she said.

"So far, so good." Stu took a swallow of his juice and listened, knowing full well she wouldn't be telling him about this one if the relationship hadn't affected her strongly.

"I would take vacation time twice each year and fly down and stay with him and work in the field, shooting photos."

Stu tried not to add pictures of his own.

"When I quit social work, I went to stay with him for a few months, sort of a retreat," she continued, reaching out to rest her hand on the goofy scarecrow figure. "That's when I acquired this and the shark and the various tikis and gable ornaments around here. Karl was a collector. He was very good at working out trades with the natives."

"So what happened with you and Karl?" Now she'd started it, he was bracing himself for the rest.

"He turned into the German rendition of Gauguin. He liked to cavort with the native women throughout the year, then with me when I was there," Rikki answered.

"Was he rawboned and sinewy?"

She smiled. "He definitely was. But not nearly as noble as I'd hoped."

"So you dumped him?"

"Actually we reached an impasse. He wanted to marry me, but he also wanted to continue doing as he'd been doing when he was on site. He said he didn't have the temperament to be monogamous, particularly if there were long separations when we were working on our individual projects. Frankly, I didn't find the prospect of being number one in a harem appealing. So we ended the romantic part. Now, we're friendly, but not friends."

"No unfinished business there?"

"None anywhere."

"Me neither."

"Good." She put aside the gardening equipment and glanced at her watch. "I do have some unfinished business upstairs. I've got some slides I need to work with. Do you want to come along? We can still talk. The subject may interest you."

"I'm interested in you. That's subject matter enough to get me to follow you."

"Good. That was the kind of clean communication I like, Sullivan." He enjoyed the way her eyes widened with sincere delight. And he liked the way the touch of laughter in her voice made him feel. "Sometimes I get the feeling you're very guarded about what you say to me."

"I'm trying to do better."

"You're succeeding."

He noticed this time when they went inside, she stopped then turned back, closed and locked the sliders. In broad daylight. Usually she just left the screens pulled across. That hesitation and the extra security measure she took was the first real evidence of how much some faceless stranger had affected her life. He wished he could fix things so she didn't have to pause and wonder if anyone would come in her house while she worked. But like Warnock said, the guy was a wild card. All they could do was play it cautious, and watch, and wait.

One end of her production room looked like the control booth in a small TV station. Another had sections of ceiling-to-floor humidity-controlled cabinets with rows of drawers like the ones set out on her worktable. The drawers next to the light table were filled with slides and transparencies, each upright in its own slot.

"Are all these full of slides?" he asked her, looking over the library.

"Maybe three-quarters full," she estimated.

"You have a hell of an inventory to draw on," Stu commented.

"True. Some of these are my dad's. Most are mine," she answered. "I have them all catalogued on a computer file. Fortunately I also have a very strong visual memory. I can usually remember the right image when I need it, even years after I've taken a picture. Of course, I'm always adding more. Whenever I'm mulling over a new project, I just come in here, and sift through some of the drawers, and think awhile."

"Obviously you've been doing a lot of thinking." He inclined his head toward the trays of slides she'd been sorting.

"Those are the finals," she explained. "I start with hundreds, then I keep eliminating until I'm ready to tape," she said. "I'm almost ready with this one. I've been working with a therapist on some videos dealing in weight management," Rikki told him. "Most of her clients will never be size eight, not without surgically removing large and useful parts of their anatomy. They're naturally big women. She wants to help them accept and approve of themselves as they are, so I'm working on the chubby-is-okay premise.''

He smiled and said nothing, a bit embarrassed but generally pleased. ''These are some kind of subliminal things?''

''Not really. They're more conscious tools. There's no hidden message. For instance, in this tape I'm using Paphs, Vandas, and several of the cuplike orchids like Peristeria, Anguloa, Cochleanthes, Cycnoches.'' She watched him nodding as each name registered. ''And I'm using some reggae music a friend composed as background. Trying to introduce a little nonthreatening humor into the piece. You'll see.''

Stu watched as she set up two projectors and two video cameras. ''I've got a new machine on order. One that will give me more flexibility and eliminate a couple of steps, but this is the way I've been doing it. Primitive, but it's worked so far.''

She had several screening monitors set up so she could watch what each camera was picking up, and a larger master monitor which would carry whatever image was actually being taped. Right now its screen was blank. She shot two transparencies up, slightly different views of a striped-pouched Paph. But she didn't bring the video units into the action.

''Should I be quiet or what?'' he asked her.

''I'm not taping. We can talk. I have to work a bit more on the timing and organization,'' she said, explaining what she'd be doing. ''I found some Phalaenopsis I want to work in too. And some shots of people and wildlife. What I'll eventually do is fade in and out from one shot to another, overlapping for just a few seconds. Then I add the music to help it flow.''

''And you use all these slides?''

''Briefly. The whole tape is edited to eight minutes.'' She adjusted a couple of connections. ''It has to move right along. I can alternate or overlap or fade one into the next, but for about five seconds you'll get one picture. That's quicker than I usually work it. Generally I hold an image for eight or ten seconds and slow the dissolves and fades. That's enough to let an image saturate without giving someone time to get impatient.'' She motioned him toward an armchair, picked up a notepad, and sat next to him. ''This will give you a sense of what I'm after." She dimmed the lights, turned on the music, then set it at "pause."

The first projector and the reggae music started simultaneously.

For the next few minutes, they stared at the twin screens as the two machines alternated, automatically putting up slide after slide. He saw her jot down some notes. They didn't speak until the music ended.

"I like that."

"I like it pretty well myself." She made another brief note. "Needs a little fine tuning, but it's getting there."

"So what happens when the tape is done? How does someone get one?"

"A colleague of mine, a therapist, supervises the distribution and does follow-up," she explained. "This is a relatively experimental concept. Right now, they're issued by individual therapists who are conducting studies. Statewide, a number of family counseling centers have access to them. Some women's clinics and safe houses have certain ones."

"But how do individuals, like the chubby women you mentioned, get a copy of their own?"

"They're made available by therapists as part of a treatment program." Rikki leaned forward. "A client can have a copy on hand, so if she feels off balance or negative or just uneasy, she can stop and take time out for herself. The tape helps a client focus. They're like relaxation tapes, the kind you listen to with earphones, only these are visual as well. They impact more senses. They're used in conjunction with counseling and support groups. They reinforce therapy. They don't replace it," she explained carefully. "Janelle's ongoing studies show they're producing very positive results. And clients like the idea that they have some control, something they can turn to. Or in this case, turn on."

"Could I see some of the finished ones?"

Rikki smiled and shrugged. "So far, they're kind of specialized, and primarily for women clients. I'll let you look at this one eventually, if you'd like." She turned off the projectors and put the sound tape on rewind.

"I'd like that. When will you do the videotaping? I've run a videocamera. Maybe I could be useful." It looked like a two-man operation.

"I appreciate the offer, but when it's ready to go, I'll have Juli to come in to work the cameras with me. We have a work-study deal, tied in with some babysitting.'' She tapped her pen on her pad then wrote down a few phrases. ''It's not quite right yet. But it will be. Maybe this weekend.'' She leaned back and stretched her arms. ''How about taking a break. Hot tea for a change?''

''Sure.'' He'd thoroughly enjoyed seeing how she worked.

''While we're up here would you like to see the new orchid? It's in my bedroom. Down the hall.'' She stood up and waved him along. ''Come on. You haven't seen this part of the house anyway.''

He was familiar with the floor plan from the window placement and what little he could see through the binoculars. Eager to get a more personal insider's view, he followed her out into the hallway, along the gallery that overlooked the high-ceilinged living room, then turned past the kids' rooms toward hers.

Her bedroom-sitting room ran the entire depth of the house from front to back, with balconies on either end. The room was big and spacious with streamlined furnishings in honey-colored wicker, cushioned with bold geometric fabrics in indigo, red, and cream. Two huge paddle fans were turning slowly overhead, but it was the breeze coming in from the gulfside that made the floor-length curtains sway. A circular stairway of teak led up to the shutter house and the sundeck that formed the uppermost floor.

Tall carved tikis, like palace guards, stood by the sliders that opened to the back balcony; shorter, squat ones propped open the hall doors. Handcrafted hangings and animal carvings lined the walls. All sizes of carved masks, grinning faces inlaid with shell, peered out from between the books on a huge built-in bookcase in one section of the room.

''Looks like the hideaway of a world traveler,'' Stu observed, pleased by the strong colors and the genuinely lighthearted feel to the sunlit room.

''It is. It's my favorite room.''

''I would have guessed that.''

Several tall plants in ornate pots and three of her own large orchid photos along the far wall softened the overall effect. She'd put the new plant from Steele Currey on the glass-topped wicker coffee table that doubled as an ottoman for a huge armchair. Small framed pictures of the children and Swede and Ivey were set there too. ''I bring some of my orchids up here from time to time just to pamper myself.

It's nice to wake up and see something so lovely first thing in the morning.''

"I bet. This is beautiful." Stu tried to give the bright red Masdevallia the attention it deserved, but his concentration kept drifting as he looked at the king-sized bed, with the bright cushions and indigo spread, deep and serene and inviting. His thoughts of waking to something lovely in the morning had nothing to do with flowers.

"You said you were married. No children?" She asked as they started back down the hall.

"Right. No kids. If we'd stayed married, I guess children would have been part of the plan," he said, shrugging. "But then we divorced. I was glad we hadn't started a family yet. Since then, I haven't given much thought to having any of my own," he continued, choosing his words carefully to make sure he didn't color his response to please her.

"How do you feel about my children? Would having racially mixed children like Lara and Jake make you uncomfortable?"

He hesitated a bit at that one. He had to give her credit, she didn't beat around the bush. "I like your kids. Another set of kids might make me real uncomfortable, racially mixed or otherwise," he offered. "But so far, they strike me as two bright, curious, reasonably pleasant people. Unless you count the times Lara lifts her eyebrows and makes me feel like an idiot," he added with a grin.

"She does do that rather well, doesn't she?" Rikki commented. "I think she stands in front of the mirror and practices." They passed the landing and kept going through the living room into the kitchen. She filled the kettle and plugged it in. He sat at the bar-height counter watching her move back and forth getting teabags and milk, feeling somewhat soothed by the quiet domesticity of the goings-on.

"How old are you, Sullivan?"

"Thirty-eight." Part of the conversation was feeling like a confession, part like a job application. He considered asking her age, then decided not to push it. If she wanted him to know, he had a feeling she'd tell him.

"If you ever married again, would you expect to have more children? Ones of your own?"

"Since we're talking specifics here," he leaned forward slightly, propping his cast on the countertop, "that means we're discussing you and me. If it came to the point where Lara and Jake and you and I became a family, I'd have kids. Two. Them. Two kids is plenty. At least that's how I feel now. I have nothing to prove by having more. Why? How do you feel about biological motherhood at this point in your life?''

''Biological motherhood.'' Rikki repeated what he'd said, smiling at him while she filled the sugar bowl. ''I like the way you put that, Sullivan. I'm thirty-five. I think I have experienced motherhood, biological or not. I was an only child, and that had its upsides and downs. Having two kids is nice, and more than enough to handle. I may want to reconsider somewhere along the line. But I'm happy with the two I've got.''

''That does mean you're still willing to continue going through the motions, doesn't it?'' Stu added, trying to amuse her.

She laughed. Softly. He liked the way that sound warmed him.

''We're both healthy. I think the sex part for us will be very good.'' Rikki said it softly, nodding while she untangled the strings on three teabags. Stu felt an unanticipated shift to attentiveness. She'd moved on from a lot of ''if's'' to a ''will.''

He liked the ''very good'' projection.

''Sex is the easy part.'' She looked up at him. ''Talking through all this isn't to kill the romance. We're simply heading off any serious problems, so neither one of us is disenchanted later. Personally I'm all for romance.'' She set out teacups—large, flowery sturdy ones with colored botanical drawings on them.

''Me too. So let's keep talking so we can get to the good stuff.''

She looked up.

''Only kidding,'' he insisted. ''Well, mostly kidding,'' he corrected himself.

''Okay. Then let's talk about important people in your life. Tell me about your mother.'' She sent the conversation whirling off in another direction.

They finished the tea and went upstairs again and she did another run through of the slides. Rikki sat forward, studying each frame, still not satisfied. Stu was exhausted. His shoulder had started to tense up and pulse, and his backside was tired from sitting. He was almost nodding off, not from boredom but from sheer lack of sleep. Despite it all, he was willing to hang in longer.

"This may not have been such a good idea after all. I think I'm putting both of us under too much pressure." She let out an impatient sigh. "I have to get out on the water a while. It helps clear my head."

"I could use a shot of fresh air." Without protest, he followed along. He been drifting off during her slides, remembering the tattoo and thinking about the indigo spread and the patterns on the cushions in her room. He couldn't help imagining how nice it would be just to stretch out with her and snuggle for a while, not for the sex, but for the closeness. He definitely needed a time out, but he was too stubborn to leave her.

"Sullivan, you look like you could use a nap."

"I think you read my mind."

"So why don't you take one?" She stopped to get the sail from behind the Sulka mask. When she turned back, she caught him staring at her. For the moment, there was something very warm, very exciting, and pleasantly sensual between them.

"Would you be interested in joining me?"

Rikki just stood there, looking at him, her expression breathtakingly soft and inviting. "I think we're dangerously close to getting some of the issues and urges confused," she responded with her jarring honesty. "We've got the luxury of spending time together in a way most people never do. But this kind of access is deceptive. I'm not so sure this situation is balanced enough."

It wasn't what he expected her to say. "What's not balanced?"

"Your part in all this. For me this is a typical workday, and it's been reasonably productive," Rikki said, still not moving. "For you, this is a forced holiday, a convalescence. You're here, you can't work, and you're making the best of it. But that's what bothers me. A whole segment of your normal existence is missing. You know the stories about patients falling for their nurses. I'm not your nurse, but the situation here is conducive to that kind of thinking. It's tempting to fill up the empty space with me."

"I didn't think I had an empty space until I met you."

"I didn't think I had one either."

"So what's the problem?"

"I'm not sure. Part of it is just a feeling. Like I need to slow down. I know you're very tired, and I'm very tense. We've covered a lot of territory today. I guess I just need some time to let it all sink it. I think you do too."

"You want me to go home?"

"I think you need to get some rest. I think you need to touch base with the rest of who you are. Have you even considered how I would fit in with that other life of yours? The real one out there, not this version?" She shook her head. "I'm not able to sort all this out. I'm going to get wet." She patted the black shark spirit and hoisted the sail over her shoulder. "There's no reason to push this, Sullivan. Or push yourself. Relax."

"Relax. Speak for yourself," Stu muttered as he headed home, feeling vaguely rejected. "Okay, I'll touch base." He took a couple of aspirin and made a few phone calls. One was to the deputy chief, the fellow sitting in for him as fire marshal, who caught him up on what was going on there. His brother Brian was glad to chat but warned him to stay away from the nursery. "Don't even think about coming out here. You'd just start poking around and end up lifting something you shouldn't. I'll try to get away and come out to see you. Sounds beautiful out there. Enjoy it. Just relax," his brother told him, echoing what Rikki had just said. "We've got everything here under control."

He checked his messages at home. He took a pain pill just before he returned a call to his mom. She said she'd bought a nice steak and invited him over for dinner. "I'm beat. I need to get some sleep. How about tomorrow?" he begged off. She agreed to settle for that.

Before he crawled into bed, he went out on the balcony and watched Rikki through the binoculars. She was still out on the sunlit water zig-zagging across the channel, totally in control. Close to the wind, just as she liked it. He knew she'd been right on target. They both needed to slow down. He was out of his element here, and she was tempting. And he had been trying too hard, pushing himself to keep up with her. She was the one with sense enough to know that something wasn't quite right.

He stood there trying to be objective about building a relationship with her, fitting in with her generally serene life and her beautiful children once this Trasher thing was over. They'd all been getting along just fine without him, the three of them together out there in their own paradise. What the heck did he have to offer her?

She already had it all. Plus she had the freedom to come and go as she chose, to work or visit or take out the sailboard for as long as she wished. She had no set structure or rigid routine. He hadn't really thought through how she would fit into that other life of his. His real life was more regimented. Officially or otherwise, he was always on call. Women, he'd found out, need more.

"If she knew the truth," he brooded, wondering if she knew the demands of his profession, how willing would she be to adapt? Like her, he was very good at what he did. Like her, he found his work demanding, exciting, sometimes addictive. Occasionally dangerous. He couldn't turn it off when the workday ended and come home like other men. Sometimes an arson investigation kept him going at all hours for weeks and tugged at him even in his sleep. Sooner or later, she'd have to know that other side of him.

He wanted to clear the air. He wanted to tell her he was more than a plant man, more than a conscientious neighbor. He was a trained investigator recruited by her father to keep her paradise secure. But Sloane said not to tell her or anyone. Warnock agreed. Officially there could be one heck of a stink if it looked like one of the Hilton Nine was getting preferential security. With a tight election coming up, Sloane didn't want this to erupt into something political. Even with Stu off duty, someone could make it look bad.

"If she knew the truth . . ." He didn't like the way those words knotted up inside him. Even as straight as he was being about his feelings, he was still editing and evading. And she sensed it. But they were on the brink of something extraordinary, something he hadn't felt in a long long time. She sensed that too, and the look in her eyes could send his hormones raging and his spirit soaring. He could be honest, when the time was right.

On Saturday morning, the first sound Stu heard was the chortling of the boys outside. "Shit." he struggled out of bed, frantic that he'd let the entire night pass without being on guard at all.

Outside the fruit was already spread out on the balcony, half devoured. Someone had remembered and already been there. That made him feel better instantly. If the Trasher had struck during the night, he doubted Lara would have been trotting over with food for the parrots.

He leaned on the railing and stared down at Rikki's house. Her kitchen lights were on. He saw a flash of green pass the window, like the robe she'd worn the other night. Then the lights went off. He watched and waited, guessing that Rikki had been the one who made the trip over with the boys' breakfast so her daughter could sleep in. He'd apparently had a chance of waking up with something lovely after all and missed it.

He stayed out on the balcony a while longer, looking and listening for any signs of activity across the way. The boys were still munching away behind him, but at her house, nothing stirred. At six-forty-two, alone, on a Saturday morning, he figured he might as well go on back to sleep.

Midmorning he called over there. No answer. When he checked the garage, her van was gone. He phoned his doctor. The bandages around his rib cage were still damp from the shower he'd taken before he came. He'd let the hand-held showerhead slip and had soaked himself and most of the bathroom before he could recapture it. "I smell like a wet dog," he told Marr's receptionist. She spoke with the doctor and arranged to have his Monday appointment moved to that afternoon instead.

"You're driving your car? A stick shift? Shifting left handed?" Dr. Marr wasn't impressed.

"I'm used to it. It fits," Stu kidded with him. "But driving it would be better if you left all this tape off. It pulls. Worse yet, it stinks."

"If you want to come in every day, we can put on fresh tape." Marr knew that wasn't the solution Stu was after.

"It would still pull. It's uncomfortable. And I don't want to drive in here every day. That might slow my recovery," he reminded the doctor. "I'd like to be able to stand under a shower," he grumbled. "I've got a jacuzzi at the place I'm staying. If you take the bandages off, I could use it anytime. If I started aching, it would have to help. I'm tired of hurting and I don't want to keep taking pills. They make me woozy. Ditch the bandages and I'll be careful," he promised.

"All right. All right." Dr. Marr was nodding more in surrender than in agreement. "I can leave off the tape and give you another kind of body brace. One that comes off,'' Marr proposed. ''But it won't do any good if you don't wear it most of the time. Especially in bed.'' Stu had already complained that the brace he had was uncomfortable to sleep in. He admitted he'd left it off a couple of nights since he'd moved in to Ash's house.

''Okay,'' Stu persisted. ''I'll try the brace. Anything. I just don't want to stink, period. This cast is getting rank enough.''

''All right. We'll try it a week with the new brace. But you may need a little help getting in and out of this one.'' The doctor wasn't at all convinced that Stu would follow through with the midriff brace, but he figured the benefits of the jacuzzi would compensate by helping with the recovery process in other ways. ''Just don't exert yourself,'' Marr cautioned him.

''I won't,'' Stu said solemnly. Marr was closing in with a pair of crooked scissors in his hand. Stu would have said anything to get the white-haired bone man to start clipping away at those bandages.

On his way into Mangrove Place, Stu was pulling through the gate to the compound when he saw Rikki and the youngsters coming in the van on their way out. She waved and pulled her vehicle onto the shoulder to let him pass.

''Nice car,'' Jake called out his window as Stu eased the 'Vette between them and the palmettos.

''Thanks,'' he responded. ''And thanks to whoever came by and fed the boys today.''

''Mom did it,'' Lara piped in, crowding her brother so she could get a look at Stu's low convertible. ''On weekends she said she'd do it.''

''Thanks.'' He aimed the comment toward Rikki. ''I hadn't thought about weekends being a problem,'' he added apologetically.

''It wasn't a problem,'' Rikki assured him. ''I simply made a detour on my way out to get the paper. I made coffee, then crawled in bed again.''

Instantly he imagined her up there reading the paper in her room. Indigo. Masdevallia. Carved faces. Something lovely in the morning. He wished he'd been awake. Better yet, he wished he'd been there.

''I checked earlier. You were out? Everything all right?''

''Everything's fine. We had some errands. We're going to

my dad's condo at the beach for the afternoon,'' she told him. ''I left you a note so you wouldn't be concerned that no one was around. I thought we'd better keep each other posted. The note says a little more.'' She hesitated, glancing over her shoulder at the kids. ''Okay, back in the seatbelts,'' she reminded them. ''We'll be back after dinner. Maybe we'll see you then.'' It wasn't quite an invitation to come over for the evening, but it would do.

The note she left in his mail slot was more specific and direct and it had a key taped to it.

My dad is worried that since it's a weekend and it's been a few days since the last incident, the Trasher might cause trouble. He and Ivey have invited us out to their place for the day. If you can, I'd appreciate it if you'd take a stroll around so it looks like someone is there. The key is to the new lock on the slathouse. There are a few new leads showing on the Cattleyas you might like to see. I left a gourd and some nuts and seeds out back. If you shake the gourd, the boys will come in for a treat. They're much more playful when they aren't starving. You might enjoy it too. I just don't want them worrying either. Will call later to see how you are. Here's my dad's number, if you need me. Rikki.

He was vaguely disappointed. When they talked in passing, she'd mentioned keeping each other posted and said she'd left the note. He'd hoped the note would have been more personal. Then he read it again. It was like her. Straightforward, thoughtful, but reserved. She cared enough to keep him informed and the birds from worrying. She was going to Swede's to ease her dad's concern. She would call. If he'd expected more, like kisses and smiley faces, he wasn't going to get them from her. But who else would leave him a note to watch a new bloom spike or set out gourds and seeds and nuts so he could have a close encounter with some birds?

He didn't even glance at Swede's phone number. He knew that one by heart. And he knew why he and Ivey had been so insistent about having her and the kids out there. The timing was enough to make any father real nervous. The art show was trashed on a weekend. Lyman Franklin was pelted on a weekend, a couple of days after the Rodriquez woman was doused. On top of that, it was a full moon. The crazies would be out.

"Could we pass on dinner tonight?" His mom called and bailed out next. He'd forgotten they had a date. She'd been asked to sit in as a last-minute fourth for bridge, taking the place of a friend too ill to play. "You can come over tomorrow and have dinner," she suggested. "It just means the steak will be more tender."

"No problem. Enjoy your bridge," he told her, somewhat relieved. "Tomorrow will be fine." He really didn't want to leave the place tonight, just in case Swede was right.

Stu spent a while in the slathouse. He started grooming a few of the plants, cutting off old spikes and dead leaves. Then he took on a section of orchids that needed dividing and repotting. He didn't stop until he felt a twinge in his upper arm. He decided to take the hint. The rest of the afternoon, he sprawled out on Rikki's lanai with an ice chest full of diet sodas and a radio, contentedly soaking up the sun. No brace. Just the cast, propped with a towel to mop up the sweat.

Late in the day, he rattled the gourd she'd left him. A few streaks of green came soaring in one at a time. First came the lovebirds. He shook it again. Then the bigger birds came soaring. They bobbed and paraded, whistled and fanned their wings. But there was no crowding, no screeching. It was more like they'd dropped in for a congenial visit with friends. Some even came close enough to eat out of his hand.

When the supply ran out, the birds still sat awhile, preening and gossiping. As the sun began to set, they sailed off, some alone, some in groups. Stu found himself smiling as he hosed the deck after their departure. Calm like this, the boys weren't half bad company.

He circled the house on the way home, stopping to recheck the slathouse and darkroom doors. Both were locked. "Son of a bitch," he muttered to the man who'd made that precaution necessary. It just chilled him that it would only take one oversight, one unlocked door to let the bastard in.

"Dad and Ivey want us to stay over. I know they'll feel better if we do." Rikki's message was on Ash's answering machine when he got in. "I need you to feed the boys in the morning. Use Harrison's emergency key, let yourself in. Their fruit is in the refrigerator. See you tomorrow."

He already knew which key on the row of hooks in Ash's cupboard was hers. Ash had each one neatly labeled in his small, squarish handwriting. Stu had slipped the slathouse key she'd given him onto the same ring. He got the fruit and turned on a few lights. Then he locked the door, hurrying back in case she called again.

She didn't.

He thought of calling her at Swede's but he suspected it would be difficult trying to carry on a conversation while she had family all around. He fixed a salad and a sandwich, sat out on the balcony awhile. He got the binoculars and looked around. At least with some lights, her place looked lived in. Just because she was away didn't mean her house was out of jeopardy.

He pedaled the bike, took a shower, watched the late news, then went back over to Rikki's house. This time he walked through it slowly, taking the pleasure of imagining her in every room. Upstairs, he sat on the indigo bed and pressed his face in her pillow, inhaling traces of her. He sat in her chairs. He looked at all the photos. He even stood in her walk-in closet and looked around, slightly surprised that there were rows of filled hangers, with clothes he'd couldn't quite envision her wearing. And shoes. In his mind, she was always barefoot. He stopped at her dresser, picked up a bottle of spray perfume and spritzed it on himself. Then taking her with him, he switched off the lights one by one, except for one bathroom light, so it wouldn't be totally dark. She was still with him when he slid into bed. Even with the new brace on, he was able to sleep.

On Sunday, it rained. Rikki came home with the kids. Once she got them settled, she came over carrying a big umbrella. "Hot blueberry muffins." She handed him a small warm package. "I wanted to see you and thank you for all the new pots of orchids you started." She stood under the porch roof, letting the umbrella drip.

"You're welcome. How about coming in?"

"I can't. Juli is coming over to help tape. I'm ready," she said simply. "If I get this done today, I'll feel like I've accomplished something worthwhile this week. How about coming over later for dinner?"

He almost groaned. "I'm having dinner with my mom."

"Good. If you see the lights on when you come back,

come over if you feel up to it.'' She popped the umbrella up again and headed back across the yard.

The rain had stopped and it was dark when Stu got home from dinner. Her lights were on. He parked his 'Vette under the carport, next to Ash's Buick. Rikki was in her front yard, talking with someone on a motorcycle. Except that it was a Sunday, not a Wednesday, and if it hadn't been for the legs, Stu would have figured the biker was Eddie Sordo. But these legs, encased in skin-tight denim, were decidedly female.

Rikki looked over and waved. ''If you have a minute, come on over. I want you to meet someone.'' Relieved that he didn't have to pretend he wasn't interested, then skulk around and try to watch them from inside, he strolled over to meet the newest addition to his list of people who were apparently safe to have visit the peninsula.

''Olivia Mello. This is Stu Sullivan. Olivia is one of the artists from the show.'' Rikki introduced them. ''She came out this afternoon to make sure we were all right. Stu is staying in Harrison Ash's house while he's in Costa Rica.''

The small, shapely woman in the leather jacket and helmet looked him over, her china blue eyes hesitating at the sling and cast along the way. Up close, he could see the wisps of bright red hair framing her face inside the helmet. ''Nice to meet you.'' She promptly thrust out her left hand to shake his good one. There was a raspy quality to her voice. ''Damn nice car you got. Classy. It's a '60?''

'' '61.'' Her handshake didn't match the legs.

''It's beautiful.''

''Thanks.'' He groped for something else to keep the conversation going. ''I guess you're like the rest of us, waiting for the Trasher's next shoe to drop?''

''Everyone's waiting. I'd love him to drop it at my place.'' Olivia's red bow-shaped lips curved into a slight smile. ''If that sawed-off fucker shows, I'll stuff that shoe up his ass for what he did to my friends.''

Stu's polite how-are-you smile was frozen in place. He thought he noticed a sliver of amusement when he looked at Rikki, assessing her reaction.

While Olivia added another terse character evaluation of the Trasher, Stu managed to inhale and try to reconcile the loading-dock language with the cute, upturned face of Rikki's colleague. It was as if some foul-mouthed ventriloquist were stationed just out of sight, spewing out the dialogue while sweet Olivia simply moved her kewpie-doll lips.

But then he saw her glance up at Lara, who was watching them from the balcony. Stu saw the lethal glint in her eyes soften.

"He'd better not bother that baby," she hissed. "Or he'll wear his balls for earrings." He had no doubt if the Trasher showed, Olivia could do precisely what she described.

"I'd like to be there for that particular occasion." He recovered, managing to smile and make a good-natured response. "Either of you heard anything today?"

"Not about him," Rikki responded. "Olivia has some good news, though. She's having some of her larger works in an outdoor sculpture exhibit in two weeks," Rikki told him. "Sort of a garden-party kind of thing out at Victor Chambers's house. She needed something dressy, so we've been going through my closet. I loaned her an outfit of mine."

"I don't do dresses," Olivia said, with a slight grimace. "And I don't do garden parties. But this is business." She secured Rikki's dress in her cargo compartment. "They've got the money, honey, and I've got the bills." She made it sound like an apology for selling out.

"Victor wants to capitalize on the media attention we've been getting and give Olivia and some other regional sculptors an opportunity to show their larger works," Rikki explained. "Things he couldn't fit into his gallery. A lot of corporate people will be there. He's invited reps from city government, the utility companies, various business and industrial complex developers. Anyone with a large space to fill."

"Doctors and lawyers and Indian chiefs," Olivia chimed in.

"He hopes that if these big pieces are set up and lighted in his gardens, the guests will find something they like to make their grounds more beautiful."

"And make my bank balance healthier," Olivia added. "I could use a few extra zeroes before the dot, if you get my drift."

"I get it," Stu replied, increasingly disarmed by the petite woman with the whiskey voice.

"Rikki says you and your brother are in landscaping. You got any big-bucks friends with wide-open spaces that you'd like to invite?'' Olivia eyed him speculatively. ''I gave Rikki some extra invitations, just in case.''

Stu chuckled. He liked the way Olivia got straight to the point. Despite her blunt language, he could understand why Rikki liked her.

''I'll try to think of some,'' he promised. From Olivia's comment he gathered they'd been talking about him before he arrived on the scene. That pleased him. It also made him wonder what was discussed besides the business he was in.

''You really should bring him to this thing,'' Olivia told Rikki point-blank. Both she and Stu looked at the tall blonde woman.

''Do you want to come? You might enjoy it,'' Rikki said, turning the question back to Stu. ''Two weeks from Thursday?''

''Sure.'' He was so eager to be included, he answered before he realized what he might be letting himself in for. Not only did he know Victor, but the garden where the party would be held was one he and Brian designed and planted for Chambers several years earlier. They still replanted and upgraded it from time to time.

He also knew a lot of developers and people in city planning. And they knew him. Over the past few years as fire marshal, he'd been involved in a number of community programs. He'd been on television. He'd spoken at a few civic clubs about fire regulations, arson, and security measures. He'd done career days at area high schools.

Even in civilian clothes with his on-leave longer hairstyle and a nicely developing beard, he could be recognized. The broken arm was a giveaway, for sure. Then he'd have to explain to Rikki the part he'd omitted about himself about being chief fire marshal. That would lead to other questions. And if it leaked out that he was her watchdog, the mayor would be pissed.

But with the rambling walkways and tiered terraces at Chambers's estate full of sculptures and artists, the focus would be elsewhere. At night, at a dressed-up garden party, he'd be out of uniform, out of context, and out of the spotlight. He might get by. Besides, in the two weeks or so until the event, the Trasher could be history. He may have been able to tell Rikki everything by then. One way or another, he decided, something would work out.

''You got a black tie?'' Olivia said, half-teasing. ''Apparently that's all they want you guys to wear. Black tie only. Says so right on the invitation. The tie-only business sure will separate the haves from the have-nots,'' she declared with a sly grin. "But it also might keep away the haves who have very large bank balances but very little to flaunt under their black tie.''

"Olivia can be selectively literal,'' Rikki said, smiling.

"I'm just quoting the instructions.'' The red-haired woman rolled her eyes. "I was tellin' Rikki to be sure to bring her camera. You know how she is about capturing natural things in natural settings.''

"I'm sure I don't want to capture anything like that on film,'' Rikki said, laughing. "That isn't the kind of nature that interests me.''

"It interests me.'' Olivia mounted the cycle and cranked up the motor. "See ya' at the event, if not before. Keep an eye out for the spineless marauder,'' she cautioned both of them. "He'd better hope the cops get his ass before I do.'' She gave Rikki and Stu the thumbs-up sign and rumbled off into the night.

They could tell she held the high-powered cycle in check until she cleared the crushed oyster-shell surface of their private road. Then she hit Midnight Pass and roared off toward the north. After the noise faded, Stu stalled.

"A bit of a paradox, that one,'' he offered.

"She's that, all right,'' Rikki acknowledged. "Olivia does big, exquisite, graceful metal pieces. She works with helmets and welding equipment and has her own mini-foundry. A lot of the material she uses is salvaged from junkyards. Last year she constructed the entire stage set of a Shakespeare in the Park production out of the recycled parts of wrecked automobiles. She's remarkable.''

"I'll say.'' He paused, looking up at the sky, hoping Rikki would talk awhile or maybe invite him in. Almost without thinking, he reached up and cupped his hand over his shoulder, kneading it. Occasionally it helped.

"I'm curious. Has your doctor said anything about whether a massage or sitting in the hot tub would do some good?'' Rikki asked him. "I know it helps my dad.''

Self-conscious, Stu lowered his head. He hadn't been trying to look pitiful. "He okayed the Jacuzzi. He didn't say much else. I know I have to start some therapy on the arm in a few weeks when they switch me to the removable cast.''

He liked the idea she might be offering some hands-on comfort. "He did give me a body brace instead of the tape I'd had so I could shower. He didn't say not to try a massage."

Rikki smiled. "I'm pretty competent at giving one. I thought you might like to sit in my spa out back and talk and I'd work on your shoulder."

"Sure. When?"

"How about now?"

"Tonight?"

"Might help you relax. You'll sleep better."

He remembered the old saying about the gift horse. He wasn't about to turn down an offer like this. "I'd really like that." The possibility of skin-to-skin contact with her excited him. "Let me get my trunks on. I'll be right over."

"I'll turn on the heat. Meet you out back."

She helped him slip a plastic bag over the cast, then prop it up on a rubber float so he could sink up to his neck and bubble in the warm water. She'd sat across from him, chest deep, her head leaning back, looking through the latticed roof of the gazebo at the stars and the moon the few pale stripes of clouds overhead. In the corner, the beaming Sulka mask stood with its hands raised heavenward.

It had been blissfully peaceful. They hadn't talked much. The aerator sent the therapeutic bubbles gushing out. The ruffling sound and the proximity to her were relaxing and friendly, and the bubbling screened out any street noises that tried to encroach.

"Ease out for a while. You'll overheat." She turned down the system. He sat up on the ledge, submerged only to his knees, while she came around behind him, poured scented oil into her palm, and started the massage.

"Relax. Just let everything go."

He tried. But he knew how much it hurt if he moved the wrong way, and he clenched his teeth, waiting.

"Come on. Open your fists. Keep your fingers relaxed. Let your head and jaw drop." She massaged the back of his neck, working her thumbs up behind his ears. "Breathe in deep, through the nose, then let it out. Like waves. In and out. Again."

The breathing made it easier.

"Talk to your body. Tell the tight places to let go. Tell every muscle that it's okay to loosen up," she coached him gently, her movements soft and rhythmical.

"Out loud?"

"No. Just in your head. You've got a direct in-house line," she told him. "And visualize. Imagine all the sore places are coiled springs of metal. You and I are smoothing them out, taking out the kinks. You do it with your thoughts; I'll do it with my fingers."

"Okay." He pictured the coils. Unwinding. Dark circles, like ribbons. Lacy ribbons, like the band around her leg.

There was something exquisitely intimate about feeling her hands on his body. Not totally sexual, although that undercurrent was definitely there. The contact was comforting and personal and close.

He couldn't stop grinning. Everything about this time together with her felt good. Deliciously exclusive.

"Relax."

He stifled the grin. He kept sending his muscles the messages, just as she suggested, but the image of the lacy band kept coming back. From time to time she'd whisper "relax" again and he'd try to concentrate on coils.

"This feels great." He had to tell her.

"Good. I have a friend Tracy who does this professionally," she told him, never slowing the steady motion of her hands across his upper back. Firm, purposeful, the movements found the places that felt like taut ropes and began working them loose "I used to get backaches from lugging around my camera gear. Then I started exercising and getting a massage every few weeks. I learned how to do this from her."

He sat with his chin almost resting on his upper chest, half-listening, feeling incredibly pampered. He hadn't realized how much muscle strain he'd suffered with the injury. Besides overloading the muscles supporting the weight of the cast, he was also overworking the other side to compensate for the uselessness of the right arm. Driving and shifting cross-armed had taxed them even more. Everywhere she touched, he flinched, stiffened, then gradually surrendered.

"I do the kids and my dad sometimes. And a friend once in a while. I like the dynamics it produces between two people. I like the way it diminishes borders."

"Uh-huh," Stu responded, adrift somewhere. After a while, he was sure she must have heard him purring.

"You want me to do your feet?" When she asked, he'd

been almost dozing while her hands circled and stroked and warmed his back.

"No. This is fine." He hated for this part to end. He could imagine doing this to her. Feeling her muscles under his hands.

"It will feel great. All kinds of good things happen with a foot rub. There are pressure points in feet that help you unknot. If you're uncomfortable about this being so one sided, pay close attention. I'll show you how to do it, then you can do mine one day." He looked at her, a bit chagrined that she had almost read his thoughts.

"Do it," he agreed, pivoting and holding out one spa-warmed foot.

She worked the muscles of his feet with the same strong movements, only this time, she knelt waist deep in front of him. He could watch the lattice pattern of the moonlight on her skin and the way the shapes seemed to dance in her pale hair. With half-closed eyes, he studied the graceful curve of her arms and shoulders, the slight sideways motion of her breasts, the way she tilted her head as she talked, and the gentleness of her expression. He tried to ignore the natural response his body made.

Silently, he kept thanking whoever was in charge that he'd come across someone so remarkable. Watching her and listening, and talking very little himself, he understood the dynamics she had mentioned, the unspoken bond between the one who ministers and the one who yields. No one had simply touched his body to make him feel good. No one had offered comfort. There was always a motive and an urgency. And then usually sex.

This kind of touching wasn't that foreplay-performance kind of contact. This was caring and giving pleasure, easing pain, without the edge of sex as the next step. With her, there was no hidden agenda, no payoff, nothing to prove. She had his feet and calves feeling incredible. He had no doubt that when he went to bed, he'd be alone, but he'd feel her hands on his body even when he slept. The gentleness of it all was incredibly moving.

The tears and the choked-up feeling came from nowhere and caught him by surprise. He was just watching her, feeling amazingly at ease and protected. He'd been smiling. Then his chest got tight and his eyes brimmed with tears.

He blinked them back, but she must have felt the change or heard his breathing pattern shift.

"That happens sometimes," she said, looking at him briefly, then going back to working on the second foot, so he would have some semblance of privacy. "Massage therapists see it all the time. It's just another level of release," she explained. "Tracy said clients often bottle things up. When the body finally relaxes, our mind does too. Our stiff upper lip goes off duty. We're able to let go of some old pains, emotional ones as well as physical. It's part of giving up the control, muscle by muscle, pain by pain, memory by memory. It's just another coil smoothing out again."

"I don't even know what started this." He croaked out the words. He swallowed and wiped the back of his hand under his nose, not feeling as foolish as he would have if he'd been with anyone but her.

"I'm not sure that matters. It could be something you buried years ago. We grow up, trying to be so tough and so much in control all the time. We bury a lot of hurt inside. Even the arm and shoulder injuries gave you pain you probably didn't dare express."

He nodded. When the beam hit him, the pain and the sound of his own bones breaking had been sickening. He'd done just as she said, he'd kept calm and walked out of the rubble.

"As kids, we're allowed to cry. We get hugged and caressed and comforted when we're hurt. As grown-ups, we have to gut it through. We're expected to act calm and unemotional. But the hurt is there. Why don't we stop and wonder where does the crying go?" she said softly, not really expecting an answer. "And how long does the crying have to stay in there?"

Stu shook his head, caught up in the memory of the accident. He was recalling how stupid and angry and embarrassed he felt on the scene, investigating an obvious arson, when the overhead beam dropped and caught him. He was the chief fire marshal. He had to handle himself like one in front of his men.

Later, he'd thrown up in the emergency van on the way to the hospital, but that was reflex. He hadn't whimpered or complained. He'd been a model patient for the two days they kept him in. And afterward he'd just gone home, taken the prescription drugs, and slept. No one hugged him. And he hadn't cried.

"Your body must be feeling less stressed. You've let down some of your defenses, so the other stuff is escaping too. That's part of the way massage therapy diminishes borders." She smiled as she spoke, but her eyes when they met his now were solemn and concerned. "You just let it all go. It's like spring cleaning."

"I don't know what to make of it. You definitely uncoiled me."

"This emotional release has very little to do with me," she cautioned him. "It has to do with you. I'm just a pair of hands. I helped your muscles relax. It's your mind that has allowed the tensions to ease so old feelings can surface. You can practice on your own. When you go to bed tonight, close your eyes, breathe easy and deep, and feel yourself letting it go again," she coaxed him. "Give it to the waves. After you've done this massage and deep breathing routine a few times, you'll know when things start knotting up and you'll learn to head them off. At the end of the day, you'll find it easier to cut through the clutter, to unload and unwind. You consciously unburden yourself. You'll reach a level of serenity and relaxation that is healthier for you. The carryover effect on a deeper level is that you'll start to feel real clear inside."

"I feel pretty clear now."

"It will get better."

When he went home alone, Stu felt more cushioned than clear. She sent him off feeling slack and soothed and sleepy. "Don't stay up tonight," she told him. "I'll make sure everything here is locked up. Remember to lock your door as well." He'd nodded and turned toward Ash's house. She'd gone upstairs and stood out on her balcony, watching him cross the grassy expanse in the dark.

He looked back and saw her still there, making sure he made it in all right. " 'Night." It didn't matter that she couldn't hear him from that distance. "Thanks." He waved.

She smiled. He had a feeling she got the message he intended.

Inside, he made a quick circuit through Ash's house, turning off the remaining lights. Then he aimed for the bedroom and sprawled out on the covers.

"Close your eyes, breathe easy and deep, and feel yourself letting go again.'' He couldn't have made a fist if he'd had to. He couldn't think of a problem to unload. All he could think of was the strength of her hands, the softness of her voice, and the fact that for the first time in weeks, he didn't hurt at all.

''Anything?'' Stu began the next day with the now-familiar, cautious question when he found her in the slathouse in her bathing suit. She'd turned on the overhead sprinkler system that filled the enclosure with a fine, gentle mist. She was simply standing in there with the orchids, letting the moisture surround her, as if it were a perfectly normal way to begin the day. For her, he had a feeling, it was.

''All's quiet on the western front. I guess we should all be thankful.''

''But you aren't?'' He leaned against the door jamb, watching her. She had water sparkling all over, even on her eyelashes.

''I'm trying to look on the bright side, but I'm not succeeding. I talked to Olivia. She's a little off kilter too. We all are. It will be a week tomorrow. It's never been this long before.'' She walked from bench to bench checking the new growth on each plant.

Even Joe Warnock sounded more frustrated than usual when Stu talked to him that morning. The detective had nothing new to say either, and he made the same comment. The Trasher was overdue.

''It could be over,'' Stu said, wishing it were true.

''Or not.'' She took a breath. ''I've just got to get to work and get out of this funk.''

''How about getting out of that rain forest and having a cup of coffee with me first?''

''You made coffee?'' She walked up to him with a grin of amusement.

''No. But I made biscuits. My mother's recipe. I hoped we could work out a deal.''

''I think we can.'' She passed him on the way out. Even wet, she smelled good.

She put on her big green robe while the coffee brewed. ''You sure must feel better. Up early? Baking?''

''I just wanted to catch you before you got busy. The

massage helped. So did the philosophy,'' he added. ''Thanks.''

''We can give it another round anytime you'd like. Ivey and I have been taking turns giving my dad the same treatment, at least the massage part. I think it will help you heal faster.''

''Just tell me when you have the time. I can make my schedule fit yours.''

''Well, my schedule today is a corker. I've got to start editing the tape we made. It may take me most of the morning, or longer,'' she conceded. ''I'm having a little trouble concentrating.''

''I don't doubt it.''

''I'm picking up the kids at school. They have appointments at the dentist. Then we've got to shop for shoes. The weather gets cooler, then all of a sudden, nothing fits.'' It was the kind of conversation he remembered his folks having over coffee and biscuits when he and Brian were kids.

''Sounds like a busy day.'' He was almost relieved. He'd picked up a laptop and some paperwork at the office in the hope of working through some of the backlog that was stacking up.

''It keeps going. Tonight there's a parent–teacher meeting at the school. The dust should settle around the kids' bedtime.'' Rikki added a hopeful note. ''We can shoot for that.''

''I'd think you might have had enough by then. You'll be the one needing the massage.''

''I'd be happy for some grown-up company.''

''Am I grown-up enough?'' He wanted to see her smile again.

''I sure hope so, Sullivan.'' Deep in her eyes, Stu could see a spark of humor. ''I'm not into perennial adolescence.''

''Ah. Perennial adolescence, of course. Brian and I use them for edging in gardens. Purple things with low silvery leaves?''

''I've got to get to work.'' She was grinning while she cleared away the coffee cups. ''Go home. I'll see you tonight.''

The next day started out the same way. No attack. No news.

Stu spent the morning testing out the bionic ear, a piece of surveillance equipment he'd brought in and started to set up the day before. She was editing again. It rained off and on. Most of the time the house was very quiet. But once in a while, he could hear the reggae music as she holed up in her production room trying to get the sound right.

When the kids came home, he tried a clear shot at the kitchen window. He could hear their voices and laughter as they fixed a snack. Professionally, he wanted to fine tune the adjustment so everything would work just right. Personally, he wanted to go over there and get in on the fun. He knew Rikki would be teaching her class that night at the Art Institute. The neighbor had a card game down the Key. Juli and kids would be alone. He couldn't cover all the bases, so he'd have to stay put and concentrate on home plate. If the guy was after her art, he'd find it there.

For two and a half hours, Stu paced and watched and waited, trying not to get too coiled in the process. Across the way, they were watching something on the Disney Channel. He'd turned on Ash's set and matched the sound.

"She home yet?" Joe Warnock called, sounding just as edgy as Stu felt.

"Nope."

"Should be soon. I sent a patrol car through campus. They said she's on her way."

"Good. So what's the consensus? You think he's given up?" Stu asked. He kept reaching for that shoulder, kneading away, as they talked.

"If it's over, I doubt if he'd be nice enough to drop us a note."

"Maybe he's noticed there's more cops around. He may not want to risk another move."

"Or he may think this makes the game more interesting. He may consider it a challenge," Warnock replied, quickly bursting that fragile balloon.

"Right. I think I'll take another look around," Stu answered dully.

"I think a lot of us are looking around tonight. I sure don't like this feeling."

Stu was out on Ash's balcony, pedaling the bike, when Rikki got back. She waved and started over. "How's the back?" she asked when he met her downstairs.

"A little tight." So was the neck, the jaw, and even his chest muscles. He wasn't about to tell her otherwise.

"I figured that might be the case." He'd come out and was looking past her, scanning the shadows as they stood on the stoop. "How about a round in the spa? I was going to sit out there awhile anyway. I'd be glad for the company, and I could give you another massage if you're interested."

He definitely was.

That after-dark session by the spa was easier, physically and emotionally. Less self-conscious now, he settled into the massage procedure as if it were a familiar ritual, one he didn't try to resist.

Once they were both sufficiently simmered, she started with his neck and shoulders and ended with his calves and feet. He didn't choke up this time. His entire body felt better. And there was a sexual tension that he simply didn't fight. He didn't act on it either. Afterward he even took a turn and rubbed her feet, doing the best he could one handed.

He went back to Ash's, sat out on the deck until long after her house was dark, watching for any movement. He stayed alert until almost two, then he decided to call it quits. "Close your eyes, breath deep and easy." It was almost as if she were with him, he could remember her hands so well. He thought of indigo and orchids and could feel himself letting go again.

"Used to be a nice little drive," McIver reflected as he drove into Venice. He'd eaten dinner at Conroy's, watched the sun go down, then cut inland and headed south. He'd avoided the Interstate and took Route 41 instead. Bad choice. It was as fucked up here as it was up his way. Franchise row. McDonald's. Wendy's. Mindless shit.

He'd made the same ride twice already. Once it was raining. He was wearing his black custom Church's and hadn't felt like getting them soaked. So he'd kept on going to Englewood and checked out Jessup as well. Pool in the backyard. Wall around it. Could be a studio upstairs. He'd have to think about that one. The downpour had continued. He put in another CD, aimed inland, and took the Interstate home.

The next time, he came earlier, dressed in shorts and tennis shoes. He parked down the street, sprayed himself with water so he looked real sweaty, put on a headset, then came loping past, like he was cooling down after a run. Stopped at the corner to retie his shoe. Abel-Smith and her girlfriend had company. Six of them. All females. They were out in the backyard. The Hyphen's girlfriend was cooking something on the grill. Four were playing badminton. One had a hell of a smash shot. He decided to pass. But the Hyphen had the garage door half open. Ventilation, he guessed. He could see the kiln outside and figured out his target.

The third time was easy. The converted garage on one end where she made her pots was dark. He'd managed to circle around through a neighbor's yard and get a good look before he started closing in. She and the girlfriend were holed up in a room out back, watching TV. They were eating their dinner on trays, staring zombielike at the screen. All they needed were a few candles, for atmosphere. And no phone calls. He was going to oblige.

This would be a quick one, he'd decided. He hadn't had a drink in hours, but one would be waiting once he made his move. All he had to do was pop a window, slide off the outer coat, snap the flare, and pitch it in. It would automatically light. He'd practiced once, holding it under water in his sink, so he would get the feel of it. If he worked fast, he figured he could get two in and take off over through the back hedge. He'd brought two extras just in case he had a dud.

The first one he pitched in on the garage floor simply lay there. The second one fizzed and spat. But the time he got the third one in, the whole place lit up like some damn disco from hell. Hot pink. Eye-blinding bright. Streaming out every crack and window, pulsing like crazy. And the stink reminded him of being downwind on the Fourth of July.

He bounded for the bushes and didn't wait. The whole yard lit up. By the time he reached the car and changed, he could hear the sirens. When he drove by the end of the street, he could see the neighbors already in their yards, staring at the eerie sight. No flames. Just that quivering pink glow and a stream of rich dark smoke.

Four down. Five to go. That deserved a toast.

* * *

Wednesday, Eddie Sardo arrived in full biker regalia, ready to cook. Jake and Lara came out to the slathouse to tell Stu he was needed elsewhere.

"Mom says you have to come in and help if you want to eat. She'll make you wash your hands," Lara said, seeing the color they'd become. Stu had taken fern bark and charcoal and was mixing it with his hands into potting medium. Next time he came over, he was planning to move some rootbound plants to larger containers.

"They'll come clean," Stu assured her. He dunked them in a bucket and rinsed before he went inside to give them a more thorough scrub.

The dinner routine had a smoothness this time that made him feel more useful. He knew where things were. He had sense enough to carry things on trays. He could pitch in without having to be given directions. He even helped with dishes afterward while Jake and Eddie scraped the plates and bagged the scraps. Later Eddie and the kids played a game on the kitchen table, with needlelike fishbones, bleached and carved like ornate pick-up sticks. Then it was bedtime. The kids went upstairs, Sordo took his compost home, Rikki and Stu secured all the sliders and windows and went outside to soak.

"I'll think we'll have to do a rather quick massage tonight," she said. She'd been working in the darkroom all afternoon, processing black and whites from the class the night before. "I'm tired." She reached up and rubbed her neck.

"We could pass."

"I'm not that tired. Besides, once you start loosening up, it's easier to keep it that way if you don't let too much time pass between sessions."

"Looks like you could use some loosening up yourself. Turn around and let me take a shot at this," he insisted. "Just don't expect me to do it as well as you do."

"Okay. But you're next." She moved close enough for him to work one handed.

It was almost ten o'clock when Lara came down in her pajamas to tell her Mom she had a telephone call. Rikki was turning off the spa and hadn't heard it ring. Stu was at the far edge of the deck, toweling off. Lara had gotten out of bed to use the bathroom and had answered.

"I should have brought the cordless out here," Rikki

muttered, sorry the youngster had been disturbed. The closest phone was in the kitchen.

Stu stayed outside, leaning against the deck railing. He could see the change in her expression and her body language as she took the call. He couldn't hear what was being said, but he knew the news wasn't good.

"He did it again," Rikki came back out to tell him. "That was Olivia. The Trasher hit. In Venice. He set off some kind of flares in the garage Lynda Abel-Smith uses for her pottery studio."

"Was anyone hurt?"

"Lynda's in the hospital, but she's not injured. Smoke inhalation, apparently." She'd crossed her arms over her chest, and she stood there wrapped in her towel, looking almost childlike. "Olivia said there was a lot of smoke damage. Lynda was at the opposite end of the house. Her neighbor had to come over to tell her something was on fire. Her phone line was cut. It was mostly smoke so she went in to open the windows and doors."

Stu shook his head in frustration. He knew how deceptively innocuous smoke could be. He'd transported charred bodies of people who'd made the same mistake. They didn't see flames and thought they could run in for a moment and got killed by the fumes. The risk was never worth it.

"Her roommate called Olivia. She said she'll be okay. She's staying overnight for observation." Rikki's dark eyes were preoccupied and cold. "I have to phone Thayer Kern and Rudy Jessup. We promised each other we would network and make sure everyone knows. I guess it's too late for them to mention it on the late news. If they do, I hope Dad and Ivey aren't up watching." She walked back inside to make the calls.

Stu stood out there, feeling helpless. He watched her pull it together, erect and energetic when she conveyed the message to two of the remaining artists. Like her, they not only felt concern for Lynda Abel-Smith, but realized the list was shorter now. Abel-Smith was out of danger now. They weren't.

His heart ached as he noticed the slight sag in her shoulders after each call. When she wasn't buoying up the other guy, the real weight settled in on her. What he wanted to do was to hug her and make it all go away.

Instead, he focused on security. That was something he

could do something about. He studied the Caribbean-style house with broad decks and balconies and sliders that made so much of the outdoors accessible. With all the glass windows and doors around her house, breaking one and lobbing in a flare would be relatively simple. But getting to her workrooms was something else.

Her darkroom had no windows. It was like a small fortress, except that the door didn't lock from the inside. Put a flare with the chemicals and they'd have a disaster. Upstairs was the jackpot. In the production room, she had the video equipment and an irreplaceable library of slides. If the Trasher targeted the second floor, he could end up hurting her and the children.

In either scenario, the location of the house made any attack tricky. He'd have to carry the flares into the compound. He'd have to get close enough to throw them. And after they were lit, the guy would have to make his getaway, and there was only one road out. "Unless he came by water . . ." Stu turned and stared.

Stu walked back and forth brooding, trying to figure out something he could rig up to ward off an attack and slow down any retreat. He could give the Trasher a dose of his own medicine, and improve on it. He'd brought his flare gun from his office. He already had the handgun. One would illuminate the entire peninsula. A few shots from the other would stop him in his tracks. There was certain authority to a gunshot warning. Stu figured if that didn't work, he'd aim lower. There were other options. One thing was sure—until this guy was stopped, he and Warnock wouldn't be sleeping much at night.

By midmorning Wednesday, Lynda Abel-Smith had been released from the hospital. Detective Warnock came by to give Rikki the same talk he'd given the others. "He targeted the artworks, not the artist," he pointed out. "Don't risk your safety by trying to rescue some piece of art or combat whatever damage may be done. Take care of you and the kids first, then call 911." He also advised her to move anything really valuable out. "The whole library should go," he suggested.

Stu called him later while Rikki took a vanload of slides to one of Victor Chambers's storage rooms behind his gallery, the first temperature- and humidity-controlled location he'd felt comfortable suggesting.

"So where do we go from here?" Stu asked the detective.

"Beats me. He waited a week on this one. And he's moved south," Warnock noted. "We've got one in Englewood, and one in Fort Myers, except that guy has gone. But the Trasher could still go after the house. Even if he's from here, he could just swing down the Interstate, do a job, and come back. He hit about eight o'clock last night. In the dark again. Only lights on were at the opposite end of the house where the woman and some roommate were watching television. Looks like highway flares. Snap and glow. Three."

"You don't think he intended to hurt anyone, though." Stu tried to salvage something comforting from the situation.

"If you want the truth," Warnock replied, "I don't think the guy gives a damn either way. But, in this case, no. I don't think he intended to hurt the woman. But what that jerk intended sure doesn't help her a hell of a lot."

"I get the picture. Thanks. Keep me posted," Stu said before he hung up.

By the time he got Ash's Panama hat on and was heading out the door, Swede and Ivey had arrived. She was carrying several boxes. Stu had already heard about them earlier, shortly after Swede learned about the Abel-Smith news. "We've got to do something," Swede started right in. "I've got a lock and two of those damn motion-sensing lights for her. She could probably use another two. I've got underground wires laid all over the place, mostly for a pool we didn't build. I'm going to hire someone to tap in and put the damn lights up. You just back me up on this if she asks you," he said. "And let me know if there's anything else she needs. We gotta' do something, damn fast," he blustered on.

Stu let Swede and his daughter iron this one out themselves. He busied himself elsewhere, cutting across to the Simons woman's house to check the grounds there. He'd gone over the area before, but now he intended to memorize every inch of the little compound so he'd know his way around it, in daylight or in the dark, or whatever lighting conditions Swede was negotiating.

An electrician rolled in an hour later, followed by a second van as backup. Sordo came in next. Stu followed them with the binoculars as Swede and Sordo walked around the yard, pointing while the electricians prodded, locating the underground conduits. Then they started digging.

"Lots of action out here today," Stu said after everyone had gone home for the day. He'd seen her crossing into the slathouse and cut across to visit.

"I'm being floodlit," Rikki said, not pleased at all. "My father insisted. He seems to think that having these things all over will help keep this guy away."

"It probably will help."

She nodded, then dug both hands into the charcoal mix he'd made and scooped some in a pot. "I just don't like a lot of bright lights around outside. I like sunlight and moonlight and twilight. But not megawatts." She loaded another pot, a bit more vigorously than the first. "Part of what makes this peninsula so wonderful, especially when we're outside, is the feeling that we're living in nature on its terms. When it's dark, it's dark."

He handed her a few more empty pots to fill, then he gave her one of the Phales that needed to be moved into one of them. Gently she shook off the old potting medium and settled the Phale in place. He handed her the next one. "Maybe you could consider the floodlights as a temporary thing. When this is over, don't use them."

"That's fine for me. But there are birds and frogs and opossums and things that feel safe here at night. I'm not sure how they'll adapt if the place lights up every time something moves. They don't understand 'temporary'." She was calmer now than she was when he came in. "But I do. When they finish installing them, I'll give them a try. My dad said I have to make some concessions to protect the kids if I plan to keep them here. He also made it real clear that if I want to be around for them in the future, I'd better take more precautions myself. So I'm going along with this for now."

Stu nodded, appreciating the persuasive strategy Swede had used.

"But I still get angry that this guy can muck up my place, whether he comes here or not."

"It's only temporary," Stu said, passing her another crowded Phalaenopsis.

Thursday Stu went over early to help her pick out some plants to take over to the Safe House. "My friend Claire at

Selby is the one who is really into horticultural therapy. She and Janelle got me interested in the Safe House because of the work they've been doing there. I like to keep some orchids there to help the atmosphere.'' She carefully chose several different orchids with spikes not quite in full flower. "We'll need a few that aren't this far along, too.''

"Like this?'' he picked up one covered with tight buds.

"That's good.''

"You're sure you don't want something showier?''

"We're into several stages in the process here,'' she explained. "Growing. Budding. Blooming. The people who come in there are at a low point. I like to show them something beautiful and hopeful, something renewing itself. Not just for the flowers. With all the plants I have here, we cover the range of developing.''

"You think these actually help?''

"I hope so.'' She went on with her selecting. "There's a pretty sun porch there where we put these along with watering cans, misters, fertilizer, and directions. Sometimes the residents aren't ready to talk yet or to listen. They're scared. They're numb. The counselors encourage them to help with the plants.''

"And they blossom? Together?'' Stu guessed.

"Sometimes they do,'' Rikki replied with more seriousness than he expected. "I'm convinced that flowers can communicate in a nonthreatening way. Their fragility is something a frightened youngster or a battered wife can understand.'' She lined up two boxes to hold the ones they were going to take. "A victim of abuse may not trust words, but a touch or a scent of something beautiful can get past all that and start them healing. That kind of sensory reinforcement can make them strong enough to talk about a problem.''

Stu hadn't quite known what to say. He'd seen her take a few orchids from her collection the week before and then return with ones past their peak. Seeing these close up and knowing their destination made him uneasy.

"Some of these are very valuable plants.'' He didn't mean it as if kindness had a price limit. He simply knew those particular ones were unusual species or ones now restricted from import. "I'd hate to see someone walk off with anything rare.''

"It's never happened. I've had no problem getting them

back," Rikki replied. "I tell the people staying there that when they're settled somewhere else and they want one of their own, to call me. I'll give them one and help them learn how to grow it."

"And have they?"

"Some have. I've given away about fifteen of them in the past year to women I've met there. They all have a clear sense of what it means to care for something. They know what neglect can do. I've turned a few thumbs green," she said with a smile.

"I'm impressed," Stu admitted. He started setting in the ones for transport.

"Me too. I've given the counselors there a few of my videos, for the same general reasons, but nothing beats the real thing, one on one." She picked up one box and headed out.

"I was hoping there'd be a connection." He followed with the second. "Speaking of one on one, how are you coming on resensitizing me?" he'd asked, trying not to watch her backside while she loaded the plants in the van.

Rikki looked up suddenly, grinning at him. "We're resensitizing each other, Sullivan. We're trying to be compassionate and open and true to ourselves. I think we're doing pretty well, in spite of all that's been going on around us."

"Does that mean I can take you out to dinner one of these days? One on one? Not because you need entertaining or that you're underfed," he kidded her, "but because I'd like to. I haven't had a real date in years." He'd been thinking about how insular they'd become. The Trasher was always out there somewhere and they had become veritable prisoners in the evenings, constantly on guard.

The new lights would make the situation easier, he hoped. Enough to risk leaving the kids with a sitter. He wanted to find out what it would be like to get her out of there, off the compound, and out in neutral territory where she wasn't glancing over her shoulder all the while, somewhere he wasn't always scanning the bushes, looking for trouble in a ski mask.

"Dinner would be nice."

"You're serious?"

"I'm serious."

"When are you free for an evening?" He felt a peculiar

pleasure asking her, despite the fact he knew most of her week's agenda by heart.

"Saturday evening Dad and Ivey were going to have the kids and me over for a cookout and a swim at their condo. Nothing fancy. Just hamburgers," she explained. "It'll be after the beach pickup, so Jake and Lara may be pooped. I can skip the dinner part, visit awhile, then let the kids stay there overnight. I could be ready about eight." She seemed as eager as he was to make it a special evening, with neither of them distracted.

"Good. With the kids stashed away, you won't be worrying about what's happening here while we're gone."

"The place won't be abandoned," she informed him. "Pat is having friends over for a party that night. She's borrowing some of my lawn furniture," Rikki said. "I doubt if the Trasher would pull anything with cars and people around. If he does, she'll call the police."

"Hell of a way for all of us to have to live," he muttered. "This nut case is like a black hole, sucking away our time and energy. I find myself waiting then rushing out and rushing back, never knowing what I'll find. I'll just be glad when this is over."

"Me too." He put his arm around her and gave her a hug. It was the first non-massage contact they'd had and it felt good. "Go. Deliver your plants. Talk to your friends there," he told her. "And don't hurry. I'll be here. If it gets close to school bus time, I'll meet the kids. And I won't be too charming to them," he added with a lopsided grin.

"Thanks. Thanks for being so careful with this," she said simply. And that soft, warm look was in her eyes, making his throat constrict and other parts react as well. "Thanks for being careful with all of us."

Stu stood there smiling, his heart pounding like a teenager, while she went inside and got her keys and purse. And when she got in her van, she gave him that approving look again, nonverbal, instantaneous, full of hope and promise, like the flowers she was taking across town. After she left, he went to Ash's house, turned the stereo up, and danced, all by himself.

"Fucking son of a bitch. Motherfucking son of a bitch." Muttering and cursing, David McIver paddled his Fiberglas canoe south on the Intracoastal Waterway, staying close enough in toward the mangroves so that he'd be screened by the fringe. He didn't want to be seen. Or heard. But he was in misery.

It was just a test trip to her house to time it all out. He figured that on a Friday night she'd have everyone locked in tight as a tick. They'd be like a bunch of Indians huddling 'round the campfire, while outside the circle, wolves and wild things stalked. Tonight he was the wolf.

"Nine little, eight little, seven little Indians . . ." He'd kept cadence with the oars.

He wanted to see how many lights would be on. Or if she'd have company. Or if she'd be like the dark-haired skinny potter, the Hyphen in Venice, who had the whole place dark except for her TV room.

It wasn't his fault she'd tried to go in and put it out. Or tried to rescue her damned clay things, or whatever the hell raku was. But the Hyphen had tried to save them. And the paper said she hadn't been able to get the windows open so that she inhaled too much smoke. Too damn bad. He hoped it scared the piss out of the other ones. Rikki Lundquist particularly.

Bambi's house and yard had looked like a damn landing strip, big floodlights going on, then off again, then on. Yellow candles lined up along the deck. On the south bank, the Simons's house was almost dark. He coasted in beside her dock. He watched the lights a while and picked out a path, close to the mangroves lining the shore. Crouched against their dark branches, he'd be just another shadow when the high beams glared.

He circled around the back so he could get a good look at the water side of the place. She and some guy were out back sitting in the spa in her gazebo. When he got out, McIver almost laughed. The guy had his arm in a cast. The best she could do was snag a hairy crip with a beard. They talked. They went inside. They started watching something on the wide-screened TV downstairs. He crouched there, wondering if she showed her boyfriends her sexy videos to get them hot. Maybe they'd start groping and end up in bed. He could feel a tingle in his crotch.

But she got up and went into the kitchen. The crip did too.

Instead of screwing, they made popcorn.

He'd moved in closer, keeping low. When the light went

on, he rolled against the deck. He lay very still. Eventually the light went off. Then he followed the line of the deck, creeping into the dark shadow of the gazebo.

He pressed against the lattice side and waited and watched. They were back in front of the TV.

"Fuck her," he coached the idiot in the cast. The crip got up and crossed into the kitchen. Getting her a drink.

"Jesus Christ," McIver muttered. The domestic bit was enough to make him puke. He shifted his weight, bored shitless. This was worse than watching Mary Poppins with his kids. "Fuck her, for God's sake." Then his feet caught fire. At least it felt like fire.

Holding his breath, McIver tried beating off the cluster of fire ants that he'd moved into. He bit his lips to smother his whimpering. "Fucking ants." His shoes and socks were alive with them. He could feel them crawling up higher in his leg hairs. "Fucking ants." He stamped and slapped and stumbled. In his frenzy of flailing limbs, his elbow slammed into the wall of the gazebo. He heard a couple of her flowerpots fall. Dull thuds. "Fucking plants."

He righted himself, cupping his hands over his face to stifle his sniffling while tears of pain half-blinded him. He shook one foot and then the other, not daring to make a sound.

The light went on. He froze. Listened.

But no one came. So he took off. This time he took a shortcut, ducking through some fruit trees that picked and scratched and slapped. The light blinked on. He kept going toward the Simons woman's dock, aiming for an open space where he could put his feet in the water.

By the time he waded in, all the way up to his crotch, his feet were throbbing. He grated one foot against the other as he yanked off the ski mask and pitched it in the canoe. Frantically he scooped salty water on his face and neck.

Then the nausea hit. He covered his mouth. He vomited anyway. His hands reeked. The smell triggered another wave. It was in the water all around him. He had to get out of there.

Dry heaving as he paddled away from it all, McIver rowed back toward an unoccupied house on Siesta Key. It was one of his luxury listings, where he'd parked his car. His feet were swelling so bad he'd had to pry off the shoes. He'd thrown the ant-encrusted socks overboard.

Shivering and feverish, he pulled the canoe ashore and made it to the car, wincing with each step. He wanted to kill her. Bambi. The fuckin' Lundquist woman had started it all.

She'd turned his life to shit. Twelve grand he'd spent on a fuckin' greenhouse, and it ends up sitting in crates. And now she'd done this. Trembling, McIver groped for his car keys. He wanted to kill her. He wanted to get the gun out from under the seat and blow her away. Her and the asshole crip with the cast. He could walk right in and kill them both. Kill them all, including her imported brats.

She'd humiliated him. She took his wife and kids away. Because of her he had to wonder if Sandra's dad was pissed enough to nudge him out of the brokerage. Pissed enough to get his buddies to exclude him from the movers-and-shakers functions at the yacht club. Or the country club. No one had called him for a game of golf since Sandra had him served with papers. In real estate, making contacts was the name of the game.

His stomach lurched again. But it had nothing more to offer. He braced his forehead on the cool roof of the car while he rifled through his pockets.

Sandra had to go to that fuckin' counseling center. Tight-assed bitches, all of them. Just like the Lundquist broad. They were all like her. Interfering bitches. And bastards. The fucker who called himself a mediator was male. Probably gay. They were all telling people what to do with their lives. Making Sandra and the kids turn on him. Helping them to go away.

He'd said he'd stop drinking. He said he'd stop hitting. He'd even bought the goddamn greenhouse. But Sandra gave up on him because of her. Lundquist and her fuckin' video.

He'd get her first. He'd like to get them all. Every one of those smart-assed counselors who stuck their nose into his private business. But he'd settle for Bambi. And he'd find Sandra and the kids. Then he'd kiss up. He'd bring them back. No one would be left to scheme behind his back.

For now, his attorney said not to make a false move; he was already in deep shit. Her lawyer had filed for separation. Threatened to get a restraining order. His guy bargained for a cooling-off period. But McIver had to play the penitent. Some judge decided how much he had to pay. Lay off the booze. Go to counseling. And don't make waves.

But he'd love to cut all their throats. The lawyers included. He hated having to sit back and let two shysters with law degrees play their little games.

He could play games too.

He found the keys. His fuckin' wallet was soaked. Real fuckin' eelskin. He couldn't stop shaking. Her fault. It was all her fault. He got the key in the lock and eased himself inside. It hurt to bend his knees. The foot on the gas pedal felt like a stump. Dead wood. Only hot inside.

McIver's teeth were chattering. His body temperature was richocheting from hot to cold. He needed a doctor. But that would mean questions. He'd just go home. Take something. Benadryl. A shot of whiskey. Soak his feet. Anything to stop the fire. And the pain.

"Easy," he cautioned himself as he backed out of the darkened driveway. He inched his way out to the main street, waiting at the crossroad a long time before pulling out into traffic. Last thing he needed was to get picked up by the cops, not with a box full of flares in his trunk.

"Sons of bitches. Motherfucking sons of bitches," he hissed. He wished the stupid broad in Venice who'd sucked in all the smoke had died. One less interfering bitch putting out propaganda that could pull a family apart. His stomach wobbled and the streetlights glared and dimmed with the pulsing in his head. Just like Bambi's yard. "I'll kill 'em. I'll kill 'em all." But the first one to go would be the blonde.

Someone was sobbing.

It was him.

Chapter 4

"Easy. Hold on." Stu squinted and checked his watch. The band of parrots and macaws had descended on Ash's desk as usual. They were grumbling and pacing, then individually and in concert began their cacaphonous screeching. "Just shut up and eat," he told them and flopped back on his pillow. Then he listened again to how they sounded and bolted out of bed, wondering what had gone wrong.

Since Rikki and the kids had the beach cleanup that morning, he'd gone home relatively early the night before. The first weekend of every month, she said, a group of volunteers gathered, armed with garbage bags and spiked sticks, to clean a section of the public Gulfside beach. They picked up plastic six-pack rings, fast food packages, drink containers, natural debris, and any other unsightly litter that made the white-sand strip less beautiful.

She'd said she'd handle the boys today before they left, but there was no sign of food outside.

"Shit." He hobbled out in his sheet and looked over toward her house. The kitchen light there was on. He phoned over. "Are you guys all right?"

"We're fine. We're running a little late, as you've probably noticed. I'll send Lara over in a few minutes."

The boys weren't interested in apologies.

Stu rummaged through his refrigerator, gathering up some limp carrots, a couple of apples, some bread, and a few Oreos, just to buy some time. "Hors d'oeuvres," he told the eager flock, figuring that would stall them a while. "Sort it out yourselves." He tossed it all out his bedroom sliders, then headed back to bed, waiting for the youngster to show up.

He lay there, half-dozing, half-dreaming about the evening ahead. "A real date," he mused, pleasantly eager. The kids would be staying at the grandparents' overnight. He'd have her all to himself. He couldn't help speculating how the evening might end, and where. She'd invite him into her bright, airy bedroom with its deep indigos and vivid reds, not to see her orchid this time. She'd help him out of his shirt and run her hands over his chest. The scenarios became increasingly erotic.

"Mr. Sullivan?" She didn't need to be so formal.

Then he heard the downstairs door and checked his watch again, realizing the voice was Lara's. He must have drifted off. Part of him was obviously alert. Hastily he rolled on his side and fluffed the sheet covering him to camouflage the effects of his reverie. Then he pretended he was still asleep.

Lara Lundquist took her usual forbidden shortcut through his bedroom, saw the litter outside, and knew he'd already been out there.

"Sorry, Mr. Sullivan," she apologized, suspecting he was playing possum. "Mom's sorry too. We all got confused. We could see that the boys were on the deck eating. She figured she misunderstood and you already fed them. She wanted to know if you had enough?"

"Not really. I just gave them something to hold them over."

"I saw the Oreos. They really shouldn't have cookies. Mom says everything has to be raw." She was shaking her head, grimacing, as though he'd broken a major commandment.

"I didn't have a lot to choose from." He turned toward her and started working his way into a sitting position, groaning and huffing a bit, yanking the sheet to make sure he stayed covered. Sleeping naked had never been such an inconvenience before.

"Are you angry?"

"No." He wished that Rikki had been the one standing in his bedroom. He was disappointed, and a bit embarassed, but he wasn't angry. He had, however, been curt.

Lara stared at the fruit in the colander she'd brought along, then looked at him with her big obsidian eyes, confused and uneasy. She reminded him of a puppy waiting to be forgiven without understanding what it had done wrong. All she needed was some sign that it was all right to wag her tail and bounce around. "Mom sent this, just in case.

Should I go ahead and give it to them too?'' Her lips were
narrowed and pressed together.

''Go ahead. Spoil them. They'll think it's a party. Maybe
we should make them all paper hats,'' he kidded her, managing a fairly convincing smile.

''Paper hats.'' She rolled her eyes.

''If it's a party, will that excuse the Oreos?'' he asked.

''Maybe.'' She almost wagged.

''Maybe we shouldn't mention it to you-know-who,'' he
suggested.

''Mom doesn't like secrets.'' Lara gave him one of her
devastating ''gotcha' '' looks.

''That's right. I'm so sorry. I'll confess.'' He hammed it
up, deliberately overplaying the part.

''That's okay.'' She hesitated, then smiled. ''If you were
up, I was supposed to ask you something.''

''So ask.''

''Mom said that you could come and have breakfast with
us if you wanted to.''

''Now?''

''Now. Before we go.''

''Sure. I'll get dressed.''

Neither one moved.

''I'll need some privacy.''

''Oh. I'll feed the boys.'' She actually skipped out onto
the deck. He grabbed his shorts and headed for the bathroom.

When he came out, he saw her with the hose and broom,
cleaning up some of the mess. ''Thanks. I owe you one,''
he called out to her.

She kept spraying.

''Enough. Lara, whoa. Leave the rest for me. Come on.
Your mom will think I kidnapped you.''

''Don't be silly. She can see me.'' Another smile, another ''gotcha.''

''How about letting her see you coming out the front
door,'' he suggested. ''That's where she's going to see me.''

''Wait just a minute.''

He didn't. But by the time he reached the landing, she
was right behind him.

By now Sordo's truck and Juli Quinn's green Escort were
parked in front of Rikki's house. His visions of a chummy
family breakfast dissipated. But the day was cool and bright

and clear, the evening ahead was promising, and he refused to let his spirits sag. "Round this way." Lara aimed him toward the back.

The table was set but no one was out there. He waved to Rikki and the others through the sliders. "Need a hand?" He held up the one he had to offer.

"No thanks. We'll be all right."

He grabbed a spray bottle. He could make himself useful and mist the gazebo plants. "Where's the blue Vanda? Did you move it?" The long-rooted, older Vanda, a blue-violet caerulea, wasn't on the side of the gazebo where he'd moved it the day before so it could catch the full morning sun. He cut across the deck for a closer look. The plant was on the ground. Two other orchids lay in cracked clay pots nearby.

"Are they dead?" Lara came over and squatted down to peer more closely at the plants like she saw him doing.

"Nope. How about asking your mom to come and take a look at this."

"Mom," she called toward the open sliders. "Eddieeee. Juliiii." Stu winced, realizing that by sending her, he'd saved on steps but not on volume.

He hadn't intended to make it a group effort, but all his instincts told him something was seriously peculiar. "Don't touch anything, just look at this," Stu cautioned them all when they came out.

"It could have been a squirrel or a cat. Or one of the opossums." Rikki tried to rationalize. But she made no move to clean it all up. "You guys get the juice glasses. We'll take care of this." She had Juli take Jake and Lara back in. "Keep them busy," she whispered.

"No squirrel did this." Eddie pointed to two vertical cracks in the lattice strips. Look." They'd been forced in until they snapped.

"It wasn't like this yesterday." Rikki's expression darkened.

"Something hit it on this side. The impact knocked the pots loose." Stu traced the action in the air.

"Pretty solid hit," Rikki said.

"Somethin' else," Eddie Sordo called them, staring at the ground farther along behind the trellis. "Remember me tellin' the kids to watch out for de fire ants. I put some dust on de mound out by the hose. They must'a moved here. Look.''

Curious to see what he'd discovered, Rikki started around his way with Stu right with her.

"Someone's been scuffin' round here." Sordo wagged his finger back and forth. In the soft edge of the mound there was a clear print of the heel portion of a shoe. The rest of the anthill looked like it had been stirred and stomped on. "Someone got a footfull." His hopeful smile stiffened and faded as he stood and checked around for more tracks. "You think it mighta' been that Trasher fella? He came 'round here to make trouble for you but de ants got 'im first?" he asked, standing and looking over the area with his hands propped on his hips. "Gotta thank de spirits for givin' 'im the what-for. Ol' Sulka over there been watchin' and keepin' you safe."

"You think it was him?" Rikki asked what they all were thinking.

"Could be." Stu stood, staring at the ant mound, wondering. If the Trasher had tried but bungled this attempt, would he leave them alone after this? "We'd better back off the way we came and have the police take a look at this."

Rikki gave the broken pots a thoughtful look. "I'll call." She checked the time on her watch. Then she smoothed back her hair, looked at the anthill, and sighed in frustration. "I'd better phone Leah and Tony and tell them we'll be held up."

"I have another idea." Stu stopped her. "I know this sounds strange, but I hate to see this mess up your day. Why don't you have breakfast and leave. I can do the rest," he offered. "You don't need to have police officers coming and getting the kids all worked up. After you folks take off, I can call and meet them here and make the report."

"I suppose that would work," Rikki answered. "Leah and Tony are counting on us to be there. Four volunteers makes a big difference."

"Then go. Makes sense to me," Stu said. "I planned to keep close to home anyway."

"I could stay," Sordo offered, a bit defensively.

"Eddie, we need you with us," Rikki told him. "Besides, you wanted seaweed for your compost. Stu can handle this."

Sordo frowned, apparently reluctant to leave Stu in charge.

"Really, I don't mind hanging around here." Stu wanted to ease the distress in the little fellow's expression. "I sure couldn't take your place on the cleanup squad, not with this thing." He patted his cast and tried to look more disabled than usual.

That seemed to make Sordo feel better. "Jus' tell 'em to be very careful. Don't want no one knocking anything down or stepping on the other plants while they look 'round. Police or no police."

"I'll do my best to keep them in line," Stu assured him.

"Okay. So let's eat breakfast, then we're off. Good. Let's get going," Rikki hustled them along. "Thanks again," she said softly, falling in step beside Stu and giving him a quick hug around his waist. For an instant he was startlingly aware how slim she felt. He wished there were a bit less of him to hug. Particularly around the middle.

Once they were out of sight, he called the police number and asked for Joe Warnock. Warnock wasn't on duty that morning. He had the weekend off. Stu called his home number. "I think we've got another possible. Come and take a look."

Warnock and two uniformed patrolmen arrived in separate cars. "Ballsy guy. Heading in with the sensor lights around. Surprised they didn't freak him out."

"They freaked us out," Stu told him. "We tried sitting out here, but every breeze and flutter triggered the damn things. We went in and watched TV and tried to ignore them. They kept going on and off all night until she finally shut them off."

"Looks like deck shoes," one officer with Detective Warnock pointed out when he studied the heelprint. "Too bad it hasn't rained this week. The rest of the ground is too hard for us to pick up where he came from or where he went."

"Contact the local doctors and the emergency rooms, just in case the guy went in for treatment," Warnock said. "Depending on how many bites he got and how his system reacts, he could end up real sick. I'd say locating someone with feet full of ant bites would narrow the field a bit," he noted, smoothing his moustache. "I don't think this guy is stupid enough to make himself conspicuous. Probably is suffering it through at home. Must hurt like hell. That's a day brightener," he added, liking that picture.

Beyond the area Warnock had marked with yellow tape, several officers were spiraling out, covering every foot of the peninsula.

"Found something. Looks like a canoe was dragged in over by the dock at the gray house." An officer who had been looking for tracks came back to report. "I spoke to the woman there. Patricia Simons. She said she doesn't own a boat of any kind. No one in that kind of boat visits there. She didn't hear or see a thing."

Stu and Warnock walked over to the Simons woman's backyard to look for themselves. "No good prints. Tide's been in since he was here. Sure looks like he must have been slipping and sliding." Warnock crouched over the few gouge marks in the softer ground near the shoreline.

"You think it's him?" Stu pressed.

"No way of telling." Warnock shrugged. "It's like the Greville thing. He didn't cut the phone lines. But he did it at the Abel-Smith place. Makes you wonder." Cutting the lines had been one detail of the Trasher's routine that the police had kept out of the news reports deliberately. "Any whacko could pick a name off the list of artists, pull some kind of stunt, and think he's fooling us. All we can do is pile up evidence, and we haven't much of that. We'll take a copy of the print by the Lundquist house. But we don't have another like it from the other sites. We got a couple of dress-shoe prints out of the Tampa hosing. Some fabric fiber on the window glass. Nothing at the other places. No fingerprints anywhere. The guy must wear some kind of gloves. Not very promising," he admitted. "We have to wait for him to screw up. Or for someone to make a connection."

"What about the hotel staff? Any breaks there?" Stu asked.

"We're still asking, still hoping. Got a couple of real sharp folks there who are keeping their ears to the ground," he reported. "One manager is keeping a close tab on the time cards. He's giving us the data and we're cross-checking with any Trasher action. If anything matches up, we're keeping track of it. Nothing yet."

"So we wait."

"You got it." Warnock agreed. "Not that you should bitch. Hell of a nice place to wait," he noted, turning back toward Rikki's house. He shielded his eyes from the mid-morning sun as he looked over the grounds. "Real tranquil out here."

"It was before all this crap started." Stu saw the neighbor, Pat Simons, watching them from the second-floor deck of her house. He waved. She waved back.

"So how are you getting along with the body you're guarding?" Joe Warnock peered up at Stu.

"We're getting along all right. Very well, in fact. I'm taking her out to dinner tonight."

"That a first?"

"Yeah."

Warnock's eyebrows lifted. "Has she figured out that you're smarter than you look?"

"I'm not sure what she's figured out."

"She doesn't know you're watching her?" Warnock asked.

"She knows I'm watching. Like a concerned neighbor. Maybe more concerned than most. She doesn't know how I got into this."

"Or that you and I talk?"

"Right. She doesn't know we talk."

"I'll remember that," Warnock assured him.

"Thanks."

After Warnock left, the police technicians finished taking a copy of the heelprint and loaded their gear in the police van and drove out. Stu carefully repotted and watered the two injured orchids and hung the Vanda back in the sheltered end of the slathouse to recover from the shock. He'd just brought out a couple of replacements and swept up when he heard the front doorbell ring.

"I came to pick up some lawn chairs for tonight." Pat Simons was on the front porch. "I saw the officers leave. How are things over here?" Near-white, close-cropped hair framed her well-tanned face. Rikki updated the woman almost daily about what was going on. From the way the woman seemed quite comfortable asking him instead, he guessed Rikki may have passed on some favorable comments about him as well.

"There wasn't any damage to speak of. Nothing that can't be fixed. The chairs are out back. I'll help you carry them over." Stu offered his somewhat limited assistance.

"So the police think we had a Peeping-Tom last night? Or did they decide it was the Trasher?"

"All that's certain is that someone was snooping around." Stu picked up a couple of chairs with his good arm. Pat picked two others. "It's likely that it was him. Whoever it was left with his feet all ant bitten." He steered through the fruit trees, careful not to snag his shirt on the sharp thorns on some of the branches.

"They told me to lock up and keep more lights on. They seem to think he'll be back."

"He might be. It's safest to go on the assumption that he'll try again. He didn't actually do anything here. Not intentionally," Stu added. "No telling what he had in mind. Don't let your guard down. We'll just continue keeping an eye on each other." He hoped to make it sound comforting.

"If he tried it tonight things would have been different." She set down the chairs she'd carried over, then took the ones he'd brought and arranged them on the patio. "Some friends and I are cooking shish-kabobs. On skewers about this long." She held up her hands about shoulder width. "Stainless steel," Pat added emphatically. "He'd have more than ant bites to worry about if he pulled into my dock tonight."

"We'd all like a crack at him," he said quietly. The Trasher had definitely chosen the most overgrown area to pull into. Stu looked over at the way the mangroves screened her dock. If he'd had two good arms, he'd have brought over lopping shears and trimmed them back a bit. "Nothing like closing the barn door . . ." He nagged at himself in frustration. Silently, he started back with her for the second load of chairs.

"I worry about the children," Pat confided, bustling along to keep up with his long-legged strides. "If I were Rikki, I'd just pack them up and go away until they get the fellow."

"That's just not her way of handling this," Stu replied. "She said she doesn't want to let anyone scare her off her own place."

"That's what she told me too." Pat nodded. "She has her principles. But I do worry. Too bad we can't put out those big net things you see in the jungle movies. You know, the ones that snatch you up in a sack when you step on them.'' She smiled as they walked along, clearly relishing the idea.

''Sooner or later, he'll slip up,'' Stu said trying to sound more confident that he felt. In all honesty, as unpredictable as the Trasher seemed to be, he wasn't sure what precautions might make a difference. He'd been mulling over other possibilities himself.

They carried one more set of chairs over, then he went in and made some phone calls. The first was to his answering machine. The second one was to Swede.

''When you put in those underground conduits, was there one out to the gate?''

''Yep. The wires from it are in a PVC pipe just like the others. Extra wires as well. We were planning to put in some fancy gate lights until Rikki vetoed the idea. She likes a lower profile. Why?''

''There's been a problem.'' He broke the news about the intruder and the orchids as gently as he could. Someone had been there. He might be back. Swede was absolutely silent for a few seconds after he finished.

''So much for the damn outside lights.''

''They might have had some impact. Any deterrent helps.''

''Hell of a deterrent,'' Swede muttered. ''You got any better ideas?''

''I'll just try hanging around there as much as I can,'' Stu said, ''and keep the place under tight surveillance. I may put in a couple of reserve lights they could hit if anything spooks them. Something that would work if the phones were out.''

''Is that why you were asking about the gate?''

''Right. If this guy has been watching the place, he may have figured out that at night the gate is locked and the police patrols only swing in the entry pulloff and sit awhile. I think it's necessary now to leave it unlocked so they push the release and drive through.''

''As often as possible,'' Swede agreed. ''I'll ask Ned Slone to see about beefing them up.''

Stu guessed Joe Warnock would have already taken care of that. ''Problem as I see it is that a patrol car is conspicuous. If seeing them circle through isn't enough to keep him out, with all the vegetation around, he could hide and wait them out,'' Stu noted. ''If Rikki spotted him or heard him and could trigger some visual warning at the gate, they could call for backup and come in on foot. They'd have a better chance of grabbing him if he didn't see them coming.''

''Good point,'' Swede acknowledged. ''But I don't want to put Rikki and the kids at any risk,'' he stressed. ''However, I'd really like to see this son of a bitch caught.''

''My thinking exactly. I won't take any chances with your family.'' Stu had been waffling back and forth himself, torn between the need to keep them safe and the desire to stop this guy for good. Driving him off from here would only make him somebody else's problem, and that didn't set well. ''There is another practical side of this,'' Stu added. ''The kids know not to open the door if her darkroom warning light is on. This could work the same way. If she got hung up and couldn't come out to meet the bus or if she felt uneasy and needed to warn the kids off, she could turn the switch on and they could high-tail to my place. I'd go over and check it out.''

''Sounds feasible. I sure don't want my grandkids walking into anything dangerous. This is one hell of a mess. Do whatever. Do something,'' Swede's voice rumbled. ''I'll try to come up with some ideas too.''

Stu drove by his condo, checked his mail, picked up his toolbox, and stopped for the electrical supplies he needed. He was back before noon ready to get to work.

''I've been watching.'' Pat Simons came over to see what he was doing. ''You've been working very hard. I fixed you some lemonade.''

''Thanks.'' He stepped back in the shade and took a swallow. He'd set an amber dome light on the gate, one on the end of the garage facing his place, and one inside the slathouse where he planned to spend more time so he'd be close. They all went on at once from a kitchen switch or one in her darkroom. If he wasn't with her at the house, he'd be somewhere where he'd be able to see one of them, day or night.

''You shouldn't overdo it.'' Pat eyed his sling and cast with genuine concern.

He didn't admit it, but her advice came a little late. He already ached. ''I'll ease off a bit,'' he promised. But he'd been focused on doing something, anything to help. Even burning off some of the tension helped. He wasn't sure how Rikki would react when he told her what he'd done.

"Do something . . ." Swede's words mirrored his own desperation. Even if she only used it until the creep was caught, he'd feel better knowing he'd made some effort to help. No doubt, so would Swede. But from the ache in his shoulder, Stu knew he was on the verge of royally screwing up his evening if he kept at it. If any of his better scenarios for his first real date with Rikki did start happening, he didn't want to be too incapacitated to function.

The other safeguard he'd set up, the bionic ear, he couldn't mention to her at all without having to explain how he had access to that kind of surveillance equipment. But if anyone got in her house and made a noise or if any crisis arose, he could hear whatever was being said or pick up any sounds, irregular or otherwise. He didn't like the word eavesdrop, and, he was sure, neither would she.

"Stu, this is Rikki." She phoned him at four-thirty that afternoon to check in. They'd finished at the beach and had stopped for ice cream before heading on to Swede's. He'd just stepped out of a very hot shower, hoping the pulsing water would head off a problem with his back. "What happened with the police?"

He didn't take it personally that that was topmost on her mind. Logically the update had to come before romance. He caught her up quickly about the canoe marks near Pat's, the footprint in the anthill, who had come, and what was said. He didn't sugarcoat what Detective Warnock and his men concluded. He even told her that Warnock said to operate under the assumption that it was the Trasher and he would be back, maybe by water again. But since he was unpredictable and had run into one disaster there, he may use some other route.

She was silent a moment, like her father had been when he heard the details.

"I'm glad you stayed, and I'm glad we left," she told him. "It was wonderful getting out in the sun and making some real progress."

"Good." He smiled to himself, having had a similar feeling, until the shoulder twinge. Even now, he didn't regret the work he'd put in. Whether it made a decisive difference or not, he'd accomplished something.

"I guess I'd better get on to Dad's now. We can talk about this later."

"Or not," he said hopefully.

"Or not," she agreed, with a smiling sound. "See you later."

"You bet."

At six-thirty, she called again, apparently from next door. "I saw you got everything cleaned up out back. Thanks for taking care of the plants."

"No problem."

"Jake is sick. I think he could have a case of the flu." He was sorry about the youngster, but by the disappointment in her voice, he guessed the plans they'd made for the evening were shot to hell. "He may just have gotten too much sun today, or it may be all the hot dogs he ate too fast at my dad's, or the ice cream, or all of the above. Anyway, he started throwing up at Dad and Ivey's, so I decided I'd better bring both kids home and put them in their own beds tonight. I'm really sorry about dinner."

"You mean you ate already?" He wasn't ready to admit total defeat.

"No. Food isn't a priority at times like this. But I can grab something here eventually."

"Not a chance. How about you get things there settled the best you can taking care of Jake. I'll make a run to pick up some Mexican food. Chilli rellenos, fajitas, tortilla chips and cheese dip? I'll come over in a couple of hours. Eight-thirty? Out back. Just the two of us."

There was a brief silence. Then something that sounded like a sigh. "That sounds wonderful, Sullivan." She was tired and worried about her son. She was pleased he was stepping in to help.

"See you then. You need some ginger ale or anything to settle his stomach?" he asked her just before he hung up. "My mom always gave me ginger ale and potato chips."

"He might like that."

"How's Lara? Is she sick too?"

"She seems to be fine. Very tired. She's upstairs taking a bath."

"I'll get her some frozen yogurt. She likes that."

"You'll spoil her."

"I'll just bring it. You can spoil her."

"Nice maneuver, Sullivan. Thanks again." He could tell by her voice that she was feeling better than when this conversation started.

Rikki must have seen him coming. She met him at the door.

"You look great." He meant it as a thank you. He'd showed up in his shorts, sports shirt, and tennis shoes. She was wearing a dress like the one she'd worn when Prince Charming came to take her out, with a full floaty skirt and a neckline that showed off a slightly pinker tan than she'd left with. She'd pulled back her hair and twisted it so it fell in soft spirals down her back.

"You said it's a real date . . ." she reminded him.

On the deck, she'd lit the candles and set the table with a linen cloth and napkins, silverware and china plates. Everything was glistening. Two large crystal goblets were set out by a pitcher of chilled red wine with ice and sliced fruit layered in it.

She was barefoot. He liked that part the best.

She caught him up on the beach cleanup campaign while they cycled each packet of food into the microwave, unwrapped it, and transferred it to china bowls. She set out compotes of salsa and sliced chilled avocado. And she opted not to activate the motion-sensitive lights so they wouldn't ruin the atmosphere.

When they finally sat down to eat, Stu let out a contented sigh. He felt remarkably at home there. With her. He could imagine doing this again and again, for years and years. And it amazed him that he felt so settled, and they still hadn't even held each other or kissed.

Only when she thanked him for repotting the orchids did he realize he hadn't brought up the rest of it. "I was trying to cover a few contingencies we may not have considered," he began, carefully explaining the small warning lights and how they could help alert him or the police, especially if the phone lines were cut.

"I was also thinking that for the time being, the lights would give the kids a specific signal that everything is okay at home. Or not."

Her fork stopped in midmotion at that.

Rikki mostly listened and nodded. Her solemn, dark eyes didn't leave his for an instant. She didn't register any objection to anything he'd done. Somehow, he felt, the food and the cozy, almost festive atmosphere, and the fact that Lara and Jake were sleeping comfortably upstairs, made it easier to talk about security precautions. While everything was peaceful, they'd tackle that other reality.

"You think that's really necessary? I could make sure someone always meets them." Rikki stared across the table at him.

"He was here. He'll be back. This is just a little extra insurance. The lights are just backup measures. I don't think you should take any chances with this guy loose," Stu answered honestly. "When this is over, I can rip out anything that you don't want. But until then, I'm asking you to stay one step ahead of him. I don't want anything happening to you or the kids."

She leveled a thoughtful look at him. "Okay." She said it softly. With a touch of resignation. But there was a trace of something else.

"I have to tell you something."

Now his fork stopped.

"Actually, I have to show you something. I'll be back." He waited.

"This is for you." She put a box on the table. "And this is for me." She had an identical one. "My dad got them. Cellular phones. So we're never out of touch."

Stu stared at his, feeling incredibly stupid. He should have come up with that solution himself. But he'd been too focused on details to step back and consider a broader solution. He'd used muscle more than brain.

"I appreciate your efforts today. I really do." She rested her hand on his arm. "And I'll give the warning lights a try." He knew she was trying to make him feel better.

"But this is a hell of a lot simpler," he acknowledged.

"And ridiculously expensive if it weren't for the circumstances," she added. "But having the phones wouldn't be so valuable if you weren't near to pick up on the other end. You make a lot of this easier for me, Sullivan. Probably more than you realize."

He nodded. He didn't trust himself to speak. He'd gone from feeling ridiculous to ecstatic in the time it took to draw a breath.

"Regardless of all the precautions you and my dad have initiated, you've been my safelight around here, Sullivan. I'm not totally comfortable with that. But it's true."

He could live with that just fine.

Shortly before eleven, they'd started clearing away the dishes when the upstairs light went on.

"That's Lara's room." Rikki went in to check on the youngster.

When he shuttled some leftovers into the kitchen, Stu could hear her talking to someone, a toilet flushed, water ran, and she didn't come back right away. He went out again and waited. When she did return, she was more subdued than she'd been through dinner. "Looks like it's Lara's turn," she announced. "Whatever Jake had seems to have hit her. I'm glad you brought the extra chips and soda." He studied the concern etched in her face.

"Is there anything I can do?"

She shook her head and noticed he'd cleared away the remnants of their Mexican feast. "No. I'm just glad that whatever she's got held off this long. This was really lovely. And I wish it didn't have to end like this. But I think I'd better go up and sit with her awhile."

"I'll lock up downstairs and clear this away. I think I'll turn on the strobes before I go home," he offered. "I can handle that much."

"Thanks. You're a good man, Sullivan," Rikki replied. "I wasn't sure about you at first. But you've turned out to be a real softie. I'm really glad you came along."

"Me too."

She reached up and gently stroked the side of his jaw, trailing her fingers over his trimmed beard. "Thanks for tonight. And thanks for all the work you did around here today. See you tomorrow." She reached up and brushed her lips, feather light, across his. "Don't forget to take your phone home and read the directions."

He watched her turn and go inside. Most of what he'd done earlier had come naturally, out of some genuine concern. But much of it was selfishness, simply wanting to spend time with her or wanting to please her. If that translated into being a "softie," then the role was becoming instinctive.

He blew out the candles, carried in and rinsed the dishes and put them in the dishwasher, turned on the motion-sensitive floodlights, and locked the door behind him when he left. He even left a note that he'd taken some fruit for the bird squadron's breakfast Sunday so neither she nor Lara would have to worry about getting up early the next day.

But he didn't sweep or take out the garbage. There was such a thing as being too good to be true.

On Tuesday afternoon, Stu got a call from Rikki on his cellular phone. He had it with him on Ash's sundeck while he oiled and adjusted the stationary bike and kept watch on the compound. She was in her darkroom.

"Hi. Can you see the bus stop?"

"Sure can."

"Is Juli out there?"

"Nope. I thought she was working with you. Her car's still there." Juli Quinn's car had been there since eleven that morning. They'd been working together, finishing up some photos for Rikki's class at the Art Institute class that night.

"I know she didn't leave. But I asked her to fix the kids a snack and meet them at the gate. Not necessarily in that order. I just wanted to make sure she got out there before the bus arrived."

"She didn't."

"Would you . . ."

"I'm on my way."

"Hi, guys." Stu greeted the youngsters at the gate. "Your mom asked me to meet you. How about we call her and let her know you're coming in. She's in the darkroom." He handed the cellular phone to Jake.

"It's busy."

"What number did you call?"

"The old one."

Stu tried the cellular number. No one answered.

"I think you two had better come cool your heels at my place while and I'll go on ahead see what's up over there. Seems to be a glitch in our connection." He said it casually, calmly, without giving them any indication of the alarms going off inside him.

He let the youngsters in and pulled out a bag of grapes and two sodas. "Stay here and fix yourselves a drink. I'll be back." He stuck the cellular phone in his belt and left, pausing long enough on the way through to pick up a five-iron from the bag of golf clubs stored in Ash's hall closet.

"Hi. It's me again. Did you just try to get me?" Rikki rang him up before he'd made it halfway there.

"Yes. What the heck happened? One line was busy. And

you didn't answer the other.'' He felt as if the rollercoaster he'd been on just banked and dropped speed. ''Are you all right?''

''I'm fine. I had my hands full. Sorry.'' He could hear her moving something. ''I used the other phone here a while ago. I guess it wasn't sitting flat on the cradle. Have you got the kids?''

''They're at my place. I didn't know what the hell was going on over here.''

''You haven't seen Juli yet?''

''Nope. I'll take a look around. You stay put.'' He circled the house cautiously, peering in the windows, stopping to listen for any sound. He saw no one, and noticed nothing out of place. He crossed the lanai. The back sliders were locked. He checked the slathouse, locked as well. Finally he came almost full circle along the walkway past the kitchen window. He tried that door. It opened.

He raised the club over one shoulder and slowly pushed the door open. ''Juli?''

''Watch out! Don't come in.'' Juli Quinn called out from somewhere inside. His cellular unit beeped. He reared back.

''I'll call you back,'' he answered and clicked off.

''Juli, are you all right?'' He shoved the kitchen door open wider with the golf club. Even then he couldn't see her. ''Where are you?''

''I'm down here.''

He stepped in, not knowing what he'd see.

It was more ludicrous than tragic. She was on her hands and knees with wads of soggy dishtowels and a roll of paper ones, trying to dam up a pool of milk. Several wet sandwiches, like whole-wheat islands, were scattered across the floor. ''I had an accident.'' She was spattered with milk. ''I had everything on a tray and was trying to put the milk away. I set it on the top of the fridge and pulled the door but the jug toppled, caught the edge of the tray, and sent everything all over.''

''What's going on?'' Rikki came charging from the darkroom. She had her tripod battle-ax again. ''Did you find her?'' She came up behind him.

''She's all right. Some milk spilled.'' He let out a burst of air, exasperated with both of them. ''You were supposed to stay in the darkroom just now.'' He turned and snapped at Rikki. "You could have run smack into this lunatic who's lurking around."

"So?"

"So damn it, you could get hurt that way," his tone was both tense and aggravated.

Her jaw took on a firmer set. "Two people I care about could have been in danger," she said with unexpected calm. "Don't kid yourself. I'm not going to sit back and wait while anything happens to either of you. I could have helped."

They stared at each other across a sudden silence. There was something in her tone Stu hadn't heard before, something distinctly Olivia Melloesque, without the Kewpie lips. The anxious, determined look on her face told him she was apprehensive, but she wasn't about to back down, not to him, not to anyone.

"Did the kids get in all right?" Juli asked in a small voice. "Please say they did."

"They did," Rikki told her, with just a trace of breathiness.

"Sorry." Juli scrambled to her feet. "I should have left this. I got so flustered I started cleaning up instead. I did something dumb, didn't I?" Juli wrung her hands. They smelled like peanut butter. "I'm sorry." She grimaced.

"It's okay," Rikki reassured her. "Stu was there to come to the rescue. He went and got them. But next time, leave the mess. Leave anything. Just go for the kids," she stressed. "Or let me know and I'll go for them. We're all in this together. We can't make mistakes. We can't leave anything to chance. And we have to back each other up. There are no other rules at times like these."

Stu felt the tension suddenly go out of him. She was right. Keep the kids safe. Back up your friends. Despite the possible danger she could be in, he had no right to stop her from coming to the rescue, his or anyone else's.

"I'd better get the kids," Stu said. "I'll tell them it's all right. We just seem to have a few bugs in the system." He took a couple of steps toward Ash's house where Lara and Jake were waiting. "I'm sorry I snapped at both of you. I was out of line." He strode off to get the youngsters.

"That man really likes you a lot," Juli said once Stu was out of earshot. "He was almost shaking when he talked to you. He was really worried. It's so romantic."

"He is rather protective. A bit like my dad in that respect," Rikki replied, watching the backview as Stu strode across the grassy area between her house and Ash's. Barefoot, shirtless, broad shouldered, he reminded her of pictures she'd seen of Swede on some of his early expeditions. "I think the tension is getting to all of us."

"I'll say. I'm not usually such a klutz," Juli said, glancing with apparent distaste at the puddle on the kitchen floor.

"At least we've got our work to get our minds off this Trasher business once in a while. He doesn't even have that kind of diversion. He doesn't even have his own furniture or whatever to go home to." Rikki reflected a moment. "I'd really like to see him in his own surroundings. Partly for his sake. Partly for mine."

Juli gave her a quizzical look. "How's that?"

"You can tell a lot about someone by looking at where he lives and where he works."

"Why don't you ask him? Ask him to take you to his house," Juli said simply. "Or to that nursery business he has. You like places like that."

"I'd rather he'd ask me," Rikki replied. "Someone has to want to let you in. He's the one who has to make the effort." She was still watching Stu with her steady, contemplative gaze. "When it's important enough for him to fill in the empty spaces, he'll do it. He has to make the move and invite me into his home and his business. He has to decide when it's time to have me meet his friends."

"I just don't have your kind of patience," Juli groaned. "I'd look his address up in the phone book. I'd at least drive by."

"I've already done that," Rikki responded with a sly grin. "I'm not that complacent."

"So . . . ?"

"Nice condo. Second floor. It has a garage underneath. Overlooks Phillipi Creek. Pretty location. Only one name on the mailbox."

"Ah-hah!" Juli crowed. "You do like him."

"I like him," Rikki acknowledged. "I just have the feeling that there's a lot more to know about him. I hope that when I find out what it is, I like it too."

"You've always had pretty good instincts about people," Juli noted. "I think it's just awfully hard to have a romance in a war zone. Especially with the kids to worry about."

"It has been interesting around here," Rikki acknowledged.

"If there's ever anything I can do to help, just ask," Juli offered. "If he doesn't get around to taking you home soon and if you ever need privacy here, you know, just the two of you," she said, wriggling her eyebrows, "I'll be glad to sit on the babes at my place some night. Mom would love it if they could sleep over."

"I may take you up on that. Here come my babes now." Rikki glanced at the trio sauntering back toward them. Whatever Stu had said to them had certainly dissipated any anxiety Lara and Jake may have had over the phone business. They were grinning and talking, one on either side of the tall, broad-shouldered, bearded man. Stu had something in a brown paper bag.

"Speaking of babes, for an older guy, Mr. Sullivan is still pretty much of a babe, in a cute way," Juli observed. "The beard is definitely sexy."

"I think it's a relatively new addition. Or maybe he just isn't real adept at trimming it one handed."

"I wonder what he'd look like without it. Or if he'd act differently with it shaved off?" Juli speculated, fluttering her hand to her chest dramatically. "You know, like maybe he has different beard and no-beard personalities, like a werewolf, or Jekyll and Hyde."

"Down, girl. You're getting a bit wound up over this," Rikki cautioned her. Lara broke loose from the others and bounded toward them.

"Maybe the beard covers a scar. Like the mask in *Phantom of the Opera*?"

Rikki shushed her again.

"Mr. Sullivan said this was like having a fire drill at school," Lara said excitedly. "He said we did really good. But he said we needed refueling with ice cream."

"He did?" Rikki laughed. She didn't have to ask what was in the bag as she led the entourage inside.

"And cookies," Jake added from behind her. "He brought chocolate-covered fudge Oreos. He says ice cream isn't decadent enough without cookies."

"I figured its better they eat them than I do," Stu said in self-defense.

"What does decadent mean?" Jake piped up again.

"It means beyond-your-wildest-dreams-super-incredibly

good," Juli proclaimed with an elaborate flourish of hands and elbows. "It means it's so good that anyone who knows what you're eating absolutely sweats with envy, wishing they were you."

"Really? Mom? Is it?" Lara asked.

"When it comes to food, I think that's a reasonable approximation of decadent," Rikki said, laughing as she held the door open wide and let everyone pass through. "Watch the milk," she called out, just a few seconds to late. "Forget it. We'll get it later," she said, bypassing the whitish trail of footprints.

The first time Rikki noticed the low bass boat out on the Intracoastal, she'd gone up through the shutter house above her bedroom to water the pots of asparagus fern she had set out on the rooftop sundeck. She glanced down at the boat when the fellow steered it close to shore and slowed a bit. Fishermen did that. They putted in close, looking for a place to anchor or occasionally drift. Still, she hated the tremor that something so familiar could set off.

Downstairs later, she noticed him coming back the other way. At least the motor sounded similar. He kept going. By the time something nagged at her to look more closely, her view of the craft was obstructed by the mangroves.

The third time, she'd just walked into her production room upstairs to work with some of the slides from the beach the day of the cleanup. She started spreading them out on the light table, peering at them through a glass loupe. That same droning motor insinuated its way into her consciousness, lingering there, not like one of the powerful outboards that stayed well out in the channel. She'd learned to tune them out since they passed quickly.

This one putted along. Aggravating. Persistent. And familiar. She checked her watch, then she picked up one of her cameras, one with a 300mm telephoto lense. She had a clear line from the bedroom.

She focused, bringing him close enough to recognize the logo on his baseball hat. Buccaneers. He wasn't carrying fishing gear. And he was looking at the house with binoculars. She felt her stomach constrict. It was schoolbus time. She took three shots, just in case, then ducked behind the blinds.

"Stu. This is Rikki." He recognized her voice, only to-day it was almost whispery and a bit anxious.

"What's up?" He glanced at Ash's wall clock. It was almost time for the kids to get dropped off. He figured she might be calling from the darkroom to ask him to meet them for her.

"There's a guy in a boat out back. No one I recognize. He's got an orange Buccaneers baseball cap on, no gear. He's gone by a couple of times. He was looking up here with binoculars. I took some pictures. He just went by again." She paused, listening.

"What's the matter?"

"He cut the motor off. He's behind some mangroves, and I think he's drifting back, coming in. Will you meet the kids again and keep them from coming here?"

"What are you going to do?" he asked.

"I'm not sure. Watch him and see what he does, I guess. Take a few more shots with my telephoto. Even if he's just looking around, I want his face as proof that he was here. He's not being particularly sneaky, but I don't want to take any chances."

"Me neither. Let me help handle this," he insisted. "You just lock yourself in. I'll get the kids settled then I'll be there. We'll check him out together."

"Gotta go. I can see him. He's at the dock." She hung up.

This time, when he met Jake and Lara at the gate, Stu wasn't as calm as he'd been before. "Hustle." He grabbed their books and made them run.

"Is this another drill?" Lara huffed and puffed.

"Sort of," he moved them along quickly. "Nothing major. Just someone snooping around the dock. Your mom's safe." He got the kids in Ash's house. "You know the routine. Help yourselves. Just stay put." While they were busy getting drinks, Stu slid his handgun in his sling with the cast. If this guy had balls enough to come in by daylight and ignore the "Private" sign on the dock, Stu figured the level of combat may have escalated. He wasn't going in underarmed. "I'll be back." He locked the doors after him. He dialed 911 on the way over, so the kids wouldn't hear the call.

Rikki had locked the production room, then inched her way down the stairs with the camera in one hand and a tall but solid Tiki in the other. From where she was, she couldn't tell how close to the house the stranger had come. She was pretty sure the sliders were locked, but she didn't want to walk over there and find out otherwise. She'd wait for Stu, then they'd confront him together.

She sat on the lower landing, hoping to fire off a few more shots if he stepped into view. Evidence. That's what Detective Warnock said they needed. If she could, she'd get him something sufficiently incriminating.

She could see the shadow on the back deck. He was there, out by the trellised gazebo that enclosed the spa. The interior blinds along the sliders on that end obscured the view.

"Damn him," she muttered. He was with her orchids. Again. She gritted her teeth and moved closer, dragging the Tiki along with her for protection. Then she heard men's voices. One was Stu's. She moved closer to the doors. More talking. Quieter. Not angry. And a laugh. So she came out into the open where she could see what was going on.

Their stance was too relaxed to suggest any conflict between the two. The other man, sandy-haired like Sullivan, was almost as tall. Now that he was standing and had his hat off, she didn't think he fit the Trasher description at all. Stu saw her and gave her a thumb's up. "It's okay. I know this guy. He was looking for me."

Rikki left her camera and the Tiki on the dining-room table and tried the doors, relieved that she had actually locked them as she'd hoped.

"Rikki, this is Brian. My brother. Rikki Lundquist. Brian Sullivan. I'd told him I was housesitting out here," Stu explained as he introduced them. "I was just chewing him out for not giving me a call so I could have met him."

"It was sort of spur of the moment. Friend of mine has a place across the way and a boat. I knew I'd found the right peninsula, but I wasn't sure if it was this house or the next one. I couldn't see his car," the slightly younger, slimmer, and clean-shaven version of Stu apologized. "I was being careful coming in. I figured he'd have the whole place booby trapped."

"Not likely," Stu said, quickly, seemingly anxious to get off the subject.

"Sure you don't have a couple of closed-circuit TV cameras planted somewhere?" Brian looked up and waved at the rear security lights, pretending they were being taped.

"No cameras," Stu said stiffly. He could hear the crunch of car tires on the shell drive out front. "But I called the cops." He'd left the gate wide open for them. "We'd better go out front and talk to them," he said, catching his brother by the arm. He sounded anxious to whisk Brian off.

"You mind if I look around the slathouse later?" Brian called over his shoulder. "Stu told me about your orchid collection."

"Sure. Look around. We need to let the kids know everything here is fine. Should I call over?"

"I'll take care of it." Stu grimaced, realizing he'd forgotten about the youngsters. "I'll round them up and send them home. Come on, Bri." He urged his brother along. "I wanted to give Brian a look at Ash's house anyhow." Stu took a few steps then paused. "Bri, let's go."

They met one officer coming around the side. "Nothing wrong after all," he told the man, explaining that his brother docked at the wrong house and was the stranger Rikki had spotted.

A second officer had gone around the other way and came up behind them. "No problem," the fellow agreed. But they both seemed more disappointed that the Trasher wasn't there than they were put off by a false alarm.

At Ash's, Stu introduced his brother to the kids and gave them a less dramatic rendition of the goings-on, then he watched them as they crossed to their house. "Heck of a location," Brian observed, looking out the kitchen windows.

"I've got binocs up on the bedroom deck. Go up and take a look." Stu steered his brother toward the stairway. "Incredible view. I'll be right up." Stu put his handgun back in the kitchen cabinet, got a Diet Coke for each of them, and followed.

"Okay, what's going on. Why the rush?" Brian nailed him when his brother joined him up top.

Stu tried giving him a blank look along with the coke. It didn't work.

"You almost yanked me off her deck. Then you run me upstairs. What's up?"

"Nothing."

"Are you afraid that if I talk with the blonde, I'd say something in front of her that might cramp your style?" Bri guessed, only part teasing.

"Of course not." Stu gave him one of his slightly bored expressions.

"What's the story?" he said, studying Stu's immobile profile. "My guess is . . ." He drew it out, hoping to see some emotion register. "You're in deep water and going down." He paused long enough to take a long pull on the cool soda. The comment made his brother's jaw muscle dance. He took that as a yes. "So. Talk to me. Or is it just that you're embarrassed to claim me? You don't want her to know the black sheep of the family?" Brian dogged him.

"I thought I was the black sheep." Stu kept staring out over the trees at a low cigarette boat cruising past on the Intracoastal Waterway.

"That was last year. Odd-numbered years, I'm the black sheep," Brian countered amiably. "And don't get side-tracked by technicalities. What's the story on you and the Nordic Princess?" Stu had used that term to him, almost three weeks earlier, during the negotiations with Swede Lundquist, the mayor, and Harrison Ash. In the phone calls since, Brian had detected a distinct shift in his brother's attitude. "Does she always dress like that?"

Stu had become so accustomed to seeing Rikki in a bathing suit top and tropical print pareu, he hadn't registered anything unusual about the outfit she had on today. Mostly purple, as he recalled, but it was the same style wrap skirt and bandeau top she generally wore to work in at home. "Just around here. She wears other clothes when she goes out."

"You've gone out with her?" Brian prodded him.

"Nope. Not yet."

"But you'd like to?" Brian took another sip of soda. "Come on, Stu. Make this a little easier," he said simply, tiring of playing question and no answer. "What's with you two?"

"I'm not sure. Nothing has happened yet."

"Nothing has happened? You came around the corner like a grizzly back there. Then you give me the rush job? And nothing's happening? Come on. Have you got her in the sack yet?"

"Nothing like that. Let's just say I don't want anything to mess this up."

"So she hasn't exactly told you no? But she hasn't said yes." Brian grinned. "You think it's the beard that's putting her off?'' He kept ragging him, good naturedly. ''Think she might like the smooth *GQ* look better?''

''It's a bit more philosophical than that.'' Stu licked his lips, choosing his words carefully. ''I really like this woman. We've been talking mostly. She doesn't play games. She won't let me confuse sex with intimacy.''

''Aahh.'' Brian took off the baseball cap, smoothed his hair, then put it back on. ''Are you in deep shit. A real grown-up,'' he commented, this time without the joking overtone. ''That's how Vicky operated. Once all the signals went off and the hormones started dancing, she put on the brakes. There was no fooling around. She wanted to be sure I was serious before she put any time into getting involved. It took me a while to come around. You know how I was.''

Stu nodded. He remembered very clearly how his younger brother had been. Good looking, a good athlete, a good dancer, but a student who sidestepped the rules, Brian had gone through high school with a string of girls, assistant principals, and coaches after him. He'd squeaked by with mediocre grades in everything but science and phys. ed. He'd been voted most popular, largely by the female vote.

In his first semester at junior college, he'd met Vicky Anne Calvert, a slim, intelligent, pretty young woman who told him not to bother her until he grew up. He decided he was wasting his teachers' time, withdrew, and joined the Navy. Three years later, he came back from his hitch in the service and called Vicky Calvert again. He'd taken some college classes in the Navy. He'd made all A's. He was starting over at the junior college, studying botany and planning to go into the landscaping business. This time, she figured he was serious enough. She'd taken a chance.

''I was wrong about the Nordic Princess bit,'' Stu said, spacing his thoughts. ''She's not cold or aloof. The princess part was close. She's got class and money, but she's real down to earth.'' He kept talking, still focusing on the strip of water between Siesta Key and the city of Sarasota farther east. ''She used to be a social worker. She worked with a lot of abuse cases, so she knows life isn't all rosy. She wasn't tough enough for the job. So she uses her photography for something she calls visual therapy, to help people who've been abused physically and emotionally.''

''That's what the sensual art thing is all about?''

''That's it.''

The two of them stood there for a while, saying nothing.

"Mom said she thought something was different with this one. She could hear it in your voice. Then you talked a lot about the work the Princess did. You don't usually get that interested," Brian remarked. "Easy come, easy go." He gave the exercise bike on the deck a long look, tapped the diet drink, then grinned. "Women . . ." he sighed, then took a long drag from the can. "You going to let Mom meet her?"

"I think so."

"Any time soon?"

"Depends on how things go here." Stu could see Rikki out back by the dock where Brian's boat was tied up. She was setting up her sailboard, ready to go windsurfing a while. Getting close to the wind.

"Would help if they caught that guy."

"That would take the pressure off her. Off both of us." It was one thing keeping Brian updated on the investigation, the nocturnal trespasser and the anthill. And a possible re-match. But he couldn't put into words yet how much this woman mattered to him.

He couldn't tell his brother that he stayed up most of the night watching her house. And sometimes he went down in the dark and sat on the lanai, smelling her orchids while she and her children slept. Or that without her knowing it, he'd stood guard in the dark when she went skinny dipping in the waterway at night. But not lately. That late swim was something she'd given up since the night the orchid pots were knocked down. He still had vivid memories of her climbing out of the water, wet and naked, with the black tattoo around her thigh.

He couldn't tell Brian how he could feel her hands all night after she'd given him a massage, or say how good it felt to rub her feet and talk and go home and shower to cool down from wanting her.

He had a feeling Brian would have understood, though. He and Vicky had been married twelve years, and they still held hands.

"What's the thing on her leg? Brian said quietly. He had the binoculars up, watching Rikki on her sailboard, cutting across the wake of a boat.

"A tattoo."

"Never saw one like that."

"It's almost a religious thing. From the Pacific. It's a tribute to her mother."

Brian watched her a while longer, then caught a sidelong glance at the way Stu was following her path, his eyes narrowed.

"Like moving to the major leagues?"

"I'll say." Stu smiled.

"Love's a bitch. But it sure beats the hell out of everything else."

Stu nodded.

"You take care of yourself while you're taking care of this one."

"I'm trying."

"So I see." He'd found out what he'd wanted to know. Now he was ready to check out the flowers.

"Tomorrow night we can try again," Rikki promised Stu when he tried to schedule an evening out to make up for the night the kids were ill. "I'll tell the Gramma and Grampa they can have the little dears for the night."

"Great. What do you want to do until then?"

"I thought we'd just stay home and do something low key. The kids need a little close time here at home."

"I can understand that." He needed a little close time too, with her, anywhere. Everyone was tense. The Trasher hadn't hit in nine days, a longer space than any of the previous ones. It had been almost a week since the fire-ant incident out back. She and Olivia Mello had been calling each other a couple of times each day, checking that everything was tranquil and to offer some words of support. But they were all apprehensive.

"Do you want to come over? We've got a Disney film and popcorn, nothing exciting. But if you don't mind loafing around in front of the TV, you're welcome to watch the movie with us."

"I'll be over. Thanks."

Throughout the evening, Stu made sure the back blinds were open and the lights were on. He walked back and forth to the kitchen a few more times than necessary, deliberately pausing in front of the windows in case anyone was looking in. Cast or not, he was a big man, an added obstacle to deal with. Rikki was no frail female. Either one could take on someone the Trasher's size. He wasn't likely to move on both of them.

"Everything's locked. Leave the sensors on outside," he cautioned her when she let him out the door late that night. "I'll feed the boys tomorrow. You and Lara sleep in. I want her going to her grandparents in real good health."

"Will do. See you tomorrow." Rikki locked the door behind him and left the front light on and all the motion sensitive ones, just as he'd suggested. As he crossed the clearing, Stu noticed Pat Simons outside lights were on as well. Bright patches of light surrounded her place, illuminating the ground and the under side of the house. But the bright patches made the dark periphery seem much darker. Outside those harsh, unnatural blotches, the surrounding shrubs and trees looked more ominous, more solid, more dense than before.

"Son of a bitch." He headed home for a late date with his binoculars and the bionic ear. "Son of a bitch." Stu was still muttering as he gathered his surveillance paraphernalia and headed upstairs. They were waiting for the next shoe, again. The guy had a closet full.

By midnight, Stu was wrapped in a blanket, huddled in a lounge chair on the upstairs balcony with the big ear aimed at her house. He heard nothing. When he caught himself nodding off the third time, he knew he wasn't going to be able to stay awake all night. Not even out there.

He took the key to her house from Ash's row of hooks. Carrying the blanket and the cellular phone, he wound his way through the yard to her house. The floodlights had been blinking off and on for hours. He didn't even try to duck them. He just let himself in with it like he'd done before when he came to get the boys' fruit. Then he locked the door again.

Inside, there was only one way for an intruder to get to her and the kids, by the open curving stairway from the foyer to the gallery above. So he padded a space behind the lower stairs with a couple of pillows from the sofa, set the alarm on his wristwatch for five-thirty in the morning, sprawled out, covered himself with the blanket, and closed his eyes.

Stu wasn't sure what made his skin bristle or what had prodded him from sleep. But when he opened his eyes, he knew someone was in the house. Moving. He listened.

Upstairs, the toilet flushed. He thought it might be one of the kids. He settled back, trying to sleep again, then he realized that something else was making him uneasy. He'd fallen asleep with the outside lights flicking on and off erratically, making the closed blinds across the back sliders glow. Now those lights were off, the blinds were pulled back, and Rikki was standing in the dark, looking out. She turned and walked into the kitchen.

She had nothing on except the pareu, this time tied over her breasts so it floated all around her. But when she opened the refrigerator door and stood framed in the light, the filmy garment turned transparent. Stu watched, vascillating between wanting to say something and wanting only to enjoy this strangely tranquil time.

If he spoke up now, he'd scare the hell out of her. He'd have to explain a lot. Like how the heck he got in. Even he didn't like the idea of saying he'd taken Ash's key and used it to come into her home in the dark, without her permission. He scooted on the blanket back into the stairwell so she wouldn't see him when she went back up. And he stayed still.

She came back and stood by the back sliders a long time, sipping orange juice and looking out toward the dock.

She paced. Like a caged lioness, tawny and beautiful. He guessed she was thinking about swimming, about going out alone and diving in. She rinsed her glass and came back. She was carrying a towel and the cellular phone. She picked up the Tiki figure from the table, unlocked the slider, stepped out on the lanai, stood listening a moment, then she carefully closed only the screens behind her. She patted the prong-tailed Oscar.

Stu scrambled to his knees, stunned that she'd take any risks at all at this point. But she stayed close. She took a sharp right, settling for the spa instead of the Intracoastal.

There was an edge of defiance to her actions, but he had to admit she wasn't completely reckless. She stayed nearby. She had the phone with her. And a Tiki for a battle-ax if it came to needing one. She didn't turn on the heater or the bubbles. There wasn't a sound. She peeled off the pareu and slipped in, keeping the Tiki and the phone next to her on the ledge.

She only stayed in a matter of minutes. Then she stepped out, wrapped up, and came back in, carrying all her paraphernalia with her. Secure inside, she left the wooden sculpture by the door and shook loose the damp pareu. When she passed him on the way upstairs, with the pareu dangling from one hand and the phone in the other, he could still see stripes of water on her naked body. The black tattoo gleamed like a beaded jet garter.

He listened to the footsteps growing more faint and he knew she had gone back to her indigo bed. He was left in the dark, wide awake, his heart racing, staring at damp footprints on the stair tread.

It had been fascinating watching her. At first, there was a sense of unreality to it, an element of theater, like seeing a pantomine on stage. But ultimately the beauty of it was darkened by an undeniable edge of violation. The star of this show wasn't an actress, and she hadn't been aware that she was being watched at all.

He'd become a voyeur, he accused himself. Now it was over, the ethics of this one-sided drama tonight made him distinctly uncomfortable. She had once said, quite clearly, she liked men with noble feelings. He thought he had a few of them. Even now. But regardless of the nobility of his intent, he'd let the Trasher and his own fear push him farther than he had the right to go.

McIver had a few quick shots of scotch before he drove to Englewood. He tucked the bottle under the front seat and took it along. He passed through Jessup's subdivision just as it was getting dark, making a quick appraisal of the situation there. Lights in the front were already on. Except for a couple of globe lights that were primarily decorative, the pool area in the back was unlit. That suited him just fine.

He only planned to dye the pool. Maybe bat a couple of flowerpots in as well. Jessup had a row of them at regular intervals in niches along the outer wall. Supposed to look Mediterranean.

Property damage, period. No contact. He was even prepared to lob the dye over the fence if it looked too well guarded for him to get closer. He cruised the neighborhood until he saw a house with several cars parked along the street. The addition of his would only make it look like someone was having company or a party.

Someone was, a block away. He just didn't know it yet.

He took another shot, just to brace himself. Then another

to calm his nerves. One more for the road, he told himself, filling the glass half full another time.

His hands were shaking as he walked up the driveway of one place in his sports shirt, acting casual, as if he were visiting there. He even carried a grocery bag, so it would look like he was bringing snacks or drinks. Then he promptly ducked between their carport and a low hedge and pulled on his dark sweater and mask.

Now he matched the night. He even had a piece of three-inch PVC pipe he'd picked up at a pool-construction site, that he'd encased in a black sweater sleeve so it would blend with the shadows as well. But if he ran into a dog or a neighbor, he'd have something to negotiate with.

He was squatting there, wishing he had another drink, when he saw the patrol car cruise by, circling Jessup's area. They shone their spotlight along the walls of the pool enclosure, cut up the alley behind his house, stopped a moment longer and checked the grounds there, then drove on.

In a matter of seconds, McIver managed to cross the rear of the yard, get his foot in one of the wall niches, and scale the pool enclosure, panting but excited by the exertion. He came down flat footed, wincing as he landed. His ankles were still swollen slightly from the ant bites and his feet began to itch. He rolled onto his side, close against the rear wall so he'd disappear into the darkness there.

Then the guy came out and prissed around in the dark. European-style bathing suit like a damn jock strap. Butt cheeks hanging out. Skinny legs. Bald head. Took a leak by another flowerpot. Shook it. Shook it again like he enjoyed it. Dove in and started swimming laps. "Asshole."

Then the bald head in the water bobbed toward the tile steps that connected to a jacuzzi swimout. The little drops of water on his tophairs caught the light coming from the ornate globes, just enough to make them shine. Reminded him how all the little ant bites bubbled up and hurt like hell. He'd scratched a few of them until they popped, then he poured on alcohol to keep them from becoming infected. Burned like hell. The fucking things filled again and still itched. Even now. He was clutching the PVC and sweating all over.

Suddenly McIver was the batter and the pitch was in his zone. It just seemed right. When the Jessup guy's head cleared the ladder, McIver stepped up, and he swung. The guy sprawled forward on the pool deck.

The hollow noise when the wide pipe connected sounded like a native drum. Clear. Primitive. Incomplete. A tom. Needing another tom.

So he gave it one. And another.

Incomplete again. Another.

Something just gave way inside, and he couldn't stop. Caught up in the sound and rhythm, he'd kept on tom-tomming, swinging furiously again and again at the shiny head or any part of the guy that got in the way, until Jessup stopped flopping.

The stillness scared him. Gasping for air and trembling, he clutched the pipe, his ears pounding with the sound of his own heart. Tom-tom.

He still wanted to hit him. But he'd calmed down enough to know he had to stop. The man was alive, but barely conscious. His eyes were puffed and closed from the beating. McIver rolled him back in the pool onto the fancy broad-tiled stairs, poured in the whole bottle of inky dye, and turned everything blue. Including the guy.

Panting and exhilarated, he had the presence of mind to take the pipe and dye packs with him when he left. But his heart was racing. Tom-tom. He'd taken too many chances. Tom-tom. He'd been too loose, too angry, and had lost control. Almost.

"Asshole." He kept replaying it.

He laughed all the way back home.

Chapter 5

The phone woke Stu midway though the morning. It wasn't the cellular's inoffensive beep-beep sound. It was the harsher ring that lately meant someone other than Rikki was on the line. "All right . . ." His mouth felt dry and his eyes were burning from too little sleep as he tried to discern which bedside phone was which. He'd dragged himself home about five fifteen, before the sky had begun to get light. He'd thrown the boys' food on the deck then and collapsed across his bed.

He groped and grabbed the right receiver, wishing he'd never given the number out to anyone. It was Detective Warnock, and it wasn't a social call.

"Sullivan. It's Joe. Bad news."

"He hit?"

"Right."

"Who'd he get?"

"Jessup. The guy that does watercolors. In Englewood. He went south again, out of town."

"How bad was it?"

"Real bad. He beat the shit out of this guy. And dyed him blue. I think this creep is losing it." Warnock's voice cracked with weariness. "I'm at the hospital in Englewood now. They're checking Jessup over. The guy whomped him with a length of PVC pipe. Repeatedly. May be a concussion. I'll tell you more in a couple of hours. He didn't touch the phone lines but the guy got a glimpse of him. Looks like we may have a match with a footprint from the Rodriguez place. I just wanted to let you know this much. Keep watching your girl."

"I'll watch her," Stu promised, letting out a breath. The waiting was over, at least for the guy in Englewood. Four left. Three locals, and an empty house in Fort Myers.

Stu stood staring out the window, trying to figure out

what to do. He considered going to bed again to get a few more hours' sleep. But if the Trasher were losing it as Warnock thought he was, he might move in again soon. Tired or not, he'd knew he'd better call over there.

He dialed on that phone. Her regular line was busy. He tried again and got her on the cellular. "Are you all right?"

"I am. I'm on the other line with Olivia. There was an attack last night. Rudy Jessup. He was badly beaten."

"Take your call. Let me clean up. I'll be over."

"Janelle is on the way. I've got a few more calls to make. We're okay. Don't rush."

"Okay, I won't." Rushing at this point for him was almost beyond the realm of possibility. Stiff and fatigued, he could barely move.

He'd brought the bionic ear downstairs again and was just spot checking the equipment before he headed over there. He really hadn't intended to listen to the conversation at Rikki's beyond the first few words. He'd recognized Janelle Givrey's car when he saw her pull in. He'd heard Eddie Sordo arrive on his cycle. He was sure the forces were rallying in support. He expected Swede and Ivey and Olivia Mello to come charging in as well. He felt he should be among them. They all had cause to be upset.

He'd had another update from Warnock, more detailed than before. This one was a trashing with a darkly ironic bent. The scenario Detective Warnock pieced together was that the guy probably came to dye Jessup's pool. Then Jessup came out. Something went haywire. The Trasher jumped him. He'd beaten the artist until he was unconscious, then shoved Jessup onto the steps. He'd ruined the pool and turned Jessup blue as well.

He watercolored the watercolorist.

He could have drowned him, Warnock said.

Stu didn't need to hear it all rehashed at Rikki's, but he wanted to be there to help her and the kids in any way he could. But first, he just wanted to test the pickup quality on the ear so it would be ready for immediate use.

The first few words he caught were "something sexually explicit." Abruptly he was remarkably alert, fine tuning the device.

"After all the controversy about some of these pieces being sexy, and our explanations to the contrary, I find myself in a peculiar situation," Janelle was saying. "We're getting inquiries from therapists as well as clients, ones that I have to respond to. I need some videos that deal with lovemaking, explicit lovemaking.''

Rikki said something he couldn't quite catch.

''We're not talking genitalia and orgasms here,'' Janelled insisted. Her voice rose and faded as they changed directions. The rest of her comment was lost. He guessed they were moving from room to room inside the house, or at least facing away from Stu's location. They had obviously discussed Jessup's plight and moved on.

There was no sign of Eddie Sordo. So he figured the fellow must be somewhere else on the premises, maybe doing something with the plants out back or in the slathouse.

''. . . about this before,'' Rikki was saying. ''I told you then that I couldn't figure out a way to do it comfortably.'' She said something else. Stu changed windows, aiming the big ear at the kitchen, but the reception was broken. He could hear ice cubes clinking into glasses then the refrigerator door closed. The conversation was drowned out by other sounds.

''We know these tapes work. At least they help. But they only go so far. Several of us who deal with sexual dysfunctions have hit the same problem,'' the Givrey woman maintained. ''We need powerful, positive visual reinforcement.'' She stressed each word. ''The material isn't for everyone. This is for a highly specific audience, rape victims and incest victims who want to have normal relations with men. They want to be resensitized. They want positive sexual experiences. But you know what they have to deal with. They have negative images, demons in their minds, they can't always fight them off. When the dark memories come crashing in, they need something on hand, right there, so they can pull out a tape and watch it. Maybe watch it over and over. Something strong, to help them drive back the demons, so they can reclaim that part of their lives.''

''I understand all that,'' Rikki acknowledged, her voice barely audible. Then she said something while she ran the juicer. Stu wished he could hear the rest.

''. . . suggested they rent some so-called erotica, or soft porn. Whatever it is.'' Janelle Givrey was talking when he could pick up the conversation again. ''But those commercial things are so stupid. It's bad theater, poorly done. Awkward. Crude. These are emotionally fragile women. They can't relate to strangers screwing and salivating over each other. That's about all those things turn out to be. The actors look bored or stoned. The physical act is all gymnastics. Not intimacy. There's no . . ."

Brrrrrrr. Stu tried adjusting the volume, but all he got was a dreadful whirring sound over the voices. It wasn't the low growly sound like the juicer. Then he looked out and saw the black motorcycle helmet gleaming in the sun. Eddie Sordo was under a grapefruit tree with a stepstool and a gas-powered chain saw, trimming up the branches. The gas engine on that thing was drowning out whatever was being said.

For a while Stu walked from one window to the other of Ash's house, pointing the ear at Rikki's but hearing nothing coherent. Then there was a break when Sordo shut off the motor and moved on to another tree.

". . . movement is too intense, too threatening," the therapist went on. "I like the still images on your tapes. It's very serene and poetic. I think you could do that with people. Lovers. Like statues. That stillness is something that would give these women some sense or control. I don't want anything performance oriented or tacky," she stated.

"Even getting still shots . . ." Rikki said something too hushed for pick up. ". . . without someone having to act for the camera and without me and my equipment invading that subject's privacy. I can't go into the bedroom and watch, waiting for a particularly good shot. Or make suggestions. I only manipulate images in the darkroom or during production, after I have the shots . . ."

Stu was hooked now, caught up in the argument, tantalized.

"But if they agreed to do it, and if they actually were lovers . . ." the Givrey woman suggested.

"I wouldn't feel comfortable even then," Rikki argued.

Outside, Sordo started the loud machine again.

"Shut the damn thing off," Stu muttered, wishing the guy would find something quiet to do. Or go home. Instead, Sordo came out from under a tree, looked up at Ash's house, flipped up the visor of the cycle helmet, shaded his eyes, and stared his way again. Stu ducked away from the window. He didn't want to be caught with earphones, propping the big ear in the opening.

Sordo was still waiting, still looking when Stu peered out

again. He shifted floors. By the time he reached the new location, Sordo had apparently given up and gone on about his work, moving around the far side of the house.

". . . just soft and pretty shots of lovers touching and kissing and embracing between some of your flower photos. Maybe not quite in focus. Misty and artsy. Something they can project themselves into. You know how you make petals look like arms and torsos. Like dancers." The words faded out. ". . . romantic music and . . ." From the way the sound kept getting weaker this time, he guessed they were going out back on the water side to continue the discussion.

From somewhere around the south side of the house, the roar of the chain saw started up again. Stu gave up on the electronics. He figured he'd have a better chance of getting the jist of the rest of the conversation if he went over there. He and Rikki had talked about her work. She might let him in on this. If not, she might tell him later. He could at least find out what Sordo was doing and maybe intercede on the behalf of a few defenseless trees.

He put on Ash's straw hat and deckshoes and started over. He could smell the gas fumes from the chain saw when he stepped outside. Gas, and citrus. Somewhere that saw was biting into an orange tree, maybe a lemon. He just hoped Sordo knew what the hell he was doing. Many of the trees were laden with a new crop of green immature developing fruit and there wasn't much sense in sawing off whole limbs now before they came ripe.

The first human noise he picked up over the chain saw's growl was a sudden desperate yelp. The saw motor raced, roared, sputtered, then stalled. With it came the thud and the rapid woosh-puff-groan sequence that sounded like somebody hitting ground.

Someone had.

"Are you all right?" Rikki called out to someone.

Stu guessed at once what had happened and started running. The combination of helmet, footstool, and chain saw was sure disaster. All he could hope was that Sordo hadn't taken the saw down with him in the spill. Then he heard the cursing, or something sounding like cursing, in a language he couldn't decipher. In Sordo's voice. Stu zig-zagged around the dismembered tree limbs.

When Stu cleared the corner, Sordo was flat on his back, spread eagle in the yard. The footstool was on top. A good-size limb still clung to the tree by a strip of bark. The saw was a full arm's length away. Despite his grass-stained pant-legs and scraped elbows, Sordo caught his breath and scrambled onto his feet.

"I'm okay. I'm okay," he insisted, in surprisingly good spirits. Rikki was already with him. His visor was cracked. "I was taking down a limb that didn't drop right." It had come through like a pendulum and knocked both him and the gas-powered tool flying.

"I should have come out and helped you." Stu was thankful that the man wasn't gushing blood. The chain saw cut off when the limb connected. Fuel had spilled out on the ground.

Sordo brushed the dirt off his shirt. "Saved my pretty face, this thing," he joked, talking off the helmet and wiping it clean of grass and dirt. His expression vascillated between a grin and a grimace. He was clearly in more pain than he was letting on.

"Let me see this." Rikki knelt and lifted his left pantleg. Stu eyed the bloody scrape she uncovered along the front of Sordo's shin. The metal nut that held the footstool brace had sliced along under the surface of the skin. A flap of bloody tissue hung from a thread.

"I think we should clean that and put something on it fast, before it swells," Stu said.

"I'll get some ice." Rikki didn't flinch at all. "Just keep the pantleg up."

Stu and Janelle Givrey helped the fellow over to the deck and yanked off his shoe and sock, which were getting soaked with blood. Rikki came back out less than a minute later with an ice pack and a clean damp towel.

"I can do this," Stu said, taking the ice pack and placing it on the scrape. "We'll need peroxide, cotton balls, anti-biotic ointment if you have some, tweezers, gauze, and scissors. Butterfly bandaids, if you have any. If we clean it and close it, I don't think he'll need stitches."

"Okay." Rikki went in again and brought the supplies. Janelle winced and watched him apply the ice, then gently clean the area with the towel.

"Nice job," Rikki told him later. She crouched beside Stu, handing him what he needed, while he put the finishing touches on the gauze covering. He'd managed to pull the skin back in place and hold it there with the flaplike bandages he'd improvised from adhesive strips. "You took a good first-aid course somewhere," she commented.

"I've taken a few." Stu carefully reapplied the ice pack to keep the swelling down. "Keep it elevated awhile," he said.

Sordo didn't protest. Despite the pain, he was enjoying being the center of attention. They'd moved him to a chaise. He was sitting with the injured leg outstretched, with Ash's hat, borrowed from Stu, shielding his face. Janelle had brought him a glass of juice. Lara and Jake had carried out pillows and extra towels to tuck under the leg. He was using his cycle helmet as an armrest. Everyone sat back now, relieved the crisis had passed.

"I wouldn't touch a chain saw for a while," Stu suggested. "Certainly not standing on a stool again. Why are you working on them now anyway?" he asked.

Sordo looked up from under the wide-brimmed hat. "I was tryin' to clear out under them so Miz Rikki can see out better from the house. Don't want to give this guy anywhere to hide."

"You just can't hack away at citrus this time of year," Stu told him. "You'll set them back and lose a lot of fruit. Maybe a few branches can be thinned," he conceded. "And that hanging limb needs to be dropped. I'd help you, but I can't run that thing one handed."

"I can run it." Sordo was on his feet, apparently intent on showing him that fall was a fluke.

"You shouldn't even be up."

"I'll be okay. I used to work all week, cutting hedges and edging lawns with a machete. I've had worse," he insisted. "How about helping me with a couple of limbs?" he asked, hobbling along next to Stu.

"Let's just clean up the mess so far," Stu suggested. Sordo frowned but went along. "We can haul the branches into a stack and cut them into sections." Each of them went after the limbs, dragging them into a pile. Sordo started drifting across toward the front of Rikki's driveway. When he reached a clump of oleanders, about five feet tall, near the mouth of her driveway, he circled and stopped and bent to pick something up.

"Wait. What did you find?" Stu called out, changing his direction as well.

"Nothin'. Just some litter," Sordo replied, holding up a piece of colored paper.

"Let me take a look," Stu insisted. He came up behind the smaller man, frustrated that the fellow hadn't left the paper laying there.

"It's just a candy wrapper," Sordo opened his hand and showed Stu what he'd wadded up. He shrugged and stuffed the paper in his pocket.

Stu bent down and looked at the flattened area where the paper had been. Further in, at the base of the bushes was an aluminum soft drink can, pushed back in.

"Someone's been standing here." Stu broke off a twig of oleander and poked it in the open top of the drink can, carefully upending it without touching it with his hands. "There's another wrapper. How 'bout you holding this." He held the stick out to Sordo. "Don't touch it. Just hold it." He bent down and plucked a second wrapper, like the first, from between the branches. He held it up, barely touching one corner.

Sordo stood there, stone faced, dutifully holding the skewered can.

"I bet the bastard did come back. But this is too far from the house for him to have done anything but look." Stu shook his head and peered at the front of Rikki's house. "There's enough bush so he wouldn't be seen. I just wonder how the hell he got into the compound. And when."

Sordo stared, shook his head, and said nothing.

"I don't think we should say anything about this to Rikki. I'll get it taken care of. No reason to worry her," he insisted, not wanting to add anything more to what she was already dealing with today.

"So what are you goin' to do with this?" the fellow asked as he handed the can back to Stu.

"Put it in a plastic bag. Same with this." He dangled the wrapper. "Give me the other one too," he suggested, holding out the hand on his broken arm to take the crumpled ball Sordo produced. "I'll give it all to the cops. Let 'em see if they can pick up any prints or saliva or whatever. They keep saying that sooner or later, this guy is going to make a mistake. If this stuff is his, he may have nailed himself."

Sordo stared intently at the soda can. He was favoring the

scraped leg again. He looked like he wasn't feeling very well.

"You should get off your feet awhile and stick that ice pack back on," Stu advised him. "I'll take care of this. I'll just put these things away. I'll be back as soon as I finish up."

Sordo shrugged. Then he turned and left.

Stu watched as the fellow limped around the corner of the house. Then he made a quick crossing to Ash's house. He placed the evidence he'd gathered in bags, then tagged and sealed them.

"Picked up something outside the Lundquist house that your lab team might be able to work with." Stu phoned Joe Warnock before he left. "Looks like someone spent some time watching her house. Coke can shoved in under a bush. A couple of candy wrappers. The grass is bent over. I bagged the pieces."

"Good. Just hold them. I'll pick the stuff up tomorrow. We'll check them out." He didn't sound like he was in a hurry. He just sounded tired.

"I could drop it off. I have some errands. Besides, I'd rather not have her see a police car here, even unmarked," Stu added. "She'd wonder what was going on. This may not pan out. After what happened last night, she doesn't need more to worry about."

"Okay. Bring it in whenever. Just have 'em call me from the front desk," Warnock told him. "I'm here, waiting for some calls. By the way, while I got you on the line, looks like we got a lead."

"What kind of lead?"

"That's what I'm waiting on. One of the young kids from the hotel said he has a buddy on the maintenance staff who simply took off this morning. He freaked after he heard about the Jessup fellow getting beat up in Englewood."

"So?"

"So the kid at the hotel said this guy, his name is Donnie Rhule, works in maintenance. Rhule apparently made a few cracks about some of the women at the art show when it was going on. When he got loaded a week ago, Rhule was saying he was scared. He said he did the stuff at the art show. He also called the TV station. But he claimed he didn't do any of the attacks since. Our informant said at first he figured the guy was running his mouth. Until this morning. He said the Rhule guy was hitting everyone up for money so he could leave town. He's heading to Miami to hide out with a brother,'' Warnock said. ''We got his Hilton ID picture and have a BOLO out statewide.'' That meant every officer would be on the lookout.

''Finally, a real not-smart move,'' Stu muttered.

''He's afraid to admit to trashing the show because he's scared he's going to get hit with all the other charges. He's petrified he'll go to jail. So I've got a friend on the Miami force checking out his brother.''

''Any chance the Rhule guy could have been here last night? This could be his garbage I picked up?''

''Can't say. We don't have any prints on file, so we've got nothing to match,'' Warnock noted. ''Not yet, anyhow. If we pick him up and take prints, we can run a comparison. If they match anything you've got, he'll have some explaining to do.''

''I'd like to see his feet.''

''Ant bites.'' Warnock was already banking on that one. ''Regardless, I'd like to talk to him. Could be he's telling the truth. If he is, that means we've got someone else out there doing the trashing. Meanwhile, looks like the Trasher wore rubber gloves again for the Englewood hit last night. But we'll work up the stuff you found. We'll hold it with the fibers and the footprint. Part by part, we'll put him together.''

''Have you told Rikki about the lead on Rhule?'' Stu asked.

''Nope. But I told the mayor. You can bet with all the press this has been getting, the honorable Ned Sloan's been breathing down my neck for some break on this. And he's thick with Lundquist's father. I don't have to tell you how aggressive her old man is. Not that I blame him,'' Warnock noted. ''If my kid was on this guy's list, I'd be camped out close to home. Which, of course, is where I am now,'' he added dryly. ''Anyhow, Swede knows the latest. Whether or not he tells her is another thing. Face it, all we know is that this kid says he didn't do any of it but the art show. We're going over his schedule seeing if he could have been to each of the places on the night the Trasher hit. So far the smudge pot in Venice looks like a no-go. His car was dead. But maybe he borrowed one. Or had a friend take him. We're checking.''

Stu nodded. He'd run his own detailed investigations before. He knew the tedious, nit-picking routine of checking and cross-checking every scrap of information, every lead. "Keep me posted. I'll drop my stuff off later today."

"There's something else." Warnock caught him before he hung up. "We're setting up a task force with a special state investigator. Suddenly, with the Jessup case, we've got a budget. Since you have sort of a unique perspective on the situation, I'd like you in on this. Usual setup. Any information you get, you bring in. Anything you find out from us is confidential, of course."

"Of course."

"Mom. It's Grampa."

Stu had come back and found a tuna sandwich waiting. He barely bit into it when Lara called Rikki to the phone. Janelle Givrey had already left by the time Stu got over there. Eddie Sordo insisted he had things he needed to do at his greenhouse. Despite her protests, he'd taken off on his cycle. That left the four of them. Until Swede called.

Stu felt like he was chewing sawdust, sitting there eating with the children and waiting for her to come back. With all the commotion already today, he figured there'd be a change of plans for the night ahead. No date. No quiet evening alone.

"That was my dad." Rikki looked more bemused than anything when she returned. "He said he'd been given two tickets for a dinner cruise tonight. I thought that meant he was canceling out."

"You mean we can't spend the night with Grampa?" Jake groaned.

"Mom . . ." Lara rolled her eyes.

"You can spend the night," Rikki said quickly. "It's all set."

Stu looked up.

"Dad said his sea legs weren't stable enough to go out on a boat and he and Ivey made plans with the kids anyway. He wondered if I wanted his tickets. He suggested I take my neighbor. That means you," she said, settling down across from him. "I think he's grateful."

"He's not the only one," Stu said, swallowing the lump that had been spoiling his lunch. He couldn't believe their date was still on.

"You think you can manage a cruise with your cast?"

"What's to manage? I can eat pretty well one handed."

"There's a band. Actually, a very small band," she said with a smile. "But they play well. And there will be a place for dancing." Rikki looked at the dingy fabric on his cast. "If I dig through my sewing supplies and come up with something less cumbersome, do you think you'd like to dance? Or aren't you much on dancing?"

"You mean we might get physical enough to dance?" Stu said, grinning over at her.

"We could try."

"Call me Baryshnikov," he answered in a low, seductive voice. "Just remember." Stu qualified his statement. "Old guys like us still have the technical know-how but we may be a bit slow on the grand jettés."

"She's not talking about that kind of dancing. He's being silly, isn't he?" Lara asked, following the exchange with obvious amusement.

"I think so," Rikki said gently.

"I think I'll go feed the fish." Jake popped up, ostensibly bored with the entire exchange. "You're as bad as Gramps and Gramma Ivey. He says dumb things and she just smiles and lets him." He'd eaten the middle out of his sandwich and had been sitting there, rolling the remaining bread into little dough balls. "You want to come?" he asked his sister.

"I think I'll feed my crusts to the fish too." Lara scraped all her bread crusts into a neat stack. "I think you're funny," she informed Stu as a parting comment.

Stu waited until after Lara was well on her way toward the dock. "Funny is all right, isn't it?"

"Funny is fine. It's when you cross into smartass that you have to start being careful."

"Let me know when I get there," he kidded her.

"I think it was last Wednesday," she countered, managing not to smile.

Swede had left a message on Ash's answering machine for Stu to call him right away. "Did she ask you about the cruise?"

"She did. We're going. Nice of you to offer."

"No problem. Figured she'd been under a lot of pressure. She likes the water. And she likes to eat. So I called up and made arrangements."

"I thought you'd been given the tickets?"

"You think she would have taken them if I told her I bought them especially for her?" Swede chuckled as he answered. "Not a chance. She'd think I was up to something. This way, she'll use them because she hates anything to be wasted."

"Well, whatever the reasoning, thanks for including me."

"You're welcome. After this Jessup fellow being hurt like he was, I'd feel better knowing she won't be anywhere alone. One of the damn problems with having all that privacy out there is that there's no one around. Most of the time, it's great. Time's like this, it sure as hell isn't. Stick with her."

"I'll do that." Stu thanked him again. "Anything else?" He was wondering if Swede would mention anything about the lead on Donnie Rhule.

"Nope, that's all. You have a good time. Take care of my girl," Swede concluded.

"Will do," Stu answered, feeling a bit uncomfortable. He doubted the evening he hoped for with Rikki would fall within the parameters her father imagined.

They returned to the house that night just after midnight. He'd parked the 'Vette conspicuously out front so it was evident she had company.

"Let's take a walk around and look it over, before you go inside," he suggested. Part of his concern was for her safety, but mostly he wasn't ready for the evening to end. He liked this quiet, hand-holding part a whole lot, just as it was, and he wanted to string it out a little longer. And if that were all they did that night, he'd be content.

On the cruise-to-nowhere, they had dined and danced and sat out on the deck watching the lights on shore. They'd been by far the youngest couple amid the group of retirees and winter visitors aboard, but they hadn't minded at all. The dance floor had been small and crowded and like everyone else there, they'd stayed basically in one spot, holding each other, swaying to the music. Then after the boat had docked downtown, Rikki had asked him to drive along the strip of beach she and the other volunteers had helped clean up the week before, after the anthill and orchid incident.

"I didn't even know this was still here." He'd pulled off into the parking lot and stopped. Beyond the asphalt car park was a band of grass, some sea oats, and a pine-rimmed strip of public beach. It was still holding on against the incursion of box-and-balconied condos that were crowding in, replacing smaller cottages and quaint houses that had once been typical of the keys off Sarasota.

"Let's get out and see how it's doing," she'd suggested. Rikki had taken off her shoes and helped Stu peel off his socks and shoes so they could walk along the damp sand at the water's edge. Small waves swept onto the shore and shuffled the tiny shells there as they broke and rippled over each other and slid back out again.

"Looks like we need to make another sweep through here," she'd said, pausing to pick up an empty cigarette pack and a cracked plastic sunscreen bottle. She almost stepped on a pair of discarded sunglasses with only one lens. She picked it up as well. "It doesn't take much to keep it looking beautiful here." She scanned the area, collected a few more bits of litter, then plopped them all in a trashcan.

"Makes you wonder why the jerks who dropped the stuff didn't take a few extra steps to dump it." Stu nudged a half-buried styrofoam burger container with his toes, working it to the surface. He picked it up and pitched it.

"Makes you wonder," she agreed, standing on the pale sand, smiling as she looked at the improvement they had made. "But the next people here will get to enjoy it like this."

"Thanks to you."

"You too. Maybe this will inspire someone we don't even know to help keep the place neat," she said hopefully. She'd held up the hem of her skirt and waded out, almost to her knees.

"Maybe," Stu responded, not at all convinced that the next folks along would even give a damn about beach litter. But like she said, they might. She had a way of looking at things that was a lot more positive than most. And probably better on the blood pressure.

She'd put their shoes in the backseat. He'd driven home in bare feet with the top down. He hadn't played any of his CDs. Just the wind seemed music enough.

"Wait. Stick with me," he cautioned her once they were home and started around her house. Rikki slipped her arm through his like she had on the boat and at the beach.

The pressure of her body against his arm felt good. The

evening so far had been easy and comfortable and fun. "If this is it, just shut up and be grateful," he told himself as they circled around to the back. He could be blissfully happy saying good night and going home. He just hoped everything out back was still standing. Unharmed, undyed, undamaged.

It was.

Both of them let out an audible sigh of relief, then they looked at each other and grinned, realizing that the worry had been a shared one.

"Sooner or later, they'll get him," Stu said.

"I just wish he'd stop. When I heard what he'd done to Rudy Jessup yesterday, I got very nervous about having the kids here. Not just tonight." Her solemn face looked sculpted in the harsh outdoor light they'd left on when they left. "I mean anytime."

"Would you feel better if you let them stay with your dad and Ivey for a while?" he suggested. "Maybe you should all stay there."

He didn't like the idea of being separated from her. But the Jessup case was assault with intent to do bodily harm. Just because the fellow wasn't sufficiently incapacitated to drown didn't mean the Trasher didn't hope he would.

"I've thought about it," she conceded. "I hate to have to hide them away. But I couldn't forgive myself if anything happened to Lara or Jake because I was too stubborn defending my principles to put them somewhere safe."

"They're somewhere safe tonight," he said, quietly assuring her. He was anxious to push that faceless phantom back into the shadows and let her keep the night as perfect as it had been for him. "You're safe too. He can't touch us tonight."

"I was giving him too much, wasn't I?" She turned and looked up at him. "You're right. He can't mess up tonight, unless he wants to take on both of us," she said, looking at him with a touch of mischief and a little defiance in her expression. "I'm going to get my suit on and take a swim. You want to come along? Soothing salt water? Just you and me and the dolphins?"

"It isn't fair to tempt an injured man," he answered glumly, reminding her of the cast. "I'll watch."

"You don't have to do that. Watching out for us is Oscar's job. We'll pat his belly and he'll protect us," she insisted.

"We'll bag the cast and we'll seal the top with duct tape. I have the perfect sleeve for you—heavy, watertight, and long. It came with some camera equipment. Anyway, it's an improvement on what we used in the spa," she said in her matter-of-fact way. "The only drawback comes when we take it off. The tape might pull out all your arm hair."

"I'll suffer. Get the bag and the tape. It may take me a while to get out of this and into my trunks." It had taken him a full thirty minutes to work his way into his sports shirt and jacket and slacks on his own.

"Just get the bathing suit and bring it over. I'll help you do the rest," Rikki said in a tone that started the heat rising.

"Right. I'll be back." He waved his good arm and hurried home zig-zagging and occasionally high-stepping around the shrubbery.

Having an extra pair of hands made the change into trunks relatively simple. The difficult part was trying not to stare too intently at the curve of her breasts as she stood in her twisted top and bikini bottoms and undid his buttons. She helped him strip to the waist, then undid the pants and left him to make the change into trunks while she got them each a large beach towel. She also brought back a razor and some soap and deftly shaved a smooth band around his upper arm. Not as permanent as her tattoo, it still would be there in the morning to remind him of this night.

Encapsulating the cast was a quick and uncomplicated procedure. Rikki tucked in the top of the bag and taped it snugly to his skin. He followed her to the dock. For once he didn't have to figure out all the moves. He wasn't trying to conjure up new ones. He was simply following directions and enjoying the view.

"I'm going to put the sailboard in so you'll have something to balance with. You can rest the cast on it and drift." Rikki hoisted the board above her head then set it at the end of the dock. Then she sat on the dock and set the board afloat, holding onto it with her feet. "Come on." She patted the space next to her. "Sit here and I'll help you get in."

Somehow she made the transfer happen gracefully. He'd been worried that he'd go off the end like ballast thrown overboard, and sink, then maybe bob back up like a cork and look ridiculous. She didn't let that happen.

"Just keep your knees a little bent, then turn and drop in

front of me.'' She held the board and the dock. He braced his good arm on the end, sliding off where she directed, his back to her. Somehow she had her legs under him, slowing him down so he settled in gently, right against her, like nesting spoons. Before the arm went under she'd brought the board close enough to catch the cast and keep it up. He was sure there were rub tracks on his back where he slid down over her breasts, and the contact with all that skin made him gasp.

"It's cool, but once you move around a bit, you'll warm up." She slipped an arm under his, holding him to make sure his position was stable.

Skin. Everywhere. He wasn't concerned about the water temperature. He didn't have to move to get warm. In fact, moving any distance from her was the farthest thing from his mind.

She stayed there, one arm on the board, for a few moments, while they drifted into deeper water. Gradually the motion of the water went back to the easy rhythm of not-quite waves. These were more subtle rises and falls. Swells without sound. Unless a boat or a wind disturbed the surface, the Intracoastal was usually calm like this at night.

Then she was gone. She slipped under and away and left him in his much-reduced cocoon of body warmth. He heard her surface further out. He scissored his legs, pumping against the water so he turned toward her. She came up, pale and lovely and wet, facing him, with only the board between them.

"Beautiful, isn't it?" she kept her voice down to a whisper as if she didn't want to disturb the quiet that surrounded them.

"You're beautiful," he said simply, not caring at all if it sounded too contrived. The words were simply there.

"Thanks." She met his steady gaze and grinned. Then she slipped her hands under his, and with the board between them, they drifted some more, saying nothing.

"Cold?" She asked when she felt him shifting weight.

"The shoulder. It's a little uncomfortable." He'd tried not to spoil the tranquility by complaining, but it was beginning to ache.

"You start chugging us into shore and I'll come around and rub it."

He began the scissorlike kick again, upright, as if he were

walking submerged to his armpits, with the cast high and dry on the board. She came up behind him, gently working the flat muscles below his shoulder blade. He could tell by the regular soft warm breath on his back and the sway of her body that she was helping to kick, matching his leg movements with her own.

"Better," he almost groaned as her strong, sure hands worked the sore spot and eased the tension in his upper back. She stayed behind him, her hands gliding over the skin under water or scooping up handfuls to rub his neck and upper arm. Sometimes her leg would brush his, or a thigh, or her breasts would sear a memory across the skin of his back.

They kept chugging along until his feet touched the soft bottom nearer shore. As each step brought them nearer to the dock, the feel of her so near to him was all he could think about. He wanted to turn and hold her. But if he slid the cast off the sailboard, he'd either strain the shoulder trying to keep it above water, or it would sink.

"Come around the front." He didn't even get the words out before she was there. She slid one arm around his neck and ran her hand into the thick damp fringe of hair that touched his shoulders. Clasping it, she held on and lifted herself so her mouth met his. Stu wrapped his good arm around her, pulling her against him, trying not to lose his balance as he lost himself in her.

They kissed for a very long time. And then he felt her hands moving, touching his body, caressing his chest and his sides. Gliding everywhere.

"One of us had better hold on to the end of the dock." Rikki's voice was hushed and heated and thick.

"I want to hold you." Stu had only one arm to work with and it was around her. The salty water was all over her skin. He wanted to suck it off with kisses.

"You hold it, I'll hold you," she promised. He let her go and got a good grip on the dock about the same instant the bikini bottoms landed there next to his fingers. Then the top. He half-stood, half-floated, buoyed up by the sailboard under his right arm with the cast and clinging for stability to the dock. This time, when she went under the surface, he felt her grasp his trunks and tug them down.

"Yes." He almost cheered. "Thank you, thank you," he

said aloud, feeling foolish grinning like he was, but unable to hold it back.

She came up for air, her pale hair streaming water and gleaming like burnished platinum. Smiling, she pitched his trunks onto the dock. They kissed again, this time with nothing at all between them.

"I like this. I like this very much," Stu murmured. She held him close and kissed him again. Then with her incredibly gentle touch, she sank chin deep in the water, caressing his chest and sides, surely moving her hands lower. He held his breath and gripped the dock in anticipation. When she disappeared under the water again, all motion above the waterline slowed.

Almost soundless, she emerged and was there, facing him again. "Don't let go or we'll both go under," she whispered, turning his knees to liquid with her exquisitely tender touch. He kissed her again and again slowly, savoring the taste of salt water on her lips.

He tried to talk, to tell her how wonderful it felt to be touched like this, but all that came out between slow kisses was her name and a contented moan. Or the moan, and then her name, murmured, with awe. All his senses were focused on the movement of her hands beneath the water and the softness of her lips on his neck and chest. Then she twined her arms around his neck and lifted herself to kiss his mouth again. He felt her smooth-muscled legs slide up and close around him, enveloping his hips. As she drew herself close against him, he had to clench his teeth and concentrate to remember to keep his grip on the sailboard and the dock.

Almost weightless in the salty water, Rikki lifted and lowered herself, pulling and and releasing in rhythmic opposition. Her breasts rose above the surface then went under, sending out ripples as Stu rocked his hips toward her to increase the intensity of the contact.

For a while all outside time and sensation was suspended. The universe seemed centered where her body embraced and enclosed his. Every sinew of muscle strained for release. But in the clear, bright fire of passion, he clenched and unclenched his hands, able to touch nothing but wood and plastic wrapping. Exquisite and exciting as this contact was, it was not all what he imagined making love with her would be. He wanted to touch her.

Before this moment, they'd had close physical contact

without it being necessarily sexual. They had touched and massaged each other's backs and legs and feet. She had taught him to receive and to give gentle, hands-on therapy, seeking and smoothing away tension. Now his hands were restricted and he needed to touch her to make this skin-to-skin contact more complete. Sexual release wasn't enough. It wasn't the point. Not with her. He wanted more.

"Whoa. Wait. I have to talk to you."

She leaned back, looking at him with soft and luminous eyes.

"So talk."

He liked her breathlessness, and the touch of humor. He liked it that she held him close to her, allowing no apartness while he framed what he wanted to say.

"I don't think this is balanced enough," Stu managed to speak at last, echoing something she'd once said to him. 'It's too one sided. I want to be able to touch you and kiss you just like you're touching me. I want to do things with you. To you . . .'' he floundered for the words to describe his peculiar sense of dissatisfaction. "Don't get me wrong. This feels absolutely incredible," he went on, not wanting her to think he was complaining. "But me hanging here like this . . . it's limiting . . . it's too passive." He hoped she understood what he was feeling. "I really want to make love with you. For days, I've hardly been able to think of anything else. But I don't want it to be like this, not without being able to use my hands when I want to. I want my hands all over you."

"I know the feeling." She stroked his damp beard and smoothed back his hair with one arm, not releasing him at all. "I want to feel your hands on my body too, Sullivan. And your mouth," she said in a way that made his skin turn to goose flesh. "And I want to make love with you and fall asleep beside you and wake up and feel you close to me in the bed."

He swallowed. That was a part of it he hadn't even got to. The thought of melting into her, then holding her, and touching some more, and going to sleep. And waking in the same bed to find that he hadn't dreamed it at all.

"You want to come home with me?" she asked. "We can sleep late?"

He didn't doubt for a second that she knew he'd go anywhere with her. "You can sleep late. You don't have anyone to feed. In the morning. The boys," he reminded her. The bird brigade would be there between six and seven, shrieking like banshees if he didn't get up and feed them. They'd have the neighborhood in an uproar.

Pat Simons and anyone within earshot would have a pretty good idea what had transpired. He wasn't sure Rikki wanted to make any part of their relationship that public yet. Running across to feed them, then hurrying back across to bed didn't sound appealing either.

"Let's turn on your answering machine and you come to my place," he said, knowing Ash's house was neutral territory. He didn't want any morning-after uneasiness or phone calls or bird calls or the Trasher or anything else to spoil this first time together. "I just wish we could get there without having to move." He wasn't completely joking.

"We'll just have to get there and start all over," Rikki commented, amused as he was by their dilemma. "Or we can try to remember exactly where we were and we'll pick up where we left off."

"Believe me, I'll remember this," he assured her.

Each wrapped in a big towel and carrying the wet swimsuits, they hurried indoors. They crossed through her house, making sure everything there was locked for the night. Stu paused on the lanai long enough to give the shark spirit an extra belly rub, more from gratitude than as a safeguard for protection on his journey. Then they wound their way to Ash's house and locked the doors. Stu put on a stack of CD's, pushed the random button, and went upstairs, followed by waves of music.

He barely felt the tug when she pulled the heavy tape that had sealed the bag around his cast. He'd sat on the side of the bed, his good arm free, stroking her backside and legs as she stood, uncovering his other arm. He glided his fingertips over the dark tattoo, feeling an uncanny flutter in his chest each time he crossed that delicate boundary. The tattoo and her breasts, naked, gently swaying just above his forehead were distraction enough when she yanked off the last strip of adhesive.

The cast was still awkward, but he could touch her with both hands. And he could embrace her, and kiss her anywhere. He could trace the contours of her body with his tongue and lips. And when he did, he heard her sighs of pleasure.

He felt her touching him again as they rolled onto the wide bed, legs and arms intertwined in full body to body contact. Later, when she knelt above him, to spare any unnecessary pressure on his arm and shoulder, and began that rhythm again, he could feel the delicious balance of power and the tenderness as they brought their bodies into harmony. Then they were locked together, gasping, reaching, damp with each other's sweat. When he heard her soft, compelling gasp, deep in her throat, and felt the tremor inside her, his body answered. Holding her, trembling himself, he almost laughed out loud with sheer delight, and almost wept for joy.

Stu woke up several times in the night, mainly from the pressure of the cast upon his chest or the dull ache in his shoulder. He usually wore the brace and propped up the cast with pillows. But tonight all the pillows but one were tossed out on the floor, well out of reach. He knew what a production it would be to roll out with the cast wobbling to get them. He would move his hip or arm or leg so she would stir, just enough to slide closer or turn onto her side or blink at him sleepily and turn her face to his for a warm and gentle kiss.

Then he'd lay there, listening to her breathe, wondering why he hadn't said he loved her. It had been easy enough with other women, other times. But she wasn't other women. No words seemed large enough for what he felt with her. And he knew when he had the right words for her, they'd come out. Right now, he had to let it settle and try to get back to sleep.

Then he woke up one time and she was sitting up watching him.

"You were groaning. Let's get you comfortable." Still naked, she'd rounded up the extra pillows and helped him wedge them under the cast so he could sleep the rest of the night at ease. She covered him over, then snuggled in on the other side and glided one leg over his.

"I like this." He remembered murmuring.

"I like this too," he heard her say. Her arm came across him and her hand lightly settled on his chest.

Chapter 6

Stu awoke to the dull groaning sound of an offshore motor passing the peninsula. It was already light outside. He was in the bed, alone. Before he started generating answers for what had happened to her, he spotted the note Rikki had left pinned to the pillow she'd propped beside him.

"Sleep. Enjoy. Message from Claire on my answering machine. She has some new blooms. Had to go to Selby to do some photography. Don't want to miss them. Call you when I get back. R."

Since it was nine-thirty and all was quiet on the eastern deck, she'd apparently gone ahead and fed the boys so they wouldn't make their usual racket.

"Thanks," he said to no one there, grateful for more than the bird feeding. He lay outspread, smiling drowsily up at the ceiling fan rotating above him, drifting off again until the doorbell chimed down below and prodded him into action. It rang a second time, insistently, as he rifled through a drawer for a pair of shorts.

"Coming. Just hold on." He struggled with the zipper as he lumbered down the stairs.

The door ringer didn't hold on. The bell rang again.

"I'm coming," Stu barked in response. His mellow afterglow was vaporizing. This was one hell of a way to start a day after a night he wanted to savor.

Eddie Sordo, without the Robo-Cop motorcycle helmet, was the first thing Stu saw as he opened the door. Sordo didn't look up. With him was a vaguely familiar tall, clean-cut, young guy who seemed to be in charge. Even before the fellow took out the badge and showed it, Stu knew he was a police officer.

"Detective Maurer."

"Some kind of trouble?" Stu asked, glancing at Sordo from head to foot to check that he wasn't injured.

"We just need some information to help clear up something," Maurer said. "You're Stu Sutherlin?"

"Almost. Stu Sullivan." He glanced at Sordo again, guessing the butchering of his last name was his doing. "Eddie, what's is this about?"

Sordo remained silent.

"This is your residence, Mr. Sullivan?" Maurer asked.

"No. I'm housesitting. For Harrison Ash. He's out of town." Stu didn't like the way the gardener kept avoiding his eyes. "Anything wrong with Rikki or the kids?" He felt a momentary surge of panic.

"Nothing like that," Maurer assured him. "It's about some Coke can. This man says you found a Coke can and some wrappers on the neighbor's property and turned it in to the lab for fingerprinting."

Stu nodded. "Right. I turned them in to Detective Warnock. I dropped the stuff off at the station yesterday. Bagged. It looked like someone had been hiding out in the bushes, watching the neighbor's house. The neighbor is Rikki Lundquist, one of the artists under threat in the Trasher case."

Detective Maurer studied his face and nodded, expressionless.

"I figured if there were any prints on record that matched the ones on the can or the wrappers, they'd help make an ID," Stu went on. "If a suspect turned up, this could link him to the place. Like I said, I dropped it off. Yesterday afternoon. Warnock came down to the desk and picked it up himself. Is there a problem?"

"The lab guys didn't have them," Maurer replied.

"Then maybe Warnock still has the bag. He had some other lead and wasn't in any particular hurry with my contribution." Stu still didn't get the point of the house call. "So what's going on here?"

Now the officer inclined his head toward Sordo. "This guy came in and confessed that the can and the wrappers were his."

"Why the hell didn't you say so?" Stu stared at Sordo. "And what the heck were you doing out there in the bushes?"

Sordo didn't answer. He still wouldn't look him in the eye.

"Come on, man. What's going on?" Stu demanded.

"Easy. Can we come in and talk this through?" the officer suggested.

"Sure." Stu stepped back. "I'd like to hear this."

"Before we get into what Mr. Sordo was doing," Maurer proceeded, "there are a few things I'd like to ask you."

"Ask," Stu said impatiently. Whatever afterglow he'd had moments before was long gone.

"Do you have in your possession and do you operate surveillance equipment on these premises?"

Stu straightened. He looked at Maurer, then at Sordo. He remembered when he'd stood in the window with the bionic ear aimed at Rikki's house wishing the gardener would shut off his chain saw. Stu wondered then if he'd been spotted. Apparently he had been, and so had the ear. "Why?"

"I don't think you quite understand what the procedure is here." A shadow of annoyance darkened Maurer's expression. "With your cooperation, this conversation can be relatively simple. I ask questions. You answer," he said with exaggerated patience. "We get this resolved, and no one has to go down to the station."

"Maybe I'd better set a few things straight." Stu softened his approach and started over. "If you call Joe Warnock and tell him who I am, you'll have some answers you need. I'm not one of the bad guys."

"Okay. What are you, then?" Maurer pressed with a contained, show-me attitude.

"I'm the chief fire marshal for the city. This one. Sarasota."

The officer eyed Sullivan's beard and collar-length hair. Neither fit any department standard. "Really."

"I can pull my badge if you'd like to see it. It's upstairs." From his own experience in interrogation, Stu knew better than to go after the badge first and leave the officer wondering what he was doing out of sight. He didn't want Maurer thinking he might bolt or return armed or pull any number of possible stunts someone under questioning may attempt. "I'm running surveillance on the Lundquist woman to make sure she's safe with this Trasher loose," Stu elaborated. "Her father and the mayor contacted me. Since I was off on recuperative leave and had some time on my hands, I said I'd do it. I'm even on the task force, for Pete's sake. Ask Joe."

Sordo's dark eyes widened.

"And I do have some surveillance equipment here. On loan from the department." Stu covered Maurer's earlier question. "Detective Warnock will verify that he knows all this." He laid it out with official precision. However, calling Rikki "the Lundquist woman" got the point across but implied a distance that didn't feel comfortable. Particularly not now as he stood there in shorts without underwear, still scented with her body perfume.

"Warnock. Okay. I'll check with him. You got a phone handy?" Maurer scanned the foyer and kitchen area for one.

"In here. On the wall. Help yourself." Stu led Maurer into the kitchen. Sordo stayed back by the door.

"Stay put," Maurer told them both.

"How about we sit?" Stu pointed to the chairs surrounding a small table at the far end of the sunlit room, overlooking the water.

"Sure." Maurer waved for Sordo to come in.

"Diet soda?" Stu offered.

Neither man responded.

"Iced tea?" Stu tried again. Sordo looked at the refrigerator and nodded. Maurer was already dialing.

"I need Joe Warnock." The young detective stood, listening. "Joe. Mike Maurer. What do you know about a Stu Sullivan on Siesta Key?" He loosened his tie and tugged at his collar.

Stu got out a pitcher of tea, dropped some cubes into three glasses, and poured. He handed one to each of the other men. Maurer nodded and kept listening to what Warnock was saying.

Sordo was watching Maurer, nervously cutting Stu an occasional sidelong look. Maurer asked a few more questions, but he was almost smiling. From the set of his shoulders, he was more relaxed than he had been when he came in.

"Okay. So far, so good," Maurer said when he hung up. "Warnock backs you up completely," he told Stu. "No need to be alarmed, Mr. Sordo. This man is on your friend's side."

"What about him going into her house at night?" Sordo pressed. "Miz Rikki didn't know he was there."

"He's supposed to be guarding her." The detective shrugged.

Sordo still had a stiffness in his manner. "He really is chief fire marshal?"

Maurer nodded. "Sure is."

"He's okay?"

Maurer nodded again. "Detective Warnock says he's watching out for Miss Lundquist. She just doesn't know the specifics. Apparently her father was worried and thought that if she knew he'd hired her a bodyguard, she'd balk. The mayor can't authorize preferential security. So Mr. Sullivan was advised not to tell her his connection with the city."

"The Swede is really in on this?" Sordo ruminated a moment then managed a weak smile. "Miz Rikki likes to do for herself," he said, arching his eyebrows. "She wouldn't put up with a bodyguard." He was bobbing his head up and down, adding up the pieces. "I wondered why the Swede wasn't 'round here more himself lookin' out for her. It's because of you." His smile widened into a grin.

"That still doesn't clear up what you were doing hiding in the bushes." Stu started in on the can-and-wrappers incident. "What's that all about?"

"I was watching out for Miz Rikki too," Sordo replied with a slight straightening of his stance. "I been a friend with her a long time. And I wasn't sure about you. Miz Simons, cross the way, she wasn't sure either. We thought you were up to somethin'. I saw you with binoculars," he declared, narrowing his eyes accusatorily. "And she saw you with a headset thing on your ears and that round thing you aim at the house. Then I saw you with it and I got worried too. We just wasn' sure what you was up to. Somethin' wasn' right." He wagged a finger at the much taller man. "She thought you may be one of those kinky fellows. Then I saw you use the key and go into Miz Rikki's house one night. You were there a long time. And I saw her movin' about, so I knew she was all right, but I know she didn't see you."

Stu sighed and rubbed his temple, not at all comfortable that anyone had witnessed the night he'd trespassed and huddled by the stairs. It wasn't one his more heroic episodes.

"Now, I don' mind you puttin' in the little lights or havin' that special phone," Sordo conceded. "But I started thinkin' that nothin's there to stop you. And I kept worryin.' So I came to watch you again."

"Again? You came more than once?"

Sordo nodded.

"When?"

"Couple of times."

"Last night?" Stu asked.

Sordo nodded. "Last night."

Stu almost winced. The vivid image that flashed in his mind was of him and Rikki and the sailboard encounter when they came back from the dinner cruise and swam naked. What went on between them he'd assumed was private. "Where were you?"

"Differen' places."

Some subtle shift in the wiry Melanesian's expression started the heat on Stu's neck rising.

"I came a few other nights too. Miz Simons watched from her house sometimes," Sordo answered. "We been takin' turns. We been watchin' you and lookin' out for that Trasher. The Swede is not the only one who wants to make sure Miz Rikki is safe." His chin jutted out as he spoke.

"When you did stand guard, did you stay out there all night?" Maurer asked Sordo, more from personal curiosity than from any official interest.

"Just some of the night." Sordo gave Stu a quick, uneasy look.

"When were you there last night?" Stu asked, feeling slightly dry in the mouth.

Sordo hedged. "I wanted to see her get home safe."

"But what time of the night were you around?" Stu had a sinking feeling he wasn't going to like the answer.

Sordo shrugged.

"When did you leave?" Maurer asked.

"I watched till I saw Miz Rikki go home early this morning and I was sure she was all right. Then I got cleaned up and went down to confess."

"She stayed here last night?" Maurer glanced at Stu, realizing the fire marshal had been observed guarding the Lundquist woman more closely than he'd anticipated.

"I didn't watch everything," Sordo blurted out unconvincingly, trying to be diplomatic.

"Really. And what didn't you see?" Maurer kidded him.

Sordo pondered the question, furrowing his brow to disguise his flush of embarrassment.

"Don't answer that. Just ignore him," Stu insisted, patting the gardener on the shoulder. "Just drop the subject. And do me a favor and don't say anything about any of this to Rikki. I'll tell her the whole story eventually. Well, most of the story.'' He qualified his assurance to Sordo. ''I just have to pick the right time.''

''No problem. I won't say a word. I just care that you aren't no kinky man. I'm happy she is safe.'' Sordo smiled openly now, as if a dark cloud had risen. ''But I must tell Miz Pat. She's worried too. Miz Pat would want to know Miz Rikki is in good hands.'' Sordo hesitated, not liking the phrasing that slipped out. Maurer was grinning because he was blushing again.

''Tell Miss Simons not to say anything to Rikki either,'' Stu reminded him. ''Once this Trasher is caught, we can all relax. But not yet. The guy is real unpredictable.''

Sordo was nodding. ''You keep on watching her real close. And I won't do no more peeking,'' he promised, shielding his eyes with his hand for effect. ''Very sorry about this.'' He turned to the officer, bobbing and shaking Maurer's hand in apology. ''Sorry for the trouble.''

''No trouble. You did the right thing under the circumstances. You're a good friend,'' he declared sincerely. ''This woman is fortunate to have people like you who care about her.''

''Thank you. Back to work.'' Sordo grinned and bobbed again and hurried out toward the front door.

''I'd appreciate your not saying anything either,'' Stu said after Sordo was gone, aiming his comment at Maurer. ''Nothing even to Warnock, other than the necessary details.'' He knew the kind of comments that could get bounced from department to department.

''What's to say?'' Maurer shrugged, subdued his smile, and took a sip of the iced tea Stu had given him. ''The fellow said he wasn't watching everything.'' He took another slow drink. ''Must have been one hell of an 'everything' to fluster both of you this much.''

Stu ignored his statement and stuck to business. ''You could tell Warnock not to bother wasting lab time processing the can and wrappers. No sense pursuing that angle.''

''Will do,'' Maurer agreed. He finished the last of the drink and put the glass back on the counter. ''But I do suggest you run past Warnock the somewhat unorthodox technique about going in the Lundquist house with a key and without an invitation,'' Maurer cautioned him now that

Sordo wasn't privy to the conversation. "Doesn't sound like it falls into the job description."

"It doesn't. I did it once. I won't do it again. It stunk," Stu said bluntly.

"My sentiments exactly. See you around." Maurer gave him the thumbs-up sign and let himself out.

"Don't worry about us. We'll be fine." Juli Quinn stood barefoot in the Lundquists' front yard Thursday night waiting for Stu to pull across from his driveway and pick up Rikki for Chambers's garden party. For the trip onto the mainland, Stu had the ragtop up on the 'Vette so they wouldn't arrive there windblown. "Pat Simon is bringing over brownies and we're going to lock ourselves in and all watch 'The Little Mermaid' again. Eddie said he'd come by and check on us later on."

She'd observed Rikki all afternoon as they worked together in the developing room. She knew her friend was uneasy about leaving the kids and her in the house for the evening, even for Victor Chambers's gala outdoor sculpture exhibit. But with lights on, doors locked, cars in front, Sordo coming on his cycle, and an occasional police patrol, there'd be enough safeguards to discourage any prowler. "Tell Olivia I hope the party goes well and she sells lots of her sculptures."

"I'll tell her." Rikki glanced back at the house. All the rooms were lit-up shadowboxes beyond the windows in her house. "Remember to close the blinds."

"Look at that sky. It's a great evening for a garden party," Juli said, determined to keep up the cheerful campaign so Rikki wouldn't change her mind and stay home after all. "Supposed to be a great moon. Not full, but close. Real romantic."

Rikki looked up at the darkening, cloudless sky. Her long-skirted, floral silk dress fluttered about her legs like an apricot haze in the evening breeze. "Okay. I get the message. Just you make sure all the doors are locked. Turn all the floodlights on. Turn off most of the indoor lights and close the blinds so no one can see in." She was running through some mental checklist.

"We're well fortified. It will be a no-man's land out here. No sweat," Juli said confidently. Suddenly she shifted her line of vision and let out a loud wolf whistle. "Wow. Don't you look handsome," she called to Stu as he pulled up and stepped out of the 'Vette. "Definitely European. Like a count or something."

He'd picked up his tux and all the accoutrements in town earlier in the day. He'd even had his beard neatly trimmed and his hair styled. Not cut. Barely shaped and edged. Having it was a luxury he intended to enjoy until he had to go back to work again. But he did look better now that a professional had tamed the hair. Even the cast was different than the cumbersome one he'd been wearing earlier. This was smaller, lightweight, and made of fiberglass. He'd had his tailor open the jacket sleeve seam so he could pull it over the new apparatus.

"You do look very elegant," Rikki agreed, stepping forward to greet him. "What's this?" She tapped her finger on the shiny blue rim of the cast, poking out like a cuff below the jacket sleeve. "New style in formal wear?"

"Actually its a reprieve of sorts. It's an air cast." He held it out so the women could get a better look. "The doctor said the arm was coming along so well that he gave me this early. It's lighter. It's got an inflatable inner layer. He put it on and pumped it up to fit. He said I can take it off to take a bath or shower and put it back on. Carefully."

"That means you could paddle around a little out there, sans the armor?" Rikki tilted her head toward the salty water of the Intracoastal. "Or sit in the spa? Like maybe later tonight?" For a few seconds their eyes met and neither one spoke.

"I could do that," Stu responded, unable to stop grinning at her.

Juli didn't miss the tender, faintly eager edge to the wordless message.

"By the way, you look great." His expression softened. "That's a very pretty dress." It was a simple design in pastels, with near-transparent layers of silk in a desert print of peaches and apricot and cream. "Reminds me of a real soft sunset."

"Thanks. Judy Rodriguez painted the fabric. I thought it would be appropriate for tonight. You look very handsome yourself." She sent an approving look right back at him.

"Okay, you two. Enough. I'm jealous. Why don't you beautiful people get in the car and leave? Shoo." Juli wriggled her fingers to hurry them along. "Not only are we well fortified, but we've got tomatoes in the refrigerator and a few pots of fern on the sundeck. If the Trasher shows and gets through the first line of defense, we're armed and ready. We're talking bombs-away time.''

''If he shows, use the cellular, call 911, then let 'im have it. From a safe distance,'' Stu said, shaking a finger for emphasis.

''Check the back sliders,'' Rikki reminded her, still anxious. It had been eight days since the pool-bluing. Rudy Jessup was still in the hospital. The lock-in, lights-on routine had become second nature for the ones still left on the list.

Juli sighed. ''Please. We'll handle this. Leave,'' she insisted. Across the way, Pat Simons stepped around from the back of her house, wearing oven mitts and carrying a baking pan. ''See. We're all ready. You can go,'' Juli declared.

''She's right. Let's go. We may need to worry about parking space if we don't hustle.'' Stu went ahead and opened the car door. Rikki followed and waved at the oncoming woman with the oven-warm treats. ''We'll be back fairly early. Don't leave until Stu and I can walk you home.''

''I'll stay put,'' Pat Simons promised, giving Stu the once-over with somewhat raised eyebrows. ''Very nice,'' she concluded with a wink. ''You two have a lovely evening.''

''Washington Drive on the north end of St. Armands.'' Once they were under way, Rikki gave him the address of Chambers's waterfront home, assuming he didn't know precisely where the garden party was being held. ''It's a big estate set back from the road just before you cross over to Lido Key.''

''I know the place.'' He didn't elaborate. He was nodding and smiling as they drove away, but his hands were slightly damp with a strange mixture of excitement, nervousness, and dread. He cranked up the air conditioning.

This was the last time he'd duck the truth. He'd already warned Swede and the mayor that he was going back on their agreement. He had to tell her the rest of it. But he hadn't told her anything all week. He'd been busy, then he'd put it off, he had meetings, she was busy, and finally he'd let time run out. The truth was, with Chambers's party coming and everyone on edge about whether the Trasher might sabotage it or strike elsewhere, it was easier to let it ride.

"You will keep staying there and looking out for her?" Swede had asked.

"I'll do anything to keep her and the kids safe. But she'll have to call the shots. If she wants me out, I'll go."

"She can make some pretty tough calls," Swede cautioned him. "But she likes you. She might wrestle with it all a day or two. But she's smart enough to think it through. Ultimately she'll understand that we were just doing the best we could. Just don't tell her before the party. When she ruminates, she gets real quiet. And she holes up in her darkroom and works a lot. Wait," he advised Stu. "Olivia and her artist chums need her all glowing and happy."

"So do I," Stu muttered after he hung up the phone. But he called Victor Chambers and worked out the drop-off routine and a few other possible kinks to an otherwise smooth evening.

At Chambers's house, Stu handed their invitation to the guard at the gate and pulled up the long driveway, ostensibly looking for a space to park. He knew the drive that looped back into itself was most likely full. He'd have to circle back for an open place.

Chambers was on the front terrace greeting guests and keeping an eye out for the 'Vette. As soon as he spotted them, he'd agreed to come out for Rikki himself. Stu would insist on dropping her off so she could go along with Chambers and mingle while he went on to take care of the car. If it proceded as planned, there wouldn't be much time for introductions. The two men wouldn't have to act like strangers or explain that they were friends.

Rikki would draw attention when she entered. The press would be there in force. But this way the tall, willowy blonde artist could make her entrance on the arm of her host and give whatever interviews she chose. Stu could ease in on his own later inconspicuously. If he stayed back on the fringes, he figured he'd be unlikely to be noticed in a sea of near-identical tuxes, and he'd have fewer explanations to make. The only explanation that counted was the one he'd give Rikki when they got home. She deserved a night full of smiles and friends.

Stu made the dropoff without any complications. "See you inside," he told Rikki then pulled off. He followed the directions of a uniformed patrolman onto a section of a side yard designated for parking, but he pulled his 'Vette out in the open, hoping he wouldn't come out and find it covered with bird droppings.

"Stu? Is that you? What on earth are you doing here?"

He almost dove into the hibiscus hedge. He turned slowly and tried not to look like he had anything to hide. He recognized the voice. "Terri. Nice to see you." He greeted his ex-wife with limited enthusiasm, dropping the "Lynn" like she'd done in recent years. She'd recognized his car and pulled her vehicle onto the grassy area next to his.

"My goodness, look at you. With a beard? And a tux?" Her voice went up with each word. "Since when are you interested in sculpture? Or are you shopping for something for your office at the department?" She was smiling. And patting his coatsleeve and looking him over with a distinctly proprietary air. He could smell her perfume.

"I'm not shopping. Just here to browse," he answered, not quite certain whether to talk there or to start walking up the tree-shrouded drive toward the house where there was a chance Rikki might see them. If he stalled there, Terri would most likely misinterpret the delay as an indication of interest.

She was a very pretty woman. Dark hair and near-black eyes. Just a touch of Spanish blood on her mother's side, enough to add interest and elegance to her not-so-perfect features. The slim-fitting dress she was wearing looked expensive. It was probably right off the pages of some high-class magazine for professional women. It showed she was neatly rounded in places women look good rounded.

"And how's the arm coming along?" Her dark eyes shifted lazily through half-closed lids from his cast to the longish hair and beard then down the tucked shirtfront and below his beltline. It was a familiar signal of sorts that once would put him into overdrive. "When I heard that you were hurt, I called and left a message or two on your answering machine. I even called your brother to see if you were recuperating there. He said to leave my message at your number again. I thought you must have dropped off the face of the earth. You look very suave. Where have you been?"

"I've been busy here and there." He decided to start walking briskly. "Are you here looking for some sculpture?" He was eager to get the focus off himself.

"My boss, Brad Miller, the head of data processing, was

invited. He's on the corporate aquisitions committee, and they're interested in a piece for the entry of the new wing. He wanted a woman's opinion. I told him I'd meet him here and give him my input.''

He had no comment. He'd heard that Brad Miller gave her some input, though not in public, from time to time.

She walked fast, trying to stay in step beside him despite her high heels. "Slow down, Stuart. This is a party, not a track event." She tugged at the sleeve of his tux.

"Sorry." He slacked the pace a bit. They were approaching the front terrace. He didn't want her clinging to his arm or doing a nosedive on the pebbly drive. Nothing that could draw attention. He could hear the music, gentle jazz, played on guitar and clarinet, coming from behind huge potted Frangipani. Stu and Brian had rescued the plant for Chambers when he'd spotted it near an old downtown house scheduled for demolition.

The outdoor lights, old-world lanterns with beveled faces, were already lighted, adding their mellow glow to the fading sunset off toward the Gulf. Stu looked over the crowd of people out there and didn't see Rikki among them. But he did see Warnock in a tux and he spotted a couple of other police officers from the task force in tuxes as well. He knew there were more.

Warnock said they weren't taking any chances with security. A friend of Chambers who owned a tux rental shop agreed to supply outfits free to the undercover officers working the event. Stu nodded to Warnock in passing and headed into the front foyer with Terri dogging him step for step.

"Diet Coke? You?" Terri gave him a patronizing pat on the arm when he told the bartender what he wanted. "Must be a woman somewhere in all this," she guessed. "Or do you have a department physical coming up?"

"I've developed a taste for the stuff." Stu stood there, preoccupied with his own thoughts, watching the flow of guests passing behind her as she talked about her job.

"Come on. Let's see who's here." She took his arm with an air of expectation that he'd willingly comply. But he felt none of the old urges, and none of the tugs of anger or envy that had taunted him over the years. No interest in showing her what she was missing. He'd been thinking how good it was not to feel anything too personal toward her at all.

"I'm going to take a stroll around myself," he said simply. She let go. "But here's to buried hatchets," he raised his glass and tapped hers. "Hope you and the Miller fellow find something you like."

Terri simply looked confused. She'd apparently mistaken his politeness for something else.

"So long." Stu patted her shoulder and stepped away. He joined the easy flow of traffic out to the rear lawn, where Chambers had said most of the statues on display were situated. He was remarkably at peace. He'd found a totally different kind of woman. One whose optimism and serenity were contagious. Someone more womanly than merely feminine. Tall and solid and strong. With a touch as soft as a flower petal.

First, he'd make the rounds and take a look at the sculpture so he'd be able to say something intelligent when he and Rikki finally got to talk. There had to be almost two hundred guests spilling out from the upper terrace across the gardens, most of which he and Brian had landscaped. Another jazz quartet was playing in one quadrant of the yard. Three portable bars and several tables of hors d'oeuvres were located strategically along the walkways. With night muffling everything and the lights becoming more distinct in the increasing darkness, the whole scene took on a lovely fairy-tale quality.

He could see Rikki now out in the lower grounds, talking with Olivia Mello and some other folks. One fellow had a pair of deep brown Labrador retrievers on a split lead. They lay like elegant sphinxes at his feet.

Occasionally a light flashed as someone, most likely press, took a photograph. Taller than most of the guests around her, he could follow Rikki's pale hair as she moved from place to place, accommodating the requests to stop and pose again. Just watching her smile and clasp a hand or touch a shoulder in her gentle way sent a warm feeling through him.

No jealousy. Not like it had been with Terri, back when she was Terri Lynn. All he felt when he watched Rikki was a distinct pleasure, a sense of affirmation that the world was a better place because she was in it, and a thankfulness that miraculously their lives had touched.

He didn't need to seek her out and tag along, especially not while she and the other artists there were the center of interest. After his walk-through, he planned to stand in a corner, like the big-eyed Sulka at Rikki's house, minding his own business. He'd keep checking that she was all right. Eventually, she'd come his way.

"Stu Sullivan. Hardly recognized you, man." One of the police inspectors he'd worked with on several fire investigations came over to shake his good hand. "Say, how's the arm?"

"Coming along fine. How are you, Ben? Are you here for the art or are you on duty?" Like Stu, the officer was wearing a dark tux and black tie.

"Security," the man responded. "Partly because of the Trasher business, partly because these damn statues are expensive. Mr. Chambers doesn't want any one messing with the guests or with the artworks."

"No harm in being cautious," Stu said, nodding and moving on.

Several other city and county government officials he knew simply passed him by. Out of context, out of uniform, longer haired, tanned and bearded, Stu simply didn't look like his old self.

Olivia Mello, barely recognizable herself in the gauzy dress she'd borrowed from Rikki, came across the terrace and noticed him standing by one of her sculptures. "How ya' doin', Stu? Boy, don't you look pretty." On her, Rikki's dress almost touched the ground. "Rikki said you were here somewhere. We were wonderin' where you were."

"I've been looking around. You look very lovely."

"I do, don't I," she acknowledged. "I surprised a few folks," she added with a smug look.

"I'm sure you did." He kept easing back out of the flow of guests.

"You're not really into this stuff, are you?" Olivia guessed. She was repinning her special engraved nametag, one identifying her as an exhibitor. The tag was one of the classy touches that Chambers never overlooked.

"Actually I like the sculpture. I'm just not into crowds. And I'm not really into this kind of socializing."

"I'm with you. I'm happy with a blow torch and a beer. But I'm not complaining. Is this straight now?" She patted the nametag. The petite redhead stood barely shoulder high next to him.

"Left side is lower. Quarter of an inch, maybe."

Olivia readjusted it. "There are some slick folks out

there. Knowledgeable. Really interested in quality. Chambers says we've sold several pieces. I was just comin' in to check which ones. He says there's been no bitching over the price. He sure knew the high rollers to invite.''

"It's a great turnout," Stu agreed.

"Hope this shows the little fucker who started this crap a thing or two. I figure he's too chickenshit to show here.''

Stu nodded. He'd almost forgotten Olivia's tendency toward colorful language.

"By the way, who's the bimbette eyeing you from the bar?'' Olivia asked, turning her shoulder so Stu could glance past her toward the woman she meant. "Dark hair. Pricey squeeze-of-New York look,'' Olivia said narrowing the possibilities. It was Terri.

"Former wife.''

"You're kidding?''

"Really. Past tense.''

"She looks interested. In you. Present tense.'' Olivia's pretty bow lips pursed in a tight, disapproving arc.

"She has been from time to time. I'm not interested,'' he said succinctly.

"Good. I don't want anyone fuckin' with my friends or fuckin' with their friends. Rikki likes you. If that broad makes a wrong move, I may have to corner her and rip her tits off.''

"I really wish you wouldn't.'' The situation with Terri was under control. Then he cut his eyes toward the bar again. Terri was smiling, scoping out Olivia's backside, and coming their way. "I think she wants to meet you.'' He kept his voice low.

"Sure she does.'' Olivia said, deliberately easing closer and slipping arm through his possessively. "She just wants to check out the competition. Let's pretend I'm it.''

"Careful. She's with Florida Power. Corporate money. They're here looking to buy,'' Stu said deliberately before Terri worked her way close enough to hear.

"Stu. Hello again.'' She cruised up, giving Olivia a brief look. "Have you seen anything worth mentioning?''

"Just me,'' Olivia replied in her whiskey voice. Now she had Terri's full attention.

"You're one of the sculptors exhibiting tonight?'' Terri asked, spotting the distinctive nametag. Despite the polite veneer, her granite gaze absorbed every detail of Olivia Mello's stance and appearance.

"Olivia Mello. I have a number of creations in the gardens tonight." She introduced herself without relinquishing her clasp on Stu's arm.

"You didn't say you knew one of the artists," Terri chastized him, trying to sound playful. "Obviously you do."

"Rather well." Olivia blinked her big blue eyes and lifted them to meet his, lingering enough to make the gesture effective, but not so saccharine that it smacked of melodrama. "But this is hardly the place to discuss relationships," Olivia answered for him. "Tonight is primarily professional," she added with a breathy sigh.

Terri's smile stiffened as she looked at Stu for some kind of confirmation that Olivia wasn't putting her on.

He took a quick sip of his soft drink, wondering if Olivia's restrained language would shift to a more earthy level of communication if Terri persisted. "How about you and Mr. Miller? Have you seen anything your company might want to purchase?"

"I haven't seen everything yet," Terri responded a bit evasively.

"If you're interested in viewing a few of my pieces, I'd be delighted to discuss them with you." Olivia promptly abandoned her combative stance and shifted into her businesswoman's mode.

"I would like see which ones are yours." Terri's gaze narrowed perceptibly. Stu licked his lips.

He considered mediating. Or running interference. Olivia did have a way of expressing herself that might give Terri more than she bargained for. But any problem between them, if one arose, wasn't his concern. He just wanted to find Rikki and feel that sense of connection between them again.

He could see her crossing the terrace with the fellow with the chocolate Labs. They were heading toward the house. "I think I'll look around this way," Stu excused himself. He hoped he could intercept her there.

"I was wondering where you were." She was alone, on her way out with a glass of white wine when he reached the terrace doors. Her hand slipped into his so naturally, he wasn't sure which one of them reached for the other or if the gesture was simultaneous. It just felt right, public or not. "See any interesting things?" she asked.

They moved out of the traffic pattern, against one wall. "I saw a lot of interesting things, including you occasionally. Usually surrounded by people. I like this up-close view the best."

"Did you see Olivia?"

"Yes, indeed. We chatted." He considered letting it drop at that, then thought of all the other half-truths between them and decided not to add another one. "My ex-wife is here. Terri Lynn. Actually Terri. She zeroed in on Olivia and me and was trying to get a fix on our relationship."

"Yours and Olivia's?"

"Right. Let's say Olivia intimated there was one," Stu said, shaking his head. "Anyway, they went off together to discuss her art, but I have a grim feeling Terri had better tread lightly or Olivia might . . ."

"I can guess," Rikki interrupted, smiling. "I gather none of this worries you?" She was studying his face.

"You mean seeing Terri? Or her seeing me?"

"Either?"

"Not at all. I told you, no loose ends there," he said with more clarity than he'd ever felt. "I'm only concerned about you," he replied honestly, smiling at her. "How are you doing?"

"I'm fine."

The feel of her hand in his was warm and familiar and exciting. He had a strong desire to kiss her right there in front of everyone. "How long before we can go home and take off our shoes and see if this damn cast comes off?" The thickening in his voice made her smile.

"First I'd like to introduce you to a few friends. I want you to meet Victor Chambers, for one." Rikki stood on tiptoe and looked over the crowd.

"I met Chambers already. Are you sure we can't mix and mingle some other time? Preferably in fewer numbers?" he asked. He really didn't like crowds. But he also didn't want to spend the rest of the evening ducking acquaintances, watching strangers, making polite conversation, or spending time apart from her. "I'm more comfortable one on one."

"I noticed." Rikki squeezed his hand. "Okay. I'll let you off the hook. I won't drag you around introducing you.

But I have a few friends down there I still need to see.''
She pointed to a lighted area in the lower section of the
lawn where several large pieces were illuminated. Terri and
Olivia were standing talking not far from one of them. Neither one seemed to have her claws bared.

"You go ahead. I'll get a soft drink and catch up with
you," he insisted. "You mingle. I'll be fine."

"Okay." She gave his hand another squeeze, then went
on.

The next forty minutes they spent weaving through the
guests, mostly separated by groups of people, but near
enough that their eyes would meet. Occasionally they'd exchange a look of subtle amusement past intervening shoulders and heads.

Stu was stopped by a city councilman and a member of
the school board, both of whom he'd dealt with on fire investigations over the years. Other guests whose faces he
recognized didn't recognize his under the circumstances and
passed right by.

Socializing incognito made cocktail-party chit-chat easier
than he'd found it in the past. The beard and the tux gave
him a cushion of anonymity and a look of sophistication.
From Rikki's conversations with Juli Quinn and with him
from time to time, he'd picked up more about art and design
and composition than he realized. Now when he overheard
comments and assessments, he understood ones that would
have otherwise gone right over his head. He even looked at
the flowering plants along Chambers's walkways and the
baskets of orchids suspended in trees more closely, not from
a botanical viewpoint, but from an aesthetic bent, because
of things he remembered Rikki saying about the sensuality
of petals and leaf textures. Even without her physically near,
he didn't feel cut off from her.

"You look like you're enjoying this," Rikki said one of
the few times they came face to face and clasped hands
again.

"I am. You've taught me a lot about this art stuff. I'm
surprised how much I'm getting out of this." He stepped
aside to leave the pathway clear for other guests. "Thanks."

"For what?"

"For inviting me here. And for taking the time to show
me how to see things more completely."

"You're welcome."

He leaned toward her, lowering his voice. "I appreciate a number of other things you've taught me as well," he added quickly with a suggestive shift in tone. She was close enough that her breast pressed against his upper arm. "I'm looking forward to an opportunity later in the evening to express my appreciation."

With a slow, easy smile, she let him know she understood. "Just a while longer. I've got a few more people I need to visit and offer a little moral support, then I'll be ready to go."

"I don't mean to rush you. Really." He stroked her upper arm, feeling the curve of solid muscle beneath the velvety surface. Even touching her like this was a sensation that brought an instant tremor of passion, a reminder of the physical range in their lovemaking from tenderness to pure physical urgency. "Your friends need you here. I know that. You've also taught me a good bit about patience," he said softly. "I want you to myself, but I'm not so anxious to grab you that we have to leave. I may moan now and then," he admitted with a grin, "but I'll do it quietly. Go. I'll enjoy watching you while you make your rounds. There's something to be said about knowing you'll be going home with me. I'm happy as a clam."

"I wasn't worried," she assured him. "I saw you chatting with some folks. Meeting some old friends?" Something more than casual curiosity seemed to trigger her question.

"I've seen a few people I know from jobs I've been in on." He didn't say which jobs. If she'd seen his encounters with the councilman or the school board member, she'd assume they were clients from the landscaping and nursery business. "I like hearing what folks say about these sculptures."

"Good. But if your patience really starts to fade, come and get me."

"Will do," he promised, watching the flutter of her dress and the outline of her legs as the fine fabric clung to her body while she strode away.

McIver knew from the invitation his father-in-law had received from Victor Chambers that the sculpture exhibit was tonight. He'd considered going, just to get a look at them all up close. It had been over a week since he'd decked the guy by the pool in Englewood. Then he reconsidered. He figured the invitation signaled a propitious time to move again. Time to throw them another a curve so they wouldn't know what to expect.

He doubted Bambi would miss the affair. Those artist types were thick with each other. The Hilton Nine, perhaps excluding Jessup, would all be out in full force. Like Chambers, they had to be shrewd enough to know the value of all that free press coverage. She'd probably show up for the garden party event in one of her sarongs and float around, sashaying up to the field of well-heeled businessmen Chamber had recruited, trying to line up a few commissions.

All of the "Hilton artists" had become local celebrities of a sort because of him. Even *USA Today* had run articles about the trashings. McIver knew he'd helped them get the kind of exposure that even expensive marketing couldn't generate. And each time he hit again, he stirred up a new dose of sympathy for them. He wasn't going to be at Chambers's house watching them bask in all the attention and he wasn't interested in their art. Her art, those damn so-called therapeutic videos, had been what kicked off his divorce in the first place. He intended to get even. And then some.

Tonight, he'd hit her house. He'd create a nice trash-abstract work of his own, especially for her. He'd let her think now her turn had come and gone. She was off the hook. He'd let her have a while to sigh in relief while all the attention would turn to the remaining ones. Nine little Indians, reduced to four, soon to three. Tom-tom.

He liked keeping them all on edge. All he'd need to do was hit one more or maybe two after her, then he'd back-track, get her for good, and quit. They'd be left waiting, guarding the survivors, wondering when the next strike would come. It wouldn't.

He had to make this round look convincing. He wasn't going to use the canoe again. This time he'd ride up Midnight Pass on his ten-speed. He'd driven that trip a few times by bike already and found a place shielded by trees where he could pull off real quick. He'd stash the bike in the bushes just inside the hedge, clip the wires on her gate, and come in the front way. He'd even used the aerial shots from the office files to plot his route.

And he'd coat himself in bug repellent. No way he was

going to get eaten up again. His feet and legs still were spotted with scabs and raw where the clumps of little oozing blisters from the ant bites were slowly healing. Some ended up infected. Like leprosy.

He had the ski mask and the tools in his backpack. Gloves. Wire clippers. WD-40. A small crowbar. A towel. The short, heavy sledgehammer. Enough to do some serious damage. If she had stayed home, he'd have to rein in the urge to go in after her there and then. No drinking before he made the attack. Not like with the Englewood guy. He'd knocked back a few stiff ones before that one, and that bit of lubrication had taken him right to the edge. Maybe a fraction over.

He'd come real close to killing that one. He'd just got too revved up, just like with the little guy he'd cornered in the darkroom. Once he started in hitting on him, all the anger came flooding out like a tidal wave.

So he wouldn't down a few drinks for courage tonight. He couldn't afford to make a mistake and let the rage take over. When he went at her for real, he wanted to be completely in charge. Total control. Afterward, he'd watch it on the news on TV and celebrate.

From Harrison Ash's backyard, McIver could see the Lundquist woman's minivan was parked by her house. There was a small green car next to it. Looked like she'd skipped Chambers's soirée and stayed home. Even invited company. The sporty classic 'Vette that he'd seen at Ash's house was gone, but the Buick was there. The door of the garage across the way was closed, lights on upstairs, security light flooding the area below, so he figured the neighbor woman was in for the night. He stood enveloped by the dark, smearing on insect repellent, trying to place the number of people in the Lundquist house. He saw one kid, the boy, cross through the downstairs into the kitchen. Then he went back again toward the lighted room with something in his hand. Probably watching TV and decided to raid the fridge, McIver concluded. His boy would do that.

A low wail deep inside began rising. His boy. His son. His Bobby.

He usually managed to block it out.

Since Sandra left and had him served with papers, he'd had to kiss the mediator's butt even to get to see his own kids. Some counselor said that the kids told him he hit their mom and he'd hit them. Hard. So he got supervised visitation. But his lawyer told him that was how it was done when abuse was alleged. Limited contact. A show of remorse. And he'd been warned not to touch a drop of liquor beforehand.

He'd been allowed two afternoon visits with the kids each week. The encounters took place at Sandra's sister's house, supposedly neutral ground. He didn't think Sandra was even there. The sister stayed around, usually off in the next room, and kept monitoring them like he was some kind of a slug who'd temporarily been allowed out from under his rock.

Today's visitation with Bobby and Tia had been particularly terrible. The boy acted funny. Peculiar. Frightened. Brainwashed by the bitches, McIver guessed. They both were stiff as boards when he hugged them. By the time he finished fifteen minutes with the youngsters, he was soaked with perspiration from being cheerful and carrying on all the conversation himself. He hung in a while longer. He finally left. Didn't stay the full hour. He couldn't stand it.

On the way home, he'd had to stop in at Conroy's, his favorite watering hole on the beach strip. He got a couple of quick drinks to keep from screaming. Then he picked up a bottle at the liquor store in a strip mall further on and knocked back a couple of swallows on the drive home.

He bet her boy didn't skulk around just out of arm's reach, afraid of his shadow like his Bobby. He bet her little girl didn't keep looking for reassurance from someone listening just outside the door.

Both his kids were polite to him, but they said goodbye with sad, accusatory eyes. They'd been getting an earfull, and they were maybe even more relieved than he was when the visitation was over. It was her fault, Lundquist and the other bitches, for filling Sandra with that codependent crap. Damaged spirit, my ass. They kept at her until she got her back up and decide to call it quits with him. He was left with a twelve-grand greenhouse still in crates and a stack of cement blocks in his garage.

He'd get even. He'd make it real uncomfortable for all of them. Including Lundquist's kids. Mixed-breeds. Not even real Americans. He'd give them a taste of what it's like having their perfect little world upended. He'd have them cowering and crying and scrambling for someone to rescue them. Then he'd rip their family apart, just like his had been. All in good time.

McIver pulled on the ski mask, shouldered the backpack of tools, and moved very slowly along through the side yard. He watched the few lighted windows, stopping and listening, making sure he wasn't walking into a trap. By now they all were taking precautions.

One of the remaining four, whose studio on Anna Maria Island looked like an auto repair shop, had a biker with a studded jacket and arm-length tattoos staying with her. Walking anachronism. The guy in Bradenton, Thayer Kern, had installed metal grids on his first-floor windows and had decals showing that the building was monitored by some security company.

The guy in Fort Myers had moved out of his house and was "on an extended vacation"—at least that was what he'd heard from a fellow realtor when McIver called and inquired about the house. He wasn't interested. He had enough to do closer to home. But they were all scared. All cautious. All targets. All because of him.

He loved it.

McIver was cutting through a moonlit space next to her garage when his foot caught something near the ground. He lurched forward, shoulder first, toward a Spanish bayonet plant. He thrust out both arms to block the fall, but one needle-tipped point jabbed through the wool mask and caught the side of his neck, slicing the skin.

The cut stung like a razor knick, only meaner. McIver hissed in the air between his teeth in pain, rubbing his neck with one hand while he worked his foot out of the clay flowerpot. A fucking flowerpot. He could have lost an eye.

He reached in his sack for the wire clippers and severed the phone line with one low, brittle snip.

He liked the touch of cutting the phone wires first. After the initial panic, she would grab the phone to call for help. And for that moment, she'd hear nothing. She could reach no one. She'd be cut off like he was from Sandra. From his own kids. Incommunicado. Trapped.

Across the way, near the neighbor woman's house, some wild bird squawked. He heard wings flapping. On that side, one of Bambi's big lights went on, flooding the area. Several other startled birds squawked again and fluttered skyward in a flurry of bright colors. It excited him that she'd been worried enough to have motion-sensitive lights installed. He lay flat for at least a minute, wedged in against her house. Finally the light went out.

If one went on again, he'd roll into the shadows for cover. It would take them a few seconds to get up to look out at what had triggered it, if they bothered at all. By then, he'd be motionless, blending in with the dark.

Through one set of glass sliders where the vertical blinds weren't shut enough, he saw the kids go up to bed, their bare feet showing through between the suspended treads of the staircase. Poked over the end of the sofa facing the TV, he saw a pair of shoeless feet he guessed were hers. And he spotted the old broad sitting in the armchair, facing the TV. He figured sooner or later one of them would follow the kids up and check that they were in bed.

Sandra used to do that, he recalled. She'd go up and tuck the kids in and make sure all the lights were out. Just thinking of that near-forgotten nightly ritual brought a tightness in his throat. It was still going on without him wherever she was living now. He huddled in the dark, hearing that internal wail begin again, trying to recall how and why it all started going wrong.

Focus. Beginnings didn't matter, endings did, he told himself, half-embarassed that he'd been playing that "poor-me" head game again. Endings mattered. He had a few more rounds before he ended this one.

He didn't want any heroics from her or any confrontation. The face-to-face stuff would come later. He picked up a bench from the back deck and set it on its side across the sliders. She'd trip over it if she dared to come out. He rearranged a few of the chairs in a second row close by, like an obstacle course, in case she made it through the first barrier.

He used the crowbar to loosen the braces that connected the gazebo to the wall of the house, spraying them with WD-40 and using a toweling pad to cushion the tool. He got inside it, stretched up, and loosened some of the roof supports as well, without making a significant sound. He'd seen her fussing over the plants out there. There was a poetic justice to bringing her prize posies crashing down, since her stupid video and all her work was full of flowers. Once he had it all loosened, he packed up the crowbar again, set out the sledgehammer, and steadied himself, running it all through once more in his head.

"Let's do it." He grabbed one of the heavy stone dwarfish figures perched by the steps and heaved it at the glass doors. The tiki thudded and shook the doors, sending spiderweb fractures out on all sides as it ricocheted off and thudded back toward him.

They'd be up on their feet now.

McIver picked up the tiki and slammed it at the sliders again with all his strength. Tom-tom. It hit and dropped. This time the whole house seemed to shudder at the impact.

Someone in there screamed.

The third time, the tiki smashed hard enough to break through into the house, taking the center of the slider with it in a shower of diamond shards. The rest just hung there.

They'd be heading for the phone. Maybe one of them was on the way up to save the children. Tom-tom.

He had to move quick now. He took the sledgehammer, and swung at the frame of the orchid trellis over the spa end of the lanai. Tom-tom. He beat at one corner until he knocked loose the support. Tom-tom. Tom-tom. Faster. The voice inside him was screaming now, a shrill war cry. "Kill her."

The huge black fish thing hanging across the outside edge that extended out above the doors wobbled. The whole structure vibrated. Pots and baskets of plants shuddered and crashed to the ground. He slammed the hammer down on the ones within range.

He leaped around to the opposite corner and used the sledgehammer again on the next upright. Tom-tom. Throwing his whole weight into it, he made the entire canopy list, tilt, and finally sink. He beat it down. Tom-tom. The leading edge stretched out toward the dock and the Intracoastal. More pots and baskets clattered and rolled. With a series of brittle splintering sounds the structure collapsed slowly on top of the spa. Long spikes of orchids quivered and fluttered, pinned under the debris.

Tom-tom. Tom-tom.

The screaming now was from the floor above. Children. Hers. Afraid. He wished he could see her face. And smash it.

Tom-tom. Tom-tom.

Somewhere along the key he could hear a siren.

Tom-tom.

Getting closer.

Tom-tom.

Run. Get out of here.

Panting, McIver pulled himself back.

Enough.

Get out.

He did.

"You're awfully quiet," Rikki commented as Stu turned onto the bridge that crossed from Sarasota to Siesta Key. "Are you okay?"

Stu had been driving, lost in thought, plotting strategy for the next part of the evening. They needed to talk. Actually, he needed to talk. He just wasn't sure when to start.

They still had to relieve Juli Quinn from her babysitting duties. He would walk Pat Simons to her house while Rikki went up to check on the youngsters. Hopefully they'd be sound asleep.

"I'm okay. Just enjoying the ride." That part was true. There was a three-quarter moon and only a few clouds. The October night air was cool and refreshing and felt good on his face. Leaving Chambers's party, he'd tugged open the neck of his shirt and pitched the tux jacket and cummerbund in the back of the 'Vette. Then he'd stowed the car top and simply let the night sky embrace them.

"Victor did a wonderful job with the arrangements," she said, turning in her seat to look at him.

"Nice function," Stu agreed. "I hope it works out well for the artists, moneywise. Heard plenty of good comments." He glanced at her warily, feeling like she was waiting for more. At the party, he'd looked up once or twice from conversations with acquaintances and caught her watching him from a distance with that strange, faintly curious look in her eyes. Almost as if she were puzzled and pleased, but not quite sure about something.

"You're sure nothing is bothering you?" she asked, reaching over to rub his shoulder. "You seem a bit tense."

"I guess I am, a little," he admitted, mustering his courage as they turned onto Midnight Pass Road. "I've got a few things I need to clear up. Things I need to say. I'd just like to let it wait until we've got everything taken care." He broke off, narrowing his eyes at the flashing red and blue lights in his rear-view mirror. Reflexively, he lifted his foot off the gas pedal and checked his speedometer. He hadn't been speeding. The oncoming police car swerved out, overtook, and passed him, lights on but no sirens.

Rikki followed its taillights, stiffening in her seat. Far ahead, she could see other lights, other patrol cars. An orange and white ambulance came toward them, only using headlights, not hurrying anywhere. No passengers apparently.

"Some kind of accident ahead maybe," Stu guessed. Then he realized how close the action was to the turnoff to the cul-de-sac where Rikki lived. Simultaneously they both reacted.

"Please, no," she whispered, leaning forward, tensing like a cat ready to spring. The patrol car that had passed them swerved onto the shoulder and stopped.

Stu accelerated.

She gripped the dash, her eyes locked onto the cars ahead. They were all pulled off to the side, blocking the entrance to her gate.

Stu followed the route of the police car onto the wrong side of the road, pulling up behind it on the shoulder. "What's going on?" he called out, starting out of the car.

"You have to move," an officer shot back. "Move on."

"We live in there. What's wrong?" Stu demanded, looking around for a familiar face. Before anyone responded, Rikki was out of the car, making a straight charge for the mixed hedge of sea-grape, palmetto, and hibiscus that fringed the property.

"Hey. Lady. You can't go in there," the officer yelled, aiming the beam of his flashlight at her and pinpointing her backside.

Rikki ignored him. She pulled her full skirt into a tight bundle under one arm, leaped the low wall, and plunged through the underbrush.

"Stop her. Call in and tell 'em someone's coming."

"Her kids are in there," Stu bellowed to get the officer's attention.

"It's the mother. She's on the way," the patrolman relayed the message.

"I have to get in there," Stu insisted. He dug in his pants pocket and produced his badge. "Fire marshal. Sullivan. Now, tell me what the hell's going on. Anyone hurt? And get one of these cars out of the way and let me through,'' he barked orders.

"No one's hurt. Vandalism. Windows broken. Plants smashed. People scared, but okay.'' The officer who'd been using the radio seemed to be supervising the blockade. He was signaling for the other officer to pull his car back so Stu could turn around and pass through.

"Who's the officer in charge there?'' Stu asked as he got back in his car.

"Detective Warnock. Just arrived.''

"Shit,'' Stu muttered, knowing the Trasher must have hit, otherwise Warnock wouldn't have been the one called in. His tires sent a spray of gravel pelting officers and cars as they gripped and skidded. The 'Vette roared down the serpentine roadway into the peninsula.

Her house was surrounded.

Two TV station vans were parked in the middle of the road close to Ash's house. He bypassed them and drove across the grass, flattening a few low shrubs along the way.

Rikki was already in the house when he parked in the front yard amid a crosshatching of emergency vehicles and marked and unmarked police cars. Circling on foot, he could see her in the kitchen with Juli and Pat Simons and the kids, all talking excitedly. Faces pale. Eyes wide. Mike Maurer, the young cop who'd come to his door with Sordo, was in with them. No one seemed hurt. Whatever anxiety had been keeping him from breathing let up.

Maybe this time the bastard had made a mistake.

Since most of the action seemed to be out back, facing the waterway, Stu made his way around, showing his ID to a couple of investigators who stopped him en route and didn't recognize him with the hair and beard and his tux shirt. Two videocam teams from the mobile news vans were shooting footage. Several other folks with cameras, most likely from the newspapers, were standing, talking and watching.

Out back, police had roped off the section for the crime lab team. The entire rear of the house was lit up with flood-lights and alive with personnel. What glass remained in the shattered sliders hung in saberlike spears or jutted up like stalagmites. The trellis of the lanai that had covered the deck and spa area looked like a forlorn pile of sticks. Orchids and broken pots were strewn all around. The tail of the long black shark poked out under one corner. It vaguely reminded him of a scene from the Wizard of Oz, after the tornado hit. Stu guessed the Sulka mask was flattened somewhere under there as well. Whatever protective magic they had apparently hadn't worked tonight.

Warnock stood amid all the commotion, quietly unruffled. "Looks like the Trasher was doing his trick-or-treating a couple of weeks early," the detective noted when he caught sight of Stu. "Your lady friend inside?"

"She's with the kids."

"Good. They were scared. They all were scared. He cut the phone lines. The creep must have figured he could take his time. Then he started with the door. They thought he was coming in after them and headed upstairs. No telling what else he planned," Warnock added. "They got 911 on the cellular. The Simons woman could hear the sirens and caught a look at him from the upstairs window as he took off on foot down the road toward the gate. Ski mask. Some kind of bag."

"No sign of a vehicle?"

"No one saw one," Warnock shrugged. "We tried to get you at Chambers's house but you guys had already left. Good thing you came straight home. Must have rattled the place like a sonic boom."

"At least no one was hurt this time," Stu said, looking at the damage that was done.

Warnock smoothed his moustache and drew his hand slowly downward to pat his tie thoughtfully. "You know, to be quite honest, your lady comes out of this pretty good, comparatively." He inclined his head toward the collapsed lattice work. "This kind of damage can be fixed. He stayed away from her darkroom and the studio upstairs. And from what I hear, she's got quite an orchid collection in that slathouse. She's lucky he didn't know enough about plants to hit it instead of the ones out here."

Stu was rubbing his shoulder, nodding.

"Brought his own tools. He cut the wires on the gate on the way in. It had to be opened by hand. Everything was real calculated. Just pisses me off that he scared the kids," Warnock added with uncharacteristic vehemence. "Rotten thing to drag the young ones into this. I told you I have a bad feeling about this guy."

"He's a real bastard, all right." Stu bit off the words. A

cold fury had taken hold. With all the publicity about the art event at Chambers's house tonight, the Trasher would have to suspect the security at the party would be tight. So instead of going after the grown-ups, he'd waited until little children were home without their mom. Like some monster, he'd rattled the walls and brought the roof down. The whole intent was twisted. And Stu was angry at himself for not figuring it out and staying home, on guard, one more time.

"So we're down to three," Warnock said with a frustrated sigh. "And nothing much to go on."

"What about the kid you're looking for? The one who was supposed to be heading for Miami? Maybe he didn't leave. Maybe he did this"

"We're still working on the brother, trying to locate Rhule. Obviously if he's in Miami, he isn't our guy. But he could be down the street and still not be the one who did this. My reading from what his buddies and his ex-girlfriend say is that he's just a scared, wise-ass kid. I don't think he's the kind to pull off anything this nasty or this dicey."

Stu caught another glimpse of Rikki, the kids, Maurer, and Juli in the kitchen. Despite the goings-on around them, Rikki was squeezing them juice, passing out apples, dispensing hugs, and getting things back on a familiar, soothing level. Nourishing their senses. Juli Quinn was still talking to the cop. Pat Simons was nowhere in sight. He guessed someone had escorted her home. Then Rikki paused by the glass sliders to look out and spotted him out there in the harsh light with Warnock and the others. She gave the rubble a dismayed shrug and then nodded, conveying instantly that at least inside, things were basically okay.

"So where do you go from here?" Stu asked the detective.

"We wait. Again. We'll go over the area here for a while. Probably come back in the morning for a thorough going-over. We'll increase patrols on the remaining folks. If it were up to me, I'd move them all out and put in some decoys. In our district, we're down to Mello and Kern. I don't think we can afford to take any risks, not with civilians. I'll run the decoy idea by the powers that be," Warnock stated, narrowing his too-close eyes. "I'm not sure how this will fly."

"I don't see that there's much choice now," Stu agreed. "If you don't act and he hurts someone, the press will hang the department. If you put in decoys and nail him, I can think of all kinds of angles that would look real good. Might even get reenacted on one of those true-crime TV shows. The mayor will like it. The council will like it. Makes the city and its employees look good.''

''Maybe. This sure as hell won't look good,'' Warnock observed grimly, anticipating the coverage tonight's attack would get. Scared children. Women alone. The photographer from the police lab was putting away his gear, but several others from the press were apparently waiting around for Rikki to come outside long enough to get some shots of her with her exotic plants in shambles.

''What about tonight? Got anything to move on?'' Stu asked.

''Nothing much yet. A couple of footprints. No fingerprints. The guy is still wearing gloves, it seems. Like I said, we'll be back tomorrow to comb the place in the daylight.''

''At least Rikki and the kids can get back to normal,'' Stu said, watching her in profile through the kitchen sliders as she stroked Lara's dark hair. Jake was sitting farther over on the counter ledge in his pajamas, munching away contentedly on an apple. Maurer was taking notes and talking with Juli, who looked considerably more animated than she had when he arrived.

''You can get back to normal too.'' Warnock came back at him. ''Your job here is done. No more bodyguard routine,'' he went on, nudging a shard of glass with the toe of his shoe. ''You can pack up and move in to the mainland. Get back to work in the real world like the rest of us.''

Warnock's words settled like a cold weight in his stomach.

Stu liked this world and the people in it a whole lot. He'd been there less than a month, and it already felt like home to him. The prospect of going back to his condo, of not being able to see her or work with her every day, pushed aside whatever relief he felt about her being out of danger.

He'd miss the family feeling. He'd miss puttering around the place. But mostly, he'd miss her. Between them, so much was still in the potential stage. Growing. He wanted time to move it ahead to something permanent. ''Harrison Ash isn't due back for two weeks. Just after Halloween. I think I'll try to hang around here until then,'' he told the detective. "Maybe help her rebuild this and get her plants back in shape."

"Sure. You look like a real Mr. Fix-it." Warnock cut him a grin, tapping his knuckle on Stu's fiberglass cast.

Stu was studying the wreckage of the lanai. "I've still got some things to clear up here." He wasn't only thinking of the cleanup work involved in rebuilding it. He and Rikki still needed to get a number of other things straight between them.

"Hey, I wouldn't want to leave either. I wish you luck," he said sincerely.

"I have a feeling I may need it."

Warnock followed Stu's steady gaze into the large kitchen where several more people were now part of the lighted tableau. Eddie Sordo was there. Swede Lundquist and Ivey had arrived and were milling around, taking turns listening to the kids and peering outside at the debris. Swede, navigating on only one crutch now, caught sight of Stu and the detective and headed toward the door to come out and talk. Sordo bustled along behind him.

"I think I'll leave Poppa Bear and his sidekick to you," Warnock mumbled, ambling off toward the yellow-taped area.

Stu shook his head. This was not the way he'd visualized the evening ending. There would be no quick check on the children, no stripping off the fancy clothes, no shelving the air cast and sinking into the Intracoastal together under the three-quarter moon. There would be questions and explanations, but not in private, where he could speak his heart.

Chapter 7

When Stu came out to observe the investigation team in the morning, Joe Warnock stepped back into the shade a few paces from the others so they could talk.

"Found a broken clay pot and some scuff marks over by the slathouse. Looks like it flipped the guy into a Spanish bayonet. Unfortunately not enough to stop him. But it looks like it may have grazed him. One of the lab techs came up with some skin and some fiber. Might get a DNA profile." He sounded encouraged. "We'll see what else shows." The lab team was processing part of the hedge area by the gate they'd sectioned off the night before.

"Find something here?" Stu asked.

"Yep. Versatile little son of a bitch," Warnock noted. "Looks like this time he came on a bicycle. Apparently he stowed it here while he strolled in to do his crash-and-bang routine." Warnock pointed to the tire tracks and footprints left in the sandy soil. "Somehow he ducked the incoming unit." He glanced up and took a closer look at Stu. "You must have had a rough night."

"I did."

"You 'fessed up?"

Stu nodded.

"She didn't like being spied on?" Warnock guessed.

"She wasn't thrilled," Stu conceded dully from behind his mirror-lensed sunglasses. He hadn't slept much. He'd paced and churned away what was left of the night. After the police left her yard and the kids were put to bed again, in a postmortem of sorts, he and Swede told her what had been going on the past four weeks. She was tired and emotionally drained but still characteristically calm.

She became far calmer as he and her father talked.

"You don't have to like the technique I used," Swede had told her. "But my motives were good. Stu's were too.

He was locked into an agreement with me and with the mayor not to say anything to you. Now you're out of danger, so it's time to clear the air.''

They both could see Rikki retreating behind a stiff-faced expression, one neither of them could read. Swede told him it just meant she was absorbing, suspending judgment, getting all the details ingested. Bristling too. He said she'd get quieter and take time to sort it all out. He had that part right.

Stu admitted straight out he'd become overzealous. He'd told her about the binoculars and the bionic ear. Even about taking Ash's emergency key and slipping into her house and staying by the stairway overnight. He'd held nothing back. Not even the part about Sardo watching him watching her. And watching them together. And calling the cops.

She hadn't said much afterward. Neither had Swede, who gradually realized there had been far more going on than he'd known about. Everyone felt awkward under the circumstances. But when the confessions and the accompanying apologies wound down to a long heavy silence, it was three in the morning.

Rikki simply pulled out extra bedding and told her dad and Ivey to pick a couch and go to sleep. Stu, she sent home. "Please go now. I'll talk to you when I can," she'd told him, her voice barely more than a hoarse whisper. Her shoulders sagged. She still had on the sunset-colored dress, its skirt ripped in places from her shortcut through the underbrush. Without another word she let him out the front door. He went alone to Ash's house, worrying as he went if he'd said enough, or perhaps too much.

He hadn't told her he loved her. But sliding that into the rather somber conversation didn't seem right. He considered calling, asking for one more minute with her alone. But her bedroom light was already out when he got inside and looked across the way. So he'd sprawled out on the bed and watched the ceiling fan rotate and ruminated until his eyes burned.

Standing out there with Warnock the next morning, he caught a glimpse of her watching from the upper level of her house. Like him, she was wearing sunglasses. She was leaning on the railing surrounding the open sundeck, watching them and the action below. Behind her, the shutters of the airy Caribbean-style rooftop sitting room were open. He guessed that since Swede and Ivey's car was gone, they'd probably taken the youngsters off with them to their condo to stay awhile. They'd said the night before they thought it was best to get the kids out of there. Besides having the police and the debris as grim reminders of the attack, once the story hit the news, there might be some curious onlookers coming to stare. It was better to give the kids some peace until the attention died down. Most likely Rikki had come up top to distance herself from the devastation and the gathering of evidence as well.

"How's it look out back?" Stu asked. He'd seen Sordo's truck over there and wondered what was going on.

"Like it did last night," Warnock said. "I told her until we were finished processing the scene, she couldn't touch a thing. The sidekick was here early though. They've got the place draped."

Warnock said she'd called in Eddie Sordo to help her protect all the flowering orchids trapped under the roofing and scattered over the lanai. He'd apparently been there at dawn with wide rolls of dense mesh shade cloth. Together he and Rikki had stapled the fabric to the east side of house, tenting the entire deck area to keep out the hot rays of the morning sun. Stu knew how difficult it must be for her to look at the mess and to hold off on the cleanup and salvage efforts. She hadn't even been allowed to pull the shark or the Sulka mask out from under the debris. He just wished that when Detective Warnock gave her the go-ahead, she'd let him help. But she'd called Sordo, not him. Stu felt like a leper, excluded, uncertain whether to go over or continue to wait until she was ready to say something.

He didn't want to crowd her. Swede had cautioned him that she couldn't be rushed. But Stu knew how gently one had to handle repotting flowering orchids, especially damaged ones. You didn't simply stuff the roots back in a basket or a pot like they were in before. You babied them. You opted for a slightly larger size, plucked away the fragments of the old container, and you eased them into the new one, without disturbing or crowding or pinching the roots or trying to repack whatever medium had been used. For mature, well-developed specimens like hers, it took more than one pair of hands to do it right. He knew he could be helpful if he were welcome to join the effort.

"I'm goin' out to get the wood to get ready to rebuild the

trellis.'' Sordo stopped his truck on the roadway to clear his exit with Warnock. "We won't move anything until you say so,'' he added hastily. "But I got a couple of friends who will help once we get the go-ahead. If I get the wood here, we can take away the old stuff and get the new frame installed in a couple of hours, 'specially once the sun moves to the other side of the house.''

"No problem.'' Warnock gave the officer at the gate a signal to let the fellow continue on.

"Morning.'' Sordo looked at Stu and shrugged, apparently uncertain what else to say. Then he drove through.

While Warnock crossed over to Rikki's house to join the officers at work there, Stu went back inside Ash's house, returned a few phone calls, talked to his brother again, drenched his eyes in Murine, and stretched out on the downstairs sofa. The next thing he knew, he was being prodded from sleep by the doorbell. It was almost eleven. He'd been out almost an hour. Trying to rub some life into his face, he made it to the door, expecting to see Warnock with an update. He squinted at the sun-framed figure on the step. It was Rikki.

"I can't hang around any longer and do nothing.'' She was wearing the kind of outfit he hadn't seen her in before, a distinctly non-native business suit, pale gold silk skirt and jacket with an ivory blouse. Her hair was pulled back softly with some kind of clip at the nape of her neck, with an elegance that made him think of a ballerina.

"Come in.'' He held open the door so she would step inside.

She did. "I don't like being suspicious,'' she told him. "I had a feeling something was missing when you talked about yourself. And I wondered why you didn't tell me what it was. Or why you didn't let me spend any time with your brother when he came to see you. Or why you didn't take me to any of the places special to you or introduce me to any of your friends. The pieces you gave me about yourself just weren't enough to flesh out the picture. You know how I feel about being lied to. Omitting crucial details is just as bad. I've felt very uneasy about you, Sullivan.'' She rested her hands, overlapping, on her chest in a poignant gesture of comfort and protectiveness.

"I know. I'm sorry.''

"I'm not interested in sorry.'' The weariness still in her

voice made him want to hold her. Instead, he clutched his cast and crossed his arms over his chest, keeping his hands to himself. "I'm interested in piecing the real Stuart Sullivan back together. The old version won't hold up, and after last night, what there was of it has simply fragmented. I need some sense of who you really are."

Her expression was still stiff, guarded, and composed. But the glimmer of pain in her velvety brown eyes held no challenge. It spoke of a need to put an end to the questions that must have nagged at her for the past weeks. "I kept waiting for you to open your outside life to me, and you wouldn't do it. You would go so far, then you closed me out. I can't work this through without some help."

"What can I do?" He flopped his good hand in the air, wishing he could touch her, but not daring to in case he might unsettle whatever tenuous set of circumstances had brought her to his doorstep.

"Let's start by taking a look at where you work."

"My office?"

"Right. I want to know who you are away from here."

"Fine. When?"

"Now."

"All right." He tried to sound more enthusiastic than he felt. "Give me a few minutes to get civilized." He turned and headed upstairs to change from his faded shorts and tee-shirt into slacks and a jacket and an open-necked sports shirt. Unfortunately it was a Friday. Almost midday. Most of the downtown offices at the administration complex would be vibrating with employees trying to wrap up business for the weekend and others simply stalling for the workday to end so they could unwind afterward.

His staff became more gregarious as Friday dwindled away. They looked out windows, they made phone calls, and they found excuses to zig-zag into hallways and stop to talk along the way. Walking through the city administration building adjacent Station One with this leggy blonde at his side wouldn't be as likely to draw attention if it were a weekend with only a skeleton staff around. On a Friday, the word would fly. They'd come swarming out of the wood-work to take a look.

"Hey, Chief. Is that really you?" The voices started coming from all sides once they stepped past the heavy glass

doors. Stu walked straight to the security desk and started
to reach for his badge.

"Welcome back, Chief."

The uniformed woman on front-desk duty obviously recognized him, longish hair, beard, and street clothes not-
withstanding.

"Hello Lisa. This is an unofficial visit," he noted.

The woman handed Rikki a visitor's tag to clip to her
lapel. "I guessed as much."

Two fireman came out the elevator ahead. "Hey. Chief
Sullivan. Love the new look."

"This is Sarasota, not San Francisco," the taller of the
two kidded him as he approached.

"I don't think that beard and all that purty hair is going
to pass the safety inspection. Not unless you're giving up
your line personnel status." The first one picked up the
beat, talking to Stu but studying Rikki with a frank and
admiring look.

Stu basically ignored the comments, greeted the men by
name, then once they were past, took a quick step and held
open the elevator door for Rikki. He knew as the doors
closed that someone would be phoning upstairs where the
fire marshals' offices were to tell them that he and "some
blonde" were on the way.

He could tell that the word was out by the unnatural quiet
when they stepped out of the elevator on the second floor.
People started ambling out of doorways and cutting across
the hallway to take a look. Then one staff member's face
would disappear, there'd be a flurry of not-quite-audible
comments, and another equally nonchalant staff person
would cross their pathway.

"Rikki Lundquist. Inspector Ben Kopitsky." Stu made
introductions as they moved through the hallway which was
filling like an obstacle course with secretaries, inspectors,
captains, and even the deputy chief. "Kathleen. Captain
Prichard. Bonnie. Rikki Lundquist." He dutifully left no
one out.

"Aren't you the lady who's been on television. The photographer? With all the orchids?"

"That's me," Rikki acknowledged as Stu kept his distance, letting her talk as long as she wished and trying to
resist the urge to steer her toward a doorway further on.

"Saw the news about your house last night. Glad no one was hurt."

"How are the kids handling it?" The questions and comments flew as soon as they all realized she was one of the Trasher's targets.

"Jenny. This is Rikki," Stu told the angular gray-haired woman waiting at the end of the hall for them to make it through to the small outer office leading to his inner sanctum. "Jenny is my indispensable overseer."

"Nice to meet you. Come in. Catch your breath. Would you like some coffee?" Jenny scanned the tall blonde from top to toe with a faint light twinkling in the dark eyes behind her bifocals. Her pencil thin eyebrows arched a bit higher.

"Just water will be fine," Rikki replied sweeping the outer office to Stu's domain with a curious look. Besides a beautiful cluster of lavender-pouched Paphs on Jenny's desk and another white-with-rose-throat Phalaenopsis on the table between two comfortable looking chairs, there were several tiers of riblike Vanda orchids hanging in baskets by the windows. Below, a row of leafy indoor plants were crowded together like a jungle fringe underneath. The greenery almost succeeded in blocking out the drab view of the parking garage next door.

"I have a stack of reports that you might want to review," Jenny told Stu with quiet efficiency, apparently covering some ongoing business. "You look tired," she added with a slight motherly softening in her tone.

"I'm okay," he insisted. While she relayed several other pieces of business about permits and safety inspections, she filled Rikki a glass of iced water from an insulated pitcher nearby. "How serious was this Trasher business last night?" Jenny aimed the question at her boss.

"Bad enough. Could have been worse. Police were there till late." He took a file she handed him and studied the printout inside.

Jenny's desk phone rang. "Sure is. Certainly. I'll ask him." She was nodding as the caller spoke. "It's the Deputy Chief." She gestured with her thumb, indicating the call was coming from the adjacent office. "He heard you were here. He doesn't want to intrude but he wants to know if you need to see him or if he should go ahead to lunch."

"Tell him to go ahead. I'm not here on anything official."

"Captain? Go ahead. Enjoy your lunch. Don't forget you

have a meeting with Bates from Code Enforcement at three. Right.'' The woman relayed the message.

"Jenny keeps us all looking more efficient than we are,'' Stu said, smiling for the first time that day.

"Now about that hair . . .'' Jenny narrowed one eye and looked at him. "And that.'' She leveled a finger at the beard. "Should I be scheduling an appointment for you somewhere to be properly shorn?''

"I've got two more weeks. Besides, I like it.'' He smoothed the neat sandy-colored growth of hair on his jaw a bit self-consciously. "Don't panic. It'll go before I'm back in uniform.''

"Me? Panic?'' Jenny peered at him with amused wonder.

Rikki doubted that this slim, efficient woman ever lost her serenity. She had that same unflappable manner that she remembered her mother having. Even when Swede was cursing at his equipment or flying off in all directions during a photo shoot, her mother could locate and pass him the correct lens or film or filter, tape record the notes he was dictating, douse them all with insect repellent, and hand out peanut-butter sandwiches to her daughter. Jenny seemed to have the ability to maintain her orientation and balance in the midst of turmoil with a similar gyroscopic precision.

"I must have had a momentary mind lapse,'' he joked back, still looking closely at the pages she had prepared for him.

"I'm sure this has been dreadful for your family.'' Jenny shifted subjects and faced Rikki with a more somber expression. "How much damage did he do to your home?''

Rikki hesitated, grim faced. "He did quite a job. He shattered a glass slider. He brought down a gazebo and a lattice roof over the back deck. I'm not sure yet if the spa is cracked. I had about twenty baskets of orchids, all in bloom, hanging out there. We're not sure how badly the plants are damaged.''

"The good news,'' Stu spoke up, "is that no one was hurt. And the guy left her slathouse untouched. She's got a remarkable collection there with some really rare and beautiful plants. He just hit the ones out back on show.''

Rikki gave him a slightly surprised look.

"Joe Warnock and the lab team are still there investigating,'' Stu continued. "They're combing the whole place for anything that might help nail this guy. Might have a skin sample from a Spanish bayonet. We haven't been given the go-ahead to start cleaning up yet.''

"Well, when you do get to rescue the plants, the Green Thumb Wizard here can do wonderful things with them,'' Jenny said, tilting her head toward the bank of lush green trailing pots behind her desk. "Those are his doing, not mine. I just water when he tells me to.''

"Rikki's orchids will take some special handling.'' Stu glanced at her, hoping she'd take his comment as an offer to do some of the handling with her.

She'd moved over by the window and was taking a closer look at the mini-rain forest he'd created there. Across the top, a canopy of philodendron were fed by a clear plastic tube connected to a squeeze bulb. Next came the Vandas in the stronger light. The lower plants were situated in a plastic tray to protect the carpet. They'd catch any spillover when Jenny watered the hanging plants above.

"I need to drop off a few things down the hall,'' Stu said deliberately. "I'll be back in a couple of minutes. Look around all you like. Is that all right?'' he asked them both, guessing it might be a good idea to let Rikki have some time to herself in his office and with Jenny so she wouldn't think he was monitoring what she saw or heard.

"It's all right with me.'' Rikki gave him a quick smile.

"We'll manage,'' Jenny said, smiling.

"Fine.'' He hesitated, collected a few other folders, almost as an afterthought, then left.

He stayed busy in the vacant inspector's office several doors away, making a few phone calls, checking on the progress of a recent safety-code inspection, and stalling. He wanted to be sure Rikki had time to chat with Jenny and absorb whatever she could from his official surroundings. From the traffic in the hall, he guessed several of his staff were still finding reasons to go into his office and have another look or a chance to talk with her as well.

"So. How did it go?'' he asked, a bit nervously when he finally went to retrieve her. Jenny had left an open file of news clippings on her desk in which a clean-shaved, occasionally moustachioed Stu Sullivan was pictured over a period of years. The top one showed him in his dark windbreaker with the official patches just before he was promoted to chief three years earlier.

"It helped. Quite impressive.'' Rikki indicated the file

she'd been looking through. "The people in the office here really think a lot of you," she told him. "I like that. They've had a lot of nice things to say about you."

"Good." He didn't know why hearing her say it made him relieved. He hadn't expected anything negative to surface. There wasn't anything particularly negative to say. Except perhaps that he had a temper. Sometimes he came down a little hard and loud when he thought something wasn't done according to his standards.

But he cooled off quickly, he didn't hold a grudge, and he didn't expect anyone else to hold one either. He'd worked hard to develop his staff and keep a good relationship with all of them. He was quick to hand out praise for work well done. Admittedly, he could be obsessive on an investigation or hard-nosed with a safety check. Occasionally he lost track of when it was time to go home at the end of a day.

Socially he was a bit of a lone wolf. Since his divorce, he knew he was rumored to have a procession of women interested in him. He'd avoided entanglements and he'd never been involved with anyone connected with the department. Rikki was the first women he'd ever brought up and introduced around. But he had nothing to hide.

"So where to now?" he asked, clearly encouraged.

"I want to see where you live."

"Okay. It's just a condo. Two-bedroom unit over a garage and utility area."

"I'm interested in the ambience, not the architecture."

"Okay."

"Roommates?"

"Not likely."

"Any pets?"

"Nope. With my schedule, they'd have to spend too much time in the place alone. Didn't seem like a good idea."

"But you do have plants?"

"A few. All the good stuff that I've collected is out at the nursery. Brian and Vicky are there all the time so they keep up with them."

"So let's go there next."

"Fine. You interested in some lunch somewhere along the way?" He hadn't eaten anything since he'd chased a banana with a Diet Coke that morning.

"I could handle a salad. How about you?"

"Just as long as it has a steak sandwich on the plate next to it. Rare."

After the lunch stop, Stu walked her through the two-bedroom apartment, one bedroom of which still had boxes of books and memorabilia that he had neatly stacked but hadn't unpacked since he'd moved in after the divorce.

Rikki strolled from room to room, looking at the rather Spartan interior, all in cool, soothing shades of gray.

"Who chose the colors in here?"

"I did. I wanted it sort of quiet."

"It's nice. The grays are very soothing," she said. Next to the cushioned sofa she saw the headset with large earphones and paused. "Are these part of your surveillance equipment?"

"Nope. Those are for the CD player," he explained quickly, swinging open the louvered doors of a shelf unit, exposing his sound system. "I like to play it late sometimes, and I don't want to blast out the neighbors so I use these."

She nodded, then stepped close enough to read the names on the three tiers of CD's. They were arranged in alphabetical order. She skimmed the artists from Aerosmith, Jimmy Buffet, Bizet, Robert Cray, the Doors, through Lyle Lovett, Bob Marley, Mahler, Wynton Marsalis, Paul Simon, Segovia, and Rod Stewart, Vivaldi, Yellowman, and ZZ Top.

"It's an eclectic assortment," he admitted. "A little of everything."

The thought of Stu stretched out with the earphones, listening, brought that slight softening of her lips again. However, throughout the tidy condo with its windows overlooking an overgrown strip of land and a wide creek, the only notable omission, for someone who loved plants as Stu did, was the touch of nature indoors.

"Maybe you could use some pictures. I have a few you might like. Maybe some nice flowers," she noted with a suggestion of a smile. "Ones that don't require looking after."

"I like your work. I'd like to get a couple of prints. I just didn't quite know how to approach you."

"Consider me approached," she said quietly scanning the walls with a thoughtful look. "You might want to look through my files and find something that appeals to you."

''I'd like that.'' He licked his lips, relieved again. He'd take her offer as a sign of progress in their mending process.

''Okay. Let's go to see Plantworks,'' she said next. Stu simply held open the door, like a well-trained chauffeur. He'd drive her wherever she wanted to go.

The acreage where Stu and Brian Sullivan had their land-scaping and nursery business was once on the northeastern fringe of Sarasota, on slightly rolling land that had been a vast citrus orchard. Gradually the city had grown out around it, swallowing up the groveland in large bites. Except for a few orange and grapefruit trees that the former residents had maintained, the orchard was long gone. Stu drove in the entryway marked by a neat permanent sign and parked by the low, air-conditioned building that was part office, part laboratory for propagating plants.

Several hundred yards off to the east on the rise beyond a series of sturdy slathouses, shade houses, and geometri-cally sectioned plots for shrubs and ornamentals was a pretty blue-shuttered old farmhouse, beautifully restored even to the extent of using tin roofing like the original would have had. It was surrounded on three sides by a shaded verandah. ''That's where Brian and Vicky live.'' Stu gestured toward the house. In various locations, workers were busy watering plants. In one open building Rikki could see a stocky older woman rotating by hand one of several mounted oil drums in which rich compost was being processed.

''Brian should be in here,'' Stu said, waving at another woman employee who was maneuvering a big-wheeled gar-den cart under one compost drum.

They barely got the office door open when Brian Sullivan came out from behind his desk to shake hands. ''Good to see you, Rikki. Heard about your lanai being smashed and your orchids being downed. Stu said the guy hadn't touched the slathouse.''

''That was fortunate,'' she acknowledged.

''He called this morning to say that you guys were all right.'' He chatted with them a moment then offered her a personal tour of the nursery operation. He left Stu in charge of the office and had him go over some landscaping plans he'd been drafting.

''Last time he wouldn't let us talk,'' Brian said, eager to visit with her. ''Vicky, my wife, was wondering if he'd bring you out here. He doesn't do this, you know. He's never brought any woman here. His wife despised the place. And he doesn't usually say anything about who he's seeing. But he sure has talked about you. Funny you should show up like this. I'd just called your house and Ash's to see if you guys needed some help with the plants, but I only got answering machines. I guess this is why.''

"Coming here wasn't actually Stu's idea." Rikki told him about the revelations and late-hour confessions of the night before and why they were making the rounds of Stu's haunts.

"So this is a crash course in the true character of my brother . . ." Brian was genuinely amused. "Then you'll have to talk to Mom when she gets back. She lives in town closer to the action. She's got scrapbooks about him. About both of us. She grew up not far from here. Her house is gone now, cleared away for a housing development. But this property used to belong to some friends of hers. They grew oranges. The nursery and growing exotics was a hobby of theirs, not really a business. Stu and I used to help out here in the summers and sometimes after school. Then the wife died and the fellow sold off some of the land. He wanted to sell the rest of it, so Vicky and I bought it with Stu as a partner. Obviously, we've done a lot with it," he said proudly. "We keep expanding. You probably already know how addictive growing plants can get. We've added on quite a bit."

"I'll say," Rikki replied as she followed him into the first of the well-tended plant houses. She breathed in the healthy, earthy aroma. The soft moist air circulated around them, pulled by giant fans set in the end wall. Overhead she could see neat rows of white PVC tubing with tiny sprinker heads set on the underside at intervals.

"Stu." Brian pointed at them. "He's pretty good at mapping out and setting up misting systems." She remembered seeing a similar setup in Stu's office, only without the small spray head. "We're putting in a couple of new units in the spring mostly for display space," Brian noted. "We've got plenty of unusual, mature plants that we don't plan to sell but we need to house them in better order. Vicky has been reading up on propagation techniques and flasking, so we'll be expanding and updating our lab too." He was checking the dials on the watering system as they walked end to end through the center of each plant facility, surrounded by tables of plants at various stages of growth. "Stu says when he retires he's planning to do some traveling and ship plants home from all over the world to build on our collections. Maybe do some cross-breeding in the lab. Until this arm injury put him out of circulation, I couldn't imagine him taking a decent vacation, much less retiring. He really likes what he does. Both jobs. Here and with the fire marshal's department. He likes to make a difference. Mom taught us to do that.''

"I'd like to meet your mother."

"I'm sure she'd like to meet you too. She'd heard about you, that's for sure." His whole face spread into a smile. "We all pay attention when Stu talks about meeting a woman with smarts," he stressed. "But Mom has taken off for the weekend with some chums of hers from her condo complex. They've gone over to Palm Beach to an antique and jewelry show, then they're going to some play at a dinner theater Burt Reynolds owns. In Jupiter Beach. She likes theater. Of course, she likes Burt too. If she and her buddies got a peek at him, it would be a kick. But I think Stu was planning to get you two together when she comes back. He must have mentioned something to her.''

Rikki was already thinking that the mother of these two sons sounded like the kind of woman Swede and Ivey Currey would enjoy meeting, someone her mother would have liked as well. Family was important to her. Suddenly she was mentally expanding their separate connections to include brothers and children and stepmothers and other possibilities she found vaguely exciting. She hadn't been looking for anyone. She'd felt no void in her life. Like Stu, she'd adjusted to the independent, single life she'd built for herself, and she'd been busy and happy in that life with just the children. But meeting Stu had changed her. Now some disquiet inside suggested that there would be an emptiness without him. An affinity for a special person was enough to cause her to pull out and examine the old conventions. She was mentally dusting off the options to determine which ones could be adapted into a life-style that could encompass both of them. And their families. And their work.

"Brian . . . honey?" A pretty, dark-haired young woman came in the opposite end of the high-roofed plant house. "I called the office and Stu answered. Then he said you were here somewhere with Rikki. I couldn't wait to meet you." As she came nearer, Rikki could see the slight roundness under her oversized tee shirt and remembered Stu had said once that Brian's wife was pregnant. She slipped her hand into her husband's.

"Vicky, this is Rikki. Sounds like a nursery rhyme," he joked. "And this is my daughter," Brian included the expected child with an encompassing sweep of his hand. "Or perhaps my son," he added with an agreeable shrug. "Either way, we're calling the kid Stormy."

Vicky's color deepened. "It has to do with the tropical storm we had last May when all the electricity went out. We had candles and champagne . . ."

Rikki nodded, guessing from the timing that Vicky was in her fourth month. "Stormy Sullivan is a great name. Rather dynamic."

"We'll see," Vicky said, obviously not in total agreement with her husband's name choice. "I'd hate for this one to spend her life explaining where we got the name. I hear you have two kids? How old are yours?"

Before Rikki could answer, Brian shrugged and flung up his hands good naturedly. "So much for the tour. I think I'll leave you two talking about mother things. Vicky has known Stu for years. She can probably tell you things about him I don't even know. Just come back and pick him up before too long," he cautioned Rikki. "You probably know how he is. If he hangs around here, he'll start nosing around, trying to help, and he'll end up lifting things. The doctor doesn't want him doing any heavy stuff for a few more weeks. The only way I could keep him from it was to make the place off limits until the cast comes off."

"We'll be back in a while," Vicky assured him. "I'd like to show her a few things up at the house." With that she turned and led her companion the opposite way, off toward the charming old homestead on the rise.

Just as they promised, the two women weren't gone long. They arrived back just as Brian was chewing at his brother for loading some orchid baskets in the back of his 'Vette without waiting for him to help.

"They're light. Gimme' a break." Stu was bent over, arranging the cargo, muttering right back at him.

"He figured you might need some new clay pots and hanging baskets, replacements for when you get home." Brian looked up and started explaining to the women why they were loading them. "You know, for repotting the ones that fell."

"You didn't have to go to all this trouble," Rikki started to protest, but Stu stood and looked at her. She could tell by the droop in his shoulders and his crestfallen expression that this had been his way of helping. He hadn't forgotten there were injured plants at home needing care. He'd even packed extra wire and support ties.

She changed tack instantly. "I probably would have had to make all kinds of extra trips for supplies. These will be great. I really appreciate this. It will save us a lot of time when we get back." She hoped Stu felt included in the "us" without her having to make an issue of it. From the way his smile blossomed, she knew he did.

"So. Let's go home," Stu suggested, eager to mend more than latticework and damaged orchids. "We've got work to do. I called Warnock. He's out of there. He told Eddie he could start."

"What's the book?" Brian asked when he saw Vicky slide a thick album onto the passenger seat.

"Scrapbook. One your mom put together. I thought Rikki might like to thumb through it."

Stu gave his sister-in-law a pained look. "That's the one with everything, including high school?"

Vicky ignored him. "When their mom gets back, we'll all get together and talk," she said to Rikki in a low, conspiratorial voice, sufficiently loud for Stu and Brian to hear. "She was very curious to meet you. We were all interested in seeing some of your photographs. From what Stu says, they must be quite remarkable."

"They are." Stu was nodding and wedging in another basket. "They're very profound and peaceful. They have a real eloquence." Stu said it offhandedly, surprising himself with the aptness and passion of his observation.

"Thanks, Sullivan." Rikki tilted her head in a nod of appreciation for the critique. "And thanks for the tour. This is really a nice setup here. I'm glad I got to see it," she told Brian and his wife. "And I'm glad I got to talk with both of you." There was a slight shift in pace now, as if she'd found what she'd been searching for, without realizing what it was she wanted. Now she was ready to go home.

Wordlessly Stu set the last of the cedar-strip orchid baskets snugly behind the driver's seat then opened the passenger door for Rikki. "Thanks. See you guys." He waved before pulling away.

"Call us if you need more pots or baskets or help with the plants," Brian called out. He and Vicky stood arm in arm watching the sporty 'Vette pull up the driveway, pause, then purr out onto the paved roadway.

It was almost three in the afternoon when Stu pulled up to the gate on Siesta Key. The electronic wires were taped off so they wouldn't be dangerous, but they weren't reconnected. The gate had apparently been closed by hand. "I'll get it."

"Stay put. I'll do it." Rikki got out and pushed it open easily.

"I'll come back and fix that." Stu drove through and waited for her to close it behind them and get back into the car.

"I'm more anxious about the orchids. Let's take care of them first." She was sitting a bit forward in the seat, gripping the scrapbook Vicky had loaned to her. The police van and the cars that had been there earlier were gone. Eddie Sordo's truck was nowhere visible but two other cars were pulled up on the lawn along the side of the house. A third was parked out front.

"That's Claire's car. My friend from Selby. She probably heard about the plants and came to lend a hand."

Once Stu pulled up beside it and stopped, they could hear voices and music coming from the back deck area. "Sounds like they've started the party without us." He slid out and grabbed a couple of the replacement baskets. Rikki picked up several of the larger ones, stacked them on top of the scrapbook, and carried everything around toward the action.

Eddie Sordo's truck was backed in close to the deck. The entire truck bed was already filled with the debris, shattered baskets, strips of splintered lattice, and plastic buckets loaded with broken glass from the doors. Now that the sun had passed over and started to drop behind the house, Sordo and his helpers had taken down the shade cloth so it wouldn't get in the way. He and his two friends were taking a break, sitting with their backs up against the house in its shade, drenched in perspiration, drinking lemonade and assessing their next move.

So far they'd just cleared the perimeter so they could safely

move in to dismantle the collapsed roof. Claire and whichever orchids had been flung farther out onto the deck were
nowhere in sight. The big black shark was propped on his
pronged tail near the door into the kitchen, relatively un-
scathed despite its ordeal. However, the Sulka mask, the
spa, several deck chairs, and most of the orchids were still
pinned under the main rooftop.

"You came at the right time." Sordo greeted them. "We
think we can lift this thing in sections out in the yard then
Carlos can pull it apart while Barry and me start framing in
the new roof."

"I'm game." Rikki put down the baskets. "Let me go in
and switch to work clothes." She was still in the pale gold
and ivory suit she'd worn on her rounds with Stu.

"Me too. I'll be right back." Stu was already depositing
his baskets on the deck, freeing his hands so he could join
in.

"No, not you with the cast. This part doesn't include
you." She wagged a finger, warning him. "You aren't supposed to lift."

"I can use one arm," Stu argued.

"Use it to point," Rikki countered uncompromisingly.
"Or to pot. We need your expertise with orchids, not with
this part of the operation."

"Your lady friend in the slathouse said she is strong and
she will help," Sordo spoke up, looking nervously from
one to the other, trying to avoid any argument. "I think we
can manage just fine."

"So do I. Just don't do anything until I change." She
stopped abruptly and looked at the open space where the
broken slider had been. Then she reached out her hand.
There was no glass in it.

"Don't worry about the door," Sordo called after her.
"I'll staple shade cloth over it to keep the bugs out later if
I have to. I measured it and talked to the Swede. He told
me to go ahead and call a building supply place. They're
delivering a new one sometime this afternoon. If they get
here early enough, Carlos knows how to put it in."

By now Claire had heard the voices and realized Rikki
had returned. "Great. Bigger baskets. Just what I needed."
She came out of the slathouse to get the ones Stu had put
down. "You must be Stu," she noted, her glance lighting

on his cast as she reached out her left arm so they could shake hands. "Claire Hailey."

"Nice to meet you, Claire." He was pleased to put another face to another name on the list of Rikki's friends that Swede and Ivey had given him. "Rikki said you work at Selby. Beautiful place."

"Sure is." Claire nodded.

"She's told me a bit about the plant programs you have. I especially like getting troubled kids into gardening. Good exercise. Helps build a real insight into caring for something."

Claire's eyebrows lifted slightly, indicating she agreed. "Rikki said you're good with plants yourself. I could use a hand in there." She nodded toward the slathouse. "And since you've got one that works . . ." She left the statement unfinished and grinned at him.

"Glad to help." He instantly liked the woman's directness.

"I'd like to get this first lot done before they lift the roof off the others." Claire started outlining her plan of action as Stu followed her with an armload of supplies.

Later, Stu stayed back and watched while Rikki and the others lifted sections of the old lattice covering out into the yard. Then Eddie Sordo and his men went to work erecting a new frame while Rikki, Stu, and Claire ferried the broken pots and baskets into the slathouse and worked salvaging the orchids that had been pinned underneath. The big fan inside the slathouse provided a steady breeze and hummed in gentle opposition to the sharper sounds of hammering and sawing on the lanai. There was little need for words. Each of them was sufficiently experienced to coordinate with the others almost instinctively.

"Bruises, some broken leads. Crushed a few back bulbs. Not pretty now, but lots of healthy pseudobulbs with good roots. Most of them stand a good chance of pulling through." Claire summed up her assessment of the destruction. She was busily plucking out pieces of broken cedar from the root system of a vintage Vanda that had held a cluster of pink-hearted flowers.

"I just never thought he'd come after the plants," Rikki said. "I figured it would be the darkroom. Juli and I pulled everything of any real importance out of there, except the processing equipment. We even moved all the slides out of the production room.'' She finished tying one cluster of long-limbed Dendrobiums upright within the four wires suspending the new basket. ''The shock may set these back a bit,'' Rikki said with more relief than sadness, ''but they're doing better than I expected.'' She looked up to find Stu watching her closely. ''I guess I am too,'' she added on his behalf. They exchanged quick simultaneous smiles and went back to the remaining casualties lined up on the worktable between them.

Just as the sun was setting, Swede and Ivey and the children arrived bearing containers of carry-out food for the inside and outside workers. ''Okay. Time out,'' Swede declared. ''Everyone stop and dig in.''

Eddie Sordo and the two men, Carlos and Barry, dove off the dock to cool off first. Then they all gathered under the skeletal structure, draped again with the shade cloth for the next morning's sun. Talking and laughing, they picnicked on hot chicken, spicy red beans and rice, fruit salad, and gallons of iced tea.

''Oscar looks pretty good,'' Lara said, walking around and patting a few of the familiar objects that had been resurrected from the rubble.

''I think the Sulka looks better fat,'' Jake noted. The rattan mask had come out of the chaos flattened, but now stood looking unusually robust propped on a wood support Sordo's friend Carlos had tacked together. His sides were all puffed out. Stu had packed him with of wads of crumpled newspaper, hoping to stretch out his folds and creases.

''Are you still mad at Grampa?'' Lara asked point blank between bites of chicken.

Swede stopped chewing and gave his granddaughter a distressed look. Obviously there had been some talk circulating at the condo about her mother's reaction to what had been going on with Stu and the surveillance and keeping secrets.

''I'm not mad,'' Rikki answered after a pause. From the stillness around her, she had everyone's attention, except perhaps Jake's. He was absorbed in eating his food. ''I was upset,'' she conceded. ''It's really uncomfortable thinking one thing is true and then finding out you only know a tiny bit of the story. It's like suddenly having everything shift all out of focus. But I'm beginning to clear up the fuzzy spots now," she said. "It's going to be okay. Different, but definitely all right."

"Does that mean you aren't mad at Stu?" Lara persisted, just wanting to be sure. "Grampa said you were."

"I'm not mad at Stu."

"Good," Lara reached next to her and patted Stu's arm. "Mama likes you," she told him. "Grampa said so."

Swede sighed and shook his head. "I talk too much," he muttered.

"Sometimes you do," Ivey chuckled, stroking his shoulder. "If I were you, dear, I'd remember that's a trait that your granddaughter may share with you."

"That's my girl," Swede replied, giving the youngster a hug.

Later in the evening, Swede and Ivey took the children with them back to the condo for the weekend so they wouldn't get in the way when the construction resumed. But Rikki suspected it was also to give her some time alone with Stu.

After dark, the two of them climbed to the shuttered enclosure on top of her house, then sat out on the sundeck with their feet propped on one rung of the railing, looking over the treetops at the lights across the Intracoastal. Cloud cover had obscured the moon and stars so the surface of the water was black and silken and still. If it didn't rain the next day, Sordo and his men would be back, working on the lanai trellis.

"A lot of things make more sense now," Rikki said, staring out over the water. "I have to admit that I was a bit put out when you seemed content to drop me off and keep to yourself at Victor's party. I almost felt that you were uncomfortable being with me in public. I wondered if you had a wife or a fiancée or a girlfriend or any combination thereof tucked away somewhere and you didn't want to get caught two-timing her."

"I don't have anyone. I was ducking a few associates," he admitted. "But even if I weren't, at an event like that I'd still be happier cruising in the background."

"I know that now. But I was nervous. I could sense you were holding back something. I told you about my old flame Karl and his native harem," she reminded him. "That kind of revelation leaves scars."

"I have a few scars myself. But no harem." He reached over and took her hand.

"However, I'm not thrilled that you steered away simply because you didn't want to be recognized and blow your cover," she said, with a trace of a frown.

"There were other reasons. I didn't want to complicate the evening. The event was for you and the other artists. I wanted to keep an eye on you. But I should have told you what the story was," he reconfirmed what he'd said before. "I didn't like keeping things from you."

She was silent a moment. "Don't do it again."

"I won't."

They sat in peaceful silence, holding hands, staring at the night sky.

"I liked seeing parts of your other life today." She broke the stillness.

"Good."

"Now I've had a chance to think about it, I also like the fact that even with your cover blown, you still didn't treat me like a trophy." For a few seconds she was silent, engrossed in thought.

"A trophy?"

Rikki blinked, suddenly shifting back into the present. "You don't parade me around. Some men I've gone out with have to show me off in public. It isn't that they're so interested in people meeting me. They want people to see them with me. You know, flaunting the blonde. Ivey's son Steele calls it the 'trophy broad syndrome.' He sometimes gets it in reverse. He gets paraded around. Then it's the 'trophy stud syndrome.' "

"I'm not sure I understand."

"The message in either case is 'Look what a babe I've got with me. I must be hot stuff.' The flashier the trophy, the more important or desireable the other person feels."

"I chased some girls just for their looks in my carousing days," Stu admitted, realizing without regret how subtly that part of his life had shifted into past tense. "Unfortunately, I caught one."

"But you weren't that way with me. Or to me. Whichever," she stressed. "I would have flushed you if you'd pulled the trophy broad routine with me. Even today, you could have shown me off all around your office building, but you didn't. You do your job. Apparently well. And you don't seem to care about impressing anyone.''

"Whoa. I want to impress you," he countered. "I still do. But I won't fake anything to make me look good. I want you to feel comfortable with what I really am. I liked a lot about my life before you came into the picture. I wasn't looking for a change.''

"I wasn't either.'' For a long moment she looked at him, studying his expression feature by feature, her own face lighted by a pensive smile. "I've been doing a lot of mental shuffling because of you. Because of us.''

"I know.'' He reached over and took her hand, cupping it between his larger ones and kissing the back of each finger with almost unbearable tenderness. "Believe me, I've been shuffling too.''

She leaned toward him, gently running the fingertips of her free hand through his sandy hair. "When are you moving back to your place on the mainland?''

"I haven't decided. Ash doesn't get back for a couple of weeks. I figured I'd hang around and keep an eye on the place. I hate to leave the boys. They'd miss me.'' He had her hand pressed against his chest, still cupped between his, trying to read her expression.

"I'd miss you.''

"I hope so. I'm a decent sort of guy. You should think about keeping me around.''

"You do have possibilities,'' she conceded, moving close enough for their lips to brush softly, then linger, then meet again, the kisses more heated this time. "Do you think we could get this thing back on, if we took it off?'' Rikki asked softly, tapping the fiberglass air cast. "We could take a swim.''

"I'm willing to risk anything . . . everything with you.'' His voice was suddenly thick.

"Let's risk unencapsulating you.''

"Please do,'' he moaned, standing and gently tugging her to her feet.

"Should we call Eddie Sordo's house first and make sure he's home?'' Rikki asked, smiling as they walked arm in arm toward the shutter house. They closed its door, then followed the circular stairway down into her bedroom level.

"After all the hours he put in here today, I doubt if he's ambulatory. Besides, he said he didn't see everything that night.'' Stu sighed and shook his head, still embarrassed by the incident. ''He only watched because he was worried about you. I don't think he's worried any more.''

''He isn't. He called me aside and put in a good word for you this afternoon,'' she confided. ''He wasn't the only one on your side. You have some very caring friends. And relatives.''

''They all stuck up for me? I told you I was a decent sort of guy.''

''So far the vote is unanimous. However.'' She qualified the statement with a playful lilt in her voice. ''I haven't polled my dad. After some of the things you had to say in front of him and Ivey, I'm not sure if he's put off, pleased, or simply in shock.''

''He seemed all right at dinner. He didn't kick me under the table or anything. Let's just assume he's happy if you're happy.''

''If that's the case, leave the cast. Take off the clothes.'' She halted at the foot of the stairway and waited for him to reach the last step. ''I have a couple of suggestions for making me real happy,'' she purred. The touch of her hand sent shivers of anticipation running rampant.

''Just be gentle,'' Stu pleaded, grinning as he embraced her.

Chapter 8

Saturday morning, Stu woke at five-thirty to the soft beep of the alarm next to Rikki's bed. It was still dark outside. Rikki reached out instinctively and pushed the "off" button. "Sorry. I don't know why it went off."

Stu cracked and eye and groaned. "I set it. Stay put. I'll take care of the boys and be right back," he whispered. "Didn't want to forget to feed them." He left her dozing there on her side while he pulled on a sweatshirt and shorts and jogged across to Ash's house to set out the usual fruit fare for the parrots. When he finished, he went downstairs and checked the answering machine. There was one message. From his sister-in-law, Vicky, apparently left over from the night before. It simply said to call her and Brian if they needed help with the plants, and to take real good care of the romance. "Classy lady you got there, Stu." Vicky left any further advice unspoken.

"Classy's only part of it," Stu acknowledged as he loped back to Rikki's house. He was careful to keep the mending arm held in close against his side so it wouldn't bounce.

The October chill in the heavy air made his skin cool and damp, and the grass underfoot was wet with morning dew. He let himself in, locked up, and left his damp deck shoes downstairs. He stood next to Rikki's bed, shivering slightly and peeling off his clothes, smiling at her long, curved form under the sheet, her back still to him. When he slid back under the covers and cupped himself against her naked body, the electric contact of her heat against him made him draw in a sudden breath then sigh.

"Hmmm. Is that you, Sullivan?" Her languid, amused tone as they lay together with her buttocks against his upper thighs made him chuckle.

"You're damn right it's me." He reached over her, slid

his hand up her tummy, and cupped her breast, snuggling closer.

"Now that part is vaguely familiar," Rikki responded, gently undulating her hips, stirring and arousing both of them.

"If you'd turn this way, I could make it less vague," he offered. Entwined, they rolled and kissed and laughed and kissed again, pulling the bed coverings over and around them. Tented, they caressed in total darkness, surrounded now by the warmth of each other's breath upon their naked skin.

"You are exquisite," he gasped between deep, almost desperate kisses, fired by the sheer energy between them. "This is exquisite."

"Yes. Exquisite." She lifted her hips to intensify his rhythm. The unhurried passion of the night before was far more tentative, more restrained than the urgency and lustiness of this dawn encounter. All they could hear were each others soft sighs, deepening and escalating, as their bodies gave and received, coaxed and responded. Finally, breathless and drenched in mingled sweat, no longer merely playful, they were caught up and suspended in a rush of tremulous sensations. Scented by a shared perfume, they collapsed in each others arms.

"Nothing vague about that," Rikki said in a low, rich whisper once she could speak at all.

Stu looked at her and burst out laughing. "I'll say. Nothing vague at all," he agreed, flushed and grinning and breathing unevenly. They lay together, smiling, holding each other. They fell asleep embracing as the room slowly filled with the pale glow of a new day.

When Stu checked the answering machine on his next trip over to Ash's house midmorning that day, Swede had left a message. "Word is they got the Rhule kid. In Miami. They're sending him back. Call me. I want to know what's going on." Swede ended it. Obviously he was still nosing around in the investigation, pumping his connections, and he didn't want to leave the message where Rikki might hear it and get her hopes up.

Instead of calling him back, Stu phoned Joe Warnock first. The officer who picked up at Warnock's extension said Warnock was out of town. When Stu identified himself, the fellow paused.

"Right. Sullivan. Your name is on the list I'm calling about a task force meeting today." The officer became more expansive. Warnock had flown to Miami and was flying back, with a suspect in custody, about four that afternoon. He added that the task force was to meet at four-thirty.

"Which airport is Joe coming into?" Stu asked, doubting that Warnock could make it from Tampa International at four to downtown Sarasota in time for a four-thirty meeting, and he didn't intend to sit around the station an hour or more, waiting.

"City airport. Private plane." The officer explained that Victor Chambers had offered his private jet for the pickup. Warnock and his suspect would be coming into the Sarasota airport, direct flight.

Stu unstrapped the air cast. He took a shower, somewhat reluctant to talk to Swede, even by phone. The problem now was professional as well as personal. He wasn't about to discuss task force business with anyone. Swede was treading on another set of ethics by trying to get information from him now. He hadn't even dried off when Swede called again, more anxious than before.

"Been wondering what you were up to. Have you found out anything?"

"Nothing yet."

"Me neither. Something's fishy. Everyone is bein' darned closed mouthed about what's going on with this character. When he gets here, I want you to go down and take a look at this Rhule. Talk to your buddies at the station. I'd like the real scuttlebutt, like if this is really the guy who's been jumping around the area doing these things. If they caught him in Miami, I'm wondering if he was even in town here Thursday night. If he didn't wreck my daughter's lanai, someone else did. Who's the someone else? The more I think about it, the less any of this makes sense."

"I doubt if they'd let me in on anything until they're ready to make it public. I have no official connection."

"Bullshit," Swede shot back. "You and I both know better. You have your ways to find out things. I have mine. Right now, mine aren't particularly productive. So give yours a shot." He hesitated.

"Swede, I can't do that."

Silence. Stu knew the man understood his position.

"Just tell me whatever you can. Please." His manner changed abruptly. "See what you can find out. I just want to be sure this mess is really over." Without his blustery facade, he simply sounded like a worried father. "Even if Rikki is off the hook with whoever this Trasher is, she still has friends out there. I'm concerned about them too. Is the pressure off these folks or isn't it? I just don't think any wiseacre kid is behind this."

"I'll go down to my office awhile. I'll make a few stops. Visit a few friends." Stu tried to sound reassuring. "But I can't pass on restricted information." He agreed that Swede's gut instincts were sounding all the correct alarms. Like Warnock, Stu doubted that the Rhule kid was the person responsible for any attacks other than the Hilton art trashing. That was a one-shot, hit-and-run deal. Vandalism. The subsequent crimes were confrontational. Calculated. And the malicious edge to them suggested someone else, someone volatile, was out there, possibly planning to strike again.

But Warnock was methodical. Rhule was the name they had, so they'd check him out. That was how investigations worked. Warnock would pursue every angle, including tracking down Rhule, even if it were only to eliminate him as a possibility. Meanwhile, the task force was going over details, reinterviewing neighbors, trying to round up witnesses. The plan to use police personnel as decoys for the two remaining artists was being put together. Look-alikes were being matched to Mello and Kern's physical stats. Apparently they would all meet today. Something was definitely up. And Rikki's father was on the outside. "If I have something for you, I'll get back to you," he promised Swede. "I don't like this any more than you do."

A vehicle with three women pulled into the driveway just as Stu was leaving Rikki's house for the third time that day. "If you're looking for Rikki, she's around the back," Stu told them, instead of them trying the front. He'd gone back over to tell her he had some business in town, which was essentially true. The task force was essentially business.

The driveway already had four other vehicles, including Rikki's van. Juli Quinn was there to do some work in the darkroom. The detective, Mike Maurer, had stopped by to see how she was doing. The two carpenter friends of Sordo's were hammering away, finishing the lanai latticework out back. The kids were still safely out of the way at Swede's and Ivey's for the weekend. Rikki had been going back and forth, doing laundry, keeping up with Juli's photo work, and checking the progress of the restoration. Stu had been watering and ministering to the plants awhile in the slathouse, helping wherever he could. He'd already lined up the ones with new flowers or full buds so they could be moved out to the gazebo when space was ready. There had been a pleasant, productive bustle as they all went about their work. Now his business was elsewhere.

Even the three women visitors had a purposeful edge. They exchanged polite passing comments with him, lifted two pots of orchids from the backseat of the car, and went around the house toward the back just as he indicated. The two women, bearing plants, he didn't recognize. The third woman, leading the procession and carrying an attaché case, was the woman from the conference, Janelle Givrey. He'd listened to her on the bionic ear, urging Rikki to do more explicit videos. He hadn't heard the outcome of that broken conversation, but from what he'd heard that time, he figured Rikki had said no. Now he wasn't so sure. He hesitated before driving off, hoping this was a social call. But the attaché case the Givrey woman brought made him suspect it was a shift in tactics, with reinforcements.

Like Swede said, Rikki was stubborn. If Givrey and the others were ganging up on her, that would most likely make her dig in her heels, or retreat. But maybe, he argued, like Rikki's other friend Claire, the women had just come to see how the repair work on the house was progressing, sympathize, restock the orchid supply, and offer their friendly support. If that were true, Rikki would be pleased. Either way, Stu would be on safer ground elsewhere. So he left.

"You already know Michelle Sands," Janelle said, introducing the taller of the two women with her when they spotted Rikki out back. "This is Holly Morrison. She's an actress from Asolo. Holly was one of my clients."

Tanned, broad shouldered, with a firm handshake and a relaxed smile, the young brunette almost curtsied as she shook Rikki's hand. "I'm very pleased to meet you. I can't tell you how much I appreciate the video you made. I used it a lot when I was in therapy. I still have it."

Rikki studied the young woman's radiant expression,

wondering which video she had used and what kind of therapy Holly Morrison once had needed.

"Holly was in my group of teens with eating disorders. Almost four years ago." Janelle explained the connection as if she'd anticipated Rikki's curiosity. "I gave her a copy of that first tape you did for positive imaging."

Rikki nodded, remembering how diligently she and Janelle had worked on that pilot video. She and several other therapists and the musician Fuzzy Haight had met and offered their input. Claire Hailey had been getting into horticultural therapy then and had given them access to any of the plants in Selby Gardens to photograph.

"Holly was bulimic. We almost lost her." Janelle's expression sombered briefly with the grim memory of how frail Holly Morrison had been when she'd finally agreed to come in for treatment. Now the actress was lovely looking and ostensibly in good health.

"I'm so glad that the tape helped," Rikki said. It wasn't often she came face to face with one of the clients. She rarely even knew the names the ones who had benefited from her work. Most of that information was confidential. The follow-up and feedback about the tapes was usually passed on to her second or third hand by whatever social worker or therapist had used the material Janelle had recommended.

"That tape even went to college with me," Holly said. "I still watch it a couple of times a month. It's like an old friend."

"That's great." Rikki felt a distinct pleasure that something she'd made so long ago still had such an effect.

Janelle Givrey had said the tapes would have that kind of impact. She'd felt from the beginning that television was a cultural given, a natural for therapeutic use. Most young people grew up with TV and VCR's as standard household equipment. Music videos were a way of life. Supplying a client with a personal copy of a therapeutic tape made sense. Music and the beautiful images were always just a touch away. Instant reassurance. Shorthand for countless conversations in counseling sessions.

"We didn't come here simply to say thanks, but that's a good starting place," Janelle noted, eyeing her other companion. "We came to say we're sorry that the Trasher damaged your property, but we're awfully glad no one was hurt.''

Michelle Sands, the second therapist, handed Rikki one of the orchids they'd brought. "We got them at Selby. Janelle asked Claire to help up pick out something."

"Wonderful."

"But we do have another issue altogether we need to bring up," Sands admitted hastily. "Now the Trasher has been here, you don't have the pressure of impending doom upon you. We have to make a pitch for something for someone else."

"I had a feeling," Rikki muttered. She'd guessed Janelle had reassessed the first turn-down and was sufficiently tenacious to come back with impressive reinforcements to press the case.

A beauty-shop strawberry blonde, soft featured, almost matronly woman in her early forties, Sands had a sound reputation for working with sexually dysfunctional clients. She also had her doctorate with a concentration in sex therapy. She'd been one of the specialists who had asked for a more explicit, more erotic video for her clients. Rikki didn't know the third woman's connection with this campaign.

"Janelle said you were not too receptive about the new project she suggested for a number of reasons. I hoped you'd consider a division-of-labor approach to making the video we need," Sands said. "We just would like to make our pitch. Please."

"Come on in." Rikki didn't want to try to carry on a conversation about sex therapy with the two men hammering or laying the last strips of lattice above them or trying to listen.

Inside, the new heavier glass slider that Carlos had installed muffled the construction sounds. "I'll listen, but you have to understand my position hasn't changed. I'm not comfortable with the dynamics," Rikki stated evenly. She didn't want them to mistake her sympathy with their cause for any encouragement that she may reconsider doing the photography. Naked people weren't her forté.

"I talked over your reservations with Michelle. We both know how awkward a situation this is," Janelle said, proceeding with the others into the kitchen after Rikki. "But we don't know anyone else with the skill or the sensitivity to do it right. You do good work. So that's how we came up with a compromise of sorts.''

"Juice?'' Rikki offered.

"Please.'' All three replied at once.

"Janelle said that one problem you addressed was the idea of staging this kind of thing for the camera. It's awkward. I can appreciate that,'' Michelle Sands pressed on. "Janelle said she'd suggested involving actual lovers, but you felt uncomfortable with that solution.''

"That about sums it up.'' Rikki shrugged slightly, then busied herself setting out glasses and getting ice cubes. The three women sat on the stools facing the counter. By now, Juli Quinn had come in from the darkroom. It only took a moment for Rikki to make the introductions and catch her up on the drift of the conversation so far. She'd already heard about the earlier one.

"What if the couple you are photographing are ones who would not feel particularly inhibited or exhibitionistic under the circumstances?'' Michelle Sands suggested. "True-life lovers who just happen to be experienced performers professionally? Serious actors.''

Rikki looked over at Holly Morrison, who was studying her reaction closely. Now Rikki had the missing piece. "You would do this?''

"Yes. I'm volunteering. Actually my fiancé and I are,'' Holly declared. "I've benefited from visualization therapy. I really would like to give something back.'' She eased forward on her stool, eager to add her part. "I know firsthand how valuable these resensitizing videos can be. One of yours helped save me from destroying myself.'' She spoke in earnest. "When Janelle mentioned this new project to me, I felt as if a light went on. I can do what you need to photograph.'' The young woman accentuated her words with her graceful hands. "I talked to my boyfriend about it. Greg is an actor too. He has a really wonderful awareness of the body as an instrument of expression. And our personal relationship is very solid, very intense.''

"He wouldn't mind other people seeing you two together?'' Juli asked.

Holly's face radiated with joy as she spoke. "He knows this is for a very restricted audience. Greg is very interested in all kinds of communication. He's seen the video I have. He understands how it reinforces my self-imaging. He feels very strongly that we should do this if it could help other people express their love and rediscover their sexuality."

Rikki paused between pouring glasses of chilled juice, considering Holly's comment. She understood quite clearly the young woman's desire to make a positive contribution. But part of her was still backing away from the realities such a shoot would entail.

"I thought of something else," Janelle added. "I was remembering some of the time-lapse photography you've done." She opened her briefcase and brought out a series of six small photos, identically framed and matted, side by side in a horizontal frame. It showed a pale yellow Paphiopedilum orchid gradually blooming. Rikki had called the series "Good Morning" and had given her the set for her birthday two years earlier. Janelle had hung them on her bathroom wall, above the vanity, so she would see them every day when she brushed her teeth and put on her makeup.

"This time-lapse kind of thing could work here," Janelle insisted. "You could set up several cameras. Focus up to a point, then set some kind of automatic timer and leave. Holly and Greg could turn on some music to cover any sound of the camera shutters. Just let the cameras shoot every few seconds from several sides of the room."

Rikki looked at Juli, who was leaning against the doorjamb, taking it all in. She was nodding. A timed shoot was feasible.

Obviously, since their last conversation, Janelle had given the dilemma a great deal of thought. "Holly and Greg are career performers," she noted. "They're trained to be at ease on stage or in front of a camera. So they won't be too affected by the camera paraphernalia. To make the circumstances as close to natural as possible, they said you can set up in their bedroom, in familiar surroundings."

"You wouldn't have to direct or prepare the subjects. I would do that." Michelle Sands added another reassurance. "I would meet with Holly and Greg and give them some ideas about what I believe I need for the clients I'm counseling. I don't want to script this thing, but I also don't want the emphasis to be on gymnastics. Just simple, sincere lovemaking. This has to be romantic. Gentle. I'd like a lot of caressing and embracing and kissing. Hands are crucial." She sat with her own, palms up, extended.

"Most of us respond to touch as a means of establishing intimacy." Janelle spoke up. She rested her hand on the files she'd brought. "These are excerpts from counseling sessions. They describe the aversion to any physical closeness these victims have to overcome. We're after a tenderness that encompasses the entire person. We want these women to experience a variety of skin contact as sensual and loving and acceptable, not just the usual target areas."

Janelle described the type of lovemaking Rikki could relate to quite vividly. Her skin tingled as her friend's words stirred the remembrance of her night with Stu. It had been all encompassing and exquisite. Hands, caressing. She felt the heat rise.

"All factors considered, I think this team approach is worth a try," Sands said.

Janelle fixed her friend with a bright, hopeful look. "Surely with several cameras and lots of rolls of film, you'll get enough to work with. Once you have the photos developed, you can look it over. Then decide if you want to go on."

"Your reservations about this project only substantiate the fact that you have the sensitivity to do this right," Sands added persuasively. "We all know what elegance you instill in the final product. We need that elegance here."

Janelle was nodding. "True. I think this is as close to the real thing as possible without suggesting anyone hide and shoot pictures without telling the subjects, which none of us would consider ethical or humane," she added emphatically. "This way we each do our part. Everyone just has to give a little."

Rikki stood there, sipping her juice and musing over the idea. She and her father had done similar time-lapse remote shoots before in the wild. They'd set stationary cameras on automatic to capture a process in a sequence of stills: the gradual flowering of a plant, the emergence of a butterfly from a chrysalis, the hatching of birds in a nest, the feeding habits of timid animals who would have balked at a human scent. She and Swede caught some remarkable shots using this technique, zeroing in on a site, then coming back later to pick up the cameras. Time lapse used a lot of film, and hundreds of shots were junked, but the loss was inconsequential considering the remarkable pictures they'd obtained over the years.

"Let me think about it," she said at last, trying to concentrate solely on the technical expectations. She was calculating how many cameras she and Swede had between them and what kinds of lighting and film and lenses could get the effects she wanted. That part was familiar territory.

"Good. You think it over. Take your time." Janelle eased back on the stool, more relaxed than she'd been when she arrived. "If you want to get a feel for the people you'll be helping, read some of these. I was careful to omit the names, so there's no breach of confidentiality. But these women say some very powerful stuff." She left the files and the Paph pictures she'd brought spread on the counter, visually reinforcing the proposal. With the variables reworked, she hoped Rikki would at least be willing to make a trial shoot.

Outside, the sound of hammering had stopped. A truck door slammed. Eddie Sordo's voice could be heard, praising the work the other two men had done that day. "Miz Rikki," he called to her.

"I think this must mean they're done." Rikki rounded up three additional glasses and a pitcher of iced tea for the men. "Eddie said they'd all help put it back in order when they finished. We need to bring out some plants and hang Oscar back in place."

"We'll help too," Janelle offered, recruiting her two companions to join in.

"Janelle said you had a wonderful greenhouse filled with orchids." Holly Morrison stood up, eager to get a look out back. "I can't grow anything with a flower, but I absolutely love to look at them."

Janelle grinned. She'd made that statement herself on occasion. It was the kind of comment Rikki would pick up on and transform into quite the opposite sentiment.

"Growing orchids is easy, especially in Florida," Rikki would insist in her soft, reassuring way. And she'd make it easy for a beginner to succeed. Among the many smaller pots she'd divided from established ones of her own, she'd surely find a healthy plant or two for Holly. She'd probably offer Janelle some new plants as well. With a little coaching they'd get their first bloom, then she'd soon have them collecting more varieties, noticing the different growth patterns.

Blooms alone weren't the only source of pleasure or sense of promise in the slathouse. There was always some kind of show. It could be watching the green-tipped roots of a Vanda reach out and overrun its basket, or checking as the spike on a Phalaenopsis sprouts a cluster of buds that stretch and turn over on their stems before they open; or monitoring the sleek sheaths of Cattleyas as they peek out, plump up, and finally unfurl their spectacular blooms. Rikki had a way of convincing the most hesitant gardener to try. Orchids could thrive on minimal care and would offer in return lasting, exotic beauty. And each would flower again, on its own schedule, when it was time.

"Plants of all kinds can restore a very personal connection with beauty and health and the positive energy in the world around us," Rikki had said weeks before at the conference at the Hilton. "But orchids have a unique and distinctive presence. They instantly uplift the spirit and fill the surrounding space with their serenity," she stressed with conviction. "They are survivors who prevail with undeniable grace." Then she'd played one of her videos to demonstrate.

Like a caravan, Janelle and the others carried pots and baskets of soon-to-flower orchids from the slathouse to the latticed lanai where Eddie Sordo and the two carpenters were setting them in place. As the accumulation of plants covered the side walls, the place lost its bare, new appearance. Once the wood weathered a bit, it would look like the tropical refuge had been there for years.

"I have to bring more of this feeling to my house," Janelle declared, realizing she'd neglected adding any new plants to her own surroundings in the past months. "Let's take another look at your works in progress," she suggested, trooping back with Rikki for another load.

"Browse around. Read the tags. It tells what color they bloom. You'll find something that appeals to you," Rikki told her.

"I like the look of that one." Janelle pointed to a plant with a burst of fiery yellow-orange spikey flowers.

"That's Brazilian. A Laelia," Rikki told her. "That particular species is Cinnabarina. Here it flowers from late summer into winter. I have a couple of divisions in pots farther back, ready for new homes. You'll love having it around."

"Do you have anything that blooms in the early spring?" Janelle asked, intent on having her seasons covered.

"I've got several possibilities. You haven't tried a miniature yet." Rikki plucked up a piece of bark with a tiny plant secured to the side. "Hang this in a slightly shady place. Just mist it every couple of days." She glanced farther back at the ones Stu had watered earlier. "If you'd like something splashier, there's another kind that will have huge sprays with clusters of tiny, tiny blooms. They're called Dancing Ladies. The flowers look like little bonneted figures in full-skirted ball gowns. I have one in bloom back here." She headed deeper into the warm, moist environment of the slathouse with the others eagerly tagging along.

"Problem?"

Joe Warnock wasn't smiling when he joined Stu and the others on the task force for their late-afternoon strategy meeting.

"I'll say. As far as the assaults go, the Rhule kid is a washout. He's taking a polygraph. He agreed to it. He admits to defacing the art at the Hilton, but he swears he wasn't involved in any of the hits on the artists. And I believe him. He isn't real smart," he stated slowly, for emphasis. "And no ant bites."

"Any motive?" someone asked.

"Not really. He'd been dumped by a girlfriend. Apparently someone delivering plants at the Hilton pissed him off. He says he did the whole thing with the art show, including calling the TV station, just so he could get his face in the news and impress her. Apparently he made it on TV, standing in the background on some of the shots. But the girlfriend wasn't impressed. He's still dumped. I have the area stations rounding up the footage."

"So where do we go from here?" One of the other officers who'd been first on the scene of the Judy Rodriguez dousing shifted in his seat.

"We go ahead as we planned. Set out the decoys," he said, shrugging. "What we've got here is a twist on the copycat thing. Someone else is shopping with Rhule's list, even picked up the ski mask idea, figuring we'd think whoever did the show did the rest as well. If the guy out there hears we have Rhule booked for vandalism, he might figure it's a great time to stop, make it look like Rhule must have done all of it. His trail disappears and we'll never know who he is."

Several heads in the room were nodding.

"So we're not letting it out that Rhule is in custody," Warnock stressed.

"So the Trasher will hit again." An officer from Bradenton reaffirmed the point.

"Right. We need him to make another move. Only we have to be waiting," Warnock said in his quiet, efficient way.

"So when do we start?" A female lab technician who'd volunteered to double for Olivia Mello asked.

"Right away," Warnock stressed. "Right now, Rhule is willing to cooperate. We're just going to have him disappear for a while. We'll say we're still looking for him and figure he may be back in the area. Then we'll move in the decoys and wait. I've talked to the police chief from Fort Myers. Wallace, the artist there, has already pulled out. But the police have a watch on his place in case the Trasher or some other fool tries to damage the property."

"Well, I'm ready to get on with it," another woman, small and redhaired, declared. She was one of two selected to rotate in Olivia Mello's place. The other was the darkhaired technician who would wear a red wig on decoy duty. But Stu had been glancing at this one, the redhead, from time to time, imagining her appearance out of uniform. With the right makeup and some tighter clothes, she could pass for Olivia without question. Even the jawset and the animation in her movements were right on target. But the technician would need some coaching besides the wig and clothes to capture the right look.

"Tomorrow is Sunday, so you folks spend the morning with your families or simply relax. I've got a file for each of you, sort of a bio on the artist you'll be replacing. We want you in here tomorrow afternoon, ready to meet your counterpart, get briefed, and get into costume. The first team will start in and take over that artist's routine Sunday night. Monday they'll run the story that our prime suspect is still loose. That should be invitation enough to get something going. The next group switches in Thursday, for the weekend. You can work out between you, who goes first."

"When have most of the hits happened?" One of the men chosen to pose as Thayer Kern, the Bradenton plastics artist with the chocolate labs, leaned into the conversation, obviously eager to pick the prime action shift. Slim, wiry, balding like Kern, he had a more aggressive style than the soft-spoken artist. He'd have to tone down his act.

"Can't really help you on that one," Warnock said, shrugging. He didn't even glance at his notes. "There is no set pattern. The time between hits has varied. He's hit every day but Sunday."

"But the October ones have been more toward the end of the week," one officer noted. "And about a week apart."

"Right. But don't try to figure this guy. We have no idea what's influencing him on his end. Pick a shift and take your chances," Warnock suggested. "As soon as we think we've got a pattern, he'll pull something different anyway. The bottom line is that he isn't stable. He's a damn time bomb waiting to detonate. So I want to grab his ass now, before we have another beating like the Jessup case. Or something worse."

Warnock passed out information folders, fielded a few more questions, then officially ended the meeting. "Have some coffee or a soda. See me if you have any questions. Thanks for your time."

Bodies shifted. Someone eager for a cigarette stepped through into the outer office. Almost instantly, Warnock's phone rang as his secretary put through the first of the calls he'd asked to be held. He let it ring twice, then he picked it up.

"Hold it," he barked above the rumble of conversation in the room, waving everyone back into their seats. "There's a fire in progress at Kern's studio in Bradenton."

Everything came to a standstill.

"Kern wasn't there. Go on." He listened, stone faced.

No one moved.

"His dogs were inside. The bastard torched the place. Shoved some kind of flares in between the window bars. They set off the plastics and chemicals Kern had all over the place. Two chocolate retrievers were trapped. They're fried." His face, taut and pale, was rigid as he passed, in installments, what he was hearing.

Like most of the others present, sobered by the announcement, Stu said nothing. A few cursed, encapsulating for them all the prevailing attitude.

Warnock put the phone on its cradle. "Sorry guys. Revamp time. Let's get Olivia Mello under wraps. I don't want anyone else dealing with this guy. He's a fucking psycho."

His hand trembled. "If Kern had decided to work this afternoon, he could have been asphyxiated. Or torched. Or both. Damn this guy."

"Sure didn't skip a beat this round," one officer commented.

Warnock muttered a few more softer damns, then as suddenly as he'd begun the outburst, he checked the anger and became exactingly calm. "All right. Those assigned decoy duty for Mello make a quick study and get ready to move in. I'll call Fort Myers and advise them to tighten up." He drew a breath and smoothed his tie. "None of you talk to the press. I don't want any of you saying a word about anything we discussed today," he cautioned them. "He has two targets. He can have his pick. I want to encourage him to pick ours. Let's start figuring out how."

Stu had already begun to work his way around the room and was waiting by the door. He was shaking his head, frustrated, like Warnock, at another unnerving shift in events.

"Where are you going?" Warnock demanded, as if he already suspected the answer.

"Bradenton. To check out the fire. That's something I know about," Stu replied.

"Mind some company?" Warnock threw all his papers in a pile. "I'd like to hear what you have to say when you see it."

"Then let's get moving."

"Call Fort Myers," Warnock delegated the job of notifying the other jurisdictions. "I'll touch base with them later. The rest of you think strategy. How do we get this guy? Wait," he called out to Stu who was already on his way out.

Stu didn't even slow his pace.

Rikki had already heard the news about the Bradenton fire when Stu called her from the 'Vette on the cellular phone. He could tell from her voice that she'd been crying. She'd already heard that Kern's beautiful twin Labs, Pyramus and Thisbe, had been killed. Even before it made the news, a friend of Kern's had called Olivia Mello, who in turn had called her. The network of the Hilton Nine had quickly passed the word among themselves.

"He'd left them there to guard the place while he picked

up some fiberglass material in Tampa. Thisbe was pregnant and he didn't want to jostle her around in the car. He was only gone a couple of hours,'' she said, barely able to keep from sobbing. ''He must be devastated.''

''I can imagine,'' Stu sympathized, recalling how proud Kern was of the big gentle dogs that followed him around. They had sat, framing his legs like mahogany parentheses, at Victor Chambers's garden party.

''I thought I'd try to drive out to his house and see him. All I get when I call is his answering machine.''

''Don't do it,'' Stu told her. ''No one knows what else this guy might pull next,'' he cautioned her, knowing Kern's house was only a few blocks from the studio that had burned. ''He may be hanging around there like a damn pyro, watching the action, getting his kicks. Or he may be watching Kern's home. Don't you come near either place. I'm going to take a look. I'll call you back. If Kern is anywhere around, I'll tell him you're thinking of him and would like to get in touch. For now, there's nothing you can do. But for sure, don't come this way,'' he stressed.

''I need to do something. I was supposed to pick up the kids at my dad's, but I can't go over there all upset like this.'' He could hear her sniffing. ''Jake and Lara would know something awful has happened. I can't talk about it, not to them, not yet,'' her voice faded. ''I'd better call Dad and tell him what's going on.'' She was choking up again. ''I don't want them to find out about the dogs on the news.''

''I'll call. You put on your answering machine.'' Stu figured that as soon as the story came out, Rikki would get a barrage of calls, including the press wanting a reaction from 'the Nine.' ''Better yet, just lock up your house, take the cellular, and get out of there for a while, away from the other phone. Go across to Ash's house. Lock up below and go upstairs and unwind. I'll call your dad and tell him what's happened. He and Ivey can make sure the kids don't catch the news on the TV. I'll pick them up on my way back. It may be a while.''

''Okay.''

''Just in case there's any problem . . .'' He added the next part cautiously, remembering what Warnock said about the Trasher being a psycho. ''There's a gun in the kitchen cabinet over Ash's microwave. It's mine and it's loaded.

Take it upstairs with you. Don't answer the door. I'll come home as soon as I've done whatever I can do here.''

"Okay."

"I love you." He'd known it for a while. He'd planned on telling her on some warm and intimate occasion, not over a cellular phone when they were miles apart. Or with Warnock sitting next to him, stroking his moustache, trying to appear disinterested.

"I love you too, Sullivan."

"Good." That made his saying it both better and worse. He hated that the Trasher had robbed them both of the chance to whisper those words to each other this very first time, somewhere safe and beautiful. "Now get out of there. Take care of yourself." Despite the tightness in his throat, he said it without a catch in his voice.

"I will. Thanks." Then she hung up.

Warnock didn't say a word. He simply sat staring straight forward, as inobtrusive as possible in the confines of a two-seater Corvette.

The fire was out by the time Stu and Warnock arrived. He parked down the street from the blackened studio, behind several official vehicles and a TV remote van. Because of the possibility of toxic fumes, the neighborhood had been evacuated. "Wait," he cautioned Warnock before either of them got out and moved closer. Then he saw the firefighters moving about without masks, and he knew the air was safe. But the stench when he stepped outside was the distinct smell of burnt flesh and death.

On the way home, he picked up the youngsters just as he said he would. "Help me take the food in, then you guys give me a few minutes while I go round up the mom."

"She's not at home?" Jake asked.

"She came over here for a while," Stu answered, trying to divert them from asking too many questions by loading them with packages of food to carry. He'd parked the 'Vette conspicuously at Ash's house so anyone could see he was there. He'd also stopped for fried chicken at a fast-food place on the trip back, thought better of it, and called ahead to a deli-restaurant for a Greek Salad and spinach-cheese triangles to go.

He wasn't particularly enthusiastic about food under the circumstances. He doubted that Rikki would be either. But he knew they all had to eat. He figured something cool and vegetarian would suit them all tonight. The desserts, rectangles of baklava, thick with nuts and honey, were a treat for afterward.

Swede and Ivey had kept the TV off, so the kids had not caught the news about the fire or Kern's dogs. But they'd have to be told eventually, and Rikki would pick the time to do it. He just wanted to get the youngsters settled for now and see for himself how she was doing.

"How about you guys taking some bread scraps and going down to the dock and chum the fish? Give your mom and me a few minutes to get organized?"

"Sure," Lara spoke for both of them, giving Jake a series of nudges. Jake grimaced, getting his sister's the message that the grownups needed some time alone to talk in private and maybe even to get "mushy." Both children dutifully followed Stu into the kitchen, put the packages on the counter, then took the bag of bread end-pieces he'd saved and headed for Ash's dock.

"How are you?" he asked when he met Rikki coming down from Ash's second floor. She walked right into his arms.

"I'm okay. It was a good idea to come over here and to get away from the phone."

"You're cool," he noted, feeling her forehead against his cheek.

"I put some ice on my eyes. I was all puffy. This whole thing with the dogs just knocked the underpinnings out from under me. I keep thinking of those beautiful dogs trapped in there . . ." she broke off the sentence, pressing her lips together to maintain her composure.

"I know." He held her and stroked her shoulders as she leaned against him. For the moment that was all he could think of to say or do.

"Do I look all right? I don't want the kids worried because I was crying."

"You look fine." He grinned at her convincingly.

"Okay, then." She took a steadying breath and looked up at him. "Where are they?"

"They're out back."

"They don't know any of it?"

"Not a bit. They probably think we're fooling around in here. Come on. I've got salad. Help me with the drinks.

We'll have dinner while the sun sets,'' he said, hoping to get her mind off the dogs at least for a while. He'd be there to help smooth things out for the remainder of the evening.

"You're a prize, Sullivan." Rikki gave him a friendly pat on the rump. "Thanks for running interference today.''

He thought of several comments he could have made in response. Some might have shifted things into a more romantic mode and brought her back into his arms a little longer. The kids were already convinced something like that was going on between them. But despite the temptation, he knew she'd feel better outside, close to the wind and water, with her family, so they could all reconnect.

"Let's get hustling. Plates, napkins. Ice," he gave the directions like she usually did, prompting himself as well as her into action.

She nodded and started filling the glasses, still preoccupied. "Now that this has happened to Thayer, I'm more worried than ever about Olivia. I tried calling her, but she had her answering machine on. I left a message. When I talked to my dad earlier, he said something about Detective Warnock picking up a suspect," Rikki said while she loaded ice cubes into four glasses. "Is something going on?"

Stu shook his head, regretting that Swede hadn't been as close-lipped as he could have been. "Something is going on, but I can't say what." He wanted to tell her that the Rhule deal was a washout as far as the direct attacks on the artists were concerned. And that the real Olivia Mello would be out of touch for a while. Warnock and the Fort Myers police were sending in decoys immediately. When either one did return a call, it would be from some location other than their home. The nut was still loose, but Olivia would be out of danger.

"Believe me. You don't need to worry," he assured her. "I'd like to tell you details, but I can't. Not yet."

"Sounds a bit like your agreement with my dad." Her dark, intelligent eyes narrowed. He caught the uneasiness in them as they shifted out toward the back where the kids were sitting, making dough wads and dropping them into the water.

"Your dad isn't involved. This time the ethics are totally professional ones."

"Professional ones?" Her eyebrows arched slightly.

"Right." Everyone on the task force had been forbidden

to talk about strategy. Warnock had been particularly adamant in Stu's case, since there were children in the home. They might overhear and pass on information that could tip off the Trasher about the decoys and inadvertently alert him that a switch had been made. Rikki couldn't be told either, he'd insisted, for a similar reason. Once that information hit the network, it could spread like wildfire.

She gave him a long, thoughtful look, then the browline and the jawline softened. "Okay," she said tentatively as she glanced out at the children again. He could tell she wanted to know more, but she wasn't going to ask.

"I'll stick close for the next few days," he said, wishing he could erase that apprehensive edge that still lingered in her expression.

She nodded. "Do that." She smiled with a slight stiffness and concentrated on the glasses she was filling. "Stick close."

Chapter 9

Sunday morning after he swallowed six aspirin and a couple of Rolaids, Dave McIver chased them down with another scotch and water. He'd eventually lost count of how many he'd had the night before. The first one he'd downed in a quick swallow at Conroy's, a gulfside restaurant with a panoramic view of the water. He'd ordered the second with a platter of raw oysters at the counter area of the outdoor bar. He lined up the basket of crackers, extra hot sauce, and settled in on the far end to watch the six o'clock news on the overhead TV behind the bartender. From where he was sitting, he could catch the sunset during the commercial breaks.

It started out as a celebration. He'd carefully landed a dollop of hot horseradish sauce on his oyster, slid it onto a cracker, then popped it in, munching away, loading up another as he waited to hear how they'd handle this one.

The news media barely had time to recover from the Lundquist hit. He'd gone ahead and slipped this one in real fast. Partly because it pissed him off to see Bambi's face in the paper again. He wanted her checked off the list and out of the limelight fast. Past history. So he showed the guy in Bradenton what a joke those expensive barred windows were.

"Another?" The female bartender on the sunset shift was a familiar fixture, one who knew how to keep pace with the regulars. And McIver was a regular. She was one of those skinny, angular women of indeterminate age, more interesting looking than attractive, who could handle a steady flow of serious drinkers with straight shots and clean glasses and still fizz up the ones with umbrellas and frosted edges for the lightweights and the tourists.

Too heavily tanned, with too much eye makeup and spikey blonde hair that made her look like a female version of Rod

Stewart, on weekends she kept the drinks coming with few comments, mostly wisecracks. On weekday nights, same shift, she was a bit more laid back, stopping to talk and offering to be more social. But McIver never picked up on it or her. He was too conscious that a client or some associate might walk in and spot him being overly familiar with the service help. That wasn't good for business. He drank, carried on limited conversation, but he kept his distance.

"Sure. Go ahead." He emptied the glass and pushed it forward for a refill.

The evening news began with a few national headlines then shifted to the local headline he expected. Another of the Hilton Nine had been victimized. McIver knew that already. The commentator mentioned that the latest attack, a studio fire, had claimed two victims. Then the station cut to the usual opening graphics followed by a commercial. McIver sat staring at the screen, immobilized. Victims. The oyster and cracker mixture he was chewing felt like it was swelling in his mouth.

Then the commentator came back. He said the two victims in the studio fire were dogs. Purebreds. Labs. Some woman broadcaster, in a taped report on the scene, talked about the chemicals Kern used. And the fact that because of the volatile plastics, the interior of the whole place virtually melted from the intensity of the heat. Contained, she said. The damage was limited to the studio. It hadn't spread into any neighboring structures. But it had immolated the two dogs and caused the neighborhood to be evacuated because of the fumes. The reporter did the voice-over of some file footage of Kern and the two animals from coverage taken at an opening at Victor Chambers's gallery earlier in the month. The Lundquist woman was in the background of that one, smiling.

Then they showed the communal body bag carrying the two dogs.

McIver left the remainder of the fresh-shucked oysters untouched. He drank two more rounds and headed back across the causeway toward town. He pulled into the first liquor store he spotted to stock up on the way home. He'd sat, flipping through channels with the remote, drinking, until eleven. Then he heard it all over again on the late-night news. Even the body bag. The blonde was still smiling. He drank some more.

He liked dogs. Particularly Labs. Good water dogs. His had liked to swim. He'd had a Lab as a kid. Not purebred chocolate like Kern's pair. His was part mutt, part Lab. An accident. They called him Hershey. After the candy bar.

Hershey had to be put down when McIver was a senior in high school. Old by then, the lab had developed arthritis in his hips. It was sad toward the end, watching old Hershey wince when he tried to get up and down or wobble when he walked. In his prime, Hershey used to race along the beach and dive into the surf, or take off like an arrow, nail a frisbee in midflight, and bring it back, head held high and proud, tail wagging. Toward the end, he was like a different dog altogether. Slow. Crippled up. Almost embarrassed. McIver was seventeen then, too cool to show much emotion. He'd gone to a buddy's house and gotten drunk the morning his folks took old Hershey off to the vet. He drank all day. And after his buddy had gone to bed, McIver had sat in the john alone, throwing up. Between bouts of the heaves, he cried.

He was alone and crying again now, staring at the TV, mourning the two dogs he didn't even know. But mostly he was mourning the one he'd let die in the vet's office without his being there.

He hadn't intended to hurt Kern's dogs. He didn't know they were in the place. It just pissed him off that the guy had bars installed close together on all the studio windows and thought they would protect his precious supplies and his works in progress. The windows behind the bars were left open, like he didn't have a worry in the world.

McIver showed him. He just walked up the back alley, carrying a newspaper, with the flares tucked inside. He lit them and popped the sticklike flares between the bars, refolded the newspaper, and kept on walking. Like one of the neighbors passing by. He hadn't intended to burn the place, just fill it with dark, sooty smoke.

He'd outdone himself this time. But so had Kern. The security bars had turned the studio into a death trap. If it hadn't been for them, the dogs could have leaped to safety. They'd have been fine. That part was Kern's fault.

The attack itself was because of her, the smiling Lundquist broad. When the news ran her story, even in the midst of all the rubble behind her house, she looked too good. The TV coverage showed her standing there in some light, flimsy dress. It fluttered in the breeze. Revealed a lot of leg. Damn sexy. McIver didn't expect seeing her would kick off that kind of a reaction in him. But suddenly, he had a hard-on. And he tried not to think about how long it had been since he'd been laid. Weeks. Before Sandra left. That last time didn't even count. It was after another fight. They were making up. She'd been crying. And he wasn't able to finish.

So after Lundquist, he'd pushed ahead with the next trashing to throw them all off, the police and the press. He'd picked an easy one. This one had been just for show, a diversion for Bambi's benefit. He just wanted to draw the attention somewhere else. So he'd zeroed in on another one on the list, one he'd passed over before. After Kern, all the coverage would be focused on the two artists still targeted. The pressure was really on so the police would be all over them. But mainly, he wanted the Lundquist blonde to drop her guard. He wanted her to feel secure, out of danger. Like Kern had with his damn bars and his security system. Secure enough to leave his dogs there.

Suddenly all McIver could think of now was dog eyes. Hershey's big brown eyes. He remembered that plaintive look in them as he helped his dad lift the old pooch into the station wagon for his last ride. McIver had refused to go along. Claimed he had other plans. He just couldn't stand the thought of watching Hershey die.

The way these two died was horrible. Pyramus and Thisbe. McIver even remembered their names from the news reports. The woman said they came from some play. Doomed lovers. Fuck.

McIver took another swallow and pressed his eyes closed. Maybe the fumes got them first. Put them to sleep, before the flames. He took another drink, hoping something would let him look in the bathroom mirror without imagining some poor ol' pup staring back with anxious, pleading eyes. Like Hershey.

Maybe another shot of scotch would help.

"I see she's out recharging her batteries," Swede said, standing on the back deck of Rikki's house Monday evening. He'd got himself a cool drink on the way through. He paused next to Stu, watching his daughter cutting across the wake of a passing boat on her sailboard. Her long hair, pulled back in a braid, lay close against her neck. Her entire body, wet from the salty water, glistened like polished wood. The leg tattoo was barely visible from that distance. "I see she's had everyone out here gardening too." He waved the hand with the glass of juice toward several large pots filled with small, leafy plants, each pot raised on square platforms fitted with casters.

"Oriental vegetables. They're seedlings from Eddie Sordo's private stock," Stu responded. "We took the kids out there yesterday to load up, then we hit a couple of farm-supply stores for some less exotic things. Tomatoes. Beans. Bell peppers. We came back with the van overflowing. We spent most of the afternoon back here setting in everything." Stu pointed to several neat rows of seedlings in the dark strip they'd turned and weeded alongside the walkway to the dock. "Broccoli and beans. Tomatoes and onions are around the side. But for these," Stu said, indicating the potted Sordo specials, "Rikki wanted the caster setups so she and the kids can roll them inside if the weather gets bad."

Swede was nodding, eyes slightly narrowed, taking it all in. Stu had seen the same expression on Rikki from time to time.

November was only two weeks off, and that shift to fall weather usually meant rain, cold nights, and sometimes hot afternoons. Winter vegetable gardens usually did well in Florida. However, wide fluctuations in temperature and moisture were not particularly auspicious conditions for some of Sordo's Asian plants. It made sense to make their containers mobile.

"She's recharging, all right." Swede spoke at last. "Spinning on all tracks. She called yesterday and asked to borrow a couple of my cameras. I figured she was up to something. Sounded real preoccupied." Father and daughter had spoken by phone earlier that Sunday morning, after the city section of the morning paper arrived carrying a long article about the fire at Thayer Kern's studio. Since Jake sometimes went out to pick up the newspaper from the drop-box at the gate, his grandfather called, concerned the youngster might open it on the way back.

"Watch out. The piece is pretty graphic," he'd warned her.

Rikki had already been up and got the paper. She'd seen

the piece and tucked it away so the kids wouldn't run across it in their search for the comics section. She said she'd baked muffins and was carrying them up through the shutter house onto the top sundeck. She and the children often started a weekend or holiday morning having a leisurely breakfast up there, leafing through the paper. She'd decided that was the time and the place to tell them what had happened to the dogs. Swede said she'd sounded calm, like she always did when she had thought something through, mustered her courage, and was ready to do what had to be done.

When she called him later about the cameras on Sunday night, she'd sounded more relaxed. She told Swede the talk with Jake and Lara had gone well. The children were understandably upset at first, but they were rebounding. She also said the kids had been working on something at the house to show him. And she was asking for cameras and tripods. He'd taken all that activity as a good sign. So he'd told her he'd come over Monday, just about the time the kids got home from school for show-and-tell.

"Has she been working today?" he asked Stu.

"She moved all the slides back in from Chambers's place. She was upstairs in the production room sorting, I guess. Juli came over for a while to help. I went in to the office for a couple of hours. Went over the fire site again with one of the investigators. Not much to go on. No witnesses have turned up."

"Too bad." Swede's comment had that trace of weariness Stu had heard in Detective Warnock's voice. He guessed it was in his own as well. They all wanted this ended. "Looks to me like she's still got something brewing," Swede observed, nodding out toward the water. "Since she was a kid, she's sorted out a lot of things out there on that board."

Stu nodded too, watching Rikki sailboarding out on the water. He understood what Swede meant about her recharging her batteries. She was visibly coming out of the slump that she'd been in since the fire. But she was still working at it.

She'd spent all day Sunday steering the children into several projects. They were positive, replenishing things to help ease the mourning over the dogs. Planting the vegetable garden was one project that Stu had helped with. Baking bread was another. Planning a party for Halloween was a new one, still very much in the early stages.

Stu had gone home, untaped his air cast, and had taken a long shower. He'd hoped she'd come over for a while, once the kids were asleep. Or call him and invite him back. He wanted to hold her. But when he looked out from Ash's house, he saw the towel out on the dock. Then he got the binoculars and spotted her swimming, naked, in the Intracoastal. Recharging. Alone.

He wasn't surprised, just a little sad. He'd overestimated how well she'd bounced back. But even now after a full day's work, Rikki was out there sailboarding, all alone, recharging again, or perhaps still exorcising some lingering demons.

"Brought the equipment you wanted," Swede told her when she finally came in.

She strolled toward them with a towel draped around her hips. "Thanks. Where's Ivey?"

"She didn't come."

"Who drove, then?" Rikki paused and propped one hand against her hip, a gesture that Stu knew meant trouble.

"I did. Ivey is out doing some shopping with a friend. I figured I could handle this." He'd obviously ignored the doctor's orders to wait until the knees had finally healed. "One of my neighbors helped load the equipment. I thought Stu or you or the kids could help bring the gear in," Swede added hastily, studiously ignoring his daughter's disapproving look. He was still walking with a cane, a concession of some significance considering his hardheadedness. And he'd been sufficiently cautious not to push his luck and risk damaging any cameras by moving them unassisted.

For a few seconds father and daughter stood in silence, each measuring the set of the other's jawline.

"Jake and Lara are due any minute," Stu said, abruptly setting his glass on the table. "I'll go meet them," he offered, willing to let father and daughter hash over the business of Swede's premature driving exploit in his absence. "We'll bring a few things in on the way back." He tried to make his hasty exit appear as casual as possible.

"So, guys, how did it go today?" Stu asked the smaller twosome as the school minivan pulled back into traffic. Neither Jake nor Lara were smiling.

"Not good. Everyone knew about the fire. We talked about dead pets. A lot," Lara said emphatically, pouting out her lips and looking as if she were on the verge of tears.

She tilted her chin down so her long dark hair partially hid her face.

"A couple of guys on the bus were real jerks about it. They made jokes. Gross ones. About hot dogs and crispy critters and things like that," Jake elaborated, resting his hand on Lara's shoulder in a rare show of brotherly comfort.

Lara trudged along solemnly, not looking up at either of them.

"I've met a few jerks like that in my time too," Stu responded. "People can say some pretty cruel things, thinking they're funny. Sometimes they're just real uncomfortable."

"And stupid." The small voice came from behind Lara's veil of dark hair.

"That too," Stu agreed, unable to suppress a chuckle. "I'm glad you're home where you don't have to put up with any more of that." Stu reached out and offered Lara his hand to hold. "Come on. Your Grampa's here. You can show him the new garden." Without a word, she took the hand and stepped up the pace a bit.

Stu kept talking as they walked toward the house, just like Rikki would be doing if she'd been the one who met them and heard about the jerks, the jokes, and the hot dogs. He told them there was camera equipment that needed unloading, urged them not to mention anything about Swede driving all by himself, and caught them up on the antics of the birds that morning. He also reminded them to check a couple of the orchids that were getting ready to bloom and to water the new plants before nightfall. Distractions. He gave them something different to think about and some time to let the wiseacre comments lose their sting.

When Stu and the youngsters paraded in, each carefully toting a piece of Swede's photo equipment, Rikki and her father had apparently reached some truce. They were hunched, shoulder to shoulder, at the kitchen counter with one of her cameras, a timer, and several lenses in front of them, talking intently in technical terms Stu didn't comprehend.

Swede looked up, stopping to inspect Lara's hands as he relieved her of the camera she had brought in. "My dear child, there seems to be something peculiar about these little thumbs," he observed with great seriousness. "They seem to be unusually green. And here's another green-thumbed grandchild.'' Swede greeted Jake with a great hug. ''I hear you two and your thumbs have been busy.'' Instantly, the camera paraphernalia was abandoned, and the two children treated the Grandpa to an in-depth tour of Lundquist Gardens.

By the time the trio returned, hot and thirsty, Ivey had arrived and was waiting in the kitchen, having iced tea with Rikki and Stu. She'd returned from her shopping, discovered Swede and the car missing, called Rikki trying to locate him, then had her friend drop her off there so she could drive the vehicle and her stubborn husband home.

''We'll talk about this later,'' she said simply, with an uneasy mix of relief and frustration. ''You know better.''

Swede simply kissed her cheek and launched into a discourse praising the garden under way outside. Then he insisted that the kids juice up, then take Gramma Ivey on a tour as well.

After Ivey and Swede departed, Rikki put everyone to work on dinner. Stu washed and sliced vegetables. Jake made rice. Lara set the table. Later, while Stu and the youngsters cleaned up, Rikki made several phone calls. Stu couldn't hear any of the comments, but he could see her expression shift as if some nagging concern kept preempting whatever conversation was going on. Between calls, he watched her scanning some of the notes she'd jotted down from time to time.

Once the children had been sent upstairs to get ready for bed, he and Rikki walked out to the lanai and stood, hand in hand, looking up at the clear night sky. ''Thanks for helping tonight,'' she said softly. ''I've had a lot on my mind.''

''Anything I can help with?''

''You're already helping.''

''Good.'' They stood saying nothing for a while.

''I was wondering what you'd think about inviting your brother and his family and perhaps your mom over for dinner one night this week.'' Rikki spoke at last. ''I think my dad and Ivey would like to meet them. I'd certainly like to meet your mom.''

''I think that goes both ways. She'd like to meet you. It's a great idea.'' He'd been watching her all evening, wondering what was going on inside her head. Even now, he felt they were only touching on one level, and she had other ones still churning with issues yet to be resolved. But there was a relaxed, familiar softness in her smile, and he knew if she was ready to have a family gathering, she was feeling better than she had in days. "I've got a gas cooker back at my apartment. I could steam up a bunch of shrimp for starters," he suggested. "I'm good at that."

She gave him a sidelong look, somewhat amused. "Sullivan, my guess is you're very good at a lot of things. You probably have a lot of talents I still haven't discovered."

"I'm willing to be explored," he insisted, holding his good arm up in gesture of total surrender. Her smile widened. She shook her head, almost laughing.

He liked the way that look made his whole chest feel warm. Approval. Connection. It was all there instantaneously. He hadn't felt that good or drawn such a clear breath since the Kern fire had left its poisonous dark cloud over all of them. Some part of her was fighting back. Part of her was holding on, waiting for him to tell her it was over. He couldn't do that yet. He couldn't tell her anything. He just had to help her get through one day after the next until the Trasher made a mistake, stepped into a trap, and was caught. But tonight, at least for a few moments, that darkness in her expression was gone.

"What does your family like to eat? I was wondering what to prepare."

"Basically, like the rest of us, they're grazers and carnivores," Stu answered with a slight hint of laughter in his voice. "They prefer veggies raw and meat cooked. I'd say do a salad. Let Jake fix a pot of his great rice. Maybe some of that spicy marinated chicken you and Eddie make. That way we can all sit out here and cool off and peel shrimp while the sun sets, then we can do the rest buffet style. No one gets stuck off somewhere cooking."

"Good plan," she said, nodding. "I wouldn't want to miss out on any of the conversation. Besides, peeling shrimp is a good icebreaker."

"When this group of folks get together, I don't think you'll need an icebreaker. You might need a whistle to blow an occasional time out," he noted. "There are a lot of heavy talkers on my side. And your dad and Ivey aren't exactly shy. Then there will be an extra kid. Wait till my nephew Todd gets trooping in and out after Jake and Lara. He'll love this place . . . stairs to climb, all the decks, the dock, and fish to chum. Maybe we'll need someone from traffic control to help out.''

"We can manage," Rikki said, smiling now, pleased at the prospect of having her house full of voices and laughter and good feelings. She'd been trying to focus on positive things. Still, the smell of new wood on the rebuilt lanai or a glimpse of one of her bruised orchids in the slathouse would put that faceless intruder there, stalking her. Terrifying her children. Damaging her home.

Innocent victims. Left with their lives changed. In the next millisecond, she'd remember Pyramus and Thisbe, trapped, dying. No life at all. Then her mind would ricochet off in several directions at once. How would Jake and Lara have fared if this maniac had thrown flares inside the house that night instead of the heavy tiki. She could have come back to a far more devastating scene. Like Thayer Kern's gutted studio. She'd knot up inside, worrying about Olivia.

"Something is being done," she'd remind herself, trying to put the brakes on. Stu assured her that her friend would be safe, he just couldn't discuss details. Anxious, she would call Olivia to offer her support. But she'd get the answering machine.

Eventually Olivia Mello would phone back to return her call. She said that she was fine. "They've got me covered. Don't sweat it, babe." No details, but not to worry. Rikki would take a breath and brace herself. She'd try to rechannel her energy. She'd do some processing in the darkroom. She'd hole up in the production room and work. She'd spend time with the kids. She'd be close to Stu for a while.

And when she couldn't stand the tension, she'd pat Oscar to keep the evil spirits at bay and go out on the sailboard. Then when everything inside her was stronger and quiet, she'd go upstairs alone, and read through the files that Janelle and the therapist, Michelle Sands, had left with her. She'd confront the other evil spirits who kept pushing other women into the dark abyss of fear.

Those victims, one after another, talked about the aftermath of rape: about the anxiety attacks triggered by something in their surroundings or even some subconscious connection. They talked of being caught up in a rush of terror and disgust, of seeing the face, hearing the voice, reliving the debasement, and desperately wishing to tune it all out. These women wanted to put the brakes on too. They wanted to reclaim what they once were. They wanted to make love again, with a husband or a boyfriend. Even the thought of lovemaking could generate all the wrong signals, set off the emotional alarms, and shut down all the healthy, responsive systems.

They needed an override system, something to intercept that one mental tape loop, the one that would rewind and replay the ugliness without invitation. They needed something beautiful and powerful and positive to help them fight back.

Rikki understood the violation these women felt. She felt their longing for control, for a return to normalcy, better now than she had before. She'd been stalked. Her friend was still under threat. Planting the vegetable garden with the children, planning a gathering with her family and Stu's, and feeling the drive to produce some work of significance were part of her own healing. They were her tools for reclaiming her equilibrium. She knew her tapes could help those other victims heal and strengthen and regain control. If they had the right one.

Janelle was clear on that point. Rikki was the one to do it. She had a unique combination of knowledge and sensitivity: the technical expertise with the equipment, a social-work background, and personal experience as an artist, as a lover, and now as a victim. She could do it. She would do it. With strength and elegance. She could help strip away the power of the perpetrators to contaminate the present and in the process satisfy her own sense of justice.

But she couldn't photograph an unknown, two strangers, and that was precisely what Holly Morrison and her fiancé were. And regardless of how beneficial their professional training might be, they were still performers. To get the truest images on film, Rikki had to work within her own experience, and that meant here. And it meant her, and Stu.

The setting-up part would require extensive preparation, not just setting up the physical location with the equipment, but getting herself into the proper mindset to do what had to be done. What showed on film had to have all the nuances of lovemaking that she wished for those women to feel. Like Michelle Sands said, it was the emotion, not the gymnastics, they were after.

For this project, Rikki didn't want one false note, nothing held back. She had an audience that needed the undeniable impact of witnessing the passion and sensitivity and intelligence between lovers. Unself-conscious lovers. With the honesty so intense that it was breathtaking. Rikki felt her throat turn cottony and dry at the thought of her and Stu being those lovers, then telling him afterward what she'd done, and why.

"I have some more reading to do," Rikki said simply before they made the final downstairs rounds, checking that all the doors and windows were locked. She had wanted to ask Stu to come up with her. She would have liked to let go of everything that had been on her mind, and let their love-making peel away the layers of care. She wanted to feel warm and safe and connected. And womanly.

Saying yes tonight would have been easy. They had held and kissed each other in the moonlight. She had felt that welcome intensification of sensation, that remarkable melting effect where they couldn't seem to get close enough, no matter how they touched. Where everything but skin against skin seemed restrictive and unnatural. The fire was there, in every touch.

But for now, for her, making love would have been an escape of sorts, not the celebration she wanted it to be. It would be a compromise. And she wasn't good at compromises. Instead, holding off, waiting awhile, was making her appreciate how delicious, how powerful, and how special lovemaking was with him. And how precious. Something that these other women no longer knew.

These files made her acutely aware how these women felt. Neutered. Desexed. They needed the affirmation of passionate, caring exchange. Rikki empathized with that abridged feeling. By sensitizing herself to the victim's pain, she'd know better how to annihilate it.

She owed it to the nameless women to be honest. So she'd take time again and again to slip into their skins and confront their horrors, absorbing and assessing. She would read another interview, feel another woman's sorrow. Then she'd read another. Their outrage, their anguish would help her do what had to be done to overcome her own need for privacy. But nothing would make invading the privacy of someone else more palatable. Certainly not the privacy of someone she loved. That, she knew, was wrong.

"Okay. See you tomorrow," Stu had said, giving her one lingering kiss. "If you change your mind or get lonely, call me. Even if you just need to talk.'' She could tell by his expression that he'd hoped the night might end differently. But there wasn't a trace of impatience. He seemed to know something was still unresolved in her mind. But he also seemed comfortable with the idea of waiting until the time was right. He wasn't pushing for half-measures or compromises either.

''He made me feel dirty.'' Rikki read that phrase again and again, from woman after woman, young and old, all victims of sexual abuse or rape. ''I take a lot of showers, but I can't get clean enough.'' One woman had bathed and scrubbed compulsively until her skin was raw. Still, months after the rape she'd suffered, she despised her own body, she didn't feel clean.

''Rough, Clumsy. He made noises like an animal.'' Rikki let the grimness settle in until it lay like a leaden mantle over her shoulders, weighing her down. Then she put away the interviews. She padded down the hallway, barefoot, and opened the drawers of pictures she and her father had accumulated. She pulled out several drawers of transparencies and began spreading the chosen ones out across the huge illuminated surface of the light table.

Dirty. Dark. Evil. The absence of light. Black. That seemed to be the color of the abyss into which memory sucked the women. Rikki would counteract that darkness with light.

She chose an assortment of creamy, feathery, delicate orchids at first. Nonthreatening color. Innocent. Pure. Gentle. Some rounded and shell-like, Anguloa and Cochleanthes; some elegant wispy ones, Brassavola and Aerangis.

Then she thought of the entire process, the escalation of feelings as playfulness and romantic caressing intensified into more impassioned embraces. The bravado. The exploration. The pleasure. The teasing. The urgency. The ecstasy. The breathlessness. The afterglow. Falling asleep in each other's arms. She could feel the heat from her neck and cheeks rising as she visualized capturing Stu and her at timed intervals in this process.

The ivories and whites were only a beginning. A prelude. The spectrum of lovemaking would have to encompass a spectacular range of color. Rikki looked more closely at a photo of several pinkish-peach Masdevallia, their kite-tailed shapes looking strikingly like rounded bare buttocks. Female, not male. Hers. On film. Then the artist-technician part of her clicked back in charge. To get a shot like that she'd need cameras on the bedroom ceiling as well as surrounding the bed. Her cheeks felt hotter.

"First the flowers." She concentrated, refusing to anticipate or plot out the people shots, frame by frame. For them, there would be no script. They would come later, naturally. In one shooting session. From six cameras on timers, strategically placed. Afterwards she'd develop the film. She'd decide then if she could use them. They would tell her if she could produce the quality of resensitizing tape she wanted. There would be no retakes.

She'd decided that studying the flower shots in advance, and selecting some at least tentatively, would provide a visual base to work from. A foil to play against. In the production phase, having an assortment somewhat organized would help her maintain a certain artistic detachment when she had to deal with the other shots.

To interlace the material, she'd have to retain her objectivity. Surrender any modesty. The flower shots were familiar, professional pieces. They would help keep her on track, so those very private shots of her and Stu would seem less personal, more universal. They would simply be lovers. Figures without names, conveying emotions that were ageless.

The white orchids and the pastels, however romantic and beautiful a beginning, were the prelude. Rikki placed page after page of color transparencies over the light table, refusing to deny these women the passion, fire, and energy of the more intense shades. There were deep purples and vibrant reds. Passionate and sensual. Sharp, impudent cerise. Fiery orange cinnabar. Crimson. And afterward . . . golds, yellows. Contentment. Peace. And the fragile-looking lavenders, and blues, even cool and elegant greens. She'd let the grace of the flowers and the variations in shades speak eloquently of texture, and tension, and vibrant life.

Rikki looked at a series of shots she had taken in Burma with her father of an undeniably erotic yellow Coelogyne pandurata, the flower curiously called the "black orchid" in Hollywood movies. It wasn't black. It was saffron yellow. Its pale, elegant petals framed the labellum, a single deep blackish-green feathery stained lip with the column arched at its base. The name itself "Coelogyne" meant "hollow" and "female," describing the opening on the column. That single dark-patterned lip, the labellum, derived its name from the female form as well.

Seductively, the interplay of lacy black across the orchid's ruffled lip and open throat slipped right past her analytical mind-set and touched off a flush of desire, warm and sweet and tantalizing. Distinctly womanly. She smiled, pleased and reassured that even looking at her own work, she could be stimulated to so primal a response by a powerful image. She set that one aside as a definite "yes." Hopefully it would whisper its message to these other women as well.

"Music," Rikki murmured as she turned off the light table, ready to call it a night. She glanced at her watch. 3 A.M. Too late to call Fuzzy Haight and talk about his "tunes." She knew he had countless unnamed, often unfinished pieces he'd composed. She would do what she had done before when she needed music for her work. She'd call and tell him what she had in her head so far. He'd listen to the rhythm implicit in her description, think about it, then he'd come over with several tapes. She'd listen. They'd talk some more. He usually brought along a keyboard and some other equipment so he could improvise on the spot. Then they'd come to an agreement. He'd go home and work it through again in his sound studio, alone. Like she would do in hers.

Only this time, she needed the music up front. Before the shoot. She wanted to play it the night of the shoot, in the room, to help cover up any camera sounds. She couldn't bring Fuzzy in later, in the editing stage, and have him preview the work in progress and rerecord some transitions or lengthen the piece like she had on other occasions. She'd edit this one totally alone. But Fuzzy's composition would be the music for the final tape, so for that night no other music would do.

Tuesday night, Dave McIver went straight to Conroy's again after work. He couldn't face going home alone. Not until he got something to eat and a comfortable little buzz on. Then he wouldn't feel the emptiness so much.

Tuesdays, Adella the maid came and cleaned the house. He used to like it all neat like she left it. Like something out of *Architectural Digest*. All the rugs groomed like a putting green, all the glass tabletops polished, wood smell-

ing of teak oil, and the raw-silk cushions on the sofas
plumped and lined up just like they were when the designer
set it up. Impressive. Whenever he and Sandra had guests,
everyone commented on how beautiful the house was and
how elegant the furnishings. It had cost him enough.

But the rest of the time, Sandra used to complain that the
new decor was too stiff and formal for a family, especially
with young children. Day to day, she didn't keep it up the
way the designer planned it. She left magazines and books
around. She stuck framed pictures of the kids right next to
pieces of expensive art. She taped their school papers to the
kitchen cupboards. Then she started bringing in some plants.
And she let the kids roughhouse everywhere. McIver used
to hate it when the kids played in the living room and left
cushions on the floor and everything slightly askew. He
hated finding their shoes and socks and toys all over. Their
clutter spoiled that elegant look.

He didn't have to worry about their clutter now. They
took most of that with them. Tuesdays Adella would put the
place in pristine shape. She'd even have a vase of cut flowers, just as he liked. But he would wander from room to
perfect room, with a drink in his hand, feeling the terrible
emptiness.

Because of the dog thing, he'd stayed drunk most of Sunday. But he'd managed to pull himself together enough to
get into the realty office both days that week, work his way
through a stack of papers, make his usual round of phone
calls, and keep his appointments. The divorce attorney said
to minimize the drinking. He knew he'd better keep himself
in line. But no one would know what he did in the privacy
of his own home. Out in public, he had it under control. He
kept a package of Rolaids and breath mints in his attaché
case along with a flask of scotch that he could refill from
the bottle in his office whenever he or it ran low.

"How are ya' today?" The same spikey-haired bartender
stopped stacking clean glasses and came over to take his
order. "You're early today. You feeling all right?" Her
mascara-ringed eyes narrowed, but the red lips were smiling.

"Had a round of the flu." He lied. He knew his eyes
were watery and red. His color, last time he looked, was a
bit gray.

"Lot of that going around this time of year. Last year,

about this time, it hit me. Halloween night, there I was home sick, all alone, and the doorbell never stopped ringing. I kept bobbing up and down, getting worse by the minute. I finally put all the candy outside with a note and let them help themselves. The little shits took off with two porch plants and the basket I put the candy in.'' She set a dish of roasted mixed nuts out for him. ''Things just aren't like they used to be. Scotch?''

McIver nodded.

''When my kids were young, I went with them trick-or-treating. Only went to the houses of friends. We always stopped to visit and show off their costumes. Trick-or-treating was a fun, neighborly thing. Now kids run wild. No supervision. Half of them don't even bother to dress up. It's just how much can you grab.'' She was shaking her head as she brought back the drink. ''I'm glad I'm working Halloween night. I'd rather put up with the foolishness on someone else's premises. You want some oysters?''

McIver shook his head. He couldn't face a naked oyster yet. ''Maybe later.''

''How about a burger? Char-broiled, no grease? That strike your fancy?'' There was a persistent, almost maternal edge to her questioning.

McIver thought about the burger a second, then nodded. He hadn't eaten anything all day.

''Tomatoes, lettuce?''

''And cheese. The works.'' He figured he might as well make a meal of it.

''Good. I'll call it in. Just give me the high sign when you need anything else.'' She smiled and headed off to buzz the kitchen and get a refill for a fellow further down the bar.

McIver was still sitting there when the six o'clock news came on. Only now, almost every seat in the inside bar was filled, mostly with younger, well-dressed business types, singles, chatting and laughing and eyeing each other. He was sure some were looking to get laid. Some others nearby were talking computerese and exchanging business cards. Networking. He knew the ritual well. But tonight McIver didn't want any part of it. He stared at the TV screen, pretending to be interested in the news. There was the usual political lead-in. Earthquake somewhere.

The blonde bartender made a pass, refilling nut dishes

and picking up empty glasses on the way. McIver still had his third one half-full and his burger half-eaten.

The local lead was about the damn dogs again. Kern had a funeral for them in a pet cemetery east of town. Private ceremony. But the press was there, showing them from a distance. Four folks were with him. One had brought a lab on a leash. "Family of the deceased," McIver guessed, silently trying to amuse himself.

The Lundquist broad wasn't present. But the little redhaired one, the Mello woman, was. In a short black dress. Real short.

Afterward Kern avoided the reporters and ducked back into his car, but the Mello woman stopped. Her sweet bow-lips curved into a polite smile. With his usual bluntness, the reporter asked how Olivia Mello was handling the pressure of being one of the remaining artists on the Trasher's list.

"Me? I'm fine." The big blue eyes blinked. "I really doubt that this guy has the balls to come after me face to face." Mello looked straight into the camera without changing her kewpie-doll expression. "I'm concerned," she declared. "But not for my safety. I'm concerned for his."

McIver took a swallow of scotch.

"In what respect?" the reported asked, then thrust the microphone back under her chin.

"Whoever this guy is, he obviously needs help." She spoke with a curiously raspy, almost sultry voice. "I'd bet the poor thing is sexually repressed. There is some reason for the hostility. Perhaps jealousy. Or substance abuse. Perhaps he's a low achiever who can't erect anything of his own, much less create a piece of art. No normal grown-up would run around in a ski mask, doing these things. I think he's a sick person. This all just got out of hand. He's hurt and crying out for attention. He certainly has ours." She arced one hand in a flourish toward the burial area. "Now, I think he should turn himself in and get some counseling, while there's still room to bargain. Therapy is better than jail. He's not supposed to be a big guy. You can imagine what would happen to someone like him if he ended up in jail. There are some real big guys there. Not too sympathetic."

McIver couldn't tell if she were sincere, or simply baiting him. He had the feeling she was enjoying every minute on screen. Then the reporter stepped in and did a wrap-up. The Mello broad must have left with Kern and the others.

"She's a hell of a lot more generous than I am," the dark-haired woman with her back to McIver said to her companion one stool further down the bar. "I'd like to see him end up in jail and let those big guys have at the little bastard." He didn't turn his head, but he heard some guy nearby say something and laugh.

The blonde bartender had stopped just inches down from McIver to watch and listen when the Mello woman came on screen. "Bad all around." She shook her head. "Sarasota has gotten a lot of real bad press over this," she said solemnly.

McIver said nothing. Except for the dog business, he'd been generally pleased with his campaign of terror. He'd made them all look like fools because they couldn't catch him. "Bad press is right," he said out loud.

He took another swallow, then kept looking at the images on the TV, trying to remember exactly what the kewpie-doll in the black dress had said. Part of it had made his neck burn. All that half-baked, psychological bullshit. He'd loosened his tie. He remembered bits of it. Calling him a poor thing. Low-achiever. She should see his house. And his car. She was living in some barn with a biker and calling *him* a low achiever. But what really pissed him off was the "repressed" part and the sly way she worked in the comment about not being able to get it up, "can't erect anything." She was wrong about that too. A good fuck was all it would take to set her straight.

He tapped his glass, signaling for a refill. Fucking anything sounded good to him.

"You planning on driving anytime soon?" the blonde asked before she poured him another. Despite the flow of people, she'd been keeping track of his consumption.

McIver considered telling her to fuck off. He hated it when anyone said he was drinking too much. Sandra used to whine about it, and he'd backhand her. But that was at home. This one was in public and she was in charge of the bottle. He felt like someone underage nailed for swiping a beer. He didn't even want to look her in the eye.

"Traffic is pretty light now that the rush is over. You could probably make it home safely." Without having that other drink, she meant. She managed to get her point across without saying he'd had too many or sounding patronizing. She was giving him an out. He had to give her that. She'd probably had to do this same routine a hundred times. If he shut up now and just got up and left, McIver knew he wouldn't look like a jerk. He knew how to handle himself in public.

"Thanks. Good idea," he answered. "How about a bill for all this." While she went to total it up, he picked up the remaining part of the burger, cold now, and forced himself to take a bite and get it down. Acting casual, in case anyone was looking.

"Take care. Hope you feel better." She put the bill by his glass.

McIver took another bite. She may have a point, but she wasn't going to rush him. He wiped his fingers on the napkin, studied the total a few seconds, pulled out some bills, and slid them under the edge of the glass. He left a decent tip. Didn't want to short her because he was pissed. Or overdo it so she'd think he needed mothering or was apologizing in any way. Then he stood, smiling, steadied himself, and worked his way toward the door.

Outside, he sat in his car in the parking lot a moment, keys in the ignition but not turned on. "Repressed, my ass," he muttered, checking out a few of the women, new arrivals, on their way in. Skirts up to their butt cheeks. He could fuck any one of them. He could even fuck the redhead. He considered going back up the beach toward the Mello broad's place, just a reconnaisance to see what precautions she was taking. He'd bet she or the cops had to have her barricaded in there, despite her comment that she didn't think the Trasher had the balls to come after her face to face.

McIver's neck was getting hot again. Surprising they let Mello get by saying balls right on the news. He wanted to slap her right across those little-girl lips. Or slide up that little black skirt and screw her every which way but Sunday. He had balls enough for any of them, Bambi included. The one he wanted was the leggy blonde with the cool, classy look. If it hadn't been for her, none of this would have happened. He'd have someone there at home, someone he could fuck whenever he wanted. Lundquist was the one who had started all this.

Maybe he should drive by her place. Then he remembered it was Tuesday. He'd followed her once on a Tuesday.

She taught some class at the community college. He'd called the registrar and asked about it. Photography. Seven till nine. She wouldn't be there.

He reached over and snapped open his attaché case. The flask was tucked under a few papers. A car pulled in the parking slot beside him. Man and and a woman. He lowered the flask onto the seat beside his leg so they wouldn't see it. The woman gave McIver a curious look as she got out the passenger side. Like there was something wrong about just sitting there in Conroy's parking lot. Alone.

He propped his elbow on the door, like he was kicking back, waiting for someone. He'd feel foolish having someone spot him taking a drink out there in public, in a parking lot, like a wino with his paper sack. Bad enough if it were a stranger. Worse if it were someone he knew.

Once she got out of sight, he'd go home. At home, he could change out of his suit and cool off, think it over. Figure out someone to call for a quick fuck. Or not. At home, he could drink his scotch out of a crystal glass, with a film of Drambuie on top. He could look out past his bird-caged pool, his powerboat, and his dock over Hudson's Bayou. Real class.

Amid the usual stack of mail waiting just inside his door, there was another thick packet of legal papers dropped through the slot. His attorney's return address. More legalese. McIver left it all laying there, and went in and peeled down to his skin. Pulled on his silk dressing robe. Filled a glass. Baccarat. Scotch. Drambuie. He stood, looking out at the bayou, sipping the drink and licking the traces of Drambuie that clung to his lips. Insulated, he finally picked up the envelope and opened it.

"Okay, what does she want now?" He glanced over the cover letter. His attorney reminded him that these petitions are extremes, beginning bargaining positions, not to take it as fact. He took that as a grim warning that he wasn't going to like what was attached. The first of the long documents following was a financial statement. He had to list all assets, income, debts. His accountant could do that. The other pages listed demands from her lawyer. Health insurance. Alimony. Child support. Then he got to the kicker.

Sandra wanted the house. This one. Immediate possession. And she wanted to keep it until the youngest kid was eighteen. He'd make the payments. She'd live in it with the

kids. Then when the kids were grown, McIver could sell it
and they'd split the proceeds. Or he could buy her out of
her half. At current market value.

"This is bullshit," he squawked. She didn't even like the
new house. She said it was pretentious. She said she liked
their old one better. That one was comfortable. They still
owned it. McIver had kept it as rental property. He'd told
her sister that Sandra and the kids could have the old place.
He'd even have the crates with her new greenhouse taken
over there and set it up for her. He figured that was generous.

But she wanted this one. And she wanted him out. Now.

It wasn't fair. He'd found the property. He'd made the
deal. He'd worked with the remodeling contractor, the land-
scaper, and the interior designer. He'd hired the best in the
area, and he'd turned the old Hudson Bayou property into a
showplace. In ten years, the market value would be astro-
nomical. If he bought her out then, he'd get burnt on both
ends. He'd paid for the improvements, then he'd get to pay
half of the market value for the property he'd improved.

"Fuck her. It isn't fair." McIver gulped down the drink
to keep from bellowing in rage. He'd always been real good
to Sandra, moneywise. And she had money of her own. She
had some trust left by her mother. All kinds of stock. Her
father had more money than God. And since they'd separated, McIver had done just like his lawyer had said. Paid
everything he'd been required to pay.

She'd moved into one of her father's condos just to make
a big show that she needed the security to protect her from
him. He wasn't sure which unit, but he knew which development. There was a guard at the entrance to the grounds
screening all visitors. You couldn't get into any one of the
buildings on the compound without speaking to someone
upstairs and waiting till they pushed their button to release
the door. And everything was monitored by a camera. He
figured she was set for a while there, at least until he could
get the renters out of the old place. He was sure that Daddy
wasn't asking for any rent.

But now she was pulling this stunt. And some judge would
go over it all and decide what each of them deserved. Sandra
didn't deserve his house. He wanted to belt her. He wanted
to strangle her. He was pacing now. Maybe he could make
a deal to buy her out now, for half of what he'd paid for the

property, before improvements. If he could get her to come home again, make up, and keep things smooth a while, he could set it up so she wouldn't have a chance to pull this next time.

"Don't get mad; get even." He'd played by that rule for years. "The best revenge is living well." Credos that made sense. Maybe if he asked Sandra out to dinner, just to talk. Maybe if he took her some place very public, very pretty. Told her he was sorry. He was going to AA. Said he wasn't drinking. Then he could pour on the charm and get romantic. He could fuck her. Make her feel good.

Instead, he poured another drink. He would just sit awhile and think it through. He'd plan it out so she'd come back. He couldn't afford another mistake. Like the dogs. The big, sad-eyed dogs. He couldn't keep them away. And Hershey was suddenly in his head again. Young. Runnin' for the frisbee. Doing bellyflops into the water. Then looking out the window, on the way to the executioner. Alone.

Listing slightly, McIver took the bottle and headed down the hall to his room. He set the alarm for ten-fifty. He wanted to catch the red-haired bitch if she showed up again on the eleven o'clock news. He wanted to hear it one more time. Everything she said. He wanted to get it right. Then he'd think it through. And he'd get even.

"I shou'da been in the thee-ya-tah," Olivia Mello proclaimed when she returned Rikki's call Tuesday night.

"You had to be out of your mind to come on TV and say that with this guy probably listening," Rikki said. She'd made a call-back sound urgent when she left the first message on Olivia's machine earlier. "What if he doesn't turn himself in and comes after you for what you said about him?" Rikki had caught the first broadcast just before she left for her photo class. She'd called then to warn Olivia that the Trasher was unstable as it was. He was dangerous. He may not respond to her peculiarly mixed message in any rational way.

"It's all right. Either way, we're covered," Olivia assured her friend. "Personally I think the sawed-off cocksucker should be hung by his nuts," Olivia added. "I don't have any sympathy for the little bastard at all. I just want his ass caught and kept off the streets." She started whispering. "Don't worry. I shouldn't tell you this, but all the stuff on the news was scripted. Even the funeral. Thayer really had the dogs buried at his home yesterday.''

Rikki listened, dumbfounded. The brief glimpse of the funeral on the news had upset her all over again. She hadn't known it was scheduled. She would have been there to help comfort her friends.

"The funeral on TV was Detective Warnock's idea." Olivia kept her voice low, and spoke quickly as if someone else were there and could be listening to their conversation. "So was the interview. It was a setup. Deliberate. To pull the guy's chain. If he turns himself in, that's great. If he comes for me, even better. Warnock is just keeping at him so he doesn't take too long to move. These guys can't sit and wait forever."

"What guys?"

"Not supposed to tell. But you'll love it when you hear what they're doing."

"You're sure you're safe?"

"No sweat. They put a stand-in at Wallace's place. We're both covered. These cops are on the ball. You'll love it, when you hear what they're doing," she insisted. She dropped her voice again. "They don't want me runnin' my mouth, but I hate knowing you're worrying like this. Think decoys." She paused. "Body doubles." She paused again. "I'm not even at home. They've got a cop there, dressed like me," she blurted out. "That's why I don't answer. I'm not there. Everything has to be relayed to me."

Rikki stood with the receiver pressed against her ear, saying nothing.

"You still there?" Olivia asked.

"I'm here. Where are you?"

"So how's Romeo? Still tall, hairy, and gorgeous?" Olivia's voice got louder and her tone changed abruptly. She also didn't answer Rikki's question.

"Stu? He's fine," Rikki replied absentmindedly, still re-adjusting her thinking. Body doubles. Decoys. Now she understood why Stu said that Olivia and the others were safe. He couldn't tell her about the decoys. Policy again. No one, not even Olivia, was supposed to talk.

"I'm so glad the plants are doing fine." The conversation now was making no connections.

"Olivia, is someone there?"

"You bet."

"Is that why you didn't tell me where you are?"

"Got that right."

"I'm just relieved to know that you're somewhere safe."

"That makes two of us. Still, it would be fun to be there for the last tango." The raspy edge of defiance was back in Olivia's voice.

"You're better off sitting this one out. I certainly feel better knowing that some police officer will be doing the tangoing," Rikki responded. "Thanks for telling me. You did your bit on TV very well," she added, considerably cheered by the unauthorized explanation Olivia had given her.

"I thought so. If I fuck up as an artist, I may have a career in film." Suddenly she was whispering again. "I just hope the little chickenshit is watching and decides to make a move. Any move. Then we can get on with it. I had a new piece of work going."

"You're not working?"

"Not this week." From the artificial lilt to her voice, Rikki could tell Olivia once again had another audience she was playing to.

"That's a relief. I was worried about you with all the welding supplies you have." Like the materials in Kern's studio, Olivia had cylinders of gas, greasy rags, and other volatile substances in her workroom.

"I know. Right. Not a good time to be intimate with flammables. Or is it inflammables? So what are you working on?" She switched to talking shop, a common ground.

"I'm getting ready to shoot a new series for a tape."

"We could probably all use one after this," Olivia quipped. "More flowers?"

"Actually I'll be doing people."

"Bit of a switch. What's the concept?"

"I'm not ready to talk about it yet. I'd rather work on it awhile, and then tell you." Now it was Rikki who was holding back. "It's an idea that is still in the formative stages."

"Ah, I know the feeling. Far be it from me to muddy your creative waters," Olivia said good naturedly. "Speaking of waters, I think I'll go soak in the hot tub a while. You know, I could really get to like this."

"Enjoy. And thanks for calling. Thanks for telling me what's going on," Rikki said sincerely.

"I never said a word," Olivia replied. "Just remember

to tune me in at eleven. I think the six o'clock version was edited. Seems to me they should have had a great shot of my ass getting into Kern's limo. Warnock insisted I wear a skirt. And pantyhose. Lots of leg. He's got a sick mind. I could get to like that man!''

"Take care. Call me whenever you can. Miss you, buddy."

"Me too. This too shall pass," Olivia proclaimed with apparent melodrama. "Meryl Streep, eat your heart out," she ended, cackling as she hung up the phone.

Rikki glanced at her watch. Ten o'clock. She still had an hour until the late news. Smiling, she took the stairs two at a time, kissed the sleeping kids, changed to her swimsuit, patted Oscar, and headed out toward the dock.

She hadn't been night-sailing in a long time. Lately she slipped down there, swam instead, and stayed close to shore. But tonight she felt the pressure leave her. Tonight she had some real sense that there were people out there, professionals, who knew precisely what they were doing. They were protecting her friends, taunting a crazy, and luring the Trasher into a trap. That knowledge gave her a welcome rush of adrenaline. She could rechannel the energy that had been draining off with worry. Now she could concentrate on what she was good at, take care of her art and her business, without glancing over her shoulder or dreading the next newscast.

She could tell by the way her smile felt that the difference must show. She didn't want to see Stu just yet, or he would see it too. She couldn't tell him that Olivia had talked and she knew about the decoys. And the newscast. And that traps were set. But she could go out on the water, slice through the dark night on her board, and laugh at last to the moon.

Chapter 10

"This was a great idea." Ivey Currey spoke from beneath the wide-brimmed sunhat she'd worn to Rikki's party. The Wednesday night affair had suddenly blossomed to include a few more than family, and it had taken on an increasingly festive air. After working with Rikki on the music for her video, Fuzzy Haight had agreed to come and play his tapes. He'd brought several of his unnamed, upbeat pieces, along with some of the more symphonic compositions he'd put together on his synthesizer. He'd also set up two extra sets of speakers and run wiring out to the deck so the entire yard was filled by the pleasant, subdued sounds.

"Sounds like something I remember from the islands." Eddie Sordo paused and listened. Then he continued on, dancing to the rhythm as he carried out the huge salad he'd made from an assortment of greens and root crops from his garden.

Juli Quinn had contributed something she called a "dump cake," a dark chocolate single-layer the size of a lasagna, with tart cherries, marshmallows, and chocolate chips throughout. When Rikki was inviting a few extra friends to the outdoor buffet, Juli had persuaded her to add to the list Mike Maurer, the young detective she'd met the night the Trasher hit. The chocolate cake was a not-so-subtle hint to the officer that she had a domestic streak.

"My mother got the recipe from her 'outrageous' file. She figured if I like him, there's no sense being coy about this," Juli explained. "And I definitely do like him."

Stu had retrieved his steamer pot from his apartment in town and had seven pounds of unpeeled shrimp turning pink in the hot and spicy water. His mother, Helen Sullivan, had brought three bowls of hot sauce, ranging from mild to incendiary. "The boys like theirs so fiery it makes my eyes tear just to sniff it," she'd warned the others before they

started peeling and dipping the shrimp into the red ceramic
bowl on the end. "Try the yellow or the orange bowls first,"
she suggested. A slim, no-nonsense woman with a broad
smile and short salt-and-pepper hair, she'd oohed and
aahed over the rambling Caribbean-style house. Then she'd
pitched right in helping Ivey squeeze lemons in the drawn
butter while they chatted about the new season at the Asolo
theater in town.

"I told you we wouldn't need an icebreaker." Stu sat,
feet propped up, peeling shrimp for Rikki and himself.
Swede, Eddie, Brian, and Fuzzy Haight were all bunched
together around a bowl of shrimp, talking about water short-
ages in the area. The morning paper had announced new
restrictions until the fall rains began.

"This isn't something that will go away," Brian noted.
Stu and he had been to several seminars over the past two
years hearing about water conservation in Florida. Brian
was advocating alternative landscaping, replacing high-
maintenance grass lawns with drought-tolerant plantings that
didn't require such extensive watering.

"Right. People are moving into the area in such numbers, putting demands on limited resources. We can't keep
on using water like we used to," Swede agreed. "We're
going to have to think more like islanders. Start catching
and storing rainwater like they do."

"My grandmother used to collect rainwater. She had a
cistern behind her farmhouse," Fuzzy recalled.

"In Bermuda, they have rippled white roofs with down-
spouts to catch the rainwater. Every house has an underground tank," Swede noted. "We could require all new
developments here to do something similar. Build storage
tanks under parking lots to hold water for maintaining the
landscape. Recycle used water to flush toilets. We're waste-
ful. Irresponsible."

"And short sighted," Brian agreed. He was hunched forward, nodding, peeling shrimp and dropping the shells in a
garbage sack Eddie Sordo had put between them. When the
evening was over, Eddie would add them to the compost
ingredients he was taking home.

Vicky was on the dock with the kids, soaking her bare
feet in the water and keeping an eye on her son, Todd, who
at three found whatever the older kids were doing fascinating. Lara was teaching him to roll little doughballs and drop

them off to chum the smaller fish. Jake had brought out a fishing pole and had his line out with a red-and-white bobber riding the surface of the Intracoastal. Todd would stare in one direction, then the other, squealing when a school of tiny minnows swarmed the doughball or when some unseen force tugged Jake's bobber under. Occasionally a boat would pass by and they would all wave at the driver and passengers or stop to watch a skier cut across a wake.

Juli Quinn and her detective friend had pulled their chairs over near the edge of the deck facing the Intracoastal like Rikki and Stu had done. They sat with their feet resting on the railing, talking and enjoying the music and the view, with a bowl of steamed shrimp between them. From time to time, the groupings shifted, plates were filled, then emptied and refilled, and tours were made of the production room and the slathouse, all very low key and relaxed.

"This has really been nice," Stu said, corralling Rikki in the kitchen for a moment. The sun had set, and a coolish breeze had sent everyone in search of sweaters and sweatshirts. But the night was clear and the lights across the water and the serene music brought the adults outside again to talk and finish off the dump cake. Jake and Lara were curled up with Stu's nephew Todd inside, watching a favorite videotape, delighted to have a new kid to share it with. Rikki was making coffee, and the aroma had touched off a special homey feeling that had brought Stu inside after her.

"I needed this." She sighed with pure satisfaction watching the dark coffee drip into the pot. "It's been very peaceful and friendly and invigorating."

"Invigorating?"

"Right. I could feel the good energy," she elaborated. "Everyone clicked with everyone else." She was setting out coffee mugs on a tray as she talked.

Stu was nodding. He started counting out the spoons. "So . . . did my mom tell you anything to scare you off?" he asked, giving her a curious, sidelong look. He'd deliberately left the two of them alone a few times, just to let them talk more freely. He'd seen them coming out of the slathouse talking in earnest, then smiling and laughing at various times as the dinner progressed. It had made him feel good to watch two women he loved, apparently enjoying each other.

Rikki smiled, filled the creamer, and put the sugar bowl

on the tray. "She seems pretty pleased with you. Unless she's holding out on me."

"She looked like she was pretty pleased with you too," he countered. "Not that it's a requirement or anything," he added, almost as an apology of sorts. "It just makes it nice."

"I know what you mean," Rikki assured him. In a similar way, she liked the comfortable relationship her father and Ivey had developed with Stu. "I really enjoyed talking with your mom. She reminds me a bit of my mother. She has a commonsense approach to things. And she's so smooth with the kids. She stepped in and steered them through a few potential feuds and accidents at dinner without any of them losing a temper or an ice cube. She said she developed that kind of radar from raising two boys. So I guess that means you weren't perfect."

"I'm still not."

Rikki was still smiling but her expression was slightly more pensive than before and a bit preoccupied. "I especially enjoyed listening to your mom and Ivey and my dad talking about Sarasota years ago. It's remarkable that they all lived so close for years and never met."

"Like you and me? Ten miles apart by road, three as the crow flies?"

"Something like that." She and Stu had gone to different schools in town, at different times, and different state colleges afterwards. Stu had been back in Sarasota, starting at the fire department, about the time she left as a freshman for Florida State. Throughout her school years and afterward, Swede had regularly spent part of each year abroad with his family, traveling and shooting photo assignments. "Over the years, Helen and Ivey must have been to all kinds of performances and exhibits at the same time and simply passed each other."

"I'm glad we're not still passing each other," Stu said with a faint shift in his voice as if some unexpected emotion had touched him. "Sometimes I get a bit angry that it took this long and it took this kind of trouble to get us together. Kind of like we've been cheated. I can think of a lot of years I'd rather have spent with you close to me."

"If we'd done things differently, we wouldn't be the people we are now," Rikki replied with a slight shrug. "We may not have even liked each other five years ago, or even two," she added, stepping near enough to hug him. "You didn't like me when we first met, as it was," she reminded him. He'd told her that he'd been reluctant at best when Harrison Ash brought him over to meet the Ice Queen in the flowered pareu.

"I got over it," he answered, chuckling, remembering that first day together, discovering that Rikki wasn't at all like he'd imagined. "I got smarter. Now, I love you. Today. Tomorrow. Next year. Till I breathe my last breath. Maybe after that, if I'm lucky." His voice was low and warm.

"I love you too, Sullivan." She stood on tiptoe, so she could touch her lips to his in a light, feathery kiss. "Nothing that happened before we met has been wasted." Then they kissed again, gently, without the burning intensity of other times. But this kiss had a special sweetness and a sense of confirmation that they would both remember.

This was the kind of moment, without the edge of sexual hunger, without any urgency, that he'd have chosen to say he loved her the first time. Instead, he'd blurted it out over his cellular phone, with Warnock sitting next to him. This was the feeling of newness that he'd thought the Trasher had taken from both of them. But it was strangely new again, and richer since they were standing, hugging, in the kitchen of her house, smelling the vanilla-flavored coffee, with all their family and some good friends just outside and three sleepy youngsters trying to stay awake in the next room.

Later, after everyone else left, Stu helped clean up the serving dishes while Rikki oversaw the bed-teeth-bathroom routine upstairs. "I really like this," he said aloud, to no one, in the big country kitchen that had become so familiar over the past weeks.

His mom had driven back with Vicky and Brian, with Todd belted in and sound asleep next to her in his carseat. "I'm glad to see you so happy," she had whispered when she hugged him before she got in. "And you make her happy too. I can hear it in her voice when she mentions your name. And I can see it when you look across the room at each other. There's a real solid feeling between you. That's good. Not that I don't suspect some real racy shenanigans go on when no one's looking," she added with her typical flash of wit. "But I'm not interested in details," she insisted, grinning all the while. "I just want you to know you've got this one right. This kind of thing doesn't happen often in a lifetime. You're blessed if it happens at all.''

"I know." He didn't have to say any more. The look in his eyes said it all. As she drove away, with her younger son and his family, Helen Sullivan knew they would all sleep with a full heart tonight.

McIver stayed away from the booze all day Wednesday. He went to his AA meeting and said all the things he knew he should say, just as he promised when he talked to his lawyer midafternoon.

"The house deal is negotiable," the attorney had declared in that easy, confident, slightly patronizing voice that made McIver's butt muscles constrict and his toes curl. It was the used-car-salesman tone that he could turn on himself at will. He just didn't like being on the receiving end.

"You just get together the information about the improvements you had done," the attorney directed him. "Pull all checks and receipts. She's just got herself a hard-ass attorney and he's starting out by asking for the moon. He and I have faced off before. Relax. We'll get this ironed out before we go to court," he promised.

But McIver had felt like his sphincter muscle wouldn't dilate until he'd gone home and poured that first drink and looked out at the bayou and the boat on the davit, waiting to go. Out on the water, he was in control.

There was still some light in the sky when he took the boat out for a cruise. The roar of the motor and the ruthless way it cut its path straight out to the channel always made him feel like a biker on a road trip. Tough. Free. He hadn't planned to swing south and cut in close to the Lundquist place. But the night was clear and cool and he had nowhere else in mind to go.

He liked the fact that there were people at her place. Lights on out back. Not the big floods. Kind of pretty. Meant she figured she was safe. He went on by, cut the motor off, and drifted back, rummaging in the side compartment for the binoculars for a closer look. At first he couldn't find them. But with the roar gone, he could hear the music. It came floating out over the water toward him. He finally located the binoculars in the underseat storage, along with a bottle of Dewars that still had something in it. He just sat there awhile, shifting hands, looking and sipping and slipping past on the current.

The salt air smelled like fall. About time. October was almost over. Good time of the year for entertaining outdoors. He remembered how it was when he and Sandra had parties. Lots of friends and business buddies. Lots of food. A bar full of everything they could want. He knew how to lay out a spread. He hadn't pulled anything together like that since the housewarming six months back. That night he'd gotten pretty loaded. The crowd started thinning early. Sandra was pissed. Said he'd been laying it on a bit too thick, bragging about the new house.

He remembered taking several of the guys into the bathroom to show them the fancy fixtures. Gold plated. Imported, he'd told them. Maybe Sandra had a point.

The boat had drifted well past the house where Lundquist lived. McIver waited a while longer then pitched the empty bottle overboard, started the motor, and steered back into deeper water, heading home. Something about all those couples there was beginning to get to him. Some of them would screw tonight. He wouldn't. Even Lundquist would probably get laid. And he'd be home, alone. With no one but Lady Thumb and her four sisters. Beating off. If he could. He hated it.

But he wasn't repressed. The red-lipped bitch had said that. Twice. On yesterday's six o'clock news, then again at eleven. And the morning paper had picked it up and printed it, editing out some of her other comments. Seeing it in print had pissed him off all over again. The paper made a big deal about the police being willing to "seek medical assistance" for the Trasher if he'd turn himself in. Psychological evaluation. More bullshit, McIver concluded. It was that kind of mumbo-jumbo that made Sandra finally leave. Only her buzzwords were "co-dependency" and "enabler" and "denial."

McIver's instincts said there was something phony about this "offer" from the cops. It was just too damn civilized, too pat. They were fishing, hoping for a miracle, since they didn't have a clue. McIver didn't trust any of them. And he sure as hell wasn't about to turn himself in.

He had one more trick-or-treat to pull. Then he'd quit. And he'd leave them all looking stupid. He just had to stay cool. Let this weekend pass. Wait for the next. Then he'd give Lundquist a surprise.

He got the boat docked and moored. Unable to resist checking if there was any Trasher story tonight, he poured a drink and turned on the late news. Thayer Kern was back on. This time smiling and holding a new pair of Labs. Pups. Some kennel owner from Georgia had heard the broadcast about the fire and had flown down with two newly weaned chocolate Labs. Free.

The camera zoomed in on the droopy-eyed dogs, drooling and licking Kern's cheek. Then he put them down on the grass and they rolled all over each other, all big feet and knobby legs and that beautiful dark smooth puppy shine. It brought back the first time McIver had brought Hershey home. They'd played like that in the yard, rolling over each other.

Hershey had slept in his room in a box that night. With a clock and a jar of hot water wrapped in a towel so he wouldn't get lonely. At least he wasn't supposed to. But the pup kept whimpering and moaning. Every time he looked at it, it would wag its tail. Wagged its whole body, in fact. And pissed all over itself. So McIver had picked it up and tucked it next to him under the sheets, and they both slept the rest of the night.

McIver was out of scotch by the time the sports came on. He was thinking about Hershey, and Sandra, and going to bed alone. He glanced at his watch. If he hurried, he could make it to a liquor store before it closed. There was one by the supermarket on the Trail that stayed open till midnight. He needed cereal anyway. And milk. It wasn't like getting liquor was the only reason he had to go. But he pulled on his shoes and found his car keys. It didn't hurt to be prepared in case later, if he stayed up and watched a movie, he might feel like a drink.

He'd already put the liquor in the car and was standing by the ice cream cooler with a pint container, looking for something else to go with it, when the blonde-haired bartender showed up next to him.

"I see we have the same late-night vices." She began chatting away, just like they were old friends. "I'm usually into Cherry Garcia but this time of night, anything with chocolate will do." She'd apparently read the container he had and was scanning the remaining labels. He had the last

Cherry Garcia in his hand. "How have you been doing?" She loaded three different flavors into her cart.

"I've been fine." He glanced over at her. She was wearing one of those spandex exercise outfits that looked like it had been spray-painted on. McIver had to admit, for an older broad, she had good legs and buns, at least when they were held tight by a second skin of shiny black. Not much up top, he noticed, trying to remember if he'd ever known her name.

"It's usually safer when I stop in here right after work. Then I'm not so interested in food," she went on. "But on the nights I go to the gym, I come away starving. Then I end up with things like this." Besides the ice cream, she had bagels and cream cheese and a small microwaveable gourmet pizza. On Cuban bread instead of a regular crust.

"Pizza looks good. I could go for one of them myself," he said, feeling somewhat magnanimous all of a sudden. "Where'd you find it?"

"I'll show you. This particular kind is tucked away on the bottom, near the cheescakes. I almost bought one of those while I was at it," she confided, laughing as she pushed her cart along.

McIver fell in step beside her. He liked not roaming the aisles alone, especially late like this when the store had more employees than customers around. Sandra had always bought the groceries. He'd simply open the freezer or the refrigerator and there would be food. But since she'd left, he'd pretty much limited his shopping to the deli counter, the dairy section, and the liquor store. He ate out a lot. Especially for dinner. But that got old, even when he rounded up a buddy from work or went to a place like Conroy's, where there were always people around. Sometimes he'd simply go through the drive-in window at a fast-food place and eat while he drove. But eating alone sucked.

"If you really want to make these luscious, you can add some extra cheese," the blonde was saying. "And if you set it up on one of those little racks, the crust will come out crisper."

He nodded, not sure at all if his microwave had a little rack. "Can't have a pizza without a lot of cheese. Where do you get that?" He was leading her on a little, testing her. If she pointed, that was one thing. But if she took him there and showed it to him, he figured she was being more than helpful.

"Over here," she led the way. "Usually they use mozzarella, but I've tried topping it off with provolone and it's really delicious."

"Provolone." He held back and let her pick it out of the case for him. She had smooth tanned arms.

"Now all we need is some cold beer. I always drink beer with pizza. Where's the beer in this place?" He was playing helpless for sure, letting her steer him around, and he was enjoying it. Apparently, so was she. He just wished he remembered her name.

"Heineken. Good stuff. You drink dark beer?" he asked her.

"I love dark beer." She had that wide-eyed, idiotic look that females get when they figure they're on the verge of being asked out.

"Look, I don't know how to cook this thing." He plunged on, figuring he might not be ending up sleeping alone if he played his cards right. "How about I get all this stuff, and you come over and do them both at my house? We could have a few beers, maybe pick up one of those cheesecakes. I really hate to eat alone. And I'd probably screw this up anyways."

She hesitated. He was afraid she'd say it was too late. Then he'd feel like an ass for hitting on her. And he'd feel like an ass every time he went into Conroy's after that.

"I'd really like to, but I'm still in these workout things. I could use a shower and a change of clothes."

"How about you just pick up a change of clothes? I've got a shower and a pool. Bring a swimsuit. You could cool off there." He made it sound so casual and practical, but he knew if she took him up on it, he could bet on getting laid. He hadn't been laid in weeks. This one looked like she could really make the ride a wild one. His palms were sweating. He felt like a fucking kid, hoping to grab a little tit.

She paused again. Then she smiled and shrugged. "Sure. Sounds good."

He swallowed. He'd done it now. No turning back. He deposited the beer and pizza, the Cherry Garcia ice cream, and the extra cheese he was carrying in her cart. "Let's pick us up a cheesecake,'' he suggested, once again letting her lead the way.

He paid for the groceries. He had them put her ice cream and bagels in a separate bag. Then he loaded his bag in his car and waited for her to get into hers. He followed her to her apartment complex less than a mile further south, a few blocks off the main road. He'd opened the scotch from the liquor store on the way and took a few drinks right out of the bottle.

''You want to come in?'' She came to his window to ask.

McIver was already uneasy. He'd slid the scotch beside him when he saw her coming and rested his arm on the seat above the open bag of groceries to screen the bottle. ''I think I'd better just wait here.'' He really didn't want anyone to see him, not here, not with her.

''Right. Wouldn't want the Cherry Garcia to melt,'' she said, eyeing the grocery bag. ''I'll put my stuff in the fridge and make it back quick.''

She did. In a few moments, she returned with a fresh layer of makeup and a carry-bag with her clothes and whatever else she needed. ''You go ahead, I'll follow you,'' she told him. McIver nodded and pulled out, grateful she was taking her own car so he wouldn't have to drive her back afterwards, whenever that happened to be. He swung out onto the main road, beginning to get apprehensive about the whole thing. He lived in a very classy neighborhood. People had garage-door openers and put their fancy cars inside. Half his garage space was filled with the fucking crates full of Sandra's greenhouse. He couldn't leave a strange car out front.

He could let the blonde park inside and he could leave the Mercedes in the driveway. ''Bad idea,'' McIver said out loud. The neighbors would wonder if they saw his car left out all night. And he sure as hell wasn't getting up later on to move his car to let the blonde pull out. Her damn economy hatchback would be sitting out, wide-ass-visible in the wee hours when anyone could see it. They might watch and figure out what was going on. They might take down the license number and tell Sandra. He didn't need to hand her the ammunition to blow his ass out of his own home.

McIver pulled into a parking area in a strip mall. He was sweating again. The no-name blonde pulled in behind him. He capped the scotch and put it back in the bag.

"How about you dropping off your car here and riding with me," he said, trying to sound relaxed and friendly. The scotch was finally taking the edge off. "I'd be glad to bring you back whenever you say. I just feel damn peculiar taking you to my place by convoy. I figure if you ride with me, we could crack a beer and talk on the way. I'll even spot you cab fare if you don't think you can trust me to get you back on time. I'm not real smooth at this kind of thing, but this separate-car business just feels . . . kind of uncomfortable."

He figured she knew he hadn't been doing the single bit for long. She'd also never seen him hit on anyone in the bar. She could interpret that line about being uncomfortable any way she wanted. He hoped she'd take it as a kind of appealing confession that he preferred the old-fashioned way of dating, where the guy and gal rode together. Not that this was a date. But at this time of night, they both knew that unless they didn't hit it off at all, they weren't just going home to eat and chat.

The blonde shrugged and turned off her ignition. "I'm not worried. I don't work tomorrow anyhow. One way or another, I'll get home all right." By the way she said it, she was leaving their options open. They might not screw at all tonight. But most likely, they would. And if things worked out between them, she could stay longer. Maybe all day and the next night as well. He could even put in an appearance at the office, then come home early. She'd be there waiting, recovering, and they could screw all over again.

"Repressed, my ass . . ." McIver felt himself getting a hard-on as he watched her get out of her vehicle and come around to the passenger door of his. The black spandex glistened as she moved. He had wanted a woman. He'd wanted to fuck the Mello broad, or Bambi, even Sandra if he could persuade her to come home. But tonight he had someone who looked like she could outfuck all of them. He was ready to give single life a shot.

McIver kept hitting the remote button all down the street, urging the electronic garage door open the second the signal reached home. He just swung the car into the drive, then straight inside without having to pause and let anyone see he had a passenger. At twelve-thirty on a Wednesday night, he doubted anyone would be up and looking anyhow. Still, he felt less tense when he'd pulled in and the door slid shut behind them.

In the bright fluorescent light of the garage, the blonde looked even more leathery than he remembered. She'd drawn the red lipstick beyond the natural outline of her mouth and it had smeared onto her chin from drinking beer out of the bottle. Still, he hoped she might do things with that mouth that Sandra always refused to do. Besides, he wouldn't have to look at her while she did it.

"I've never driven into this area. I never even knew there were houses like this back here," the blonde said as she stood there waiting for him to let them in through the door to the kitchen. "Wow." She registered the kind of reaction he liked when she stepped inside. She walked right over to the glass sliders across the back of the kitchen and looked out at the deck and the pool, a slice of dark lawn, and the bayou, still and shiny in the moonlight. "This is quite a view."

"I did some major renovation when I first got the place," McIver began explaining, turning on a few house lights from the central panel.

"Must have cost you a mint." She turned and smiled, plopped her carrying bag on the cooking island, and started moving off into the living room. He got another look at those lips. And the near-white hair with the dark roots starting to show through at the back. Her open-back shoes clicked against the terra cotta Italian tile floor, then made a duller sound on the wood in the adjoining room. He followed.

"This is really pretty," she said, surveying the Florida-formal living room with the huge overhead paddle fan. All the pastel raw-silk pillows were lined up along the sofa just like Adella left them. The collection of lead crystals and the glass-topped tables gleamed. The carpets were perfect. McIver usually made a point of stepping on the hardwood around the carpets so he wouldn't disturb their manicured effect.

She walked right onto one and left footprints. And her "pretty" assessment hardly did the room justice. She picked up a crystal obelisk, turned it back and forth so the faceted edges caught the light, then put it down, not where it had stood before. Steuben. Over a grand. She had no comment.

McIver felt his stomach knot.

He'd made a mistake bringing a woman like that here.

"How about a drink?" he asked her, hoping to coax her back the other way.

"I'm fine with the beer," she answered, dangling the bottle by its neck as she strolled toward the hallway leading down to the bedrooms. She paused to look at the framed pictures of his kids.

"Yours? Cute."

When Sandra left, he was sure she'd left the photos out just to spite him, but he hadn't put them away. Adella could testify to that. Like a devoted dad, he kept his kids in view. But he didn't like them getting tangled up in what was going on tonight.

McIver dropped some ice cubes in a glass and sloshed the scotch over them. "Now how about that pizza? You said the provolone goes on top." He spoke quickly, and a bit too loud, wanting to stop her from going any farther. She turned back toward him.

"Is there someplace I could change and take a shower?"

"Sure. How about getting the pizzas started, then you can change while they cook?" He wasn't a bit hungry now. But he needed to slow things down a bit, to buy some time to figure how to get her out of there without making a big stink. He didn't want a scene. He just wanted her gone. He wanted everything erased. He didn't even want to know her name.

The Cherry Garcia was dripping and soft when McIver stuck it in the freezer. The blonde had poked through Sandra's cookware and found a rippled tray she said would work like a rack to keep the bottoms of the pizzas from getting soggy. She set the rectangular pizzas side by side on it and layered them both with provolone. "Now we just set the time," she said, poking the panel that programmed the microwave, "and we wait."

McIver hated the way she included him in that "we." He'd told her once the food was started that she could use the poolside guest bathroom. Now that the LED numbers were counting down, he took his drink and showed her the way.

Outside, the cool night air bit through his clothes. He'd been perspiring again, all over, and the shift in temperature only underscored that clammy feeling.

"The pool sure looks nice." She was swaying her shoulders as she walked, with her back all stiff, like some beauty pageant cutie on parade, trying to make the most of the little boobs she had. Only there was nothing cute about this one. He figured she had to be forty, maybe forty-five, a few years older than him. In the garage, she'd looked even older.

There was more mercy in the dark.

She slid off one shoe and poked her toes in the water. "It feels warm. Is it heated?"

McIver nodded. "Solar. Just finished getting the system up and running."

Like she cared.

"Are you going to take a swim later? I brought my suit, just in case."

"You go ahead. I may pass." He figured he had no choice but to let her swim if that's what she wanted. He was the one who'd told her to bring the damn swimsuit in the first place.

His jaw ached from trying to keep from saying anything more. He didn't like this woman asking him questions. He didn't like her dropping hints or pulling any of the other maneuvering that went on between strangers, pretending to be friendly, trying to get laid.

He needed a refill. He went back in.

While she was changing, McIver took a kitchen towel and wiped off the faceted crystal obelisk in the livingroom and put it back in its place. He even brushed the rug with the cloth, removing the indented marks her shoes had made. He only regretted it wasn't as easy getting rid of the woman itself.

"Maybe I could fuck her." He stood, staring out the open sliders, speculating, trying to work up his courage. The blonde was still switching clothes. He'd had to admit, it would give him a perverse kind of pleasure screwing her in Sandra's bed. Then one day, maybe if Sandra came back and he was calling the shots again, if she ever got out of line, he'd tell her just that. He'd fucked somebody in their bed. Maybe got a blow job, too. He could imagine the expression on her face when he dropped that one on her.

He must have been grinning. When the blonde came out in her swimsuit, she looked his way, saw him staring, and smiled back. Probably thought he liked what he saw. McIver felt his face stiffen. She was wearing the kind of suit he'd seen in magazines. The two-piece kind where the bottom part was little more than a waistband with a strip attached. The cheeks of her ass hung out. Some guy in the office had called them butt-floss. Just enough to cover the crack. There wasn't any alternate tan line to make him think she'd just put on the skimpy thing for him. That was her regular suit.

And she had those damn shoes on again. Flapping with each step.

"How's the pizza doing?" She came toward him.

"The thing just beeped." That was almost the truth. It had been a while.

"Plates?" She looked at the wall of cabinets, then back at him.

He pointed.

"Napkins?"

He hated this. Like she was nosing into everything. He got out napkins and forks and knives. "You want another beer?" he asked.

"I sure do."

He got her one. "You want a glass?"

She didn't. He got one for himself.

"Looks good. How about we eat out back?" He took his plate, his beer, his napkin and utensils, and stepped out toward the pool again.

The pizza might as well have been sponge for all he tasted it. He cut it in bite-sized pieces, packed it in, chewed and swallowed, and chased it with the beer. He didn't have to talk if he kept eating.

She must have said a hundred times how pretty it was out back and how gorgeous it must be at sunrise. There must have been some other bits of conversation, but all McIver could do was think about getting through the next hour or so, maybe getting laid, and dumping her off at her car. He didn't want her there at dawn.

"I'll be back in a minute." McIver went in to get them both another beer. He kept on going and took a leak in his own bathroom. He'd had a lot of scotch before they ate, and he wasn't feeling real good, so he figured switching to the beer might help. It only made him need to pee.

"Do you have any vodka?" the blonde asked. She was already in the living room in that suit and those damn shoes when he came back through the house. He'd barely got his pants zipped. There was a tightness in her expression that hinted she wasn't enjoying her evening as much as he'd thought.

"In here." He showed her the liquor cabinet in the kitchen. "I guess you don't want the beer?"

"This goes in the beer. Just adds a little kick. You have a highball glass? And Tabasco sauce?"

He got her both.

She mixed the drink and stirred it. Then she tasted it, tapped a few more drops of Tabasco sauce on the top, and let it settle in. "You have a towel?"

He got one out of the kitchen drawer and held it out.

"I mean a bath towel or a beach towel. I thought I'd take that swim now."

He nodded. "Sure. Outside. In the changing room. There's a linen closet."

"Okay." She clopped across the tile floor again, drink in hand.

"Round two," McIver muttered, knowing that the evening had to play itself out. After the swim, there was still the cheescake. And the Cherry Garcia. And the fuck. He wasn't sure of their order on the agenda, but he wasn't up for any of it. He'd been drinking, alone and otherwise, for hours, and was feeling weighted. He was also bloated and gassy from having forced down the beer and pizza.

"However . . ." He brightened somewhat, realizing if he were drunk enough, obviously too drunk to drive, he'd be able to bow out gracefully. At least bow out. At Conroy's earlier in the week, she'd stopped serving him to keep him from driving all liquored up. With her ass in the car, she sure wouldn't want to take chances. She'd seen him drinking tonight. He could put on a convincing act. He would simply tell her he was loaded and was going to bed. He could give her cab fare so she'd figure she had to leave. He'd be off the hook.

He poured another scotch and took this one out with him.

He waited until she'd finished the swim, dried off, got another of her beer-vodka-hot sauce brews and came back out to join him by the pool with it.

"I'm not feeling real well," he said, blinking and staring at her like he was having difficulty focusing. "I hate to admit it, but I'm toasted."

"We all get that way one time or another," she answered good-naturedly, not quite getting the implications he intended. She sat down in the patio chair next to him, crossed her legs, then settled back with a satisfied sigh and gazed out over the bayou. She looked wide awake and refreshed.

McIver sat there a few seconds, then tried again. He was sweating. He mopped his face and throat with a napkin. 'I'm not doin' well at all. I think I'd better go inside and fall in the rack.''

She looked at him intently, with that same matter-of-fact scrutiny he remembered from the bar. ''Take a few aspirin before you lie down. It might head off a hangover. Chasing it with soda water would help.'' She didn't seem the least perturbed.

''You'll close up and catch a cab?'' He figured he'd better spell it out for her.

''Sure. No problem.'' She wasn't giving any indication that she intended to hurry. She just sat there with her drink, making herself at home, like she was planning to take her time. Or maybe not bother to leave at all.

''I'll put a twenty on the kitchen counter.'' He figured he'd make the first move. He braced himself on the arms of the chair and rocked forward.

The first time, he couldn't get enough thrust to lift off. He inched forward and tried again. As soon as he was on his feet, it hit him. All at once, he got hot and wet and whoozy. In slow motion, the room slowly started to shift like it did sometimes when he ended up with his face on the floor. This time he wasn't acting at all.

''Let me give you a hand.'' She was suddenly out of her chair, right beside him, propping him up.

''I can manage.'' He couldn't even get his mouth to make it the right number of syllables.

''Easy. Let's walk you down to bed. You can sleep this off.'' She hooked his arm around her neck and caught him by the waist. His knees wouldn't hold his weight like he wanted them to.

''I'm all right.''

He wasn't. But he remembered being worse. He remembered mornings when he'd couldn't even piece together what happened after this. But at least this part was working. She knew the party was over. They were moving down the hallway. He'd flop across the bed, and she'd go home.

He threw up before he got there.

He felt it coming. She must have figured as much. She

started moving him faster. They made it through the bathroom door, then all hell broke loose. He lurched toward the double vanity and threw up into the first sink. Sandra's sink. Then he braced himself and hit the next one. His. Only he got it all over the back of his hands. He stood, propped up, heaving. Cold with sweat.

Then he felt the hot spot lower. "Fuck," he groaned. He hadn't realized how bad off he really was. Here he was, peeing all over himself. He couldn't stop. He didn't even have a hand free to unzip his pants. "Fuck." This time it came out like a sob.

"That's all right, honey. Just let it go."

McIver wanted to belt her. He felt stupid enough as it was. He didn't need her fucking permission to pee on his own floor. Another wave of heaving hit. When he was steady enough to look at his own reflection in the mirror, he saw hers there as well. She was standing just inside the door, watching him. He wiped his mouth and spit.

"Let's get you out of all this." She was shaking her head.

"I can manage," McIver snapped, trying to camouflage his embarrassment. He tried unbuttoning his shirt. His fingers groped at the buttons but they kept slipping free.

"Let me give you a hand." She stepped over the puddle on the floor and came around to the far side, by the shower. He hated it when she touched him. She reminded him of Sandra, all self-righteous and motherly and disappointed.

"I said I'll do it. Fuck off." He shoved her. Planted his hand square on her breastbone and pushed. She rocked back and hit the shower door.

"Easy. Lighten up." Her voice lost its ever-so-patient, cajoling sound.

"You lighten up," he barked, swinging at her again. This time when he flung his arm out, he wacked her across the face. It was an accident. But he liked the sound.

"Easy. Back off." She squared her shoulders.

"Back off yourself." He flicked his hand, splattering the front of her bathing suit with spots of half-digested gourmet pizza and provolone. She'd made such a fuss over it, she could have it.

She didn't even wipe it off. "Just get out of my way. I want to leave. Move." She was waiting for him to clear the path.

"I don't take orders in my house." McIver planted himself between her and the door.

"And I don't take this kind of bullshit from anyone," the woman growled. "Move your ass. I want out." She clenched her fists.

He punched her then. Maybe it was all of them he was punching. Sandra. Lundquist. The Mello broad. The smug-faced lawyers. Suddenly he swung. Straight in the mouth. He missed and caught her nose. It made a dull, soggy sound when his fist connected.

She grabbed her face. Then there was a weird, long silence. Her eyes widened. He could see the blood starting out from under her hand, trickling down her neck. She turned and moved the hand far enough away to get a look at it. Then she wheeled and took a look at herself in the mirror.

She screamed. Her shrill voice echoed off the tiles.

McIver grabbed towels off the rack and started thrusting them at her. "Here."

She wailed louder.

He had to make her stop. How would he explain this one to the neighbors? Or the cops? Or Sandra's hard-assed lawyer? He had to make her stop.

He kicked the bathroom door shut to trap the sound inside. "Shut up. Shut up." He kept shoving towels at her, pounding them, and piling them up, driving her back into the large shower cubicle.

"Get the fuck away from me," she rasped, swinging both fists at him. He jerked aside but she landed a hard shot on his ear. Another caught the side of his neck so hard his teeth rattled.

McIver had never been in a real fight. Not one where someone struck back. Certainly not with a woman. At first he was so startled, all he could do was cover his head and block her punches. Then he managed to ram out one arm and shove her back.

She had blood all down the front of her face and neck now. It covered both hands. "Let me go." She came at him again, trying to push him against the john so she could get by.

"No!" McIver grabbed her by the hair. She tried to knee him in the balls, but he jerked her head and yanked her backward. Hard. She lost her footing and went down, arms flailing as she hit the shower door.

That other sound was back again. That tom-tom sound. McIver's heart was pounding like it was going to come right out of his chest.

Tom-tom. He was over her now. He couldn't stand to look at that face, eyes wild, the rest of it smeared and flattened, oozing red. He didn't want her touching him again.

She tried to yell.

"Shut up." He packed the towels over her face and pinned her to the floor with his knees. "Shut up," he said over and over as he banged her head again and again against the tile. Tom-tom. Tom-tom. He had to make her stop.

He wasn't sure when she quit thrashing. Or how long after that he'd kept on thudding her head against the shower floor. Wet with perspiration and gasping for each breath, he finally slowed to a stop and crawled off her.

Tom-tom. The beats gradually came farther apart and grew quieter.

She wasn't moving at all.

Tom-tom. He couldn't even lift his arms. Tom-tom. For a long time, McIver sat on the cool floor, propped between the commode and the open shower sliders. He stared at the bare legs just inches from his own. He'd stopped her. She wasn't screaming now. The room smelled of vomit and urine and sweat. He smelled of vomit and urine and sweat.

When he finally was calm enough to move, McIver crawled forward for a closer look. He didn't really think she was still breathing. He didn't know what he'd do if she had been. But she wasn't. That narrowed his choices.

"No one knows she's here," he told himself, bracing against the commode as he worked his way upright. He grabbed her ankles and dragged the rest of her into the cubicle. Then he rearranged a couple of towels that had shifted, completely covering her face again. He spread a clean one over them to cover the blood spots. He didn't want to see them.

He peeled off all his clothes and threw them in on top of her. He even made a weak attempt at mopping up the floor with a bath towel and piled it in there too. Then he closed the shower door. He wasn't in any condition to deal with it now.

Naked, he lumbered into the next bedroom and used that

shower to wash away the stench. He scrubbed his hands
with Ajax cleanser. He stood under the hot spray, coating
himself with the scented soap that Sandra always put out for
guests. "No one knows she's here." He showered a long
time, trying to convince himself that much was true. They'd
left the supermarket in separate cars. They'd left her apartment complex the same way. They'd come home late, too
late for anyone to be looking. He'd driven right into the
garage. He'd hit the button so the door closed right away.

She lived alone. She had the next night off. She wouldn't
be missed for a while.

McIver checked the time. It was nearly three. He set the
alarm for eight. He would sleep until it went off. Then he'd
call the office and tell them he'd be out all morning. He'd
have to clean up in there. Between the two of them, they'd
made a real mess. Tomorrow he'd figure out what he would
do with her.

"No one knows she's here." He kept repeating that part,
calming himself, knowing he was too strung out to think
things through right now. Before he did anything, he had to
lie down and sleep off the booze.

"A few aspirin. Might head off a hangover." He remembered what she'd said. Even now, she was bugging him.
Telling him what to do. He took four Tylenol instead.

Rikki and Juli Quinn spent most of Thursday afternoon
and all day Friday setting up the shoot. Using one of Swede's
suggestions for suppressing sound and eliminating tripods,
they'd used bags of sand to "nest" the cameras on shelves
and low tables. "Can you hear it now?" Rikki would ask
from time to time while Juli sprawled out on her bed, listening for the sound of a camera shutter beneath the cover
of one of Fuzzy Haight's tapes. Most of the time, the music
and the paddle fans overhead blocked the sound.

It didn't work for Rikki to take a turn listening. She'd
been concentrating so intently on setting each timer that it
seemed she'd developed an internal timer of her own. Some
heightened sense made her pick out the sound no matter
how carefully they adjusted the music to screen the me-
chanical whirring noises.

"I sure hope you aren't this tuned in when you do the
shoot," Juli said, genuinely concerned that the noise from
the cameras would distract her. "I don't think you really

hear them. I think because you know they're coming, you anticipate each click. I really don't think anyone else would catch them," Juli declared, without mentioning Stu's name at all.

Once Rikki made her mind up that Friday would be *the* night and she couldn't install and test the setup alone, she and Juli hadn't spoken much of the personal implications. Primarily they'd approached the setup from a purely technical aspect. They worked with six separate cameras. Each had an electronically triggered motor drive that was wired into a central control by the headboard. Each camera was loaded with the best quality color-slide film for extremely low light. Each had to be focused precisely, then equipped with special diffusion filters to create a romantic haze.

"I want soft-edged images," Rikki had insisted. "These women don't need anatomy lessons. They need something with a touch of fantasy. As a matter of fact, so do I," she'd added with a tense smile. She still wasn't sure how she would react to having some lights on in the room. But even pushing the film beyond its normal range, she had no choice between leaving on lights or shooting with a flash.

"We're lucky this bedroom is so big," Juli had commented when they were well into the installation. To test the lighting, they'd closed the push-out Island-style shutters and taped blackout paper to the windows. To conceal the cameras, they'd brought in extra plants and fabric panels from other parts of the house. They'd rearranged the furniture so it wouldn't seem crowded.

"I usually shift plants and art pieces around from time to time," Rikki had said, making a mental note to mention to Stu in advance that she was doing some minor redecorating. "I'll just shift a few things downstairs as well."

"Be sure to tack the corners of the rug down," Fuzzy Haight had cautioned her after he finished running several wires underneath one end. "We don't want anyone tripping." Like Juli, Fuzzy had to be told what the filming entailed so he could get the wiring and the music right. Once he understood the intimate content, he'd been completely professional, speaking only of "the subjects," and tactfully avoiding mentioning Rikki or Stu directly.

He'd been called in for his electronic expertise as well as his musicianship. He'd spent much of Thursday afternoon making phone calls, tracking down parts, and picking up components to install the equipment she would need. Besides figuring out the master switch for the timer system, he'd help them set up his sophisticated tape player and station several extra speakers around the room. The sound would come from all sides, closer in than the cameras, and act as a buffer. He'd even set up a second player farther out with an ongoing tape of "white noise" that sounded like a constant breeze.

He knew they were not recording his sound. Not yet. The music part of the final video would be added in later, in the production room down the hall. That finished work would only be eight minutes long, and it was clear Rikki couldn't get the shots she needed for the visual part in just eight minutes of actual shooting time. The best shots couldn't be rushed. So sustaining a certain atmosphere was crucial. Haight had worked up about two hours of similar mood music for the shoot so inside that cocoon of sound, "the subjects" would be insulated from extraneous noises.

"It will loop back into the actual video theme periodically." Fuzzy explained what he had done. "I retaped a number of pieces, wove in the theme music, and added some transitions so it would play without a break. I tried to keep it all real fluid so it wouldn't be intrusive." On some subconscious level, the music would enhance the continuity.

Friday, they tested and retested the system. Lights. Sound. Cameras. They'd even sprayed the air with Rikki's perfume to draw in another sense. They did several run-throughs with Juli and Fuzzy standing against the wall or sitting cross-legged on the floor in the environment they'd created, listening and looking, critically appraising the results.

Rikki had come into the bedroom, just as she would that night. She turned on the switch that started all the timers, then took her place, center stage. Alone. Later, she'd developed the test film from each camera, mostly showing her, reclining or sitting on the bed. Occasionally she would turn from side to side so the cameras could catch another angle.

"Looks good to me," Juli said, crouching over the light table in the production room, studying the quality of the numbered transparencies from each camera. "Real artsy effect," she murmured.

Rikki nodded. That was the look they were after. "I think we've done all we can," she agreed, peering through the loupe at the results. Technically, they had it right. "I guess we reload the cameras, tidy it all up, and call it quits." She glanced at her watch. It was almost dinner time. "Stu said he'd have the kids back in thirty minutes."

"Then we'd better get moving," Juli replied.

They had the schedule worked out well in advance. Stu had met the kids after school and had taken them out to the nursery so he and his brother could show them around his other business. They were going to stop in at a produce stand he knew and pick up a few pumpkins for Jack-o-lanterns for their party Sunday afternoon. Mostly he was trying to be helpful and give her a couple of hours extra to work.

Rikki had told him she and Juli would be setting up an involved photo project all day. Then Juli was driving the kids to the grandparents for a sleep-over. But Rikki and Stu had a real date scheduled for later. They were going out to a Chinese restaurant for dinner. Just the two of them. Then they were coming home together, to an empty house.

"Break a leg, or whatever it is one is supposed to say at a time like this," Juli said with a slight hesitation before the two women went downstairs.

"Thanks, I think," Rikki responded with a weak smile, trying not to let the nervousness show.

McIver waited until it was dark Thursday night to get rid of the bundle. It had taken him most of the day to move her and get the mess in the bathroom cleaned up. She'd pissed all over herself. And crapped. He'd gagged the moment he opened the door on the shower stall and the smell hit. He'd turned on the exhaust, backtracked, and shut the door. Before he tried again, he made a face mask from a tea towel and sprinkled it with cologne to filter the stench. He'd rounded up another fan and a can of Lysol spray. And he'd grabbed a bucket and some brushes and a mop. He'd step in, spray, work awhile, then come out gasping for air. Afterward, he rounded up all the rags and cleaning cloths with the clothes and towels he'd thrown in with her the night before and put them in heavy-duty garbage bags. He figured he could drop them in a dumpster somewhere closer in to town. Getting rid of the body was something else.

He brought in a tarpaulin and some plastic sheeting from the garage, both leftovers from the house renovation. He wrapped her up. He used clothesline to truss it tight. Then he'd dragged the bundle through the house. He'd left her, wrapped and tied like the garbage, in the garage beside the crates with Sandra's greenhouse while he scrubbed and bleached the bathroom tiles.

At first, the grout between them wouldn't come clean. That made him furious. He'd had that big shower with the jets on all sides custom designed. The tile was special ordered. He didn't want anything to spoil the look. And he sure as hell didn't want Adella fussing over the stains.

He ran through every combination of disinfectant and cleaner in the cupboard before he finally brought in the chlorine and muriatic acid from the pool. His hands were red and sore before he found Sandra's rubber gloves and put them on. Then he alternated sloshing the pool chemicals over the shower floor, holding his breath all the while to stop from breathing the fumes. He'd go outside and air out and let them sit. He'd come back, run the shower to flush it out, then try it all again. He didn't go into the office at all.

By midafternoon, he had it all under control. His eyes burned. His head throbbed. When he swallowed, he tasted acid. The skin around his fingernails was raw. He ached all over. He showered in the guest bathroom, retreated to his bedroom, and spent the remainder of the afternoon stretched out in the air conditioning, waiting for night to come.

The drop itself was relatively simple. No one could see the boat dock for the tall podocarpus hedges on either side out back. He used the wheelbarrow to get her to the boat. He loaded in several concrete blocks intended for the foundation of the greenhouse. He simply turned on the running lights and rode out into the Intracoastal like he'd often done at night. Only this time, he didn't swing south toward the Lundquist place. He kept going west, out through the channel that linked Sarasota Bay to the gulf, found a spot he knew was deep, cut the motor, wired it all together and rolled her off.

"Shark bait," he muttered, remembering complaints surfacing in the newspaper from time to time about fishermen and cruise boats dropping their refuse in that part of the channel on their way in. The practice was drawing sharks into waters they hadn't frequented before. If they didn't mind it wrapped and aged a bit, he'd just added a few more pounds to their latest buffet.

He had his first drink of the day when he got in. He cracked open a new bottle, poured it out, and took a sip. It went down smooth. Then he caught the acid aftertaste. "Fuck it." He took another swallow and shrugged, pleased at how easy it had been. He just had to pitch the lighter bags, show up at Conroy's and pretend to be surprised Friday night when the blonde bartender didn't show. No problem. He'd put in a day's work, drop in at the bar for happy hour, eat some oysters, and watch the sunset, just like he'd done before.

He poured another scotch. Then he strolled over to the refrigerator, interested in food for the first time all day. He didn't feel like cooking. He eyed the cheesecake they'd bought and hadn't got around to eating. Then he remembered there was ice cream in the freezer section up above.

"Here's to you." He stood by the back sliders, holding the container, raising a spoon of Cherry Garcia toward the boat dock and then to the Bayou and points west. He still didn't know her name. He could have found out if he'd wanted to. He'd felt her wallet jammed in her carrying bag with her keys. But he'd left it there and shoved it all in one of the trash bags in the garage. It was less personal if he didn't know.

"Bon voyage." He took a second spoonful, savoring the way it cooled his throat. He dug right into the center and lifted out a chocolate hunk. This is all he'd wanted. This was what he'd been after when she'd come butting in at the supermarket the night before. Cherry Garcia. The last pint left. He took another spoonful, and angled the container toward the light so he could find the lumps. He hadn't liked the idea of having to share it, anyway.

Rikki wrapped a sheet around herself and stepped out on the balcony beyond the open doorway of her bedroom, letting the cool fresh air sweep around her. If she and Janelle Givrey and Michelle Sands had worked out a script for the evening, it couldn't have been more perfect. She and Stu had come back from dinner, undressed together in the house, wrapped in big towels, and taken a swim, without the air cast. Without anything at all. They had gasped at the chill in the water, laughing and kissing and holding each other, trying to get warm.

"Be careful, I've moved a few pieces of furniture," she

warned him after they'd bundled up in towels again and hurried inside. They locked up below and headed through the house in total darkness. "And don't bother getting out of bed in the morning to feed the boys. I'll do that." Before he got a good look at her bedroom by the light of day, she wanted to make sure a few things were out of there.

All Fuzzy Haight's electronic wizardry had produced flawless results. The remote button worked. On cue, the music played, the white noise whispered, and the cameras functioned at whatever intervals she'd designated. Best of all, she hadn't heard anything beyond the first hushed clicks. After that she concentrated on the feel of skin and hair against her fingertips, the way their cool skin warmed on contact with each other, and the delicious sweetness of each kiss. Gradually, that excluded everything else.

"I wish this for you." She held in her thoughts those nameless women who would watch the two of them one day. "I wish you courage, and happiness, and love." She could almost feel their presence in each touch. "This is yours . . ." She exulted in the gentleness and tension as she and Stu caressed and whispered and sighed. They were drawn along by the music, slowly, sensuously escalating with its rhythm and melody, then becoming more subdued, more languid as a familar strain slipped through again.

Leaving the low lights on only made the contact more intimate, more exquisite. It underscored an honesty and acceptance, a reverence for each other's physical presence as it was, without reservation. They had made love before in the pale light of dawn. But this interior glow introduced a suggestion of boldness, an edge of playfulness, and a feeling of seclusion and abandon. It made the lovemaking clearly an occasion in itself, not a passing interlude in the dark that preceded sleep. Making love in the light was an affirmation that between lovers all touches, all kisses, all embraces were powerful and elegant and positive. Nothing was hidden. Or needed to be. This was the celebration she had hoped it would be.

"As you are . . ." Rikki almost wept as she saw in Stu's eyes the unqualified love and felt the delicious tenderness in his touch. "As you are . . ." He had been so patient all week, so kind, so careful with this precious bond between them. Since the killing of Thayer Kern's labs, Stu had been there, like a gentle bear, to help her and the children recover. She could feel her love flowing back to him, without any desire to hold back, without the shyness or awkwardness she'd anticipated.

Afterward, they had looked at each other, teary eyed and breathless, both moved beyond words by the eloquence of their bodies and the frankness of their passion.

"I love you," Stu had whispered between soft kisses. "I never imagined anything could ever be like this. I don't mean the sex part," he murmured. "It's the whole connection. I could feel you become part of me. Like you'd chosen to live inside me." He patted his chest, grasping for words enough to express the complexity of emotions he felt. "Unbelievable." He simply held her close, whispering over and over that he loved her.

Standing on the balcony alone afterwards, Rikki knew how fortunate she was. Out there in the night, there were countless other women, some frightened, some bitter, some disillusioned, but all of them were aching to be loved and to love someone.

Someone worthy.

So much of it came down to chance. So much depended on a certain kind courage. It was risky to explore the possibilities, to drop the defenses and make oneself vulnerable. One had to persevere to make a love grow strong and true. And even then, it could work out all wrong.

"But when it's right," she mused, moved to tears herself by the quiet strength, the solid decency of the man inside, asleep in her bed, "it is worth the waiting." Once again she turned toward the distant lights on the mainland across the waterway. "If I had one wish," she let her words be carried by the wind. "I would wish you love."

Chapter 11

"We're going to give him another jolt tomorrow," Detective Warnock announced at the Task Force meeting Saturday afternoon. "One of Olivia Mello's artworks has been purchased for the Women's Center. Kind of an embryonic thing. Victor Chambers and some friends bought it and said they'd donate it. I suggested they do it now. The newspaper will run a piece on it tomorrow. Next Thursday there's going to be a ceremony for the installation. The media will cover that story as well."

"Sounds like a good deal all the way around." Stu remembered seeing Olivia's smooth ovoid sculpture at Chambers's garden party. He thought it resembled a partially hatched, stylized egg. Warnock's choice of "embryonic" was a much classier description.

"Won't someone have to keep an eye on the artwork? Won't this give the guy an easy target?" an officer from Bradenton asked.

Warnock peered at him. "Precisely. But we'll have that covered," he assured them all. "First of all, it's steel. Basically indestructible, unless the guy has a tank to drive over it. Secondly, the electronics shop across the street from the Center has volunteered a video unit to monitor it. Their staff will keep tabs on it during work hours. At night, they'll tape whatever goes on. Besides, several volunteers at the Center have offered to take shifts at night sitting in the shop, watching the screen. At least for a week or so. They'll call 911 if anything looks peculiar. And we'll have patrol cars cruising by anyway." He was bobbing his head up and down, clearly satisfied with the precautions they would have available. "Frankly, I wish the guy would come after this thing. It doesn't burn and it doesn't bleed. And it's wide-ass out in the open."

"So it might piss him off if he reads about it," one fellow

noted, well aware that the press coverage of the sculpture donation wasn't aimed at the general reader. "If he's pissed, he may get reckless."

"Exactly." Warnock smoothed his moustache and tugged at his tie. "We want to keep nudging him."

"I'd like to do more than that," one of the fellows muttered.

"You'd have to stand in line," Warnock countered. "There's a lot of folks who would like a round with this guy, beginning with me. Personally, I'd be glad to let one of this Mello woman's buddies go first. She has some very large, very motivated biker friends. But enough wishful thinking," he added with a quick head shake, focusing back on business. "It's been a week since the Kern fire. Tomorrow they run the article about the sculpture. Four days till they put the thing in place. Two days after that is Halloween. No way of knowing when he'll strike. Lots of possibilities. We just have to hang in there. If we're lucky, someone might see something or remember something that will help, before he hurts anyone else."

"I'm betting he tries it Halloween night." The Bradenton officer sounded eager.

"Anytime he chooses. We're ready," Warnock stated. His youngish face showed signs of weariness from the long hours he'd been putting in. "The sooner the better."

After the meeting ended, Stu kept an appointment at the doctor's office to have the arm and shoulder checked. "I'll be going in to the office half-days this week," he told the white-haired doctor, the department's orthopedic specialist. "Next week, I'd like to get back to my regular schedule. In uniform. How about it? Can we ditch this thing?" He tapped the air cast.

"You can have it off the end of this coming week," Dr. Marr had said, putting it back on after the examination. "That's pushing a bit, but everything looks real good. Just don't plan on doing any lifting for a while," he cautioned Stu. "It takes a couple of months to get the strength back." Then he sent him on into the medical center for an hour of physical therapy he'd scheduled.

When he came back late Saturday afternoon, Rikki was unloading a large box marked "B&B Photo-Video" from her minivan. He pulled in under Ash's house. By the time he walked across to help her, she already had it to the front door. "New equipment?" Stu asked her. "You need a hand?"

"Just with the door. I've been waiting for this. It's my new processor. Couldn't find one here, but they called from Tampa and I drove up to get it." She'd said she was heading straight into the darkroom when he left earlier. Apparently her plans had changed.

"So what does it do?"

"It helps edit transparencies and transfers them to video." She carried the box singlehandedly while he held the door wide enough to let her navigate through the opening. "This goes upstairs. How's the arm?" she asked as she continued on toward the stairway.

"Good. The cast comes off in a week." He felt helpless, following behind while she hauled the sizeable box by herself.

"Olivia called." Rikki stopped at the landing and rested a moment, balancing one side of the box on the railing. "She said she wanted me to go to a dedication at the Women's Center next Thursday. One of her sculptures is going there. Do you want to come along?"

"She's going to be there? In public?" There was a chance the Trasher might hit during the ceremony. Stu was sure Warnock would be using the decoy. He knew better than to put a civilian in jeopardy. Now he'd have to check that part.

"Of course she'll be there. It's her work. She seemed pretty excited about the whole thing. She asked me to take some pictures." Now Rikki was concerned, wondering if she'd misunderstood Olivia's hurried announcement or if she'd blurted out a confidence she should have kept to herself. Olivia's call had ended abruptly, but she said she'd call back. Despite the decoy system, Rikki had assumed that for an important presentation, Olivia would be there herself, albeit suitably protected.

"She may be thinking it will be all over by then," Stu offered. "If it's not, it may be dangerous. Either way, I'll go. I don't want you to miss it. And I sure don't want you there alone."

"I guess that means I'd better not take the kids."

"Better not," Stu agreed.

In silence, Rikki got a grip on the box again and finished the climb to the second floor.

"So tell me, how does this thing work?" Stu asked, trying to shift the subject to less sensitive ground.

"It connects into the TV and the VCR, so I can see each picture just as it will appear on a final tape." She had the carton on the floor between them. She slit the packing tape and started sliding out the styrofoam inner liner that encapsulated the equipment. "I can preview slides or transparencies of any size, crop, zoom, balance the color, adjust the intensity, you name it. Then I zap it. I just hit a button and the corrected image is stored on videotape. Like a library. The tape saves it, I work on the next shot. Whenever I choose, I can pull up the adjusted images for a final edit."

"So this helps make a good picture better?" he thought he had the point.

"This thing can make even a poor-quality picture come out beautifully on tape. It's more technical manipulation than it is art," she conceded. "The processor gives you a second chance to modify what you get on film."

"But it doesn't actually alter the original picture?"

"Right. The original stays the same. What's recorded is the new, improved version. Sort of an eerie concept." She set the desktop-sized processor on a worktable and pried off the white foam housing. Stu watched while she unwrapped the heavy clear plastic cover. "I'll be able to take a single transparency, use the processor to alter the composition or play with the color, and get something considerably different each time. Still, it's only on tape," she stressed. "It's like freeze-framing a fantasy."

"So you could go back through all the transparencies in your library and rework them?"

"That's right."

"We're talking endless possibilities here." He started looking around the production area noticing the drawers of slides already out on work table.

"Exactly. But first of all, I'm going to teach Juli how to use this thing and simply document everything here, just as it is. A two-hour tape can hold fifteen hundred slides at five-second intervals. We could get all of this duplicated and put copies in storage, in case there's ever a disaster." She said it all so smoothly, Stu would have missed the edge of uneasiness if he hadn't been watching her. He caught the way her eyes narrowed and grew suddenly grave.

"You mean a disaster like a hurricane?"

"That. Or a fire." The matter-of-fact tone in her voice made it clear that what had happened to Thayer Kern's studio the week before had prompted more than sorrow over the loss of the two labs. The devastation had made her question the ongoing security of her collection.

"These photos are irreplaceable," she noted. "Some of the flowers and plants we found in the wild have become extinct in the years since the slides were taken. Logging and cattle ranching have destroyed many native habitats." She'd stopped the setup procedure and was scanning the cupboards lined with drawers of her slides and her father's as well. "Some of the plants are rare specimens that have survived only in private collections and a few botanical gardens around the world. Some aren't so irreplaceable. But they represent years of work. I can protect them from dust and humidity and heat. But I can't protect them from a fire. So I'll create a backup, a family archive, somewhere besides here."

"In a way I'm sorry that you have to think that way," Stu said quietly.

"So am I," Rikki acknowledged. "But it needs to be done. It's always needed to be done. Now I have the equipment to do it, and the motivation. There is a positive side to all this," she stated, with the sense of conviction that Stu had come to recognize as an essential part of her character. She'd obviously come to terms with a certain vulnerability that affected her work as well as her home and family.

"So does this mean I won't see you much for the next few days or few weeks?" Stu asked good-naturedly.

"This could take a week," Rikki estimated. She was going to have a very tight schedule to complete what she needed to get done by then. Besides helping Juli put the files on video, she planned to use the new processor herself to work on the still-undeveloped transparencies from the night before. She wanted that particular tape finished to show to Stu before he moved back to town. Seeing it within the now-familiar boundaries of the quiet peninsula would somehow keep it in perspective. She hoped.

She had six days. Harrison Ash had faxed confirmation that he'd be back the next Sunday, the first of November. Stu was planning to have the place cleaned and be out on Halloween Eve. But there were other events in the meantime that would take her time and attention. One afternoon and early evening was for the children's Halloween party. One afternoon was Olivia Mello's sculpture dedication. And Saturday night was the time for trick-or-treating.

"Will you be working any evenings?" Stu asked, trying to camouflage his growing uneasiness by trying to sound casual. "I'd like to take you out to dinner. I'll only be back at work half-days, so I can juggle my schedule."

"We could eat out. But I really liked the time you brought home Mexican food."

"We could do that too," he said, knowing he sounded like he was trying to book up every free minute she had. "I'd just like to have some evening to spend out together, somewhere nice, if that's okay with you." Even that sounded stiff, he felt. The easy access he had taken for granted was slipping away.

Throughout the previous week while she'd been putting in a lot of hours with Juli and Fuzzy Haight on one project or another, he'd been easing back into his own office to do some work. All unofficial. Despite his secretary's prodding, he hadn't shaved the beard or had a haircut. Somehow those were symbols of a world he wasn't quite ready to relinquish. But he had managed a couple of productive sessions with his deputy and one of the inspectors he'd trained earlier in the year. And he had gone over every bit of evidence gathered from the fire at Kern's. That professional contact had felt good.

But he was still coming home to Ash's house when he was finished. He only had to cross a strip of lawn to spend an afternoon or evening with her. Now he felt both their schedules filling up with other responsibilities. Part of him resisted giving up those quiet times together. And time was running out before he moved back to the mainland.

"I'll try to knock off when the kids come home. If you're home then, come over. We'll talk or swim or water plants. We don't have to make any of these next few days special occasions," she added, wanting him to know she was struggling with the same sense of apprehension as he was.

"Some things are going to be different," she acknowledged. "But the essentials won't change. I love you, Sullivan. There isn't an end to that. So let's just take this transition business day by day, and we'll do dinner together like we usually do. We'll find time for some other things too," she added, slipping her arms around him and giving his buns a friendly squeeze.

"I hope so." He let out a slow breath as he wrapped his arms around her. Holding her made a lot of things seem better.

The Trasher still hadn't struck again by the morning of the sculpture dedication. "I think we need to discuss this event today." Stu came over to talk to Rikki before he left for work. He'd just got off the phone with Warnock after getting an update on the way things would be run. His version and Rikki's didn't match.

"I guess there's no way to keep her from noticing it's a stand-in," Warnock had conceded. "So tell her. She may not even want to show up when she hears it won't actually be Mello." But Stu had a feeling Rikki would want to be there to show her support for Olivia's work regardless whether the artist herself was in attendance.

"Is something wrong?" Rikki had been outside, hosing down the plants in the lanai and finishing her coffee while she waited for Juli Quinn to arrive.

Stu came around the corner near the slathouse, looking semiofficial in his white shirt and fire-department windbreaker.

"Warnock said Olivia won't be there today. It's too dangerous. He's having someone who looks like her there instead."

"I see." Rikki kept watering.

He watched her, waiting for some additional reaction. There was none. "So do you want to change the plans? Do you still want to go?" As it stood, they'd agreed that she'd come to his office building and pick him up in her van. He'd go with her to the installation ceremony, then they'd stop for a late lunch. She could drop him back at the office afterward.

"I still want to go."

"I thought you would. So I'll see you about two?"

"Right. Juli will be here all day. She said she'd take care of the kids until I get back."

"Great."

"See you then." Rikki aimed the hose the other way and came over to give him a quick kiss. "At two."

Stu walked away feeling more at ease than he had in a

while. She'd taken his announcement about Olivia in stride. She hadn't registered any disappointment at all. As he trudged along, he began to think about that part. By the time he reached his car, the uneasiness was back. She hadn't registered surprise either.

"What does she know that I don't know?" he wondered, speculating whether or not he should go back and ask her straight out. As if by tacit agreement, the two of them had tapdanced around any mention of Olivia for days. "Dammit," he muttered, putting it all together. "She's going to be there." He just knew that was why Rikki was so unperturbed. Somehow or other, her friend had slipped her the inside story. Olivia Mello wasn't planning to miss the event at all.

Stu considered calling Warnock. He'd mentioned to him earlier that he thought Olivia and Rikki had some signals crossed. Perhaps then, they had. Warnock had told him that he'd get it all ironed out. At the time, Stu had felt like a kid telling tales. He hated getting caught in the middle. But from Rikki's nonreaction today, he guessed that whatever Warnock had ironed out was one sided. The women had their story straight. The ones with crossed signals now were Warnock and his men.

"Dammit." Stu knew he could be totally off base. After all she'd been through, Rikki could just have steeled herself for whatever happened next. Keeping Olivia away may have simply made sense to her. He didn't want to stir everyone up just because she didn't get upset. He'd let it sit. He could say something when he and Rikki got there. Besides, Warnock had plainclothesmen coming to the installation. There would be uniformed officers around. Even if Olivia Mello did show, she could be whisked away.

"Sure," he muttered, failing to convince himself. He couldn't imagine anyone whisking Olivia any place she didn't want to go. "Joe . . ." He relented and called Warnock from the car on the cellular. "Just a feeling I have . . ." He went on to tell him what he feared might happen.

"Not a chance," Warnock countered. "The Mello woman, some of our personnel, and her buddy, Terminator Three, will be watching it all on video from the shop across the street. If trouble breaks out, she's covered."

"Okay. I just didn't want two of her there. Not with the press coverage."

"Thanks for the call anyway," Warnock added. "I know this must make you feel like some kind of double agent," he sympathized.

"Something like that," Stu grumbled.

"We're on top of this," Warnock insisted. "He'll get edgy. He'll make a mistake. This will be over soon."

"I hope so." Stu put the car phone back in place. He shook his head, still worried that Warnock was underestimating the little red-haired artist and her friends.

Victor Chambers and his cosponsors had a festive blue-and-white-striped tent set up on the Center green. Volunteers were serving lemonade and pretty pastries for the guests and staff members assembling outside in the bright sunshine. A solid blue cover blanketed the sculpture itself so it could be unveiled at some point in the proceedings. The ceremony began precisely at two-thirty with Darlene Jacquemin, the executive director of the Women's Center, making the introductions.

"Pretty convincing double," Stu said, leaning close enough to whisper in Rikki's ear. The Mello lookalike was standing next to Jacquemin, also petite, also smiling. This one even had the same blood red bow-lips that made Olivia Mello look deceptively innocent.

"I guess so." Rikki responded with that same calmness that had made him suspicious in the first place. He noticed that she'd brought one of her cameras, but she hadn't taken any pictures.

Jacquemin began explaining that in the next few weeks, a patio and landscaping and several benches would be installed, not immediately surrounding the sculpture, but farther back so the public could enjoy sitting there and contemplating the piece of art. "We hope anyone wishing to pass some time out front can rest in pleasant surroundings," she added in good-humored reference to occasional demonstrations protesting their abortion services.

Jacquemin noted that the parklike setting would contribute to the overall beautification and humanization of the predominately business area. She went on to thank Chambers and three other contributors for their generosity and showed the audience a metal plaque that would be set into the patio, bearing the name of the sculpture, the artist, each of the benefactors, and the date.

Stu kept watching Rikki throughout the brief talk, following her gaze. She was scanning the crowd of perhaps two hundred, a number of whom Stu recognized as police officers. Two Bay-area television stations had their remote crews on hand. Several attendees were videotaping. One of them, filming the audience, he knew was a cop.

Chambers and the Mello stand-in did the honors, each pulling a cord that unveiled the sculpture. Rikki took several photos of that. There was applause. While the principals posed for pictures, Jacquemin invited everyone to enjoy the refreshments. Officially, it was over.

"So. Ready to head back?" Stu asked. He was rushing her a bit, but he hoped she'd seen enough. Now there were too many people milling around. One of them could be the Trasher. He just wanted her safely out of there.

"Not quite yet." Rikki hesitated. "I'd like to say hello to Victor and Darlene."

"You know her?"

"Of course. We went to school together. You should meet her. Come on." She took the lead and started winding her way toward the sculpture where Jacquemin and the others were still talking with the press.

"I should have guessed this wasn't going to be easy." Stu was nodding and muttering, working through the crowd after her.

Someone grabbed his ass. Firmly.

"Nice ass, Sullivan." She spoke before he did. The voice was familiar. He turned and came face-to-flowers with a short woman in shades, jet black hair in a Prince Valient haircut, and a picture hat with hot pink chrysanthemums around the brim.

"Olivia?"

"Damn straight. You should'da been a cop," she answered.

"Does Warnock know where you are?" He kept his voice low. The dress she was wearing was so frilly and feminine, he almost choked.

"Slack off. You're sounding like one of them. And smile." The upturned lips were fuschia, like the flowers on the hat. "Our detective friend thinks I'm across the street." She tilted the flowered hat toward the electronics shop.

"You just walked out?"

"Honey, I ambled," she drawled. "My friend Bobby is covering for me. And I did dress for the occasion. I also used the loading dock exit," she added with a quick grin. "The real me is in here." She patted a huge purselike bag she was a carrying. "Along with a canister of mace."

"Olivia?" Rikki had retraced her steps and come back looking for Stu.

"How ya' been, kiddo?" Olivia reached out and clasped Rikki's hand.

"Better now. I was wondering where you'd be."

"Here is not a good place," Stu spoke up.

"True. Could we cut out of here and get a Greek salad? Or are you two busy? I've been living in a hotel, having a lot of food delivered. If I see another burger or box of chicken, I'll puke. But I'd kill for a big salad. With dark olives, lots of feta cheese. And hot peppers."

"Don't you think we should tell Warnock you're all right?" Stu asked, wondering at what point someone would report her missing.

"Jus' you stay calm, honey," she cooed. "I'll tell him. I wouldn't want the little fella' to worry. Wait here." They watched her saunter off toward the refreshment tent where Warnock had stationed himself in the shade, inconspicuously studying all the passersby. The other Olivia was sticking close to Victor Chambers and some fellow from the task force.

The big hat screened their view of Warnock's reaction. Olivia stayed only a moment, then came back smiling. "He was not happy at all," she reported on her return. "I assured him I would be back at the hotel by four."

"But he said you could go?" Rikki asked.

"Actually he mentioned something about putting me in handcuffs," she commented quite casually. "But I told him I wasn't into kinky stuff. We chatted, and he decided it was wiser to let us drift away quietly than to make a scene. Smart move."

Stu had to agree. He wasn't sure he wanted to know what the "chat" between Mello and Warnock had entailed. He was convinced that Olivia's side of it was straight to the point. But now he kept glancing at the crowd apprehensively, looking for anything or anyone that could mean trouble.

"Let's go now." He ushered the two women toward the parking lot, figuring it would make Warnock's job less complicated and his own jaw muscles less tense if they were well away from the area, out of harm's way.

"So . . . how's the new equipment working out?" Olivia asked, stretching out her legs and kicking off her shoes as Rikki drove off. She started yanking garments from her bag. Stu kept glancing back, scanning the exits, checking if any car came out behind them. None did.

"The processor? It's great." Rikki answered. "Juli is home using it now. We're making a backup copy of every slide in the library." Stu adjusted the right hand outside mirror so he could watch the traffic behind them.

"Good idea. And how about the kids' party? How'd it go?" Olivia asked. "I considered making a break and coming. I make a damn good ghoul. But I figured today was pretty important, and I couldn't pull a slip on these guys twice. But the party was what gave me this Scarlett O'Hara idea."

Stu kept his eyes frontward while Olivia ditched the hat and peeled off the dress and pulled on more casual attire. Rikki kept talking, telling Olivia the blow-by-blow of the Halloween gathering the previous Sunday afternoon. Juli and Mike Maurer and Eddie Sordo and Stu's Mom had helped with all the food and games.

"Okay, I'm decent, Sherlock. Did anyone follow us?" Olivia tapped the back of Stu's seat.

"Doesn't look like it," Stu shrugged.

"Great." She pitched the hairpiece into the back of the van with the other things, raked her fingers though her red hair, and let out a sigh. "Okay, now let's get serious. Let's eat."

Dave McIver didn't go to the ceremony for Mello and her sculpture at the Women's Center. He wasn't about to play their stupid game. They'd have cops all over, waiting for someone to make a move either there or at her studio. Neither one really interested him. He wanted to string it out, keep them all wired and anxious, have them spinning their wheels, wondering what came next. He'd catch it later on TV. While they were covering her ass, he'd be covering his. And when her little party was over, he'd have one of his own.

He went to work all day. He stopped in a Conroy's after work and had a couple of drinks. He wanted to show up there, like he had twice that week already, and make the point that nothing about his routine had changed.

They had a new bartender, a guy, but with him, everything was business as usual. Scuttlebutt in the bar was that the cops had found the blonde's car empty, abandoned. McIver knew that must have been in the parking lot on Tamiami Trail where they'd left it. They'd apparently checked her place, then Conroy's. No one in either place knew where she was. The bar had flyers printed up with her picture saying she'd disappeared, asking for information. At least they were making an effort to help. The police weren't doing anything, as far as he could tell.

In the televised coverage of the Women's Center event on the evening news, they didn't mention having cops there for security, but McIver spotted a couple of guys he knew who were on the force. The place must have been crawling with them. With all the publicity the Trasher series had generated, there was no way the cops would risk letting anything go wrong. They didn't want to come out looking like fools in the media. But he saw that the Lundquist broad was there. She was tall enough to stand out in the quick pan of the audience. And it amused him that she felt safe enough to come out in public to give the other bitch a boost.

"Cunts. They're all cunts," he'd muttered while he sat in front of the TV, loading his gear in the backpack and sipping his scotch. Soon there would be one cunt less. He waited until the weather came on. Cold front was moving in. Cloudy. Twenty percent chance of rain. Fifty percent tomorrow. Good. Overcast. That meant it would be real dark that night.

"Cooler for the weekend." That part was intended to warn parents to bundle up their kids. Saturday night they'd be out trick-or-treating. McIver didn't care. His trick-or-treat visit would be all over by then.

He loaded the gun. It was one he'd bought several years ago when they were living in the old neighborhood and there was a prowler scare. Paid cash. No papers. No record. Now he was the one on the prowl. And he was going to do this one cool and easy. No chance for error at all. This wasn't going to turn into a slugging match like the battle with the bartender.

With the gun, they would all do what they were told. It would be calm, slow, and precise. An execution. He'd be totally in control. He'd thought it all through step by step. He'd round them up, one by one, whoever was in the house. Lundquist first. Gag her and tape her to the bed. Then he'd find the kids and tape their mouths and wrists and ankles. Tie them down with sheets.

When he was through with her, he'd soak the place with gasoline and torch it. But he planned to shoot the kids first. He couldn't stand the thought of letting the fire get them. Not like it got the labs. He'd make it mercifully fast for the children. But for her, he'd drag it out as long as possible. He'd fuck her. Then he'd blow her brains out so there would be no chance in hell that if somehow someone put the fire out, she'd survive.

The unknown factor now would be the boyfriend. McIver wasn't sure how tight the two of them were. He might be sleeping over. But if he were there, McIver would have the gun to keep them both in line.

He'd even thought his way through that part to minimize any risk to him. It was like the old parable of the fox, the grain, and the chicken. He'd make her tape the boyfriend's feet first. Then he'd get the guy to tape hers, to hobble her. Then she'd tape the boyfriend's hands. She could wrap a length of tape around one of her own wrists. All McIver would have to do was finish wrapping it. After he'd gone through the rest of the house, he'd come back. He'd shoot the boyfriend, with her watching. Make her squirm. Then he'd take care of her.

On his way out, he'd simply light a match, and they would all disappear.

Throughout the week, he'd been able to watch her place with some regularity, right in broad daylight. McIver and his people had been showing condos at a high rise in Siesta Cove, a little less than a mile along the Intercoastal. He'd driven over in his powerboat and docked it there every day so he could take prospective buyers out to show them the impressive water view. It was a very effective sales technique.

Mornings, nothing around there moved. The neighbor's red 'Vette and the Simons woman's station wagon would be gone by the time McIver and any clients rode past. He usually couldn't see Lundquist's van at all. Often the little Escort that he'd noticed there before was parked in front most of the day.

In the late afternoon, there was more action. The kids would be home from school. Sometimes they were out on the dock. They'd wave. Wednesday some guy in a truck came and worked on the yard. The boyfriend with the cast helped water plants.

Another day she was out with her sailboard. He slowed down and she cut across his wake. The boyfriend came out and shook some kind of gourd thing on the back deck. Some birds squawked and flocked toward him. He and the kids let the things eat right out of their hands. Parrots. Wild ones. McIver's passengers loved it. He played along.

But he hated the whole thing. There they were, like something out of a magazine. All together. Having a lovely time. And he was working his ass off, going home every night to an empty house, and worrying that some judge would tell him he had to move out. He wanted to kill them all.

McIver used the remote to turn off the TV. He slid the gun back into its leather case and snapped it closed. He put it in his backpack on top of the three rolls of silver duct tape, some lengths of nylon cord he'd cut and wound into neat bundles, and the lighter. He already had a full can of gas stowed in the storage area at the condo site. He was ready. Friday night, regardless how many of them were there at Lundquist's house, they would all eventually be inside in the dark. And so would he.

Stu was upstairs sweeping some potting soil off the back of Harrison Ash's deck when he heard Rikki calling him from ground level. He'd brought a flat of cascading petunias and three large hanging baskets from the nursery and had filled and set them out for Ash to enjoy on his return. "Come on up. I'm just cleaning up the deck before the rain starts up again." The sky was gray and overcast and periodic showers had punctuated the afternoon. From the grumbling far to the north, a major storm front was still working its way down the coast.

"These are going to be beautiful," Rikki said, coming out to look at his handiwork. "Harrison will be thrilled. I noticed the basket out front too. Quite a homecoming gift."

"I hope he thinks so." Stu finished whisking the last traces of soil and started gathering up the tools he'd used. He'd already had a cleaning woman come in and put a thorough polish on the house. He'd packed and moved most of his personal things downstairs. He'd even restocked the refrigerator so the essentials would be there.

"I figured since I enjoyed his place so much, I'd add a little something to show my appreciation. These will flower all winter and they'll smell great. I bought him a hose extension with a cutoff valve so he wouldn't have to stretch to water them." He pointed to a goose-necked piece of aluminum pipe with a spray head that slipped into a storage clip he'd mounted to the wall. "I put one downstairs too so he won't have to run it back and forth."

"He's not much for gardening, but he'll love this. Nice idea, Sullivan."

Stu gave a nod toward the videotape she was carrying. "So, does this mean you've finished what you've been doing all week?"

"It sure does."

"These are all the library slides? On one tape?"

"No. Those are done too," she replied. "There were almost nine thousand slides. They took up six tapes. I sent copies of them to my dad and put a duplicate set in my safety deposit box. This is the other project," she said, showing only the slightest apprehension.

"Does this mean you're already to celebrate?" He glanced at his watch. It was almost seven, and he hadn't eaten since lunch. He'd been waiting to hear from her. "We could go out. Or do you just want to knock back, stay in, and take it easy this evening?" he asked.

She'd already said she wanted him to leave the night open to spend with her. It was his last night housesitting, and the kids were out to the condo with Ivey and Swede. He'd been hoping that meant they would have an entire night together like they'd had the week before. Just the two of them.

"I haven't had dinner yet." She sounded tired. "I have a couple of steaks marinating. I figured we might do them later. But I'd really like you to take a look at this." She held the tape out to him.

"You mean now?" He wiped his hands on the sides of his shorts and took it. "I was thinking of showering off and getting dressed. The steaks sound great. I'm starving. Are you sure you want me to watch this whole thing first?"

"I'm sure. It's shorter than it looks. It's just eight minutes." She said it with a quiet urgency he found disconcerting. "I brought you a six-pack of cold sodas and some cheese nachos. They should hold you until later."

"There will be a later?" he stressed, not quite joking.

"I hope so."

He didn't like the peculiar formality in her expression. "That sounds a bit ominous."

"This is important. It's not ominous. I want you to see this. Then I want to know what you think about it."

"If you insist."

"Making this one was not an easy decision. Just keep in mind that sometimes I have ethical dilemmas too," she said softly. "And in his case, I had to do what I did, the way I did it, to get what had to be there. I think the results are valuable. What happens after this is up to you." She let out a breath, as if she'd thought out her comments beforehand and had said only what she felt was essential. "Don't rush. Just let it sink in. Let it settle. I'm going home now. Whenever you feel like coming over, I'll be there."

She left him standing, bewildered, staring at his unmarked tape. The steak dinner and an evening alone with her now were prefaced by a "whenever."

He wanted to run in and slam the tape in the VCR immediately and see it thorough. But something about the way she said it was "important" and the part about ethical dilemmas made him real nervous. Too nervous to rush into it. He decided to go in and take that shower. Long. Hot. Partly because he wanted to clean up after his gardening endeavors. But mostly just to slow down the acceleration he felt all over. Like a panic reaction.

He knew the kinds of tapes she'd done before. He remembered how Janelle Givrey had come to talk to her about something stronger, more explicit. From what he could catch of that conversation, he assumed Rikki had declined. Then Givrey had come back with two other women. He was guessing now this was what they'd talked her into doing, and wondering why it was so "important" what he thought.

She'd never asked him to critique her work before. She had an innate standard of excellence that was indisputable, without anyone's input but her own. But if all she needed was a simple outside opinion, she wouldn't have brought it to her and ended that way, with the comment that what happened next depended on him.

"Just get all the crap out of your head," he warned himself, remembering what Rikki had told him. She'd said he should view art without a lot of preconceptions. "Let the piece speak for itself," she'd suggested before they went to see the art her friends had done. But he wasn't at a gallery now, or in Victor Chambers's garden. He was home. Almost. Alone. And this artwork wasn't something by a friend.

"Relax," he coached himself, hurrying through the shower despite himself. He wasn't even hungry now. He just slipped the cassette into the VCR and pulled up the ottoman. "Okay. I'm ready." He aimed the remote at the player and pushed "power."

By the time it had played through completely, Stu felt that eight-minute tape had run at least an hour. Like someone anesthetized, he had to make a determined effort to stop staring at the screen long after it went gray. He hit the power button again to shut it off. Then he still stared.

He couldn't believe it. She'd taken pictures. Of him. With her. Touching. Kissing. Making love.

He recognized the music. At the time, when they were alone, he loved it. And the lights. It had all been more erotic, more exciting than anything he'd experienced. He'd sat, unmoving, stunned that she had set him up like that.

As private as he thought she was, he'd never have believed she'd bare it all on film. This was the same woman who'd told Givrey she couldn't even bring herself to be on the other side of the camera. But what was worse was that she'd put his private parts in view as well.

"Keep in mind I have ethical dilemmas too." He remembered her words.

"Dilemma, my ass," he muttered, stalking off to the refrigerator for one of those cold sodas she'd said she'd brought him. They were even diet. Caffeine free.

Beneath the anger and the hot flush of betrayal, he had to admit, it was powerful stuff. He stood, downing the drink in several long pulls. Then he opened the second soda and went back to rewind and watch it all again.

This time, now that the initial shock was over, he tried to be more analytical. There was nothing crude about this piece of work. It was nothing like some of the things he'd seen in college or even at the station. Late-night TV was more graphic.

There was a gentleness to this one. There was a sense of action, although nothing moved. The frames just changed.

Flowers faded in, then slowly faded out, staying only a few second before they blended with limbs and torsos and disappeared completely, leaving the lovers there instead. Hair and arms then faded into leaves and petals and another flower emerged. Then the flow continued, with one image supplanting another, slowly, with an enchanting interplay of line and color and mood.

The faces here were not fine focused and gaping into the camera or at each other like he'd seen in other films. These were all misty and soft edged and subdued. Mostly it was heads and shoulders. And hands. With some degree of relief, Stu saw that it was not as revealing as it seemed the first time through. Some part of his mind had been filling in the graceful fades with intimacies he remembered on his own. Then there'd be petals and flower segments again, some subtly colored, some vibrant, but all velvet textured. And lots of skin on skin.

She'd taught him that part. Caress the whole person. With your whole body. Skin on skin. Inner arms against a naked back. Strong smooth shoulders against a cheek. His chest, rough with body hair, against her smooth breasts.

She taught him patience, the gradual immersion of two people into each other. There was lots of gliding and stroking and holding and kissing. Hands touching. Not just in places that were supposed to excite, but everywhere. He'd left his cast off again that night and she had massaged that arm gently for a long time. He'd felt cherished. That was a feeling he'd never felt before.

He loved to feel her hands on him. He loved the clean scent of her hair and the feel of it streaming through his fingers or brushing like an angel's wing across his chest. She liked to sit astride him while he looked up at her and ran his hands from hip to shoulder then down her sculpted arms. There had been lots of other intense contact that night, none he'd ever want to share with anyone but her. But he realized how discretely she had edited those parts. The suggestion of what happened next was there. But he was the one who kept filling in those missing scenes, so vividly that the recollection made him sweat.

"Why, this? Why now? Why me?" he groaned.

He'd already had a lot of conflicting emotions building as the week drew to a close. Saturday, he was planning to shave off the beard and get a haircut so he could go back to work in full uniform the next Monday. This casual look would be gone. He was moving back to his apartment, away from that everyday ease he'd developed with her and the kids and the boys. He'd dreaded that in the transition, some of the magic would slip away. Now she had handed him a memento of that remarkable time, like a farewell to an interlude too beautiful to endure anywhere but in a dream.

Rikki had said the new processor could freeze-frame a fantasy. She was right. The technical maneuverings had transformed this experience into something far more idealized and graceful on screen than he knew it had been in real time. A hazy light pervaded each scene. A misty periphery blurred everything beyond the central image. The sequence of movements were stilled and subtly altered. The skillful interweaving of the elegant orchids had made this fantasy powerful stuff. The music and the pictures reached right through the anger and the embarrassment and touched some deeper sensibility.

Here he was, sitting with a dripping can of soda in front of the TV, listening to the music. Tears were streaming down his face, and he was becoming increasingly aroused by the images shifting before his eyes. With her, that night and always, it had been exquisite.

He remembered what Janelle Givrey had said to Rikki, trying to persuade her to do something more explicit. "What if the two were actual lovers . . ." That was the part that really came across. These two were lovers. Not actors. He could feel the heat between them like hot sunshine burning his face and eyes as he sat mesmerized and ran it again and again.

"I had to do what I did, the way I did it, to get what had to be there." He understood now what she'd been bracing him for. A lot more than sex was going on between them. That time there was a special intimacy. He'd felt more open, more connected than he'd ever imagined possible. He trusted her. Still, what made his mouth feel dry and his stomach knot was that she wanted others to see it and feel it too.

He knew she was waiting to hear his reaction. But she had told him to let it sink in. Let it settle. Not to rush. He needed time to sort it all out. He couldn't begin to articulate his feelings. He could hardly catch his breath.

He took another shower. He paced. Outside, distant thunder rumbled. He reran the tape and played it through another time. It was already past dark.

The rain came again, a bit heavier this time. He stared out at her house. Her living room lights were on. His own, except for the glow from the blank screen of the TV, was dark. He made a sandwich and got himself a glass of milk. Then he sat down and watched it all again.

It was late when he looked out again and saw that she'd turned out the downstairs lights. There was only a gentle sprinkle outside now. Everything was clean and hushed. Her bedroom light was on. So was the one in her bathroom. He guessed that meant she would be showering then she'd go to bed. Maybe it would be best for both of them to let it rest for the night.

He peeled off his shorts and stretched out on the bed. He remembered he'd promised the doctor he'd keep wearing the cast at night, so he got up and put it on. The fiberglass felt sticky against his skin. He tried propping it up with a pillow. Then he gave up, pulled the Velcro strips, and dropped it off the side. He still couldn't sleep.

The phone rang. He picked it up, knowing it had to be her.

"Hi. This is Rikki. Don't say anything. I just wanted to tell you good-night. I love you. See you tomorrow." She gave him the message, then hung up. She'd even told him who she was, like his heart wasn't in his throat when he heard her voice. He lay there a while longer, thinking about calling her back. Then he got up and looked out the window. With the exception of the porch lights outside, the place was dark.

This time McIver wasn't crawling through any mangrove tangle. And he wasn't going to come up on the place the way he had before. He sure as hell wasn't going to row any more than he had to. But the off-and-on drizzle that had shrouded Sarasota and its offshore keys in dull fall gray couldn't have been better timed. At night, that gray would turn to black and the drizzle would muffle everything.

He pulled on raingear and used the big boat to tow the canoe up from the condo dock at Siesta Cove, following the Intracoastal, to just below her place. He didn't really mind the rain. But he'd stowed a couple of towels and a change of clothes back at the condo sales office before he locked it up. When it was over, he'd come back and shower there, so he could go home dry.

He slowed the engine and idled past, peering through his binoculars for signs of life. The Simons woman had already gone upstairs for the night, it seemed. The one upstairs bedroom light and the outside security lights were on at her house. There were lights on in Lundquist's living room, a dim one in her kitchen, nothing upstairs.

At first he thought no one was home at Ash's house. Then he caught the bluish glow in the downstairs room and figured the TV must be on. It was about nine o'clock. If they had plans for the evening, he wondered what had screwed them up. Maybe it was the rain. Or they could have had a lover's spat. Perhaps what they had in mind for the evening didn't start until the kids were all asleep. Whatever the story, he'd come prepared for anything he found.

The drizzle let up about the time he anchored the big boat. He pulled in near shore amid the mangrove cover on a strip of undeveloped property further north so the current would carry him back. Then he shifted the gas can and the loaded backpack into the smaller boat, peeled off and stowed the raingear, climbed in, and drifted, using the paddle as a rudder.

He stayed close in. The cloudy sky covered the moon and dulled the surface of the water, turning the shadows of the overhanging trees into inky pockets that he could slip in and out of without a ripple or a sound.

Ash's dock was simple to negotiate in the canoe. McIver ducked and the boat glided right under. Then he secured the canoe, unloaded his supplies on land, and pulled on his mask and gloves. Clad all in black, he moved from one bit of vegetation to the next, working his way closer to her house on the waterside where he couldn't be seen by either neighbor if they happened to look out.

Somewhere far off a storm cloud rumbled. He felt the wind pick up, making the palmettos shiver and whisper in expectation of more rain. He tried to hurry then. Once he got up there, on the top, he could hide under the overhang of the shutter house and relax awhile. He might even get to watch a lightning show if the storm kept moving south over the mainland. He'd brought his flask. He would have a drink or two to keep out the chill, and he would wait.

Out back, through the expanse of glass, he could see she

was still in the living room, apparently alone, reading. Closer in he could hear music that didn't sound like anything on TV. He crept within a few feet of the lanai, took off his shoes, then went on, in stockinged feet, across the deck into the spa enclosure. She never looked up.

He left the gas can under the skirt of the straw figure in one corner and moved the wooden bench so he could use it to stand on. Then he pushed his backpack onto the roof of the lanai and lifted himself up after it. From there it was an easy stretch to grasp the railing of the second-floor deck and pull himself up and over.

All the bedrooms opened out onto that deck. All were dark. He tried each set of sliders and found the third one unlocked. He smiled. If he'd had to, he could have popped it with a crowbar. Or he could have looped one of the knotted ropes over the railing of the sundeck and pulled himself up to that floor. This was less dramatic, but a lot easier on the hands.

He crouched low, set down his pack for a moment, and took out the gun. If he came face to face with anyone now, he wouldn't be the one surprised. And he'd have a hostage, human leverage to keep the others in line.

Soundlessly he entered and stood absolutely still, listening, until his eyes adjusted to the room and he could tell there was no one else there. Then he grabbed the backpack and closed the slider behind him. He padded to the hall door, then he zig-zagged from room to room, like a moving shadow.

When he'd looked around in every room, he came back and stood a long time on the second-floor landing, listening for some sound of conversation down below. The kids weren't in their rooms. All the beds were made. He heard no voices.

"So it's you and me, babe," he concluded, vaguely disappointed that she was there alone. All his contingency plans, it appeared, were unnecessary. "But the night is young . . ." He hoped the boyfriend still might show.

From her bedroom, McIver followed the circular stairs up to the shutter house and out onto the sundeck. He ran a piece of tape across the doorcatch so when he opened it later, he wouldn't have to turn the handle to make it retract.

From his aerial post, he had a spectacular view of the entire peninsula. On the land side, he could see both neighbors' houses, the barrier of trees that screened them from the main road, and the roofs of houses on the other side of Midnight Pass. If it hadn't been so overcast, he could have seen all the way to the gulf.

Both houses down below looked dark now, except for their porch lights. But on the waterside, the only lights were distant ones on the mainland across and away. Occasional stabs of lightning lit the sky like crazed fireworks. It took five or six seconds for the sound to reach him, which meant the storm was about a mile away.

Between the flashes, it was very black, very still. He could hear the puff and whistle of dolphins. Then the drizzle began again. He backed in so the overhang would cover him, pulled out his flask, squatted with his back against the wall, and watched the deck grow slick and dark in the gentle, steady rain. The wind kicked up, and the rain came harder, moving across the Intracoastal like an audible wall. McIver moved back around to the landside, pressing against the shutters so the house and overhang would protect him from the storm.

He didn't hear her come upstairs. He raised the flask and suddenly noticed the pale stripes of grayish white on his sleeve. She'd moved up to the bedroom, and that light was shining up and out through the shutter slats. He ducked lower and listened. He thought he heard the shower. Then he heard her talking. Briefly. But no other voice responded, so he guessed she was on the phone. After that, he heard nothing but the rain.

When the light below went out, he took another drink.

Stu stood in the glow of the refrigerator, staring in, trying to figure out what else to eat. He sure couldn't sleep. He tried a glass of milk. Then he found a chunk of cheese and started looking for the nachos she'd brought him. He found them sitting on the counter. Cold. He dribbled some extra salsa on them, crumbled the cheese he'd found on top, and stuck it all in the microwave while he got himself a Diet Coke.

He took it all upstairs and stood staring out awhile, looking at the storm. Then he'd pace, stare out at her house awhile, and pace again. In one lull between rushes of rain, he thought he saw a glint of something metallic on her sundeck. He strained to see if she was out there. Restless. Per-

haps, like him, she was a storm watcher too. But nothing
moved.

He got the binoculars and returned to peer at the place
for most of an hour. Disappointed, he decided she must be
asleep. Then he swore he saw the door to the shutter room
open and close.

She had said "whenever . . ." If he called and she were
still up, he'd go over. They could talk. All he needed was
a light or a sound. A toilet flushing. Maybe she had her
music on. Anything would do. He hurried downstairs where
he'd stacked all the things he'd already packed. He grabbed
the bionic ear, unwrapped the earphones, and carried it all
upstairs.

Rikki didn't know what made her suddenly snap to attention. She'd lain in bed a long time, eyes closed, breathing
regularly so she would at least physically relax. She knew
she must have finally drifted off to sleep. But then she woke
with all her antennae up, like she sometimes did when
one of the kids had a bad dream or felt sick. They'd only
have to whimper or cough in their sleep, and somehow she
would hear. But they weren't in the house tonight. Some
other alarm was sounding the alert. She slit her eyes, deliberately not moving, and tried to scan the room. She couldn't
see a thing. But every fiber of her body said that something
was wrong.

She tried to make it all right. Perhaps it was just some
apprehension triggered by the storm. But she'd slept right
through far worse weather out in a rain forest in a string
hammock. This was something else.

She clenched her teeth and held her breath to keep from
screaming when she saw the legs coming down the circular
stairs from the shutter house. Somehow she suspected that
even if she opened her mouth, no sound would come out.
"Thank God the kids aren't here." That was the first coherent thought. The second one was that this intruder was
alone. The ski mask and the dark clothes and the moderate
build fit the Trasher. One on one, she'd give him a real
contest. Then she saw the backpack and the gun.

A gun meant he was ready to kill. He may not use it. But
she wasn't going to play along, let him get control of the
situation. "Get angry, get moving, and get the hell out of
there." She remembered that from some anti-rape seminar

in college. Fear could incapacitate you. Anger is not what any attacker would expect. Get angry first.

Judy Rodriguez. Lyman Franklin. Lynda Abel-Smith. Rudy Jessup. Pyramus and Thisbe. She summoned up all the bottled-up feelings. Jake and Lara and Juli. "Now or never, you son of a bitch," she swore silently, trying not to freeze up.

She waited until he'd set his bag down and came closer. He had a roll of some kind of tape in his hand. The gun in the other. She was going for the gun. Without it, he'd have to deal with her on her territory, on her terms.

"Get out, you bastard," she barked and swung at the same time, coming up out of the bed like an apparition in white. She slammed her forearm against his hand. The gun arced through the air and hit the floor near the door. The man yelped, nothing intelligible, just a squawk of surprise, then she landed an elbow on the side of his head and rocked him in the opposite direction.

She lunged straight across the bed and reached for the gun just as he tackled her. Still she managed to fling it out in the hallway so it ricocheted off the gallery railing and skittered on down the hall toward the stairs.

"Get off me." She rammed an elbow back at him. This one caught him on the cheekbone with a solid crack. His grip on her slacked off. Scrambling on her hands and knees, she went after the gun again, determined to keep it out of his hands. He grabbed her ankle, and yanked her leg back. She landed on her chest.

"If you have to fight, *never* fight like a lady." The long-unused admonitions of that speaker at the rape seminar came back. "Get angry, get moving, and get the hell out of there."

Rikki rolled over and kicked him square in the face. That gave her enough of a head start to grab the gun and pitch it off the landing out toward the sliders downstairs. Then the phone rang. It was the cellular, back on the charger by her bed. There was no way she was heading back.

It had to be Stu, ready to talk. Whether she answered it or not, he'd come over, especially if he thought she was outside, swimming, unwinding like he'd seen her do at night. She bounded down the stairs in the dark. Her best bet was to get the gun and herself out of the house completely and buy some time until he got there.

* * *

Stu stood with the bionic ear aimed at her house, trying to adjust the reception to make out the sounds beyond the soft swoosh of the rain. He heard something clunk. Or was it thunder? Then some other dull noises, like someone stamping on a wood floor. Or hammering. Or banging a door. He looked more closely at the shutter house again. Then he heard the distinct clatter that made a brittle sound.

Whatever she was doing in the dark, she wasn't sleeping. So he called. One ring. Two. Three. Four. He was looking out the window at her bedroom, waiting for her to answer.

She didn't pick up the phone. It just kept ringing. She'd been waiting all evening to hear what he had to say, so she'd know it was him. He aimed the binoculars at the dock, half-expecting to see her towel there. Maybe because of the rain, she was just out back in the spa. "Whenever" was enough of an invitation to go over and hash this videotape thing out face to face. He pulled the cassette from the VCR and took it along.

Rikki vaulted several pieces of living-room furniture, grabbed the gun, and unlocked the nearest slider before the guy in black had even made it down the stairs. She bolted out and threw the handgun over the gazebo as far as she could into the darkest sector of the yard. Then with it gone, suddenly she stiffened, realizing who she had inside.

"You bastard. You came back," she muttered, looking around for something to use as a weapon. She wasn't going to run and hide and let him get away. She was going to stop him, for Thayer Kern, for Lynda Abel-Smith, for Judy Rodriguez, for Rudy Jessup, and Lyman Franklin. For all of them. For Pyramus and Thisbe. For Olivia. For herself.

"Get angry, get moving, and get the bastard," she panted, changing the litany. Hand to hand, she might get hurt but she could probably take him. Then she saw Oscar, dark and slick from the rain. "*Never* fight like a lady." Together they could corner the guy and hold him until someone arrived.

Rikki lifted Oscar down from his hooked mounts, braced him under her arm like a battering ram, and moved in, slamming the slider closed behind her. She still didn't turn on any lights. Even in the dark, she could see the masked man across the room. He was struggling with the locks on her front door. He wasn't even coming her way. He was trying to get out.

"Stop! No you don't," she yelled, lunging toward him. "Get away from the door. Get your hands up."

He wheeled around to face her. He grabbed the tiki by the door and raised it, ready to swing. "Stay back," he warned her, staring at the weapon she was carrying. "Just stay back." He started inching around the other way, aiming for the sliders behind her. "Get out of my way."

"Not a chance." She squared her stance, not doubting for a moment that if he kept coming, she would hold her ground.

"Move," he growled at her, his voice tight and frantic.

"You're not leaving here," she warned him, bracing the wooden shark, ready to jab at him. "Just put that down and raise your hands over your head."

"Fuck you." He leaped behind the kitchen bar, using it as a barricade. Now he was glancing behind him the other way, measuring the distance to the side door.

"You'll never make it," Rikki warned him, closing in on him.

Still clutching the tiki, he bobbed it back and forth like a batter eager to hit a line drive, then took a wide sweep with it. She stepped back. He broke away, aiming for the side door after all.

Determined to immobilize him, Rikki charged right after him. She aimed the prongs of the tail at his buttocks. "I said stop." She jabbed at him, one quick hard poke that dug in his upper leg. She could feel the flesh give when she yanked it back.

"Aaaahhh!!" He squalled, grabbing his backside as he whirled away and hobbled back out of range. "You're fuckin' crazy," he screamed. "Get the fuck away from me. You fuckin' stabbed me. I'll kill you."

Suddenly Stu was there beating on the kitchen door. "What the hell is going on in there? Let me in."

The guy swung at Rikki. She blocked it with the rump of the shark, but the impact staggered her sideways. He leaped past her, heading for the glass doors across the deck. Only Stu now came thundering up the back, white faced and anxious. He pushed open the sliders and stepped in his way.

"Stay back." The masked man was screaming now, but

he stopped. Silhouetted by the moonlight, Stu towered above him.

"Rikki?" He took a look at the masked man, then caught sight of her with the shark levelled chest high at the man.

"It's him," she panted. "Call the police."

"No . . . get out of my way," the man yelled, with a frantic ragged sound.

Stu still blocked the exit. "Give it up, man. It's over. Don't push your luck." His voice was loud and firm and shook with anger. "Put that damn thing down."

"Let me out." The guy kept coming with the tiki pulled back.

"You're not going anywhere." Stu reached back with his left hand and gave the heavy slider a shove to shut it. The guy drove in and took a swing.

"Stu," Rikki yelled, but not in time for him to dodge the blow. The Tiki caught him on the bicep of the newly healed arm and dropped him to his knees.

McIver came at him again, weilding the tiki like a battle-axe, intent on crushing his skull.

"Duck," Rikki screamed. Recoiling, and sick with pain, Stu rocked back. This time the thing grazed his cheekbone, making an ominous whoosh too close to his head. He couldn't focus. He doubled over, clutching his arm, and trying not to pass out.

Ricki drove home another hit, catching the guy in the upper arm and rolling him off as the prongs raked tracks across his shoulder.

"Fuck," McIver whipered, then raised the tiki to slam at Stu again. Like a cornered beast he was frantic, frightened, and out of control.

"Get away from him." Holding the five-foot shark like a pitchfork, Rikki jabbed it at him again. This time she got a solid hit, ramming the sharp points of the pronged tail into his back. He screamed, stiffened, and staggered out of range, letting the tiki drop to the floor with a dull thud.

"Get back against the counter."

"I'm bleeding."

"Get back." She was trembling, on the verge of losing control herself. "I'll ram you again if you don't back up." She aimed him toward the kitchen while she moved between him and Stu. "Stu? Can you get up? Can you call 911?" She could tell he was still moving, but she wasn't sure how badly he was hurt. She wouldn't take her eyes off the man in black.

"Can't," Stu groaned. "I'll try . . ." His breathing was labored.

"Never mind. Just stay still." She could hear the near-hysteria in her own voice. "You. Just keep backing up," she said shrilly, advancing menacingly at the man. He was hunched over, limping, clutching at his wounds and trembling too.

"Just let me go," he begged. "I'm hurt." He rubbed his back, gasping at the pain. His hand came back bloody. "Please."

"You listen very carefully," she ordered him. "Because if you don't"—she was speaking very slowly, very precisely, like she was wound too tight and ready to spring—"if you don't do exactly as I say, I will run you through with this, in a heartbeat. You have to stop." She was gasping for air, just as he was. "This is the end. Don't piss me off. Don't say another thing. Just turn around. Now."

He was whimpering and clutching at his back with both hands. But he did as she said.

"Walk, slow. If you make one false move, I'll pin you to the wall. Just don't fuck with me," she warned him.

She reached over and picked up her keys. She hit the light switches, illuminating the kitchen and the sidewalk just outside. She unlocked the door. "This way." She walked him out the kitchen door. "Remember, move slow."

She aimed him straight for the darkroom. "Against the wall." She unlocked that door with the key. That was the only place with no outside windows, no other exit, and a deadbolt on her side. "Now, you get in there." She stood behind him. "Go." He reached out for the knob and hesitated. "Don't even think of trying anything," she warned him, biting off each word.

He turned the handle. It freewheeled.

"Jiggle it. Then push and turn." The directions sounded silly, considering the context.

But he followed the instructions. Jiggle. Push. Turn. Again. This time the temperamental doorknob caught and worked. "Go." He went inside.

Rikki didn't put down Oscar until she'd locked the deadbolt. Even then, she carried the big wooden creature cradled against her, as she hurried back inside.

"Just take it easy. I'll get help," she promised Stu. She went into the kitchen and dialed 911.

"Tell them to get Joe Warnock," Stu told her.

She yanked several pillows from the sofa and used them to make him more comfortable, cushioning his head and back and the injured arm. He was sweating and pale but conscious. Between carrying him water and applying ice packs to try to keep the swelling down, she also took a sidetrip upstairs and brought down the cellular phone.

"Call your dad," he reminded her as he lay there. "And Pat Simons." He didn't want Pat to be alarmed when the police converged on the site. After that she phoned Olivia Mello's hotel room. Then Thayer Kern.

Within minutes the whole peninsula was jammed with patrol cars, emergency vehicles, marked and unmarked units from all departments, and hordes of personnel.

"He's still in there. In the darkroom," one of the first officers at the scene told Warnock when he arrived. "Not a peep."

"Good. How's Sullivan and the Lundquist woman?"

"He's still inside. Paramedics are with him, but he won't leave," he reported. "She's doing real well, considering. Put up one heck of a fight. She's out back, showing some of our men where she threw the gun. The satchel he had is upstairs, in her room."

Warnock was nodding. "I'm going to take a look around and talk with her awhile. Call me if he says anything." On the way over, he'd radioed ahead and told the officers on the scene not to unlock the door. Just let the Trasher sit. As far as they knew, he wasn't armed. He was wounded. Stabbed in the back. Speared in the leg. He'd been kicked in the face. And he was locked in a room with one exit. There wasn't any reason to move fast or to risk anyone getting hurt. They had him. The rest was just a matter of details.

"Now what does that yellow light by the door mean?" Warnock asked when he had Rikki sketch out the darkroom layout for him.

"That's the safelight. It means he's found the light switch inside. It's not very bright, but it's enough to see by. There's a regular light as well. It's on the opposite side of the door."

"Okay." He had her mark the location of every workspace, each piece of equipment, and all the chemicals. Then he went outside and knocked.

"Okay, you in there. This is Joe Warnock. I'm with the police force. I hear you're hurt. How're you doing?" he began, starting in easy.

There was no reply.

"Look, we got some paramedics out here. Maybe you'd better have someone take a look at you. Looks like you lost a good bit of blood. Any chance you got a punctured kidney? Maybe a lung?" That part was an exaggeration. There were drops and splotches on the sidewalk and the kitchen floor, but nothing that suggested the pronged tail had hit a major organ. But Warnock figured the guy inside couldn't see the wounds very well. If he hurt like hell, with a little encouragement, he'd imagine they were far worse then they were.

Again, there was no reply.

"Hey. If you're conscious, let me know. We don't want you bleeding to death in there. Besides, some of those chemicals and things in there are damn toxic. If the fumes don't make you sick, you could get something smeared in a wound and develop one nasty infection. For God's sake, don't light a match for a cigarette." He waited, with his ear close to the door. "Look. I know you're scared. I know things look real bad from where you are. But we can work this out. Just tell me one thing, can you hear me?"

There was a long pause. "I can hear."

"Good. Real good." Warnock rubbed his moustache. "So you're all right?"

No answer.

"Hey, fella. I just want to make sure you're all right," Warnock pressed. "Are you all right?"

"No. I'm hurt."

"I'm worried you might be in real bad shape. I saw the blood. You want to do something about it? Have a doctor look it over?" Warnock suggested.

No reply.

"Listen. You take it easy. Think it over," Warnock told him. "No hurry. If you need anything, just call out. There'll be someone within earshot. I'll be back." He walked away and went in through the front door.

"Okay, so this is how it looks," one technician began covering what they'd found so far. There were shoes and a gas can on the back deck. Prints on the darkroom door handle. Blood samples to match with the smear from the Spanish bayonet. In the midst of the conversation, one of the outside team came in. They'd found the gun.

"Someone named Mello at the entrance. She wants in. Says you'll know who she is." One officer with a hand radio called out to Warnock.

"It's the redhead."

"Decoy duty." Several officers nearby immediately placed the name.

"Might as well let her through," Warnock gave the order. "I'd prefer having her here where we can see her, rather than say ''no'' and wonder where the hell she might turn up."

"What about a Swede Lundquist?" The officer relayed another request.

"He's this one's father. Let him through," Warnock replied. "They both can come in. Have someone meet them and escort them both right in the house," he told the uniformed patrolman who would radio the instructions back.

"So, How's it going in there?" Warnock began again. "You need a pain pill or something?"

Silence.

"Look. We may as well start working on this. There's nowhere to go. We could camp out here with coffee and doughnuts and wait all night," he contended. "Or we could keep changing shifts for days and starve you out. We're not interested in any heroics. We're real patient. The question remains, how long do you want to sit in there? Face it, you aren't in a real strong bargaining position."

No reply.

"Look. I'm trying to make it easy on you. How about we just unlock the door. You come out with your hands held high. Nice, clean, neat," he persisted. "No one is going to hurt you. You're already in bad shape. We know that. We just want to get you looked at, and then we want to talk."

"I want my lawyer."

Warnock hadn't expected that one. "Fair enough. Who's your lawyer?"

"Richard Watson."

Warnock's eyebrows shot up. Watson was well respected and expensive, but he was primarily a family law practicioner who dealt in divorces, custody cases, and estate settlements. But if this guy wanted Watson, it was worth a call.

"You know Watson?"

"I know him."

"I'll phone him right now," Warnock offered. "But it's the middle of the night. I can't promise he'll come unless I tell him who wants him. You think he'll recognize you by name?" He waited. "We need a name."

The guy didn't offer one.

Warnock shrugged. He walked back and forth, pacing his next move.

"Put yourself in his shoes." Warnock pressed for some response. "Some cop calls you in the middle of the night and says some guy is holed up in a darkroom and wants him there or he won't come out. Then I can't tell him who you are. Watson doesn't do freebies. I doubt he makes house calls. You'll have to give me some name if you want to get him here." He waited, hoping the fellow inside would speak. "I can see that it might be real valuable to have a top notch lawyer walk you through all this. But from his standpoint, I sure couldn't blame him for passing on this one."

"Tell him it's McIver. David McIver." The voice on the other side sounded almost embarrassed.

Warnock had already written it down and was sending officers out to call the name into their computer files. "Okay, McIver. Sit tight. I'll make the call."

"I've never heard of him," Rikki said when Warnock came in to tell her that the man may still be faceless, but he now had a name. David McIver.

"Me neither." Olivia Mello shook her head.

Stu shook his head. "Doesn't connect." His color was improved now, and the arm sling was back, along with more ice packs. Both were temporary measures, but along with several pain killers, they would hold him a few hours. He wasn't leaving until he saw this guy in handcuffs. Then he'd go for X-rays and have his bone man start all over again.

"Real estate." Swede had headed straight to the phone book. "He's got an office number and a house one."

Warnock called the house number just in case the guy had simply picked out someone else's name. No answer. Then he called Richard Watson and got him out of bed.

"I know him. I'm representing him in a pending divorce case. I can't believe this is the David McIver I know," he declared.

"Let me ask him if he can give us anything else," Warnock suggested, carrying the cellular phone outside. "David," he called through the closed door. "I have Richard Watson on the line. He knows the name, but he needs to be sure that it's you. Anything I can tell him to convince him?"

He hesitated before he replied. "I just gave him some financial statements he'd asked for. He knows I want my house. The one on Hudson Bayou. Sandra, my wife, she's fighting me for it. Is that enough?"

Warnock repeated the message, word for word, to the attorney. "He says it's you, all right. He's not in criminal law, though. He wants to know if you'd like him to refer you to another lawyer in his firm who does that kind of thing."

"I know him. I want him."

"He wants you," Warnock said simply back to Watson. "He's been hurt. It's late. You may be able to help us do this real smoothly. I'd appreciate it if you'd give it a shot." He added his own remarks to McIver's message. "Okay. He says he's coming over," Warnock announced. "It may take awhile. Thirty minutes. Can you hold on that long?"

"I can wait."

"Good." Warnock took the phone back inside.

"Hey, Mr. McIver. Do you want a cup of coffee?" Warnock had the officer at the door call in that offer. Sometimes something simple and familiar like a cup of coffee could make a holdout more cooperative. Rikki had made a pot for anyone who wanted a cup while they waited. Warnock had his in hand.

"No."

"Anything else. Coke? Juice?"

"No."

"How about something to eat? We could unlock our side of the door and slide it in."

No reply.

"Okay. Have it your way. But if you get hungry or thirsty, give us a holler." Warnock let him dangle for a while.

When Richard Watson arrived, Warnock had a quick conference with him. Then he let the attorney talk to McIver through the door. McIver had asked them to let Watson in to talk. "I can't come in." Watson repeated what Warnock had told him to say. "You could be armed. You could use me as a hostage. They won't let me take that chance. So you'll have to come out. You have to show them that you don't have any other weapons.''

"Right. You'll have to come out," Warnock insisted. "Simple as that. You come out. Mr. Watson is waiting. He knows what needs to be done. He'll also verify that you're being treated properly." Warnock directed Watson back inside then. He had police sharpshooters stationed on the balconies and roof. If they all were wrong and if McIver were armed, they could drop him before he hurt another soul.

"Okay."

"Okay. I'm unlocking the deadbolt. All you have to do is come walking out."

They waited. Nothing happened. Then Warnock gave the signal for the officer nearest the door to try the handle. It turned, it caught, but the door itself didn't budge.

"He's locked it from the inside," Rikki said when they came to her with the latest update. "Stu put a slide bolt in for me, to keep anyone from bothering me when I was working."

Warnock sighed, reflected, and decided to face this development head on.

"Okay, McIver. Our side's open. You've locked your side. That wasn't necessary. We aren't going to storm the place. We don't have to," Warnock informed him. "If we wanted in, we have numerous options. We could just undo the door hinges. Or we could cut right through the lock," he declared. "Or cut a hole in the wall. We've got a lot of toys we haven't used. We could run some gas in there. We've got the kind that makes you puke. Or the kind that sears your nasal passages and makes your eyes burn. Some stuff just makes you sleepy. But what makes the most sense is to get this over with. With some kind of dignity. You're only making yourself look bad by dragging this out."

They heard a crash then. And another crash. He was busting up the place.

"Hey, McIver. Take it easy. Are you okay?" Warnock called out, beating on the door, hoping to distract him. "Don't go getting all worked up. Save your energy. You've lost a lot of blood. You don't want to exert yourself too much. You might cause a hemmorhage or something."

Everything inside was silent.

"Look, McIver, you've got to be exhausted. It's almost two in the morning. You don't want to keep this up till dawn. What good would it do anyway? Why don't you just call it quits? It will go easier on you in the long run." Warnock kept at him.

"Is Watson there?" McIver demanded.

"Sure. Does this mean you're coming out?" Warnock asked, signaling frantically for someone to bring Watson out long enough to make some reply.

"If Watson's there."

The attorney came bustling out. "I'm here. Everything is fine. No one is going to hurt you."

"What do I have to do?"

"Just keep your hands up. Show these men you are not carrying a weapon." The attorney delivered his part precisely, then Warnock waved him off to safety again.

There was a long silence. Then the inside slide bolt clicked. Slowly the handle turned. Jiggled. Caught. The heavy door pushed open. No longer hooded, David McIver stepped into the open and lifted both hands.

"Step forward. Easy." Warnock's voice was the only sound.

McIver moved into the light.

"Now freeze."

The police were all over him in a fraction of a second. Warnock read him his rights while he was cuffed and searched. He tried to block a view of his face with his shoulder as he was led off toward the paramedic van.

"So . . . ever see him before?" Warnock asked the civilian contingent who'd come out to get a look at the face behind the mask. Rikki shook her head first. Olivia said no. Stu had even come out to take a look. He didn't recognize him either.

"I've seen him. Somewhere," Swede said, more subdued than usual. "Can't begin to remember where."

"It's damn crazy that someone you don't even know tries to kill you," Olivia muttered. "Who the fuck is he, anyway?"

"The pieces will all come together eventually," Warnock assured them. "It just takes time." He went over to talk with the suspect while the lab team moved in.

Gradually all the civilian cars and vans and most of the police vehicles moved out. Swede went home. Olivia said she was camping out in Jake's room for the night and went upstairs.

"I think we should get you to the hospital. You need someone to take care of that arm," Rikki said, standing next to Stu watching one of the TV remote units follow a patrol car out.

Stu looked at the sky, finally clearing now after the storm front had passed through. Everything smelled wet and clean and new. The last place he wanted to be was a hospital, surrounded by the antiseptic smell.

"They've got me iced and numb. Let's take a look at the damage in there first," he suggested. He was deliberately stalling, sidetracking her by aiming for the darkroom. In all the commotion after McIver emerged, they hadn't had a chance to look inside.

The small warning light outside the door was still on, but the interior of the room was dark. Rikki went in and took a flashlight from one drawer. "He broke the bulbs," she said, "and whatever else he could get his hands on." She shone the light around the interior.

Stu stepped in with her, flinching at the crunch of broken glass beneath their feet.

"Here. Get that part out." She gave him a pair of plastic tongs to wedge in the socket and unscrew the old base. She got a new bulb from a drawer. He reached up and screwed it in. Now the room was filled with that familiar amber glow.

"Well, he made a real mess," she acknowledged, now able to see more clearly the enlarger that he'd smashed amid the clutter of trays and empty cylinders. "But nothing that can't be fixed or replaced." He could hear relief as well as weariness in her voice. "Good thing I wasn't keeping anything that important in here. All my work is upstairs."

"Not all your work." Stu moved closer to her, cupping his good arm around her shoulders. "This evening, before we were so rudely interrupted," he said, "I was coming over to talk about your tape."

"I'd forgotten about that."

"I certainly will never forget it," he assured her.

"It's intended for therapy. It's part of a program for women . . ."

"Whoa. I figured that part out," he stopped her. "I never doubted your intent. After I survived the initial shock, I got the point. It was very personal, very powerful." He licked his lips, wanting to get this part right. "You captured an incredible range of feelings. And you made a very erotic statement. It took me several replays to realize that about fifty percent of what was on the screen were flowers.''

That observation made her smile. "I was more concerned about your reaction to the other fifty percent."

"That's what shows. Your concern, your care, your tenderness," he told her, hoping that would ease another element that hadn't been resolved. "I just hope that any other person watching feels that goodness of heart as strongly as I did."

"Thanks." Her voice was soft. "I wouldn't let anyone else see it unless you said it was all right."

"It's better than all right. You do beautiful work." He paused and let out a long breath. His chest hurt. His shoulder ached. His arm was starting to throb. "Just don't ever do anything like that again," he stressed.

"That was a once-in-a-lifetime, one-time deal."

"I'll make you another one," he said, grinning at her, despite his pain. "Once in a lifetime, one-time deal . . .''

"I'll take it. Now quit stalling. Hospital." She led him out, flicking off the safelight on the way.

"I hate hospitals. I hate having my bones shoved around," he groaned.

"I'll stay with you." She had her arm around him, trying not to squeeze anywhere that hurt.

"For how long?"

"How long was that deal for?"

"Forever," he said, grinning at her.

"I guess until they come up with something better, it'll have to do."

New from the #1 bestselling author of *Communion*—
a novel of psychological terror and demonic possession. . . .
"A triumph."—Peter Straub

UNHOLY
FIRE
Whitley Strieber

Father John Rafferty is a dedicated priest with only one temptation—the beautiful young woman he has been counseling, and who is found brutally murdered in his Greenwich Village church. He is forced to face his greatest test of faith when the NYPD uncovers her sexually twisted hidden life, and the church becomes the site for increasingly violent acts. Father Rafferty knows he must overcome his personal horror to unmask a murderer who wears an angel's face. This chilling novel will hold you in thrall as it explores the powerful forces of evil lurking where we least expect them. "Gyrates with evil energy . . . fascinating church intrigue."—*Kirkus Reviews*